THE LAST VOYAGE
OF
SOMEBODY THE
SAILOR

THE LAST VOYAGE OF OF SOMEBODY THE SAILOR

JOHN BARTH

LITTLE, BROWN AND COMPANY

BOSTON TORONTO LONDON

FIRST EDITION

This is a work of fiction and the characters and events are imaginary. The
author is, however, indebted to the nautical explorer Tim Severin, who appears in this
book as a fictional character and whose own voyage and writing provided some of the
background information about Sindbad's voyages and certain travels of the main
character, Simon William Behler, as he recreates them. With this exception, any
similarity to real persons, living or dead, is coincidental and not intended
by the author.

LIBRARY OF CONGRESS CATALOGING-IN-PUBLICATION DATA
Barth, John.
   The last voyage of Somebody the sailor / John Barth.—1st ed.
   p.   cm.
   ISBN 0-316-08251-1
   I. Title.
   PS3552.A75L37   1991
   813′.54 — dc20   90-44991

              10 9 8 7 6 5 4 3 2

                        MV-PA

Designed by Barbara Werden

Published simultaneously in Canada by
Little, Brown & Company (Canada) Limited

PRINTED IN THE UNITED STATES OF AMERICA

for Shelly

CONTENTS

THE LAST VOYAGE
OF
SOMEBODY THE
SAILOR

THE FAMILIAR STRANGER

The machinery's rusty, I acknowledge to my half-expected guest, but it hasn't seized up altogether. "I could tell you one about the death of Scheherazade. . . ."

"I've heard it."

"Not this version."

My visitor crosses her nyloned legs with stern self-assurance and smooths her skirt-pleats. I was rather expecting an elder man, cordially disposed but skeptical, like my late uncle Josh, or like Sindbad the Sailor's old navigator, my friend Mustafā mu-Allim. The young woman eases back — sits back, anyhow — in the room's one chair. "I've heard them all."

"Those were King Shahryar's very words," I declare to her. "In fact, his *last* words. Age eighty-five, the story goes, and healthy as a horse till just a few months before. Then bingo: perforated ulcers with complications. Queen Scheherazade was standing by, sixty-eight herself by then and a grandmother several times over. The king had been delirious for three days: uremic poisoning, complications. He had got to thinking he was thirty-five again, back in the days of his thousand and one nights. 'By Allah,' he would say to whoever was in the room, 'I won't kill her till I've heard the end of her story,' and the busy nurses and orderlies would say, 'Right.'"

My caller's eyes are greener than her hospital tunic: an almost reproachful green. She turns them from me, not for long.

"Finally Scheherazade got the doctors to catheterize him and change his prescription. That same night his head cleared, but it was too late to save him. He recognized his wife in the dark, gave her hand a squeeze, and said, 'Anyhow, I've heard a mess of stories. I guess I've heard them all.' She kissed his turban and sent word for their two grown sons to get there fast. The king died quietly just as the muezzins were calling from the palace minarets that prayer is better than sleep. A good death, all hands agreed — but those last words of his were wrong."

Down the line, some poor devil or his victim is howling again. My visitor fiddles with her stethoscope as if it were an amulet. "Sounds familiar."

"So it sounds familiar. You *look* familiar."

Those eyes are on me again, through me, briefly. She gives her auburn hair a toss. "I'm in the halls."

"Anyhow, that wasn't Scheherazade's death yet, right?"

She regards her fingers, interlaced in her lap. No ring. "You're the storyteller."

Regarding her, I twist my own ring, charmed, bemused: "Once upon a time . . ."

Now she checks her wristwatch, one of those multifunction digitals. I used to do that, plenty, whether I was in a hurry or not; but mine's an old-fashioned analog with a calendar window that you have to set forward in months with fewer than thirty-one days; also a rotatable bezel for measuring elapsed time. In better days I've used this watch for everything from navigating sailboats to barbecuing lamb. This watch . . .

Do you know where you are? she's asking me. What day is today? What's your full name?

The days go by, I could tell her: Tuesday, Saturday, the American century. My watch isn't right. Do I complain? On with the story! Test me on the general time of day, I could say to her; you'll see I'm compos mentis. Evening shift ready to punch out, right? Graveyarders punching in but not on the halls yet. Century ending, maybe ended by now. Luckier folks asleep.

But listen, Doctor, I want to tell her: you're more than welcome. Sleep isn't what it used to be. I have a daughter your age, I want to tell her: biologist, married, out on the Coast. I don't suppose you're her, or here is there? There's a rivershore out front of here, right? Big tidewater river, running out just now, and crossing that river a two-mile bridge, which it would be useful indeed to know whether is to our left or to our right, for position-fixing, as there's more than one kind of hospital along this shore — but don't get up. And once upon a time (Saturday, Tuesday) I had a lover *her* age, handsome as yourself; even strikingly beautiful, as they say, and sharp and spirited as a young Scheherazade.

Another story — of the sort once told by Simon William Behler, a.k.a. "Baylor," the once-sort-of-famous "New Journalist," of whom you may . . . never mind.

I had half imagined you would be a chorus or a jury, maybe a spectrum of my major women: dear Aunt Rachel, Crazy Daisy Moore and her green-eyed sister Julia; my first wife, Jane, I suppose, and maybe Juliette — our biological daughter, so to say. And Yasmín, Yasmín, Yasmín. Plus one other: the one who, in fact, young lady, might tell us my proper name, might even have told "Bill Baylor," before he dropped out of the American century and into Sindbad's, who he is.

Was?

Another story. Baylor calls this one (stop him if you've heard it)

THE DESTROYER OF DELIGHTS

or,

The Last Story of Scheherazade,

as Told by the Narrator of the Foregoing

She had done her thousand and one, Ms. Scheherazade had, and then some — told them all over again for the scribes after the king made an honest woman of her and she an honorable man of him, cooked up all new ones for their children's bedtimes and retold *them* to each grandchild in turn, plus recapping her fans' old favorites at state dinners: Aladdin, Ali Baba, Sindbad's seven voyages. And more than once, in their middle years, she and King Shahryar had pretended in bed that her life was on the line again, as it had been for those first thousand nights of their story — a touch of the old fire, the familiar terror of once upon a time.

But by when Shahryar was translated, as they say, to the ruth of almighty Allah, his widow was told out and no regrets. She was a handsome, healthy-enough woman still, though rich in minor physical complaints. She lived on and on in the palace until she wasn't so handsome and healthy anymore, and on and on after that until she was a bedridden, pain-wracked crone, and on and on after that. The Destroyer of Delights and Severer of Societies, as folks spoke of him thereabouts, had paid a call decades before upon her youngest son, always the least robust of the three, and then upon her father, the ex–grand vizier, and then upon her old husband, as aforenarrated, and later on upon her younger sister, Dunyazade, not so young by that time, and presently upon *her* husband, and after that upon one of the other grown-up sons and even upon one of the grandchildren, not to mention the house staff and any number of ordinary citizens. It seemed to Scheherazade that that dismal fellow came to and went from the place more often than the painters and the plumbers. Several times in latter years, when pain and pointlessness were roughing her up more than usual, she had caught sight of him going by in the corridor and called out to him, the way you yell for the nurse who's supposed to bring your pills and doesn't. But his appointment was always with somebody else.

"For pity's sake," she had proposed one late evening years ago, when he came for her first granddaughter: "take me instead!" He had smiled her way, not triumphantly, and shaken his head. Nowadays it was "For pity's sake, take me, *too!*"

No deal.

The night it finally occurred to her, through the noise of her misery, that her current situation was just the reverse of her original one, she must have cried out to him in a different tone; he actually paused, silhouetted by backlight, and leaned his shoulder against her door-jamb. Right away the racket quieted. Her body felt thirty years younger, a healthy sixty-at-most, and she was able to speak and register things almost normally for the first time since who knew when. It struck her, for example, now that she could see him, that the fellow looked tired, though he is famously tireless: an elderly, gray-bearded, serious-faced chap after all (the sort "Baylor" had expected, gentle listener), neatly dressed but rumpled, the way travelers get on the final leg of their journey or medical residents toward the end of their shift.

A little break in his rounds.

When she had put her case, he said, "What do you mean, 'die'?" His tone was . . . oh, challenging but not unsympathetic. "You've been kaput for years. When was the last time you told anybody a story?"

"Who's left to tell to?" she came right back, warming to it, and gestured toward the bedside miniatures of Shahryar, Dunyazade, the other dear departeds. "Job enough to get my bedpan changed."

8

"Forget bedpans," her visitor advised. "You're through with all that. Mind if I sit."

She *didn't* mind, in fact, but he hadn't put the question as a question. She sat, too — up, in bed — understanding in her bones that she was indeed through with all that, hallelujah, and that there remained now only a bit of bargaining, an exercise in negotiation. She straightened her hair and the neck of her gown, said, "I'd offer you mint tea, but it's the maid's day off."

She saw his tired eyes follow her movements. "No mint tea, Scheherazade." At mention of her name — a long while since she'd heard a male voice sound those syllables! — she was aware for the first time in ages of the city round about her: a late-summer night in the busy town she had once saved with her young-womanhood. A town that now, no doubt — absorbed in new, more glittering distractions — scarcely remembered those old tales and their teller.

"Once upon a time," she said, inspecting her wedding ring with a disingenuous sigh, "I could have offered more. But that time's long past."

She paused for acknowledgment: who could say what such a man's tastes might not include? When he agreed with her — a tiny wince of the eyebrows — she went on smoothly (delicious, once again to go on smoothly): "And the coin of the realm, I assume, is not *your* coin."

"No."

"So, then." She clasped her hands in her lap, looked him full in the face with those once-again-astonishing eyes. "What's my ticket price?"

And wearily, but not *simply* wearily, he returned that look. "You know as well as I do, Scheherazade."

"You're not serious. Well, you are, if anybody is. But what a thing to want, this late in the day!"

"It may be earlier than you think." He consulted his wrist. "However, if the well really has gone dry . . ."

"Just you hold on, now. This particular well ran out so long ago that nobody's checked lately to see what's what." She . . . sighed. "So: the shoe really is on the other foot."

And he . . . shrugged, okay? "If it fits, et cetera. But listen: no Ali Baba and company. Your first audience wanted virgin girls and hand-me-down stories. What your last one's after is a virgin story."

"From a hand-me-down teller. But Allah preserve us: a virgin story! There can't be anything *you* haven't heard!"

He put his hands on the chair-arms. "Then I won't keep you."

"I bet you've even heard the one called The Last Voyage of Somebody the Sailor."

He smiled, turned down the lamp, sat back, and crossed his legs, twitching his already uncreased trouser-crease out of harm's way. "If I have, you won't stop me."

"And if you haven't," said Scheherazade, more confident with every sentence, "then this last tale of mine will be a virgin story in both respects, for it's *about* virginity, too, you might say, as was my own story . . . once upon a time . . ."

We may imagine then, you and I — may we not? — that she goes on to tell *her* familiar stranger (with a little help from yours truly, ma'am: "Baylor" the Taler of Behler the Failer) the whole time-straddling story of

THE LAST VOYAGE
OF
SOMEBODY THE SAILOR

The story goes (in its official version) that the *next*-to-last voyage of Sindbad the fabulous Seaman — as recounted by that fortunate fellow himself to his dinner guests at the end of the holy month of Ramadan for the benefit of the beggar called Sindbad the Landsman — was little more than a replay of the five voyages before it. He goes down per usual from the city of Baghdad to the port of Basra. Per usual he sets out (but this time with a particular urgency, explained anon) with a clutch of other merchants, to score in the silk-and-spice trade, or whatever. Their captain loses his way, per usual; the usual storm disables their vessel and piles her up on some uncharted island. Most of the passengers and crew go under, but old Sindbad, as he'll tell it, is so accustomed to this routine by now that as soon as the skipper admits they're lost, he climbs into his faithful laundry tub, his Tub of Last Resort, and waits on the afterdeck for the squall and the foundering. He makes it to shore, as always, this time with a handful of others, whose next job in his story is to die and leave him the sole survivor.

No need to tell *them* that: let them praise Allah for their deliverance from the Destroyer of Delights and for the fact that the shore is strewn with supplies and merchandise from other shipwrecks, enough to open a bazaar with if there were any customers besides themselves. Let them marvel to their hearts' short-lived content that the beach they're stranded on has jewels for pebbles: they'd all be wealthy men if they weren't the wretched castaways they are.

So all except Sindbad pile up the goods, each man guarding his hoard day and night and looking for a chance to pilfer his neighbor's. Seasoned old Sindbad, however, ignoring them and theirs, patiently gathers spars and lashings from the wrecks. His erstwhile shipmates laugh at him, ha ha, and catch castaway's colic and die. Each new victim's pile is scrabbled after by the survivors, until the last of them besides Sindbad has the whole inventory to himself.

He kicks, too. Whereupon Sindbad loads the raft he's just completed per program with as much of the stuff as it can safely carry and sets out, not to sea but up the tidal estuary he has long since spotted on his beachcombing expeditions. It leads into a cave in the nearest mountain and thence (he presumes from past experience) to some marvelous realm where he'll either cope ingeniously with monsters or become the king's favorite (also his financier) or both, but from which he will in any case make his way eventually back home with yet another fortune.

Turns out it's the King's-Favorite scenario — by far Sindbad's favorite scenario, too, this late in the story of his life. No rocs, no cannibals, no giant serpents; Sindbad regales the king-of-the-moment with travelogues of his six times out and anecdotes about his hometown caliph, the great Haroun al-Rashīd, Commander of the Faithful, until the king takes the hint and proposes establishing diplomatic relations between the Caliphate of Baghdad and this Magic Isle of Serendib. He dispatches our man to do the job, with a royal present from king to king and Sindbad's treasure stashed in the hold. No navigational problems this time, because if S. the S. doesn't always know where he is or where he's going, he seldom loses sight of where he's coming from.

And the story goes — one of the stories, anyhow — that the old hustler's *last* voyage, undertaken reluctantly indeed on direct orders from Haroun al-Rashīd, was back to Serendib, to deliver a reciprocal gift from the caliph to the island king.

So far, so good: but (here comes *our* story) it wasn't Sindbad the Sailor who made that final voyage. Sindbad the Sailor had no quarrel with the caliph's project, though he'd never before set sail with any motive nobler than restless greed. As he knew from hard experience, however — and will presently declare to his dinner guests, at the end of their monthlong fast — you don't reach Serendib by plotting a course for it. You have to set out in good faith for elsewhere and lose your bearings . . . serendipitously.

Another tempest, another shipwreck, at his age! But one doesn't say no to the Commander of the Faithful.

So: the chap who, late in this story, will set all-but-solo sail sidewise for serendipity will be that *other,* self-styled Sindbad, that nobody whom folks called (for convenience' sake) the Landsman, and he must have got more or less where he was going, or he wouldn't have survived to be telling you Scheherazade's story of his life. But he has never since returned to Baghdad except in dreams. And the chap's real name wasn't Sindbad the Landsman; it was . . . something else. Somebody took that name because then and there, at the time we tell of, he was a streetwise castaway from the Here and Now who happened to know a thing or two about S. the So-Called Sailor, this wealthy Baghdaddy who'd been teasing his guests for a lunar month with hints of his adventures on the bounding main. Rocs, cannibal giants, sea monsters! His audience didn't necessarily believe him, you understand, but whether his exploits were real or not, his wealth was, and likewise his hospitality. He bought the willing suspension of your disbelief with the promise of more where this came from, plus an upcoming banquet of first-rate food and wine to break your fast with. No doubt your several hungers helped his hints reach harbor. True sons of Islam, for the whole of Ramadan you had fasted faithfully, taking only your ritual bowl of barley soup at day's end. Under tonight's new moon you would be fed a feast fit for the Prince of Believers himself.

Trouble was, you had to be a rich friend to get a dinner invitation. In fact, you had to be so rich and friendly that you'd invested money in your host, and that means rich, friend, since old Sindbad had so much of his own that he scarcely needed yours. He would borrow it more to oblige you than to smooth some minor perturbation in his house's cash flow, which flowed on like the Tigris and the Euphrates. Lest you think he *needed* what you pressed upon him, he'd oblige you with half the going interest rate, if you asked for interest at all; the goodwill of Haroun's chief import-export man and de facto emissary to Serendib was usually interest enough for you.

But that's you (let's say), and you're somebody, hacking your harira and not asking too many questions about those big birds and one-eyed giants and diamond coastlines. Never mind what really went on in voyages One through Six, you figure, if the old pirate will let you buy into number Seven: Serendib Limited. Then along this midsummer evening came Somebody Else: Somebody the Nobody (yours truly, in truth), a fifty-plus foreigner in those days with not two pennies in his pocket or a name to his name. When he found the right address, he took a load off his back and sat himself down beside it on a bench before Sindbad's entrance gate with a growing crowd of bona fide beggars, all hoping for a handout when the new moon rose. He was currently pretending to be a poor porter, was our Somebody; with his next-to-last dirham he had rented that load for half an hour from an even poorer porter, now one coin richer, just around the bend.

"Another mouth," his fellows said, looking him over. He was taller than they, less dark of hair and skin and eye: a foreigner, though every bit as lean and, by the look of him (if I may say so), not much less cagey.

"Shush," he said, sniffing the air and cupping his ear toward the gate, the wall, the window overhead.

"Your mother, gharīb," they replied. But they shushed.

Somebody heard from inside the familiar sounds of tambourines, pipes, and mirthful voices, also songbirds glorifying God in sundry tunes and tongues. Through the gate he saw from a familiar distance the familiar courtyard (you're guessing he's been here before), the pages and other servants moving about their service. He smelled the familiar fragrance of harira and the fresh aromas of bastilla, braziered lamb with cumin, newly baked pita, dates and figs both fresh and dried — and like the other beggars', his eyes watered, his empty stomach sang to those perfumes. Raising his face to heaven and his voice to the open windows of what he knew (though he had never yet been in that particular room) to be the banquet hall, he praised Allah's mysterious justice, first in prose and then in verse.

"So be it," the beggars said as one.

Somebody bade again, "Shush."

"Yours."

Noting that the voices in the hall above him had quieted somewhat, he next cleared his throat and sang:

> *We all commence our journey as a little sperm and egg;*
> *Yet some wind up as millionaires, while others have to beg.*
> *Some plot the course and give commands that others must*
>   *obey.*
> *Some live a hundred years; some die before they've lived a*
>   *day.*
> *Some reach safe harbor; some are cast away or lost at sea.*
> *To Allah this makes perfect sense. I wish it did to me.*

"Hear, hear," his companions muttered.

"Shush."

"Yours."

He paused long enough to confirm that the voices inside had gone quite silent, then sang on:

> *The Author of our story understands His story's plot;*
> *We characters can't fathom who's the villain and who's*
>   *not.*
> *A wretch like me might be the hero, from Allah's point of*
>   *view;*
> *But if you were I, milords, you'd wish like me that I were*
>   *you!*

And hearing the murmur of amused curiosity he had hoped for, he concluded high-heartedly:

> *There is no god but God, but there are Sindbads by the*
>   *score;*
> *Praise Him who made that Sindbad rich, and this poor*
>   *Sindbad poor!*

Ignoring his fellows' grudging applause, he then reshouldered, in no hurry, his heavy load (he's trim and tan, hard and healthy, our Somebody is, but fifty-plus is fifty-plus) and, without waiting for his share of scraps, in no hurry made as if to go his way — which would have been back around the corner he had just turned, from where the true poor porter kept a watchful eye upon his leased-out burden. He did not depart so busily, however, that he failed to hear a page coming gateward from the feast to find out for his master what was what. See our man pause now to let the fellow catch sight of him; see him begin to unburden himself even before the expected summons from the gate; see him make with thumb and forefinger a circle at the watching true poor porter and kiss his fingertips at the beggars, who, fearing chastisement, had pointed him out to the page.

Then he barefooted back (once upon a time) in his raggedy loincloth and soiled turban — both torn from a caftan that had been fresh fine linen just the month before, when (unknown to the host) he had last been in Sindbad's house — and made a little bow to the page: "Salaam, Salīm."

Taken aback, the chap asked, "You know my name? I've been sent to learn yours."

"Your errand and mine," Somebody sighed, "are the same." From the crotch of his loincloth then he fetched forth his final dirham, which he thrust first under the page's nose, then into his palm. "Call me Sindbad, lad: Sindbad the Shipwrecked; Sindbad the Simoomed."

"Sindbad the Shusher," one beggar suggested.

Somebody winked. "Sindbad the Lubber of the Land. Lead on, Sayyid Salīm. Don't keep my namesake waiting."

This particular page (Somebody happened to know from direct though distant observation) — a bead-eyed, mocha-skinned, kohl-curled, furtive-faced scamp — was more used to deliveries in the rear from certain of his master's guests than dirhams in the palm from barefoot beggars. But we sense he sensed that this Somebody was something else: he pursed his lips as he pursed the coin, which he had been holding by its edge; he gave his head a toss, this way, and led into the familiar court.

There we pause, as did this second Sindbad, just for a moment, to marvel at the changes wrought in that courtyard since its famous owner's sixth and recentest return. Its centerpiece, a great empty wooden tub, was still in place, but the pools and fountains whose plash our Somebody had savored from his singular retreat were now waterless, filled with sand. Where hibiscus and oleander had flowered through the month of Sha'ban were now cactus and other desert plants. A camel, even, browsed and shat contemplatively midcourt, in the dusty shade of new young date palms. Above and beyond this strange aridity, Somebody espied the latticed window from which, through as sweet a short season as he'd known in his half century, he had first beheld all these.

Nobody home up there. No doubt she was in dutiful attendance at the feast.

On, he motioned to Salīm, who led him then leftward into the wing of old Sindbad's spread where he knew the banquet hall to be, and there it was: richly carpeted and hung like an enormous Bedouin tent; radiant with light from the high windows at which he had pitched his lamentation; furnished forth with inlaid hardwoods and soft embroidered cushions; flanked with servants of every sex and shade, the comeliest of whom now served table or stood by to entertain the guests with music and dancing. These latter fortunates, nine in number, were (Somebody knew) ranked by creditorship in a certain order down both sides of the low banquet board, at the head whereof (on a cushion and a half) sat their portly, silver-bearded and red-silk-turbaned, merry-faced but shrewd-eyed host, Sindbad the Soi-Disant Sailor himself, while just then rising from the foot — or, rather, not rising but making as if to rise and then, catching sight of Salīm's Somebody . . .

Stunned yet unstartled, she sat. Stricken but half smiling, too, she stared. All eyes but his own were on Somebody the Singer, of whose voice she was more certain than of his proper name. His were on hers, and had his been yours (listener, reader, familiar stranger), you would have seen one seriously beautiful woman at the end of her twenties, robed in a scarlet djellaba. She was unveiled, thus presumably unmarried, thus presumably not the old man's young wife. Contrary to custom, she was seated with the all-male company and, though scarcely touching the food and drink before her, bidding the others to set to. Again contrary to general custom, if not to the custom of her father's house (you've guessed she's Sindbad's daughter, the only child of his late and only local wife), she had half risen to greet the stranger whom it had been her father's whim to summon forth, but seeing that he was exactly who she feared he might be yet hoped against hope he was, she recushioned herself. Her hands gripped the low table-edge; her upper body, shrouded in that thick, loose garment, was half turned Somebody's way. In lieu of veil, perhaps, at his approach she'd hooded her head; unlike a veil, that hood now hid her emotion, not from him (and perhaps not from Jaydā, her aging overseer, standing behind old Sindbad, or from the scamp Salīm, just behind Jaydā) but from her father and his guests. From under that hood, from over her right shoulder, from that sun-browned (contrary to custom), uncosme-ticked, so-grave face hooded further in dark lustrous hair, she trans-fixed our man yet again with her perfectly astonishing gray-green eyes, which flashed so in every light that he still found it hard to believe they didn't shine in the dark.

But those eyes were hers, So-and-So's only his, and *he* saw little with them except that brace of marvels, Yasmīn's eyes. She did not even mouth her darling version of his name; she merely regarded, with whole alarm and utter gravity (and just a trace of mischief), his soul.

"By Allah," that soul now said, looking about him with pleased wonder, then back briefly at Yasmīn. "Here is a piece of Paradise, brothers: a slice of Serendib itself, such as I scarcely dreamed I would see again!" Not to sail overclose to that particular wind, he then bore off boldly to the tented table's head, where Salīm was already whis-pering in the master's ear. He kissed the carpet beside who sat there and, having made as it were his narrative move, waited with bowed head to see what this story has next in store for him.

Our setting is a Baghdad evening; we're coming onto an Arabian night. The head of the house, when he was ready to, said, "Rise and sit, stranger. Sit and be washed; be washed and eat with this good company. And when you've eaten and drunk your fill, repeat your name and sing again those verses that took our ear. Yasmīn."

At her dad's low-keyed command, that grave-faced beauty rose from her place and — followed by all male eyes in the room except those of Sindbad, who brightly scrutinized our interloper, and those of that interloper, who dared not look where aimed undeviatingly the compass-needle of his heart — taking a basin from Jaydā, herself knelt before the ragged visitant and washed his hands, all the while transfix-ing him with those hooded eyes of hers. Not even the faithful near the table's head, used though they were to their host's grand gestures, had seen such hospitality lavished upon a nobody. As for Somebody (who, truth to tell, could not have met his washer's gaze again without giv-ing himself away), he raised his eyes in God's presumable direction and repeated, "Surely this is Paradise, or some king's court! I'm only a poor shipwrecked porter, gentlemen, who knows the streets of Baghdad better than I know my name; yet I've made a wrong turn and strayed onto Adam's Peak, or into Heaven itself!"

Then, as he was in fact not fasting but starving, he fell to with the others as directed, seated incredibly in Sindbad's daughter's very place, upon the cushion she had shaped and warmed. The young woman herself stood by and tended his wine cup, which by some magic she was able to fill with her gaze fixed level (and still incredulous) upon his face. The company, while they ate, chatted about their host's hospitality and about his momentous projected voyage, back to that fabulous island which he alone among Baghdad's citizens had both adventured to and returned from, and which, since his return, had become so legendary that even nameless beggars now invoked it.

Presently the fullness of Somebody's stomach approached that of his heart. The host tapped for attention upon a wide, shallow, empty wooden tub immediately behind him, smaller than the great one in the courtyard. Then he ordered slops sent out to the other beggars and with narrowed eyes repeated his request: "Your name, Brother, and your song."

"For that song," our man replied after duly resinging it, "I ask your pardon; for my name I may not. Some while back I was dubbed Sindbad the Shipwrecked by one who found me stranded in the marshes below Basra, where the Shatt al Arab meets the sea. Fate had set me there as naked and nameless as on my birth-day, and not for the first time. A local fisherman kindly gave me mullet chowder to postpone death with, a clean rag to cover my nakedness, a name to be called by, and simple directions to Baghdad: 'Upstream till you're there,' he said, 'where derelicts before you have found good harbor.' Upstream I went, and here for hire I tote others' burdens when they're there to tote. When not, I shoulder my own by begging, as I beg you now to excuse the impertinence of my lament."

He salaamed. The guests approved. "We suspect, Brother Sindbad," declared their host, "that your directions were more particular. But in any case, praise Allah, from whose perspective it's no coincidence that my name is yours and that your fate has more than once been mine." He gestured around the company. "As your song says truly, in Allah's eyes we are Sindbads all, and whether we sail first class or steerage, the same port finally awaits us, every one. Yasmīn."

Without changing either her expression or the direction of her gaze, his daughter topped up every wine cup in the room in a particular order, beginning with her father's and ending with his namesake's. Nor did she spill a drop, though her hand was seen by some to tremble at the end.

"Sindbads all," her father said again, this time by way of a toast. The company drank. "But some perhaps more than others," he went on. "I myself am that Sindbad called the Sailor, after whom your rescuer seems to have named you and to whom I don't doubt he sent you. The Basra boatmen know that my condition hasn't always been as you see it now."

To the company at large he continued, "Six voyages, friends, each harder and more harrowing than the one before, have paid for what I share with you! Six several times I have thought myself sunk and drowned, or cast away beyond hope of rescue! And yet — Allah be praised! — though on every voyage I've lost my whole investment and despaired of my life, I've come back each time to Baghdad more wealthy than the time before. Nowadays the very smell of salt water turns my stomach; the sound of surf, of seamen's chanteys and slatting sails, makes my mouth go dry, my blood turn cold. From past immersions I've become so hydrophobic that I yearn for the desert. I've drained my fountains; I wash only with perfumed oils; I piss into a vessel of sand, so as not to hear the splash. I can't bear even to water my wine. Yet though I'm scarcely dry from my sixth submersion, I must set out a seventh time, old man that I am! Set out once again, and sink and soak . . . Allah preserve me! And preserve me He will, I don't doubt — marinate me in that brine He has seen fit to pickle the earth with. As surely as steam rises and dry wood floats" — again he tapped the tub behind him — "Sindbad will come back up the Tigris older and richer yet, though not a bit happier or more wise."

So moved were the dinner guests by this speech that it seemed to Somebody they could scarcely restrain themselves from putting their purses altogether at their host's disposal. Boldly from the table-end our man called, "Brother Sindbad!" The astonished guests fell silent. "Had you no more than excused my doggerel, I'd have been your debtor! But you have plucked this stranded nobody off the street and wined and dined him beyond his dreams. You've set your own daughter, the flower of Baghdad, to wash and serve me like a houri in Paradise. What right have I to further favor?"

"None," his host affirmed at once, and then amiably gestured for him to continue.

"But as it happens," Somebody said, "*this* Sindbad, too, has sailed six several voyages, though they fetched me not to wealth and peace and joy but to what you see before you: a derelict in even more ways than may appear. For that reason, when I try to conjure a fit finale to such a feast as this, I can imagine nothing better than the tale of your six successes. What entertainment!"

The guests regarded one another, their wine cups, the backs of their hands. Yasmīn carefully regarded Somebody — as (renarrowing his eyes and stroking his beard) did ruddy Sindbad. There was throughout the tented hall a holding of breath. Salīm alone, standing out of his master's view, dared roll his eyes Allahward.

"I had meant to have Kuzia Fakān and her friends amuse us," Sindbad said. He smiled toward two slender, veiled women standing by with pipes and tambours, and a plumper, handsome third — unveiled, black-eyed, barely costumed under her half-opened robe — standing behind them with folded arms and a skeptical expression. "But we Sindbads agree that the only entertainment better than a story is half a dozen stories. The ones you crave, however — which, despite their seasickening aspect, happen to be my very own favorites as well — these patient gentlemen have heard already, in bits and pieces."

Discreet exhalation; sips of wine. But Somebody protested, "What can that matter? A story first heard is a virgin bride, who so takes us with her freshness that we care nothing for her style. A good tale retold is a beloved wife or long-prized lover, whose art we relish because no novelty distracts us. Tell, this beggar begs you: from start to finish, tell, and while these worthies relish your grace notes and flourishes, my worthless ears will hang on the tale's mere melody. Do tell!"

Were the diners polled, Somebody sensed, it would be he who'd hang, not his ears. And from both ends of the table — Sindbad before him, Yasmīn behind — he felt a voltage rise at his mention of brides and mistresses. The old man paused and pondered, glanced particularly at a red-faced, red-bearded, beefy banqueter perspiring immediately to his right, and then with a hand-wave bade the three women sit. The unveiled one (Kuzia Fakān, Somebody happened to know) sniffed and tossed her head. Several gentlemen for several seconds closed their eyes.

But then what the senior Sindbad said was "No: a tale told too often is a jade whose bawdries only postpone sleep." All eyes opened. "Not a man here," he declared, "but has heard me from time to time, through the lean and holy month just now behind us, resail those voyages: my first, to that floating island that was a monstrous fish; my second, to the valley of serpents and diamonds, the island of rocs and rhinoceri; my third, to the mountain of apes and cannibal giants; my fourth, most dreadful of all, to God knows where, where I myself was obliged to deal death or die, and I did not die; my fifth, no easier, to where I was pissed on head to foot by the Old Man of the Sea — ai!"

As on his right hand he ticked off these terrors with his left, Sindbad the Sailor grew finger by finger more distressed; this fifth fetched tears from the teller, nods from the told. "Who can shake him?" Sindbad wept. "I feed him wine to loosen his grip; it loosens his sphincter instead, and once more Sindbad's drowned! I killed him, brothers, but he rides me yet, and night after night I am bepissed! Yasmīn."

But without waiting for her cue, already by the rocs and rhinoceri his daughter had moved himward behind the dinner guests, who dutifully wept with him. As he wiped his eyes now with the red hem of her djellaba, and each guest his own with the sleeve she then offered turn by turn in the same order as the wine, she fixed hers — tearless, smileless, knowing, waiting — upon our upstart second Sindbad, who said now, "The sixth, sir, the sixth: praise be to Allah, who in His mercy follows Five with Six, and will follow Six with Seven!"

"Hum," said Sindbad. The company hummed. "Our virgin listener turns out to be less than virginal."

The company fell silent.

"The fame of Serendib," Somebody said, "and of Sayyid Sindbad's recent visit there, has spread even to Serendib itself. God grant you a dry return from your second going, sir, and a rich return from your rereturning. Sweet Serendib!"

All eyes were on him. Asked Sindbad carefully, "Can it be you've been there?"

His daughter by this time had sleeved all hands' tears save those of Somebody, who had been dry-eyed as herself and beside whom now she resumed her stand. "Where your tales and travels end, sir," he declared, "is where my story in this world begins. Sweet Serendib!"

"You've been there," Sindbad said. He frowned. "Yasmīn: your sleeve for our visitor."

She offered it as bidden but for the first time turned her eyes away.

"More than once," Somebody swore, and under the pretext of dabbing his eyes with it, he kissed that sleeve. "It's from there I came here, though not directly, on my own last voyage but one. And it's to there I would give anything to return, if I had anything to give."

The host fingered his beard. Appraised his wine cup. "On the strength of our common name, Brother, I had planned to give you gold and good-bye. But the story of how you got from Serendib to here is one to which we're virgins all." Again he glanced at the plump young redbeard beside him, then back at his namesake. "Very well, sir: that virginity of ours is yours. Tell your tale, and then we'll have Kuzia Fakān. But look here," he then demanded, "what shall we call you? Not the Shipwrecked; not the Simoomed; not the Survivor: those are me, Allah be praised."

Somebody smiled; Somebody bowed. "Call me Sindbad the Still-Stranded, at your orders."

His reply appeared to please. "Still-Stranded? So are we all! And at my orders? Then I order you, Still-Stranded, to tell us of Serendib, and how you came from there to here."

Somebody said, "With pleasure. It is a tale that involves the house in which I now find myself as well as my long-lost own, to which I pray the telling may return me." To the company at large then he went on: "Know, sirs and ladies, that there are several Serendibs, not one. There are the Serendibs of our childhood, our youth, and our mid-manhood, from each of which I made a voyage and was lost and found. There is the Serendib of late maturity, in very sight of whose Adam's Peak I drowned to the world I'd known. Yet a fifth Serendib there is: the one I next woke to, aboard Sayyid Sindbad's ship *Zahir* (its master's daughter aboard, her father not), which was then captured by the Qeshmi pirate Sahīm al-Layl. . . ."

Before the company's consternation at these names, Still-Stranded paused. His host went turban-red; the red-faced fellow on his right went white. Yasmīn drew the red cowl of her djellaba about her face, and old Jaydā her black one likewise. Only the dancer Kuzia Fakān appeared amused by the general alarm, while the page Salīm (like our narrator) sized up the scene.

"Serendib Six," Somebody said, "is truly where I sit." He patted the silk-embroidered cushion under him and carefully did not glance at its former occupant. "Sweet Serendib, to which I fetched (who knows how?) and where I now find myself still stranded! But sweeter yet, sirs, is the seventh: crossroads between the world of my first four voyages and the world of my latter two, in which, in my flawed but heartfelt Arabic, I speak words like these. *That,*" he declared directly to Sindbad the Sailor, "is the place voyaged to by you and from by me: the Serendib to which we would return."

When the company calmed, disconcerted Sindbad said, "Speak for yourself, Sayyid Still-Stranded. But in so speaking, speak to us, and more plainly. It's not your Arabic that gives us trouble, but your in-direction. Kindly begin at the beginning."

Unabashed, Somebody countered, "Again I pray you, Brother: be-gin at yours, and let me match you voyage for voyage until our twelve voyages become one — to Serendib!"

At that rate, Sindbad observed, there would be neither Kuzia Fakān nor sleep. Since even an Arabian night must come to morning, he counterproposed (weary as he was of all things nautical) that they rehearse their separate voyages one by one, at the rate of one apiece per evening, till it be discovered how they interweaved and ended at their common starting place: right here, right now. Moreover, he in-vited the assembled — in particular the now once more tomato-faced gentleman on his right, but the others as well — to be his dinner guests again and again till those tales were told, for they clearly bade to bear upon business present and to come.

In a tone compact of invitation, command, and threat, Sindbad then proposed to Somebody the Stranger that he strand himself upon his namesake's hospitality until their narratives reached common harbor.

Our man bowed his head slightly and turned up his palms. "So be it. But let Sindbad the Somebody speak before Somebody the Nobody."

The host nodded. "Yasmīn."

Since the mention of *Zahir* and the Qeshmi pirates, Sindbad's daughter had not uncowled her face, but only rocked slightly where

she sat, and where Jaydā now comforted her. At her father's command, however, she put back her hood, wiped her own tears with
the sleeve she had earlier offered the company, and dutifully, with
downcast eyes, refilled the wine cups in the same complicated order as
before: first she served her father, then the young redbeard on his
right, then a very old man at her father's left hand; then she went
down-table to the diner at what had been her own right hand before
Somebody took her place, and filled his cup; after that she served
the man across from him, at Somebody's left; then she moved up
to the man at Redbeard's right, two seats down from Sindbad; then to
the man across from him, two down on her father's left; then to the
man two down from him; then to the man third down on Sindbad's
right; then to the man more or less across from him; and finally to
Somebody the Still-Stranded, at whose left hand, having filled his cup,
she demurely sat.

As she performed this busy service, Sindbad said, "I need not
repeat what all here have heard before — that I first got into the
voyaging-and-trading way because as a young man I squandered in high
living the fortune inherited from my dear father. That when I set out
from Basra on my maiden trading voyage to recoup that fortune with
my fellow merchants, the first island we paused at was no island but a
whale of such enormity and sluggishness that like a dark, luxurious
dream, in the floating ages of his sleep he had grown trees and rocks
and beaches on his back, and had thus disguised himself without intention to deceive. Innocents innocently thus gulled, a party of us
went ashore and strolled as if through Eden. Anon our cookfires
burned through the dream to the dreamer, who, half wakened, dived
for deeper sleep, extinguishing our fires and most of us as well. A few
reached ship; I saved myself in a wooden laundry tub and watched
those luckier comrades panic off without me. Alone then in Allah's
ocean, I quite gave myself up for dead but managed to tub it to another island — which, half eaten though I was by the citizens of the
deep, and desperate for dry land, I would not set foot upon till I saw
campfires burning safely on its beach. Once ashore, I contrived to
become King's Favorite; but as I would not trust myself even then to
the island's interior (lest it prove after all to be but a larger dream,
with a longer waking time), he appointed me his port minister. Never
out of sight of the sea — which, dreadful though it is, is what it is — I

dreamed my own dreams in a small boat moored in the harbor, my lines always singled up for quick departure, my Tub of Last Resort ever at my side, and spent my waking hours aboard the larger vessels clearing customs. Either this island was real or this whale a sounder sleeper, for when one day, like a dream redreamed, my original vessel called at that port — and I persuaded its captain that I was Sindbad the erstwhile Sailor, and reclaimed and sold my goods, and returned to Basra enriched both by my profits and by a good-bye present from my friend the king — I left his sea-girt kingdom as fixed as I'd found it.

"From this maiden voyage, my friends, I learned four things." He tapped his tub with his left hand, from which our man now observed that parts of two fingers were missing. "That some shores may be less solid than the sea. That a dream long dreamed may grow a real geography, unsuspected by the dreamer, and that we who therethrough wander wake such dreamers at our peril. That the castaway who would become King's Favorite must first not only abandon hope but feed a portion of himself to his ultimate devourers. Finally, that he who would regain his lost goods does well to become registrar of cargoes. Yasmīn."

Through a chorus of approval, Sindbad's daughter made her complex rounds, recomposed enough now to suspend Somebody's soul once more in her sea-green gaze. The company's attention moved with her (all but Redbeard's; he was recounting Sindbad's lessons on four fat fingers) and thus ended upon our narrator, Still-Stranded. . . .

Who, in his odd but not unfluent tongue, now told a version of the tale of

Somebody's First Voyage

Once upon a time I was twins; my other half didn't quite make it into this world.

I remember her.

Like many another solitary though not unhappy child, young Simon William Behler invented playmates. "Bijou" especially, with her tidewater eyes. We two had long conversations, high adventures; no doubt they've colored my memory from this distance. But we were together back there, more or less conscious through the last trimester, and my kid sister (I've never thought of her otherwise) was game for anything. In our liquid world we slid and turned like a brace of young otters. We even told stories — I did, anyhow — about what we imagined was going on: what was out there, who we were, who *they* were. In these tales of adventure, love, and mystery there was no *Once upon a time*. Our language had no tenses. My stories were perhaps no more than a rendition of what took place.

In the last of them, Bijou and I make ready for what four decades later will be called Extravehicular Activity. The pressure's on. We know it's risky, this shift from one world to another; we're edgy but eager.

A comradely last hug; then I thrust myself headfirst into the Passage. My faithful friend and audience is right behind me. See you there, Bijou! Two. One.

He awoke in the strange though familiar bedroom of his older brother, Joseph "Joe Junior" Behler, in the family house in East Dorset, Maryland. Sunday morning, July 1, 1937: Simon W. Behler's seventh birthday.

Bijou's, too.

"Familiar" because our parents had lived in that house since before we were born; "strange" because the night just past was the first I had slept in my brother's room. Today they would bring Mother home: my birthday present, Aunt Rachel said. (Bijou's, too.) But she was still too sick to sleep in her and Dad's room, and so yesterday Dad and Uncle Josh had moved my twin bed back into Joe Junior's room. Today we would move the rest of my things, and Mother would take the spare twin.

Neither my brother nor I was happy with this arrangement. Joe Junior was thirteen and wanted privacy; I was used to rocking myself to sleep and talking to Bijou. But it was for Mother's sake, and just for a while.

Those twin habits of mine, however, were of long standing and not easily put by. I rocked on my left side; all my pajama tops wore through at the right shoulder from friction against the bedsheets. When I was mostly awake, talking quietly to my sister or telling our stories in my head, I had a way of rocking that made nearly no noise. But as sleep took over, sometimes I would rev up enough to set springs and bed-frame going. On the door between her and Uncle Josh's room and mine (and Bijou's), Aunt Rachel would tap "Shave and a haircut" — tap tata tap-tap — and say, "Sy?"

"*Okay*," I'd answer. Wearily. For a while then I would lie still, and sometimes fall asleep without further movement. But well into my teens I woke up rocking. What would I do, I used to wonder, when I had college roommates? When I had a wife right in bed with me?

Now my brother said, "Quit rocking." Joe Junior's room had an odd rank smell, not sweat not dirt not garbage. Matter-of-factly he declared, "You got to quit that now, big baby," and added in a singsong, "Happy birthday to you happy birthday to you happy birthday dear Simon happy birthday to you. Amen."

The room was hung with his flying model airplanes, rubber-band-powered, their hand-razored balsa frames painstakingly tissued, doped, decaled. Testors glue and banana oil were part of the smell, but not all of it. Spad, Fokker triplane, Flying Jenny, Ryan trainer, and my favorite: Stinson Reliant, with its ring of nacelle blisters around the navy-blue engine cowling. An airplane pilot was what I was going to be.

He went down to breakfast with the family.

On weekends the black and chrome breakfast table was moved mid-kitchen from its nook to make room for the six of us, lately five. Dad and Uncle Josh, at its ends, were deep into the *Baltimore Sunday Sun,* cigarettes, coffee. Dad and Aunt Rachel smoked Camels; Uncle Josh, Chesterfields in a black holder. The men tapped their ashes into smears of corn syrup on their willowware plates, Aunt Rachel hers into the sink beside which she worked. My uncle came to Sunday breakfast pajamaed and robed: with his silvering hair and rimless bifocals, jaunty chin and cigarette holder, he looked like his hero, President Roosevelt, especially when he tipped back his head to laugh or focus on the newspaper. Our father always came down fully dressed except for his suit coat, whether by personal inclination or because as a town councilman and volunteer fireman as well as a businessman, he was much summoned from the house. Even on hot summer weekends Dad wore his suits, white shirts, solid-color neckties; I had never seen him in short sleeves, much less swim trunks or pajamas. The front section of the *Sun* was reserved for him; I knew they were on their second coffee because he was reading the "Maryland" section. He folded it neatly twice the long way, as Aunt Rachel told us New York City subway riders do, so as not to take up more than their share of space. Our father was lean and tall and bald, long of nose and ears and fingers, hard-of-hearing from a condition that made his nose run always, and farsighted. Without his reading glasses, he liked to say, he couldn't make out a headline at arm's length, but street signs and license plates he could read from half a block away.

Our kitchen was the family's pride and a showpiece of our business: ample and modern, fluorescent-lighted, chrome-and-leatherette-furnitured, replete with white cabinets and appliances, black imitation tile halfway up the walls, a black-and-white checkerboard floor of genuine rubber squares that any careless motion of our sneakers marked, a nonticking electric wall clock with a red sweep second hand, and, beside it, a built-in fan to carry off cooking odors and cigarette smoke. When Joe Junior and I came in, Aunt Rachel was scouring one of the stainless-steel countertops with Bon Ami cleanser, by which she swore. On its red and yellow label are a newly hatched chick and the company's motto: *Hasn't scratched yet*. My brother liked to ask her, "Yet?" Aunt Rachel would make a show of examining the countertop closely before answering, "Not yet!"

There was a strong family resemblance among the Behlers, which skipped my brother but passed to me. With her ears lengthened even further by dangling rings, her dark hair braided and terry-turbaned, her lank form robed in plum satin, my aunt looked to me like a Gypsy lady or a Turk. Tap tata tap-tap, went the near-empty can of cleanser; "Happy b-day, Simon B.!" called out Aunt Rachel, and with Bon Ami in one hand and sponge in the other, she came around the table to kiss me seven times in the hair. Joe Junior availed himself of that opportunity to whale me seven good ones across the backside plus one for luck and one to grow on. "Not too hard there, Joey," said amused Uncle Josh around his cigarette holder, and my father, "Happy birthday, son."

"Bijou, too," I reminded them, not insistently. My brother groaned. My uncle returned to his newspaper. My aunt said, "You're the birthday boy," in a tone meant at once to humor and gently to reprove. My father didn't hear.

Birthday or not, Joe Junior had First Goods on the funnies, to catch up on Buck Rogers and Flash Gordon. The scorchings on the egg-yellow field of my French toast made a false-color map of our tidewater county, whose labyrinth of salt-marsh necks and islets, creeks and coves and guts and tidal meanders, had harbored escaped slaves before the Civil War, bootleggers during Prohibition, and moonshiners even yet, Dad declared, in the hard times that were upon our nation.

The talk at table — as my brother and I ate and Aunt Rachel cooked, served, scrubbed, sometimes even sat, sipping coffee all the while and lighting one Camel after another — was of the current, sometimes violent strike at the Albany Brothers canneries, whose workers were protesting their employer's ban on national labor unions. My family's sentiments were mixed: my father — who had been a carpenter's helper for *his* father and then an appliance delivery-man and repairman for Sears and Roebuck before opening his own little shop and gradually expanding it into Behler Maintenance & Improvement — thought the Albanys were entitled to their motor yachts and large waterfront houses; for "Captain Philip" Albany, our only native millionaire, he was proud to have done the most elaborate kitchen cabinetry to be found outside the more imposing downriver estates of minor Du Ponts and Chryslers. The striking workers were biting the hand that fed them; better to take pay cuts in these lean times, if necessary, than to shut down the plant to protest layoffs and call for even higher wages. The unions were killing the goose that laid the golden eggs. It was all the fault of outside organizers.

Uncle Josh, born and raised across the Chesapeake, in Baltimore, had himself been laid off as a bookkeeper at Maryland Drydock and therefore took a less benevolent view of Albany Brothers and their product, Dorset Brand vegetables and seafood. But in his earlier life he had been variously a merchant seaman, a groundskeeper for a fancy golf club, and an assistant purser on an ocean liner. Aunt Rachel had met him in that last capacity on a trip to London, England, with some girlfriends before the Depression. Though the couple had been obliged to give up their city apartment and move in with us till times improved, Uncle Josh played golf and hunted wild geese and went on fishing trips when not bookkeeping and estimating for Behler Maintenance & Improvement and tending bar on weekends for the Chaptico Country Club. We regarded him as something of a sport: a good-natured dependent whose opinions were indulged like his black cigarette holder, his bright bow ties, his maroon Nash coupe and deer-skin driving gloves. He subscribed to *National Geographic* and *Field and Stream.*

Aunt Rachel was the family favorite. Her service as a Red Cross nurse in England during the world war and as a registered nurse at Union Memorial in Baltimore afterward, her return visit not only to England but to France as well in the Roaring Twenties, her marriage to a city man and their residence in a city apartment building rather than a house with porch and yard, even her and Uncle Josh's childless-ness — all gave her the aura of an adventuress in our eyes. She and Mother "got on famously," as Aunt Rachel liked to say, and it was

well that they did, for Dad's business, his deafness, and his involvement in civic affairs left him little time or taste for recreation beyond
our ritual Sunday drives. Every day he read the morning and evening
editions of the *Baltimore Sun,* also the *Philadelphia Bulletin* and the
Dorset Daily Democrat, and on Sundays the *Philadelphia Inquirer* and
the *New York Times.* He was concerned about Benito Mussolini and
Adolf Hitler, and likewise about the New Deal, for which there was
much to be said but which went too far. After dinner with the family
he was off to town-council or fire-company meetings, or responding
to the fire calls themselves at all hours, or scouting more contracts for
Behler Maintenance & Improvement, whose business had so declined
with the decade that only our repairs department kept us afloat. Or,
still dressed in white shirt and tie, on weekends he would rake leaves,
simonize our black LaSalle, mix unslaked lime to spray the caterpillars
on our Chinese Cigar trees. But Aunt Rachel made even grocery shopping an adventure: she and Mother used to go off in the maroon Nash
like chuckling conspirators and return laughing with baskets of canteloupes they'd talked down the price of at some roadside stand, baked
goods from a church benefit, saltwater taffy for Joe Junior and me
(and Bijou) from a State Hospital raffle. Older than Dad, she freely
teased him for his stick-in-the-mudhood, and thus we learned that he
was a stick-in-the-mud. Before Mother took sick, the two women had
played double solitaire, even contract bridge with Uncle Josh and a
fourth from among Aunt Rachel's nurse friends down the street at
Dorset General. Despite our father's standing in the community, he
and Mother never entertained or went socially to others' houses, only
to Democratic bull-roasts and fire-company ham-and-oyster suppers.
Uncle Josh and Aunt Rachel, on the other hand, went almost weekly
to dinner at friends' houses (invitations that, I realized much later,
they were in no position to return), to the movies at Schine's Bijou
Theatre with Mother and us, to Ocean City for the day. They even
went dancing at the country club on Uncle Josh's occasional Saturday
nights off from bartending. Though he was not a regular member, he
was on all-but-equal terms with the membership, who by and large
were not socially superior to him and Aunt Rachel, only more fortunate economically. Those minor Du Ponts and Chryslers belonged to
other clubs, elsewhere.

In her amused and scoffing tone Aunt Rachel declared that strike or no strike, the union didn't have a Chinaman's chance on the Eastern Shore of Maryland, which still considered itself deep Dixie and would have nothing to do with anything Union.

"Rachel," our father said.

No, really: she knew East Dorset people who wouldn't be caught dead in Union Memorial Hospital, just because of its name. And had we ever heard of a union organizer from Richmond or Charleston? she asked Joe Junior and me. Of course not: they were all from Pittsburgh or worse, and it was time for us to get out of our pj's and off to Sunday school.

His family was indifferent to religion. Except that Dad, perhaps out of civic-spiritedness, went regularly to men's Bible class at East Dorset Zion Meth-Prot while we boys attended Sunday school. But we "went to church" only on special occasions, did not say mealtime grace or bedtime prayers, and never spoke of God, Jesus, the soul, the hereafter. Probably we thought that Uncle Al, mustard-gassed in Belgium in 1918, waited to rejoin us up there somewhere, meanwhile looking after Bijou. But our disposition was entirely secular. Joe Junior and his buddies spent their Sunday-school hour teasing girls, twisting the words of the hymns, and making plans for the interval between the 10:50 benediction and our one-o'clock Sunday dinner. I myself took more interest in the exotic but vaguely depressing world of the illustrated lessons — camels and palm trees, figs and dates and anointing-oil, sandals, robes, unbarbered hair and beards — than in the strange agonies and paradoxical imperatives of the lessons themselves, presided over by cheerful matrons of the neighborhood: *Whoso loseth his life shall find it,* and the rest. *Let the lower lights be burning,* we sang together at the end:

> *Send a gleam across the wave.*
> *Some poor sinking, suff'ring seaman*
> *You may rescue, you may save.*

Joe Junior and his friends changed *sinking* to *stinking,* adding the *t* just lightly enough to escape detection. Since boats and beacons, unlike palms and camels, were the daily furniture of our tidewater lives, I wondered as always why the hymnist called for lower rather than higher lights. A forward range light, perhaps — but in that case, why more than one lower light? It was only a hymn, Mrs. Travers explained.

In the ten-minute break between Sunday school and church, as others mingled and chatted in the steamy shade of maples out on the bright sidewalk, my brother's gang and I made our way back along Maryland Avenue to Maple Street, past rows of crabfat-yellow clapboard houses, mean but tidy. I hurried ahead to say hi to Mother. But though the rest of my bedroom furniture had been moved, she had not. The fire-company ambulance had been called to a drowning up by the Chaptico River bridge; its crew had not yet delivered the victim to Dorset General, whence they would drop off Mother en route back to the firehouse.

Good: we would get to see the flashing red Cadillac stop importantly before our porch, perhaps with siren purring. Aunt Rachel guessed not: Mother's homecoming had been scheduled for when most of the neighborhood and family were at Zion because she disliked being the center of attention. We boys were to change clothes now and go off to play until dinnertime, as usual; Mother would be waiting for us when we came back.

What was usual for my brother was not so for me and Bijou; *we* usually played in our room, ours no more, or about the yard, or, at farthest, along the seawall before Dorset General, at the end of our street, where I skipped flat stones and oyster shells, narrated to my invisible sister (in third-person italics, I would later come to understand), and looked for washed-up bottles with messages. Joe Junior's gang played on the Island, in the mouth of Island Creek, over by the other hospital. I was a compliant child, but I resisted Aunt Rachel's suggestion that today I go with Joe Junior, who I knew didn't want my company, either. My Ingersoll Mickey Mouse watch — a gift from the family one birthday past — kept good time; moreover, this was supposed to be my day. Why could I not seawall it alone and promise not to come home before a quarter till one?

"'Cause you'll snoop," my brother declared matter-of-factly, having arrived in time for this question.

"Will not!"

Normally then we'd have Will/Will-notted, Will/Will-notted until either we were shushed by authority or one or the other of us tired of the contest. Today, however, far from carrying on his taunt or objecting to my company, Joe Junior agreeably offered as part of my birthday present to take me riding on his Silver King, his own birthday gift from the whole family two months past.

I perched sidesaddle on the crossbar, and we labored up Maple and down Maryland. My brother stood on the pedals to get his one-geared bicycle up to speed — hot work on a still tidewater forenoon in July — but then drove the two of us without difficulty across our gradeless neighborhood. First stop was the foot of Bridge Avenue, where the two-mile Chaptico River highway bridge linked our poor salt-marsh county to its drier, more prosperous northern neighbor, to check out the drowning. Despite the stinging sea nettles that infested the estuary after June, this was East Dorset's bathing place: the narrow brown beach had been widened with dredge-spoil from Dorset Creek, and a stretch of it was shaded by the bridge. The river bottom was firm and mostly weedless. The agile could scramble onto and dive from the concrete piling bases; the daring — in defiance of clearly posted prohibition — used the bridge itself, some twenty feet above the surface at the eighth piling out, a doubler.

This Freddie Mulligan had done, one of Joe Junior's friends told us, and had not been seen to surface. His older sister Mary had gotten hysterical; someone had run to the nearest house and telephoned the fire company; the ambulance had been dispatched before Freddie appeared from behind the *ninth* piling, to which he had swum underwater to alarm his friends. There being no two-way radio for such purposes in those days, the ambulance crew could not be recalled. By when they reached the scene, scared Freddie had bolted; no one believed his protestations that he had been only resting out there, not hiding.

"A hiding's what he'll get," my brother and Andy Travers agreed, chuckling soberly. I concurred, feeling truly older to be in on the conversation. "And I know where he's hiding till he gets it," Joe Junior added. Andy Travers exclaimed, "Hey, yeah!" and asked were we going there now.

Tapping a forefinger on my head, my brother said, "Directly," which meant the opposite.

He and I went then, not on up the rivershore to Island Creek and the Island, but up Bridge Avenue, the county's only stretch of four-lane highway, toward Albany Brothers, to have a look at the strike.

The word *pickets,* lately much spoken in our house, I associated with the fenced camps of migrant Negroes who picked tomatoes all summer for Albany Brothers, but the ones we saw now outside the first cannery building, standing in dungareed groups or walking up and down with placards, were white men. I was thrilled and frightened: the pickets had beaten workers and truckdrivers who had tried to cross their lines (I envisioned a literal line on the ground, such as East Dorset schoolboys drew for certain challenges); they had in turn been attacked by Captain Philip Albany's guards, and some of them arrested by the state police. Joe Junior had already broken a family rule by riding his Silver King on the dual highway; I thought we should not also go close to the pickets.

My brother mildly replied, "Big baby," and pedaled us right along the highway shoulder opposite them. UNFAIR, their placards read. One of the pickets called to us across the road, "Not carrying any tomatoes on there, are you?" "No sirree!" I called back. I could see no line on the ground.

At Washington Street we turned right, at Dorset Avenue right again, winding among cannery buildings on both sides of those streets. The most pickets were at the main plant entrance, but as it was Sunday, not much was happening there. On the Dorset Avenue wall of one particular building, however, was a machine we called the Lifter, which in peak season we sometimes saw in action even on Sundays, on our afternoon family drives. The device was no more than a vertical conveyor for carrying cases of Dorset Brand from truckbeds to the upper story of the warehouse, but we always pressed Dad to drive by to "check the Lifter," to see whether it was working and, if it was, to stop the black LaSalle for a minute so we could watch the cartons rise and disappear inside the building. "Watch now," I would instruct Bijou. Once in a while the loaders' rhythm lapsed and an empty riser would appear among its loaded neighbors like a missing tooth. Then we would proceed.

That we could now ourselves go check the Lifter, on Joe Junior's Silver King, seemed to me a prodigious, adult freedom.

"Hey, hot dog!" To pump us back up to cruising speed after turning from Washington onto Dorset, my brother was standing on the pedals again, and so saw before I the overturned tomato truck surrounded by pickets at the foot of the idle Lifter. Like a gutted elephant it lay on its side in the hot sunshine, its ripe load hugely spilled and stinking. Squashed early tomatoes flooded the macadam from shoulder to shoulder; baskets both shattered and intact were scattered everywhere. The truck's windshield panes, we saw as we approached, were smashed into twin webs of cracks, like the eyes of comic-strip characters stunned or killed. Pickets milled among the mess, some gingerly, others heedlessly.

"Pee-yew!" Joe Junior and I agreed. Two brown-and-yellow state police cars idled on the far side, flashers flashing. Some altercation was going on, either among the pickets or between them and the troopers; both seemed to be struggling with a man who wielded his UNFAIR sign like a bat till other pickets wrested it from him and yet others pinioned his thrashing arms and legs. Except in the movies at Schine's Bijou, I had never seen grown men fight. My blood surged; I hoped the struggler would be arrested, so that I could tell my parents and aunt and uncle (and kid sister) that I had seen a man arrested. But the state troopers seemed interested only in clearing the avenue for traffic. We saw a tow truck rounding the corner some blocks down.

"Neat-o!" I wanted to watch the dead truck be righted, but Joe Junior was eager to tell his friends what we'd seen. Several times between the Lifter and the creek he even used the term *we*: "Don't tell Dad and Aunt Rachel we rode up Bridge Avenue, you hear? Tell 'em we stayed on side streets and never got close."

I promised and let my fancy embellish the role of kid brother. We would exchange confidences from bed to bed; Joe Junior would advise and stick up for me.

On Island Point, the sandspit where Island Creek meets the Chaptico, we parked the Silver King in reeds and, as my brother's friends had not arrived, threw oyster shells for a while. The cupped bottom shells skipped more times across the still surface of the creek; the flatter upper ones could be sailed straight up into the air, almost out of sight if you had a good arm, and would slice back into the water with no splash, just a kind of *shck*. A good skipper made five, seven, eleven touchdowns before it sank, leaving a row of spreading rings progressively smaller and closer together. Joe Junior could sail the nearly flat shells, inside down, clear over to the small wooded island halfway across the creek mouth. This he did, to learn whether his friends had swum over there already.

They had not, or they were playing possum like Freddie Mulligan, so he gave me the next part of my birthday present: another secret to be kept from the family (except Bijou), like our having biked right up Bridge Avenue. I would never be old enough to join their club, whose name was known only to its members, because Joe Junior and his friends would keep on being six years older until they grew tired of the club and disbanded it. But under oath of secrecy he revealed to me three of their initiations and demonstrated the first. Unbuttoning his fly and fishing forth his pee-tom, he wrote his name on the sand with pee in two-foot block capitals, J-O-E B-E-H-L-E-R, and had enough left to underline it. I was astonished.

"That keeps girls out," he declared, and with little knee-dips he joggled his writing equipment back into place as he rebuttoned. "Do yours."

Dismayed, I protested, "Mine's longer."

"Like fun it is!" He was fortunately so taken with this joke that instead of insisting on my performance, he explained that Freddie Mulligan, for example, had been allowed to do his in smaller letters; even so, they called him Mullig because he hadn't managed his AN. Anyhow, JOE was longer than SY, ha ha.

The second initiation could be done only on an ebbing tide, and just now the water was slack. On the nuthouse side of the Island was an oarless, abandoned old skiff that would still just barely float if you bailed it constantly. Any aspiring member of the club was set adrift in midafternoon on the outgoing tide, facedown in the bottom of that skiff with nothing but a rusty quart tomato can, one side flattened, for a bailer. He had to go where the gentle current took him, bailing as necessary but neither sitting up to see where he was nor calling for rescue until the sun set behind Turkey Point, downriver. So far, either wind or countercurrents had set every candidate ashore not long after the skiff passed under the Chaptico bridge (the initiate's only landmark), half a mile downstream. My brother himself claimed to have been carried to the Dorset General seawall and the foot of our own street. But he believed that if you got yourself fetched as far out as the channel buoys, nearly a mile from either shore, the tide would never bring you to land; you would drift up and down the Chaptico without food or water until some other boat rescued you. And Mullig believed that beyond Turkey Point the current strengthened and would carry you right out into the bay and down to the Atlantic Ocean like a message in a bottle, and good-bye. They'd find your bones washed up in Portugal.

I was impressed but skeptical. How did a person know, without peeking, exactly when the sun went down?

"You can *tell,* dumbbell. Hey!" My brother was much pleased with his unintended rhyme. "And you know why I went the farthest? 'Cause I'm a natural-born *bailer!* Get it?"

I skipped a shell. "How do you get the rowboat back to the Island? I bet there isn't even any rowboat."

Twisting my arm up behind my back, he invited me to reconsider that bet: "Is there or not, big baby?" But taunt and torture alike were edgeless, a half-attended reflex; my brother was more interested in the club's third initiation, a swimming test.

"You get stripped and blindfolded, all right? And we walk you out by the red day beacon till you're up to your chin. Then you have to swim fifty strokes out — real strokes, not baby strokes, and we count 'em off from shore. Then you have to somersault twice underwater and spin around three times when you come up. *Then* you have to swim a hundred strokes before you take your blindfold off, unless you touch bottom first. If you look to see which way you're going, you're out."

The idea was to watch the disoriented novice swim off in the wrong direction and have to wade or swim naked all the way back. Andy Travers, who had told us of Freddie Mulligan's faked drowning, had swum bare-assed into a throng of girls bathing off a small beach halfway down toward the bridge. Mullig himself had come ashore upriver, at the nuthouse, right in front of the Violent building, where signs said NO BATHING OR BOATING FROM THIS BEACH. As for Joe Junior, he had raised his blindfold at the permitted time to find himself well out in midriver, and what with the tide and the sea nettles, he had darn near not made it back to the Island. I could try it now if I wanted to, closing my eyes in lieu of a blindfold and stopping at a couple dozen strokes, since I was little and this wasn't a real initiation. I needn't even strip naked; the thing was, it was neat not to know which way was home.

"I can do a hundred easy," I declared, "and then some." This was the best ordeal I'd ever heard of, and sea nettles or no sea nettles, it was a rare East Dorset child who was not at home in that warm green water.

"Not *three* hundred, you can't," my brother reminded me: the distance out and back, should I go the wrong way, plus the distance to and from my starting point. Besides, who wanted to wait for me that long?

"Fifty, then," I proposed, already boldly stripping to my jockey shorts. "It's my birthday."

Since it was my birthday, Joe Junior replied, I ought to swim in my birthday suit, ha ha. But fifty strokes only, from the starting place; he had a club meeting to go to. Still feeling kid-brotherly, I decided to take his joke as a dare. I folded my khaki pants and blue polo shirt and left them atop my sneakers in the reeds beside his Silver King; then, having waded out waist-deep on the shoal toward the red day beacon without spotting serious sea nettles, I shucked off my undershorts, squeezed them into a dripping ball, and pitched them shoreward.

"No tricks," I demanded. Joe Junior said back, "No tricks your own self. Keep your eyes closed, or it doesn't count." I was gratified to see him step out of his shoes and pants to retrieve my shorts from the shallows and stand watch: my idea of an older brother. It was my first time naked in the river; though I worried about nettle stings on my pee-tom, the free flow about my hairless crotch and cleft was interesting. At the chin-deep point — only halfway to the red day beacon just now, as the tide was in — I stood on tiptoe and called "Two! One! Zero!"

Joe Junior, down to his own jockey shorts, stood knee-deep holding mine. He waved me on and strode ashore. I was pleased to hear him shouting the count as I swam half a hundred easy strokes out into the river.

The overall salinity of the Chesapeake estuarine system, Uncle Josh had once remarked at our dinner table, is the same as that of human tears. Its waters therefore never sting the eyes, as do those of the ocean or a freshwater lake or a swimming pool. We children had never swum in lake or pool, but it was true that at Ocean City we had to close our eyes when we ducked under a wave, whereas in the Chaptico we always swam and dived with eyes open. To swim out now blind was disconcerting, even a bit alarming — to reach my starting mark and know only from my brother's distant voice (and from what sense remained of my initial bearing) which way was landward.

At fifty, as I treaded water, he called out, "Okay! Two somersaults and three turnarounds!"

The underwater somersaults alone, while easily executed, were enough to remove any lingering sense of direction; it took me a moment after the second one even to determine which way was up. The three subsequent turnarounds were approximate as well as redundant; since Joe Junior now said nothing to give away his position, I had no way of knowing when a rotation was completed. And it was, as he had promised, gratifyingly scary then to strike out in the dark, so to speak — dark green, as it seemed behind my tight-closed eyelids — for all I knew right out toward the distant draw and trestles of the Chaptico bridge.

Nevertheless, I narrated silently to my sister, *young Simon Behler swam on, determined not to stop and open his eyes at fifty strokes but to swim on and on until his hands or feet touched bottom, even if he had to swim all the way across to Avon County.* Which, in fact, I intended to do as soon as I was old enough to get my parents' permission and arrange for someone with a boat to stand by. Nobody I'd heard of had ever swum the Chaptico at Dorset, either nonstop or resting on the bridge piers from time to time, but already by my seventh summer (eighth, if you counted 1930 as my first) I was so able a swimmer and so effortless a floater — a regular muskrat, Aunt Rachel called me — that I felt sure I could go on all day, swimming and resting by turns, without touching bottom.

At forty-two or -three strokes, however, my left hand touched soft mud. I veered right, thinking to make my way as if accidentally back into deeper water and on. But then my right hand touched, and something brushed my leg. I jerked away reflexively, fearing sea nettles; my foot felt bottom. I had swum into weedy shallows and had no idea now which way was out. So as not to embarrass myself as Andy Travers had done, I opened my eyes and found myself disappointingly near my starting place: inshore, just a bit downriver from the day beacon. Joe Junior was nowhere in sight: around the point, maybe.

His uncanny homing instinct, I reported to Bijou, *had guided young Behler back almost to where he had started.* Taking care to remain waist-deep, I swam and waded across the shoal. Nobody to be seen along the creek mouth or over on the Island, but now I saw other bicycles stashed beside the Silver King, other piles of shoes and clothing beside Joe Junior's and mine.

Instead of coming ashore, I recrossed the shoal to where I had first touched bottom, and fooled around for a while there in the tepid water. Eyes open, I did the facedown dead-man's float, regarding my murky arms and legs, my pendant pee-tom, white on green. Then I floated on my side, one eye above the surface, one below: different worlds. Holding on to a waterlogged tree limb on the bottom, I imagined myself seized by a giant South Seas clam, unable to surface, and tried to see how long I could make myself stay under.

There was an indentation in the shoreline nearby and likewise in the stand of tall spartina behind the pebbled beach, which, being leeward of the northwesterly storm winds, was strewn with driftwood. At the one-foot depth the bottom was smooth clay and mossy flat stones, pleasant to lie prone upon, propped on my forearms, amphibian. From within the indentation I could see neither bridge nor day beacon nor — I realized with a little thrill — any other sign of human habitation. There were no cans or bottles on the beach, no boats out on the Chaptico, no channel buoys in sight, and the wooded farther shore from where I sat now, cross-legged in the wavelets stirred by a light new breeze, was unbroken by fields or houses.

A desert shore. I had tucked my wristwatch into my sneakers for safekeeping, and I wore no ring or other ornament; when I boldly now stood and walked ashore, I was as truly and completely naked as the beach itself. *Only by S. W. Behler's short haircut might an observer have guessed that he was a twentieth-century American boy.* But there was no observer.

Ensconced in my cove of reeds, I sat on the smooth beach pebbles, resting my back against a half-buried driftwood tree trunk. While racing Amelia Earhart across the Pacific, Bijou and I had developed engine trouble; our Stinson Reliant had gone down in shark-infested waters near an uncharted tropic isle. I had stripped off my flight suit, plunged into the clear lagoon, and, calling to my kid sister to follow me, by sheer good fortune reached shore unscathed. The sky was cloudless, brilliant. There was not a sound besides the rustle of spartina on three sides and the wavelets' soft lapping before me. The little breeze moved sweetly on my drying skin.

Where was I? Languorously I fiddled with my crotch; found myself; let my hand remain there. Slowly, experimentally, I retracted the foreskin of my pee-tom, exposing the pink gland like a thumb-tip through a driving glove.

Promptly from over my left shoulder came a rising howl: the East Dorset fire siren, loud for its distance, followed a moment later by the chorus of its counterparts in our town's other wards. It achieved and sustained a single note that went on and on, then subsided to a growl and then to nothing: the noon whistle, against which I often checked my Ingersoll. But today was Sunday, and by now it was past noon. Another ambulance call, then.

I found myself again.

Surrounded by used white handkerchiefs on the screen-porch glider, Dad was reading a section of the Sunday *Times*. Aunt Rachel was at work in the kitchen; Uncle Josh was off in the maroon Nash but would be back soon. I hurried upstairs through the odors of roast chicken and cigarette smoke to see Mother.

She was propped on pillows in the spare twin, wearing a light bedjacket over her nightgown despite the heat. She looked sick, all right, and the room smelled different. She had her glasses on — I used to think she looked prettier with them on, like a pretty schoolteacher — but the magazine section of the *Times* was lying beside her on the bedsheet, open to the untouched crossword puzzle. On my maple nightstand were a small white enameled basin, a box of Kleenex, and a pencil for the puzzle. My wastebasket had been set in front of the nightstand; quite a few used Kleenexes were in it already, and a couple more were on the floor beside it.

"Mother's *so* tired," she said after we had carefully hugged and kissed and she had wished me a happy birthday. "She wasn't able to go shopping for you this year."

That was okay, I told her. The powder on her cheeks was thicker than she used to wear it; you could see it caked on, as if new powder had been put right on top of old. I sat on the edge of the spare twin, holding her wrist as she held mine. On hers was still the name-bracelet from the hospital.

"Is Joe Junior home?"

"He's coming."

He and I would have fun in the back bedroom together, she assured me. Would I promise her, now that I was seven, to try not to rock in bed?

I promised.

She really was tired. We didn't say anything else for a while. Presently, however, I asked her whether she could tell me something about my sister.

"Your sister!" She laughed a little, in her chest, and that made her cough, and she had to spit into a Kleenex and close her eyes and lie back against the small headboard. "There's nothing to tell, honeybun. She didn't quite make it into this world, is all." She considered. "We called her BeeGee, for Baby Girl Behler, 'cause she didn't live long enough to get a real name. Then you took to calling her Bijou after Schine's uptown."

Those things I knew. "Was she born alive and then died, or born dead?"

Mother had squeezed my wrist while she coughed; now she patted my forearm. "Some of both, I guess. Once in a while it happens that a baby gets hung up being born, and that's what happened to little B. G. Behler."

I had more questions, but Mother was so tired, and I heard my brother taking the steps two at a time, calling "Mom?" Anyhow, I had learned a considerable piece of news.

I should have *told* him I was going home, Joe Junior complained as soon as he saw me; he'd had to go looking all over the Eastern Shore of Maryland for me. How could I have told him when he was over on the Island with his club? I could have left a note on his Silver King, for pity's sake. Well, it so happened I didn't carry a pencil and paper around with me. Then I should have written it on the *sand*, for pity's sake.

Mother whispered, "Boys."

I went down to help Aunt Rachel set the dining-room table and asked her what made a baby die being born. "Now *there's* a nice Sunday-dinner question!" she scoffed, in her way, but then she explained while stirring gravy that sometimes the belly-button cord gets twisted around a baby's neck and strangles it while it's being born. Dr. Fowler and everybody had been upset, but there wasn't a blessed thing anybody could have done. They had been relieved then that I came out okay, because with two of us swimming around in there, she guessed things could get right tangled.

I was astonished. Hadn't I been born first, as I'd always been told?

"No no no no no," Aunt Rachel scoffed, and she tapped her stirring-spoon smartly on the edge of the roasting pan: tap tata tap-tap. "Who ever told you such a thing as that?"

"Everybody!"

Good-humoredly but positively she declared, "They never did! You got that idea from being older than your sister ever since. But she came first and she went first: 'Girls first!' "

This second revelation, more momentous than its predecessor, made me almost dizzy. I could not, in fact, recall ever having been told in so many words that I had been born before "BeeGee" — though surely I had never been told otherwise, either, and that omission struck me as extraordinary, even somehow culpable. I urgently wanted verification, but Mother was resting now, and with Dad you had to say things too loud, and Uncle Josh wouldn't know any different than Aunt Rachel. I summoned the family to dinner and on the way back from the screen porch asked my brother whether *he'd* known that BeeGee was born first.

Nonchalantly he asked back, "What's the difference between a duck?"

The talk at table was of the strike again, of how much better off were the Albany Brothers cannery workers than the people in war-torn Spain and China, who would count it a blessing to eat spilled tomatoes right off the street and would give their eyeteeth for a dinner of stuffed roast chicken and succotash and mashed redskin potatoes with giblet gravy. That was a Christ fact, Uncle Josh had to admit, but even so.

"I heard another truck got turned over," Joe Junior announced loudly to our father. "And a picket was beaten up and arrested."

"I doubt he was beaten up and arrested both," Dad said. Uncle Josh chuckled and said, "It happens." Aunt Rachel thought they should arrest them all and ship them off to the U.S. Army.

"*Nothing can stop the Ar-my Air Corps!*" Joe Junior sang out, with a grin that meant he was in on something I wasn't. Aunt Rachel crooned admonishment — "Joe *Jun*-ior . . ." — pitching the second note higher, like our door chime. My brother said "Tee hee" and made a neat volcano of his mashed potatoes, with gravy lava. "Isn't it some-thing to have Mother back for your birthday!" Aunt Rachel asked me, and I agreed it was, and Aunt Rachel said to Uncle Josh in a knowing tone, "The poor thing's tired, though."

Over tapioca pudding the fire whistle blew again. My scrotum tightened. When the sound had risen and fallen once and then rerisen, Joe Junior told Dad, "Fire whistle," and Dad said, "Hah," and excused himself to go to the fire, blowing his nose as he left the house. Almost an hour later he telephoned to say that the fire had been at an Albany Brothers warehouse and now there was an emergency town council meeting and he didn't know when he'd get back. We had cleaned up dinner and were all on the screen porch waiting to take our Sunday ride, which Mother had insisted we ought to go right ahead with, never mind her. It was the first time I could remember Dad's ever telephoning home.

"Well!" Aunt Rachel said when she came back out on the screen porch. In her cheery-scoffing tone the word whooshed out with lots of breath: "*Hwell!* We'll just take our little ride in the Nash, the four of us."

Joe Junior said, conversationally, "Yippee."

We didn't *have* to take a ride, I offered. "'Deed we do," Aunt Rachel replied, "and it's a pity Mother and Dad can't come along, 'cause it's your birthday surprise. Howja like *them* apples?"

"Eee-urr-*room!*" Joe Junior went, imitating first the sound of a diving Spad and then its chattering machine guns: "Khuh-huh-huh-huh-huh-huh-huh-huh!"

Uncle Josh said mildly, "That'll do, Joe," and folded his section of Sunday paper.

"You have a good time, honey," Mother bade me when I went upstairs to say good-bye. "Mother's sorry she can't go with you, and you'll love your surprise, I know." She was lying down now, her glasses folded beside the basin and pencil on the maple nightstand. I bent over and was weakly hugged and kissed. While her hands were pressed to both sides of my face, an awful question occurred to me, so important that I went ahead and asked it despite her being sick and Joe Junior's standing right behind me:

"Was it her own belly-button cord that Bijou got tangled up in, or mine?"

"Jeez, Sy!" my brother objected. A blush scalded over me.

But Mother didn't seem to mind. She laughed, airlessly, and shook her head. "The things you think of!" Her hands were on my shoulders now; she squeezed and wearily let go.

Joe Junior crowed to our aunt and uncle, "This *drip!*" We were turning off Maple onto Maryland in the maroon Nash, Uncle Josh driving with his deerskin gloves even in July, his black cigarette holder between his teeth. "He *asked* her that, while she's sick in bed!"

"Mother didn't mind!" I said hotly. But I was impressed both by the accusation of tactlessness — which, once I heard it, seemed shamefully justified — and by my brother's superior discernment, which clearly impressed him, too.

"I'm sure Mother didn't mind," Aunt Rachel said soothingly. "That all happened years ago, and there wasn't a blessed thing any soul could do."

Seven years ago *today,* I thought, stinging. And *I* could have gone first.

"*Nhow!*" Aunt Rachel declared. "What we need to know is what Simon William Behler intends to be when he grows up."

Joe Junior at once replied, "A bigger baby," but not in his really needling tone — more as if he were still rolling his eyes at my dumb question to Mother.

"A famous pilot," I answered, glumly. They all knew that very well, in general.

But Uncle Josh grinned in the rearview mirror. "A *famous* pilot?"

Aunt Rachel approved. "That's the ticket."

What had happened was that the first time Joe Junior had declared at table his ambition to be an engineer, and I mine to be a pilot, the grown-ups had pointed out to us that there were many sorts of each: highway engineers, electrical engineers; harbor pilots, coastal pilots. When my brother then specified locomotive engineer and I airplane pilot, they had good-humoredly chided us both: such people (Dad and Aunt Rachel, especially, maintained) were no more than glorified truckdrivers. We should set our sights higher, make a name for ourselves. Joe Junior subsequently decided he would be the other kind of engineer, the kind that designed and built locomotives; that way he'd get to drive them as often as he wanted to, to make sure they were okay. For a while I reckoned I would do the same with airplanes. But "aeronautical engineer" sounded too close to what my brother would be doing, and I had in mind to be a lot more important than he would be. So, without mentioning it till now, I had revised my ambition.

"Get a load of Charles Lindbergh," Joe Junior mildly jeered. I blushed but was pleased to sense that he was envious of my having thought of celebrity. I was ready to point out to him, when necessary, that there *were* no famous locomotive engineers, in the desirable sense: who wanted to be Casey Jones? But it was not necessary yet.

There was something going on.

"My father's father was a famous pilot," Uncle Josh remarked around his cigarette holder.

Joe Junior laughed. "Was not!"

"Sure he was," our uncle insisted. Aunt Rachel smiled at him.

All we knew of the Vernon family was what we had been told. "He was a farmer!" I insisted, considering however that in those early days a person might somehow have been both. "Was he a crop duster?"

"Some people might call it that," Uncle Josh allowed, twinkling. "But actually he was a manure pilot: *Pile it here; pile it there. . . .*"

As we duly groaned, I saw that we were about to turn left off Maryland onto Bridge Avenue, toward the river bridge itself and Avon County, instead of right, as usual, toward the canneries and lower Dorset. "Hey, what's up?"

"The price of eggs," cracked Joe Junior.

"Price of tomatoes," Aunt Rachel predicted, "soon enough."

"*Airplanes* are up," declared Uncle Josh, cocking his cigarette holder at a jaunty angle as we headed north over the blue Chaptico.

"What goes up must come down," my brother said, and he made his dive-and-crash noise: "Eee-urr-room-*pulghhh!*"

His family had arranged a marvelous birthday surprise.

"Where're we going?" I demanded, beginning dizzily to suspect. Aunt Rachel said, "You'll see, birthday boy."

We were across the bridge and headed for Avondale, where the region's only airport was. As often as I could persuade them to, my parents took me there to watch the planes take off and land, but that was not often: our father always said that the Eastern Shore began at the south bank of the Chaptico, and he had no interest in prosperous Avon County, with its gentleman farmers and waterfront estates.

It was these that the Avon airport largely served: there were no scheduled commercial passenger flights, but many of the "C'meres" — people from Washington, Wilmington, Philadelphia, and even New York who "came here" to their vacation or retirement properties — owned private airplanes or hired air taxis to and from the city. Sometimes we would sit for half an hour among the Pipers, Cessnas, and Grummans and see no planes move at all. Once, however, we saw a trimotored Ford "Tin Goose"; another time, just a few weeks past, a brand-new Douglas DC-3.

But merely being taken to see the airplanes again, so soon, was not likely my birthday surprise. I became uneasy. *"Are we going up?"*

Uncle Josh steered smiling through Avondale. "You couldn't get *me* up in one of those things!"

Always-game Aunt Rachel said she would give her eyeteeth to go up again; years ago she'd had a beau who was a barnstormer. (He was that, Uncle Josh agreed.) But we would just see.

"You're going, aren't you?" I asked Joe Junior anxiously.

"What's the matter, big baby? Cold feet?"

As we approached the familiar corrugated-metal buildings on the far side of town — and the windsock, the beacon, the grassy runways — those brightly painted airplanes parked in rows no longer looked like large gay toys. They were formidably real and not particularly friendly machines. Where we lived there were neither mountains nor tall buildings; I had traveled no farther from home than Baltimore, once, and there had not been time then to go up in a skyscraper. The highest off the ground that I could remember ever having been was the top of the Ocean City Ferris wheel.

"It'd better be a Stinson Reliant!" I said. "I guess if it's not that blue Stinson Reliant, I'd just as leave skip it."

Joe Junior chortled. "Listen to the big baby!"

"I don't *have* to go!" I made clear. "It's *my* birthday!"

"Boo hoo hoo!"

"Peace on earth good will to men!" Aunt Rachel chided us. "I'd go up in a raspberry Model T if somebody offered!"

Uncle Josh said he bet she would, too.

The blue Stinson Reliant I had admired on other visits "belonged to somebody," they guessed. Anyhow, it did not take passengers up for hire. What kind was it, then, the one they'd rented? Incredibly, to me, they didn't know: a regular little one, they supposed. Nor had they rented it, quite; on our last ride over here, the family had seen a sign for airplane rides, and Aunt Rachel had phoned ahead this morning while we were in Sunday school, to confirm. The pilot was expecting us.

"Manure pilot!" said Joe Junior. "I'll go with you, big baby."

I was much relieved. "But I can decide, okay? When I see what kind of plane it is."

We did not go from the maroon Nash right out onto the airfield, but into a small office entered from the grass parking-lot side of a nearby hangar, where a red-on-yellow hand-lettered sign advertised AIRPLANE RIDES $5. The office was floored with worn-through green linoleum; a chipped oak desk was strewn with grease-soiled manuals and papers, box and crescent wrenches, ashtrays filled to overflowing; the walls were hung with finger-smudged maps of Avon and Dorset counties and calendars from spark-plug companies, with all-but-naked women on them. A thin-faced man in yellow sport shirt and slacks and red porkpie hat swiveled his beat-up desk chair to face us, mouthing an unlighted cigar. An ancient black oscillating fan stirred the humid air.

It was me he looked at. "You're the feller wants to be a pilot?"

I cleared my throat. "Yes sir."

"It ain't no way to get rich!" he laughed to Aunt Rachel and Uncle Josh.

My aunt informed him, with mock asperity, that I was going to be a *famous* pilot.

"Oh, well, then!" The man's laugh loosened phlegm. He spat into a rusty metal wastebasket beside his desk and said, "'Scuse *me*."

"Wiley Post!" my brother offered. "Eee-urr-*pulghh!*"

"Well, I'm Howard Garton," the man said, shaking hands with me and then with Joe Junior, "and I say don't let *no*body make fun of your wantin' to be a pilot."

My uncle said that that was the ticket.

"What kind of plane do you have?" I asked Howard Garton, and he said why didn't we all just go take a look. Then he winked: or did I want to leave Big Brother behind?

In the same tone he had used, I said I *guessed* Joe Junior could come along. We were going simply to inspect the airplane, I imagined, after which we would return to the battered office to discuss the flight plan and I would make my decision. But Howard Garton led us through the small, empty, dirt-floored hangar behind his office and out to a Bellanca four-seater, red and yellow like his clothes or Aunt Rachel's Bon Ami can, with painted flames streaming back from the exposed cylinder heads and the wheel pods. He opened the thin door on the passenger side, tipped down the right front seat-back, and said to Joe Junior, "In you go, bud. We'll let the birthday boy ride up front. You coming along, Ma?" he asked Aunt Rachel, and he explained to Uncle Josh, "Can't sit but four of us."

"You bet your bottom dollar I'm coming along!" Aunt Rachel scoffed, and then she added, "How 'bout three for the price of two?"

Things were happening too fast. Where were the helmets and goggles? The parachutes? I thought of offering to wait on the ground with Uncle Josh. But Howard Garton chuckled and said, "Make it twelve-fifty," and Aunt Rachel said to Uncle Josh, "Kiss me good-bye, love; I'm off to the wild blue yonder," and let Howard Garton help her up into the rear seat beside Joe Junior. I didn't have nerve enough not to climb in too.

It was better when Howard Garton threw away his wet cigar, stepped up into the pilot's seat, and stashed his red porkpie into a stretchy pocket in the door. His head was bald, bumpy, freckled. "All right, sir," he said. "What's your first name?" I told him. "Let's you and me fasten our safety belts, Mr. Simon, and Mom and Brother do the same, and we'll see if old Bessie feels like running today."

"Aunt Rachel's our aunt," Joe Junior reported. As if in a spirit of mere inquiry, I asked, "Where do you keep the parachutes?" Howard Garton laughed. Joe Junior said, "What good are a *pair o' chutes* for four people? Get it?" Aunt Rachel told me to go ahead and ask all the questions I wanted to, and Howard Garton explained then that parachutes were used only on warplanes and maybe by stunt pilots and test pilots; if old Bessie's motor conked, we would just look around for a nice place to park. He started the engine — not nearly so loud a noise as I'd expected; like a big fan, really — and now I understood that of course we didn't need helmets and goggles in a closed cabin, any more than in the maroon Nash or the black LaSalle. The Bellanca had dual controls; I knew what every one was for, from my reading. Howard Garton let me move the ailerons, the elevators, and the rudder while we were still on the ground.

"Not when we're up in the air, though," Joe Junior warned from behind. Howard Garton said we'd just see. Now all my fear was gone; though we had not yet moved, I loved Howard Garton and old Bessie and flying. Uncle Josh stepped back and waved his gloves; we three waved back. Howard Garton advanced the throttle — I admired the way his bony, freckled hand rested so lightly upon the knob — and we rolled forward.

"Off we go!" sang Aunt Rachel. "Do you like Stinson Reliants?" I asked Howard Garton, who squinted judiciously out the side window and replied, "Stinson Reliant. They're a right nice airplane, I reckon. Out of *my* class." I declared Bellancas to be good airplanes, too — though in fact I was struck by the apparent flimsiness of old Bessie's construction. As we bumped along toward the runway, the plane seemed not all that different, except in scale, from one of Joe Junior's balsa-and-tissue flying models. Even the quietly fluttering propeller sounded rubber-band-powered. . . .

Until, in takeoff position at the head of the runway, Howard Garton advanced the throttle while braking the wheels, and the Bellanca roared and trembled and strained to go. "That's more like it!" cried Aunt Rachel. I watched the instrument needles climb; my skin buzzed. I had expected radio talk with a control tower, but there was none. Howard Garton merely looked around, released the wheel brakes, and opened the throttle all the rest of the way. As we gathered speed, the Bellanca's tail lifted; now I could see the grass runway rolling swiftly under us, the windsock almost limp above the distant hangar before which Uncle Josh waved. In no hurry at all, at a certain point Howard Garton drew toward him ever so slightly the little steering wheel on his side, as I knew he must. Mine came back in tandem with it. We were airborne.

I had not anticipated the untidy decrepitude of Howard Garton's office, the unglamorousness of the little man himself, the homely insubstantiality of old Bessie's interior appearance, but about the experience of flight itself my imaginings proved prescient, and I was as perfectly at home in thin air as in the waters of the Chaptico. My boyish ambition to be a pilot, however, fell lightly away from me with the treetops and rooftops of Avondale. Oh, I might fly a Stinson Reliant for recreation when I was grown, but commercial aviation (I realized already from this first altitude, as clearly as I had realized while taxiing that we didn't need helmets and goggles), even piloting a brand-new DC-3, was . . . *an insufficient destiny.*

Things were exactly as I had known they would be: the little airport, already well below and behind us; tree-shaded Avondale; the highway leading south through farmland to the Chaptico bridge. I was glad that Joe Junior and Aunt Rachel were behind me, glad also that they were too absorbed to speak much. In a calm, nonboyish voice I asked Howard Garton whether we had time to fly over the river to Dorset; above the engine's drone and the rush of air past the Bellanca's thin fuselage, it was like speaking to our father.

"I reckon," Howard Garton said. The steering wheel in front of me turned just a little, and we banked left on the light west wind we had taken off into. "It don't take long to get there in this baby."

Already I saw the blue-gray Chaptico ahead, so much wider below our town than above it. Just under us was the smaller Avon, its tributary, flecked here and there with sails and scored with the wakes of motorboats.

"Hey, neat!" Joe Junior said. "There's the bridge! I bet we see our house!"

I knew we would, and more, for there was the world exactly configured, a living map. There was the rivershore, the general hospital with its seawall; there were Maple Street, Maryland Avenue, and the other mapled streets and avenues of East Dorset. Our house was mostly shrouded by those maples and by our Chinese Cigar trees, but I saw part of our shingled roof, under which Mother lay ill and tired, and a white clapboard gable, and now the black LaSalle out front; so Dad was there, too, probably on the screen porch with the *Times,* deaf to the plane humming high overhead. There was the squat gray granite belfry of Zion Meth-Prot; there was East Dorset Elementary, and behind it the shiny new standpipe of our ward. There was Dorset Creek, lined with packing houses, dividing our town into East and West; the creek bridge leading to the business district, with Behler Maintenance & Improvement somewhere in it, on the street behind the firehouse. Howard Garton banked left again before I got a good view of West Dorset, where the boat basin and the waterfront park and River Boulevard and the better residential section were. But to westward, when we leveled off, I had a long view out toward the hazy great mouth of the Chaptico, miles wide where it joined Chesapeake Bay at what remained of Piney Island; and to southward now stretched the endless marshes of the lower county: a maze of reedy necks, meandering tidal creeks, and spattered low islets, like the patterns on scorched French toast. Now we banked left yet again, to head back to the airport, and I could see the poor colored ward and the spread of the Albany Brothers canneries, from one of which rose smoke. I hoped vaguely that the pickets had not burned the Lifter. There now was Island Creek with its several channel markers, the Island, Island Point with its red day beacon, exactly right. I could see where the twin creeks eventually came together, at the municipal cemetery, making a larger island of East Dorset itself. I could even see the shoal that the Island Creek day beacon perfectly marked, extending to meet it underwater, and the little indentation in the shore nearby, where Bijou and I —

To hide my sudden distress, I pressed my face to the glass. *Though this should have been her birthday gift as much as his, Simon Behler had not even thought of his sister, much less narrated to her, since the family reached Avon Airport in the maroon Nash.*

The voice was hollow now, wrong. Dismayed, I regarded upshore, beyond the Island, the grounds and buildings of the Eastern Shore State Hospital, and beyond them, where the slightly higher ground of the upper county commenced its quiltwork of woodlots and tomato fields, the new county cemetery. That was not yet where our dead lay, but it would be: the Behler plot in Dorset Municipal, where BeeGee Behler was, was full; so was that whole old graveyard, which had served our town since its incorporation two hundred and fifty years ago. Dad and Aunt Rachel had bought space for the future in the bare, newly laid-out county spread, formerly one of Captain Philip Albany's tomato fields.

"*Hwell!*" my aunt exclaimed just then, behind me. "There's home!"

"Right pretty to look at, i'n't it," Howard Garton said.

Announced Joe Junior, "I see the seawall!"

En route home in the maroon Nash, I was teased for my odd behavior, mainly by my brother. But Aunt Rachel, too, told Uncle Josh that she didn't know just *hwhat* had come over our Simon. When Howard Garton had invited me to take the wheel for a minute and hold old Bessie steady as she goes, I had politely declined, saying I was content to let him do the flying so I could just look. "It is right pretty," Howard Garton had admitted. Back at the hangar, standing beside the Bellanca's yellow wing strut, I had felt subdued, taller and more serious forever. I shook Howard Garton's freckled hand and thanked him for a good flight.

"You don't seem too het up," Uncle Josh observed kindly in the car. "Stomach woozy?"

"No, I feel great. It was great." Even to me my voice sounded peculiar. Just to hear it again I said, "I sure thank you-all." I was relieved that they pretty much left me alone then. My small dismay at forgetting Bijou had quickly passed; the exhilaration of flight remained, but I felt too serious about it and other things to join in Aunt Rachel's and Joe Junior's Did-you-sees as we recrossed the Chaptico bridge. I worried, too, that they would ask whether I still wanted to be a famous pilot, and then would think it was out of fear that I had changed my mind, when in truth . . .

On the screen porch, Dad took off his glasses, smiled, and asked, "How'd it go?" "Great!" I called back. Aunt Rachel declared that the whole Eastern Shore of Maryland looked from up there just like the fire company's Christmas garden. Except no snow, Joe Junior corrected her, and he went off on his Silver King — hollering, "Contact! Switch off! Eee-urr-*room!*" — to tell his friends where he'd been.

Still feeling tall and grave, I *ascended* the stairs to thank Mother for the airplane ride. It was the neatest birthday present I'd ever had, I said truthfully. In that room my new voice and manner seemed less affected. She held my hand as I sat on the edge of the spare twin and told her what I'd seen from up there. That was nice, she said. She believed Mother might be feeling just a little bit better.

Then I asked her whether Dad and I could ride over to the town cemetery before supper: I wanted to put some flowers on my sister's grave.

Surprised, Mother said, "What a thoughtful idea. But I know Dad's tired, honey. And we don't have any flowers."

I stood my ground. "Just to visit, then."

"Well. Ask your father, or maybe your aunt Rachel. No — she'll have her hands full with supper. And your uncle Josh has been driving already."

I could see the problem tiring her out. All the same, gratified that Joe Junior wasn't there to tease me or maybe even ask to ride along, I put the question loudly to our father.

"Cemetery?" he repeated.

Uncle Josh was on the screen porch, too, looking through the travel section of the *Times*. He raised his voice for Dad to hear: "Boy wants to say happy birthday to his sister! I'll ride him over, directly."

Aunt Rachel called from the living room, "The boy's father can drive him, Joshua." She stepped out onto the porch, wiping her long hands on her apron. "I think that's a *good thought!*" she said to me, loud enough for Dad, too. "I wish we had flowers for the whole kaboodle!"

Dad blew his nose and put on his seersucker suit coat, though the temperature and the humidity were both in the mideighties, and we went off in the black LaSalle. Even with the windows down, it was an oven inside that car until we had driven across East Dorset to the creek bridge, for Dad never parked in the shade of the silver maples, where starlings would drop all over the paint. In the black LaSalle it was even harder to talk to him; since he couldn't hear the big engine idling, he often raced it and engaged the clutch too suddenly. But when we crossed the trestled swing-bridge over Dorset Creek (which was rank even on Sundays from the mountains of crab shells rotting in the sun beside the packing houses) and lurched onto Cemetery Avenue, I saw cornflowers and Queen Anne's lace wild along the rusting fence and asked whether we could pick some for Bijou's grave.

Dad guessed not.

"They're just weeds!"

He smiled and shook his head. "They don't belong to us, son."

That was that.

We turned off the creek-side street of peeling clapboard houses and into the old cemetery, wound through its crushed-oyster-shell lanes of tombs, and stopped beside an ancient cedar. Dad took a cigarette from the pack with its desert scene like our illustrated lessons, tamped its end against the horn button, and pressed his thumb against the cigarette lighter on the dash. A clear glass bead in its knob would glow red when it was ready. "We're over by those holly bushes," he told me, pointing with the unlit Camel. "You take your time."

The air was still and steamy; already cicadas rasped in the trees. Our plot was marked by a polished gray stone the size of a single-bed headboard, lettered BEHLER. Before it the individual grave-mounds bore low footstones. WILHELM BENJAMIN, 1850–1933, and ROSA HERRON, 1855–1934: my grandparents, who had come over from Germany and whom I scarcely remembered. JOANNA PARSON SIMONS, Mother's mother, not really a Behler, 1863–1935, after whom I'd sort of been named; her, too, I could but half recall, though she had lived with us in her last years, ill and indifferent. FLORA, Dad and Aunt Rachel's elder sister, 1885–1929, who had never married or left home and had died of cancer the year the market crashed. CPL. ALBERT WILHELM — older than Dad, younger than Aunt Rachel, 1891–1918, mustard-gassed in Belgium. And BABY GIRL BEHLER, the only one of us with her last name on her stone, as she had never had a first: DAUGHTER OF JOSEPH BENJAMIN AND PAULINE SIMONS. BORN AND DIED JULY 1, 1930.

The mound above her footstone — had I ever really seen it before? — was tiny. Here is where she had been, winter and summer, while I was growing up and doing every kind of thing. I considered saying some sort of prayer for her soul, but it occurred to me not to believe in any such thing. The people in the coffins under those mounds were just skeletons now — though Grandma Simons maybe not quite, as she had died only two years ago — and their souls weren't anything. Chemicals came together to make a holly tree or a sea nettle or a person; then after a while they dissolved like Piney Island in the mouth of the Chaptico. Fifty years ago, Dad had once told us at the dinner table, Piney Island had had farms and woods and a village of three hundred people, with a general store and a Methodist church; now everything was washed away but a small stand of loblollies and the skeleton of a pier. By the time I grew up and had a wife and children, there would be nothing left of Piney Island but a shoal under the water, marked with a light.

Same with Bijou: when the time came that I forgot even how I used to narrate my life to her, that would be that. Same with Mother and Dad and Aunt Rachel and Uncle Josh, eventually, and me and Joe

Junior and whatever children *we* would have. The tide would still come in and go out; that had nothing to do with us.

Not far from our footstones was a single clump of dandelions in bright blossom. I checked to see whether Dad was looking; couldn't tell through the reflections on the windshield; went ahead anyhow and plucked the whole clump. The five or six blossoming ones I laid atop my sister's mound. Anybody watching from behind would think I was kneeling to pray. One dandelion had gone to fuzz; to make up for having picked the clump, I puffed its seeds over the whole plot.

As we crossed back into East Dorset in the black LaSalle, Dad surprised me by remarking, without turning his head, "I want you to *be* somebody, son." I supposed it was a birthday wish; or perhaps my wanting to visit the cemetery had impressed him. On the other hand, maybe he meant I wasn't measuring up. To ask, at a shout, was too awkward. Without turning my head, either, I nodded shortly.

As we passed Andy Travers's father's ice cream store and Zion Meth-Prot, my father went on, still looking forward down Maryland Avenue: "Make a name for yourself."

It was odd, that night, to look up through the dimly reflected street light at Joe Junior's hanging models, even the blue Stinson Reliant, and feel myself measurably older. Now I didn't know *what* I would be. Odd also to realize — as I could easily do now by imagining myself up there just then, looking down on us all from Howard Garton's red and yellow Bellanca — that the whole town of Dorset, asleep and awake, was *going on*. The entire world was going on while I lay there, and Joe Junior lay over in his bed, asleep already or pretending to be, and BeeGee Behler, who had gone first and was gone now, lay out under her little mound. Tigers in the jungle, Chinese people in China, whales in the oceans of the globe.

Under my head my Ingersoll wristwatch ticked. Bijou's dandelions were already dead and curled. Down by the Island Point day beacon the tide slid silently, in or out. I counted the hours back to when I had swum: it was moving in.

So that my brother, if he was awake, would think me asleep, I breathed slowly and evenly. Presently from his side of the room came a muffled slap slap, his more urgent respiration, and the smell. Some time after that I heard the breathing of his unfeigned sleep. East Dorset was by then so silent that I could hear the dinging of the Dorset Creek bridge bell, many blocks up Maryland Avenue from Maple Street. Even at this hour on a Sunday, they were opening the draw to let some vessel out upon its business. Then that sound, too, ceased.

Ever so slightly, ever so lightly, I rocked, and it was not long before I reached that state between two worlds where distances go strange and the familiar is no more. I was in black space, suspended, or as it were with one eye open above some surface, one below. Though his family little suspected it (my narrator resumed in a new voice, to a different audience), our unnamed hero verged upon an alternative and very different life, in a very different realm, to the threshold whereof his lost twin had led him, but into which not even she could follow.

Seven Interludes

1.

Although their version of his tale had been more or less in their language and on their terms, the company sat silent when Somebody finished it, studying their fingernails and the backs of their hands, perhaps glancing at one another. Yasmīn alone looked unswervingly at our narrator, he at her.

Said Sindbad presently, "Hum: mechanical birds and bracelets that measure time. Yet who would have believed a sleeping whale overgrown with trees and beaches if he had not himself mistaken one for an island and been carried under? And that business of your brother's drifting in a leaky vessel that must ceaselessly be bailed: that speaks to my condition! An admirable bit of realism in a sea of fantasy." He rapped the wooden tub behind him, either for attention or for luck, and shifted on his cushion-and-a-half. "Tomorrow evening, friends, my second voyage, no nearer-fetched than these, and this second Sindbad's second Serendib." He clapped his hands. "Kuzia Fakān!"

Yasmīn excused herself. The eyes of the assembled were divided between watching her leave the hall (in close whispered conference with her duenna, Jaydā) and watching the three performers make ready at last — especially that black-eyed dancer-in-chief. With such art then did they play and dance — in particular Kuzia Fakān, who directed her charms almost belligerently at the half-attentive host — that at music's end there was surely not a dry crotch in the hall, not even Still-Stranded's, though his thoughts were emphatically elsewhere.

Only in Baghdad, upon an Arabian night, would the host not next, once the company was dismissed, have interrogated his visitor till morning and beyond, if need be, until he had the *real* Serendib story, chapter and verse, in private. But an Arabian night was in what Somebody was stranded still — had been, as it seemed to him, for a thousand-plus — a night in which Sailor Sindbad did indeed now say to him, "You and I will talk tomorrow," but then directed the rerobed dancer herself (to the company's envious surprise) to show the guest to a guest-apartment: a room off the harem, tented like the banquet hall in silk brocade. There bright-skinned, dark-eyed Kuzia Fakān, still perspiring from her dance and plainly set down by her assignment, nevertheless laid out fresh linens and sponged and scented Somebody's body and her own, mechanically fondling each by turn and frankly examining him for evidence of disease.

"Your attention does me honor, Kuzia Fakān."

Her eyes flicked. "Be honored, then. At least *your* honor stands to my attention."

Somebody perpended this observation. "In hands so skillful, whose would not?"

"Ask your famous namesake," the woman said impatiently. "For their own lack of appetite, some blame the cook."

"Aha." During his earlier sojourn in the house, still-standing Somebody had from his secret distance more than once observed this woman (whom he knew to be Sindbad's current favorite, procured for him by Jaydā) but had not appreciated, among other things, her quickness. "Then am I your punishment? The mistress of the house is given for the night to a nameless nobody?"

"Who spoke of the night?" She perched half pouting on the bed's edge and gestured at its tentlike canopy. "Like the Bedouin I came from, I carry with me the only house I'm mistress of." Opening her muscled, clean-shaven thighs, with two impudent fingers she spread herself. "Yours to enter and begone from, Sayyid Whoever-You-Are, not to camp overnight in."

"That is a wâhât," Somebody acknowledged, "fit for the king of all the Bedouin." But he gently pressed her knees together. "Consider your penance done, Kuzia Fakān, and a good night to you." He handed her her robe and began donning the linens she had laid out for him. She looked from one to the other.

"What's this?"

"It appears to me," Somebody said, "that the owner of that royal oasis is not its mistress but only its caretaker." He indicated the door.

"Caretaker, then!" cried Kuzia Fakān. "I take care of it, and it has taken care of me, from the day my mother first sold me until the day before yesterday!" Standing with legs apart, she opened her robe to let lamplight illumine the place in question, altogether depilatoried, per custom, like her legs. "Has it suddenly gone sour as a camel's, that I can't entice either an old man or a nameless beggar with it?"

"Entice?" Smiling Somebody raised his eyebrows. "I don't doubt that you could entice the Commander of the Faithful himself, if enticement were truly your objective. Good night, now."

Wailed Kuzia Fakān, "What are you doing?" She had reluctantly closed her robe; now she flung it wide again and went to her knees on the carpet. "Let all Baghdad know I begged the beggar!"

She found herself raised up and gentled doorward. "Don't beggar your professional pride," Somebody said. "Count on me to tell your master tomorrow that never in half a century have I been so *enticed*."

With one quick hand she boldly tested that proposition. "Liar."

Somebody shrugged. "Half a century, Kuzia Fakān, is half a century."

In a different tone she asked, "Are you an agent of Haroun al-Rashīd?" Surprised indeed, Somebody reminded her that he was not even the caliph's subject, much less his secret agent — only a hapless castaway from Serendib.

"Liar," she said again, but almost respectfully. At the door at last, her dark eyes reappraised him. "Do I truly disgust you? Or are you one of those who prefer boys to women?"

"You saw me stand to your touch," our man reminded her, "even when you'd made it plain what you thought of your assignment. But

I've been thrust from one world into another like a genie through the neck of an hourglass, and I'm dizzy and spent. I've gorged myself with food and drink, I've told a long story understood by no one, and I've sat through a dance more sexual than sex itself. It's no wonder I'm too far gone for anything but sleep. Good night, I beg you."

"You're a spy. A queer. An assassin. And I've seen you before."

"None of those."

"You're an ifrit from a Jew's lamp, a genie from a sea chest. Your speech is ours but not ours. I *have* seen you before, in this place, before Ramadan. You're an agent of Prince Jabāl or Sahīm al-Layl, come for revenge."

"I am an agent of Sindbad the Still-Stranded," Somebody declared. "Find me that sea chest, Kuzia Fakān, and if I'm a genie, I'll close its lid over me and float myself home tomorrow, back to where your master says he came from."

"It's not my fault his silly amulet doesn't work!" the dancer suddenly lamented. "Yet he blames me for its failure and for his. The only love charm I believe in is desire, not rhinoceros horn and silver heartbeats."

"Of this," Somebody said, "you and I must speak further, but not now. I'm told you're Sindbad's favorite —"

"Once upon a time," Kuzia Fakān interrupted crossly. "He has no favorite now, amulet or no amulet. Unless I find a new patron or some magic trinket of my own, I'll end up like Jaydā." She took Somebody's arm. "Look here, Sayyid: I've seen more of the world than its bedroom ceilings. Whatever you are, I know you're not what you're pretending to be. Do you think Sayyid Sindbad invites beggars in every night? Do you think I do? He's afraid of you, but he's not sure why yet; that's the real reason I'm here. Help me out with him till I can plan my next move, and by Allah I'll show you what enticement is. Like my mother and grandmother before me, I *am* a professional, and proud to be."

"Who can doubt it," Somebody asked, "once having glimpsed that wâhât like a mirage among the dunes?"

"Another mocking man," Kuzia Fakān said bitterly, and she turned to go. "Nobody will help me."

"If nobody will help you," Somebody said seriously, "I'm your man. I mean that truly, Kuzia Fakān."

Muttering something in dialect, she sniffed and left, not bothering to close the door behind her. Somebody left it ajar, turned low but did not extinguish the lamp she'd lit, and lay on the bed to consider where he was and what he had learned, or been half told. Presently the household quieted, and the city around it. A single small bell dinged distantly, then ceased. Our man himself — nobody, nameless, spent, still stranded — slipped, against all resolution, into sleep.

2.

Out of which a name stirred him — one of his, hers for him — whispered from the closing door, the red-hooded djellaba in his arms already as he rose to her:

"*Sīmon!*"

Her dear version, whispered like "Seaman" by the mouth under the eyes framed by the hair framed by the hood, which now fell back; breathed into his ears, against cheeks and forehead, lips and neck, chest, shoulders: "Sīmon Sīmon Sīmon Sīmon! Sīmon! *Sīmon!*" Still she repeated it, laughing, incanting, till by and by they lay sweating their joy into her djellaba, spread like a second carpet beside the bed: like *their* carpet, on which, in which . . .

Out there in Baghdad somewhere, a dog howled sirenlike and was answered by another. Prone atop her lover, brow to brow, Yasmīn tented their faces with her fragrant hair, rolled his head from side to side by rolling hers, rode her last small waves with the help of his hands on her hips, and even then murmured, incredulous, "Sīmon!" until they slept.

3.

When presently we woke — refreshed, restored — it was as if some drug or incense cloud had cleared, or exotic curtain opened to plain air, though it was still night in the house and city of Sindbad the Sailor. We lovers moved from carpet to bed, where as we washed and kissed each other clean and toweled ourselves dry with Yasmīn's djellaba, the young woman spoke quietly of her dismay and disbelieving joy: at hearing *his* voice, of all voices, outside the banquet-hall window; at his wild imposture, his reckless return to her despite everything, including her wishes. But who knew her wishes? Certainly not herself: see her weep with delight at being with him again; hear her laugh with fear that our mad connection (which, at news of Sindbad's sudden sixth return, she had cut off for both our sakes, against her heart's whole thrust) will come to light, at the cost of what remains of her reputation and quite likely at the cost of Sīmon's life, given her father's peculiar feelings for her and the ready availability of hired assassins. But Allah spare us, there he was: her lovely, her precious, her demented, her doomed!

And there ("Sīmon" told the silky small of her back, backs of her knees, undersides of her breasts, brave underneath of her chin, her earlobes, nape) was she, whose returning of him one month past — gently narcotized and rolled in her own magical Bokhara, on which we had made such flights! — to the marshy shore where he had first remet her had brought him closer to ending his life-story than he'd come since the day he realized he'd changed worlds. There was she, of his love for whom he was more certain than of his name and whereabouts: his prop against despair, touchstone of reality amid its opposite, long-suffering fellow victim and companion in his only joy. There was his Yasmīn, for whose sake her Sīmon was now quite prepared to die.

But his Ramadan-month in the marshes near Basra with Mustafā the Navigator had given him a better idea. He made to tell her it; she stopped him with a kiss. She didn't care what it was; anyhow, whatever it was, she had a better yet. Light out, eyes closed, we made love again, more or less (Sīmon's not young). We breathed long and deeply — now in unison, now not — and told stories through our skin: long stories and short, simple and complex, realistic, fantastic, happy, sad — but every one ending, not in the peace that passes understanding, but in the most understandable peace on earth.

4.

We slept.

Prayer, the minareted muezzin called again, *is better than sleep!*
We woke.

"Love," Yasmīn sighed, "is better than prayer," and she kissed her friend here and there in the predawn dark. He held her head between

65

his hands; like the muezzin's echo, a rooster crowed. We reviewed in two sentences our plan, still tentative, improvisatory, in which Sīmon had no more than a little confidence and Yasmīn less. Who except Scheherazade ever changed her fate by telling stories? But we had not much left to lose: our lives, maybe, though probably not; each other again, maybe, though we were now determined not. Most else we had lost already, separately and together.

In the gray first light, Yasmīn slipped into her djellaba, out of the guest quarters (old Jaydā, waiting slumbrously on a pallet not far from the door, gave the interloper a single, expressionless glance), and back to her own. Her fragrances lingered in the air, on the bedclothes, on her lover's skin, which therefore for some while he would not wash.

Had Sīmon (she had asked him, hours back) noticed the plump and crimson-faced, red-bearded fellow at her father's right hand? He of the wide-open eyes, the tight-closed mouth and hands? Sīmon had, though not particularly; his own eyes had been too full of her. Then he might trouble himself tonight, she said, to notice that fellow more particularly: Ibn al-Hamrā, a wealthy merchant of the city (it went without saying) and . . . her prospective new fiancé, with whom Sindbad was currently negotiating her marriage price.

She had felt her friend go rigid in her arms. Then he exhaled, relaxed his limbs somewhat. What had he expected? Yasmīn wanted to know. Why did he suppose she and Jaydā had drugged him and rugged him off last month from her chambers (against her heart's whole thrust)? Had we not agreed long since, in our darkest hours together, that life must be not only got through but somehow made the best of? Perhaps Sīmon would make her father a better proposal than Ibn al-Hamrā's?

He had muttered "Sorry" and kissed her darkened breasts. She pressed his face between them. So: her price was being negotiated once again.

It was, and that negotiation was delicate indeed, for reasons Sīmon knew. After *Zahir's* hijacking by the Qeshmi pirates, Yasmīn's value on the bride market had been as sorely compromised as her captor had intended. Who would now believe her virginal, when her own ex-betrothed would not? Yet who could blame the young Sohari prince Jabāl, to whom she had been en route with her bridal party, for concluding that his goods had been irreparably damaged in transit? Jabāl was only following his vizier's prudent advice, and that is the business of viziers: prudently to advise.

On the other hand, what everybody assumed had never quite been proved. At the time of that first affiancement, Yasmīn's maidenhood had been attested by her lifelong nurse-duenna. Such was Sindbad's wealth after five successful voyages, and so desirable his daughter, that her father had been able to rebuff, politely, Jabāl's vizier's discreet suggestion that the fiancée be confirmed "intact" by some woman of the prince's retinue as well. Young Jabāl, in love at first sight of Yasmīn during a state visit to Baghdad, had not insisted, but there, no doubt, was sown the seed of misgiving that flowered when news of her hijacking reached him.

With her and her attendants aboard *Zahir* had been half her dowry, which the pirates had seized together with the ship's passengers. The other half was to have followed with Sindbad himself, in another vessel, in time for the wedding. That second half the pirate captain, Sahīm al-Layl, had demanded as ransom for the lives of his hostages, and as much again if Yasmīn's virtue was to be preserved along with her life. In vain Sindbad had pleaded with Prince Jabāl, for his bride's sake, to underwrite that third portion, which it would impoverish her father to pay. Jabāl's vizier had pointed out that even if Sindbad paid it all, the prince would be marrying a now dowryless woman of unverified purity. His advice to Jabāl therefore had been to go forward with the wedding only if Sindbad met either of two conditions: he must both ransom his daughter himself and restore her dowry, or, since the young prince so desired her, ransom and deliver her to Sohar (Jabāl's capital, in Oman, which happened also to be Sindbad's birthplace) with no further dowry than her maidenhead — to be examined and pronounced intact, however, by the prince's own inspectors.

Sindbad had groaned and cursed, had torn turban and caftan, but in the end had borrowed heavily to pay the additional ransom for Yasmīn's "honor" as well as her life, and she and her party had been restored to him. He would not, however — *could* not, he insisted — meet either of the prince's alternatives. To restore even half the dowry was now quite beyond his means; indeed, he must set out promptly on another fortune-hunting voyage (his sixth and latest) simply to pay off his creditors. As for the other option, he declared it an affront to both his honor and his daughter's. Indignantly, Yasmīn had agreed; likewise Jaydā, who had been taken and ransomed with the rest of the bridal party. The engagement was off.

But the truth, of course, was that Sindbad no less than Prince Ja-bāl — and most certainly Jabāl's vizier — had assumed all along that the "virtue" ransomed by that final ransom, after weeks of piratical captivity, would not likely be Yasmīn's virginity. Of that her father had not even bothered to stipulate proof before payment. At best, all tac-itly assumed, she had been spared the even further outrages she would surely have suffered at her captors' hands if Sindbad had ransomed only her life; this way, he had bought as well his own self-respect and some measure of technical honor. This last had enabled him then to denounce Prince Jabāl (anyhow, the prince's vizier) as an unfeeling scoundrel, though in his place Sindbad would have acted no differ-ently, nor for that matter would Yasmīn.

It enabled him, too — and here we rearrive at last night, for be-tween Yasmīn and Sīmon (who had been hostaged with her from the bride-ship *Zahir* and pressed into service as the pirates' navigator), all the foregoing went without saying — to exercise some limited lever-age in his current negotiations with the merchant Ibn al-Hamrā. Both parties "knew" that the ferocious young pirate Sahīm al-Layl had done to Prince Jabāl's betrothed what pirates do to their eligible victims. Indeed, the fact that Yasmīn had not returned pregnant from her or-deal (as had several of her bridesmaids and servants), far from arguing that she might after all have been spared, had put her fertility in ques-tion. The kindest interpretation of it was that she had perhaps been forced less frequently than the others. But honor forbade any of this to be acknowledged openly, even between father and daughter. It was acknowledged instead (as Yasmīn had explained last night to Sīmon, between our lovemakings) by Sindbad's offering Ibn al-Hamrā the same handsome dowry he had offered Prince Jabāl, though her new suitor was not of royal blood: in the code of their dickering, "though no less beautiful, Yasmīn was less young" than she had been at her first affiancement. It was acknowledged also by Ibn al-Hamrā's sug-gestion that — precisely because he was no prince, only a successful commoner like Sindbad himself — an even handsomer dowry would permit him to surround Yasmīn with more of the comforts appropriate to "a woman of her maturity and experience."

All this Yasmīn herself attended with pained amusement, among other emotions. As of the evening past, she had reported to Sīmon last night, her father had given her suitor to understand that an increase in her dowry might be interpreted by the cynical as reflecting unseemly doubts on Ibn al-Hamrā's part concerning the "pure desirability" of his bride-to-be; and Ibn, professing horror at the mere possibility of such misinterpretation, had proposed alternatively that a share of the profits of Sindbad's upcoming seventh voyage — fifteen percent, say? — be discreetly added to the package.

Five, her father had replied at once, plainly signaling to any true gentleman his willingness to settle for ten. But Ibn al-Hamrā had had the effrontery to suggest next that where the comforts of children and grandchildren "cannot be assumed" for one's old age, material prosperity must be their hollow substitute. Fifteen percent.

"Could I give myself to such a man?" Yasmīn had exclaimed, first to her father, later to her lover. "It's clear what he thinks of me! Ten percent tops, or Jaydā herself will regard me as nothing but a scrap of used goods, to be haggled over in the souk!"

And if your suitor agrees to ten? Sīmon wondered. But by then we were making love again (as ardently as a spent semicentenarian can, the third time in a night), and after that we briefly slept until wakened by the muezzin's early prayer call. We reviewed Sīmon's desperate and so-tentative new plan. "Do it," Yasmīn said. "At least it might persuade that red-bearded cow-pat that a virgin's wâhât is worth his coming down to seven and a half for."

5.

S. the Still-Stranded therefore made bold to say to Sindbad the Sailor, when the page Salīm fetched guest to host at the latter's midmorning summons, "Sir, your pardon: I must risk your displeasure by speaking plainly."

"Take that risk," his now orange-turbaned host advised him. In the shade of a date palm in his sandy court, Sindbad was taking his ease, oddly, in the larger version of that empty wooden tub before which he had sat at dinner. "Myself," he went on, "I sit here every morning to remind myself to risk no more." He thumped the tub's high wall. "Dry land! But who knows when it may sink, or the water rise? Serendib is what I want to hear about: the real Serendib, not last night's Never-Never Land. But speak your piece."

Somebody bowed and declared, "The pirate Sahīm al-Layl himself was no more impudent than this merchant Ibn al-Hamrā! How can the pearl of Baghdad be bestowed upon a niggling nobody?"

The old man's watchful countenance darkened. "Kuzia Fakān has been filling your ear. But that Bedou magpie was with you so briefly that I'm surprised even she found time for such gossip."

"Fifty years," Still-Stranded said in his own defense, "is not twenty-five."

"And seventy is not fifty," Sindbad replied. "But to get out of *my* tub still costs Kuzia more sweat than that."

Smiling to himself, Somebody bowed again. "Twice in one evening, sir, you set an unexpected banquet before a starving beggar. The first unmanned me for the second." In any case, he assured his benefactor, the splendid Kuzia Fakān had not been his informant. A survival expert such as himself learned to read every crack in the plaster, so to speak, and to listen with all the pores of his skin. He had known of the negotiations with Ibn al-Hamrā before last night, he acknowledged — even before he had presented himself yesterday at Sindbad's gate. Indeed, it was his indignation at the great disservice being done the lady Yasmīn — a disservice, he could only conclude, that she herself was too proud to protest — that had led him so audaciously to presume upon Sindbad's hospitality, and that led him now to presume upon it further by pointing out that just as seventy years are not fifty, nor fifty twenty-five, so fifteen percent of a projected profit is not ten, to say nothing of five, not to mention zero: the share Ibn al-Hamrā deserved of the upcoming voyage to Serendib.

"Make yourself clear, Brother," Sindbad said. "Not only about the business of Ibn al-Hamrā, which is not your affair, but about that unmentionable pirate captain as well, whose name is never to be uttered in this house. Also, if you please, about your own comings and goings from Serendib."

Somebody thereupon did just that, more or less: retailed to his near-namesake an abbreviated version of the story he proposed to tell the company in full a few evenings hence, when his recounted voyages and Sindbad's reached their crossing point. By his reckoning, it would be the story of his fifth voyage.

Leaning back again in his cameled court like a figure on a cigarette package, his solitary listener at this forenoon rehearsal heard him out with narrowed eyes, fingered beard, and no comment. At story's end he shifted on his special cushion, spat sideways over the tub's edge, and did not even question the tale, only its teller, of whom he asked simply, "You expect grown men to swallow that?"

Unruffled, Somebody said, "Grown men may swallow what a child would choke on: whales the size of islands, with landscapes on their backs! Rocs and rhinoceri! Shores strewn with diamonds!"

Sindbad smiled. "Because their appetite was whetted with greed, friend, and the marvels washed down with wine."

"As they will be tonight," said Somebody, "and tomorrow and the evening after. But in my stories there are no genies or one-eyed giants to be swallowed whole. Nature's laws are not transgressed."

"Only the laws of human nature," Sindbad replied, "which bid hungry men eat when food is in their hands, as Yasmīn was in the hands of We-Know-Whom. Besides, I brought real diamonds home, whereas the jewel *you* speak of —"

"Is tucked safely in its casket yet," declared Still-Stranded, "unless that daintiest of vaults has been forced since you ransomed it. Sayyid Midnight (so I'll call him, since I'm forbidden to say *al-Layl*) was so enthralled by the flower of Baghdad that he would not touch her without her consent, and would cut off the nose of any crewman who so much as sniffed in her direction. As for Prince Jabāl of Sohar, he let himself be viziered right out of the garden, believing that his jasmine had been plucked. As did others."

Sindbad squinted at him some while longer, clearly endeavoring to see through him and just as clearly failing in that endeavor. Half under his breath then he exclaimed, "Plucked and petaled! Stemmed! Sucked dry! Seeded, chewed, and spat!" Spitting once more over the tub's side, he said to Somebody, "Whoever you are, Brother, try that story, if and when you dare. If you are not hooted from the hall, we'll speak further of Serendib."

6.

Transported by his night and much pleased by his morning, that afternoon our man spent *scribbling:* a former trade from a former life, so far behind him now in time and space that his roughened hands could scarcely draw the letters. To be sure, in the world where they used to flow so readily that he seldom thought of them as letters, only as the ongoing line of story, they had flowed not from a goose-quill that must be redipped line by line and repointed page by page, but from an ever-sharp, never-dry fountain pen, as effortlessly as from the fountain of his youth. Even so, the old muscular cursive spoke to both memory and imagination, which together made a journey that the penman himself could not: from Here clear back to There. He set down an abbreviated version of what he had come to think of — speaking of it first to Yasmīn in her bedchamber through the month of Sha'ban and again to his baffled auditors at last night's feast — as his "first voyage," in "America" in "1937," when his name had been Simon William Behler, more or less; when he had told stories to his lost twin, acted them out with her, narrated their life and high adventures.

He mused then upon his "second," in that same realm seven years later: perhaps forty years past, as Somebody's body measured time; perhaps a thousand hence, if where he was was real. But whether two score or a thousand and one, it was more than years that divided "East Dorset" — and Crazy Daisy Moore and her Bon Ami and Joe Junior's Island — from the East of Baghdad and of Sindbad the Sailor.

7.

"Every morning," Sindbad said that evening to the assembled, "every one of us begins a new voyage, or resumes the voyage of yesterday. Men speak of Sindbad's six voyages: twenty-five thousand and six would be closer to the mark. In the holy month of Ramadan alone, since my latest return to Basra, I have sailed thrice-ten more without leaving my dear dry courtyard, as have you all without venturing beyond Baghdad. And on this morning's voyage alone, speaking with my brother the Still-Stranded" — he gestured down the low board's left side, at the midpoint of which sat Somebody — "I learned more

72

about the blessed isle of Serendib than my own landfall there ever taught me. My faith in Voyage Seven (if not my thirst for voyaging) is now redoubled, as yours will be when you have heard him. But let's address our appetites in the usual order. Yasmīn."

Robed in a fresh djellaba, this one a brilliant saffron like her father's turban, and fresh-faced herself from a long day's rest after her night of love, his daughter rose from the board's far end and smilingly served wine, Jaydā following to replenish the decanter as it was emptied. She took particular care that her father's cup, Ibn al-Hamrā's, and that of the old fellow across from him, in that order, were brimful; then she went back and forth and up and down among the company in the same elaborate order as on the previous night, filling their wine cups nearly to the top — "Still-Stranded's" last of all.

"To the two great harbors," Sindbad proposed. "Dry land and sleep, from which we venture in order to return."

The company drank. Food was then served, first to those at the main table, then to those at a small side table where sat veiled and frowning Kuzia Fakān with her piper and tambourinist as well as Jaydā and the page Salīm — not quite servants but not ranking members of the household, either, at least not currently. By unspoken agreement, the dinner talk was not of foreign lands and voyages but of matters less glamorous, though related: cinnamon and pepper futures, the market price of sandalwood and aloes, the relative merits of teak and aini wood as ship's timber. Her father's daughter, Yasmīn more than held her own in these conversations; though appearing to defer to male opinion like any properly brought-up Muslim woman, she was so clearly knowledgeable about the commodities market that all at her end of the board sought her advice, as all at Sindbad's end sought his.

"If I happened not to be a mere woman who knows nothing of the world," she would venture when asked, "and if I happened to have at Basra a fresh shipment of first-quality poon logs from Beypore, as has our friend Sayyid Talīb ibn Sahl, I would resist the temptation to sell them just now, even though the price of ship spars has peaked and begun declining. I would warehouse those logs at whatever cost till this time next year, when the caliph's new shipyard is scheduled to begin production. The demand for poon logs should then double, and their price as well. Rice futures, on the other hand, I would avoid this year like the pox, for every sign points to a good monsoon and a bumper crop, which will depress rice prices till the next drought and famine rescue the market. But what do I know?"

Boldly replied Still-Stranded, his heart full, from the third seat down on her right and the third equally from her father's left: "You know the price of things as well as their value, whether or not those coincide."

"And where they do not," Ibn al-Hamrā called approvingly from Sindbad's right hand, "may you know as well how to come to terms with the differential."

Yasmīn levelly regarded first the one, then the other, then her food.

At dinner's end, Sindbad the Sailor signaled for attention by tapping, not his Tub of Last Resort this time, though it was in ready place behind him, but his turban, with both hands. Then, as promised, rather than recounting his second voyage in detail, he merely recapitulated it, drawing the company's attention to aspects perhaps not emphasized in his previous tellings:

"Dry land and sleep," he repeated. "Also turbans: the three great things. But sleep, as my second voyage shows, is a slippery savior."

He sipped and sighed. "It was mere profligacy, you remember, that first drove me to sea and beached me upon that sleeping whale. Disturbing its dreams led to the fulfillment of my own, once I had paid the dark dues of despair and fed a bit of Sindbad to the creatures of the sea. I had been rich, then poor; I came home richer than the father whose dear death had first enriched me. With my riches I bought this house and slaves of every sex and shade to serve me, and though I lived more extravagantly than before, my fortune like a healthy muscle increased of itself by that exercise, as the fortunes of the fortunate sometimes do. What I desired, I acquired. As in a very dream of luxury, I lived high, slept late, and never waked alone. Yasmīn.

"From this dream of a life," he went on when fresh wine had been poured, "it was not want that waked me, but a double itch: to see more of that monstrous world beyond gracious Baghdad, the City of Peace, and once more to trade sharply with my fellows, a sport as delightsome to the adept as love or narrative. I bestirred myself to Basra, half hoping that the sight of ships and serious water would scurry me back to the high ground of my slave women and other sweetmeats. Alas! I saw for sale in the harbor a fine new trading vessel named *Zahir,* so pleasing to my eye, so finely joined and rigged and fitted, so fully found, so yare, so Bristol fashion — oh, my friends! Bear in mind my term as port minister in Voyage One: my eye for marine architecture had grown as cunning as my eye for cunts and cargoes, and here was a young Jaydā or very Kuzia Fakān of boats. I fell in love with her on the spot and therefore promptly climbed aboard, as had become my custom. When the most intimate inspection confirmed my first impression, I bought her straightway (as had also become my custom), loaded her with merchandise and fellow merchants, hired me a canny young captain, and bade him make sail.

"Brothers! First voyages are dangerous because we have everything to learn, second voyages because we believe we have learned everything. This time I curbed my natural impulse to befriend my shipmates, having learned that many of them must perish, and not wanting unnecessary cause for grief. Soon enough we raised the inevitable tropic isle, a very Eden et cetera, and remembering the hard lessons of Voyage One, I remained in my cabin while the captain and my fellow merchants rushed ashore, strolled about, and built cooking fires. Not until I had satisfied myself that this beast was either a true island or a truly imperturbable sleeper did I slip ashore myself. Even then I stayed aloof from the others, who had strayed too far inland for my taste; I picnicked alone in a grove of what looked like sea grapes on the beach. So sweet was that grove, so splendid the day, so delicious the feel of a bona fide island under me again, and so excellent the wine I had brought ashore to toast my solitary landfall that I sank not into the sea but into sleep, whereupon it pleased Allah to teach me the innocence of my experience. Because I had so warily held back, my captain and fellows didn't know that I had finally followed. Having abandoned myself to sleep, I woke to discover myself abandoned, my beloved *Zahir* already hull-down on the horizon.

"Hello again then to Despair: shipmate from Voyage One, stowaway on Voyage Two, and now my fellow castaway and sole companion. How I saluted him you may imagine, for neither need nor greed had brought us together this time, only idle restlessness and idle rest.

"We strolled about, he and I, waiting for *Zahir* to notice my absence and return for me, and found ourselves to be the island's only human inhabitants, a finding that closened our bond. There was no sign even of other animals: only Sindbad, Despair, and vegetation.

Fruit and fresh water abounded, enough to keep both of us alive indefinitely and unconstipated. But my companion kept asking: without wines and convivial friends and slave girls with silver chains on slender ankles, why should a man live? Unable to answer, I let him unwind my turban and look about for a convenient tree limb from which to hang me with it.

"That is how we came upon the great white dome you all have heard of, which I mistook for the alabaster temple of some barbarous faith, as it lacked both doors and windows, not to mention minarets. As I walked around it, its owner arrived to blacken the sky and teach me that temples of that sort are always rocs' eggs — a lesson I would remember on Voyage Five but neglect to teach my shipmates. Despair was for the moment frightened away; I put off hanging and hid myself instead.

"The great hen settled down to incubation and, like me in my sea-grape grove, soon drowned in sleep. Praise be to Allah, said I to myself, who never sleeps and who gave men turbans with which to solve their problems one way or another. Instead of hanging myself by the neck from a cinnamon tree, I bound myself fast to the roc's right leg, big as a tree itself, in my innocence believing what my experience had taught me — that no other place to which the bird might take me could be worse than where I was.

"Presently she awoke and flew, paying no more heed to me than to the other parasites that plagued us both. Terrified though I was, I soon beheld, with the same astonishment as my namesake here, what he told us of last night in his first voyage: the living world spread out below me like the chart of Allah mu-Allim, the Celestial Navigator. This, however, was no fretwork of marshes and meanders like the scorch-marks of fresh-baked pita, but a merciless expanse of blue water as boundless as the Seven Seas it was — as boundless, even, as the blue dome above it, on which it seemed to me my carrier must soon bump her head, so high did she carry me. Had I understood what I was overviewing, I might have seen the whole geography of my life below me, past and future, the seas of my several voyages and all their landfalls: the City of Peace, from which I had so foolishly reembarked; Whale Island and its solid neighbor, where dwelled my friend the king; Roc's-Egg Island and all the islands yet to come, including cursed Qeshm and blessed Serendib. But such names are ours, not Allah's; he puts none on his great chart.

"What happened next you know — how the roc descended into a cliffbound valley and her passenger, airsick but grateful, unturbaned himself from her, only to discover that the valley floor was strewn equally with large diamonds and much larger serpents, and that there was no more exit from it than there had been entrance to the Temple of the Egg.

"Nor any less. Though life's tuition is always ruinous, inexorably we learn. Too late now to retie myself to my roc; she had flown off with one of those sides of mutton thrown down by diamond hunters from the clifftop to be studded with gems on impact and carried aloft again by the birds. Even as I lamented (turban in hand) that my dreadful new landing place had not even a decent tree from which I might hang myself before the serpents ate me alive, I heard myself ask *One of those what?* and then remarked both the rest of the diamond-gathering operation and two better uses for my turban than suicide.

"Down the cliff came another side of mutton. Had it struck me, I'd have been squashed as flat as millet cake and my troubles ended. It struck the valley floor instead, and diamonds stuck in the fat of it like lardoons. Another great bird, this one a giant eagle, snatched it off to her clifftop aerie, whence the hunters retrieved it by flapping their turbans till she flew. They then picked out the diamonds from the suet and tossed the mutton down again. Before it hit the ground, I had my plan.

"Like most serpents of my acquaintance, these in Diamond Valley were active by night but torpid in the heat of the day. While they slept — as soundly as an incubating roc or myself among the sea grape — I loaded with the largest diamonds every pouch and pocket of my person, even the six usable orifices of my body (also my navel, which in those days held forty carats snugly), and when the sheep I counted on came whapping down, I lumbered to it with my trusty turban.

"Alas, this particular side of mutton had been so many times re-cycled in the heat of the day that now it dripped and stank like carrion. Another fell not far from it, just as rank, and another and another. I scanned the clifftop, hoping for a fresher vehicle. But the afternoon had waned; there was not a roc or an eagle in sight; it seemed that the gatherers had got their day's worth of diamonds and were discarding their spoiled bait and heading home. Nevertheless, breathing gingerly, I trussed myself under the rotten meat in hope of retrieval, and there spent the most disgusting hour of my story thus far. No rocs appeared — rocs don't eat carrion — but so many flies swarmed down that with any organization at all, they alone could have carried us off.

"The serpents began to stir. I praised Allah the Tireless Schoolmaster, who deigns to teach us lessons even when we're past applying them — and just then, in the familiar twilight of my hopes, I was birded off. Not, alas, by a roc or even a giant eagle, but by a mighty vulture, who moved in when those noble raptors had left the field.

"He took me to his nest, a place more revolting than the food he fetched there and the family he fetched it to, and what happened next I would not speak of in this room were your own dinners not securely down. A horrid mate he had and two huge chicks, by comparison to whose ugliness their mother was Kuzia Fakān herself, and their nest this banquet hall. Their manner of feeding was for the adults to rend and swallow their foul food and then vomit it into their offspring's gullets. This they set about, and in the process retaught me Lesson Three of Voyage One: as I had fed two toes and part of my ring finger to the fish before I floated to that voyage's second island, now I lost to the buzzards the first joint of my left pinkie and portions of my right buttock before I could untie myself and flap those horrid scavengers off. Their babes remained, not old enough to leave the nest but big enough to have been the end of me had they known how to bite as well as swallow. Their parents, moreover, fancied them in danger from me rather than vice versa; they swooped and reswooped to flush me from that nest. To preserve myself — your indulgence, friends — I was obliged at every swoop to duck into the swamp of regurgitation.

"Later I learned from the diamond hunters that normally they worked as a team. Six flapping turbans of assorted colors are required to frighten a feeding roc; four will serve for a giant eagle, and one for a monster buzzard. But only the poorest hunters, those who cannot afford fresh sides of mutton with firm white fat, bother with the buzzards, so nauseating is the labor of retrieval. They wait until the baits of the successful have spoiled and been discarded, and their prosperous owners gone home like the rocs and eagles; then, like the vultures themselves, they pick over the remains.

"On the day I speak of, there was but one such human carrion-crow about, and having but a single turban, dirty and colorless, he dared not approach the pair of adult buzzards until he saw *my* turban flapping at them from the nest. Then he ran up angrily, thinking me one of his kind who had beat him to his haul — and it's well he did, for by this time I was so soaked in buzzard puke and overpowered by nausea that I myself was regurgitating between swoops. These spasms — though they cost me the diamonds I had been holding in my mouth and (for reasons I need not explain) those in my bitten arse as well — saved my life. The chicks believed I was feeding them, as indeed, unwillingly, I was. The circling parents paused in their attack to assess this novelty, and my grudging rescuer finally arrived. The wrath with which he flapped his turban at me sent the buzzards scurrying long enough for me to climb out of their nest at last.

"I explained how I had got there. The fellow called me a liar. Had I not needed his direction to the nearest bathhouse and seaport, I would gladly have left him to fetch his filthy diamonds single-handed from that carrion stew, for I had plenty left of my own. Instead, I convinced him of the truth of my story with the gift of my navel-stone, bigger than any fetched up by even the freshest sheep suet. Furthermore, as I was already basted in upchuck from crown to sole, I volunteered to go back into the nest and pick out his meager take of gemstones from among the bluebottle flies while he flapped off the parent buzzards. But the fellow was too meanspirited to trust me, and so instead I did my final turban-work of Voyage Two: frightening off my erstwhile besmirchers while he mucked out his low-carat catch.

"The rest of that voyage need not concern us here. Three days of scrubbing made me presentable at last to the better class of diamond gatherers; my gifts to them of selected items from my hoard made my story plausible. My buzzard bites were a suppuration long in healing; I still bear the scars and must sit on a cushion-and-a-half. For weeks afterward I was obliged to spend hot afternoons in cool baths, for the least perspiration brought out a lingering whiff of recent history. En route home at last, I paused for a final fumigation at the Camphor Isles and there observed, but was not threatened by, further monsters: rhinoceri who lifted elephants on their horns like wagons of ripe fruit and then themselves were lifted, prey and predator together, by rocs that made my earlier ones look like sparrows."

Sindbad adjusted his well-wound turban and beamed about the table. "Perhaps you doubt me? Then look for proof in the bottom of your goblets! Yasmīn."

She made the rounds, Jaydā this time preceding her, and as each wine cup was filled by the older woman in the now familiar complex order, the younger dropped into it a gem. Even the servants found themselves included in the toast, and were convinced. To ruddy Ibn al-Hamrā, Yasmīn gave the largest stone — but mischievously dropped it in from such a height that his red wine splashed him like buzzard pabulum.

"From Voyage Two, as from Voyage One," Sindbad concluded, "I learned four lessons." Ibn al-Hamrā left off stanching his caftan to count on his fingers, as before. "First, that with respect to salvation, as aforedeclared, sleep is a soporific. Particularly when you suspect yourself to be in Paradise, do not doze off! Second, that God gave men heads not only for wearing turbans on, and turbans not only for wearing on our heads. Third, that where diamonds abound, so surely shall serpents. Fourth, and finally, that what goes down may come up — though for narrative digestion there are all-but-foolproof aids. Perpend this last, my friends, for tomorrow's voyage will put these first two in the shade. Your health!"

The toast was drunk, and many were the cross-eyed drinkers of it, careful not to swallow their persuaders with their persuasion. Some glanced in the direction of Kuzia Fakān, hoping for an intermission. But Sindbad the Sailor, as good as his word, simply extended one hand, palm up, toward Sindbad the Still-Stranded, offering his namesake both the audience and the narrative floor.

That fellow turned between pensive thumb and forefinger the diamond from his cup.

"To flavor your wine with, comrades, or my story," he said, "I have nothing like this. It must be swallowed neat or spat back like buzzard's brew."

He rose, went down to the table's far end, and smilingly dropped the stone into the empty cup of the cup-bearer in her saffron-orange djellaba. Frowns of surprise at his presumption went around the company.

"Empty-handed I came into this hall," Somebody declared, returning to his place, "and all but empty-handed I'll leave it when our tales are told, though my head and gut alike will be as stuffed with marvels as were our host's with diamonds till those vultures fouled him."

He smiled: at still-startled Yasmīn, at the dinner guests (even Ibn al-Hamrā), at old Sindbad.

"As you said truly, Sayyid, every morning begins a new voyage or resumes an old. But each night does, too: awake and asleep we sail by turns two voyages, now parallel, now worlds apart, yet at times so close that the voyager may be transported unawares from one ship to the other. One Sindbad naps among the sea grape and wakes to find himself headed heavenward; another dozes off in Serendib and wakes still stranded."

The company praised Allah, who, though He never sleeps, dreamed both their world and any others. Their present narrator then told them a version of

Somebody's Second Voyage

When Simon William Behler was thirteen and fourteen, his special friend was Daisy Moore, who lived on River Boulevard in West Dorset. It might even be said that "Crazy Daisy" was the young man's moral coach and sexual instructor.

"Oh *blyeh!*" my friend Daisy would have replied to that: her throwup sound. It was the noise she had made last night in Schine's Bijou, for example. The island chieftain's daughter, a saronged and hibiscused Dorothy Lamour, had expressed to Sterling Hayden her puzzlement at the catcalls and wolf whistles of the U.S. Navy exploration team that had come upon her swimming innocently in the lagoon: "Among my people, the naked body is a thing of dignity. It is a flower to be quietly admired, not one of your *pinups* to be whistled at."

"*Blyeh! Blyeh!*" had gagged Crazy Daisy.

"How come *blyeh?*" I asked her afterward, as I walked her home from uptown to River Boulevard. "I've heard you say things like that."

My lean and serious friend liked from time to time in these dialogues to clutch my arm with one hand, clap her brow with the other, and stop us where we stood, as if calling God and the community of

Dorset to witness her dismay at my retardation. This she did now under the streetlight on the corner of High and Holly, not far from the offices of Behler Maintenance & Improvement. "That's the *point,* 'Simmon!" (Her nickname for me that season, from *Simon* but also from the country term for persimmon: this same season she had reported to me that in the transport of ejaculation I scrooched my face as if I had "sucked a sour 'simmon.") "I *believe* it, but Lamour's talking movie-talk. 'Among my people . . .' *Blyeh!*"

Daisy Moore's speech was rich in italics, exclamation points, sound effects, and moral distinctions. Her father — a slight, gentle, almost apologetic man with silver hair and a black mustache, whose daughters affectionately called him Sam — was, by his own description, a "vice president by marriage" of Albany Brothers, Inc., the packers of Dorset Brand tomatoes, shellfish, and, lately, C rations for the U.S. Army. Her mother — the vague, wild-haired, good-natured daughter of one of those Albanys — was in and out of the Eastern Shore State Hospital. Daisy was the second of their numerous children, several daughters followed by several sons. The oldest girl, Brinsley, had gone off to college and never came home on school vacations. Especially during Mrs. Moore's sojourns in the asylum, Daisy "watched out for Sam," as she put it: she helped the housekeeper look after him and her younger siblings and the house, a pillared pile on Dorset's oldest residential street, and discreetly saw to it (she once mentioned to me) that neither she nor Julia, her younger sister, found herself alone with him in his library at day's end, when her brothers had been put to bed and her father enjoyed a brandy or two before turning in.

I asked. She shrugged. "He gets too friendly."

Upon this subject and certain others about which I was comparably curious, Daisy sometimes volunteered information, but I was not permitted to press inquiry. Though we were classmates, she was a year and a half older than I (I had skipped a grade) and uncountable laps ahead of me: in everything, it seemed to me; "In two things, 'Simmon," she would correct me, "and only one of those matters. 'Among my people . . .' *Blyeh!*"

This was the last night of June, a Friday, warm and damp and fragrant on River Boulevard, which ran its few wide blocks under splendid cottonwoods and mock oranges from the uptown business district down to River Park and the Municipal Basin. Though there was no need for it, I was wearing over my polo shirt a poplin wind-breaker, currently the fashion in our school; Daisy's sleeveless blouse and airy skirt were better suited to the humid evening. We sat awhile in the glider on the Moores' porch, dark and vast. Julia and some of the brothers played noisy hide-and-seek in the boxwood and hydrangea; from where we sat, Daisy refereed their game. Fired by the example of Sterling Hayden, I put an arm around her bare shoulders and bussed her ear, moving her long brown hair aside with my lips to expose the little pearl pierced earring in her lobe, and tautly awaited her response.

In these matters I found my friend altogether unpredictable. Nearly sixteen, she had dated high-school seniors — had even run around briefly with my brother Joe's gang — and helped raise her brothers. Male anatomy and its functions had no mysteries for her, as had female still for me. Her sister Brinsley, who had been to Daisy in the moral sphere as Daisy was to me, was known to all Dorset to have been "fast": a regular hellion, Aunt Rachel had told me, half admiringly. Even before she went away to college for good, Brinsley Moore had had to be packed off to a girls' boarding school near Baltimore for her senior year. ("*Had to be*," scoffed Daisy. "*Blyeh!* Don't believe everything you read in the papers, Persimmon.") The Moores in general were out of my social class: Sam's brandy nightcaps and university degree; Brinsley's cream-colored roadster, laid up "for the duration" in their carriage house; Mrs. Moore's easy talk, when she was home, of art museums, operas, and the novels she pressed upon me from the family's library — these were to me themselves the stuff of novels, and of Hollywood movies, with which I had larger acquaintance from faithful attendance at Schine's Bijou.

But Daisy's unpredictability seemed to me, even then, quite her own. Through the first third of *Lagoon* I had let my right hand idly dangle ever nearer the front of her blouse, my arm along her seat-back and over her shoulder, until in a moment of reaction to Dorothy Lamour's close encounter with the tiger beside the sacred waterfall, fingertips and breast made a seemingly accidental contact that I lightly then maintained. Without moving her eyes from the screen, Daisy snapped me off her with a smart flick of the fingernail, as one might send flying an errant Japanese beetle. Through the contretemps with the rowdy sailors and Sterling Hayden's subsequent demonstrations of his superior sensitivity as well as his manliness, I moved my operations to her left leg, beginning boldly not at the knee but a hand's width above it, and not atop the hem of her dirndl but straightforwardly underneath, on the smooth, slightly sweaty inside of her lower thigh.

"Jesus, 'Simmon!" she had hissed. "Lay off pestering me!"

Now, on the contrary, she grabbed my wrist and stuck my hand right into the front of her blouse, onto her little bare left breast. At a time when most girls her age were eager to wear brassieres and even padded them out with Kleenex, Daisy Moore would not. "For *these?*" she had said in May, the second time we'd swum together over to the Island. There she had permitted her very excited friend to examine and within certain limits to explore her in our special bower, formerly Joe Junior's gang's clubhouse: the first naked girl's body I had seen firsthand.

"Neat, huh?" she'd said. "But no headlights."

Moreover, to my astonishment she had presently on her own initiative "done" me (the occasion of my nicknaming), collected my prompt ejaculate in her palm, inspected and sniffed it as if disdainfully, but then with a grin lapped it up and said, *"Mnyum!"*

Then and now, I was electrified. But what had been amiss, I wanted to know, with my touching her in Schine's Bijou?

Daisy clapped her brow. "I was watching the stupid *movie!* No hiding up here, Charles Moore!" she warned a ten-year-old brother, and then she quietly observed (I was working her nipple carefully now with two fingertips, neither hard enough to hurt nor lightly enough to tickle), "Hey, Persimmon: you've got it right."

But even as that nub rose welcomely under my touch, her father ambled out onto the porch, brandy snifter in one hand, cigarette in the other. Not so abruptly as to attract his attention, we disengaged, and I saw Daisy shift her left ankle behind her right to hide my I.D. bracelet. That summer it was the custom for a Dorset High girl who was "going steady" to wear on her left ankle her boyfriend's silver identification bracelet, the heavier the better. Daisy Moore and I could hardly be said to be going steady, though neither of us was "involved" with anyone else; moreover, Daisy's father disapproved of this particular custom, as well as of going steady in general among high-schoolers, and Daisy seconded his contention that she was nobody's property.

For just that reason, however, after our second visit to the Island she had not refused the bracelet that my family had given me a year ago, on my thirteenth birthday: thinking that when I became the famous explorer that I intended to be, I might elect to use William as my first and Simon as my middle name, I had asked them to leave the bracelet unengraved until I decided, and a year later its nameplate was still blank. Daisy liked that: she declared it showed she was Nobody's property. Sometimes she wore it on her arm with other bracelets; most often she kept it in her jewelry box. Now and then she would insist that I wear it for a while. Then, unpredictably, as she had done this evening, she would demand it back and, once we had left her house, wear it in plain view on her left ankle.

"Time to come in now, Daise," Sam Moore said gently. "Is that Simon Behler? Hello there, Sy."

"Hi, Mister Moore." I admired the way he held his brandy glass, its squat bowl cupped in his palm, its stem between his third and fourth fingers.

"Game's over!" Daisy announced to the dark yard. "Ten! Nine! Eight! Seven!" Her count brought siblings from the shadows, all except six-year-old Beaufort, a famous tease.

"I'll find him," Daisy said. "Happy birthday tomorrow, 'Simmon."

Shy, befreckled Julia Moore, stringy like her sister and already as tall, had emerged from a hydrangea just behind our glider, smiling through her dental braces and framing us in an imaginary camera. Daisy caught her elbow and briskly led her off, calling, *"Beaufort Moore, we know where you are, and if you make us come get you we're going to tickle you till you wet your pants!"*

Their father inhaled his filter-tipped cigarette and watched the girls leave the porch. I was pretty sure he had noticed the ankle bracelet. Then, as if to the brandy sliding around in his snifter, he remarked, "So: your birthday, is it."

En route home from West to East Dorset across the creek bridge, young Behler paused for some moments on the draw-span to admire his hometown and to savor his really quite considerable sophistication.

Counting tonight, I had half a dozen times reached Second Base, at least briefly — and with a girl older than myself — and on two occasions had precociously achieved Third. It was Daisy herself, not my male friends, who had explained those bases to me, together with the distinction between measuring physical intimacy in such terms, which she regarded as inevitable and even useful, and boasting of it to our classmates, which she judged to be contemptible. I was certain from their talk that none of my East Dorset comrades had experienced with any girl what I had (twice) with Daisy on the Island. What was more, thanks to her carrot-and-stick coaching, I had managed *not* to boast to them of my extraordinary sessions with her, at least not directly and explicitly — though I had learned to deploy a smiling silence to good effect. If I lapsed, she had warned me, she would learn of it soon enough, however much I might swear my buddies to secrecy, for such gossip was never containable; her sister Brinsley had taught her that truth. Needless to say, between her and me, that would be that. But if (she had said one late-April night on that same front-porch glider) I actually kept my mouth shut and moreover didn't *pester* her like some absolute *drip* . . . we would see what we would see. So saying, she had moved my hand from its tentative perch on her left knee up under her skirt and snugly and exactly to her crotch, which it breathtakingly fitted — atop her underpants, yes, but so exciting was the warmth and moistness of that contour that I spontaneously fired off into my jockey shorts.

I had been twice also to New York City with Aunt Rachel and Uncle Joshua, their joint birthday gifts to Joe Junior and me in 1939 and again in 1940: to the World's Fair, the Statue of Liberty, and the top of the Empire State Building. We had stayed in a Manhattan hotel and had once had breakfast served to the four of us in our room. At Daisy's mother's urging I had read *Ivanhoe*, by Sir Walter Scott, and *The Adventures of Tom Sawyer*, by Mark Twain, and was currently attempting both that latter author's *Adventures of Huckleberry Finn* and a volume of tales from *The Arabian Nights*, unexpurgated; I was also a great fan of the adventurous Richard Halliburton, who had personally autographed Sam Moore's copies of his travel books. Very likely I was the only East Dorset kid — perhaps one of the few East Dorseters of any age — ever to have been inside the Moores' big house on River Boulevard; none of my family had been, though my father was now mayor of the town and on cordial terms with Sam Moore, himself a councilman. But I had even eaten dinner there, three times, when Mrs. Moore was in residence. Once she had served roast leg of lamb, which

I had never eaten before because my father didn't care for lamb. I had liked it all right. Mr. and Mrs. Moore sipped wine with their dinner, and Daisy and I were permitted a third of a glass each, Julia and the brothers a sip or two, to begin to learn the different flavors. Neither my father nor Uncle Josh knew that round-shouldered bottles were Bordeaux and slope-shouldered ones Burgundy, though Aunt Rachel remembered having been told that by a Frenchman during her visit to France.

Behler was not destined, my narrator intoned, to play out his part on the small, familiar stage of Dorset, as had his father and grandfather before him. Vaguely but unmistakably, some larger, more adventuresome future beckoned.

That intuition inspired in me, there on the creek bridge, a detached affection for my little city and the tidemarsh county of which it was the seat, where I had lived for what seemed to me a very long time already. I felt . . . *seasoned by experience.* Up at Dorset Creek's dark confluence with Island Creek, under the quarter moon, was the old municipal cemetery; I recalled *with wry amusement* the day seven years ago when I had last visited it, at my own insistence. I remembered my early fascination with the Lifter at the Albany Brothers cannery — nothing more than a vertical conveyor belt! — and my trepidation at Joe Junior's close bicycle approach to Colonel Philip Albany's striking workers. Now my brother was a Seabee in the Pacific theater of operations, and over the Albany Brothers cannery flew the blue and white E for Excellence for producing rations for our troops, and my father was no longer town councilman but mayor, and Uncle Josh — the general manager of Behler Maintenance & Improvement — was chief of civil defense for the town. I myself was an expert airplane spotter, the only boy in my scout troop to get a perfect score on all three parts of the aircraft identification test: Allied, German, and Japanese. In consequence, though I was a year younger than my fellow freshmen, I had served last year on the Incendiary Bomb Squad at Dorset High and hoped this year to be its chief. While the others, students and teachers alike, sat in the hallways during air-raid drills with their foreheads on their knees and their arms clasped around their legs to protect themselves from flying glass, the Bomb Squad and its faculty advisers stood watch on the asphalt-and-gravel roof beside shovels and galvanized washtubs filled with sand, with which we were prepared to smother incendiary bombs dropped on Dorset by Heinkel bombers.

(*"Pfth!"* had scoffed Daisy Moore two weeks ago on the Island, retracting my foreskin while we discussed the recent Allied invasion of Normandy. I had spoken gravely of the likelihood of Nazi counter-measures, including some sort of raid on America itself; I was proud that both the Albany Brothers cannery and the Dorset Shipyard, two blocks from our house, had been officially designated as possible mili-tary targets. "How're they going to get bombers clear across the At-lantic Ocean?" The only way America could ever be "attacked," she declared, no doubt quoting her knowledgeable father, was either by commandos put ashore by submarine, who at most might manage to smuggle a bomb into the Capitol or the Washington Monument, or else by V-1 buzz bombs somehow launched from those submarines. In either case, I and my bucket of sand would be of little avail. Didn't I realize that all this civil-defense business was just to make the home-folks feel involved in the "war effort"?

I did not, until that moment; the idea was as astonishing to me as was Daisy's candid inspection of my exposed and erect glans penis for traces of smegma — terms I learned from her then and there, as I learned of the charade of civil defense — before she said, "Looks okay," and . . . kissed it!)

Without compunction — indeed, with cool exhilaration — Simon William Behler then committed the first consciously immoral act of his life.

Just off the East Dorset end of the creek bridge was Paul's, a neigh-borhood soda fountain and candy store whose Coke sodas, we loyally maintained, were the best in town. Although it was still a good hour before closing time, the place was empty of customers. Freddy Mulli-gan, rejected for military service because of flat feet, had begun clean-ing up behind the counter. Everything about me just then gave me satisfaction: I could remember being brought to Paul's for ice cream when I was so little that Mother had to lift me high onto one of the green revolving stools, and the counter clerks seemed huge grown-ups; now, a grown-up myself in many ways, I could drop in at the end of an evening and with my own money casually buy a Coke soda from my old boyhood acquaintance Freddy Mulligan. This reflection gave me unexpectedly to appreciate what must be my father's perspective: born and raised in East Dorset in its rougher days as a poor watermen's neighborhood, the hardworking son of hardworking immigrants, he had lived his adult life in a house three blocks from the house he was born in, and though like many of his generation he had been obliged to quit school at sixteen and take up his father's trade, he had risen to be a prosperous businessman and the first mayor of our town ever to have been elected from East Dorset. How proud his stolid parents would have been had they lived to see his success! I too was proud of it, yet I understood that beyond our marshland county his name was scarcely known, and that beyond tidewater Maryland it was not known at all.

"Whatcha hear from Joe?" Freddy Mulligan asked me. He had made my Coke soda, rung up my quarter, and gone back to wiping the ice cream cabinets with a rag. A red and yellow can of Bon Ami cleanser, in use, stood near my elbow on the green marble counter.

"Nothing since San Diego," I reported, pleased with the recent huskiness of my voice. "He won't be allowed to say where he is even when he gets there."

"Bulldozing hisself some Japs on one of them islands," Freddy Mulligan reckoned. "Wish I was right there with him."

Mullig had grown fat and sported a thin mustache. The years between us, once so formidable a span, were insignificant now. I recognized that by comparison even with my brother he would never amount to much, and this understanding inspired in me a generous self-confidence.

"You been out messing with Crazy Daisy?" he wanted to know next. His back turned toward me, he was polishing the cash register. Firmly but amiably I said, "None of your beeswax, Mullig."

He chuckled and waddled off behind the candy showcase. Loyally I called after him, "There's nothing Crazy about Daisy Moore. She's all right."

From where he stooped, out of sight, Mullig chuckled again. "You ought to know."

I had finished my Coke soda and was contemplating the familiar trademark on the half-empty can of cleanser. "I *do* know," I acknowledged, and in one easy motion I tucked that can under my wind-breaker and swung off the much-taped revolving stool. "See you, Mullig."

Grunting to his feet, Freddy Mulligan called back, "See you now, Behler."

Under street-lit maples down wide and empty Maryland Avenue I strolled home, as coolly giddy as on that hot May afternoon on Island Point when I had challenged Daisy to swim with me over to the Island, though we had no swimsuits with us, and she'd said Sure, and I'd stripped to my underpants, hoping she would do likewise, and she had not stopped there. With my left forearm I clutched my stolen prize to my heart until I turned onto darker Maple Street, where I dared carry it openly.

Poor dumb Mullig!

On our screened front porch, Uncle Josh was smoking and sipping beer in the dark; I had seen the glow of his Chesterfield from the sidewalk. Nowadays he could have afforded his own house, but he and Aunt Rachel had grown used to living with us, and after Mother's death it had seemed to go without saying that they would stay on and manage. "Late," he noted mildly as I crossed the porch. I reported having stopped at Paul's for a Coke soda.

Dad was in his living-room chair, simultaneously reading his double-folded *Philadelphia Evening Bulletin* and listening to Edward R. Murrow on the radio, used white pocket handkerchiefs tucked all around his seat cushion. He could not hear people come onto the porch, but he looked up smiling when he saw movement in the room. "How was your movie, son?"

Holding the Bon Ami can lightly out of sight behind me, I called "Fine!" and went on back to the kitchen. Aunt Rachel was fixing herself a fresh-lemon Coke, her regular and frequent summer drink, to take with her out to the porch, where she and Uncle Josh liked to sit together in the dark through the eleven-o'clock radio news.

"Brought you some Bon Ami," I declared, and I put my red and yellow prize (the colors, it now occurred to me, of the only airplane I had ever flown in, Howard Garton's old Bellanca at the Avon airport) on the stainless steel countertop next to the sink. "Freddy Mulligan gave it to me for helping out at Paul's."

"*Hwell!*" Aunt Rachel feigned mutual indignation. "That's some pay!" She pretended to inspect the countertop. "*Hasn't scratched yet!*"

I saw at once a possible mistake in my having provided her with an anecdote that might call undue attention to my trophy. Just then the radio news came on — loudly, for Dad's benefit. I bade all good night and went up to bed.

After Mother's death, in 1938, my old bedroom had passed to Aunt Rachel as a sewing room. My brother and I, ever less agreeably, had shared the back bedroom for yet another two years, until his high-school graduation and immediate enlistment in the Seabees. Thereafter, as he came home only on brief, infrequent leaves, the room was virtually mine, though for sentimental reasons my brother's half was left undisturbed for the duration. Though nearsightedness had disqualified Joe Junior from flight training, the airplane models he had built right up to enlistment day still hung, dusty now, from their ceiling threads: the gull-winged Stuka dive bomber and Vought-Sikorsky carrier plane, the pursuit planes P38, P39, P40, P47, and P50. My side of the room was equally military: my spotter's sheets of winged silhouettes, my wall maps of the ETO and PTO with their flagged pins, which, as a rule, I relocated nightly after the news. I would catch up tomorrow with our Normandy invasion forces, our bogged-down campaign in Italy, and the Red Army's advance across eastern Europe. My Pacific pins had scarcely been moved for more than a year, since Guadalcanal. Some were actually rusting in our humid air. But Dad and Uncle Josh agreed that something big was brewing out there.

Wearing only my pajama bottoms in the damp heat, I turned out the bedside light, armed myself with a handful of Kleenex, and began my ritual. Rocking lightly on my left side under the sheet, I embellished the remarkable-enough facts of my adventures on the Island with Daisy Moore. Never mind that my friend had actually twice done for me what I was doing now for myself, and the second time had instructed me how to do the same for her, which I had not suspected possible; I felt obliged to destroy my hometown by fire (a surprise attack with secret new rockets fired from U-boats off Ocean City) as Dorothy Lamour's village had been destroyed by the angry volcano god. Daisy and I escaped only by swimming to the Island. Looking back grimly from its shore as Sterling Hayden had done from his retreating ship, I embraced my tearful lover to console her and myself for our loss, then led her into our bower of honeysuckle and Virginia creeper, where at last —

The ceiling light clicked on. "Where'd you get the Bon Ami, son?"

Luckily my bedsheet had worked its way down only to my waist. "Swiped it from Paul's." My treacherous voice broke in midconfession. I could not recall my father's ever having been in my bedroom before; it did not occur to me to lie to him.

"What?"

"*I swiped it from Paul's!*"

"Get on your wheel," he said quietly, "and take it back 'fore he closes." He set the can on my dresser-top and withdrew.

Asweat with humiliation, I pulled my khaki pants on over my pajama bottoms, slipped into my polo shirt and penny loafers, and went downstairs with the Bon Ami. Perhaps to spare my feelings, Uncle Josh and Aunt Rachel had moved back into the kitchen. Dad, in his living-room chair, didn't look up from his *Evening Bulletin* but said, "Tell Paul Travers you're sorry."

Joe Junior's battered old Silver King had passed to me; though the Maintenance side of the family business was prospering from the same wartime shortages that curtailed the Improvement side, there were no new bicycles to be had for the duration. I wheeled it off the porch, letting the screen door slam behind me to signal that I was obeying orders, but under protest. The night was still warm and breezeless, the street empty. As I pedaled past Zion Meth-Prot toward Dorset Creek, I conjured Andy Hardy–like scenes of earnest apology to Mr. Travers, who usually stopped by his store at closing time to check the receipts and make sure all was secure for the night. Feigning sternness but secretly amused, he would commend my strength of character and offer me a summer job; the anecdote would be retold in East Dorset when Simon William or William Simon Behler had risen to national fame, or maybe even international fame, like Richard Halliburton. On the other hand, if Mullig was still there by himself, I would take the simpler course of pretending to have forgotten something I needed and surreptitiously restoring the Bon Ami can while he fetched whatever that was.

Paul's neon sign and display windows were dark. If the store was closed, I could leave the can in the entranceway with a straightforward, dignified note — or perhaps without a note (I had no pencil or paper), but I would say I had left one. If Dad happened to check with Mr. Travers — he wouldn't go out of his way to check, but as mayor he chatted with dozens of Dorseters every day, and he had grown up with Paul Travers — I would suppose that my note had blown away.

Just Mullig would be best. I would tell him I was sleepless with concern for my brother — premonitions, call it what you will — and needed another Coke soda and a little conversation before turning in. But I had neglected to bring any money. Just some talk, then, though it wouldn't surprise me if old Mullig set up a Coke soda on the house. I would tease him, amiably, with Joe Junior's story about how he had got that nickname.

They were both there, closing up: Mullig lumped on one of the green counter stools, waiting to be dismissed, and Mr. Travers counting out the cash register. All thought of confession fled, and Maryland Avenue was so deserted that even if I tried to sneak the Bon Ami into the doorway, one of the pair would surely notice me. My face burning, I pedaled on, out onto the creek bridge. I paused where I had paused before, on the grating of the draw-span, and (making sure the bridge tender couldn't see) dropped the wretched can into Dorset Creek.

What retribution I then inflicted upon my humiliators. En route home I indulged myself in a resentment that would have been unbecoming even had I done what I had been dispatched to do. The porch was empty. Uncle Josh and my betrayer had gone to bed; Dad waited up, still reading newspapers, but though I was no doubt prepared now to lie if questioned, I made it plain in the way I stalked past him and up the stairs that I was not to be interrogated, and I closed my bedroom door just loudly enough to advertise my anger without provoking his. Too furious to resume masturbation, as I rocked myself toward sleep I summoned the *Luftwaffe* to redestroy my town, and though I managed to save most of my family with a daring at which they could only shake their humbled heads, once clear of the rubble I turned my back on them forever and went off Islandward, to where Daisy Moore (whom I had rescued first) waited for me in our honeysuckle bower.

He went down to breakfast with his family.

Though our old LaSalle had on its windshield both the black *A* and the green *C* gasoline-rationing stickers, its ponderous tires, recapped once already, were wearing smooth again, and so on weekdays my father walked uptown to Behler Maintenance & Improvement.

Saturday mornings, however, he drove to his municipal office and about his mayoral rounds, for which our *A* card had been granted. I lingered in bed until I heard him leave the house, blowing his nose and clearing his throat, racing the engine and riding the clutch as he shifted gears. Then, still shouldering the chip of my insulted pride but worried afresh that on his way uptown he might stop by Paul's to chuckle at my prankish theft and chastening restitution, I came downstairs.

Uncle Josh, in his seersucker summer robe, was clearing the breakfast dishes. Around his cigarette holder he announced, "Here's the birthday boy."

Aunt Rachel — terry-turbaned, long-earringed, light-housecoated — turned from her sinkful of suds. "Happy b-day, Simon B."

Without replying, I went to the refrigerator to get milk for cereal, though the skillet and French-toast makings were assembled on the stove. In plain view, too, on the breakfast table, was a small gift-wrapped package, the shape and size of a wristwatch box or an Eversharp pen-and-pencil set. I ignored it as well and conspicuously fixed myself a bowl of Rice Krispies.

"Uh-oh," said Uncle Josh. "Snap, Crackle, and Pop." He patted my shoulder and left the kitchen. Aunt Rachel sat down across from me, propped both elbows on the breakfast table, rested her chin on her interlaced fingers, and crooned to the tune of our door chimes: "Si-mon's *pout*-ing. . . ."

"It's not funny!" I let her know.

"No, it isn't," she mildly agreed, and she got up to put things away. "You're old enough to understand that Dad's got your best interests in mind. He wants you to be a *somebody,* not another Freddy Mulligan."

"Mullig's okay," I let her know.

"Sure he is! And twenty years from now he'll still be jerking sodas for Paul Travers. Is that what *you* want to be doing in nineteen sixty-four?"

"Nothing wrong with that," I let her know, but Aunt Rachel, confident that arguments to my ambition were unanswerable, let the matter rest. Her Saturday-morning chore was to scrub the week's scuff marks off the white rubber tiles of our checkerboard kitchen floor, which she had made Dad promise to replace with cheaper, more practical asphalt tile as soon as the war was over and things were available again. Mine, much less laborious, was to mow the lawn and spray the Chinese Cigar trees, and I would be well advised, Aunt Rachel suggested, to get the job done in the cool of the morning, as the forecast called for another stinkeroo like yesterday. But that, she agreed, was nobody's beeswax but my own.

Our yard was a small flat rectangle, easily mowed with our ancient, clattering push-mower except for the nuisance of our catalpa trees, which were to the grounds what those white rubber floor tiles were to Aunt Rachel's kitchen. For climbing, they were splendid; I could even enter and leave my bedroom via what I called the Escape Route, a thick lateral catalpa limb that overhung the back porch roof, onto which my rear window opened. But in May they littered the grass with their dead white blossoms; in June and July, unless sprayed weekly with slaked lime from our pressure sprayer, they were so infested with caterpillars that the yard was unusable; in August and September their foot-long green seed pods — the "Chinese cigars" that East Dorset children dried and attempted to smoke — turned brown, split, and carpeted the lawn with both their winged white seeds and their long, brittle husks, impossible to mow over and clumsy to rake up; and in October the leaves themselves, as big as water-lily pads, came down. This morning was still and steamy, the sky gray-white, the grass wet with dew. Walking about stirred up mosquitoes, but I peeled off my shirt and set to work, feeling especially virtuous under the circumstances, and the physical exertion purged me of my mood.

Fourteen! My body pleased me, mostly: wiry, smooth, and sunbrowned, still too thin in the chest and upper arms but already broad-shouldered and narrow-hipped and, unlike my brother's stocky build, pushing toward six feet, maybe beyond. The family predicted that I would be its tallest member. My jaw was as hairless as a girl's, subject more to pimples than to whiskers, but I had practiced shaving it with Uncle Josh's expensive prewar Gillette. I wished my voice were deeper, my muscles larger, my pubic hair thicker, my penis more imposing in its flaccid state. Otherwise, however, it was okay, and I assumed that all those improvements would come to pass before long. Pleasuring in the exercise, I mowed the grass, raked the clippings, emptied and replaced the canisters of the Japanese-beetle traps supplied free to all local householders by the Department of Agriculture and faithfully maintained by the neighborhood as a patriotic duty. Alone among the people I knew, my friend Daisy scoffed at these traps; her mother had told her that their scented baits attracted more Japanese beetles than they killed, and that the whole program was no more than patriotic busywork inspired by the insect's name. But Mrs. Moore was, in her own phrase, "part-time crazy," and the Moore family inclined to such heresies. Daisy said, for example, that her father believed the War Bond drives to be another patriotic fraud: the government, Sam had told her, would see to it that the $25 we got back in ten years would buy less than the $18.75 we paid out now. At this shocking idea, when I reported it, Aunt Rachel clucked her tongue and Dad frowned. But Uncle Josh said it wouldn't surprise him: 1954 was a long way off.

Next I mixed the white lime spray, pumped up and shouldered the heavy pressure tank, and sprayed the catalpas, pretending that the caterpillars were Japs and the sprayer a flamethrower. I was one against multitudes, but even in the steady southwesterly from a Bermuda high stalled off the coast, my accuracy was devastating. The trees were liberated. "I've got a brother out there somewhere," I modestly declared to President Roosevelt. "I was only doing what any of my buddies would have done."

By late morning the sky was sunny, the temperature climbing through the eighties. My family were all about their business; the house was empty, its doors and windows open to the humid breeze. I washed up and fixed myself a tall glass of strawberry Kool-Aid. On the breakfast table, beside my unopened birthday gift, was a note from Aunt Rachel: *Back by 2. Windows?* Burglary was no problem in East Dorset, but mildew was, and it was the summertime responsibility of whoever left the house last (in practice, always either my aunt or myself) to balance the usual possibility of afternoon thundershowers against the need for maximum ventilation and to adjust windows accordingly, especially on the north and west sides. She and I regarded ourselves as experts in this area and enjoyed conferring on its fine points, such as whether a forty-percent chance of thundershowers warranted closing the south and east upstairs windows as well, since rain could be backwinded through them in a real squall. Hence the question mark.

At the sight of it I understood that I had forgiven her, if not yet Dad, for last night — she had doubtless only reported to him what I myself had told her, and for some reason Dad had doubted my story — and that I *liked* Joe Junior's being away in the service, so that I could both miss him and be the only young person in the house. Our relations had been neither very close nor often truly adversary; I liked my brother better in his absence and wouldn't mind if he never came home again except to visit. However, if that birthday gift was what its size and solitariness suggested, I would be touched and thankful indeed. My faithful Ingersoll Mickey Mouse watch still kept good time, but I was too old to wear it; Uncle Josh's old Longines-Wittnauer, which he had loaned me, looked and ran like an antique; and no new watches were available for the duration. But Joe Junior had mentioned in a letter from California that he could get real Swiss watches cheap in the Navy Post Exchange. . . . I shook the package carefully and was gratified; its rattle was not that of an Eversharp pen-and-pencil set.

Concerning my birthday gift from Daisy I had certain hopes, and though I knew I must leave the initiative to her, I was determined to provide her with ample opportunity to take it. As a virtual only child, with few summertime responsibilities beyond such chores as I had just completed, I was freer to spend time at her house than she was at mine. In Aunt Rachel's view this was as it should be, but I wished it were otherwise, for our house was often empty for a predictable interval, as it was just now, whereas the Moores' was always swarmed. On the back of Aunt Rachel's note I wrote, *Scouts till 12, Moores after. Windows OK.* Uncertain of whether or where *Moores* should be apostrophized, I added a small, ambiguous mark directly over the *s*.

The last part of the morning I spent in the furnace room of Zion Meth-Prot with the Silver Fox Patrol of Troop 159 of the Boy Scouts of America, baling the wastepaper we had collected in a neighborhood drive the week before. Ordinarily, in the absence of adult supervision, my patrolmates and I made a leisurely job of untying the string-bound piles of old newspapers and magazines and culling choice items such as *Esquire* and *Judge* before stacking the rest high in the baler for compressing and wiring into regulation bales for the war effort. The Silver Foxes had yet to turn up anything to match the three-foot stack of illustrated *Spicy Detectives* once found and sequestered by the Otter Patrol, but this morning Freddy Mulligan's kid brother, Danny, a newly recruited Tenderfoot, had discovered a single issue of a bona fide nudist periodical, which I found the Silver Foxes examining to-gether — the first such that any of us had seen.

"Simon the Behler," Charlie Norman greeted me. He was the min-ister's son, our patrol leader and only Star Scout, working toward Eagle. "Come get a load of these headlights."

Nothing to jerk off by, we agreed: the men, women, and young children in the black-and-white photographs were just standing around naked in parks and on beaches; there were no teenagers, and almost none of the women pictured had a good body. On the other hand, these were actual photographs, not line drawings like those in *Spicy Detective,* and the people were white Americans, not the naked Papuans and Pygmies of Uncle Josh's *National Geographic.* Raucously but carefully we inspected the misshapen breasts, bellies, and buttocks, the sometimes startlingly shaggy crotches and pendulous cocks. The magazine declared editorially that if the delegates to the League of Nations had convened regularly in the nude, "with nothing to hide," there would never have been a Second World War.

"Yeah," Roger Henry commented. "They'd've been too busy fuck-ing to fight." Danny Mulligan attempted to repeat a dirty joke that his brother had told him involving Franklin and Eleanor Roosevelt, but all he could remember was that they were naked in the White House and that the last line was "Cobwebs, Franklin." "Man," Charlie Norman said, "this one's got *plenty* to hide." He pointed to an obese lady standing with others before some sort of cabin. "Who could fuck that?"

Several Silver Foxes volunteered.

After only an hour's baling I left, pleading a fictitious birthday lunch. Roger Henry singsonged, "We know where you're go-ing." Charlie Norman bet I was going to "dine at the Y." "*Eat Moore at the Y,*" Roger Henry improvised, a note of respectful envy in his taunt, and Danny Mulligan said, "That would be *crazy.* Get it?"

"Shut your lunch hole, Tenderfoot," I warned him. But I was not displeased at the general assumption. When Roger Henry (First Class Scout, like myself) called after me, "Have a nice lunch, Behler!" I simply called back, "Thanks, Rodge."

Pedaling past Paul's and over the creek bridge to the Moores' in the hot light of day reinspired my grudge against my father, a resentment that I must have imagined would somehow work in my favor with

Daisy, for I was eager to share with her the story of last night's humiliation. She was, however, busy with the family's lunch, which, at least in Mrs. Moore's absence, was an assembly-line production. Their kitchen — designed a hundred years ago for the Negro slave help, Sam Moore had once explained to me, not for the lady of the house — was much smaller, darker, and less modernized than ours. Virginia, the colored housekeeper, brought out to the main dining-room table institutional-size jars of peanut butter and two kinds of jelly, long loaves of sliced whole-wheat bread (never used in our house), half-gallons of milk, a bag of apples, stacks of plates and napkins, and a sleeve of paper cups. Warning the brothers to keep their hands off till she gave the word, Daisy dealt out a row of lunch plates like playing cards — one extra when she saw me come in — and Julia, behind her, four slices of bread per plate. Young Beaufort then, at her orders, went around spreading peanut butter on half the slices ("He always spreads it too thin," an older brother complained; "This time he won't," declared Daisy, whose authority in these matters was absolute), Charles the grape jelly on one slice per plate, and Morgan the peach preserves on another: no variations permitted at time of manufacture, though swaps might be negotiated after. Winston, the oldest boy, then assembled the sandwiches and cut them "Moorewise," as their father had once defined the family style: halfway between diagonally and athwartships. Julia poured milk, Daisy doled out apples and paper napkins, and all hands, our hands full, filed into the backyard to sit in a circle on the grass under a huge old mock orange that shaded the former slaves' quarters. There we said grace (never bothered with in my family), bartered this for that, and ate.

My friend did not look her best this noon. Her face, as thin as the rest of her, appeared at once gaunt and puffy, reddish around her brown eyes. Her voice sounded worn; her hair was turbaned up like Aunt Rachel's; she was dressed in soiled pink pedal pushers and a baggy Antioch College sweatshirt sent her from Oberlin by Brinsley, to whose ex-boyfriend it had once belonged. There was no sign of my I.D. bracelet. And her manner was, for Daisy, subdued. She neglected to wish me a happy birthday even after shy Julia did; indeed, except for automatically dealing out that extra lunch plate, she scarcely acknowledged my presence, but busied herself with confirming the boys' afternoon plans and ruling peremptorily on the exchange values of apple halves and jelly flavors when free-market principles hit a snag. Sometimes she got this way; it occurred to me that she might be having her period, the mechanics of which she herself had once explained to me.

Julia, always closer to Daisy than to her brothers, was more than usually solicitous. She neglected her own lunch to brush and braid her sister's hair into a long pigtail as the rest of us ate, and conversed with her in their private language, a version of "opp-talk" spoken at such a machine-gun clip that not even the brothers could follow it, much less I.

"Yoppou fopporgoppot toppo woppish 'Soppimmoppon hopp-appoppy boppirthdoppay."

"Noppo oppI doppidn't. Loppatopper, moppayboppe, oppif oppI foppeel loppike oppit."

"Oppokoppay."

When it had been established that Winston would walk Beaufort uptown to his piano lesson and redeliver him to Virginia the housekeeper before meeting his friends at Schine's Saturday matinee, and that Julia would see to it that Morgan and Charles and she got down to the Yacht Club in time for their dinghy-sailing class, and that everybody would be home without fail by four o'clock sharp to get themselves and the house ready for Sam's arrival at five with their mother, who might be coming home this time to stay, we trooped back through the kitchen to dispose of our trash. Daisy reviewed the afternoon schedule with Virginia (who sat plumply at the little kitchen worktable in her white uniform, eating sliced tomatoes and sipping iced tea) and added that she and I were going for a bike ride, probably.

"Y'all be careful," Virginia instructed us, unconcerned.

Behler's objective was Island Creek, Island Point, and, if possible, the Island itself.

After telling Daisy the story of my unjust disciplining, I would wish aloud that she and I could run off somewhere together, just the two of us, away from civilization entirely. With my Scout survival training, I was reasonably confident that we could manage like Tarzan and Jane. Thus would I lead her into our game, which several times already had taken unexpected happy turns. If no one was in sight, we would hide some or all of our clothes in the reeds near the red day beacon and swim over to the Island and around to a certain little spot of beach on its northeast corner, from which nothing human was visible, not even the Chaptico bridge — only woods and the wide, empty upper reaches of the river, which served as our South Pacific. The honey locusts became coconut palms, the trumpet vines lianas. Once, under my direction, we had been Adam and Eve in the Garden; another time castaways on a desert isle without a common language; yet another time Robinson Crusoe and his Girl Friday. By a tacit division of labor I was, as a rule, in charge of the story, Daisy in charge of its limits, especially when (as had become our narrative-dramatic tradition) its plot fetched us into our bower, where my friend's unpredictability was most likely to assert itself in either direction. There fantasy had twice been outstripped by extraordinary reality; on the other hand, and rather more likely, Daisy might tire of the conceit and its obvious direction. She would then quash it with her throw-up noise and challenge me to a footrace in the shallows or a swim to the State Hospital shore and back.

Today I had in mind to try Princess Wakini and Lieutenant Bailey from *Lagoon* and see where that might lead us. But Daisy's mood was still cranky. She appropriated her oldest brother's bike and did not object when I turned off River Boulevard toward East Dorset, but we pedaled in silence, and instead of riding beside or ahead of me, she trailed behind. At the uptown foot of the Dorset Creek bridge she turned aside and coasted down past the colored bakery and the oyster-dredge builder's smithy to the Albany Brothers seafood plant. By the time I noticed, turned back, and caught up with her, she had dismounted at the creek bulkhead, propped Winston's dark-red Schwinn against a mountain of oyster shells, and was skipping flat ones out into the channel of Dorset Creek.

Gray-and-white herring gulls stood about on the pilings or hovered low on the southerly over the creek, hoping for scraps from the hard-crab pickers. Instead of probing Daisy's mood, I skirted it, idly testing my hypothesis that hovering gulls cannot be hit by oyster shells. With calm and minimal evasive action, they confirmed it. To my own surprise, I heard myself say vehemently, "I *hate* this place!"

Daisy, still morosely watching the gulls, said, "No you don't," and I realized at once that the truth of my feelings was nearer the opposite of what I had declared. Anyhow, I had her attention. I reported how I had swiped dumb Mullig's can of Bon Ami to get even with him for his teasing me about her, and how instead of throwing it away I had given it to Aunt Rachel to use in our kitchen; how my dumb aunt had gone straight to my father with the story even though I'd *told* her I'd been helping Mullig at Paul's; how Dad, the Great Dictator, had waked me from a sound sleep and ordered me out of the house, back down to Paul's, even though I had told him the honest truth immediately, which I certainly needn't have done; and how that unfair punishment had made me so angry that I'd flung the damned Bon Ami right into the creek.

Through the latter part of my complaint, Daisy listened with eyes closed. Toward its end she held her left hand to her brow but did not, this time, stay me with her right. When I was done she regarded me without expression for some moments. To express my continuing resentment (and to avoid that stare) I zipped another oyster shell through the squadron of gulls, and, uneasily, another.

At last she said, "*You chickened out!*"

"What do you mean?" But I knew already what she meant. Even as I was telling my story, I had seen myself for the first time from outside it, and was abashed at the sight.

"Persim-mon. . . ." Furious now, Daisy grabbed both my elbows to make me look straight at her. My face fired up. "You'd've done the same thing!" I said, though I strongly suspected that she would not have and suddenly much wished that I myself had not. I shrugged her hands off me, but was appalled at the revelation that I was not the hero of my story. On the contrary.

Instead of denying my objection, however, Daisy dismissed it. What she would or wouldn't have done in my place didn't matter, she declared, because *she* didn't matter, any more than Freddy Mulligan mattered, or anybody else we knew, except me and her sister Julia. Herself she regarded as a lost cause, like her mother; she was therefore permitted anything. But *I* had to be honest and brave et cetera, because (like Julia, if Daisy had anything to say about it) I was headed somewhere that none of the rest would ever get to.

Why in the world did I not pick up on that "lost cause" business, a complete surprise and the closest Daisy had ever come to inviting intimate questions? But my vanity was so dazzled by what she had just said about me (I wasn't so sure about Julia) that I could think only to mumble some protest against her double standard of behavior. Exasperated, Daisy moved off toward her brother's bike.

"I'll find the damn can and return it right now!" I said after her. She cut her eyes back at me, over-shoulder. "Let's look for it!" I called. "You can stand right there and watch while I give it back to Mister Travers!"

I saw that she was interested. More forceful by the moment, I took her arm and led her up onto the bridge. The tide looked to be near flood now, I pointed out; therefore it would also have been running in at Paul's closing time last night. So as not to be seen from the bridge-tender's station, I had dropped the can over the upstream railing of the draw; it would have been carried on up the channel toward the old cemetery at the two creeks' fork and might well be lying alongshore somewhere up past the packing houses and the work-boat fleet.

"Baloney," Daisy scoffed. "It's halfway to Portugal by now." But the project appealed to her imagination. We locked our bikes together with Winston's combination lock and chain and prowled the creek-shore, looking between the moored oystering skipjacks and bugeye ketches laid up for the summer season, the tong-boats fitted now with outboard rollers for trotlining crabs, the haul seiners piled with nets. Then, shoes off, we prowled the slick mud flats farther up, where the remains of abandoned work boats made a marine graveyard before the human one.

Soon enough my bravado waned; there was so much floating and stranded litter that I began to fear we really might find a discarded Bon Ami can. I considered proposing a detour into the cemetery; I hadn't poked around in there for ages. On second thought, I proposed the more promising alternative of continuing around the fork and then down Island Creek all the way to the Chaptico. There had, after all, been a low tide between the two highs; if we reached the other creek mouth having found nothing, there we'd be at Island Point. We could swim over to the Island and check *its* perimeter as well, just to make sure. . . .

"Never mind your Island," Daisy said. "This matters; that doesn't."

As she led us back down Dorset Creek instead and across the

bridge toward Paul's, I began to worry that she would demand confession with or without restitution. I even thought of taking that moral initiative before she came up with it — and I realized I hadn't nerve enough.

At the East Dorset end of the bridge she said, "'Simmon, you wait here for me and don't dare go away, or you and I are finished. I'll be back in two shakes."

"Where're you going?"

But she sprinted off — not, I was gratified to see, toward Paul's, but back across the creek bridge to our bikes, and from there pedaled away in the direction of River Boulevard. The afternoon blazed. The breeze had waned to a damp breath, not enough to dry sweat but just enough to carry the stink of sun-rotting crab waste across from the packing houses. Clearly in for it, I waited like a condemned man in the shade of the bridge abutment, experimenting to see whether, by force of a willed neutral attitude toward nature's basic processes, I could make myself inhale that rank stench deeply without gagging or even catching my breath. I discovered that I could, after some practice. By the time Daisy returned, I had learned almost to enjoy doing so.

From the bridge railing overhead she tossed down to me a can of scouring powder.

"This is Bab-O," I pointed out.

"Never mind. Come on."

I headed with her toward Paul's as toward a scaffold. "Where'd you get it?"

"Swiped it from Virginia's closet."

"Swiped it!"

Her over-shoulder look this time was mischievous: the first good humor I'd seen in her all day. "I'm allowed to. You're not."

Almost like Aunt Rachel, I said, "Well! This is some birthday present!"

"Stop worrying about your birthday present."

It was no use proposing to Daisy Moore that we leave the can inconspicuously in Paul's entranceway. My last hope was that despite what I had said before, she might wait for me outside, and I might be able to set the can casually on the counter while speaking to Mr. Travers of something else, in such a way that the scene would look from outside like confession and restitution. To that desperate end I strode ahead of her, as if angrily, saying, "Let's get this over with."

When my hand was literally on the store's door handle, Daisy called from twenty feet behind me, "Persimmon?"

"What."

Her brow furrowed. "You don't have to."

My heart lifted, but I kept my voice truculent. "How come."

"You're *willing* to," she explained. "That's enough."

But I saw my part clearly now, and the heady savor of moral-dramatic initiative made me fearless. Without replying, I strode through the door and up to the soda fountain, where Mr. Travers was chatting with the Zion Meth-Prot organist and choir director, Mrs. Pool. He looked over when I plunked the Bab-O can onto the marble, just about where Mullig's Bon Ami had stood. "Hi there, buddy. Get you something?"

"*Two Coke sodas!*" Daisy called from behind me. "Chocolate ice cream in mine. Treat's on me," she said brightly, taking the stool beside me, and she explained to Mrs. Pool and Mr. Travers that today was my birthday.

"How old are you, Simon?" Mrs. Pool asked me.

"No sodas," I ordered. Paul Travers paused, his hand on the shelf of inverted soda glasses behind the fountain. Mrs. Pool regarded us over her Coke. Mr. Travers raised his eyebrows and wiped his hands on a rag. To keep my voice in its lower register, I spoke quietly. "I swiped this can off your counter last night, Mister Travers, while Freddy Mulligan was cleaning up. It was a dumb thing to do, and I apologize."

Mr. Travers stepped over, picked up the cleanser, and tipped his head back to examine its label through his bifocals. "Didn't come from here, bud."

Actually, I explained, what I had taken was Bon Ami, but I hadn't been able to find any Bon Ami in our house this morning, so I had brought the Bab-O instead, for him to use until I got to the A & P to get a new can of Bon Ami.

Mr. Travers shook his head and set the Bab-O back on the counter in front of Daisy. "Would the pair of you kindly scoot out of here now and take this back where it come from?" He looked over his eyeglasses at Mrs. Pool. "Kids."

* * *

Daisy Moore herself then led the way out to Island Creek, across to the Island, around to their special beach, and, finally, into their bower, and there presented "'Simmon" Behler with his birthday gift.

Though my earlier experiments both alone and with Daisy had shown me how inexpungibly, even in total darkness or underwater, we carry ourselves inside our heads — our time and place, who and what we are — my recent reading in Mrs. Moore's *Arabian Nights* had made me chafe not only at being ineluctably I and here and now but likewise at the iron constraints of nature itself, which made it quite certain that no fish would really ever talk and no genie appear from a bottle, nor would Daisy and I be magically transported from Dorset County to Samarkand or Serendib. My closest approaches thus far to anything resembling the boundary of those constraints had not been those two surprising interludes on the Island with my friend, when — even as I'd groaned and scrooched my face as if sucking a sour 'simmon — I had not for a second left self-awareness behind but had been on the contrary preternaturally aware of myself and her, the honey locust trees round about us, a twin-engine Army transport plane passing overhead (the military version of the DC-3), and two bright-blue dragonflies mating on a tendril of trumpet vine near Daisy's perspiring forehead, their long, thin abdomens arched and connected to form a Valentine heart. No: the eerie moments of a true near-ecstasy, whose scary disorientation I had learned to protract and relish, had been those rather less rare ones when (especially since I'd had the back bedroom to myself) I was able in a certain combination of drowsiness and less-than-total darkness to rock myself just beyond all usual and normal sensory cues into a charged suspension, vertiginous, electrically humming, in which the ceiling, the walls, the frames of the doors and windows, and the very bed beneath me were at once their familiar selves and unspeakably alien, their distance and configuration fluid, and I myself was no longer or not merely I but as it were the very lens of the cosmos: a sentient star of light-years more compass than anything named Simon William Behler — to whom, however, I clung in those thrillsome intervals like a man overboard to a rope, to haul myself back before I was carried past retrieving.

Something like that, I supposed, Home Plate must be: an ultimate transfiguration. There *was* a degree of transport in even masturbatory orgasm; there had been rather more (though more self-consciousness, too, as aforedescribed) when Daisy "did" me, and she had acknowledged a like sensation the time I did her, even in the absence of any literal, observable squirt. She was squirting plenty inside, she had reported, and her joints felt unglued and her muscles melting, and the inside of her head was squirting, too — floating and squirting at the same time. What I had hoped might happen today, if I could orchestrate the situation and if Daisy's mood coincided with mine, was that in our bower, out of sight of all things human except each other, she would remove even the little pearl pierced earrings she wore always, and that after "Wakini" and "Lieutenant Bailey," our eyes closed, had embraced and kissed each other into a half-trance (as had once or twice happened), we might "do" each other simultaneously, eyes still closed, and then together . . . I didn't quite know what. Levitate? Evaporate? Melt?

Cross over?

Her earlier truculence had therefore much discouraged me, but after our stop at Paul's my hopes were higher than ever. Daisy seemed almost excitedly pleased with me now; from her pants pocket she fetched out my I.D. bracelet, and fastened it around her left ankle. She rode ahead down Maryland and across Bridge Avenue, standing up on the Schwinn's pedals to pump it along faster, laughing, raising the Bab-O can like a standard, and calling back to me over her shoulder. Still in charge, I followed more deliberately on the Silver King, obliging her to pause from time to time and urge me with merry impatience, "Come on!"

At Island Point I was disappointed to see four or five youngsters from the Second Ward playing on the shore and in the shallows a hundred yards up-creek and several crab boats working trotlines out in the river, not far from shore. The kids I could cast as Polynesian natives, maybe headhunters to hide from in our jungle cave, but the crabbers and their distinctive Chesapeake work boats, chuffing back and forth on one-lung inboard engines, would be hard to work into *Lagoon*. And the proximity of both ruled out skinny-dipping to the Island.

"Come *on!*" Daisy said. She stashed her bike in the reeds, shucked off her penny loafers, and peeled out of her Antioch sweatshirt, under which she wore one of her brothers' plain white T-shirts. By the time I laid the Silver King atop the Schwinn, she was already undoing the

waistband of her pedal pushers. I embraced her from behind, my forearms just under her little breasts, and murmured experimentally into
her hair, "Wakini. . . ."

"*Blyeh!*" She hugged my arms closer to her for half a second before
shrugging them away. "No make-believe, 'Simmon. Come on."

Stepping back into the tall spartina where our bicycles lay, she
slipped the pedal pushers off, rolled them around her sweatshirt,
and tucked the bundle into a handlebar basket. Her underpants were
robin's-egg blue. As I unlaced my canvas sneakers, she half squatted
beside me to lock the bikes together and retrieve something from one
of her pockets. I bussed her skinny hip just below the panty-line.

"That tickles," she protested — but she pressed my face against her,
not away. Then, giggling, she sprinkled my head with Bab-O,
dropped the can, and dashed from the cover of the reeds into the river,
the ankle bracelet flashing. "Last one in's a rotten egg!"

I followed in my jockey shorts, checking as I went to make sure
that the Polynesian natives (who usually did their swimming up near
the crabhouse, where their mothers worked) were keeping their distance and paying us no mind. In chest-deep water off our beach —
where the crabbers were, alas, in plain view still, but busy at their
work — I overtook and embraced her again. Chuckling, she permitted
me to kiss her thin, wide lips, but when I closed my eyes and slipped
in my tongue, she drew her head back and said, "Eyes *open* today,
Persimmon!"

And that was the order of an afternoon that both fell short of and
far exceeded my anticipations. No *Lagoon* or other scenarios: Daisy
was uncompromisingly Daisy, I I, nowhere but on the Island of Island
Creek on the lower Eastern Shore of Maryland on the hot afternoon
of July 1, 1944, crabbers working the Chaptico nearby and somebody's
large dog barking intermittently up-creek, probably at the Negro kids.
Daisy's soaked white T-shirt clung close; her pink skin and dark nipples showed through. Keeping my eyes dutifully more or less open
while she rinsed the cleansing powder out of my hair with river water,
I put a hand on her breast. She clapped her forehead, rolled (but did
not close) her eyes, grinned and groaned, pressed my hand against
her, then led me by it into the trees, watching out as always for briers
and poison ivy. At our bower she let go, jumped a step or two ahead
into its moss-and-fern-lined center, and (still dripping wet, as was I)

with a toss of her braid turned to face me, smiling but serious, her legs slightly apart and arms wide open.

"Happy birthday, 'Simmon."

It was a level declaration. Even our kiss then had to be open-eyed: Daisy and me. When I slid my hand from the small of her back up under her T-shirt and then down into her underpants, and dared even to press my fingertips for the first time into the cleft of her backside, and Daisy made a murmur into my mouth and pushed herself against the front of my jockey shorts, I shut my eyes with a shudder of excitement. Still kissing me, Daisy straightway opened them with thumb and forefinger before darting her tongue into my mouth in hard little thrusts.

Encouraged by that response (which reminded me of her reaction to my initiative with Mr. Travers), after lifting off her T-shirt with her help, instead of merely kissing her breasts I boldly nursed one nipple, a thing I had never done before. Daisy said *Mm hm* and with her closed left hand pressed my head there, then presently moved me to her other nipple. Her free right hand, moreover, she cupped under my jockeyed scrotum and gently kneaded it.

When we had stepped out of our underpants I moved back from her, all nerve and willpower now, in order to move likewise from the verge of ejaculation, and asked her — commanded her, really — to take her earrings off.

"My *earrings?*" But without entirely opening her left hand, she obligingly removed them, reattached their backings, and put them atop her blue underpants for safekeeping. I relished her movements, and even more so my authority. As she stooped to secure the earrings I said in a husky whisper, "Let's undo your braid," and set about removing the tan rubber band from its end.

"'Sim-mon," she protested, but I saw that the idea interested her. She obediently turned her back to me and held still while I undid the plait, even pressed her lean little rump against the wet tip of my erection. I astonished myself by being able to draw back from her and say, "Not just yet, Daise."

She shook her hair loose and, pleased, tilted her head to one side and combed her right-hand fingers through it. "You're *weird*, 'Simmon!"

But when I knelt now to remove the final item, her ankle bracelet, she gasped and jerked that leg away.

"No!"

What she meant, I flattered myself to suppose, was that she *wanted,* just now, to be my property. But in that case she must do as I wished, mustn't she? Squatting before her, I said, "Take that off, too, Daise." But my command came out as a request, to which I added, as if sportively, "Let's get *completely* stripped, okay?"

Once more in charge, Daisy said, "We're stripped enough." She sat herself Turk-fashion on her spread-out T-shirt in a clean mossy patch a few feet away, her unbound hair falling across her shoulders, and fingered the ankle bracelet distractedly. Her brown eyes, I was surprised to see, were wet and reddening. Without looking up she said, "Come here to me, Persimmon."

I readily obeyed: stood on my knees before her and kissed the top of her head. She opened the hand she had kept closed; in her palm was a small flat packet with a picture on it of a handsome Arab chieftain. *Sheik,* it said, and other things.

She smiled wanly and knuckled teardrops out of her eye-corners. "You know how they work?"

I said "Sure," for though I'd never handled one myself, I had seen discarded ones like beached sea nettles along the rivershore and even near our bower. Moreover, certain members of the Silver Fox Patrol had once sneaked some — Trojans, they were, not Sheiks — from their older brothers for a water-balloon fight in the basement of Zion Meth-Prot, and had spoken by the way of their intended function.

"Be honest, 'Simmon!"

I understood then that Daisy was telling me that she *did* know, if I didn't. "I just slip it on, right? We don't *have* to do this, Daise."

She put her packet-holding hand to her forehead and raised her eyes briefly skyward, but then lightly bussed my shoulder and said, "First you take one out of the box."

The packet said in smaller letters: *3 prophylactic sheaths. For prevention of disease only.* There were two white Sheiks inside, tightly rolled but not otherwise sealed. I pinched one out — it looked like a model of those inflatable life rafts that downed flyers sometimes drifted in for days and weeks — and Daisy tossed the packet over to where her earrings and our underpants were. A glance showed me in which direction the thing was meant to unroll, but I did not in fact know whether one unrolled it first and then slipped it on like a sock, or what.

"Now you hand it to me," Daisy said, and taking it from my fingers, she drew my face to hers and snugged my hand onto the little mound of her crotch before proceeding with the demonstration. Her eyes were less teary now; her previous emotion, I supposed, had had to do with the momentousness of the occasion, which would leave her physically altered, as it would not me. This I understood from conversation on the subject not with Daisy (who characteristically discussed things after the fact, rather than before) but among the Silver Foxes, whose fund of sexual lore was rich in the area of defloration and its complications: infrangible cherries on the one hand, unstanchable hemorrhages on the other, panic lockups that required a doctor to disconnect the couple (how would we get to one?), sharp initial pain on the woman's part, transformed into insatiable craving once the barrier was breached.

Daisy and I were spared all that. When my excitement filled the first Sheik before my friend had finished unrolling it onto me, she gently complained, "'Simmon," removed and tossed it away among the creepers, and in a little while was able to apply the second. I promised huskily, as she drew me onto her, "I'll be gentle." Daisy said nothing but kept her eyes on mine as she first introduced and then with a surprising motion slid me fully into her, or herself fully onto me, and held me in place there for a considerable while before permitting or resuming further motion. Up-creek, that dog barked on; those trotliners chuffed away out on the Chaptico. In our bower, midges whined. A plane droned overhead: another twin-engine job, by the sound of it, flying high enough to see all of Dorset County spread out like a map. At one point a faint shout or howl floated to us from the grounds of the State Hospital, of a sort that I had heard once or twice before on the Island when the breeze was southeasterly. Daisy's eyes closed at the sound, and all her muscles tensed, but there was no lockup. As I approached my second ejaculation, the fire sirens of Dorset suddenly chorused from ward to ward. Daisy broke her own rule again by closing her eyes and turning her head aside on her spread-out hair. She made a low sound, whether of passion or of amused exasperation at the sirens I couldn't tell, but I took the opportunity to steal a glance down between us at the spectacle of my firm piston in its prophylactic sheath — aglisten, but not with blood — sliding in and out of Daisy Moore.

Then it was I who made a sound, trying not to scrooch my face as my knees and elbows deliquesced. Daisy clasped her thin limbs around me and received my weight; I felt the ankle bracelet press into my buttock.

Presently into her left ear I said, "I love you." With a deliberate motion Daisy turned to give me her sizing-up look, then eased herself out from under me. "Wrong again, 'Simmon. You just *say* things."

I was too full of pride and other emotions to object. If we had crossed no Boundary, we had unequivocally passed a celebrated milestone. Just turned fourteen, I had accomplished with Daisy Moore what the love songs really meant when they said *kiss*; what the camera turned away from after Dorothy Lamour's and Sterling Hayden's faces came together in the grotto behind the sacred waterfall; what the Silver Foxes' banter was tirelessly preoccupied with: the mysterious business at the heart of adult desire. If what I felt for my friend was less than love, it surely included affection, admiration, and gratitude. Pleased as I was with myself and with the postcoital look of my genitals — the organ itself flaccid now as I stripped off and discarded the condom, but unquestionably longer and thicker than it used to be, perhaps permanently so, and my scrotum gratifyingly looser, more dangly — I was more pleased still with the look of Daisy as she picked herself up off the ground. Her shoulder blades and buttocks were blotched and impressed from our double weight; flecks of moss and leaf-scrap stuck to her skin and in her hair, as also to my reddened knees and elbows. Whether or not I loved her, I loved watching her movements as she shook out her T-shirt and brushed herself clean: standing, turning, bending.

Fucked.

The coarse word filled me with tenderness. I helped brush the litter off her while she replaced her earrings. Daisy liked that; she let me embrace her afterward front to front for a long kiss, during which my curiosity buzzed. Was it because of the Sheik that I had felt nothing pop or tear inside her at my first penetration? Where was the fabled blood? Did she feel different inside now? Did she love me? Neither of us had gone out of our minds with passionate excitement, as I had thought we might at Home Plate; indeed, in our two earlier sessions on the Island, which had gone less far, there had been more ardent, dizzying play. Perhaps such transports would come later: the possibilities for exploration and experiment seemed limitless, and though just minutes ago I had felt utterly expended, the press of Daisy's breasts against my chest and of her bushy little mound against my thigh was already restirring me. I began moving my kisses down from her face.

"No more," she announced. "We're out of rubbers, and I gotta get home. Let's take a swim."

Later, as we dressed in the reeds, I managed to ask, "Are you okay?"

Daisy was refastening her hair. She turned to me while fixing the rubber band in place with both hands. "Aren't you?"

"I mean did it hurt you."

She went back to the little rearview bicycle mirror she was using to see herself in. "I'd'a said ouch if it'd hurt, 'Simmon."

I considered this while lacing my sneakers. "Did it feel good, then?"

Daisy raised her eyes to heaven. "Jesus peezus! That's what it's *about!*"

Uncoupling our bikes, I remarked that I had seen female cats and dogs in heat who didn't seem to be enjoying themselves, and that I was just checking to make sure, since what we'd done had certainly felt good to me, but I guessed I wasn't interested unless she liked it, too.

"We're not cats and dogs," Daisy pointed out. "Anyhow, never mind about me." She unlatched the ankle bracelet, slipped it into her pocket, and swung up onto her brother's Schwinn. Following behind, I watched to see whether she sat on it perhaps more gingerly than before. She did not. Shortly before Daisy and I had become friends, Charlie Norman had told another Silver Fox that Andy Travers had told *him* that back when she had hung around with some of my brother's gang, Travers and a couple of the other guys had once bet Crazy Daisy that she couldn't write her name in the sand the way *they* used to, and she'd said she bet she could, too, if they swore not to watch, and they'd sworn, but she'd caught them peeking and had quit after the second letter. Charlie Norman didn't particularly believe that story, and neither did I, though Daisy's tomboyish spunk had helped earn her her nickname. Andy Travers was a notorious liar, especially concerning girls. But when I remembered the story now, a new question forcefully suggested itself, and I resolved to put it directly to Daisy as soon as possible, whether she felt like talking about the subject or not. To that end, I didn't say good-bye at Maple Street but rode on with her toward the Dorset Creek bridge and River Boulevard, though she made me promise not to hang around her house: she had stuff to do before Sam brought her mother home.

The draw happened to be open for one of the small freighters that plied between Albany Brothers and the Baltimore shipping terminals. As we waited with our bicycles at the lift gates with their lights and bells, I asked Daisy to tell me honestly whether this had been her first time, as it had been mine.

"'Sim-mon," she protested. "Leave me alone."

"I need to know," I insisted — though I already knew, now, and my heart stung. "I'm in love with you. I have a *right* to know."

"No you don't," Daisy replied. Her tone was glum but positive, as if the moral question were familiar. "If you loved me it wouldn't matter, and since you don't it's none of your business. You just *think* you're in love, 'Simmon. It's fun to think that."

Everything Daisy Moore said seemed true to me as soon as she said it. But I had begun to learn from her how to respond. "I *do* think that. And you're right: it doesn't matter if this wasn't your first time. But I wish it had been."

She cut me a glance of serious appreciation and went back to pretending to watch the swing bridge close. "So do I."

Andy Travers, I said to myself: Paul Travers's son, who had failed a grade and then quit school to join the Merchant Marine after Joe Junior joined the Navy. Though not bright and known to be a ready liar, Andy Travers was an athlete, handsome and popular; my brother, I now bitterly recalled, had once teased him about being a cradle-robber who dated freshman girls, even junior-high girls, in his senior year. Andy Travers! The idea of him and Daisy doing things together on the beach, maybe even in our bower, made me dizzy, almost nauseated. I felt ridiculous, too, for having imagined myself her first lover. Those childish games of mine, which she had gone along with, humoring me like one of her kid brothers!

She must have seen something of my distress. As the lift gates rose she put a hand on my perspiring arm and said, surprisingly, "Hey, Persimmon? You're the first one I ever *liked* it with, okay?"

I jerked my arm away from her and — not quite registering what she had said — pedaled angrily ahead. What stung most, perhaps, was that except for the moment in Paul's with the Bab-O and the moments in our bower with Daisy's earrings and braid, I had been the novice, in my friend's complete and experienced, maybe even amused, charge, whereas with that cradle-robber Andy Travers *she* had been the tenderfoot, submitting to his wishes, doing at his direction things that she had never done before. I hated and envied him for that, so much so that I had crossed the creek bridge before I realized that to punish Daisy for deceiving me — for betraying me in advance, so to speak — I ought to have biked off the other way, homeward. Now it would look dumb to wheel around at Staub the Jeweler's on High and Holly, one block from River Boulevard, and head back, especially since Daisy was making no effort to overtake me but was pedaling at her own pace a block or so behind.

Awkwardly, therefore, I reached her house before she did. Various brothers were already on the porch, playing Monopoly under Julia's supervision. She gangled down the steps as soon as she saw me, her white legs too long for the rest of her, particularly in her summer shorts. Half breathless, as always, she asked, "Where's Daisy, Simon?," but then grinned past me and clicked an imaginary camera at her approaching sister.

Already, at thirteen, Julia Moore had larger breasts than Daisy. Among the Silver Foxes it was theorized that such precocious development was the result of girls' massaging their tits nightly with a Turkish towel and/or letting guys suck on them, but so shy was Julia that I wouldn't have believed that the theory applied to her even if her sister hadn't told me (with her throw-up sound) that it was baloney. Remembering now the circumstances in which Daisy had enlightened me on that point and others, I burned with chagrin and supposed unkindly that skittish Julia, following the example of her older sisters, would soon enough let some Andy Travers reach that Second Base, if she had not done so already, and quickly move on to Third and Home.

"Your uncle called a half hour ago," Julia told me. Her eyes, I noticed for the first time, were not brown, like Daisy's, but a greenish color. "You're supposed to go right home. Hi, Daise."

"Jule." While they embraced as usual upon remeeting, Daisy, still straddling the Schwinn, gave me one level look over her sister's shoulder. Then she propped the bike on its kickstand and turned her attention to counting brothers.

"Beaufort's hiding from Ma," Julia explained to her. "Hoppe's oppin Broppinsloppey's coppar."

Recrossing to East Dorset in this late afternoon of his innocence, "'Simmon" Behler indulged himself in a multiple indignation.

No doubt it was the Bon Ami affair I was being summoned home to account for, though for some reason it had been Uncle Josh who had telephoned the Moores'. Either Dad had talked with Paul Travers before I'd confessed and been excused (unlikely, considering Mr. Travers's surprise) or — it would be just like Dad! — notwithstanding that courageous gesture, I had still to atone for not having made it last night as directed. Given what had happened on the Island this afternoon, the whole business seemed petty: ancient history. If Dad hadn't spoken with Paul Travers since this morning, I would say, "Maybe you ought to speak with Mister Travers again." If he had, and expected me all the same to be contrite about last night, I would just say, "Seems to me the books are closed on that particular business, Dad."

I liked that expression, which I had in fact picked up from my father himself: it suggested mature judgment and resolution. Between Daisy and me, too, I guessed, the books were closed, or almost so. She had amused herself with me because the older fellows she used to run around with were off to war, all except Mullig the pig. Let her piss *his* name on Island Point, along with Andy Travers's! Mullig's insinuations of last night came back to me, along with the Silver Foxes' teasing earlier today. They must all know that as well as taking him up on his bet, Daisy had let Andy Travers fuck her — *he* certainly wouldn't have kept it secret. Maybe she had let them all fuck her!

Picturing that as I turned onto Maple Street, I recalled belatedly what Daisy had told me at the creek-bridge lift gates, and my nerves thrilled: maybe she hadn't *let* any of them do any such thing but had spunkily taken them up on their challenge to pee her name in the sand

(I could imagine Crazy Daisy doing that) and had then been not only spied upon but ganged up on and . . . forced.

Raped.

That supposition — more an illumination than a hypothesis — along with that cruel, exciting word, clarified everything: Daisy's inclination thereafter to a younger, more innocent and more manageable boyfriend, with whom she could set and maintain whatever limits she pleased; her obvious "experience," together with her disinclination to talk about it; her description of herself as one who didn't matter, a "lost cause"; her brief, involuntary tears at the prospect of "going all the way" again, even though this time — for the *first* time — willingly. Even her mercurial attitude toward my blank I.D. bracelet made sense now: after what had happened to her, she felt herself a nobody, unworthy to wear my bracelet, which nevertheless she treasured and would not remove for our lovemaking even at my insistence.

Now my heart flooded with belated tenderness for my friend, whom I had so insensitively wounded. Far from being closed, our books were only beginning to be really opened. By the time I reached home I was indignant for a different reason — at having to bother with such a trifle as half a can of swiped Bon Ami before I could somehow get through to Daisy and make a private apology that was enormously more important than the public one made already to Andy Travers's father.

Behler found his family stunned with grief.

Both cars were parked out front, but there was nobody on the screened porch. I allowed its door to slam shut behind me like a warning shot. Nobody in the living room, either, but as I considered whether to seek out my summoners in the rear of the house or go on upstairs and let them find me, Uncle Josh came in from the dining room, coughing softly and rubbing his forehead with his fingertips.

"Terrible, Sy." His tone was shocked, not censuring. With sudden horror I wondered whether someone might just possibly have caught sight of Daisy and me in our bower or even just swimming half naked to the Island and reported what he or she had seen. "Telegram came." He put an arm around my shoulders and, still coughing into his hand, ushered me kitchenward. The dreadful words did in fact shock, like a small current of electricity: "They say young Joe's missing."

On the dining-room sideboard was the birthday cake for which Aunt Rachel had pinched our sugar rations since Flag Day. Beside it, like a gaily wrapped reproach, lay the longish little gift-box I had disdained to open at breakfast, along with an envelope that I knew contained a U.S. Savings Bond from my aunt (inflation or no, she bought them loyally and regularly) and a second package of a size with the first: it was my aunt and uncle's custom to give separate gifts. Though I knew the thought was reprehensible — I could imagine Daisy Moore's reaction to it! — I couldn't help a moment's rueful wish that the War Department telegram had arrived a day later.

Western Union yellow, it lay importantly open on the breakfast table as in a scene from a war movie, its ripped envelope beside it along with three coffee cups, two ashtrays, a book of matches, and open packs of Camels and Chesterfields. For some reason (it would be, I realized irrelevantly, because Aunt Rachel had scrubbed the rubber-tile floor that morning) the table had been moved back into its too-small nook; it was odd to see my father tucked in there beside the wall phone, smoking and staring through the window into the side yard. He must have noticed movement at the edge of his vision; he looked around at me, his long face blank, and turned back to the window.

"Sy Sy Sy!" Aunt Rachel crooned from across the kitchen, where she was wiping her eyes with a dish towel and making more coffee. Already weeping again, she hurried to hug me. "Your poor brother!"

Uncle Josh said thickly behind me, "Doggone war."

I was as tall as my aunt already and would soon be taller. As she hugged me she cried into my shoulder, "Some birthday present!," and the thought set her to sobbing. I patted her bony back and, as soon as I could disengage myself, boldly picked up and read the telegram for myself. Less terse than the classic ones in the movies at Schine's Bijou, it regretted to inform us not simply that Seaman 1st Class Joseph Behler, Jr., was missing in action in the Pacific theater of operations but, more specifically, that the transport plane carrying him and other members of his construction battalion and their equipment from Pearl Harbor to an (unnamed) advanced base had failed to reach its destination and was presumed down with all hands.

"He could be somewheres out there in a rubber raft," Uncle Josh supposed. Aunt Rachel said, "Oh dear God!"

The phone rang. My uncle coughed and said, "I'll get it." Most calls in our house were for Dad; he could hear telephone speech rather better than face-to-face, but someone else usually took the call first. This one was town-council business; Uncle Josh said firmly, "He can't come to the phone now, Fred. I'll tell him you called," and then spoke up to Dad: "Fred Parsons! Not important!"

Dad nodded; ticked the ash off the cigarette burning in his long fingers; drew out one of his white handkerchiefs and wiped his nose but didn't blow it.

"We should get the word out!" Aunt Rachel called to him. "Doctor Norman can announce it in church tomorrow, and they can put it in Monday's paper!"

Dad nodded. To Uncle Josh, Aunt Rachel reckoned, "That means people'll stop by after services." She consulted the electric wall clock. "I better get myself to Howard Henry's 'fore he closes."

I volunteered to run the grocery errand on my bike, if she would give me a list and money. "Bless his heart!" Aunt Rachel cried, and she hugged me again, and again went off into tears, as if to do the weeping for all of us. "*Where's my Joesikins?*"

Young Behler himself remained as dry-eyed as his father.

Pressure built behind my eyes, however, when I wheeled out the Silver King to fetch an extra pound of chicory-laced "victory coffee" and two boxes of assorted Nabisco cookies from Howard Henry's little grocery down by the creek. There weren't sugar coupons enough for another cake; since mine was undecorated except for its candles, I volunteered it for tomorrow's obligation, and after a bit more weeping, Aunt Rachel agreed, blessing my heart as we smoothed chocolate icing over the fourteen holes. Full of my new maturity, I requested further that no happy birthday be sung at dinner, despite our agreement that my brother would have wanted things to go on as usual.

That verb form constricted my throat and brought the pressure behind my eyes again, as it had not at its last frequent usage in our house, after Mother's protracted dying in Dorset General. But I was too busy being grave and brave to shed tears even when, following a ham-steak and sweet-potato dinner for which none of us had any appetite but which we all managed to put away, at the family's behest I solemnly opened my gifts: Aunt Rachel's war bond, a black and gold

Eversharp mechanical pencil from Uncle Josh (I had wanted a pen, if anything in that line, but no matter: an explorer could use a mechanical pencil, too, to make notes and such), and, from Dad and Joe Junior, a fine Omega wristwatch with a thin flat stainless-steel case and an expansion band to match, wiry black hands including a sweep second hand, and stark black tick-marks instead of numerals on its brushed-steel dial. It was neither waterproof nor self-winding — I had hoped it would be both — and the band would need to have several links removed by Staub the Jeweler on Monday, but I liked it so much that I wound it, set it, and put it on immediately, pushing it up my forearm until it stayed.

Though only Aunt Rachel wept, we were all sniffling. When I called out my thanks to him, Dad nodded and said, "Your brother got that in his PX out there in San Diego." He blew his nose. "Looks like you're it now, son."

Through the heavy evening, after Aunt Rachel had telephoned our minister and Uncle Josh the editor of the *Dorset Daily Democrat* and a representative of the town council to pass along our news, we all sat on the darkened porch — the two men in wicker chairs, my aunt and I in the glider — reminiscing about Joe Junior and assuring ourselves that he might already have been rescued. Lightning bugs pulsed in the damp night air and car lights twinkled distantly on the Chaptico bridge, occulted by its concrete railing posts. In the silver maples along our sidewalk, cicadas rasped — "Calling for more hot weather," Mother used to say — and in the grass the higher-pitched crickets sang continuously. Three glowing cigarette tips moved among our voices and the agreeable, unaromatic smoke. From time to time a car rustled to or from the hospital, and once the fire-company ambulance purred by. Out on the river, I calculated, the tide would be moving in again now, off the bay, from the interconnected oceans.

The theme of my family's reminiscences, despite our professed optimism, was how tragically young my brother was to have been "cut off." But even more so than on the creek bridge last night it now seemed to me that I myself had lived a long time already, a very long time; and Joe Junior had lived six years longer yet and had been to even more places. It was true, as Uncle Josh was recalling, that although Betsy Birdsall had pretty clearly been sweet on my brother, he had never gone steady with her or anyone else; nor had he, on the other hand, "played the field." His only letters home, as far as we knew, had been to us.

"He was in no hurry with the girls. Let 'em come to him!"

But my impression was that they had not, particularly. For the first time in some while I remembered the familiar slap-slap and sour smell of Joe Junior's masturbations (my own semen, unless I stuck my nose virtually into it, was odorless to me), and it occurred to me that there was another side to his preferring the rough-and-ready camaraderie of Andy Travers and Freddy Mulligan to the more fastidious company of Betsy Birdsall: my brother had been shy with girls. Indeed, unless his Navy buddies had taken him to whorehouses in Bainbridge or Norfolk or San Diego (the Silver Foxes had heard about such places), it was possible that I had done things already that he had not — and now never would.

In the light of this possibility, his side of the back bedroom — when Dad, consoling himself with habit, went in from the porch to hear the eleven-o'clock news, and Aunt Rachel kissed me good night and wished me a happier birthday next year, and I went upstairs — had a particularly boyish aspect. In our evening's recollections both sad and merry, my brother had already taken on a half heroic stature: his bluff, often coarse insensitivity had become a reluctance to wear on his sleeve the emotions that he in fact felt deeply. At the memory of his sarcastic "razzing," often relentless and seldom witty, we tsked and said, "He really knew how to tease, didn't he?" He seemed to us to have been more than normally able, dependable, truthful, untroublesome, stouthearted, loved and respected by his friends, admired in the neighborhood. But as I made ready for bed among his not-awfully-well-finished model airplanes, his rudimentary high-school crafts-shop projects, the Boy Scout merit-badge sash (with a mere half dozen badges on it) pinned over his headboard, his blue and gold Dorset High pennant, I saw his other aspect: not especially bright or accomplished or handsome or popular (though not the opposite of those things, either); no athlete, a nondancer; he had been simply a stolid, unexceptional boy, shy with girls — and perhaps even a bit jealous of his more supple younger brother.

At this view of him my eyes watered with sympathy, if not yet real grief, for the first time since I had come home from River Boulevard.

Lying in the humid dark beneath my serious war-zone maps and airplane-spotter's charts, I imagined Joe Junior out on that trackless ocean in a life raft, maybe alone, maybe at night. No: it was daytime out there now. Maybe in a storm, then, or in a menacing calm with great sharks circling, ever less patiently nudging the soft tubes of his half-deflated raft.

I began to rock myself toward the Boundary.

"'Simmon?"

The War Department telegram had supplanted, briefly, all my thoughts of Daisy Moore, but when Uncle Josh had instructed that town councilman to spread the word among Dad's colleagues, it had not displeased me to fancy, added to my friend's other feelings for me, her shocked pity for my bereavement. In the face of this adult tragedy there was of course no longer any urgency in my wish to apologize to her for my earlier inconsideration. Even so, I liked the idea of making that apology, perhaps sometime tomorrow; to do so in such circumstances would demonstrate all the more effectively my unselfish regard for her. I rocked.

"*'Simmon!*"

It really was Daisy, calling in a loud whisper from the unlighted alley behind our house. And now a small handful of gravel rattled off the window screen between Joe Junior's bed and mine and down the cedar shingles of the back-porch roof. Surprised, I hustled up and raised the screen. In the partial moonlight I could just make out a person and maybe a bicycle down there, beyond our privet hedge.

"Daise?"

She blinked a penlight briefly at my window. "Can you come out a minute? I heard what happened."

"Hold on." I checked my new Omega — and found it nonluminescent as well as nonwaterproof. But the big exhaust window fan in Aunt Rachel's sewing room had been turned on to ventilate the upstairs, a sign that everyone was abed. Much impressed by Daisy's concern — she couldn't have been *permitted* to bike across town alone at this hour — I hurried into my clothes and slipped quietly out by my Escape Route: over the windowsill onto the back-porch shingles, into the overhanging catalpa, down to the ground.

"Hey, 'Simmon, that's neat." Daisy had leaned Winston's bike into the hedge. Now she wiped her gravel-throwing hand on the waist of her skirt — the same one she'd worn the night before to Schine's Bijou — and held it out to me. "Hi."

I made to reply and was not displeased that for one reason or another my voice failed me. I embraced her instead, sniffing and swallowing. Daisy kissed my cheek and, briefly, my mouth before breaking off our embrace to smack at her bare calf with the penlight.

"I've got bug stuff," she whispered. "Let's go where we can talk."

From a pocket in her skirt she fetched and then applied one of the new chemical insect repellents that were just appearing on the civilian market. I had never used any — our family relied on punk sticks, cigarette smoke, citronella candles, and screens — and for some reason declined when she offered it to me. She had with her also a not-quite-empty pack of her father's Parliament cigarettes, which she occasionally filched. It was exciting to set off down the dark alley with her, hand in hand, sharing a cigarette and knowing that my friend — my girlfriend — was waiting sympathetically for me to give voice to my grief when and as I wished. I imagined myself too full of that grown-up emotion to speak of it immediately; perhaps I was. Presently I asked instead, "Is your mother okay?"

"She's home," Daisy said.

I thought that a terrific reply and squeezed her hand. My new watch slid down my arm; I pushed it back up with my cigarette hand and asked her how long she could stay out. In the near-total darkness we were passing through, I felt more than saw her shrug.

"Sam's got his hands full now, but he could notice I'm gone. Is there somewhere we can sit?"

"Sure." I was thinking of the hospital seawall, just a block away, which I had prowled once before at night, alone, to try out my Escape Route. But a more adventuresome idea occurred to me. We were approaching a streetlight; I halted us the way Daisy sometimes did, but instead of clapping my brow and raising my eyes to heaven, I took both of her hands and said, "Come up to my room."

"'Sim-mon." She frowned and smiled together. "This isn't the time for that!" But she kissed me again and let me press her against me. As I did that, she said, "One of these days I'll swipe some more of Sam's Sheiks. I'm sorry about your brother, Persimmon."

We strolled riverward through lightning bugs, crickets, occasional mosquitoes. I reminded Daisy that Joe Junior was not dead for sure, only missing. They might have had to ditch the plane; he could be out there on a raft somewhere. My friend did not reply; I realized that I didn't believe what I had just said and probably shouldn't wish it: for every such crash survivor who was eventually rescued, there must be dozens for whom the "life raft" meant a lingering, horrible death instead of a quick one. It occurred to me therefore to speak next of my feeling a kind of responsibility for the family's loss. I had *enjoyed* not having my brother around, had even hoped he wouldn't come home after the war to stay, only to visit. It was almost as if I had wished him dead — and now, almost certainly, he was.

Daisy stopped us. "'Sim-mon!" It was her *Don't pester me* tone. "That's such baloney!"

I understood that it was, even before Daisy went on to explain that she herself loved not having her sister Brinsley around always, and yet at the same time she missed her like crazy. Why did I say stuff I didn't mean?

Instead of replying that I did so because I didn't yet know *what* I meant and therefore said things in hope of finding out, I walked on silently for half a block, pretending to be cross with her. Maybe I *was* cross with her. Pretty clearly, nothing else very interesting was going to happen this night.

At the crumbling concrete seawall, against which the black Chaptico chuckled, Daisy stopped us again and sighed. "Walk me back, Persimmon."

I supposed she meant back to River Boulevard. I didn't really want to haul clear over there at this hour — ten before midnight, my street-lit Omega said — but on the way back along our alley I remembered the things I had wanted to ask about her and Andy Travers, and also that I had intended to apologize for my afternoon surliness. And here I was being surly again to the friend — my *best* friend, really, as well as my girlfriend — who despite my childish behavior had come clear across town in the middle of the night to console me. What was more, when we rearrived at our hedge she said, "Good night, 'Simmon. I really am sorry about your brother," and went to retrieve her bicycle.

My eyes watered. "Daisy!" I caught her arm, and this time my throat truly clutched up. I was barely able to squeak out through my tears, "I'm such a jerk!"

Daisy hugged me while straddling Winston's bike. "Sam says people our age don't know who they are yet."

"*You* do!"

She liked that. Though she said "Hah!" she added, "I guess it's mainly boys Sam means."

Having checked to make sure that our house was still dark, I insisted now on walking her home, though Daisy pointed out that she could get there sooner on the bike. We shared another Parliament, passing it back and forth as we walked the Schwinn up empty Maryland Avenue, and our conversation now was easier. Without yet questioning her further, I apologized for having behaved badly at the creek bridge that afternoon — "Yeah," she affirmed, "that was dumb" — and let her know how much I admired her personality (I didn't yet have the word *character*, much less *integrity*) as well as her good looks and the rest.

"I'm a knockout, all right," Daisy scoffed. "*Blyeh!*" But I could tell she was pleased. As we passed Paul's, long since closed and dark, I went on to praise her openness, her nerve, her lack of phoniness, her *maturity*: a term and concept I was getting to like.

"Don't overdo it, 'Simmon." But I felt myself to be on solid ground. What I meant, for example, I declared, was things like her concern for her brothers and sisters, as well as for her father and her unfortunate mother.

"Ma's still plenty scattered," Daisy acknowledged.

At the creek bridge we laughed about the Bon Ami/Bab-O business. "Hey," I asked her, "did you put that can back in Virginia's closet?" and Daisy said, "Hell no: we left it on Island Point." I was reminded of our creekshore search, which I had initiated. On an impulse as sure as that one, I said, "Let's poke through the cemetery. I want to say happy birthday to my sister."

"'Sim-mon! You're *weird!*"

Once before, swinging on Daisy's porch, I had mentioned my stillborn twin. My present hunch was sound: despite the hour and the possibility that her absence would be discovered, Daisy turned off Maryland Avenue unhesitatingly with me, and onto the scruffy oyster-shell road that ran behind the crab-and-oyster-processing plants to the fork of Dorset and Island creeks. Julia was covering for her, she said. I wondered how — and, for that matter, how discipline was adminis-

126

tered in that easygoing household where none ever seemed to be
called for.

A stringy cat prowled by. Farther on, as I took a turn at wheeling
the bicycle, Daisy clutched my arm at the sight and sound of a water
rat scuttling along the bulkhead. But it was as if we were our town's
only living human inhabitants. I propped Winston's bike against a low
chain-link fence and climbed over into the graveyard, where I was
jumped immediately by mosquitoes in the untrimmed grass. Daisy
handed me her sandals, the penlight, and then, from her skirt pocket,
the insect repellent and a short, slender wrapped package, the wrong
size for Sheiks. She tucked the hem of her skirt up into its waistband,
thrust her toes into the fence mesh, and swung herself over.

I tried some repellent on my face, arms, and ankles; as Daisy reap-
plied it to her legs, I reached over and smoothed some between her
thighs.

"'Sim-mon. . . ." But she did not bat my hand away. "Where's your
kid sister?"

"*Twin* sister," I reminded her. Even with the penlight it took me a
while to find the family plot; I hadn't visited it for years, and we had
entered from the creek side instead of through the Cemetery Avenue
gate. There were no lights in the graveyard itself, but street lamps here
and there along the fence cast some small light inside, and the quarter
moon had risen. A slight warm breeze stirred; there was no dew.
Holding hands, we walked the weedy crushed-shell aisles among
tombstones and shrubbery until I found the old cedar I was looking
for and, nearby, the clump of hollies, grown now to small trees themselves. There was the old Behler headstone; there were the footstones
of the family (up to Mother, the first of us out in the new county
cemetery); and there was Baby Girl Behler, Born and Died July 1,
1930, whose nickname I used to conflate with the exotic name on
Schine's marquee: the Spare Twin, who had gone first.

Her little mound and the next few near it were carpeted with dandelions. After wishing her aloud a happy fourteenth birthday, I sat
awhile on BeeGee's stone and told Daisy how I used to narrate to
"Bijou" both my actual ongoing life and our imaginary adventures
together.

"You still do, sort of."

We smoked the last of her cigarettes. Daisy showed me how to hold it backward, the lighted end cupped inside my hand so no one would see it. Brinsley had taught her that, and even how to smoke it with the lit end in her mouth. Daisy was sitting on my uncle CPL. ALBERT WILHELM, 1891–1918, mustard-gassed in Belgium. So, I remarked: now we had lost family in wars on opposite sides of the planet.

"Stupid stupid stupid," Daisy sighed, sympathetically, and I realized that it was at least incomprehensible, their fighting and dying in wars half a world away, for reasons that Sam Moore claimed had as much to do with "the flag following the dollar" as with what governments told people they were fighting for. Life itself, I went so far as to suspect, was . . . not stupid, no, but scarcely comprehensible: Joe Junior's life and Uncle Albert's, for sure, but the others' lives, too — Mother's and Dad's, Uncle Josh's and Aunt Rachel's, Daisy's, even mine. Yet the universe went on, and not in quietly measured ticks like my new Omega, but in an unpunctuated streaming like the red sweep second hand of the electric wall clock in our kitchen: relentless, irreversible.

"Life's *weird,* Daise!" It came out a sort of blurt, half choked, and suddenly there were tears behind my eyes again.

My friend bent over me where I sat now on the dry grass, put her hands on either side of my head, and kissed my hair. "It sure is that."

I pressed my face into her skirt to stanch my eyes. Hoarsely into that fabric and almost to my own surprise I said, "What'd Andy Travers do, *rape* you?"

Daisy's thigh muscles tightened, and the grip of her hands in my hair. "Andy Travers!" She pushed away from me but held on to my head. "Persimmon, you're loo-oo-*ney!*" Laughing now, she pushed me backward onto BeeGee's mound and piled atop me as if wrestling, then rolled off onto her back. "Andy Travers! *Blyeh!*"

Just as suddenly she turned serious, raised herself on one elbow, and declared, "That is *it* now, 'Simmon Behler, and I mean it." To enforce her decree she kissed my mouth so hard that my teeth hurt my lips, and this time I closed my eyes tightly, opened her mouth some with mine as I embraced her, and rolled with her into the dandelioned trough between BeeGee's mound and Uncle Albert's. I prolonged the kiss beyond any previous in our connection, cutting off our breaths until my senses spun as if we were submerged or suspended, at the Boundary.

When finally Daisy pulled her mouth away, we lay huffing like winded divers. Then she put her lips to my ear — to whisper something, I supposed, but instead she took the whole ear into her mouth and moved her tongue-tip around inside. Almost frantically I tugged at her blouse; she quickly unbuttoned it, and as I pawed and nuzzled her she chuckled into my hair and asked, "What'll your baby sister think?"

Indeed, Daisy's head and shoulders rested now on BeeGee's mound, her hair fanned out as on a floral pillowcase. I rose to my knees to survey her: her blouse untucked and wide open, the front hem of her skirt pushed halfway up her thighs. She tucked her hands comfortably behind her head and smiled up at me: my birthday present. I tackled her underpants.

She started up — "'Simmon, no!" — but I persisted. With a little whine of protest she lay back again, lifted herself just a bit to let me slide the panties down, and then accommodatingly bent one knee at a time to help me get them over her feet. When I undid my belt and fly, however, she quickly moved my hand from there to between her legs and whispered, "Just your hand, honey."

That endearment, unprecedented, did it, together with the fact that Daisy's crotch was decidedly wetter than I had ever felt it before: so hotly liquid under and around my fingers that I wondered for a moment whether girls maybe sometimes peed from excitement. I would not be stopped. Urgently — when with no deftness at all I struggled my khakis and jockey shorts down over my tennis shoes — Daisy sat up and pleaded, "Let me *do* you!" I permitted her to handle me for a few moments but then firmly pressed her back against the little mound, kissed her forehead, and moved onto her.

She closed her legs and eyes and rolled her head. "We don't *have* anything!"

"I know," I said, though I was far from truly understanding. I pinned her forearms lightly over her head with mine and humped against her, covering her face and neck with kisses until at last she stopped shaking her head. She exhaled a long breath, opened her eyes, and relaxed her whole body at once. Regarding me levelly, she lifted her knees high, spread them wide.

This second sexual penetration of my life was very different from the first. I found Daisy's slippery entrance for myself and drove in so forcefully that though my friend's expression did not change nor her level gaze falter, she grunted involuntarily at each thrust. Of these there were no more than the number of my years, for Daisy's unmediated sheath was so intensely more alive that despite my resolve to withdraw at the critical moment, I could not. With a shiver, I shot her full.

"Oh Jesus," she sighed. But then with sure, slow movements under me she drew my climax vertiginously out, right to that Boundary that I had fancied Home Plate might even carry us beyond.

Whereupon the next wonder ensued. As my sweaty face pressed into Daisy's collarbone and my breath came gradually less hard, I noticed that my birthday watch had slid loose to my wrist, and my spirit flooded suddenly as if from nowhere with the truth of my brother's fate. Whatever his actual state of affairs, I saw my earlier life-raft fantasies for what they were and all my day's reactions to that fell telegram as sentimental experiments, postures, attitudinizings, for which Joe Junior had been only the occasion.

I believe that I had never before sobbed; *sobbing* was something that characters in novels did, especially women characters. But as my false grief was displaced by true, I found myself spontaneously *racked with sobs*. Between them, to let Daisy know I wasn't weeping at what we'd done, I managed to croak out my brother's name and, having found my voice, added something no more specific than "Everything's so *real!*"

Her heels still pressed into the back of my thighs, Daisy held my forehead against hers and praised and encouraged me. "Let it come, Persimmon." And as if, irrespective of my emotion's source and nature, its authenticity aroused her, she began moving under me again, at first slowly and then not, exhaling hard at her own thrusts as she had grunted before at mine. When I realized what was happening, I tried to assist her with movements of my own; in the end Daisy rolled us over and ground herself atop me quite as I had earlier atop her, until with sounds that astonished me her passion peaked.

Side by side then against BeeGee's mound we lay collecting our breath, cooling down in our perspiration, until mosquitoes stirred us.

In her normal voice Daisy fretted, "I'm gonna get *killed*." But we dressed in no hurry, punctuating our movements with light kisses on each other's mosquito bites. "That was dumb dumb dumb of us, Persimmon," my friend declared at one point, "but it was terrific. The best." I quite believed her, and so much more mature a lover did I feel myself to have become than the boy she had initiated just that afternoon, I took it as a compliment that her range of comparison was larger than mine, and kissed the nape of her neck instead of pestering her on that subject. Walking her back through the deserted streets to River Boulevard, I asked merely whether she thought we had made her pregnant. To speak that word — for the first time in my life, probably — made me feel both grown-up and frightened.

"Not likely," Daisy said. "I'm late already, but I'm never on time like Julia. What's done is done."

I myself rather doubted that at barely fourteen I could actually *knock a girl up;* it would be two more years before I could even get a legal work permit and a driver's license. In any case, I had meant to . . . pull out, I told her, but hadn't been able to when the time came.

"Sam says that's one of Mother Nature's little tricks," Daisy said.

The *reality* of these things, which till now I had only heard of and joked about with the Silver Foxes, awed me. What would she do, I asked her, if worst came to worst? Daisy shrugged, as if not very interested, then flashed me a sad sidelong smile. "We'll name it after your brother."

We turned onto River Boulevard. At the sight of a dim front-bedroom light in her house, Daisy said, "Uh-oh," but then she decided it was probably just her mother having a bad night. If Sam had noticed her absence, he'd have had lights on in his study. All the same, she thought she'd better go on alone from there. What time was it? I consulted my upper left forearm. Feeling very mature, instead of "Quarter till two" I said simply "Late," and insisted on waiting across the street from her house until she signaled me that all was well, maybe by blinking her penlight from her bedroom window. Which one was hers and Julia's?

But Daisy said no, she'd be all right in any case. And if she wasn't, so what?

My heart surged with uncertain pity.

"Hey," she said then, brightening. "I forgot the rest of your birthday present." She bade me hold Winston's bike while she fished out of her skirt pocket that slender little package. "Good night, Bill Behler." She bussed my cheek. "Open it when you get home, okay?"

Despite the hour, Behler brooded to the foot of River Boulevard, to the municipal wharf and waterfront park, to regard the night and sort out his soul.

Beyond question, Daisy Moore was my girlfriend now. We were *lovers,* maybe in serious trouble. I wanted to be with her a lot — every day, perhaps — not only to explore the length and breadth of the exotic country she had led me into, but to become closer to her than even Julia was and to know all her secrets. I ought to be anxious, I knew, that our lovemaking would be found out, and that whether or not I had knocked Daisy up, her indignant parents might call me to account before my father and themselves for a malfeasance beside which my petty thievery from Paul's was laughable. And this in the rawest hour of my family's grief, when I ought to have been stricken by Joe Junior's almost certain death! I could never in a million years explain even to Aunt Rachel, never mind deaf Dad, that I *had* been stricken, that it was with Daisy in the graveyard that I had learned true loss, along with other grown-up things.

But though I felt some concern, even some guilt, what I felt mainly was reverential excitement. A car rippled past on the bricks of the boulevard; several others were parked, with lights out, in the gravel lot down by the wharf, a favorite spot for Dorset lovers with cars and spare gasoline. Only a few months ago I would have said that the couples in those cars were *smooching,* or *necking,* not altogether sure what that activity involved once it went beyond kissing and the guy's feeling up the girl. Now I understood quite well what they were doing, and further, with chastened awe, that even some twenty-year-olds would go less far this night than Daisy had taken me twice on my fourteenth birthday. Some people went to their graves without ever experiencing what I had experienced. Perhaps Uncle Al had, mustard-gassed in Belgium; perhaps Joe Junior. Just last night I would have felt like a child among these smoochers and neckers. Now I felt benevolently more mature than they: more seasoned, further along.

Flecks of foam on the dark water moving westward past the bulkhead told me that the tide on the Chaptico had turned again and was now running out. Up-shore beyond the shipyard were the lights of Dorset General, never dark; to the left of them, one car blinked its way across the river bridge on some small-hours errand worth burning scarce fuel for. Below the bridge, the channel buoys winked their various rhythms, each regular but in shifting syncopation with the others.

I decided once and for all that there was no God, or if there turned out to be one, that I had no interest in him. Though no one but myself was watching, I shrugged my shoulders. A car started up and left the parking lot, lights out until it reached the street. A small meteor slid down the far sky across the river, over Avon County. Overhead, the stars were breathtakingly clear; my Astronomy merit badge not far behind me, I identified a dozen constellations and half a dozen individual stars, most of the former named in Greek, the latter in Arabic. The Milky Way was particularly brilliant, its black dust clouds sharply defined. The physical universe, I acknowledged, was vast, intricate, and full of marvels and mysteries in both directions, from atoms to galaxies. But not miracles.

I decided to drop out of the Boy Scouts of America. My mosquito bites from the cemetery itched like crazy. To test my self-control, I stoically held off scratching them.

I decided to open Daisy's present under the first streetlight I came to. In the box were my I.D. bracelet and an Eversharp fountain pen to match Uncle Josh's mechanical pencil. My girlfriend had been in secret touch with my family! I looked to see whether she'd had the bracelet engraved, maybe with my name on one side and hers on the other. But though just a while ago she had called me by a surprising new name, the silver plate was still blank on both sides.

Uncertain as to what its return (in the form of a gift, together with the pen) signified, I put the bracelet on my right wrist and headed back up River Boulevard toward home. The Moores' house, I was relieved to see, was entirely dark now. I wondered whether Daisy was asleep already or lying awake in her bed, maybe whispering to green-eyed Julia about what we had done. It was exciting to imagine her telling her rapt sister *everything,* and equally exciting, and at least as easy, to imagine her telling Julia nothing much at all. Would I ever fathom my deep friend Daisy Moore?

I decided that Simon William Behler would *not* be a famous

"explorer." Fancying that I would be was no more than a habit I had gotten into after reading Richard Halliburton; I hadn't really meant it for quite a while.

On the creek bridge I decided that Simon William Behler would maybe not even be my name. I didn't know who I was, who I would be. However (idly scratching after all), I decided to become not only "somebody" but somehow . . . immortal.

Six Interludes

1.

Though their version of his tale had been briefer than the one here given, when Somebody finished it the listeners were afidget. This one stroked his lips between thumb and forefinger; that one conferred with his neighbor in turbaned undertone, shrugging eyebrows, turning up palms. Some frowned into their cups as if prospecting for further gems; others shifted upon their cushions and looked to their host for cue. The elder merchant at Sindbad's left hand had nodded off in midvoyage. At its end the silence woke him; he beamed benevolently at the company and declared adversity to be a schoolmaster charged by Allah with man's improvement, and tales of voyaging to be that master's lesson-book. Yasmīn smiled at her saffron lap. Sindbad the Sailor scratched his saffron-wound head and leaned back against the empty tub behind him.

"If I may, sir," suddenly said Ibn al-Hamrā, and with a turn of Sindbad's hand he was given leave to speak.

"Though God has seen fit to favor my enterprises," he declared carminely to the company, "I do not forget that I am a mere merchant of humble origin, not a man of learning and culture. Yet in narratives of voyaging, as in other matters, I know what I like, and whereas our host's compelling and exemplary tale of his second expedition quite fills that bill, I must say that our visitor's, in my estimation, falls short."

He wet his red lips, already glistening with his eloquence. "The high ground of traditional realism, brothers, is where I stand! Give me familiar, substantial stuff: rocs and rhinoceri, ifrits and genies and flying carpets, such as we all drank in with our mothers' milk and shall drink — Inshallah! — till our final swallow. Let no outlander imagine that such crazed fabrications as machines that mark the hour or roll themselves down the road will ever take the place of our homely Islamic realism, the very capital of narrative — from which, if I may say so, all interest is generated."

Several nodded assent, none more vigorously than the speaker himself, who then asked, "And may not the same be said for a story's action? Speak to us from our everyday experience: shipwreck and sole-survivorhood, the retrieval of diamonds by means of mutton-sides and giant eagles, the artful deployment of turbans for aerial transport, buzzard dispersal, shore-to-ship signaling, and suicide (Allah forfend) as necessary. Above all, sing the loss of fortunes and their fortuitous re-doubling: the very stuff of story! Do not attempt to distract us from these ground-verities with such profitless sideshows as human copulation, which is no more agreeable to hear about in detail than are our visitor's other narrative concerns: urination, masturbation, and — your pardon, Sayyid Sindbad — regurgitation."

"*Blyeh!*" suddenly went Yasmīn, in a creditable imitation of "Daisy Moore."

"As to that," her father put in, "whatever my brother Still-Stranded's less plausible and tasteful flights, he has got that noise right. Just hearing his young concubine make that sound was enough to put me back in my nest of foul and giant vultures, which I had hoped never to revisit: a commendable touch of realism among so much unbridled fancy."

"Granted," Ibn al-Hamrā said at once, his florid cheeks perspiring. "Or should we say, rather, it *would have been* commendable if, like your hapless own excursion into filth, it had been a detour fraught with moral instruction. For what we successful merchants of Baghdad most prize in any tale, after realism, is edification. A story without a moral is like a meal without mint tea. Consider, gentlemen: our host's first two voyages yielded four pious lessons each, a projectable return of two dozen moral gems from his peregrinations to date. But from his self-styled namesake, what have we gained? *His* so-called voyages have fetched us nowhere, at greater length and slower pace than life itself. In the time it takes him to mark one boyish birthday, we listeners age seven years. We shall expire of inanition and old age before he ever reaches his Serendib, not to mention our Baghdad and the gracious house of Sindbad the Sailor.

"Moreover, he will not deign to knit the ravels of his plot. The pressing question of that young tart's maidenhead, for example, is no-wise resolved." He looked candidly at Yasmīn before continuing. "I propose, sirs, that we accept it as a given that this stranger finds himself among us in the City of Peace rather than in his barbarous native land, and that we brook no further lies about how he got from there to here. He has battened on our hospitality. We have generously heard him out. Let him go his way now, back to his self-abuse and other impious diversions, such as desecrating his own family's grave-plot like a vulture fouling its nest. As for ourselves, let us get on with a voyage more profitable than any story: to Serendib!"

In one plump pink hand he raised his empty wine cup. But though many nodded approval of his speech, no cups joined his except that of Kuzia Fakān, off in a corner, and she quickly lowered hers when she saw that she was alone. By way of acknowledging that neither the criticism nor the proposal was unworthy of consideration, Sindbad the Sailor cocked his head. Then — after a long glance at Kuzia Fakān — he looked to still-stranded Somebody for reply, as did blushing Yasmīn and all the others except her prospective fiancé. Still flushed by his own rhetoric, Ibn al-Hamrā sipped vigorously at his empty wine cup and recomposed himself on his cushion like an agitated rooster after crowing.

"Every teller," ours presently declared, "tells at his audience's pleasure. I would be most pleased if my story pleased all who heard it. Failing that, I shall be satisfied if it satisfies my host and any other whose heart is open to it and its teller. Failing that, I'll tell on all the same while I have one listener for whom I care. But hear me, friends: when I wake from this dream of Baghdad to find myself once more beached and bleached, with none but the tireless tide to talk to, nevertheless I will hearse and rehearse the six voyages that left me stranded here, for it is only by retracement of his course that the lost navigator can hope to find his bearings.

"Of which six voyages, gentlemen and ladies, the third jumps not another seven years but four times seven, to the voyager's forty-second birthday: a leap in time that should gratify my impatient critic. And it fetched me not to an island virgin but to a virgin island, where I not only reapproached the Boundary you've heard me speak of — between that world of my stories and this of their telling — but for the first time (if only for some moments) crossed it."

"By Allah," said Sindbad the Sailor, "we will not let our brother go till we've heard that story." As if to the company at large then he added, "Let any who has heard his fill not join tomorrow's feast, when we twin Sindbads will tell of our third voyages. My own, at least, is as rich in moral lessons as in island monsters, but it has not a virgin in it. Yasmīn."

Her face the hue more of last night's djellaba than of tonight's, his daughter went the wine-rounds, but this time saved for last Ibn al-Hamrā's expectant cup. Then with a small salaam she took his cup-holding right hand in her left, as if to make a joint toast. He blinked, crimsoned, smiled. Having thus steadied his cup, however, Yasmīn carefully poured the red wine half in, half out of it, onto the belly of his white caftan, which looked now like a bridal bedsheet or a shambles apron.

"Kuzia Fakān," Sindbad called at once, not urgently. Yasmīn made another salaam to Ibn al-Hamrā and yet another to her father, before whom she set down the now empty decanter. Then, with Jaydā following after, she left the consternated company as Kuzia Fakān, veiled and caftaned, came forward with her two associates. Scarcely looking up at her, Sindbad gestured toward the offending stain. Kuzia Fakān snapped her fingers three times at the musicians; they set to with pipe and tambourine, and she danced the host's amends to Ibn al-Hamrā. Stepping right onto the low table, after introductory pirouettes among the empty plates and bowls she removed her black head-scarf, flourished it at each member of the company in turn as she shook loose her dark hair, then spread the scarf like a silk napkin over

Ibn's wine-stain. Next, to an insinuating melody, she pulled her silk-sleeved arms in through the wide sleeves of her caftan and moved her hands invisibly about, all the while swaying and turning before the guests as kitchen servants cleared the table for her dance. At length, her arms resleeved, she reached down the caftan's open neck and slowly drew forth, as if from between her breasts, a short, bead-spangled vest or jumper, which she had managed adroitly to unfasten and remove. This too she brandished around the approving table, especially at the two Sindbads, before draping it over Ibn's lap.

Now the rhythm accelerated. Kuzia Fakān thrust her hands this time through side-slits in her caftan and once again busied herself invisibly, in the neighborhood of her waist, accompanying her business with thrusts and swivels of her generous hips. From one of the side-slits she then drew out a silken sash, from the other a large, brightly patterned wraparound worn like a skirt or decorative apron over her long embroidered trousers. One garment in each hand, she swirled and capered, snapping the sash (to the company's amusement) directly at Still-Stranded's face as she passed by him, and then laid these, too, in the lap of the beaming Ibn al-Hamrā.

The music slowed. Back into their caftan-sleeves went Kuzia's silken arms and moved here and there out of sight about her upper body. Never pausing in her dance, she raised the neck of her caftan briefly high enough to hide her head. When she slipped it down again, her forearms reemerged bare: one hand held the sheer long-sleeved blouse she had wriggled out of, the other a cupped and sequined halter that she wore beneath it. Depositing both on Ibn's pile, she drew back her shoulders, thrust forth her chest at each diner in turn, and shook her unharnessed breasts: deferentially at Sindbad the Sailor, contemptuously at Somebody the Still-Stranded, and most vigorously at Ibn al-Hamrā, to make it clear that under her overgarment she was now topless.

"God is great!" exclaimed the elder merchant on Sindbad's left. No one disagreed. Now the rhythm ceased; the tambourinist sustained a beatless sizzle, over which the piper wailed a sinuous, minor-keyed cadenza while Kuzia Fakān, her hands busy in the caftan's side-slits, loosed her embroidered trousers at the waist and then, her hands clasped above her head, lowered them by slow gyrations of her hips until she could step out of them and with one bare foot pitch them over to Ibn al-Hamrā. The piper continued her improvisation — half impudent challenge, half wild lament — and Kuzia worked invisibly but suggestively upon her pelvis as she danced frontally before each diner in turn. The exception was Still-Stranded, at whom for the company's entertainment she thrust her busy backside.

"In all His aspects," declared undismayed Somebody, "Allah be praised."

She ended her dance not before Ibn al-Hamrā but before old Sindbad, vibrating her hips to the piper's trill until with a crash of tambourine her ultimate underthing, little more than a small network of beads, dropped to her ankles. With prehensile toes she deftly footed it to her hand; then she snatched off her veil and, with one of those final intimate garments in each hand, raised her arms and danced triumphantly, at once stripped and entirely covered, in the table's center. At the music's close, bowing low, she presented veil and bead-string to her lord. But Sindbad took her wrist instead and transferred the presentation to Ibn al-Hamrā, to whom he said, "Be kind enough to carry this Bedou's costume to her quarters, and she will expunge that stain on our hospitality." He then bade the applauding company good night until Voyage Three and — as Kuzia Fakān haughtily ushered florid Ibn from the banquet hall — brought a final knowing smile to his guests' faces by assigning as Somebody's bedroom guide not one of the other attractive woman attendants (the piper or the tambourinist, say) but the page Salīm. That saucy fellow promptly queened it around the table in mimicry of Kuzia Fakān: he twitched his hips, pirouetted on his toes, fumbled under the sash of his trousers as if to undo his drawers, minced backward from the hall, and beckoned seductively for our narrator to follow.

Nodding calm good-night to host and guests, Somebody did in fact exit with his mocking usher. Once out of the room, however, he said, "Enough, Salīm. I know my way."

"What way is that, Sayyid? Kuzia Fakān tells us that none of *her* ways is yours, and yet you make sheep-eyes at Yasmīn."

"Good night, Salīm."

But the young man stuck to him as to a tourist in the souk. "You prefer to ride the camel?"

"No camel, Salīm."

"Fountain of youth? Shower of gold?"

"Sleep well, Salīm."

The page followed him around the dry courtyard and up the stairs to the guest quarters, trotting before him, skipping backward, catching at his sleeve. "We all think your stories are mad."

"You are free to."

"Yet they make it plain that you understand why God hung men's tails in front. Do you use yours only for shooing flies?"

"Also for flogging the impudent. Shoo, Salīm."

"You are a fool to set yourself against Ibn al-Hamrā! One day he'll be the richest man in Baghdad."

"Allah's will be done."

"He's a camel-driver, too, that one. Kuzia will be too sore to dance tomorrow."

"You speak from experience."

"You don't believe me? I could tell you about Ibn al-Hamrā."

"I am not asking."

"When he weds your Miss High-and-Mighty, he'll skewer her like a lamb on the spit. She'll think she's back with the Qeshmi pirates."

"Enough of that."

"Aha! I think you are a spy for her former boyfriend, Prince Jabāl."

"Thoughts are free."

Surprisingly then, the page said, "Listen, Sayyid: you may depend on me. Use me as you will."

"You would be disloyal to your master?"

"Allah forbid! But he has as little use for me these days as for Jaydā and Kuzia Fakān."

"For whom has he use, then?" They had reached Somebody's door. "Never mind. Leave me now, Salīm."

"You *are* a spy," the page said. "If not for Prince Jabāl's vizier, then for Caliph Haroun al-Rashīd himself. I know all the secrets of this house, Sayyid. What things I could tell you!"

"Good night, fellow."

But Salīm pushed past into the room and turned to face him. "Eunuch and pig-eating Christian!"

His curses were clearly experimental. When Somebody seized him duly by the back of his shirt, as if by the scruff of his neck, he laughed and said, "Have mercy!" And he was merrier yet when Still-Stranded forced him chest-forward over the lid of a large trunk near the bed. Far from resisting, he quickly slipped his trouser-sash and, unlike dancing Kuzia, in one swift motion presented his bare buttocks. "Woe!" he wailed. "I am a naughty camel who needs the whip!"

What he felt instead, however — and not where he expected, but edgewise against his scrotum — was a fish-knife given Somebody by Mustafā the Master Navigator, its blade so many times resharpened that it was reduced to a keen-edged sliver. Merry no longer, Salīm cried "Allah spare me!" and wondrously compressed what he had been spreading. "It was Kuzia said you're a foreskinned faggot!"

"You will now be a circumcised eunuch."

"No offense, Sayyid! For God's sake, mount the camel instead of gelding him!"

"Stop shivering, Salīm, or you'll geld yourself. What does Sindbad think to learn by sending you to me?"

"*Aiee!* Careful there! He wonders what the whole house wonders: who you are, where you came from, what you're after. He worries that Haroun will learn the truth about his last voyage and his next. *Lessim,* master! Ease off!"

"What is that truth?"

But wide-eyed Salīm declared that he could not say, even on pain of castration, for he knew no more than that Sindbad's public account of his voyage to Serendib was either not true or not the whole truth, and that behind the official project of Voyage Seven was some other, secret plan. These things he knew, as did Jaydā and Kuzia Fakān, from long tenure in the household and even longer practice at keeping his ears and eyes, for example, open. But though Ibn al-Hamrā (to name only one) would pay well to know more of these matters, the facts were known only to Sayyid Sindbad — and perhaps to his daughter.

"Speak of her quickly, or you are eggless."

"*Aooo!*" Already the page was grinning again, though nervously. "She is a miracle of fortitude and chastity! A jewel! A treasure!"

"One. Two."

"*Owow!* What do you want to hear?"

"The truth about Miss High-and-Mighty."

"Yes! Such airs, when everybody knows she was zabbed from stem-head to sternpost by the pirate Sahīm al-Layl! *Wuff! Lessim!*"

"You don't believe Captain Sahīm kept his side of the ransom bargain?"

"*Fuff!* But long before the pirates porked her, she had opened her legs for her daddy's pet, right under her daddy's nose. Stop!"

"No. You mean a certain young sailor called Umar al-Yom, who grew up in this house?"

"Why ask, if you already know? Umar took what she offered and got what he deserved."

"So you say. And this is the virgin for whom Ibn al-Hamrā dickers?"

"*Fah!* He knows what he's trading for. As late as last month, while her father was out recouping the ransom, Jaydā and I sneaked one of Yasmīn's boyfriends right into the harem, rolled up in a rug! There they went at it day and night as if the household knew nothing, and when Sindbad reached Basra we rugged the young buck back out again."

"Was that this fellow Umar al-Yom?" asked Somebody, who happened to know that Salīm had not been an accomplice in the episode.

"No, man: Sindbad got rid of Umar years ago, on Voyage Five! This was Captain Sahīm al-Layl himself! He'd given her such a taste for Qeshmi sausage that she had to have more."

"I see. And has Sindbad got wind of this?"

Salīm turned up his palms. "Who knows what that old man knows? When I offered to tell him just what he had bought with his ransom money, he put his dagger where yours is now, and the whole story slipped my mind."

Said relieved Somebody, "It seems clear to me that Mistress Yasmīn is anybody's for the taking, and that you and Jaydā are her pimps."

"Ah, well, now. . . ."

"I want a piece of her."

"Sayyid!"

"As you value these peahen's eggs of yours, Salīm, take me to her now."

Such a thing was unthinkable, the page protested. No man but Sayyid Sindbad himself — or a rare guest honored by him with the privilege, such as Ibn al-Hamrā just now — could enter the women's quarters without bringing the house down about his shoulders. Even Ibn would be taken not to the heart of the harem but to an intermediate space on the order of Somebody's guest apartment, where Kuzia Fakān would do her hospitable work. . . .

"Yet you say you smuggled the pirate Sahīm al-Layl directly to Yasmīn's bed. Do the same for me."

"I lied," the young man confessed. The pirate captain likewise, he said, had been taken to a private room of Yasmīn's just outside the harem itself, overlooking the courtyard. And it had not been he and Jaydā who had toted him there, but Jaydā and Kuzia Fakān's tambourinist, Fatmah Awād, who had subsequently mentioned to Kuzia the unusual weight of Mistress Yasmīn's new rug, whereupon Kuzia, when Yasmīn declared the room off-limits to anyone except herself and Jaydā, had speculated to Salīm and to others (but not to Sindbad, from whose favor she feared herself to be already slipping) as to what and who might have been inside that rug.

"Up with your pants and lead me to that room," Somebody demanded, "and you will learn who was there before. But if you take me to the wrong place," he added, "you may say good-bye to that camel's nipple God gave you to wet your drawers with." To our man's considerable relief, the retrousered page admitted now that he could not say for certain even which room it was that Yasmīn's lover, presumably her late ravisher, had allegedly been smuggled into during her father's sixth voyage. There were so many rooms in Sayyid Sindbad's house! He could, however, point out which room it was that Kuzia Fakān said Fatmah Awād said she and Jaydā had set the rolled rug nearest the door of.

Pleased as Somebody would have been to revisit that sanctum of happy memory, the excursion was doubly unnecessary: he had learned what he had hoped to learn, and when nevertheless he ordered Salīm to lead away, and set out with him along the obscure balcony that led from the courtyard past his door and others to he knew not where, he saw a shrouded figure coming toward them, carrying a small lamp.

"Jaydā," the page whispered. "We're fucked." Somebody thrilled to see then behind the first figure a second, making her way to him as she had the night before. At sight of the approachers, she stopped before they could make out even the color of her djellaba, much less her face. Salīm, too, stopped still, but Jaydā came on.

"Mother of Yasmīn!" Somebody saluted her (using the respectful title Umm), and he tucked away his fish-knife. "Sindbad the Still-Stranded greets you and your young lady and wishes a word with you both in this page's presence."

The duenna drew her veil closer to her face and raised the oil lamp to inspect the caller. At Salīm she frowned her eyebrows; the page pouted and shrugged his face. Yasmīn gathered her djellaba-hood over her nose and mouth. Turning to her, Jaydā nodded toward a curtained door, the nearest to hand, and followed her inside.

"You have her, Sayyid!" Salīm whispered triumphantly. "Ten dirhams to Jaydā and a little something for your guide, and I wish you a white night!"

He held out his open palm. Somebody seized his wrist and pulled him into the room, which was handsomely carpeted but otherwise unfurnished. The two women, lamp-lit, stood by. Yasmīn pushed back her saffron hood and smiled questioningly.

"This fellow," Somebody declared, "awaits his payment for delivering me to Sindbad's daughter for the night."

"Salīm!" Yasmīn redrew her hood. Jaydā scowled over her veil.

"Sayyid insisted," the page said.

Affirmed Somebody, "I did. I asked to see that famous room he told me of, where Mistress Yasmīn hid her lover Sahīm al-Layl for the month of Sha'ban while her father sailed out for reimbursement and revenge. Is this it, Salīm?"

"Ask her." The page cocked his head Yasmīnward.

"Sahīm al-Layl!" cried appalled Yasmīn. "What a thing to say, Salīm!"

"That rug wasn't empty," Salīm grumbled. "Fatmah Awād says she strained her back carrying it upstairs and then turned her ankle carrying it back down again, just before Ramadan."

Yasmīn closed her eyes. "Sahīm al-Layl!"

"Now," Somebody went on, "our friend here suggests that ten dirhams will persuade Madame Jaydā to leave her responsibilities in my hands for the night."

For the first time in this interlude, Yasmīn's guardian broke her silence: "Ten dirhams!" she scolded the page. "See if I don't wring your unwashed neck!"

Though still held fast by the wrist, Salīm shrank from her. "I swear by Allah I said fifteen!"

"Sahīm al-Layl!" Yasmīn moaned again, her hand to her forehead.

"Fifteen dirhams!" Jaydā said contemptuously. "For the whole night!"

"Say what you will," the page insisted, "somebody was in that rug. The whole house knows it, except Sayyid Sindbad."

Yasmīn hid her face in Jaydā's shoulder and murmured in the language they used between themselves. Jaydā glanced at Somebody over her veil.

"Enough of this," he said, and he instructed Salīm, "Tell the whole house, beginning with Fatmah Awād and Kuzia Fakān and the camel-driver Ibn al-Hamrā, that somebody *was* in that rug, both going and coming. But that somebody was neither Captain Sahīm al-Layl nor any lover of Mistress Yasmīn. On the contrary: it was an agent of the Prince of Believers himself, commissioned to protect the honor of Sindbad's daughter."

The two women regarded each other.

"That agent," Somebody asserted, "was with her on the bride-ship *Zahir* when its captain surrendered to the Qeshmi pirates. He was with her on the pirate ship *Shaitan* to help Sahīm al-Layl protect her from his crew while her ransom was being negotiated. He was with her in this house during Sindbad's sixth voyage, to make certain that no foxes raided the hen-coop in the farmer's absence. He is with her now."

Redrawing his fish-knife and reseizing the great-eyed page by the back of his shirt, Somebody went on: "To the most serene Caliph Haroun al-Rashīd, it is of no concern whether Mistress Yasmīn bestows her maidenhead upon Prince Jabāl of Sohar or Sahīm al-Layl or Umar al-Yom or Omār Khāyyām. She may give it to the Man in the Moon for all the caliph cares. But out of respect for her and for his loyal subject Sindbad, who has brought back six several fortunes to the realm, he commissioned me to capon any cock who offers to take before Mistress Yasmīn offers to give. I have left a trail of such upstart zabbs, separated from their owners, from Baghdad to Qeshm to Basra and back. You will now carry yours to Ibn al-Hamrā in a little sandalwood casket designed for that purpose, to let him know that what he bargains for is more than he bargains for."

Whatever the rough edges of this improvisation, there were none on the blade of the fileting knife of the master navigator Mustafā, which flashed in Jaydā's lamplight like an outsized scalpel.

"I can't bear to watch yet another of these operations," said quick Yasmīn. "I'll just step outside. Where do we keep those little sandal-wood caskets, Jaydā?"

"Where else," smoothly replied her overseer, "but under my bed?"

"Go with her," Somebody bade Jaydā, "in case she meets the camel-driver coming from his stable. This fellow's backside will serve as his little casket, for he has fucked himself."

"*Ai yi!*" Salīm wailed. "Don't let him do it, Mother!"

"*Pfwah*," Jaydā scoffed. "For all the son you've been to me, I should take Sayyid's knife to you myself. But Allah help us," she declared to surprised Somebody, "a mother is a mother, and though this scamp is neither cock nor hen, he's all I have in that line. Let him keep what he was born with, please, in the place where Allah saw fit to put it. Maybe one day he'll learn to use it as God intended."

Released, the page moved a safe distance off but did not run. To Jaydā, Somebody said, "Your pardon, Mother. Who knew that Umm Yasmīn was really Umm Salīm?" He consulted Yasmīn's face but could not see it clearly in the shadows near the doorway, where she had paused.

"She carries on like Yasmīn's mother, though she isn't," Salīm complained, his fright forgotten. "Her own flesh and blood she has no use for."

"Because from the hour it was weaned it had no use for me," Jaydā replied at once. "If I had given you a thrashing every time you deserved one for being a wretched son, perhaps you would have learned that you *are* my son. But I always pitied him and made excuses," she explained to Somebody, "and came between him and his just punishment, as I've done again tonight. For that he has become *my* punishment. Go along," she ordered Salīm, "before I change my mind and borrow Sayyid's fish-knife. This house will be no worse for having one less zabb in it."

The page turned his behind to them in the doorway, farted swiftly and roundly one two three, in turn at Yasmīn, at his mother, and at

Somebody the Still-Stranded, and hurried out. Yasmīn hooded her amusement. Lamp in hand, Jaydā stepped after him, grumbling that his father would be told.

"My father!" we heard Salīm scoff; he farted again and snickered off. The room was altogether dark.

2.

Toward where he'd last seen Yasmīn standing, our man said quietly, "You never mentioned that Jaydā is Salīm's mother."

"*Magboot*," she replied, just as quietly but from elsewhere in the heavy darkness. "That's right."

He moved over the carpeting toward her voice. "No doubt there are other things as well that you haven't mentioned."

"No doubt," she granted, speaking almost in a whisper from yet a different place. "If you and I had done nothing but talk through the month of Sha'ban, we could never have told each other our whole stories, let alone Jaydā's."

As she spoke, he moved. "We did talk, Yasmīn, didn't we?"

Her reply, when it came, came from back where she had stood at first, and she seemed to be moving as she spoke: "We did." Down by the carpet, over toward the doorway, there was a rustling, almost a jingling. "But we did not talk all the time."

"Who is Salīm's father, then?"

Suddenly close behind him, she said, "Ask Jaydā." But when he turned and reached out, she was gone.

"Why are you moving about? Where are you?"

"Over here in the graveyard, waiting for Beel Bailer to find me."

"*Bus*, Yasmīn. It's so dark in here I can't even find myself."

"Leave that to your Day-*zee*, once you've found her."

So we moved and paused, listening for each other's breath, soft footfalls, the rustle of clothing. "I have found your dear slippers," the man said presently, and the woman: "Let yours lie atop them."

A bit later, after stumbling to his knees over it: "Your djellaba."

"It longs for your caftan to cover it. Make a little mound of them, like BeeGee's grave." In a whisper then: "Good night, Beel Bailer."

"Don't call me that. Where are you now?"

"Oppovopper hoppere. Oppacropposs yoppour Boppoundoppary."

Marveling, he stalked her, half kneeling on the carpet to keep his balance as he swept the darkness with his arms and speaking no more to signal his position. There was that muffled jingle: some jewelry that sounded as she stepped. Over there, after a near catch, her faster breath: his hand had grazed a bare hip. In a corner, sure enough, he felt a small pile of silken, perfumed underthings; he added to it his own, of linen, and heard either the woman or her jewelry chuckle from the room's dark center. Moving thereward, he heard her not move off. On the scented mound he'd made he found her and hers, and was by her found.

"Sīmon."

Through our blind and ardent business then, that jingling was now up behind his head, now at the small of his back; he understood in general what it was even before Jaydā returned with the lamp. Lips to his ear, Yasmīn identified the approaching footsteps. "Sīmon" paused, would disconnect us. But she spurred him back with those ankle bracelets to his joyful work — "*Yallah,* Beel! *Yallah!*" — until her urgings rose to a muezzin-call of satisfaction: "*Tamoun, tamoun!* Oh, *jumail,* Sīmon! *Shabash!*"

When we had quieted, we heard the door open slightly and saw ("Sīmon" did, at least, and moved to cover us with some free part of his caftan but was clasped fast) the lit lamp handed just inside and set on the floor, then a water-basin and a towel, and finally a chamberpot, and the door closed. The man raised himself off top, the better to kneel beside and resavor what he had just light enough now to survey: Yasmīn's body, dusky, recumbent, perfect; naked but for silver bracelets on both slim ankles; arms overhead, as Daisy Moore's had been in 1944, and relaxed upon our mounded clothes; breasts ampler than skinny Daisy's, lifted by her upraised arms; knees bent slightly and thighs still parted, like the lips between, from our coupling.

"*Jumail* indeed," he said, and he placed one hand just under her navel. "Beautiful."

She turned her smile his way before opening her eyes. "Jaydā?"

In our month of Sha'ban, he had gotten almost used to this. Veiled and caftaned, the older woman stepped on hearing this call into the room, brought over the basin and towel, and stood impassively by while first Yasmīn sponged and toweled her lover and then he her.

From time to time the duenna would take the sponge for rinsing in the scented water or refold the towel dry side out; when it was Yasmīn's turn to be washed, Jaydā sternly brushed her hair as Sīmon sponged her skin. All through these ablutions, as was her habit, Yasmīn talked: sometimes to him, sometimes about him, to Jaydā, either in standard Arabic or in their private language. Sex not infrequently wound Sindbad's daughter up, after first pleasurably unwinding her.

Had there ever been, she would demand of Jaydā, a softer, silkier little Beel-Beel than the one she was now toweling, which just minutes past had stood like a minaret pointing her to Paradise? Really, she believed she loved it as much when it was Sayyid Tom-Thumb as when it rose and swelled like an uncorked genie — which, to be sure, it did less often and less awesomely for her, given Sīmon's age, than it must have done long ago and far away for her lucky sister Day-*zee*. And she *was* Daisy's sister, no question about it: at once her older sister (inasmuch as Daisy on *her* mound had been sixteen, and Yasmīn on ours was nearly thirty) and her younger (inasmuch as Beel-Beel, then fourteen, was now fifty-plus). How she would have enjoyed to touch him back then and see him spring up again and again like a jack-in-the-box! Day-*zee*, yes: Yasmīn understood her, and that business of the ankle bracelet, better than "Bill Behler" had. All the same, she did not quite see how Sīmon's first and second "voyages" — which had involved no vessel except Daisy Moore's little oasis (wâhât Day-*zee*) and had brought Simon William Behler no closer to Baghdad than he'd been before — bore upon what we were calling "our plan." It seemed to her that he had accomplished more to our purpose in five minutes with the inspired fabrication that he had sent Salīm to spread about the house than he had in two whole evenings with tales of his stillborn sister and of Yasmīn's new sisters Day-*zee* and Jul-*ya*, so beloved of their father. . . . "*Ai*, Jaydā! Not so hard!"

"Critics everywhere," Sīmon sighed, and he dabbed dry the damp undersides of her breasts. "What had your father's first two voyages to do with Serendib? They fetched him to his third, which fetched him to his fourth. Without six voyages there can be no seventh, and I could not be fifty if I had never been fourteen."

That was, Yasmīn replied, not quite an answer. Rather, it was an answer for critics of the redbeard sort, with wine-splotched bellies, but not for the listener who makes love to her teller and would know his tales as she knows his body. Would he please scratch her, lightly, back here? "Not you, Jaydā: him. What was that business of Beel Bailer's *scratching*, for example, at the story's end? I am not a camel-driver in search of moral lessons, but I like to know what's going on."

"Yes. Well." While Jaydā finished brushing her charge's hair, Sīmon lightly scratched her bare shoulder blades and explained both the French words *bon ami* and the hatchling trademark and slogan of the American cleansing powder so named.

"Enough," Yasmīn said: "Noppow oppI oppundopperstoppand." Her green eyes flashed approval and sought it as well. She caught one scratching hand and kissed it: "Enough of that, too. My teacher's reward," she declared, "is to watch his student turn wine into water, if it would please him to do so."

Extending one hand to him, she rose from our mounded clothing and led him doorward to the chamberpot, upon which she managed to perch herself like an allegory of grace. More than once, in the waxing of our honeymonth, she had pestered him to let her oversee those functions more private than sex, as if, after the sore indignities we had earlier suffered together aboard the pirate ship *Shaitan,* it was a solace to do such things by choice, as an act of love; and he had learned that at least in some humors it aroused her for him to reciprocate that curiosity. He hunkered before her; she toyed with his hair while daintily tinkling into the pot. Did Sīmon suppose she could write her name on the beach, as her sister Day-*zee* had spunkily attempted to do until those crude boys interrupted her? "A virgin wâhât," she acknowledged, stroking herself now with his hand, "is not the best writing instrument in Islam."

"That may be," her friend concurred. "But I believe that Sindbad's daughter could write the whole *Kitab Alf Laylah Wah Laylah* on the Chaptico rivershore if she set her mind to it — that Book of a Thousand Nights and a Night that I've told you of."

She glanced to see whether she was being teased and must surely have seen, even in our poor light, that she was but being admired. Nevertheless (perhaps at the echo, in *Alf Laylah,* of *al-Layl*) her animation vanished, as sometimes it did. All business now, she rose from the pot, turned her splendrous back to him, and patted herself dry with a cloth supplied at once by Jaydā, whom then she asked for the gemstone that Sīmon had presented to her from his wine cup at dinner. She wished to return it to him.

"It was a gift," her lover protested.

Still hind-to, she said, "So shall this be." From somewhere in the folds of her clothing Jaydā fished forth a small wooden box, of a size with those we had invented to frighten the page Salīm. As best Sīmon could see from behind her, Yasmīn took from it the stone and, pressing it into her belly, said "Oppalsoppo moppy voppeil." Looking surprised but not puzzled, Jaydā unhesitatingly provided it, and Yasmīn donned it. Then — wearing only that veil, the ankle bracelets, and the naveled jewel — she turned to face her lover like Daisy Moore in that island bower and said seriously, "Happy birthday, dear Sīmon. Come and have now what is yours."

"*Shabash!*" Jaydā cheered: the first time Sīmon had witnessed that woman merry. She even added, chuckling, "Woppell doppone, daughter!" All the same, she announced then, she was going to put out the lamp now and lie down in the doorway to sleep. She did not doubt that we two could prospect for diamonds in the dark.

3.

Prospect we did, but in virtual vain: to this second occasion, "Beel-Beel" would not rise. Our wordless work cannot have made sleep easy for the third among us, though this was by no means her first such dark audition. As in the business of the chamberpot, Yasmīn was indifferent to Jaydā's attendance on our intimacies. She would even report to her from time to time in course of them: "Allah help me, Jaydā! I am impaled!" or, in instances like this: "What am I lacking, little mother? Nothing you've taught me makes Sayyid Tom-Thumb stand!"

To such outcries the older woman made no response. Tonight, amid our busy sounds of alternative recourse, Sīmon thought he heard her snore. He would not retrieve the stone from Yasmīn's navel; prone atop him, pinning his arms and legs with hers, she did her best to transfer it directly into his without manual mediation, until we both were stifling laughter. Her other ministrations reroused Sīmon's appetite but perversely shrank Sayyid Et Cetera. "I'll tell him a bedtime story," Yasmīn decided, wordlessly but not soundlessly. "You tell *her* one, too, and never mind if Jaydā overhears it."

These twin narrations, sentenceless, achieved in time their denouement. Breath and pulse recalmed, the tellers dozed damp-faced each upon the listener's thigh. Then, after who knows how long a lull, clearly across the darkness Jaydā's voice spoke into our sleep:

"To the handsome and the privileged," she declared, as though addressing the night itself, "who can scarcely imagine being otherwise, it appears that their elders *choose* old age, for reasons as mysterious as their choosing to be ill or ugly. Servants faithful or impudent, louseridden beggars, wine-bellied fools, even munificent but crotchety patriarchs — to the handsome and the privileged it appears that all those around them have chosen, or have been assigned by Allah, the role of minor characters in the story of which they, the handsome and the privileged, are heroes. Sayyid Sīmon's father *chose* to be deaf-eared, or anyhow accepted that condition; his Aunt Rachel *chose* to be the childless, good-hearted housekeeper; his mother and baby sister and older brother all *chose* fortuitously to die, and young Day-*zee* to lie down on her back and open her legs to that one and this one — all in furtherance of the hero's first and second voyages. 'Now I make love,' young Mistress Yasmīn announces to me; 'now I make water. Now I suffer indignities at the hands of him who calls himself Sahīm al-Layl; now I rejoice in the handsome arms of the outlander Sayyid Sīmon.' And all the while Jaydā, a minor character, stands faithfully by."

Surprised indeed, we waited to hear more.

"Who *is* this creature Jaydā," Jaydā went on, "who silently hands out towels and empties chamberpots? It now appears that she has a son. Can it be that that same son had a father? Impossible, think the handsome and the privileged, for that would imply that somewhere under her black and ageless garments this Jaydā has a wâhât of her own, or at any rate had one once upon a time, and that some man somewhere once actually coveted that oasis enough to pitch his tent there! Surely then it must have been some hole-in-corner affair, of no interest to the handsome and the privileged, whose very navels glint with diamonds; whose couplings are the stuff of poetry; whose idlest pissing must be music to Allah's ears. Some itinerant tinker or passing camel-driver must have caught old Jaydā one night between the kitchen garden and the buttery, and first had and then gone his way.

When her time came on her, no doubt she dropped his spawn behind a wild oleander on the riverbank and went back to laundering her master's turbans. And while she did not go so far as to deny the little wretch her teat, it is not to be expected that she much cared whether he suckled or starved, for it was her incomparable privilege to be a minor character in the life story of one who truly mattered: she was nursemaid and governess to the pearl of Baghdad.

"Well well well: it so happens that who Allah's great story is really all about is none other than this same Jaydā, the Cairene. Cairene Jaydā is its hero, and all the others, from milady Yasmīn to Haroun al-Rashīd himself, are but accessory characters of more or less importance. The history of the world from Adam and Eve to the birth of Jaydā the Cairene is no more than that story's prologue. Its first chapter is her happy girlhood in Cairo, as the daughter of a loving and pious goldsmith who married late in life and had but one child, herself, the apple of his eye, her mother alas having died not long after bearing her. For all his grief, so grateful was her father to Allah for blessing him with Jaydā the Cairene that when she reached fourteen years of age he sold his shop and with his precious and already surpassingly beautiful daughter set out to make the hajj, the holy pilgrimage to Mecca. In the company of some like-minded fellow goldsmiths we traveled overland from the sacred Nile, which I have never laid eyes upon since, to the city of Suez, where we joined a shipload of pilgrims bound down the Red Sea for the holy city.

"And there ends Chapter One of the Story of Jaydā the Jewel of Cairo, for like certain other vessels we have heard of, this one got no farther down the coast than Râs Banâs, near the Tropic of Cancer, before it was waylaid by two boatloads of fishermen-pirates from the nearby islands of Zabargad, who regularly netted such traffic along with their mullets and pilchards. These gentlemen promptly threw to the sharks any crewman who made the least show of resistance, robbed the pilgrims of all their goods, took with them a number of the younger women passengers for their future amusement, and bid the others a safe and glorious hajj.

"First among their prizes, need I say, was young Jaydā the Cairene, whom the chief of the fishermen-pirates reserved for himself the moment she was fetched forth with the other young women hiding belowdecks. When my father saw me led away by that fierce and filthy fellow, my hair and clothing already disheveled, as if in token of what was to come, he set up a grand howl against Allah for His indifference to pious pilgrims. His caterwaul so offended my abductors, who were themselves devout, that instead of raping their young captives on the deck of their fishing boats then and there, before the eyes of parents and husbands, as was their custom, they paused a moment to slit my father's throat for his blasphemies and dispense him to the sharks.

"Then, when the grapnels had been released and the pirates raised sail for home port, they zabbed their captives all together on the open decks of their vessels, among the herring and the sardines and the booty taken from the pilgrims, who, for grief at the sight and sound of what was happening to their wives and daughters, tore their own hair and clothing as the pirates tore ours. Thus was every maid among us rudely deflowered except Jaydā the Cairene, not (God knows!) because my lord and master spared me, but because, unknown to him, the half dozen of his crew who had found me hiding with my girl-friends in the hold had been no less struck than he by my beauty and had taken turns upon me and me alone, three at a time — one here, one here, one here, a thing I had never in my innocence imagined possible — before they brought the lot of us on deck.

"And so it went now with the others, turn and turn about between the starboard and the larboard watches, one group tending sheets and tiller while the other took its pleasure, all the way from Râs Banâs to Geziret Zabargad, until every fisherman-pirate had had his way with each of the captives except the captain's favorite, Jaydā the Cairene. I was likewise spared, after the first round, the unpleasantness of being humped on deck in company with the rest; like a certain young and privileged lady in this room, I was sequestered for the captain's plea-sure in his cabin. But this evil fishing-smack was no sleek and ample *Shaitan,* nor was its skipper a once-handsome devil like Sayyid Cap-tain We-Know-Whom. What woman will deny that rape is rape in whatever circumstances? And yet here were no soft berths and clean linens and perfumed baths and gentle orders to do this and that. The place was cramped and dark and stank of fish; the man was bestial, besotted, foul of tongue and fouler yet of breath and hair and skin, as crusted with the slime and scales of fish as if he had become a creature of the deep himself. Master Sindbad the Sailor tells us that after his sojourn with those giant vultures it took him weeks of bathing to purge himself of their smell. But this second chapter in the story of Jaydā the Cairene took place more than thirty years ago, and I cannot to this hour distinguish the natural fragrance of my poor wâhât from the fishy infusions of its first befouler.

"Chapter Two ends in Geziret Zabargad, those islands in a sea made redder with the blood of cut throats and the ruptured hymens of the faithful. A number of my sisters, when they could bear no more, put an end to their shame by leaping over the side. Of the rest, some joined their predecessors as the fishermen's slaveys, cleaning their catch and bearing their spawn for the rest of their lives. Others were sold off to be sailors' whores in small ports up and down the coast. But the two or three beauties among us, including Jaydā the Cairene, though by then we had been violated uncountable times in every orifice and attitude, were refitted as virgins to be sold in the white-slave market in Jiddah, the port nearest the holy city that my father had set out for with his maiden daughter.

"Chapter Three of Milord Allah's great novel tells how its heroine, Jaydā the Virgin Cairene, reached Mecca after all and was redeflowered not a stone's throw from the holy Kaaba by her new owner, a rich and pious old Yemenite with a face like a basking crocodile's and a taste for girls the age of his eldest son's daughter. How he effected penetration of Jaydā the Cairene I shall pass over, remarking only that the spectacle of her hymenal blood so excited him that Chapter Three is the briefest in her story.

"His eldest son, who now took possession of her along with the rest of his late father's goods, was a reptile of another color. It had cost the old man dearly to buy me in Jiddah; his son resented this expenditure of money that otherwise would have passed to him. The hajj completed, he determined to exact his lost patrimony out of my arse on the overland trek back to Yemen. This he did with compound interest: a sore and busy chapter, at the end of which, his daughter being jealous, I was resold to a Somalian trader in such wares.

"Chapter Five takes Jaydā the Cairene ever eastward underneath a series of owners, through the Gulf of Aden and across the Arabian Sea to the Malabar Coast of Al Hind itself. By the time I reached that fabled shore, three years had passed since my setting out from Cairo with my father. I had been mounted upward of a thousand times, by more men than I could remember, and every time a rape, inasmuch as even when I initiated the thing myself (as for one reason or another I often did), I did so under the general duress of a condition into which I had been forced. I had by then three times been gotten with child by who knew whom and thrice been ungotten, to free me for further sport. I knew backward and forward the naughty pleasures of men both forward and backward, of all ages, from a dozen countries. I could fuck either human sex in four principal languages and two dialects, and at certain private exhibitions had been mounted as well by a very large guard dog, a small but ardent donkey, and a particularly lascivious chimpanzee, from whom I contracted a social disease. Yet so skillful were my Indian owners in Calicut that for my seventeenth birthday they cured my monkey-pox, outfitted me with a new maidenhead guaranteed to fool any but another dealer, and sold me to a certain wealthy merchant trader en route home to Baghdad after his harrowing but immensely profitable third voyage, of which we shall once more hear the tale tomorrow night.

"My expectation was that Jaydā the Cairene's new sayyid would have a go at his virgin concubine at once, as he had been long at sea and twice stranded among monsters of the nonhuman sort. Inasmuch as he was in those days handsome as well as rich and did not appear to be a monster himself, I put on my most maidenly demeanor and awaited my third defloration. But throughout our long passage up the Bahr Larwi and the Bahr Faris to Basra, though he smiled and spoke kindly to me, he showed no interest whatever in plumbing my refreshened wâhât. Nor was this his only peculiarity: he would not sleep belowdecks in the comfortable quarters in which he had installed me (almost as elegant as the pirate Sahīm al-Layl's quarters on *Shaitan,* and a palace compared to certain other cuddies and cabins I had known) but preferred instead to bed down in an empty wooden tub on deck, lest this vessel sink under him as others had. And even sleeping in that tub he would not remove his turban, which he claimed was more precious to him than gold.

"In consequence of his not forcing me, and because of all my owners he was the handsomest, richest, and gentlest, despite these oddities of his behavior I began to desire him — my first experience of that emotion, which made me feel like a maiden indeed — so much so that one afternoon when he visited me belowdecks to tell me once again the story of his three voyages, I made plain my readiness to visit *him* that night in his capacious tub, if such was his pleasure, and there present him with the maidenhead he had bought and paid for.

"'Allah forfend!' he said, with a merry laugh that I can hear yet. 'I know the merchants of Malabar from three several voyages' worth of experience with them. When they offer an Egyptian virgin pilgrim for sale in Beypore or Calicut, I take it for granted that she has been pilgrimed stem to stern from the Giza Pyramids to the Isle of Serendib, by donkeys, monkeys, monks, and men. She has borne four bastards, three of them human, been cured of two poxes, and learned to hump all the higher sexes and species in their native tongue while calculating currency exchanges and baking pigeon pie. That is why I bought you.'

"His recitation made me weep, perhaps for the first time since I had been brought by the fishermen-pirates to Geziret Zabargad. I wept both for pity at that catalogue of my degradation and for fear of what must be in store for me at the hands of a man who had paid my virgin-price in full knowledge of what he was buying. All the same, he had not spoken his unkind words in an unkind voice, and he stanched my tears with one of the spare turbans he carried like handkerchiefs in every pocket. I therefore presently took heart, told him my story from first to last, and set the record straight on the few points where he had overstated it. Unveiling my wâhât for his inspection, I assured him in particular that I was altogether free of the one pox I had ever caught (from that lying and lubricious ape in Djibouti), and I confessed that I could never get the pastry right on my pastillas, even when being violated by no more than one man at a time.

"Never mind, said Sayyid Sindbad the Sailor; he would buy himself a proper pastry chef in Baghdad when he set up his new household there. It was his intention, he then declared, to take a proper wife and to sire children upon her by way of curing a certain pox of his own: his itch for merchant-voyaging, which three times out of three had wrecked or stranded him and had come within an isba of costing him his life more times than I had ever pretended rapture to earn my keep. Because he himself had been handled so roughly by fate and had become of necessity so wily in the world's ways, he meant to marry as innocent and trusting a bride as he could find in the City of Peace and to savor her innocence and trust as he would savor the other comforts of his house after the hardships of voyaging. However, as he himself trusted no one besides himself, he wanted a particular sort of spy in his harem: a young maidservant of good family, apparently as chaste as his bride but actually as canny as himself, to serve and befriend her and become her confidante while secretly reporting to him her every word and movement.

"Even as I wondered, without asking, why he would trust a foreigner and stranger like myself with that equivocal mission, he proceeded after all to a visual and manual examination of my private parts, as deft and thorough as any physician but more gentle, all the while praising their beauty and mine, marveling that we had come through such ordeals with so little apparent damage. He promised that in his house no man would touch without my consent what he was touching just then for verification purposes only; that despite my youth he would make me chief among his womenservants if I gave him ample evidence of my trustworthiness and general ability; and that when enough time had passed to prove both my loyalty and my freedom from disease (for not even he, who had survived captivity on Ape Island in Voyage Three, knew all the ins and outs of monkey-pox), he would be pleased to accept what I had graciously offered to deliver to his tub. There was a piquancy, in his opinion, to the breaching of the revirginated — especially those of the Malabar Coast — that was lost on the credulous but prized by the connoisseur. Did I not agree?

"With my entire heart I did, as I would have agreed just then to anything that man proposed — and there begins Chapter Six of Allah's great tale of Jaydā the Cairene, for the purpose of telling which He created this world. To the young and the privileged it may appear to be no more than an interlude in their own story, an anecdote overheard in the dark between any two of their epic couplings. In fact, however, it happens to be the central episode in the main line of the plot, and the longest as well, for it began nearly thirty years ago and is not finished yet: I mean the chapter of Jaydā the Cairene's love for Sayyid Sindbad the Sailor.

"But now its heroine is weary of her own narrative and will sleep."

Throughout this extended interlude, Yasmīn's hand squeezed Sīmon's, and his hers, each of us bidding the other to hold still and listen and at the same time signaling that we were indeed all attention, astonishment (at least Sīmon was, knowing nothing of Jaydā's past except that she had been bought as a young woman to serve Sindbad's first wife and that she had raised his daughter after Yasmīn's mother died), and the particular sympathy that the rather less victimized may feel for the rather more. At its end we moved wordlessly from our original position into each other's arms. After a silent embrace, Yasmīn said quietly into the room, "I am not so very young anymore, my dear Jaydā. But privileged I remain, and high among those privileges has been your guardianship my life long."

If her nursemaid heard her, she gave no sign.

"As for me," Sīmon added softly, resting our clasped hands between his thighs, "I am no longer young at all, but privileged I am and have been, extraordinarily. And high among those privileges, Umm Salīm, has been to hear Allah's tale of Jaydā the Cairene, up to its sixth chapter, from the main character herself. May the Author grant that we hear more another night."

Whether or not she heard, Jaydā presently answered us with the heavy breath of sleep. Soon enough we slept, too: the intermittent sleep of lovers reminded of desire by every stir of each other's bodies, though not necessarily stirred to desire by each reminder. Toward night's end we dreamed separate versions of that second coupling we had not managed while awake: "Beel-Beel" (in need now of the chamberpot) stood firm; once again (in her dream) Yasmīn cried joyfully, "Jaydā! I am impaled!," and her lover (in Sīmon's dream) thought he heard presently his lover's climax-call, "*Jumail!*"

But it was the muezzin himself, sleep's enemy, summoning us all to wake.

4.

Though he could scarcely credit his own reality, let alone God's, still-stranded Somebody made his way back along night-cool corridors to his own room as if he were one more of the faithful en route to morning prayer. Hunkered dimly on his threshold was Salīm, adrowse; at the touch of a hand on his shoulder, the page woke instantly, registered who had roused him, and — once on his feet — trusted aloud that Mistress Yasmīn's maidenhead remained safe from harm.

Our man fished forth his fileting knife. More wary than fearful, Salīm salaamed.

"Sayyid Sindbad is at his prayers," he reported from just out of range. "He invites you to breakfast with him in the courtyard when you've finished your own devotions." He flashed the pretty eyes in his ferret face. "I'll tell him you've done so."

"You'll tell him I have yet to begin to pray," Somebody said, truthfully. "But I'll meet him soon."

He then washed the love-smells off himself, emptied his bladder, cleaned his teeth and trimmed his beard, donned a fresh caftan from the guest wardrobe in his room, and went to the central courtyard. There under date palms sat his host, as on the morning before, but bright-gold-turbaned now and at his ease in the great dry tub, from over the edge of which, with Salīm's assistance, he fed leafy branches to the camel standing by.

"Come aboard, Brother Sindbad!" he called, and he tapped the tub's rim. "May Allah have blessed you with a night as undisturbed as mine."

Salīm grinned and handed his master another oleander branch.

"My night's ship safely reached the port of morning," Somebody replied. "May the same be true for all your household fleet, however they navigated through the dark." He climbed as bidden over the tub's side and seated himself opposite Sindbad the Sailor. Between them were plates of bread and dried dates, bowls of yoghurt, and a pot of tea, which Salīm now poured with a flourish. For some minutes further, as the two Sindbads sipped and ate, their conversation took its shape as did the tub, from the space inside. Speaking of navigation, declared the elder Sindbad, he had named his camel Mustafā after his erstwhile navigator; for just as this could find his way across the trackless desert from oasis to oasis, so that one, in his prime, could steer the good ship *Zahir* unerringly from landfall to landfall across the trackless sea. Or almost unerringly.

"To that same Mustafā mu-Allim," Somebody now acknowledged, "I happen to owe my life several times over. Most recently, it was he who found me stranded not long ago near Basra and chowdered me back to health, and at my insistence directed me here."

"I guessed as much," said Sindbad. "And before that?"

"Another story, Sayyid, for another time."

"In a lifetime of navigation," Sindbad mused, "our faithful Mustafā made but one grave error in his reckoning — and that, he would have us believe, was not truly his."

"It was not," Somebody affirmed. "I will swear to it."

"You? I suppose you were there?"

"My fifth voyage, Brother: three evenings hence. I was there, who now am here."

"And why, exactly, are you here?"

"Yesterday's reason is still today's."

Sindbad spat a date-pit overside. "Yesterday, sir, is the day neither of us was born, and today we're yet another day older." He tipped his gold turban pageward. "You have told Salīm a story even more preposterous than the ones you tell at dinner."

"And Salīm," Somebody said smoothly, "has dutifully passed it on. May the accuracy of his reportage match its promptness."

Said Sindbad, "I know how to read this fellow. The tale you told him is not true."

Somebody pursed his mouth and nodded, as if at his tea. "If it is not, then you had better accept your prospective son-in-law's proposal before he raises his percentage of Voyage Seven from fifteen to twenty."

"Twenty percent! Leave us, Salīm."

The page grinned, bowed, and turned away with a twitch of his backside. Sindbad sniffed and said to Somebody, "Now, then, Brother: who might you be?"

With his host's indulgence, our man responded, he had addressed that very question for two evenings running and would again tonight and yet again tomorrow, as he had done for some five decades, with indifferent success. "I am one," he concluded, "who has learned who he is not, and who nightly discovers who others are not."

"Enough of that," said Sindbad. "Unless you've begun to believe your own fabrications, you know as well as I that one thing you're not is an agent of Haroun al-Rashīd, commissioned to protect my daughter's virginity. In the first place, the caliph takes no interest in such matters. In the second, there is nothing to protect, nor was there even before Mustafā made the single error of his career and led my daughter afoul of Him-Whom-We-Do-Not-Mention."

"To me personally," Somebody replied, "that is of small concern: if it is not Mistress Yasmīn's maidenhead that I protect with this navigational instrument" — he showed Sindbad Mustafā's fileting knife — "then it is her honor, and *that* has not been sullied since *Zahir's* captain (not its navigator) betrayed your trust. If the Commander of the Faithful has been misled on this point, however, it may be that he has been misled on others as well. Your most recent voyage —"

"It quite accomplished its objectives," Sindbad said shortly, "whereas *your* project in my house, so far as I can see, has made no headway whatever. Nobody understands your stories."

Somebody the Still-Stranded smiled. "Unless my own navigation is in error, that project will take a more evident step forward this evening. But it, too, in my judgment, has quite accomplished its objectives so far. Ibn al-Hamrā no more believes Salīm's report than you do, but he is not *certain* that it's false or that something like it may not be true. Very likely he suspects that you and I are in league, as in a sense we are. Very likely he smells a trick, but he's not sure what trick."

"No more am I," admitted Sindbad. "Suppose he breaks off the marriage negotiations?"

"Then he will receive his due share of Serendib Limited, which is nothing, and likewise of your daughter."

"My daughter." Sindbad spat another date-pit, but as it were reflectively, not disdainfully, and looked Somebody straight in the face. "In the month of Sha'ban, while I was homeward bound from Serendib with my latest fortune, where were you?"

"Still stranded," Somebody said, "but no longer in the hut of Mustafā mu-Allim. I was here, Sayyid." He pointed up to one of the elaborately grilled upper-level windows overlooking the court. "Right up there, to be exact, making sure that what you had ransomed at such cost maintained its value in your absence. Ask Yasmīn."

Grumbled Sindbad the Sailor, "I have long since done so," and there ended both the interview and this interlude.

5.

Pleasurably exhausted by his night and not at all displeased by his early morning, through that forenoon Somebody slept, gratefully alone in his room: a respite from search and subterfuge, delight and despair alike. Though he dreamed hard dreams and true — brother found, son lost, love spent and soured — he awoke refreshed from where he had become the successful travel journalist known as "Baylor" to wherewhoever he currently was: still-stranded "Sīmon" in the house and world of Sindbad, called the Sailor.

For his own bemusement then he fetched forth what passed in these parts for pen and paper and synopsized what he had told last evening as his Second Voyage, with Daisy Moore, to the then edge of his understanding. Were you to slip into his room right now, dear dead Daisy, as he scribbles this line (he wrote), would he know you any better? Or has your lean, mishandled person become no more than memories imaged, images rendered, a body of words?

Moving only his neversharp quill, he then leapt three decades: over two wars and how many killed millions more? Over "Korea," over "Vietnam," from the domestic fuel rationing of "World War II" to the verge of the Arab oil embargo consequent upon the "Yom Kippur War" of "1973"; from (westward the course of time's empire!) a Swiss-made wristwatch, through an American, to a Japanese. . . .

To none. Here where he was stranded out of time, his misgivings were suspended at the point above by a sudden fanfare of tambourine. Half-veiled, lithe, wiry as a brown-limbed Daisy Moore, Kuzia Fakān's percussive colleague snapped and sizzled through his doorway, spun to a barefoot halt, and made a slow salaam, all the while darting dark eyes about room and occupant with the bright curiosity of one who had lately heard from the page Salīm.

"Fatmah Awād," Somebody acknowledged.

Holding her position, she replied, "Sayyid Sīmon."

"Where did you hear that name?"

"On the tearful tongue of Mistress Yasmīn," the tambourinist declared, "when I helped Jaydā rug you out of here one month ago." She stood at ease now and looked him over. "Who could have imagined a woman weeping so over the death of her eunuch bodyguard? For so she described the burden in that Bokhara. But Kuzia tells us she has seen for a fact that you're neither a dead man nor a eunuch — only a lover of boys, she decided, and now Salīm tells us you're not that, either."

"In this house," Somebody said, "if I decline to eat a goat's eyeball, I'm called a vegetarian. What's your errand, Fatmah Awād?"

"Her errand," another woman called impatiently from the corridor, "is to bring you Kuzia Fakān's apologies for having insulted you in one or two ways and to request a few minutes' talk. But when tambourinists take solos, they lose the beat."

Somebody invited the dancer in and offered her a cushion near his own. Dressed in the same caftan under which she had performed the night before, Kuzia Fakān ouched herself down.

"This one," Fatmah Awad announced to her, "just compared your wâhât to a goat's eyeball."

Somebody sighed, but weary Kuzia waved away both sigh and slander. "If it was a goat's eyeball yesterday, it is the gouged-out socket today. *Ai,* what a Tatar! Stand watch, would you, Fatmah darling?"

"I've done nothing else lately," the tambourinist complained, but she obligingly moved doorward.

"Then I owe you the same," Kuzia Fakān called after her. She was answered with a clap of the tambourine on its owner's backside as Fatmah Awād stepped into the corridor.

"My compliments on your dance," Somebody said then, and he set aside his writing materials. "Even from where I sat, it was enticing."

With a level glance the dancer sized up this compliment, then nodded at the ink-scribed leaves. "Be sure to put that praise into your report."

"You may count on it. Has your new friend's wine-stain been removed?"

Kuzia rolled her eyes. "Allah knows it has been redeemed. Ibo was so annoyed by your lady's little prank that he swore to raise his percentage of her father's next voyage to seventeen and a half or break their engagement. I spent the night humping him down to thirteen-five, and at this morning's prayer call he weighed her insult against my reparations and held the line at fifteen."

"Well done," Somebody said, and he promised to report her accomplishment both to Sindbad's daughter and to her father.

"You may be sure that I've done that already," said Kuzia Fakān, "but it won't hurt to have it done again. Report it to your master as well, if that will do me any good. But tell your friend Yasmīn that if she spills more wine on that camel-driver before tomorrow night, she'll have to balance the ledger herself."

Somebody smiled and shook his head. "You chum the waters of our conversation with more baits than one poor fish can rise to." He ticked off examples on his thumb and two fingers: "Sayyid Sindbad's daughter is not 'my Yasmīn'; she is her own and none other's. If you are close enough to her these days to have told her of your night's work on her behalf, you will also have warned her in the matter of the wine. But I doubt that any of these is what you came here to discuss with me now."

Complained Kuzia Fakān, "You are one of those men who want to make music before our instruments are in tune." All the same, she then replied to each of those items in turn: in her opinion, Sindbad's daughter was first and finally Sindbad's daughter, more than she had ever been young Umar al-Yom's boyish conquest or Prince Jabāl's fiancée or Sahīm al-Layl's prize, not to mention her own person. For just that reason (to speak to Somebody's second point), there had been no love lost between Yasmīn and Kuzia Fakān since the dancer was recruited by the aging Jaydā, at Sindbad's direction, to replace her as his paramour-in-chief. Though Yasmīn at the time was affianced to the most enviable catch in Islam, that handsome young Sohari prince, she had been nonetheless jealous of Kuzia Fakān's regnancy with her father — not an unusual state of affairs in view of Yasmīn's privileged position as a wealthy widower's only child. And the proof of her jealousy was that it had wondrously abated since Sindbad's return from Voyage Six — that is to say, since Kuzia herself had fallen from the old man's favor. And in the two days past, since the dancer's sexual assignment first to present company (whoever he was) and then to Yasmīn's fiancé-in-the-works, Sindbad's daughter had been positively friendly for the first time — just when she might have been expected to be jealous! Surely that showed which way the wind blew.

Aware that his expression was being monitored, Somebody simply nodded.

"Mind you," the dancer went on, "I hold none of this against her. Your Yasmīn has her agenda, and I have mine, and though by day she's a rich man's spoiled daughter and I'm only a poor Bedou dancing girl, Allah has so arranged the world that once the sun goes down we hold the same cards under our djellabas. In the dark, it is her wâhât against mine, and since her little pleasure cruise with that Qeshmi pirate, their market values are not so different as they used to be. What's more, while each of us plays her cards as cannily as she can, Yasmīn has never yet cheated me, to my knowledge, nor I her. And you are right: this is not what I came here to talk about."

Ignoring all that new bait on the water, our man sat by for his visitor to say more, and soon enough she did.

"Who was it who camped in Yasmīn's rooms in the month of Sha'ban, while her father was out settling scores in Serendib with Prince Jabāl and Sahīm al-Layl? It was you."

Only half teasingly, Somebody asked, "And who is that?"

"So we all wonder. The one thing that none of us believes is what you told Salīm last night at knifepoint, and so I allow that that — like Sayyid Sindbad's rocs and rhinoceri — may just possibly be the truth."

"Kuzia Fakān," said appreciative Somebody, "even at your dance's end, there is more to you than meets the eye."

She shrugged off the compliment. "Salīm himself now claims that you're an agent of the King of Serendib, charged with seeing to it that Sindbad makes the return voyage that the king expects and that the Commander of the Faithful has commanded."

Impressed by the ingenuity of that speculation, Somebody raised his eyebrows, pursed his lips, and nodded. "But why would such an agent set up camp in Yasmīn's bedroom? Of what interest is Sindbad's daughter's honor to the Caliph of Serendib?" He watched Kuzia Fakān register the word *honor*.

"We haven't worked that out," the dancer admitted. "But when I look at Yasmīn's face and yours in the morning, and when I see you steal glances at each other in the evening, certain possibilities occur to me."

"And those," Somebody ventured, a bit disquieted, "are what you've come to speak to me about?"

The dancer shook her head. What went on in Yasmīn's rooms in the month of Sha'ban, she said, and again last night and the night before, was no more her concern than what had happened to Yasmīn and the others aboard *Shaitan,* and she would declare as much to Ibn al-Hamrā when it occurred to him to ask (no later than tomorrow, she predicted, for that camel-driver was no fool). What *was* her business, the first order of it, was the failing potency of Sindbad the Sailor, at least in connection with herself, and what that betided for her position in the house. Of this she had spoken to Somebody two nights ago. What perplexed her now was that she knew that old villain to be as keen-eyed as herself and no less skeptical, yet he had not, so far, contracted for the assassination of a man demonstrably potent (as she had attested), though of undetermined sexual tastes, who in the midst of the delicate engagement negotiations with "Ibo" spent night after night within access, at least, of the wâhât in question. Kuzia knew, moreover, that Sindbad's first business of the day, recently, had been conducted tête-à-tête in the Tub of Truth with that same privileged interloper, as if to hear a report on the night past.

"And he calls you his younger brother!" she concluded. "And he lets you call yourself by his own name! Let Ibo and Salīm and Fatmah Awād think what they please; *I* think you're an agent of Sindbad himself!"

"Really, now, Kuzia Fakān. . . ."

"I believe it!" the dancer insisted. "He doesn't trust Jaydā these days, because she's still jealous of me for taking her place, even though she chose me for the job. So he sets you to make sure she doesn't get even with him for dumping her by smuggling some boyfriend of Yasmīn's into the harem while he's cutting a deal with Ibo."

Somebody sighed. "Where in the world —"

"From Sindbad himself," Kuzia Fakān interrupted him triumphantly, "in that famous tub of his, not an hour ago. He and I used to be too busy in there to talk, but nowadays the best he can do is natter on. What he doesn't yet realize is that in giving that particular job to you he has set the fox to guard the henhouse."

"Aha," said weary Somebody. "With that *yet* we arrive at the end of this striptease." He then gently scolded the dancer for an insinuation more expectable from the page Salīm than from her: that there was something he so wished to conceal that her silence about it would be valuable to him. Let her tell Sindbad whatever she knew, suspected, or imagined about his relation to Yasmīn, he invited her; let her think him an agent of Haroun, Sindbad, Sahīm al-Layl, Prince Jabāl, the King of Serendib, or Muhammed the Prophet. The truth was less complicated and doubtless less interesting: he was no one's agent except his own, whoever *that* might be — "Sīmon" the castaway, marooned, still stranded. His first and final goal was simply to return to where he came from: that much-vexed realm that he was miscalling, for convenience' sake, Serendib. But he had no more notion of how that return was to be effected than had Kuzia Fakān of how to reinvigorate old Sindbad's desire for her. Meanwhile, derelict in her place and time, he was Yasmīn's friend and ally because she and he had survived an ordeal together. There was much he did not know about Sindbad's daughter, he acknowledged, and about her household; but he was the only one besides Yasmīn herself who knew exactly what had and had not happened in the captain's cabin of *Shaitan,* for the reason that he had been there with Yasmīn and Sayyid Midnight even at certain times when Jaydā had not. In those parlous hours, because of his peculiarly privileged though also dire position, he had been able to be of some comfort to her; she had been likewise to him, then and since, when the shoe of circumstance was on the other foot. If now she chose to marry Ibn al-Hamrā, that was altogether her affair — but the man would not get a bolt of virgin cashmere for the price of a worn-out prayer rug.

"If my efforts in this line make me Yasmīn's agent or Sindbad's as well as my own," he concluded, "so be it. There's nothing secret about such agency. I only wish the best for my former fellow hostage — and I wish no ill to my host or to you either, Kuzia Fakān."

"How is one to deal with you?" the dancer complained. "You can be neither seduced nor blackmailed, and just when I'm thinking that our instruments are in tune enough to play, you tell me that the dance is over! What Yasmīn sees in such an outlander is beyond me."

Somebody smiled. "Like you and Sindbad in his Tub of Truth, we talk."

"I'll bet you do. But not for the same reason, and not in Arabic words."

"What I suggest, my friend," said Somebody, shrugging, "is that *you* tell *me* in straightforward Arabic, with neither bribes nor threats, how you think I might help you. If I can, I will."

Straightforward Arabic! the dancer complained again. How could she trust what she had neither extorted nor paid for in her customary way, nor even haggled over? But she had no choice; she was at "Sī-mon's" mercy —

"Stop that. Neither of us is at the other's mercy."

"What a way to do business!"

"We are not doing business."

"Fatmah Awād!" Kuzia cried doorward. "This man drives me mad!"

But then the dancer did after all state her business, in the satisfied tone of one party pretending for the other's benefit to have been gotten the better of. Ibn al-Hamrā, she reported, clearly recognized in Sindbad's new "brother" a threat to his marriage negotiations, if not yet an outright rival for Yasmīn's favors. He naturally suspected the wily Sindbad of having arranged the stranger's interruption of the feast and all that had happened since; not knowing that the old man shared his apprehensions, he was as eager as Sindbad to learn just what was afoot. Inasmuch as both Yasmīn herself and Jaydā were impenetrable on this matter, and nobody trusted Salīm either to size things up accurately or to report them truthfully, both her master-in-chief and her master-designate of last night were promising her substantial rewards if she could by any means whatever learn who the interloper really was and what he was up to.

"For that information," Somebody assured her, "I would add a third reward to those two, if I had anything to add." As he did not, he could only repeat what he had told her already, which nobody believed — that Yasmīn had not been assaulted by her pirate captor, as was generally assumed, and that he himself was matching Sindbad's stories voyage for voyage in hope of learning how they had fetched him here from "Serendib," in further hope (against hope) of learning how to fetch himself back. There was the truth.

"But not the whole truth," ventured Kuzia Fakān.

"Who besides Allah knows the whole truth? Meanwhile, it seems to me that your position is enviable. Look how much you have already to report! And if the whole truth comes in installments, so should your rewards."

"I'll see to that," the dancer said. From the corridor came a low rustling of tambourine. Kuzia picked herself up, not urgently, and Somebody stood with her. "But if you've told me all you have to tell," she wondered aloud, "what is the next installment?" Over her veil, her eyes flickered up and down his height. "Surely there's *something* I can offer you in exchange for more."

Somebody touched her arm. "Your friendship?"

"Fatmah, did you hear? No man ever asked me for *that* before; it must not be worth much."

"Perhaps mine isn't, either," Somebody said. "But it's all I have until there's something more."

The tambourine rattled again, more briskly.

"Coming," said Kuzia Fakān. As she left, Somebody remarked casually after her, "I'm not yet as old as Sayyid Sindbad, but neither am I as young as your new friend Ibo. Perhaps you and I can talk next time about secret amulets instead of secret agencies."

The dancer looked back at him over-shoulder, her eyes bright. "Who's doing business now? Maybe it's Yasmīn I should have a little straightforward Arabic chat with."

As they stepped into the corridor, Fatmah Awād reported, "It's only Salīm, as usual." She pointed with her tambourine. "He slipped behind that corner when he saw me here." Over her veil, she, too, reappraised still-stranded Somebody.

"Till tomorrow?" Kuzia Fakān asked him. She held out her hand. Somebody pressed it in his own and bowed.

The two women had no sooner turned down the corridor, whispering and laughing together, than Salīm appeared at its other end. "*Psst!* Sayyid Sīmon!" he called in a loud whisper; then, glancing theatrically behind him as he approached, he assured our man that for the past hour he had maintained a careful lookout on his behalf. There was no reason why either Sayyid Sindbad or Mistress Yasmīn should get word of this little dalliance with Kuzia Fakān.

"Nor any why they should not," Somebody sighed. "Stand watch one moment longer, while I fetch my fish-knife, and I'll explain."

6.

"Swallow, swallow!" gold-turbaned Sindbad bade his guests and household that evening, when all were seated in the new places assigned them. "What joy it is to eat! Particularly in contrast to being eaten." He raised his wine cup. "Praise be to all-wise Allah, who has provided men with the means to bite, the ability to chew, and, above all, the capacity to swallow! Yasmīn."

All present joined him readily in this toast (the purport of which was not yet entirely clear) as soon as his daughter had filled their cups. Yasmīn too was dressed in golden yellow, her brilliant djellaba embroidered in reds and oranges as if to echo her costumes of the previous two nights. It could be no coincidence, Somebody decided, that his lover wore each night the daily color of her father's turban. This evening her face was radiant, her manner almost merry as she and Jaydā went around with the wine. Our man complimented himself that her demeanor might be in some measure the happy reflection of two nights of love, followed he hoped by more and better sleep than he himself had managed, but it seemed to him, too, that there was a new rapport between father and daughter. They bantered easily and wittily: teased Ibn al-Hamrā for the ample bib he sported tonight to protect his clean caftan; agreed with each other across the length of the low table that old Hasīb Alī (the eldest, wealthiest, and most respected of the company, who had previously sat at Sindbad's left hand but who was absent tonight) must have dozed off this time before dinner, as he so often did after. Still-stranded Somebody recalled Sindbad's forenoon remark that he had already questioned his daughter about her relations with him; he wondered what Yasmīn might have replied, to such benign effect.

Jaydā, on the other hand, seemed less than pleased by this and other conspicuous differences between tonight's banquet and its immediate predecessors — including the change in everyone's position at table except the host's and his daughter's. By now our man reckoned he had figured out the house protocol in this matter. The ten guests were not ranked in an order of descending favor from the head of the table to its foot, as he had once supposed: the most favored at the host's right hand, the secondmost at his left, the thirdmost at his second right, etc., down to the least favored at his fifth left (Yasmīn's first right). The actual order, both of seating and of service, was at once more intricate and more respectful of Sindbad's daughter: first and second place were as Somebody had assumed — those positions having been taken, until tonight, by the prospective son-in-law Ibn al-Hamrā and the elder Hasīb Alī, respectively — but third-favored was the seat at Yasmīn's right hand, and fourth-favored that at her left. Thereafter, he presumed, the order alternated in like fashion from Sindbad's end of the table to hers, and from "right" to "left" in turn from each one's point of view, so that the tenth and least of the company (himself as of last night, since he was not an investor in the upcoming voyage) occupied the place halfway down the table on Sindbad's left, or halfway up on Yasmīn's right.

It followed that Ibn al-Hamrā had slipped a notch in their host's esteem. In the place of honor, his former position, now sat another merchant speculator, who the night before had sat at Yasmīn's right: presumably the largest investor in Voyage Seven after the absent Hasīb Alī and perhaps al-Hamrā himself. In that enviable latter seat tonight sat yet another, who had previously occupied Seat Four, at Yasmīn's left hand: a dark-eyed, dark-bearded man about Ibo's age, but less plump than beefy, whose face Somebody had come to know, though not yet his name. Indeed, something about the cast of his features and a way he had of dropping his jaw and widening his eyes in mock astonishment at every conversational sally, whether his own or another's, put our man in mind of his brother, "Joe Junior," who in middle age had developed the same affectation.

The other regular guests had all been reseated accordingly, each moved a notch up. Somebody himself therefore was tonight in the ninth place (third down on Sindbad's right and third up on Yasmīn's left), while across from him in the tenth place, to fill out the company, was none other than Kuzia Fakān, doubtless in reward for her services on her master's behalf through the night past. Her delight in being there was evident even through her veil. But though Yasmīn (who through the month of Sha'ban had spoken disparagingly of the dancer as "Daddy's Bedou bedwarmer") smiled and made a good-humored mock ceremony out of pouring Kuzia's wine, Jaydā stood stiffly behind her and frowned over her black veil at these innovations.

"Swallow," Sindbad repeated, this time directing that invitation or command to the three women in particular. Kuzia Fakān lifted her veil, grinned, and downed her cup. Yasmīn took a cordial sip of hers. Jaydā touched her cup to her veiled mouth, set it aside, and signaled Salīm to begin serving the food.

"There is no question," Sindbad said, "that some things are more readily swallowed than others. When we are the diners, it behooves us to enlarge and improve our capacity in that line. But when we are the dined-upon, it is another story: the story of my third voyage. I urge you to practice on these easier dishes before I try you with that harder one, after which my brother Sindbad the Still-Stranded may try us with one harder yet."

That said, he and the company fell to as usual, eating, drinking, and talking of business and pleasure. Kuzia Fakān alone was left out of this conversation, whether because the merchants to her right and left (in places Six and Seven, respectively) were more eager to talk business with the higher-ranking guests on their other hand or because they associated the dancer more with the business of pleasure than with the pleasures of business. But she paid no attention to their inattention and busily pleased herself with the food and wine, now and then winking or waving her fingers across the room at Fatmah Awād and company at the smaller table.

When at last the dessert course was served, Sindbad thumped for attention on the tub behind him and declared, "Those of you who look for moral nutriment in tales of voyaging may chew on this appetizer till I serve up my story's dessert: In the dialectic of experience, what our first voyage teaches us, our second may well unteach, so that our third may then reteach it in amended form." He paused and regarded Ibn al-Hamrā, as if waiting for him to record this long maxim. But that stainless fellow sat with his fingers laced in his lap and contemplated his bib. Only Kuzia Fakān nodded her head in grave accord.

"As after Voyage One," her master presently went on, "so after Voyage Two the time came when such delights as ours tonight once again lost their appeal (as they seem to have done for our old friend Hasīb Alī), and nothing would do but I risk my life a third time for no better reason than the second. I posted the usual eunuchs to oversee my harem, bade good-bye to my usual dinner companions and to this landlubber's paradise of a Baghdad, and went down as usual to Basra to find ship and shipmates with which to seek a fortune that I did not need and the misfortune certain to attend it. You would think I had learned nothing from my hard history.

"But note: I took with me this time, as my principal stock-in-trade, a great quantity of turbans of every sort and size, thinking thereby always to have a supply on hand for survival purposes when the inevitable came to pass. And this time I looked *not* for a ship to fall in love with, as I had loved my lost *Zahir*, but rather for one of indifferent lines and merely adequate seaworthiness, so that I would not lose something of which I was especially fond, or be lost by it. On the other hand (following Moral Lesson One of this voyage, aforestated, or Lesson Nine of the lot), this time I neither closely befriended my fellow merchant-sailors, as I had done the first time out, nor held myself aloof from them, as I had done on Voyage Two. Knowing I was bound to lose them one way or another, I enjoyed their companionship while I could, troubling neither them nor myself with the inevitability of their fate.

"We set sail, and my shoreside restlessness dropped astern with my home port. As before, the first leg of our voyage took us along mainland coasts, whose ports of call were now old friends of mine, and where, in my experience, disaster never struck. In these ports I did my business chiefly for pleasure, having learned that whatever I gained at this stage would most likely be lost in the next. And no matter how fearsome the squalls that from time to time threatened to drive us upon the Arabian or Persian shore, I slept soundly through them while my fellow merchants tore their beards and shat their wuzaras, for I knew that real trouble comes not from the mainland but from islands in general and island paradises in particular.

"When therefore one fine day we saw our captain rend his garments in despair, I reckoned we were nearing our first island. I stuffed my pockets with spare turbans, climbed into my tub (whose true purpose I had concealed from my shipmates by laundering turbans in it each evening), and looked about for the tree-covered whale or soporific grove that would begin the next chapter of Voyage Three of Sindbad the Sailor.

"Sure enough, there was a palm-lined beach to leeward, which the captain identified through shuddering teeth as the shore of Ape Island, and toward which a contrary breeze was setting us faster than our miserable vessel could make good to windward. No mariner had ever made landfall there and returned to tell the tale, he told us, though the fate of those lost mariners was unknown.

"You might expect that in these circumstances I would have longed for my excellent *Zahir*, which was particularly able at clawing off a lee shore. But for the reason given, I praised Allah for our ship's leeway, and though my heart beat fast, it was with suspense more than with terror, and also with measured pity for the comrades I must now begin to lose, who, though they lacked my experience of maroonment and the like, otherwise truly spoke my language.

"The same cannot be said for the troop of hairy apes that now suddenly appeared as if from the sea around us and clambered aboard, gesticulating and jabbering at one another and us in a tongue foreign to all hands, though as seasoned merchant-traders we knew between us the languages of every Muslim nation and not a few of the infidels, as well. This of the apes was a grinding of consonants and a popping of vowels, as if words were being eaten rather than spoken; and all the while the speakers pointed at our spars and shrouds and stays, and at their island, and the open sea, and us. Yet when we shrugged our shoulders and turned up our palms in terrified incomprehension, the apes made plain their annoyance as they could not make plain their discourse. Most especially were they angered when, being true believers, we refused to join them in what looked to us like some travesty of worship, as they kneeled northwestward on our deck and called *OppAlloppah! OppAkboppar!* I can hear their feral curses still as they then swarmed aloft: *Goppo! Oppawoppay!* But instead of tearing us limb from limb or pitching us overside, they chewed up and spat out half our standing rigging, retangled the rest, set us ashore when the breeze at last beached us, and then sailed off with our goods and what was left of our ship, hurling imprecations shoreward: *Oppinfoppid-oppel! Mopponkoppeys!*

"Our captain reasoned that in their subhuman ignorance these apes had once witnessed an act of human piracy off their shore and, as apes will, had subsequently aped it at every opportunity without understanding what it was they were aping, in the same way that they seemed to themselves to be making meaningful utterances. All the same, I noted that with their shortened rig they had contrived to beat briskly offshore to windward, as we had not. Fearing that they would soon return to abuse us further, we retreated into the woods of their island and there found what my companions took to be an empty white building, as it showed to the naive eye four walls, a floor and ceiling, and a rectangular hole in one side not dissimilar to a large doorway. At the captain's bidding, all hid themselves inside, except me, who elected instead to tie myself into the top of a coconut palm with several turbans from my supply. My independence in this matter baffled my companions and much annoyed the captain and first mate (who had never much cared for my turbans and my tub), but as they could scarcely threaten to put me ashore for disobeying an order, I chose to follow my own counsel.

"Voyage Two, remember, had taught me that on islands uninhabited by humans, what we mistake for a domed temple, say, is probably a roc's egg. The squarish shape of this structure by no means ruled out the possibility of its belonging to some other species of giant bird. Moreover, through its so-called doorway I had caught a glimpse of what looked to be a strew of large bones, some of them fresh, on its so-called floor, which suggested to me another explanation for the behavior of those apes: they were regularly preyed upon by such terrible birds as those in the Valley of Serpents and Diamonds; they had boarded our ship to save themselves and had endeavored to warn us of our peril and persuade us to sail them to safety, not understanding in their animal ignorance that our ship was no good on the wind; finally, unable to communicate their messages in genuine language, they had set us ashore to appease their predators and then blundered off as best they could.

"Alas, the worst part of this hypothesis (which I kept to myself) was soon confirmed: whether or not the white structure was a giant angular eggshell, it was currently inhabited not by a roc chick but by a fearsome one-eyed ogre, who no doubt had taken possession of it as the hermit crab does an empty mollusk shell. This awful fellow lumbered home at sunset and, fortunately not catching sight of me in my tree, seized at once upon the windfall banquet in his house. Having tested each of his terrified prisoners in turn for plumpness, he chose our luckless captain for his evening meal, spitted him through from mouth to anus, and roasted and ate him like a chicken. The sight, sound, and smell of this atrocity was the more horrifying for its being perpetrated without a word from the terrible giant, whose vocabulary seemed limited to lip-smacks as he ate our captain, a great burp of satisfaction when he was done, a monstrous fart as he then stretched himself out on his filthy floor, and earthshaking snorts and snores when presently he closed his single eye and slept.

"The laments among my companions, on the other hand, were as eloquent as anything in that vein of which the language of Allah's prophet is capable. In the morning, when the ogre awoke and went his way, they streamed out of his hovel, still wailing and pounding their turbans in despair. I rather expected them to salute my wisdom in having treed myself; at the same time, I feared that they would all now follow my example, whereupon the giant must surely discover us, and I would be but one more bird in his self-snared flock. Therefore I lied and told them that my night had been as fearful as theirs, declaring that the horrid apes had returned and prowled the treetops in search of victims, grinding their consonants and popping their vowels, and only by chance had missed the palm I'd taken refuge in. Our ship's first mate, now in command, then ordered us to search the island for better shelter, and all did so except me, who instead began scouting materials for a raft. My continued insubordination so vexed the mate that when evening came without his having found a single cave or other hideaway on the island, and he ordered the company back into the giant's den for the second night, he refused to let me share that fearsome shelter with them.

"His reasoning was that in the ogre's house, one of their number was sure to die but the others would survive, whereas outside we were outnumbered by the apes and might all be killed. I pretended terror at my fate but was secretly delighted to turban myself again among the coconuts. The giant returned, and the second-plumpest of our original company, a jolly merchant from Abadan, suffered the wordless fate of the captain. The next morning, after the giant left home and the survivors came forth, I repeated my story of the apes, and while the majority were too undone by their own night's terrors to question mine, I discerned a note of skepticism in the mate: he rescinded his decree against my joining them in the giant's den, adding that if I nevertheless preferred the terrors outside, perhaps he would risk them with me.

"In this I discerned also a problem not far ahead, for the mate was now the plumpest of the survivors, all of whom began to size one another up. It did not much surprise me therefore when the larger among them began to speak of mass suicide as preferable to the foul fate of being cooked and eaten one at a time before one another's eyes. So desperate were they all that even many of the midsize merchants were in middling sympathy with this proposal. I myself argued vehemently against it, ostensibly on the grounds that self-slaughter was forbidden by Allah but actually because my chances of being discovered by the cannibal ogre would be much increased if he had to look outside his den for his dinner. The leaner of the survivors — crewmen, mostly — took my pious objection seriously, but all became uneasy, realizing that if the mate alone should kill himself, for example, the next-plumpest would be in line to be tonight's entrée and would no doubt kill himself in turn. In short, one suicide at the top would trigger another and another until the leanest was the plumpest. Inasmuch as the mate had nothing to lose (in this life, at least), it particularly behooved the next-plumpest after him to come up with a better idea.

"That fellow, as it happened, was myself, and though I had nothing immediately to fear as long as the company believed my fiction about apes in the trees, the man next plumpest after me began to voice the same skepticism as the mate. If our leader killed himself, this one announced, he intended to take his chances with me in the trees rather than submit to being spitted and roasted.

"Clearly the fat was in the fire — *my* fat, unless I came up with something quickly. I therefore declared to all hands that so certain was I of the apes' discovering and killing me tonight that I intended to take my chances in the giant's den instead, even though in the mate's absence I would be the next-plumpest. For in my two treetopped nights, I lied, I had overheard enough ape-talk to get the hang of their so-called language and had heard them express their disgust at the giant's habit of breaking his victims' necks and roasting their flesh before eating it, instead of nibbling them alive one limb at a time in the apes' own civilized fashion.

"This story took care of the movement to the trees but not my predicament. 'By Allah!' I then exclaimed. 'What sort of men are we, to talk of destroying ourselves instead of our destroyer? Let us wait till he falls asleep tonight and then throw ourselves upon him and do him what hurt we can, whether cutting his throat or at least blinding his eye to keep him from finding us so easily.'

"This proposal they received warmly — all except the mate, who pointed out with grim satisfaction that the ogre had never yet been seen to sleep before filling his belly with a Muslim, and that since he himself intended either to hang himself with his turban before sundown or to hide in the trees like certain other folk from those night-apes that nobody except me had seen, the giant's soporific meal would be myself—unless, as would not surprise him, I proved as indigestible as I was insubordinate.

"Obviously I needed to take prompt measures against this fellow, before his jibes turned the company against me. As soon as he went grousing off, I gathered a caucus of the plumper merchants and said to them, 'See here, comrades: the life of each of us is immediately in the hands of those plumper than himself, but eventually we'll all be eaten unless you follow my advice. Kill or disable our devourer we must, if we can, but that alone will not save us. Where did such a beast come from, if not from parents like himself? And if they are no longer living to avenge him, no doubt he has brothers somewhere about, or a cannibal mate, for Allah does not make his creatures in single copies. Before we attack our attacker and bring down the wrath of his kin upon us, we must build a raft on which to escape this island; and in this matter, though I am not a shipwright or sailor by trade, I have some experience.'

"I told them then from first to last the story of my escapes from the sundry islands of my two previous voyages, together with those voyages' eight moral lessons, and added that while they and the crewmen had been searching in vain at the mate's orders for hiding places, I had been scouting sufficient drift-timber along the shore to build a raft big enough for all of us, or almost all. But experience had taught me that its construction would require at least twenty-four hours under my supervision and perhaps several days under that of a less knowledgeable foreman. If they could think of some way to appease the ogre's appetite for one night more, I told them — with other food than myself — then we had a chance to save our necks. But our sacrificial victim (if that was what it must come to) ought not to be one of those presently gathered, I suggested, for the reason that, as the closest in line to be eaten, it was we who had the liveliest interest in getting the raft expeditiously built and launched. Neither of course could the sacrifice be one of our leaner shipmates, whom the ogre would simply reject in favor of a plumper. I bade them think the matter over between then and sundown, and meanwhile fall to under my direction to gather and bind our raft's main timbers. Tomorrow, if I remained alive, I would show them how to rig the mast and a makeshift sail.

"Just as I had hoped, they no sooner set about collecting the timbers I had spotted earlier and now directed them to, lashing them together at my instruction into the shape of a great tub, than our erstwhile first mate came down to the beach in a splendid rage, demanding to know what mutinies and cabals I was concocting behind his back and swearing that while he lived and had the power of speech, no one would give orders but himself. He then ordered his crew to clap me in irons, to be fed to the ogre, and to undo that ridiculous construction we had begun. Tomorrow, he declared, when I was gone, he would show the company how to build a proper raft in only three or four days.

"Sure enough, with no prompting from me or resistance from the sailors, the three or four next-plumpest merchants after myself straightway fell upon the mate and bound his arms and legs with their turbans. I complimented them on their judgment and provided extra turbans to insure the fellow's bondage as well as to gag his mouth, lest his arguments turn their minds against me or his cries move their hearts to misdirected pity. All the rest of that day we labored on our tub, merchants and crew together, and at sunset went trembling back to the ogre's den, fetching with us the unhappy mate. It was, needless to say, a terrifying hour for the teller of this tale when its monocular villain arrived to make his dreadful menu-perusal. Who could be sure how discerning his judgment was? He inspected us in his customary awful silence, passing over the skinny chaps now without bothering even to squeeze and pinch their flesh, and quickly narrowed his selection to the three or four plumpest. Of particular interest to him were myself, whom he'd not seen before, and the mate, so oddly turbaned; he picked up each of us in turn several times, squinting at us closely and squeezing various parts of our anatomy, and flung us down again, then finally weighed us against each other, one in each hand. My anxiety was heightened when the mate for very fear now beshat himself, thereby lessening his mass by half a kilo. In my own terror I readily followed suit, but what finally tipped the scales was that unlike the mate and the other survivors, I had not till this night been inside this grisly lair. The sight and smell of his recent victims' rotting bones, together with the filth of the ogre himself and the stink of the mate's terror and my own, revolted me as nothing in my past experience ever had except that nest of giant vultures in Voyage Two. *That* memory, atop the present foulness, was enough to add regurgitation to my defecation, and the two combined so unballasted me that the ogre dropped me in disgust, broke the mate's neck underfoot, spitted him through, and laid into his evening meal in his customary fashion.

"Thus did we survivors, in the manner you've heard me tell before, survive the second of the triple perils of Voyage Three: we blinded the ogre per plan with a red-hot iron when he was safely snoring and then escaped to the beach, where I kept my company too busy rigging and launching our tub to ask me where were those dreadful apes I had earlier reported. We stepped a tall mast and improvised a square sail of two dozen turbans knotted together at their corners: one from each of the twelve of us still alive, plus the nine remaining of my private supply, plus one each from the departed heads of the ogre's victims, which he had used to wipe his mouth after dining. Clumsy and leaky as our vessel was, it floated, but even as we paddled off, I saw clearly that we were too many to survive in it at sea, even if we had had food and water.

"Naturally enough, after my success with the ogre and the tub, my companions appointed me their captain and declared themselves ready to obey any order I gave them. But I knew that however much I had disguised the idea as theirs, they had seen me make a calculated sacrifice of the first mate; I could scarcely expect half their number (preferably the plumpest) to drown themselves now at my command for the sake of the rest. When, therefore (as I had predicted but scarcely expected), the blinded ogre reappeared on shore, guided by a one-eyed female no comelier than himself, and the pair of them commenced bombarding us with boulders the size of yonder camel, I took the desperate measure of ordering our turban-sail hoisted, though I reckoned that the wind might carry us shoreward faster than our paddles could paddle us off.

"This came to pass, while I kept my sailors paddling too briskly to watch where we were going. The boulders splashed about us, throwing up great waves as we drew near the beach. The ogre-woman, in particular, had a wicked right arm as well as full use of her eye; while her mate hurled his missiles blindly in all directions, hers came ever closer to their mark, until at last one fell so nearly upon us that by springing up in alarm to the gunwale of the tub at just the right moment, I contrived to make it seem as though the boulder-wave had capsized us.

"Thus did the ogres have their revenge, for all but two of my tub-mates drowned, one way or another, before we got our vessel righted and bailed. I then struck the sail, and we three survivors made good our escape to windward, out of missile range.

"Once clear of the island, we collapsed over our paddles, entirely spent, and would have drifted back to our enemies had I not recalled how the apes, in their ignorant attempt to imitate human sailors, had accidentally hit upon a more efficient windward-sailing rig than our late captain's. Though I could only guess at its details, I gave orders to my companions to imitate that rig as best we could with our turban-sail, and thus we completed our flight to freedom.

"Which is to say, we were free now to die of hunger and thirst, or to drown in the first storm that came our way (so underballasted was our tub with only three men in it), rather than being cooked and eaten. And for that we praised Allah, at the same time hoping He would fetch us quickly to a kinder shore. This He did after a mere two days and nights, which under ordinary marine-distress circumstances would have been scarcely enough to parch our throats and turn our thoughts to cannibalism. But inasmuch as we had all been starving ourselves for the three days prior in hopes of becoming less appetizing to the ogre than our fellows, by the time we piled up on the next island down the line we were reasonably emaciated and beginning to salivate at sight of one another's flesh.

"As was my wont, despite the cravings of my belly I hung back a bit near the wreck of our craft while my two tubmates rushed ashore to gorge themselves on fruit and fresh water, with which the place happily abounded. Only when I saw that the beach was free of dia-monds (and so presumably of serpents and giant vultures as well), and that there were no egg- or building-shaped structures in sight, and that those vowel-popping, consonant-chewing apes had not made the same landfall as we, only then did I join the others in eating and drink-ing what they had ingested without evident harm, and in praising Allah for our deliverance. So as not to presume unseemly upon His mercy, however, when evening came we climbed a tall tree, tied our-selves fast to its upper limbs with our turbans, and took turns standing watch — if *standing* is the right word for three Muslim merchants trussed in a treetop. Not until the first light of dawn showed safely on the eastern horizon — which happened to occur during my watch — did I allow myself blissfully to join the common sleep.

"But know, my friends, that Allah is a tireless schoolmaster who is no sooner satisfied that we have learned His last lesson than He sets us His next. I had scarcely begun to dream of dear dry Baghdad when the three of us were wakened by a horrid crunching and snapping, which at first I thought to be ape-talk but which proved to be the breaking bones of the lowermost of us as he was swallowed alive in two gulps by a serpent so much more monstrous than those in Diamond Valley that he needed not even to climb our tree to seize his meal. He simply lifted his head and upper body from the ground like a cobra rising to the charmer's pipe, and down went Mahmud the Damascene, tree limb, turbans, and all, crying 'There is no god but God!' as he consummated his martyrdom. Whereafter the beast retired.

"'As Allah lives,' my one remaining comrade and I agreed, 'it is a foolish man who believes the worst to be behind him while the story of his life has even one more page ahead.' As it was certain death to greet another dawn in that tree (our experience having confirmed that monsters seldom occur singly, and horrors never, but that even a gaunt and famished Muslim will satisfy your average monster for about a day), we risked meeting the serpent's family in order to search the island for better sanctuary, as well as for such friendly folk as that king who had made me his favorite on Island Two, Voyage One. White structures we would of course have eschewed even had we found any; caves there were aplenty, but none small enough to block that great snake's entry, and many large enough to house him or his kin. By afternoon's end the best we had found was another tree, twice as tall as the first, though not half as tall as we might have wished. My companion — a spice dealer named Amahl — was all for building a ring of bonfires around its base, despite my reminding him that nothing was more likely to awaken the sleeping whale that our island might yet turn out to be. Like that of most men with limited experience of desert islands, Amahl's view of them was insular; he could scarcely credit gross unlikelihoods other than those he himself had survived. Only by agreeing to bind myself to a lower limb than his could I talk him out of his foolish fire.

"Even so, he insisted on staying awake through the night, not because he could have done any more awake than asleep to fend off the serpent (since our respective limbs were already the two highest in the tree) but because he frankly suspected that if he fell asleep and I heard the serpent approach, I might untie and cast him down or attempt to steal just above him to the tree's limbless tip, where no man could turban himself securely but one might hold on just long enough for the other to be made a meal of. In vain I reproached him for his want of trust in the man to whom he owed his life several times over; Amahl declared that it was exactly that debt that made him fearful, lest I decide to collect it.

"Nothing for it then but that I suffer not only the fear of being swallowed alive (for I had, in truth, agreed to take the lower perch with the intention of sneaking above him once he slept) but the prayers and songs that my companion chanted hour after hour, off-key, till his voice grew hoarse, to keep himself awake. 'See here,' I called up to him when I could abide no more. 'For all we know, your songs may charm a brace of serpents our way, and we'll both be done for. In God's name give your voice a rest.' Amahl replied that he would be silent only if I spoke, so that he could keep an ear on my position. Accordingly, I launched into a tale he had heard twice already, once on Ape Island and again in our tub: the tale of my adventures in voyages One and Two, together with their several morals. Just as I had hoped, before I had gotten myself fairly cleansed of buzzard puke on Island Two, Voyage Two, I heard Amahl snoring; at the same time I heard a mighty sibilance in the darkness below, which could be nothing other than the swallower of Mahmud the Damascene.

"Pausing in my story only to indent a new paragraph, so to speak, I quickly unbound my turbans and slithered up past Amahl's limb. But either he had only pretended to snore, or else my narrative's shift of position waked him. 'False savior!' he cried, and he undid his turbans as the great hissing drew nearer and tried at once to loosen my hold on the slender treetop and to clamber past me. 'It is no false savior who has saved you two or three times already,' I told him, 'but I can save no one from inside the belly of a snake.' So saying, I clambered past him, and then he past me, each of us stomping the other down and being by the other stomped in turn as our doom hissed nearer, until the treetop began to bend under our weight.

"Now it happened that this spice dealer had been the next-plumpest after myself back on Ape Island, and though we both had lost weight while tubbing it from there to here, Amahl had in our brief time ashore engorged himself with fruit and water, whereas I had eaten and drunk only enough to restore my health, lest the food prove unsafe or there be another cannibal ogre on this island. He therefore had the better of me, heftwise, by a considerable margin, with the result that whereas I was the better slitherer and clamberer, Amahl was the better stomper. Once we were well clear of the last limb and shinnying together up the bendy tip, there was no getting by him; indeed, I was obliged to retreat lest he kick me loose. As the great snake's tongue came forking usward now from below, I commended my spirit to Allah, closed my eyes, and clung fast where I was while ungrateful Amahl grunted himself higher and higher.

"A moment later I felt the treetop bend like a bow and opened my eyes just in time to see the dealer dealt with: in his eagerness to put both me and the snake below him, Amahl had climbed to the very tip of the tip, which then suddenly bent almost double under his weight. Thus was he served like a spiced olive on a pick to the serpent just below me, who gobbled him turban-first before he could even praise Allah. I saw his legs thrash briefly as if they were the serpent's second tongue; then he was gone, and his swallower as well, leaving me the only Muslim snake-bait on the island.

"At dawn I came down to the shore with which all islands are surrounded and conferred with Sayyid Despair, my old traveling companion from voyages One and Two. As usual, he counseled suicide, as the only death less revolting than the one I was bound to suffer before I could build myself a new tub. But experience had taught me to hazard a vile death in some attempt to save myself, however desperate, rather than to guarantee an easier one at the end of a turban. Of these I had still a fair supply, having retrieved the ones I'd loaned Mahmud and Amahl for tree-binding purposes. I dismissed my dark counselor and cast about to find a new use for them.

"Turning over in my mind the unforgettable images of my shipmates' being eaten, some by the ogre of Island One and others by the serpent of Island Two, I was struck by this difference in their way of going: whereas Allah had given the one-eyed ogre two hands with which to skewer his victims from mouth to anus and then rend them limb from roasted limb for eating, He had obliged the limbless snake to swallow men whole or not at all. So considerable was his capacity that I had no hope of fattening myself beyond it, certainly not before nightfall. Therefore I looked about for other ways to render myself unswallowable, and after rejecting such expedients as smearing myself with filth (for who knew that serpent's tastes? Furthermore, I had as leave die as ever stink again as I had in the buzzards' nest and the ogre's left hand), I happened to remember, apropos of Allah's inscrutable wisdom, those apes' imposture of true worship. That memory led me to reflect upon the false religions of other unturbaned infidels: the Jew, with his six-pointed star instead of a proper crescent; the Christian, whose Savior is seldom depicted but as a suckling at the breast or a dead man fastened to a cross. . . .

"'Allah pardon me!' I here cried out, for this latter memory, together with Despair's phrase *bound to suffer,* showed me the way to self-salvation. Christian, Jew, and Muslim agree that the Lord is One, though His images differ, and so I combed the beach for drift-timbers fit for a crucifixion. When evening came I left off tub building and, using turbans in place of nails, bound myself there on the shore to one timber twice my length, crossed by another twice the span of my arms. Then — for extra insurance, as well as to avoid aping the infidel too closely — I crossed this crosspiece with another in the plane perpendicular to it, to make myself unswallowable in three dimensions rather than two.

"As you may gather from my being here to retell the tale, Allah smiled upon this stratagem, though a more fearful night I hope never to pass. Again and again the serpent gaped and struck in vain, licking me from head to foot with his cloven tongue, bathing me in his spittle, and so enveloping me in his foul breath that I might have succumbed to asphyxiation had the terrible tickling of his tongue not made me laugh so hard into the teeth of my fear that I could scarcely inhale. But swallow me he could not.

"And that was the end of my third series of ordeals, if not of the vexations of Voyage Three. The next morning, when the serpent had retired in hungry chagrin, Allah rewarded my ingenuity by sending past the island a handsome old merchant ship, which I flagged down with the same turbans that had repeatedly been my salvation — this time waving a varicolored streamer of them from one of my cross-timbers.

"My friends: there is no adventurer who is not altered by his adventures, and therefore the Sindbad who sails home is never the Sindbad who sailed forth, though they share a name. I was rescued, clothed, and fed by the kindly captain of that smart-sailing ship, which happened to be homeward bound to Basra after a long and arduous but successful trading cruise. Such pity did he feel for me after hearing the tale of Voyage Three alone that at his next port of call he offered to let me sell the goods of his vessel's former owner, who had been accidentally lost on a desert island some years before and was presumably now dead. I could keep a commission for myself; he would take another for successfully completing his late master's voyage and would pay over the balance, along with the ship itself, to that luckless fellow's family in Baghdad. I gratefully agreed, complimenting the captain on his good character. He then ordered the ship's clerk to bring up from the hold the bales and bundles of Sindbad the Sailor and asked me under what name he should enter me as trading agent.

"At the sight of my long-lost goods from Voyage Two, the scales fell from my eyes — some of the scales, at least — and I recognized this weathered but still handsome sailing vessel as none other than my *Zahir,* the same that I had fallen fatefully in love with years ago when she was fresh from the Basra yards and that had unknowingly sailed off without me when I drowned in sleep in that pleasant grove on Island One, Voyage Two. Weeping for joy, I told that story and its four morals to her present skipper, declaring myself to be Sindbad the Sailor.

"'Don't expect an old sea dog like me to swallow that whopper,' the captain scoffed, and he scolded me for repaying his goodwill with such a farfetched and greedy fabrication. He himself, he said, had been master of *Zahir* since her launching, and ipso facto when she had put in at that delightful island. The ship's owner, who had presumably been left behind (though they'd found no trace of him when they discovered his absence and made their way back to search for him), had in no way resembled me.

"'Nor do you,' I replied indignantly, 'in the least resemble Kasīm of Basra, whom I hired to captain our company on that voyage. Kasīm was a fellow as fresh and ready as the ship we set forth in — his first command and her maiden voyage — whereas you are as barnacled and weatherworn as the hull now under us. Don't ask me to swallow this rank imposture.'

"Thus did we rebuke and discredit each other, until one of the elder merchants among the passengers, overhearing our dispute, declared himself prepared to resolve it. Had I not acknowledged, he asked me, that the ship on whose quarterdeck we quarreled was the same *Zahir* in which I had loaded my bales and sailed forth under young Captain Kasīm of Basra? Or did I think this a different vessel of the same name? 'So great a coincidence as that,' I answered, 'would be too much to swallow. It is not only her name I now recognize, but every line of her hull, every detail of her rig, every move she makes under me, all of which so pleased me when she was brand-new and please me yet. I would know this ship no matter what her name, even if she were twice as weatherbeaten as she is.' 'Yet you did not, at first,' the merchant reminded me. 'Therefore recognize your captain as well, for he is no other than your servant Kasīm of Basra, as seasoned by the leagues gone under his keel as are your *Zahir* and its owner. I have sailed with him for a full year now and have seen seafaring age him as it has aged me. And you, my good Kasīm,' he then advised the captain, 'must swallow that this battered derelict is indeed your master Sindbad the Sailor, whom I met not many years ago on the Island of the Valley of Serpents and Diamonds, where like myself he was for a time in the mutton-and-gemstone trade and where he told me the moraled story of his maroonment. I will vouch that both of you are who you say you are, as am I and as is this ship.'

"Well, the truth is that I didn't recognize either this peacemaker or his name (which I have since forgotten). But as it was clearly in the best interests of each of us at least to pretend to swallow the other's story, both the captain and I swallowed his as well and embraced each other like long-lost partners. We willingly suspended our disbelief and did our business, at such tremendous profit that by the time *Zahir* reached Basra I found it no more difficult to believe that Kasīm was Kasīm than that I was Sindbad. For by then the misfortunes of Voyage Three seemed to me already as distant and dreamlike as those of voyages Two and One. And though en route home I witnessed many another prodigious implausibility, such as fish who resembled cattle and birds born from seashells, I swallowed their reality with ease, so adept had I grown at that art.

"Just so, I hope, comrades, may you all, having trained yourselves with these first three voyages of mine and the two we've heard thus far of my brother, Sindbad the Still-Stranded. For it lies to us now to unhinge the jaws of our credulity and swallow *his* third voyage — after which, this time tomorrow, we shall address my fateful fourth, more horrendously entertaining than these first three combined, and a turning point in the story of its teller. Yasmīn."

Surprised and smiling, Sindbad's daughter looked up from her gold-robed lap, which both she and Somebody had been contemplating since her father's first mention of the ship *Zahir*. "So long a voyage," she asked, rising to pour the wine, "and no further moral lessons at its end for my prospective fiancé?" She smiled sweetly but briefly at far-off Ibn al-Hamrā, then turned that smile full and radiant upon our man at her left midtable.

"Oh, those," said Sindbad, and he rattled them off casually upon his own left hand: "Where there are diamonds, Q.E.D., look for serpents, too; but where no diamonds are, watch out for serpents anyhow. Never be the plumpest chicken in the coop; in the company of cannibals, keep yourself lean and mean and in every way unpalatable. Consider that while discourse that makes no sense to us is not ipso facto nonsense, if we try to ape it we may make monkeys of ourselves. And bear in mind that it's better to speak the unswallowable and swallow the unspeakable than to be swallowed up by either. Is that not so, Brother Sindbad?"

"Brother Sindbad," responded Somebody the Still-Stranded, "it is the very truth. Though God's great serpent waits to swallow every one of us at the end of our story, we do well to render ourselves unswallowable through its middle. Your health, sir."

"And yours," the host replied, raising his wine cup first ourmanward and then in a flourish that included the whole company: "and yours and yours, my friends and partners."

"Yours," grumbled Ibn al-Hamrā, and he tossed off his drink so curtly that he splashed his own bib.

"Hasīb Alī's," murmured one of the other guests, sipping pensively.

"Mine," proposed happy Kuzia Fakān. She drank off her wine in a single guzzle, burped contentedly, patted her lips with her veil, and held out her cup to Yasmīn for refilling.

"Hers," sniffed old Jaydā.

"Hers indeed," their joint master agreed, "and there's an end to proposing this toast, or we'll never get it swallowed." So saying, he and the others who had not yet done so drank. Yasmīn went the rounds again, returned to her place, and looked brightly to still-stranded Somebody, at whom now her father nodded.

"Here is how I, too, was once swallowed," that fellow said, "by Mother Ocean, who then saw fit to burp me up again, as she has more than once done since. But what befell me when I came ashore, though it involved neither apes nor ogres nor giant snakes, I myself can still scarcely swallow."

He then recounted a version of

Somebody's Third Voyage

Through the first, or "British," half of Baylor's forty-second-birthday gift to himself — a two-week "bareboat" sailing cruise in the Virgin Islands — things had gone well enough, Baylor wrote in his travel log, *considering.*

He checked his left wrist, his reflexes forgetting again that as of yesterday afternoon he had no working watch. At the sight of the bracelet there of untanned Baylor-skin, he closed his eyes for some moments. The passenger ferry's idling diesels soothed the throbbing in his head, but (as had happened more than once last night in the forward double berth of our rented sailboat) he soon felt the approach of vertigo, a premonition as of drowning in darkness or coming un-moored in outer space, and opened his eyes wide. An electric clock on the steel forward wall of the passenger lounge read 7:53: seven minutes till *Native Son*'s scheduled departure from West End, Tortola, in the British Virgins, for Charlotte Amalie, St. Thomas, in the U.S. Virgins. Baylor's daughter, Juliette, was queued up at the aft-end food conces-sion with her uncle Joe and aunt Betsy and a commuting crowd of native sons and daughters, buying coffee and doubtless glad of the respite from her strainful parents. Jane, his wife, was off by herself — prowling the little high-speed ferry from stem to stern, Baylor bet, and seething.

The harbor at West End was as unprepossessing as its name: Soper's Hole. Somewhere among the moored yachts across from the ferry dock, our forty-foot chartered sloop, *So Far*, lay to twin bow anchors uncertainly set, their nylon lines crossed (*like Baylor's fingers,* the writer noted now in his log, *and the couple's purposes*) from the vessel's having swung overnight with wind and tide. Most unseamanlike, not to straighten things out before leaving *So Far* untended through the day; but matters were so volatile between him and Jane just now, and Baylor was in such an odd, disoriented funk since last evening's accident, that we had simply let the damned boat lie. Chances were that unless another squall like last Tuesday night's blew through, *So Far* would stay put till our return this evening. If she should happen to drag down on her too-near neighbors (mostly other charter yachts at permanent moorings, unchartered in this slack season), to hell with it: maybe the day's respite from responsibility would give Baylor the wherewithal to address the situation at afternoon's end.

With a promptness more Brit than Carib, at 0800 almost sharp the native captain of *Native Son* sounded the ship's whistle. Deckhands and dockhands called to one another in mellifluous West Indian and cast off lines; the diesels shuddered, and the motor vessel moved out. Normally Baylor would have followed the undocking with interest, to admire (and report to his readers) the crew's dexterity or lack thereof, maybe to pick up a few pointers in case the family went on with this birthday cruise. At least he ought to have made sure from the afterdeck that the wash from the ferry's propellers didn't bash *So Far's* dinghy unduly against the next dock down, where Baylor wasn't sure we had any business mooring it; a ten- or twelve-year-old whose T-shirt read I BORN HERE: TORTOLA, B.V.I. had collected a dollar from us for the privilege of our leaving the tender under his wardenship for the day ("Loving tender-care," Juliette had wisecracked) and then had promptly disappeared. But what could Baylor do if in fact the dinghy banged and scraped the pilings now, or even swamped, outboard engine and all? Tell the captain to redock and hold the ferry till he set things right?

Baylor doubted that things could ever be set right.

A Styrofoam coffee cup in each hand, here approached his jewel: lean and angular but never ungraceful, fair-skinned and -featured, short-haired and short-shorted Juliette, with her father's sharp jaw and Low-German stoicism, her mother's ultramarine eyes and Pilgrim severity of expression.

"One sugar no cream, yes?" She handed him her left cup and settled on the bench beside him, crossing her fine tanned legs.

"You got it," Baylor said. "But I'm not sure I want it. Thanks anyhow."

"Today's our present to you," his daughter reminded him. "Relax and let it happen." She raised her plastic cup in toast. "*Salaam*, okay?"

"Shalom."

She patted his left shoulder. "Happy birthday anyhow."

In the spring of her sophomore year at Boston U., Baylor's daughter, an uncertain liberal-arts major, had taken up with (been taken in by, Jane grumbled) an expatriate Omani doing graduate work in oceanography. Against her mother's wishes (in 1972, Jane was still a holdout against the permissiveness of the American sixties), Juliette was living with the fellow this summer at the Woods Hole Institute. Only her new enthusiasm for marine biology — and a private pitch from her father that her company might oil the troubled waters of her parents' middlescence — had induced her to leave her Musalām for a fortnight and join the birthday cruise. Wiry, gentle-mannered, abstemious, imperturbable Musalām — Musalām the Impenetrable, so he seemed to Baylor, who was never comfortable in the younger man's presence. Musalām the penetrator of his daughter.

Once clear of the harbor, *Native Son* throttled up for the run south and west to Charlotte Amalie. Already Tortola and Great Thatch Island were astern; likewise Jost Van Dyke, which we might sail to tomorrow if we didn't call it quits. Sunward through the ferry's portside windows Baylor saw the shadow-sloped west coast of St. John, the main cruising ground of the scheduled "American" week of our charter; ahead to starboard was the brightly dappled, camouflage-colored east coast of St. Thomas, which we would probably not bother sailing to now that we were shuttling to its capital city. The morning was brilliant and balmy, with fair-weather cumuli riding west on the trade winds: a better sailing day than yesterday, for sure, maybe the best so far.

So what? Baylor asked himself, he wrote.

Joe and Betsy Behler took up station at a window on the St. John side: the writer's bluff and florid older brother and that brother's stolidly cheerful wife, who was as usual listening while her husband held forth. "Joe Junior" — turned out for the excursion in polyester slacks, elbow-sleeved sport shirt, and green and yellow John Deere cap — was in this instance pointing to this and that on the ship, no doubt explaining their functions knowledgeably from his World War II–time stint in the U.S. Navy.

"Let's look at the world with Aunt Bets and Uncle Joe," Juliette suggested, already rising.

"Be with you shortly," her father said, and tapping his logbook, he added ironically, "Baylor needs to talk to himself for a while."

It was the family's little standing joke — sometimes, lately, Jane's taunt — that Simon William Behler had exactly half succeeded in following his father's early exhortations to "make a name for himself." From East Dorset High he had proceeded on scholarship just after the war to the state university across the Chesapeake, the first of his family to attempt higher education. "Now *that's* the ticket!" his aunt Rachel had cheered; his uncle Josh would surely have joined her applause, but lung cancer had fetched him by then out to join Simon's mother in the new family grave-plot. His father had nodded approval and blown his nose loudly into a linen handkerchief.

Encouraged by his work on the campus daily newspaper (*The Diamondback*), the young man followed his baccalaureate with a year of graduate-school journalism at Northwestern but used the excuse of his bride's prompt pregnancy to drop out of the program, which didn't much appeal to him after all, and into entry-level reportage for the city desk of the old *Washington Star,* which soon enough appealed to him even less. When the twins were old enough to be left with day-sitters, Jane went back to three-quarter-time office work to supplement their income — she had been a typist and proofreader for *The Diamondback* when Simon met her — and her husband moved from reporting for the daily *Star* to feature-writing for its Sunday magazine. The trade-off was a reduction in his already meager salary for increased latitude in his subject matter — no more city-council and schoolboard meetings! — and more time for free-lancing of a non-journalistic sort. Using the nom de plume "William Baylor" to differentiate this latter writer from S. W. Behler of the *Star* ("William" struck him as more appealing than "Simon," and the English spelling of his surname "looks more the way it sounds," he got into the habit of saying), he established in the latter 1950s a minor reputation for science-fiction fantasies with a topical-satirical twist: Joe McCarthy–style red-baiting, say, among Cold Warriors on Ice Planet Zembla, or, inversely, a gentle extraterrestrial accidentally stranded on Eniwetok just before the first hydrogen-bomb test. In the early 1960s he had rather more success with a pair of popular-historical narratives, published in hardcover by a mainstream press rather than by the science-fiction paperback houses: *The Magnificent,* about the sixteenth-century Ottoman empire of Suleiman I, financed the down payment on a modest house in the "planned community" of Columbia, Maryland; *Zanzibar!,* a novel about the medieval Arab sea trade from East Africa to China, went far toward paying Juliette's and her brother's private-high-school tuitions when the time came.

Through those innocent Eisenhower-Kennedy years, the happy first dozen of our marriage, how hard he and Jane had worked! We were laboring, both of us, not only to repay Simon's graduate-school tuition loans and to finance a house and car and to educate our children and to establish "William Baylor" as a professional author, but at the same time — almost without realizing it, so innocent were we ourselves — to change social classes: from small-town, semirural lower middle to urban professional middle middle. Yet we had energy to spare for everything: holding down several jobs (Simon taught an evening course in journalism at College Park in addition to writing features for the *Star* and the moderately successful books of "William Baylor"; Jane did telephone canvassing at home in the evenings after six hours of office work at the Bureau of Standards), repainting the house ourselves, gardening and lawn mowing, playing with the twins and chauffeuring them to after-school lessons in this and that, attending parent-teacher and neighborhood-association meetings, entertaining and being entertained by our circle of young professional friends, and making vigorous love at odd times and in odd places when our busy schedules happened to give occasion.

Yet it was not until the American sixties really hit their stride that "Baylor" found his most successful writing (and written) self.

Inspired by their author's boyhood reading in *The Arabian Nights,* *The Magnificent* and *Zanzibar!* had been worked up purely from library research; "William Baylor" had never traveled outside the United States or, except for family camping vacations, very much within them. On the strength of *Zanzibar!*'s paperback sale, however, he was emboldened to plan for 1965 — when he and Jane would turn thirty-five and the twins thirteen — a year's leave from the *Star* and our life in Columbia to visit Europe, the Near East, and North Africa. More specifically, he proposed to winter with the family somewhere mild-weathered and economical on the Mediterranean — an inexpensive villa in southern Portugal or Spain, maybe, or off-season Minorca, where Jane would housekeep and tutor Juliette and Andrew while he got cracking on a book he had begun about Iberia in the Moorish period — then tour western Europe through the summer on the cheap, perhaps in a camper bus; and finally (if *The Court of Lions* was sufficiently advanced) make a solo swing in the fall from Suleiman the Magnificent's capital city, Istanbul, down the Eastern Mediterranean coast and west across North Africa to Morocco, flying home to Maryland from Tangier or Casablanca by, say, Thanksgiving.

Young Andrew and Juliette protested: they would miss their middle-school graduation! What would they do, cooped up with their parents in some foreign shack for the entire winter, no friends no phone no television, not even any movies they could understand? On this their parents were unanimous: the experience would be important for them, and they *would* understand those movies, because the whole family was going to crash on Berlitz School Spanish starting now.

But Jane was unenthusiastic, too. The summertime camping part sounded appealing enough; God knew we were overdue for a real vacation, though such a long one would put her job at risk. But she had no head for languages and could not look forward to housekeeping through the winter in a foreign country while riding herd on a pair of bored thirteen-year-olds and supervising their correspondence-school lessons in eighth-grade math, science, history, English, and the rest — particularly if doing so meant giving up a job she liked, just when she was about ready to move into it full-time. As for that third part of the plan: in fourteen years of marriage we had spent scarcely a night apart, and now he was proposing a three-month separation — "Let's call it by its real name!" she cried — during which she was to reopen the house, get the kids established in high school, find a new job, and manage everything while he roamed footloose and fancy-free, like the middle-aged hippie he was maybe turning into, through every fleshpot and pot-pot from Istanbul to Casablanca?

Argument in this vein had lately been becoming a habit with us. But Jane undeniably had a point: since President Kennedy's assassination and Simon's move to the *Star*'s Sunday magazine, her husband had come to wear his hair and sideburns longer and had all but given up neckties. Nevertheless (he would remind her in extremis), he remained the principal breadwinner in the house by a factor of several; he had been the model petit bourgeois paterfamilias for a dozen-plus years and was not about to turn into Jack Kerouac, much less Allen Ginsberg. The times they *were* a-changing, but he was not proposing to kick over the traces; all he wanted (and by golly he intended to have it) was a sort of working sabbatical: a temporary change of scene — and, okay, "life-style" — in order to pursue a significant career move. "The day you see me wearing a gold necklace and reciting mantras," he declared, "you'll know we're in trouble." But for the good of the order he shortened that solo part of the *Wanderjahr* from ten weeks to two, abbreviated its itinerary to Morocco alone — just enough of Islam to get a sense of where the Spanish Moors *came* from, for God's sake — and moved it to the front end of the trip. He would check out Moorsville right after Christmas, cross the Straits of Gibraltar to Andalusia as Islam itself had done, rent a little place for the family on the Costa del Sol, meet them there in mid-January, and return with them around Labor Day, in time for the new school semester.

These things all came to pass, but from them William Baylor's *The Court of Lions* never materialized. On his first full day in Tangier (stopping at the old Grand Hotel Villa de France, where Matisse lived while painting his odalisques, in the city where Rimsky-Korsakov composed *Scheherazade*) he fell in with a crew of younger American hangers-on around the expatriate writer Paul Bowles — bona fide beatniks and hippies, most of them — and in surprisingly short order found him-

self both stoned and laid. Hashish, it was, in the first instance, provided (after a trial run of marijuana failed) by a winsome though
solemn Sarah Lawrence dropout in the second: granny-glassed and
Mother-Hubbarded Teri-from-Teaneck needed a place to crash for
two-three days and had a thing for straight older guys — a *father*
thing, you know? Once the dope had overcome Baylor's initial,
conscience-stricken impotence and enabled him well beyond his
norm, she fucked his brains out.

No doubt jet lag, the novelty of traveling abroad and alone, and
the exotic otherness of Islam (market-women in veils and djellabas,
men in caftans over their business suits, currency in dirhams, a predawn muezzin crying something that sounded like *Wombat! Wombat!*
from a loudspeakered minaret near the Villa de France just as he and
Teri soixante-neufed to the point of orgasmic vertigo in the pitch and
dopey, languorous but heavy-breathing dark) all conspired to overwhelm so easily his Stateside values, loyalties, inhibitions. Even when
his head and hotel room had more or less cleared, the experience left
Baylor much moved, even shaken — though not a little exhilarated as
well, and less remorseful than fascinated. He made no attempt to follow up on this initiation into "fleshpots and pot-pots." Relieved to see
no evidence of venereal infection, he stayed clear of the Paul Bowles
groupies, and of his fellow American tourists generally, and attended
to his Moorish homework like the able journalist and book-researcher
he was. He telephoned home: Jane was querulous, then testy, finally
just lonesome and looking forward to our reunion, as was he. He
reported, truthfully, that after a disoriented start his note-taking was
going well, and more equivocally, that he much missed her and the kids.

Miss them he did, positively. On the other hand, he wouldn't at all
have minded a whole month alone in Morocco and Moorish Spain, to
sort out he didn't quite know what, before settling down again with
the family. Instead of side-tripping the coast east and south from Tangier, as he had planned, he probed inland, into deeper and somewhat
less touristed Islam, to the holy cities of Fez and Meknès, and even as
far as camel-girt, throat-parching, terra-cotta-colored Marrakesh. And
he found that he could not get Teri-from-Teaneck out of his thoughts.
Not the girl herself: what did he know or care about the girl herself,
beyond her dry olive eyes and freckled little breasts and disconcerting
habit, when approaching climax, of —

Knock it off, he wrote in his notebook while touring Meknès; but he could not. It was not the girl herself, but the elasticity of time and space — hash-induced, no doubt — that stayed with him from . . . *Might as well say "from that magical night,"* he wrote in his notebook in Fez, *though love was nowise an ingredient of the magic.* Laved almost head to foot in their joint perspiration, sexual fluids, even saliva (Teri was a cat-lover and prodigious licker of her bedmate's skin); enwrapped by arms, legs, bedsheets, and the girl's long tangerine hair; particularly at that moment when the muezzin's call had rung over their muffled, mouth-full moans, he had felt a black, cosmic suspension that recalled to him certain others long forgotten: rocking in his childhood bed in East Dorset; holding on to both his breath and a waterlogged snag in the Chaptico River bottom till he nearly lost consciousness; French-kissing Daisy Moore ditto one night at age fourteen on "BeeGee's" grave in the Dorset Municipal Cemetery.

In Baylor's imagination, he wrote in his notebook in Marrakesh — for the first time referring to himself by his surnom de plume, as if to distance the Columbia husband from the stoned philanderer of Tangier — *that one-night stand with a New Jersey dropout in the Villa de France became inextricably conflated with the souks and medinas of Morocco.* The taste of mint tea or couscous, the smells of cumin and oleander (even of the notorious Marrakesh tanyards), the sight of camels and caftans and hammered copper, the feel of soft tooled leather, the sounds of goat-bleat, pipe and tambour, of spoken Arabic itself — most particularly the five-times-daily prayer call from the minarets of Islam — were charged for keeps with the illicit voltages of hashish and adultery.

No need to remind him, he wrote in his notebook now — speeding toward Charlotte Amalie aboard *Native Son* and himself reminded, by yesterday's mishap, of his Moroccan experience seven years ago — *how unfair all this was to his wife and children.* He had duly found and leased a tiny villa for them all in Estepona, still more a fishing village than a resort in those days, on the coast of what "his" Moors had called Al-Andaluz. Together we had coped with an inclement winter, warmer than Maryland's but less comfortable for want of heat and other amenities. Jane and the twins had been real troupers, seldom complaining, better at Spanish than he by the time we left, from having practiced it in their daily make-work while he tried vainly to breathe life into *The Court of Lions*. We had all then enjoyed our long camping reconnaissance of the rest of Spain (including the original Patio de los Leones in the Alhambra) and most of the rest of western Europe, and had returned home enriched by the adventure and feeling closer as a family, in nearly all respects, than we had felt before. Setting aside the Moorish project when we left Andalusia, Baylor contented himself through our grand tour with keeping a journal, or travel log, in his "Moroccan" style — *Baylor in the Court of Lions; Baylor in the Piazza San Marco, the Colosseum, Dachau, Schloss Neuschwanstein, the British Museum, Stonehenge, Tivoli, Elsinore* — registering the details not so much of those celebrated places as of his persona's reaction to them: a mainstream, midlife WASP American en famille at certain waypoints and touchstones of Western Civ; a not-quite-innocent abroad.

Teri-from-Teaneck, alas, who had not infected him, infected this journal. In the summer months especially, Europe was overrun with the likes of her and her blue-jeaned, cowboy-booted, backpacking male counterparts thumbing down the highways, sleeping in the parks and campgrounds. Many of the young women were lumpy, pasty-faced, slack-assed, altogether unappealing, but the sight of one trim and comely on the Ponte Vecchio or in the Luxembourg Gardens or the Rijksmuseum — like the sight of a Near Eastern restaurant in Munich, an Ingres harem scene in the Louvre, an edition of *The Thousand Nights and a Night* in a London bookstall — *would put Baylor stingingly in mind,* he wrote, *of TFT's muskmarine vulva* (his wife's was invariably daisy-fresh, even after intercourse) *and copper-fleeced armpits* (Jane shaved); *of Baylor's repeated and, in one instance, unprecedentedly sustained erections; above all, of that swooning sense of being not "out-of-body" but supernally* in *it, beyond the particulars of time and place.* In vain he strove with Jane to reproduce that sensation, without of course mentioning what exactly he was after. Our sex life, in consequence, was more than usually vigorous through our European sojourn, despite our limited privacy; Andrew and Juliette, feeling worldly and amused, would take long after-dinner hikes about the campground or the neighborhood of the family's pension-du-soir "in case you guys want to be alone for a while," and would loudly signal their return. But *vin ordinaire* is not hashish, a Danish family campground is not the Grand Hotel Villa de France, and one's faithful spouse of a decade and a half, however still handsome and well put together, *is not likely to be* (Baylor wrote) *a space-and-time-transcending fuck.*

At first light one morning near the end of our trip, stirred by a vivid but already fleeting dream in which "TFT" was displaced for his pleasure to the Jmaa el Fna in Marrakesh — that bustling, sensuous, somewhat intimidating "Place of the Dead" bazaar — Baylor half woke to find his bedmate fondling him in her own, evidently amorous half-sleep. In that intermediate zone we came together, so ardently that at the moment of ejaculation Baylor felt his ontological moorings slacken, almost give way. Just then an English rooster crowed; an English morning dawned, gray, rain-pattering; from belowstairs in our bed-and-breakfast outside Weymouth came the cozy smells of fried tomato, pork sausage, English tea. Smiling Jane laid a finger to his lips, to shush his groan.

Baylor's Grand Tour, the first of the "Baylor" series and the author's debut into "the new journalism," was also his first to attain the *New York Times* best-seller list: for a respectable five weeks it bobbled between number 8 and number 6 before subsiding. It was cordially reviewed in the places that count and did well in paperback, too. Though the book made no direct mention of its pseudonymous author-antihero's Tangerine sexual adventure, it dealt candidly and amusingly with his hashish initiation and with certain restlessnesses attendant on his being (Baylor quoted Dante) *nel mezzo del cammin di nostra vita.* He had spoken of these things, more or less, with his wife, though not quite in these terms, while recasting his journals into book form. Gratified by his success — Jane, unfortunately, had not found a new job as interesting as the one she had quit for the sake of our trip — she was not a little embarrassed as well, a touch hurt-feelinged and resentful, less because her husband was capable of "middlescent" stirrings than because he had thus broadcast them, even under a (transparent) assumed name. Moreover, a few particular phrasings — e.g., in the chapter "Baylor Dreams of the Jmaa el Fna" — provoked in her an unwonted wifely suspicion. Chiding herself, she nevertheless poked about in his newly refurbished writing room one winter Saturday when he was over in D.C. with fifteen-year-old Andrew ("Baylor & Son Protest Our Presence in Vietnam," for *Esquire*). On a shelf of his books and notebooks, in no way concealed, she found his travel log from the family's season abroad. Standing there among the regulated clicks and hums of their pleasant house, she read it through.

As *Native Son* throttled down from planing speed at the entrance to St. Thomas Harbor, Jane excused herself from the family group again: to get a better view of the cruise liners from across the passenger lounge, she said. But Joe Junior, prompted by Juliette and the sight of the ferry's orange life rafts, was in the midst of retelling his wartime adventure in the South Pacific, and not only had we all (his niece included) heard that remarkable story often before, but Jane found such anecdotes distressing and thoughtless in the too-long absence of any word from Drew. At least she wasn't moving specifically away from *him* this time, Baylor reflected; rather from his family in general, of whom (including Juliette, her father's darling) she had had a gutful in the last twenty-four hours.

"Honey, I *bailed* her!" Joe was declaring in a cheery holler. "Didn't I bail her?" he demanded of his wife.

"You just better believe it," placid Betsy affirmed on cue.

"That's why I still get the willies e'en on a *real* boat like this one," he confided loudly to his brother. "Never mind your tippy little dingbat Whatsitsname!"

"*So Far*," his niece reminded him. "From exotic Akron, Ohio."

He laid a red hand on her tan knee. "Lemme tell you this, hon: when your damn flying boat won't boat no better'n it flies, and then your damn inflatable won't more'n half inflate, and then your damn *island* 'bout washes away from under you, old Akron Ohio gets to sounding a lot like Heaven!"

"What'd you bail *with*, Uncle Joe?" Baylor's daughter seemed to enjoy thus feeding her uncle, who needed no feeding, and who seldom in his brother's memory had reciprocated that polite interest in other folks' doings. He left it to his wife, along with managing their house and keeping the books for Behler Maintenance & Improvement, to ask what Juliette was doing with herself this summer, and whether we had heard anything from Andrew lately, and what "Sy's" new book was going to be all about.

"Same thing I caught and ate my seagull with!" Dropping his jaw and widening his eyes in mock astonishment, he held up both meaty hands, fingers splayed. "Man gets desperate enough, he could bail this whole damn harbor with his bare hands!"

"His fingers were so cracked and bloody they drew sharks," plump Betsy said. "But his last night out there he kept seeing this *light,* low down on the water? So he kept on paddling with his two bare hands the whole blessed night, sharks or not."

"Paddling and a-bailing!" her husband roared. An elderly West Indian woman down-bench from them nodded affirmation.

Weary as Baylor was of the recitation — and still half dazed and more than half depressed from yesterday evening and last night — he still found the tale extraordinary, all but incredible, though his brother was too guileless, for one thing, to invent or much exaggerate. Joe Junior's C-46 transport, loaded with Seabees and their equipment, had crash-landed in the ocean when one engine caught fire, just as the War Department's telegram had more or less informed the family, and had sunk very quickly thereafter, carrying with it the flight crew and most of the passengers. Half a dozen, however, escaped in two sturdy inflatable life rafts, and though one man died in the night from internal injuries, the others had the marvelous luck to be spotted and rescued only three days later by an amphibious PBY patrol plane on the lookout for the overdue C-46. But for reasons unknown (the sea was calm enough for the flying boat to "land" instead of merely radioing the rafts' position to a naval vessel), the PBY on takeoff "caught a wing pontoon," according to Joe, did a violent cartwheel, sheared the caught wing, and flipped over, its fuselage broken at the waist turrets. Joe Junior (who had been "bidding good-bye to them damn rafts" from one of those turrets) found himself back in the water, bruised and neck-wrenched but otherwise unhurt; his comrades were either killed in that second crash or too injured to escape, he never learned which. The capsized plane settled and sank as he swam back toward it through a strew of debris, luckily including a life raft that was partially punctured and smaller than the one he had just abandoned (now blown too far away by the PBY's prop-wash to overtake) but better equipped.

There ensued an ordeal almost as long as the famous Eddie Rickenbacker's and perhaps more heroic, for being endured alone. For blazing weeks Baylor's brother survived on the raft's small supply of water and rations, then on raw fish and (like Rickenbacker) raw seagull and sips from his own scant urine. Sun-fried, salt-blistered, storm-swamped, shark-menaced, he paddled by hand, after losing the raft's paddle in a night capsize, to more than one hallucinated island — including, Joe Junior liked to swear solemnly, hand on heart, "the Island" in Island Creek, where he and his buddies had had themselves many a good old time when they were kids; did Sy remember it? — before following that aforementioned light to a real one. The tiny atoll was uninhabited but fortunately not treeless; on it he found nothing that could account for the light that had beckoned him there, but enough coconuts, firewood, and catchable fish to make the next installment of his ordeal — the "Robinson Crusoe chapter" — seem a beach party compared to what he had survived already.

Juliette sighed. "Boyoboy: no wonder you're not crazy about swimming and sailing."

"Honey," her aunt Betsy complained, "it's a miracle he's here. I can't even get him to Ocean City for a weekend!"

"Oh, I don't mind watching you girls in your bikinis and whatnot." Joe patted his wife's strapping, pants-suited right thigh with his left hand, Juliette's lean and bare brown left with his right. "But gimme dry land to watch from, any old time!" He tapped his cigarette pack and winked: "That's why I like Camels!"

Rejoining us but not sitting, Jane declared that if dry land was the order of the day, we had better come along and clear customs, or we'd find ourselves headed back to Soper's Hole. "Aye, aye, ma'am!" cried Joe Junior, and all but Baylor set about gathering up cameras, handbags, caps, and themselves for disembarking. He was in fact lingering half in the unretold climax of his brother's adventure (after a typhoon nearly washed him off his desert island, Joe Junior had spelled out his last name on the beach in ten-foot capitals with coral rocks and coconut husks and, praying that it wasn't Japanese, attracted the attention of a reconnaissance plane by standing at the tail of the *R* and waving a bright-orange nylon signal pennant from the raft's survival kit) and half in associated reveries, some long forgotten, some recent: "Princess Wakini" swimming nude in *Lagoon*; his wife doing likewise lately off *So Far*'s stern in the crowded anchorages of Norman Island, Trellis Bay, and Gorda Sound, and even in Soper's Hole last night with Joe and Betsy aboard. Jane had been not so much indifferent to nudity, in her husband's opinion (as were the French and Scandinavian charterers she had taken her cue from), as asserting her nakedness — Here it is; what are you going to do about it? — and, in that last instance, defying as well the cruising guide's advice against night swimming in tropical anchorages.

"It's your party," she reminded him now, obviously keeping her voice under control. "Are you ready to come?" At forty-two, Jane Price was a striking woman still, long and lean like their daughter though more amply tushed and breasted, an eye-turner yet in snug jeans and a sleeveless top that set off her fine arms and shoulders. Her sunglasses were perched stylishly atop her walnut hair, the more attractive for its seasoning with a touch of gray, as was her face for the crow's-feet forming at the corners of her eyes. Those eyes were the color but (in present company, at least) not the warmth of the Sir Francis Drake Channel, which *So Far* had crisscrossed for the past week; her tone was no warmer. Baylor's new lover — who would not likely be in Jane's shape when she reached Jane's age, but that wasn't going to be any time soon — happened to have asked him that very same question, in a quite different voice and quite other circumstances, the afternoon before he set out from Washington National with his wife to rendezvous with Juliette in San Juan and go on to Tortola. As he had done then, he replied now simply, "Yup."

It was certainly not that Jane Price didn't have just grievance, past and present. She and Simon William Behler had married comparatively young and comparatively innocent, even for the innocent American 1950s. Though neither had been virginal when we commenced our premarital affair, our high-school and early college romances had been transient and infrequently consummated. We had more or less rediscovered sex together and had relished our discoveries. We had loved each other, our married life, our babies, and our hardworking climb up the postwar American middle-class ladder. Notwithstanding that new abrasiveness in our relation after S. W. Behler left his staff job with the *Star,* who could say that we might not be contentedly married still, despite Baylor's lapse with Teri-from-Teaneck, if he had simply been grown-up enough not to let that adventure possess his imagination, and above all discreet enough not to *write it down?* Good people could lapse; good marriages survived such lapses. But Baylor had not only dwelt upon and written about his single infidelity, in a

way that made the family's European odyssey a bitter exercise in hy-
pocrisy; he had published it to the world, or might as well have. Even
Teresa Anginelli, the aspiring College Park journalist whose apartment he had lately been visiting before or after his evening workshop,
had been appalled when he told her about that; in motion astride him,
she had cheerfully promised instant reprisal in kind if he ever published a "Baylor Tries Italian." And this many years after Tangier, he
still blushed for shame, not at the incident but at his mishandling of
it, which had effectively poisoned at home the success of "Baylor" in
the larger world.

That said, however, he believed that an impartial jury would agree
that Jane's reaction had been unusually vindictive and sustained. In the
seven years between his one-nighter with Teri-from-Teaneck and his
recent once-a-weeker with Teresa-from-Last-Semester, he had been
penitently faithful, striving earnestly to repair the damage he reproached himself for having caused. After the dreadful weeks of tears,
hysterics, and virtual nervous collapse that followed her discovery of
his European journal, Jane had retaliated by screwing cold-bloodedly
first the divorce lawyer whom she consulted as soon as she was on her
feet, then the clinical psychologist from whom she sought counsel on
the lawyer's advice before taking legal action to separate, then her new
boss, when the psychotherapist advised giving the marriage a second
chance. Each time, she announced to her husband what she had done
and Baylor excused her — though he considered bringing a malprac-
tice suit against the psychologist and was not surprised when Jane's
boss subsequently eased her out of his department. A season passed
before husband and wife made love again, and if on rare occasions
something of our old ardor returned, our innocent spontaneity never
did. Jane made it clear that she would never quite trust him again or
love him as she had before. As "Baylor's" reputation grew, his wife
became ever more managerial, businesswomanlike, though her actual
office career declined to part-time stenography and filing. She quarreled with coworkers and supervisors, with maids and service people.
The couple did not quite separate, but our values did, and the voltage
between us through the intemperate High Sixties drove each further
from the middle ground than either would likely have moved otherwise. Bell-bottomed, blue-jeaned Baylor was a moderately busy peace-
marcher against the Pentagon, a critic of domestic surveillance ("Baylor

Bugged"), a civil-rights demonstrator, over Joe Junior's objections, back in their hometown ("Baylor Jugged"). Low-hemlined Jane grew increasingly hawkish and anticountercultural; thought Martin Luther King, Jr., a pious fraud and the Vietnam draft-resisters unpatriotic cowards; advocated expulsion for college activists who struck or trashed their campuses.

Of the twins, Andrew gravitated more and more toward his mother, to Baylor's disappointment. Never a scholar, the young man matriculated in prelaw at conservative Washington and Lee, did not resist the draft, and was drafted: unresolved oedipality, Baylor said to himself, stung with guilt. Juliette shared many of her father's values, but as the "oldest child" (by an hour) she inclined to conservative dress and unrebellious behavior, and strove with some success to mediate between her parents. We both credited her with, and sometimes teasingly blamed her for, keeping the household together.

And we both — Juliette, too — rather expected we would split once the twins were off to their respective colleges, but that final breach had never quite come to pass. Indeed, with the turmoil of the children's adolescence behind us, the noisy 1960s officially over, the war in Southeast Asia obviously winding toward its sorry finish, and the family's finances (thanks to the "Baylor" series) in ever better shape despite college tuitions, the couple seemed in our forties to be edging toward rapprochement. We exchanged our Columbia house for an older, more gracious one in Bethesda; we bought a vacation condominium near Ocean City and a small secondhand sailboat. Jane sometimes accompanied her husband on his lecture trips ("Baylor" was in middling demand on the campus circuit) if the place interested her, though she avoided the lectures themselves and the attendant socializing and would not read his books and articles.

In truth, those became the sticking point between us. "Baylor" was not Baylor, but more and more the invented self supplanted its inventor, who had perfected a merchandisable blend of candor and reticence, biographical fact and imaginative projection. "Baylor" idealized most appealingly Baylor's actual faults and strengths: his innocences, timidities, small vanities, frustrations; his patience and prevailing goodwill, affection for his household and concern for his country; his occasional braveries and small triumphs on the margin of history's larger text. Virtually everything in Baylor's life was grist for "Baylor's" mill, even the (discreetly intimated) strains of his marriage and the temptations attendant upon "Baylor's" increasing celebrity: "Baylor Does a TV Talk Show," "Baylor Encounters a Baylor Groupie." "Baylor's" tattered innocence reflected WASP middle America's, and WASP middle Americans warmly responded to his narration of its unraveling. The peculiar taboo in his house on acknowledging "Baylor's" existence no doubt helped sustain the enterprise, though it gave Baylor the feeling that his life was being lived Voice Over; as if the italicized narrator in his head more and more had all the lines.

Baylor Trips (1971), a collection of his articles from and about the sixties, won the National Book Award for nonfiction and was nominated for a Pulitzer Prize as well. The title piece, one of many done for *Esquire,* concerned a belated and disorienting experiment of "Baylor's" with LSD at the decade's end, representative of his generation's and class's experimentation with such other consciousness-alterers as radical politics and countercultural "life-styles." The title also alluded to "Baylor's" stumblings, and those of many of his kind: literally, in his instance, over his own feet (in a student apartment in Boston, where "Baylor" had gone to deliver a lecture and visit his daughter and been appropriated by graduate-student fans), but figuratively, too; stumbling, also, upon the realization that he was finally and contentedly "straight": a preferrer of good Bordeaux to Acapulco Gold, of struggling up to dropping out, of responsible heterosexual monogamy to "open-ended" and unorthodox "relationships." Jane had congratulated him with champagne but declined to attend the awards ceremonies earlier this year; Juliette had proudly and handsomely stood in for her mother at Lincoln Center. While he was in New York, however, his wife broke her own rule and against her better judgment read not the whole collection but the title memoir. It did not devastate her, as his old travel log had done. But far from finding it prevailingly affirmative of her own values and therefore encouraging for our future (not to say moving, funny, and brilliantly written as well), she found it disgusting. To "do" illegal drugs in his own daughter's company; to behave like an undergraduate in middle age among total strangers; no doubt to "score" here and there with promiscuous and impressionable coeds and bring home who could say what venereal infections — and then to make a public disgrace of himself and his family by bragging in print about such misbehavior . . . !

There ensued on his return to Bethesda our most scarifying quarrel in half a dozen years. Divorce was once again in the air; this time we went so far as to propose — and argue over — hypothetical divisions of property ("Baylor Pays Price," he imagined himself writing). Despite his angry protestations of innocence, Jane remained persuaded that he was an ongoing occasional philanderer and for much of the spring refused sex with him. He began to suspect that she was retaliating as she had done before, this time without acknowledgment. Indignant at her accusations — he had had plenty of opportunities and had declined them; that was virtually the point of "Baylor Trips" — he made a flat-out pass at Teresa Anginelli after class one mid-March Tuesday evening in College Park and learned that she had been wondering since Labor Day whether he would ever get up nerve enough to respond to her obvious signals. Well, he had missed them; no doubt there was a "Baylor" piece in that. Moreover, once he had got his nerve up, it took three assignations to persuade his penis to follow suit: a "Baylor" piece there, too. But when his potency more or less returned, his manhood welcomely returned with it, like a strong melody one had forgotten that one had forgotten, in the embraces of this frankly admiring fan not much older than Juliette — a fan who, despite her aforementioned threat, was amused to call herself "Baylor's Italian Piece."

Jane must surely have detected the change in him — his renewed self-confidence, his sharpened interest in all sorts of things, together with a good-humored new indifference to her — and felt her accusation vindicated. That she did not make a particular issue of it or pursue the matter of divorce reinforced his suspicion that she must have an affair of her own in progress. Thus we entered the summer, in Baylor's narrator's words, *like a couple living in (and living out) a John Updike novel.*

But however uncertain and essentially unhappy his and Jane's home life, he had seldom felt his imagination so enabled as in this year's first half. His new book-in-the-works bade to be a corner-turner as well as a page-turner, bringing together his earlier attempts at fiction and his later strengths as personal essayist and commentator on our times: tentatively titled *Baylor's Kid Sister,* it was a satirical fantasy in the vein of *A Connecticut Yankee in King Arthur's Court,* about a young American hippie feminist in 1968 (the invented "kid sister" of the title, an amalgam of "BeeGee" Behler and Teresa Anginelli, garnished with a touch of Teri-from-Teaneck), transported by drug abuse back to the court of King Shahryar and Scheherazade. Posing as Scheherazade's younger sister, Dunyazade, and returning periodically "home" for advice from "Baylor," "Sis" coaches Scheherazade through her thousand-night ordeal and saves the kingdom by curing the king's misogyny, but against her own principles she falls in love with his male-supremist younger brother, the handsome Shah Zaman of Samarkand, and only reluctantly comes back to the here and now, annealed but chastened by her adventure. It was — his editor, his agent, and his Tuesday-night lover all agreed — a winner. Accustomed to working hard (how little his typical writing students, even able Teresa, understood the professional's sustained hard labor), through April, May, and June he toiled almost feverishly: at the novel, on the lecture circuit (Teresa went with him to Albuquerque for a two-night stand, their first tryst longer than two hours), on his new syndicated newspaper column, called simply "Baylor," and (it being an election year) on a number of political-satirical "Baylor" pieces for *Esquire,* over and above.

Late in May, happily exhausted, he proposed to Jane a midsummer sailing vacation in, of all July places, the Caribbean. It would be low season down there then; yacht charters were cheaper and available on short notice; the beaches and anchorages would be less crowded than Ocean City and Chesapeake Bay, the weather no more subtropical, the scenery better. Renting our vacation condo at local high season would pay part of the freight; the balance we could easily afford (though he had privately in mind something like "Baylor Cruises Virgins in Sinking Ship" to justify charging off his share of the cost as a business expense): call it his forty-second birthday gift. More experienced sailor-friends had reported that the boat handling and inter-island navigation were well within our capacity and had recommended a reliable Annapolis agency for Virgin Islands bareboat charters.

Jane shrugged. Her latest job — volunteer office work with the American Red Cross — was going the way of its predecessors; she was convinced that the black office manager was practicing reverse discrimination against her white staff, to the point where Jane was ready to quit or bring suit or both. But was her husband prepared to miss two or three in a row of his Tuesday nights out?

She had taken, lately, to such knowing insinuations. "There are no

Tuesday nights in the summer," Baylor reminded her neutrally, hoping he would remember that line for "Baylor's" possible wry use. "School's out." We could even bring Juliette along to keep us civilized, he added good-humoredly, if our daughter can tear herself away from her A-rab friend.

Jane shrugged again and poured herself another frozen margarita from the blender.

The free port of Charlotte Amalie, St. Thomas, noted Baylor the tourist after clearing U.S. customs, *is unscruffy by Caribbean standards, rich in happily shopping Americans even in July, and in fact an agreeable place to shop: Dronningen's Gade and the other picturesquely peeling stucco alleys of the restored market area.* Remark, he instructed "Baylor," that cars drive on the left here, in the U.S. Virgins as well as in the British. Remark that homely cotton pullover tops made of colorfully labeled flour sacks from Guatemala are a big item this year with us affluent Statesiders, both male and female.

Terra firma proved restorative for all hands. Joe and Betsy were clearly enjoying themselves for the first time since deplaning yesterday morning at the Beef Island airport in Tortola: it was their first vacation ever outside the United States, and like kids turned loose in a Toys "Я" Us, they were crowing now over the duty-free booze and Japanese cameras. Juliette and Jane admired gold hoop earrings and agreed not to buy their flour-sack tops until after lunch, by when they'd have scouted the inventory. And Baylor's head verged upon reclearing for the first time since yesterday's anchoring fiasco. Taking his cue from his womenfolk, he only reconnoitered the waterproof Rolexes, Omegas, and Seikos before lunchtime, to get a sense of prices and features and of the competition among dealers in the neighborhood. By half past noon, after an agreeable hour's strolling among the gades, through cassette-taped reggae and calypso floating from Sonys and Panasonics in every market stall, he had narrowed the options to two models of Seiko and two shops well off Dronningen's Gade, where low-season prices were a few percent lower yet.

"Conch-chowder time, Aunt Bets!" Juliette pronounced the mollusk's name "East Dorset–style," the *ch* like that of *chowder*; it was the forenoon's running tease since her aunt had innocently read it off that way from a restaurant sign back at the harbor.

"I b'lieve she means *conk kowder*," came back her uncle Joe, an ever-ready razzer. "Us poor rednecks'll settle for a cheeseburger'n'a Bud."

"You will *not!*" declared Betsy, and she punched his big arm; then she added, to us, "I swear." Juliette flagged a cab — since little-girl-hood she'd had an odd gift for spotting empty taxis and cars about to vacate parking spaces before either of her parents saw them — to fetch us to the Sheraton St. Thomas, whose restaurant Jane believed she had read a good notice about in the *Times*. With a large tip in advance, Baylor bribed the cabbie to carry all five of the party, against company policy; four, however, the fellow decreed, must sit in the back. Joe Junior — the most "space-intensive," as Juliette put it — was elected to sit up front; the three women and Baylor, joking, chuckling, squeezed themselves into the rear, lean Juliette perched on her father's lap.

"Lucky mon, hah?" joshed the cabbie, and Baylor readily agreed. It was, in fact, complexly stirring to hold his grown daughter thus as the taxi wended through crosstown traffic. How many years had it been since she'd sat so? In what foul and dangerous jungle was her twin brother maybe sweating at that moment, he whom Baylor used to gallop on one knee, with Juliette on the other, the day before yesterday, it sometimes seemed, two steeplechasers taking the jumps? The recollection dizzied him; the apprehension for Drew's sake, too. At the same time, the gold hair fluffing into his face with the window breeze, the trim thighs atop his Bermudas, shifting on his lap as the cab turned corners — all felt indecently sexy. Juliette was a better-put-together young woman than Teresa Anginelli; better-looking even than Jane had been at her age. That Musalām was one damn lucky Mussulman.

Their cabbie proved to be a cheerful and garrulous native son who had once visited cousins in D.C. and claimed to be a fan of the Baltimore Orioles but couldn't recall having seen Chesapeake Bay. "God's country!" Joe Junior assured him. Betsy asked, incredulous, "You mean you never ate steamed hard-crabs?" "Ate plenty steam conch," the cabbie teased, grinning in the rearview. "Crack conch, scorch conch, fritter conch — just like home!" That subject broached, he advised against the Sheraton for lunch if conch was our objective and recommended instead a place back near the harbor.

"Native place, is it?" Joe asked. Baylor winced at his tone: cordially skeptical, as if he were back in *Lagoon* country instead of a bustling tourist port. And his brother added with a wink, "One of your cousins runs it, right?"

But the cabbie seemed unannoyed. "No, mon! Cost too dear for us! But the ladies like it, you know? Prit-ty place. Green Tree."

In the event, we were all so taken with the fellow that we bade him wait while we made a quick inspection of the Sheraton grounds and restaurant (sure enough, no conch on the menu) and the associated marina, where our driver pointed out to us serious cruising yachts from around the world, many refitting after long ocean passages.

"Boyoboy," sighed Juliette, smoothing her hair and shifting position on her father's lap. "Someday, huh?"

Then he drove us back harborward, nattering on agreeably en route about his family in response to the women's questions. His wife ("smahta than me") was a high-school graduate and worked in the customs office; another, earlier wife had taken their young son off with her to Toronto, Canada, some years ago. "Cold up there, mon!" He himself had never seen snow. At the Green Tree Restaurant, Joe Junior paid the fare, gave him another large tip, shook his hand sincerely, and declared that he was right pleased to've made his acquaintance. Betsy, too, shook his hand. Juliette and Jane thanked him for the restaurant recommendation — "Hope you thank me afta!" he said, laughing — and Baylor instructed "Baylor" to perpend that the St. Thomasians' reputation for unfriendliness seemed a bum rap: not only this cabbie but the ferry crew, the customs agents, and the marketplace salesclerks had all been prevailingly cheerful, even high-humored, so far.

Over conch stew and Heineken's dark — which even Joe Junior mock-grudgingly allowed were worth passing up his usual lunch for — Baylor decided, with Juliette's help, to buy the Seiko Sports 100 with rotating bezel for measuring elapsed time instead of the dressier fixed-bezel model, though both were waterproof, quartz-crystal jobs and God knew what he'd ever use the bezel device for. Barbecuing lamb chops?

"Navigating old *So Far* out of Soper's Hole," Joe suggested with a chuckle, "better'n you navigated us in." Though not malicious, the tease was tactless; but it also oddly reprised Baylor's narrator's use of the words *so far* a few sentences back.

"Time your lectures with it, Dad," Juliette advised — another innocently unfortunate reference, as Baylor suspected that Jane suspected he had not been alone that weekend in Albuquerque.

"I could do that," he agreed, and he turned to his wife across the table corner with what he felt to be a friendly smile. "Anyhow, I'll miss my old Bulova."

Matter-of-factly she replied, "I doubt it," and went on with her stew.

"I will," Baylor found himself insisting. To the company he declared, "I've loved every wristwatch I ever owned, starting with my Ingersoll Mickey Mouse. What a timepiece! And that Omega you sent me for my fourteenth birthday," he reminded his brother, "the same day we heard you were missing: that watch lasted me through high school and college, and it was still running fine when Jane gave me the Bulova for my twenty-first. It's in a drawer back home right now, almost as good as new."

"So why buy another one?" his wife asked without looking up. "You didn't need mine in the first place."

"Mom," Juliette protested. "That's not what he meant."

It was not, but Baylor let the provocation pass. As Joe Junior started in on how *his* Navy Post Exchange Rolex had survived the South Pacific with its owner, Baylor reflected about himself that he had likewise more or less loved every woman he'd ever gone to bed with — not a great number — and that that circumstance doubtless helped account for his inordinate postcoital preoccupation, seven years ago, with Teri-in-Tangier: a conditioned reflex of affection. Other people's wristwatches were usually replaced because they were worn out; his had characteristically been set aside, still going strong, because they were being replaced. He could almost imagine that his old Ingersoll, wherever it was, would still tick along faithfully if rewound, as it had done through the years when, having outgrown it, he wore Uncle Josh's Longines-Wittnauer. He had in fact more than once fetched out "Joe Junior's" Omega to wear while "Jane's" Bulova was being cleaned and oiled, and had enjoyed each time the old feeling that he was going back to where he'd somehow left off: rejoining some parallel track of his life, resuming some alternative plot of "Baylor's" story. In the same way — until last night, at least — he had often felt that as the hands of those successive watches wound around, and all about him aged and put their pasts behind them, there was a part of him ready like his Ingersoll and Omega to take up exactly where it had left off, as if no time had elapsed. His mortification over that stolen Bon Ami cleanser, for example, still stung whenever he saw a can of that product, as if the episode had happened last Tuesday rather than twenty-eight years ago. Visiting the Dorset Municipal Cemetery with Juliette some seasons past, he had told her the story of the dandelions on "Bijou's" grave and been moved to tears, not by that memory alone but by an almost swooningly strong recollection of his boyhood tryst there with Daisy Moore — in and out of asylums herself these days, like her mother before her. He could pick up that connection, he had felt, exactly where it had ended in 1944, except that now he would bring to it a much more seasoned understanding than he had been capable of back then. He clearly remembered lines of their dialogue on the Island, just as he could still see clearly, apropos of nothing, the "Lifter" out at the Albany Brothers cannery, the tomato truck overturned by angry picketers there in '37, the seedy office of the Bellanca pilot Howard Garton in the Avon airport, with its smell of cigar smoke and "old Bessie's" engine oil.

Baylor's Arrested Development Jumps Bail.

Through the first, or "British," half of his forty-second-birthday gift to himself, things had gone well enough, considering. Waiting for Juliette's Boston flight to arrive in San Juan, he and Jane had actually strolled the Aeropuerto Los Angeles hand in hand, "up" for our unusual vacation. On impulse he had bought in a concourse shop three pukka-shell necklaces, and though Jane had declined to wear hers, she had made no jibes about his "going hippie." Our daughter, true to form, had donned hers immediately after kissing us hello at her gate, then rehefted her seabag and set about reinforcing the spirit of happy family adventure. On the leg from Puerto Rico to Tortola, as the old BVI Airways DC-3 banked over emerald and purple water, she looked forward enthusiastically to snorkeling the reefs with her parents — nothing to it, she assured us novices; not like scuba diving — and after mentioning only once how much she missed her Musalām already, she wished repeatedly that her brother could be with us: the family adventuring together again, as we had done through Europe. . . .

That evening in our hotel in Roadtown, and the next morning at the charter-skippers' briefing and boat checkout, she had been a real pal, reviewing with her father the unfamiliarities of diesel engines, marine refrigeration, ship-to-shore radio, and battery banks (our little sloop back home had a hand-start outboard and an icebox); going over *So Far*'s galley equipment and provisioning with her mother. After making our first short passage across the Francis Drake Channel and our first Caribbean anchorage in the Bight of Norman Island, we had agreed: "So far, so good."

For some days thereafter, our weather held prevailingly fair as we zigzagged upwind from island to island, anchoring here for lunch, here for snorkeling or exploring ashore, there for the night. We became adept at plotting compass courses between landmarks on the chart; at jiffy-reefing our sails when the trade winds breezed up or a quick afternoon squall swept down the channel; at judging depths and spotting coral formations by the color of the water; at reminding whichever of us was at the helm that the occasional red and green channel buoys, like the vehicular-traffic rules ashore, were the reverse of the U.S. system. Juliette duly instructed us in the pleasures of snorkeling the rocks and reefs, dispelled our apprehensions about barracudas and moray eels, which were essentially harmless, and pointed out sea urchins and fire coral, which were not. Father and daughter did most of the boat handling while Jane read and sunned herself, but she was a good sport about lending an extra hand as needed, and she planned and cheerfully supervised all the meals. Every afternoon, following the charterer's instructions, we would anchor in one of the recommended spots while there was still light enough to see the bottom through the crystal water; we would "back down" on the anchor to set it in three or four fathoms, and then Baylor or Juliette would snorkel it, pulling themselves hand over hand down the line to make sure that the flukes had good purchase and that any sharp coral in the neighborhood would chafe against chain rather than nylon. After a swim we would sip rum drinks and nibble hors d'oeuvres in *So Far*'s comfortably shaded cockpit; then by the long orange and violet evening light or a lamp hung under the bimini top, Baylor would barbecue on the stern-rail charcoal grill whatever Jane had chosen from the fridge while the women built salads and side dishes, or we would all dinghy ashore to some little island restaurant we had radioed ahead to for reservations.

With double discretion Baylor logged for future reference his impressions of all this: so as not to restir unhappy memories, he kept his journal posting as much as possible out of Jane's view and kept Teresa Anginelli altogether out of the journal, though from time to time she was inevitably in his thoughts. There was a trade-off in Juliette's being aboard: her presence was a pleasure in itself and no doubt helped "keep things civilized" between him and Jane, but in the confines of a smallish sailboat it also gave husband and wife (*this* husband and wife, at this stage of our history) no convenient opportunity to make love, as Baylor felt pretty sure we would be doing otherwise. The water and air were so voluptuous on our skin, the sea and sky so beautiful, the leisurely island cruising such exotic refreshment, and there was Jane frequently topless on deck and nude in the water, as were some other of the women on yachts round about. Ten years ago we would have invited our daughter to take a nice little dinghy ride around the anchorage for an hour, if Juliette hadn't initiated the idea herself, so that Mom and Dad could have a bit of private time. She would still have been more than willing now to do something of that sort at the least hint, but no such hint forthcame. Even so, she would announce that she was going to swim back and snorkel the Treasure Point caves again, or dinghy ashore at cocktail time in Trellis Bay to check out the Last Resort Restaurant even though we were cooking aboard that evening. After a moment Jane would say, "I guess I'll keep you company," or Baylor, "Why don't we all go?"

On our fourth evening out, in particular. . . .

We'd had a fine afternoon's sail from Beef Island up past the Dog Islands to the far end of Virgin Gorda; we had successfully negotiated the breaking reef into Gorda Sound by way of a tricky set of sailing directions in the cruising guide (from Mosquito Rock steer such-and-such a course until Necker Island lines up with Prickly Pear, then aim due south until the "Seal Dogs" reappear between Mosquito Island and Virgin Gorda before turning to port into the Sound); we had picked up a guest mooring for the night off the Bitter End Yacht Club, where we had dinner reservations. No anchor to be snorkeled this time, but we had taken a sweet late-afternoon swim and were lounging in the cockpit over planter's punches, pleased with ourselves and the world, before taking turns in the makeshift shower and dressing to go ashore. Deliciously fatigued and utterly relaxed, admiring his wife's and daughter's handsome bodies and for that matter his own as well, Baylor realized that the day was Tuesday, and was by that realization so aroused that he had to cover his lap casually with a beach towel. Just a few minutes later, Juliette (who perhaps intuited other things besides cars about to leave parking spaces a block away) excused herself to go wash up. Still camouflaging his tumescence, Baylor moved across the cockpit into her seat, beside topless Jane, and took his wife's left hand in his right as if just amiably. How strange, that even with Juliette out of sight he no longer felt free to take her breast as well. It occurred to him to wonder, unfairly but not unreasonably, whether there was some man back home who *had* that easy freedom, once his.

"Are you glad you're here?" he ventured. She compressed her lips briefly — a flat-line smile, accompanied by a glance that asked, Are you sure you want to raise that question? — and acknowledged, neutrally, "It's nice."

"Jane." In one motion he bent to kiss her farther breast and tucked our clasped hands under his towel. His wife neither recoiled from nor responded to these overtures but sipped her drink indifferently with her free hand while he stroked himself with her other and kissed her nipple. Over his head then — in a tone more clear than intimate, and tinged as much with sorrow and perplexity as with contempt — she declared, "I don't know what to call you."

That was that. If Juliette hadn't been along, Baylor guessed we would have had something out then and there—and perhaps headed back the next day for Tortola, Washington, and separation proceedings. As it was, he let his wife's equivocal challenge hang in the air rather than blow the evening, the vacation, and what remained of the marriage. Joe and Betsy — from whom the strains in Baylor's house had distanced him further than ever in recent years, and whom on a reckless compensatory impulse he had invited to join us for the second week of our cruise, not really expecting to be taken up on the invitation — were scheduled to meet us in Roadtown two days hence; he would hate to call that off, now that plans were made and money paid. Moreover, whatever Jane had going on the side back home, if anything (but there must be something: so still-vigorous a woman, and so little real intimacy remaining between the two of us), it was likely no more serious than his Tuesday-evening affair in College Park, which he had no interest in escalating. Who could say but that by age forty-five or fifty we would have put these final growing pains behind us and, disabused of innocence, learned to relove each other and value our marriage till death really did us part? Though he detumesced almost at once, he nuzzled his wife's right breast a few moments longer, then bussed its companion and — when Jane turned her lips aside — her cheek and her fingers before releasing her hand.

"Same here," he said, just as equivocally, and he fetched up his cocktail glass as if in toast. Jane bottoms-upped hers and asked politely for a refill if he was going below.

The Bitter End Yacht Club (so named, Baylor reported to his journal, aside from the nautical allusion, for its being the eastmost developed anchorage in the Virgins and thus the turnaround point for most charter cruises) maintained shark pens under the inboard end of its dinghy dock — a half-humorous reminder that visitors not spending the night ashore should mind their alcohol intake. Juliette assured her parents that sharks in general were as misunderstood as barracudas and moray eels, and that the particular specimens lazing on the bottom under the dock lights were sand sharks, scarcely more dangerous than large catfish and doubtless kept so well fed that one could swim among them in entire safety.

"Our biological daughter," Baylor teased. All the same, the three of us stood soberly, so to speak, on the dock for some moments before going in to dinner, and again en route back to *So Far*'s dinghy afterward, regarding the black shapes below. Jane, especially, seemed lost in thought, entranced. *Suppose she should fall,* Baylor thought, watching her stand on the dock's very edge, pensively stroking her fine chin. *Or jump.* Would he leap in after her, reckless, or simply try to reach out a hand from the high dock? He scolded himself for imagining her . . . *tearfully refusing his assistance.* . . . No doubt he would miss her dreadfully, despite everything.

The night was moonless and a touch cool for late June in the Caribbean. Once away from the dock, Baylor found himself motoring the dinghy through near-absolute darkness toward the row of tiny anchor lights out at the club moorings, of which ours was the farthest. A fifteen-knot breeze piped through the slot between Virgin Gorda and Saba Rock to the northeast, and although Eustatia Reef sheltered the anchorage from waves, he was reminded that that was the black Atlantic over there, rolling vastly in all the way from West Africa.

"No stars!" Juliette called from amidships, over the racket of the dinghy's outboard engine. When Jane, in the bow, didn't reply (it was so dark that from his stern seat Baylor could scarcely see her up there), he did:

"Nope."

His wife had put away more wine than usual through dinner while Juliette gave us to understand that Musalām was not to be regarded as a passing fancy: when their Woods Hole summer ended, she would be moving in with him back in Boston, and if his postdoc studies took him elsewhere before she finished her baccalaureate, she was prepared to transfer for her senior year or even postpone her degree. There were things that Baylor much wanted to ask and advise, but he knew that Jane half blamed him for this connection of our daughter's — his "liberal ideas," his "permissiveness" — and after that standoff at happy hour he was reluctant to say anything that might provoke a family quarrel. Had Juliette chosen the moment deliberately, he wondered, or had she simply been filling the dinner-table distance between her parents? His resentment festered; once we had located and reboarded *So Far,* the family went directly to bed, out of sorts. When Joe and Betsy joined the party, he saw now, we would be a crowded ship's company for sure, even in the best of humors; for the present we slept comfortably enough in three separate berths: Jane in the forward "double," Juliette in the fold-out dinette berth, also advertised as a double, and Baylor in an ample though very low-ceilinged quarter-berth aft, from which he had ready access to the cockpit if necessary. There in the darkness he listened to the wind in our standing rigging and the wavelets slapping our waterline, twelve inches from his ear, and punished his wife with lustful reveries of Teresa Anginelli, who had likely missed him that evening no less than he her. Indeed, once he heard his daughter breathing deeply in her nearby berth, he discreetly masturbated, postponing climax while the hum of shrouds and stays increased to a whistle that rose and fell with the gusts. "Baylor's Italian Piece" was an intrepid semen-swallower whose winsome habit it was to raise her large dark eyes unblinkingly to his while he ejaculated into her mouth. As her image rendered him this service now, *So Far*'s rigging positively howled. The sloop fetched up sharply on its short tether; a shower of lightning and a tattoo of rain swept Gorda Sound.

The next two days were downhill. Intermittently squally weather stayed with us: a "norther," though the wind held mainly northeast at twenty knots and more. We spent a morning grousing about ashore, hoping the sky would clear. At an apparent near-noon break we unmoored and headed out of the Sound, carefully reversing our entrance maneuvers, only to find the Seal Dogs shrouded by a squall exactly when we needed a fix on them to make our turn, and the water uniformly gray in the neighborhood of Colquhan Reef, where we needed to see what lay ahead before our depth-sounder could tell us. Frightened, we retreated and remoored, hired a taxi, and spent a sullen afternoon touring Gorda Peak and snorkeling in light rain at the rock formations called the Baths: *like swimming in an unlighted aquarium,* Baylor told his journal that evening.

The next morning was only slightly better: overcast and even windier but less showery. As our itinerary was downwind to Roadtown, where we were to rendezvous that afternoon with Joe and Betsy at the charter agency, father and daughter voted to slog through it if possible. Inasmuch as we were the boat handlers, Jane had no real veto, but she pronounced the plan damn-foolish and sulked in the cabin. Wearing life vests over lightweight foul-weather gear, we exited Gorda Sound without mishap, powering into ever-larger seas as we entered the more open waters of Drake Channel. Just when we had reached the point where the larger waves were stopping the sloop dead in its tracks, drenching us in cold salt spray, and making Baylor wonder whether we *weren't* being maybe dangerously foolish, we managed to bear off around Mosquito Rock and put the whitecapped seas first abeam and presently abaft, on our starboard quarter.

"Yay for us!" cheered sopping Juliette. Baylor, too, was exhilarated, the more so when we were able then to crank out the jib, shut down the diesel, and tear along Tortolaward at six knots plus.

But Jane wasn't having it, even when the sun broke through and the abovedecks crew shed their life vests and slickers. At Juliette's urging she joined us in the cockpit, but she sulked against a cabin bulkhead, read a Taylor Caldwell novel she'd bought in the San Juan airport, and ignored the handsome views of the islands — Dog, Ginger, Cooper, Salt — passing by to port. She had him in a corner, Baylor fretted to himself, what with his East Dorset kin about to join the party, and she would make the most of it. In Joe and Betsy's presence she would cope amiably with the inconvenience of their company while giving him a programmatic, spontaneity-killing cold shoulder and, in whatever private moments befell us, letting him know that the couple were impossible; that he had been a fool to invite them; that his attempts to keep things high-spirited were ridiculous.

All of this came to pass. Jane stayed behind on the boat while Baylor and Juliette taxied into town to meet the new arrivals, and his heart sank at the sight of his older brother and sister-in-law climbing out of the airport jitney. They were so *big!* Their clothes cried out American Hick, and contrary to Baylor's instructions they had brought along a large Samsonite suitcase in addition to Joe's old Navy duffel bag. "Didn't have but the one," his brother would explain, dropping his jaw and widening his eyes, as was his habit, "and be damn if we'd go buy a fancy seabag for a six-day trip. Plenty of beer on board?"

Juliette's presence now was all asset. Childless themselves, Joe and Betsy had always been fond of the twins; Baylor was especially grateful to his brother for having introduced Drew and Juliette to such tidewater pleasures as fishing, crabbing, and waterfowl hunting, which he and Jane had no taste for. Though the differences between the two households — and between the brothers' temperaments since earliest boyhood — kept the adults from any real closeness, the twins had spent time all through their childhood with their East Dorset aunt and uncle, and by extension with their grandfather and their great-aunt Rachel. Juliette could argue earnestly with her uncle Joe's hawkishness about Vietnam and his contempt for civil-rights "agitators," as Baylor could not without reopening serious old quarrels. She could good-naturedly chide her aunt Betsy (as Jane could not) for wearing a 1950s-style beehive hairdo on a sailboat cruise ("Fifties-style is what I am, honey," unruffled Betsy would reply. "We won't be going in the water anyhow") and lay down the law about smoking when the sails were up. Baylor had somehow repressed the fact that both Joe and Betsy still smoked tobacco; his own household and nearly all their friends had quit. He suspected thankfully that Juliette's spiel about windblown sparks' burning holes in the Dacron sails was her tactful way of reducing the amount of smoking on board.

We were a long time getting the newcomers and their gear secured:

one had to break into Joe Junior's endless, battering, circumstantially detailed anecdotes to point out anything about the scene around us or the operation of the boat, even to move from jitney to cab, street to pier, cockpit to cabin. He clearly preferred sitting around telling stories over beer to going sailing. "Iced tea for me," Betsy called down the companionway to Juliette in the galley, "with lots of ice and a little lemon. Can we make some fresh?" Juliette told her, laughing, that she'd have to settle for canned Lipton's aboard and go easy on the ice. The couple hinted broadly, Betsy in particular, that they were more interested in exploring Roadtown than in putting out "right away" to sea. "I've never been much of a one for boats," she confessed. A quick shower came through ("Good-bye, beehive!" Juliette teased), and by the time Baylor cut into his brother's relentless narration sufficiently to make it clear that Betsy could use her portable hair dryer, if at all, only when *So Far* was hooked up to dockside AC power — which would be the case only right there right then at the charter dock — it was really too late to set out for a decent overnight anchorage. Jane poured herself a glass of white wine and regarded her husband wordlessly. He and Juliette exchanged glances over Joe's reminiscence-in-progress, and his daughter suggested that maybe it would be a good idea to stay put in the agency slip for now and start out fresh tomorrow morning.

"I'll buy that," Joe Junior declared. "Bets'll cook us up a mess of steak and eggs for breakfast, and off we'll go to see ourselves some virgins." He chuckled. "When I'uz in San Diego in 'forty-three . . ."

Through the cruise thus far, our breakfasts had been juice, coffee, and half an English muffin each. Jane said nothing. The fivesome ended up taxiing back into Roadtown proper (in two cabs, and a grim ride it was for Baylor, alone with his wife in one of them) to stroll about through what remained of the afternoon, ducking into shops to avoid the brief showers. Then Joe Junior — who had literally almost not paused in the anecdotes that everything put him in mind of, addressing most of them to Juliette because Baylor, for one, had heard them all before — insisted on buying dinner for everybody while we were right there in town, if his kid brother the world traveler knew of a restaurant that we wouldn't get food poisoning at.

Hours later, back at *So Far*'s slip, he mused loudly, "Akron, Ohio?" and tapped his cigarette-ash into the harbor. Tired Baylor explained that charter-boat companies operated on "lease-back" to minimize their capital outlay: a couple in Akron, say, would buy (and name) a sailboat through the agency, lease it back for charter and maintenance, write off the cost as a business expense over the allowable five-year depreciation, use the boat themselves for two weeks each year (claiming half their airfare to the Virgins as the cost of checking on their investment), and finally either sell it or have themselves a free sailboat.

Less loudly, as if in reply, Joe Junior observed, "Your wife don't have much to say, does she." He and Betsy and Juliette then made noisy fun out of the cramped sleeping arrangements: Baylor and Jane jammed into the forward vee, our feet overlapping in the vertex, Aunt Betsy sprawled in the dinette "double," Juliette made do in the narrow settee opposite, and Uncle Joe squeezed his bulk into the aft quarter-berth. "Feels like a gawdamn coffin!" When all the lights were finally out, Baylor called wearily from his side of the vee-berth, "Sleep well, everybody. Tomorrow we go sailing."

"Yay," said cheerleader Juliette.

"I'm for it," her uncle agreed.

Her back turned to Baylor, from her side of the vee Jane hissed furiously, "*Asshole!* You fucking *asshole!*"

The insult shocked through him like electricity. Even in her worst hysterics upon discovering his journal half a dozen years ago, his wife's language had been only hurt and wildly angry, never contemptuous. A folding door closed off our forward cabin; possibly the others hadn't heard her. Baylor's nerves buzzed. He longed to lash out; in twenty-one years of marriage he had never struck her, but she had never called him such names before, either. So as not to make a scene, however, he stayed his hand, held his tongue.

As if her reviling him had eased some pressure, in light cotton pajamas Jane amiably scrambled eggs for all hands the next morning in *So Far*'s galley, chatting with Betsy about Joe Senior's declining health while bedding was stowed and the family took clumsy turns in the head compartment. Baylor, on the other hand, still shaken by the depth and ferocity of his wife's contempt, was subdued, passive. The weather remained unsettled: many dark clouds, abundant bright-blue patches. "On to Soper's Hole!" urged Juliette: the next stop in our projected itinerary. Through the day her uncle would make heavy ribaldries with that name, wondering whether Mr. Soper had been an Ivory or a

Lifebuoy man, etc.; the jokes stung Baylor afresh with Jane's insult. It was midmorning by the time we got away from the slip. The sunshine continued off and on, but the wind had fortunately moderated, and since our course was westerly it was an easy downhill sail for the newcomers' first day. In his brother's company, it was not difficult for Baylor to remain inconspicuously quiet; his hurt feelings hardened into an amalgam of anger and relief as Jane's triumphant cordiality persisted through lunch and the afternoon. With Joe Junior she became almost flirtatious. As the midday warmed, she changed into a bikini even scantier than Juliette's, and when Joe dutifully paused in his anecdote to wolf-whistle, she struck a cheesecake pose on the cabin top. Against his own prohibition of alcohol under way, Baylor went below for a beer.

"Bring me up one, too!" his brother hollered after him. "I'm not used to such sights!"

"Well, I guess you're not," affirmed placid Betsy.

Jane pointedly observed, "I thought we never drank alcohol before anchoring time," but she neither pressed the matter nor joined the drinkers.

Despite our late start we made good enough time toward St. John and Tortola's West End to pause for lunch and a swim in the lee of Fort Recovery before the final leg to Soper's Hole. "Y'all go ahead," urged Betsy, who had not moved from her spot in the cockpit all day; "we'll just watch." "'Deed we will!" Joe agreed, and he fired up a Camel now that the sails were down. So weary of him by then was Baylor that as soon as the anchor was set and cleated he dived overboard from the sloop's bow — and in midair realized that though he had earlier changed into swim trunks, he had neglected to remove his wristwatch. He turned and doubled, held his left arm high, and surfaced immediately, but the Bulova got soaked. What was more, in his impatience he hadn't lowered the stern ladder before diving, and Jane was still busying herself in the cockpit while Juliette shut down the engine and braked the steering wheel. He was obliged to paddle off *So Far*'s transom for more than a minute, holding his wet watch arm above water, before he could get his situation reported, the boarding ladder deployed, and himself back aboard.

"Now that's a darn shame!" Betsy sympathized, exhaling cigarette smoke.

Joe Junior put on his mock-astonished face and boomed, "Absent-minded perfessor!"

"Shit shit *shit!*" Baylor said, almost ready to weep as he toweled the Bulova.

"Should we rinse it in fresh water," Juliette wondered, "and then paper-towel it?"

"Soak 'er in oil," Joe Junior recommended, "till you get 'er to a watchmaker. Got 'ny Three-in-One aboard?" He began the story of his wartime Rolex.

Already the watch had stopped: five minutes before one o'clock, as if it were throwing up its hands.

"Nothing lasts forever," Jane coolly declared, and she lowered her sleek self overside for a swim. Nor did the accident dampen her spirits through the afternoon, as it did Baylor's. In the event, he both flushed the Bulova with fresh water and dipped it in oil (Johnson's Baby Oil, from Juliette's suntan kit, was as close as he could come to light machine oil), but there would be little chance of a watchmaker's services till he was back home, by when surely the salt water would have corroded the movement beyond repair.

"That was my get-married-and-go-to-graduate-school watch," he mourned to his daughter. "It's been with me longer than you and Drew have. For twenty-one years I've never taken that watch off my wrist except to shower and swim."

"And not always then!" Joe Junior teased.

"Tomorrow's your birthday," Juliette reminded him. "If we go over to Charlotte Amalie, you should look for a new one."

"Waterproof," her uncle advised. "Like my old Rolex. One time in Honolulu . . ."

On the back of the Bulova's gold-filled case, Baylor would note in his log the next day, Jane had had engraved in 1951 her then love-name for him, which she had used with little modification until our return from Europe and never thereafter. So infrequently did he remove the watch that he seldom saw the engraving and scarcely registered it when he saw it. Rinsing and marinating the Bulova now, however, he observed that the nearly two hundred thousand hours it had measured of his life had so effaced the engraving that only one who knew that pet name (there were but two such) could make it out.

Jane, back aboard, said nothing. As we moved on to Soper's Hole, the sun came out strongly for the first time all day, and though Joe and Betsy elected to remain fully dressed in the shade of the bimini, Juliette and her mother lotioned up and stretched out on the foredeck, out of anecdote range, while Baylor steered the boat. Jane even removed her bikini top and made no effort to conceal her still-handsome breasts as she lotioned them.

The strength of Baylor's remorse surprised him, for there were things about that Bulova that he had never much liked. It was a less dependable timekeeper, in recent years especially, than his old Omega had been; it had no sweep second hand; its gold case and rectangular design were a touch formal for his taste, particularly since the midsixties. Yet he missed it already, felt *lonely* for it, as he had heard one missed an amputated member. He was not in fact an absentminded man; it was Joe Junior's oppressive presence that had so rattled him, and Jane's sulking hostility. The sight of that naked bracelet of white on his left wrist, echoing the white band of his wife's toplessness, made him almost dizzy (the unaccustomed lunchtime beer had gone to his head, too). He asked his brother to take the helm so that he could fetch sun lotion for the exposed area.

"Would you get our camera out of my stuff if you're going down there?" Betsy asked him. "I gotta have a picture of this to show Dad-Dad and Aunt Rachel."

"I'm Popeye the Sailor Man!" sang out Joe Junior at the wheel.

By afternoon's end, when we rounded Frenchman's Cay and motored into Soper's Hole, the sky was gray again, and Baylor's spirits continued to sink with the hidden sun. Jane left her swimsuit top off when *So Far* turned into the wind, but she pulled on a shirt, knotting its tails instead of buttoning it. Space proved so tight among the unoccupied yachts riding at permanent moorings that Baylor considered picking up one of the few vacant buoys rather than anchoring, but then he decided not to risk the owner's showing up later and obliging us to move elsewhere in the dark. Several times he threaded through the anchorage, conferring with Juliette and the chart on the merits of this or that spot while Joe yarned on. Here with our longer scope we would possibly swing down on the moored boats if the wind shifted; here there was swinging room, but the depth was too great for a proper five-to-one scope, not to mention a more secure six or seven to one; over there the chart showed shallower water and perhaps adequate swinging room, but if we dragged anchor even a little way we would go aground. No previous anchorage in the islands had posed such problems. As we considered and rejected one alternative after another, Baylor felt his wife's impatience building in the bow and asked his brother rather crossly to cut the monologue for a minute so that he and Juliette could think.

"Aye, aye, *sir!*" Joe Junior replied, his astonishment this time perhaps not entirely feigned.

When we finally chose the least unsatisfactory spot (one in that third category), Juliette took the helm, as had become her custom, while her father went forward to lower the main plow anchor with its three-fathom lead of chain. From her perch on the cabin top, Jane remarked uncordially, "You make such a *production* out of everything," and for the second time in twenty-four hours Baylor wanted to hit her. He signaled Juliette to reverse the engine and paid out chain and nylon line while she called out readings from the depth-sounder: twenty-four feet, twenty, twenty-two, eighteen, sixteen. The sloop's anchor line was unmarked; when he estimated that he had fed about a hundred feet through the bow roller, he took a turn around the cleat to set the anchor — and for the first time on the cruise felt it skip and skid along the bottom instead of digging in.

"Twelve feet, Dad. Ten." The boat drew six, and two had to be subtracted from the readings to correct for the location of the sensor. Prudent Juliette throttled down and shifted into neutral just as Baylor thought he felt the anchor take hold; but when we shortened scope to back down again and set it, it pulled free. Nothing for it then but to retrieve all that line, raise the heavy plow, maneuver back to our approximate starting place, and try again — and again the thing slipped and slid along the bottom.

"Right tricky business, i'n't it," Joe Junior sympathized.

The sun was low now over Great Thatch Island, to westward, and in those latitudes darkness follows quickly after sunset. Given Betsy's leeriness about boats (she had not budged from her cockpit cushion since midmorning, not even to use the head), Baylor had been particularly anxious for things to go smoothly on her first night of "anchoring out." He was relieved therefore when, at the last possible moment, the plow seemed to dig in. There remained, however, only two feet of Caribbean under our keel; in coral waters that was not a safe clearance, as it would have been in the Chesapeake or Sinepuxent bays. But if a snorkeling of the anchor revealed it to be securely set, we could take up scope into slightly deeper water for the night.

"I'll go snorkel it," he said — to Jane, without looking at her directly, and then he called back to Juliette to stand by with the engine idling in case he signaled, through her mother, for her to back down on the anchor again.

"I *swear*," Jane said, exasperated.

Ignoring her, Baylor asked his brother to stand by on the foredeck in case the anchor had to be raised altogether and reset. "Aye, aye, sir," Joe Junior said again.

The light was failing; the harbor water was gray, uninviting, surprisingly cool, but Baylor's adrenaline took care of all that. In mask, snorkel, and flippers he swam forward to the anchor line, took a large breath, and pulled himself hand over hand down its long shallow angle to the eighteen feet of chain leading from the anchor itself. The bottom was a hard gray rippled sand prowled by spiny black sea urchins and strewn here and there with dead and broken finger coral. The plow, he was disappointed to see, had dug in only the point of its blade; the main fluke was simply wedged against a small coral rock embedded in the sea floor. He surfaced above it (four times his height) and with shouts and hand-signs instructed the foredeck crew to tell Juliette to back down again so that he could observe the set. Jane was talking or listening to her brother-in-law, but evidently the message got relayed; as he dived, Baylor could hear the diesel rev up and see the slack line tighten. The anchor didn't quite break free, but it set no more deeply, either, and wobbled so against the little rock that he knew it would drag in any real blow or shift of wind. He surfaced again, his ears and lungs uncomfortable from the depth, rested a moment, and swam halfway to the boat to explain the situation and give instructions. Jane, laughing at something his brother had said, ignored him. Holding on to the anchor line where it emerged from the surface, he shouted to Joe Junior that Juliette was to ease the boat forward a bit to take tension off the line so that he could reposition the plow by hand. Joe Junior was to take up the larger slack as necessary to keep the floating nylon from fouling the propeller, but he was not to uncleat the line; then, on Baylor's signal, Juliette was to back down again slowly and Joe pay out the slack until the pull set the anchor properly.

On Baylor's end this was hard work, in ever poorer light. The anchor was heavy, even underwater, and more trouble to wrestle free of its precarious grip than he had supposed. The bottom was like concrete — no wonder we had dragged. Shards of finger coral cut his hands as he manhandled the plow to a new position, taking care not to step on urchin spines. He imagined sharks gliding in from deeper water, even glanced over his shoulder to check, but saw only their normal prey: a few black-barred sergeant majors and silver-yellow goatfish. His lungs aching now, he pushed surfaceward — three stories up! — fetching with him a bight of slack line that had not after all been taken in.

When he regained both breath and bearings, he saw that Juliette had properly moved *So Far* well forward (more so than necessary; the hull was all but atop him); indeed, with so much slack line out, the light breeze curling over Frenchman's Cay had swung the bow off, and he was able to give instructions to his daughter directly. That was well, since Joe Junior and Jane appeared to be fooling around heedlessly up forward: Baylor saw his wife turn his brother's John Deere cap backward on his head like a baseball catcher's and give him a playful poke in the gut, while so much line floated about that it really could reach back to the propeller.

"Hey, you guys!" he shouted from the water, flippering to stay in place over the anchor while he gathered up large coils of the slack. "How about some help?" It was useless at that range to scold them for their negligence or repeat his instructions to Juliette; he might just as well pay out the line himself as the sloop drifted back on the wind, and then hold on while the last of the slack pulled him under so that he could watch the anchor set. "Just don't reverse hard till I wave you back!" he called.

"Gotcha, Cap'n," Joe Junior said back, and he tipped his cigarette. Jane was perched now on the bow pulpit as if to be photographed. Despite his labors Baylor began to feel chilled, and he knew that (Juliette's pooh-poohing notwithstanding) sharks other than harmless prowled those waters, in which, the cruising guides agreed, one ought not to swim after dark or with bleeding cuts. It seemed to take forever for the boat to drift down; in the gray light he was a lonely distance from it, treading water, when finally the last loose loop pulled from his hand. As it uncoiled he shouted "Okay!" — and then realized, as he prepared to pull himself gamely under to inspect the anchor, that that loop had wrapped itself around his left ankle, just above the flipper. He felt it drawing tight, called "Wait!" and ducked under to wriggle free while he could. The line had happened to coil, alas, "bitter end under" — with the lower part running back to the boat, the upper crossing it and dropping straight down to the anchor — so that when now the last slack disappeared, the loop was cinched. Alarmed, he thrust to the surface, churned with his free flipper to keep his head briefly above water, waved both arms overhead, and shouted, "Neutral! I'm caught! *Neutral!*"

His wife was alone in the bow, maybe fifty feet distant. Joe was for some reason ambling back toward the cockpit. Baylor's arm-signal was surely unambiguous, his call audible from the bow if not from the helm. In any case, voice and movement together must have spelled distress. But his last sight through the half-steamed face mask, before *So Far*'s momentum tightened the line further and drew him under, was of Jane's calmly signaling astern for their daughter to back down hard. "Back," she called. "Back."

The anchor set, or at least it caught on something down there and held, as it had done before. Eight tons of sailboat drew taut a hundred feet of half-inch nylon, some inches of which cinched like a tourniquet around his ankle. With not even a full breath left in his lungs after shouting, Baylor was held in painful suspension halfway to the bottom. Snorkel and flippers were useless; he could move neither up nor down, forward nor back. Far off at one end of the line was the copper-painted underbody of the sloop, black now in the dimming light, the engine churning relentlessly; down at the other, nearer end he saw the anchor arrested against broken coral. Well above his head a rippling patch of greasy light marked the surface, but his kicks and yanks and flipper-thrusts got him nowhere. The anchor line was as straight as a bowstring; it felt to Baylor as though he would be dismembered as well as drowned while dutiful Juliette, at her mother's bidding, backed and backed the boat. Heart and head pounding, he clawed off the caught swimfin, which had impeded his efforts to twist his ankle free. He pulled himself frantically head-downward on the line, at the same time waggling his trapped foot; in his struggle he bumped the face mask against something — his arm, the anchor line — and it half filled with seawater. His air was gone. Suspended, he felt his last seconds run as if swept by a sweep second hand before his lungs must gasp against his will and the water choke him. Those seconds ran. He gave up clawing at his ankle bond, closed his eyes against the stinging salt water, strained to hold and hold on yet to his nonbreath as he had done in certain boyhood experiments, and found himself bidding some sort of good-bye — not to anyone up there in the world above-surface but to whatever it was that for four decades had been con-scious of itself and done this and that, and had been called variously Simon and 'Simmon and Sy, Behler and Baylor, William, Bill.

Then he died.

But just before he did, Baylor felt the line ease at last (his consci-entious daughter finally satisfied, he supposed later, that the anchor must indeed be set, or Jane that a different work had been accom-plished). One simple motion freed his ankle. No longer suspended between worlds, he thrust himself toward their beckoning interface, at once immeasurably distant and just above reach. Surfaced at last, he gasped and coughed, choked on water, breathed in air, rested faceup to the gray sky before paddling weakly to where the line surfaced, too, and he could hold on to it and rest again. His chest and temples throbbed; he spat and snotted brine; his left ankle ached — but his spirit was shocked calm. It scarcely surprised or bothered him that no one was on lookout in *So Far*'s bow, or that when at last he made his exhausted way to the stern ladder and hung on some moments longer to gather strength, he heard the three women in the cockpit discussing marinades for London broil.

"You okay, Dad?" Juliette asked mildly over the transom. Her tone assumed he was.

"I'll be up shortly," he said back.

From out of view, Joe Junior called, "Rum and tonic or a beer?" Baylor didn't reply.

"See any sharks down there?" Betsy wanted to know.

"Oh, sharks," he heard Jane scoff. "I'm going in for a dip myself before we do dinner. Anybody else?"

As he climbed the ladder (no one thought to reach down and take his remaining swim fin), Baylor understood that he would not even mention the extraordinary mishap he had just survived. "Lost a flipper," was all he said, toweling off and at last approaching normal respiration. "Damn plow's still not really dug in."

His brother hmped. "Just ain't your day, is it?"

To his daughter Baylor said, "After dinner we'll put out the second anchor, for insurance," and he went down the companionway to get into dry clothes.

"What *for*?" Jane called irritably after him. "We've never bothered with that before."

"Cap'n's orders," Joe Junior said, laughing, and he put on his favorite expression.

His wife's provocation seemed to Baylor to come from another world; likewise her warning to his brother not to peek while she slipped out of her bikini and into the water. On a shelf in the head compartment his old Bulova lay nested in a wad of paper towels. He snapped on a cabin light and saw that in just the few hours since its immersion it had begun to corrode: under the misted crystal its gold hands were blackening already in that final Y, and its white face was dramatically discoloring. He rinsed and toweled his own face briskly, to revive himself.

But if Jane's taunts had lost their power to touch him, his new unprovokability seemed to spur her. "You're just showing off!" she charged — crossly, publicly — when after dinner he and Juliette did indeed set out the second anchor, a lighter-weight Danforth, at a forty-five-degree angle to the first. It, too, Baylor was pretty sure, merely hooked behind some coral instead of burying itself, but the two together ought to hold. All the same, with a hand-bearing compass he noted the bearings of the lighted ferry dock across the harbor and certain lights on nearby Frenchman's Cay, along with the depth shown on the sounder, as a baseline against which to check whether we shifted position during the night. "He's playing *Captains Courageous*," Jane said, sneering, to Joe and Betsy. "We've never done all this nonsense before."

Juliette mildly admonished her: "Mom."

"Can't be too careful," Betsy supposed.

Baylor could have replied that Jane had never swum nude before, either, except within the nuclear family (the term seemed apt for her volatility that evening), nor had she ever arguably tried to kill him thitherto. But he was as removed from her jibes — indeed, from her — as were the fish he imagined gliding past the anchors out there in the dark. He felt down there still; something of his soul had accompanied that lost swim fin. Not only Jane but also Betsy and Joe and Juliette (who was proposing a Dad's-birthday trip by ferry tomorrow to Charlotte Amalie) seemed to him to be floating in an enclosed dark space at the far end of some line, from the low and distant other end of which he watched and heard them.

Several times that night he left the forward berth and made his way quietly aft to the cockpit, to recheck those bearings, the water depth, and the lie of the boat. The readings were not consistent, but neither were they wildly out of line with the normal swing of the sloop on its anchors and the foot or so of Caribbean tide. In all likelihood, *So Far* was staying put. Overhead in the spangled firmament the trade winds moved through unfamiliar constellations. Joe and Betsy appeared to be sleeping soundly after all in their separate berths. Once, as he passed through the cabin, Juliette whispered, "Everything okay, Dad?," as if she were a child again in Columbia and he'd been checking some noise downstairs. "No problems," he whispered back. But every time he climbed out of or back into his side of the berth, Jane would hiss "Jee-*sus!*" or "What *is* it with you?" and draw her feet away from any possibility of touching his.

Between these excursions he slept fitfully and dreamed, among other things, that *So Far* had dragged anchor all the way into the Behlers' back alley in East Dorset. He saw the sloop high and dry out there in the bright morning when he looked down from his bedroom window across the back-porch roof and his catalpa-tree escape route. Another time he dreamed of Daisy Moore and of Daisy's shy, wide-eyed sister, whose name just now eluded him, though she had become a well-known photographer. He woke with a headache and a bone-hard erection; it was gray morning in Soper's Hole, and he needed to urinate.

"Happy birthday, Dad!" Juliette cheered from her berth, to rouse the others in time for breakfast and the ferry. But in the head-compartment mirror, Baylor looked to himself like a man who had seen his own ghost. As for the old Bulova, just overnight it had sea-changed into an archaeological relic, the hands encrusted now in their last position, the face stained with brilliant greens, blues, even oranges, as if the watch had been retrieved from a long-wrecked ship.

Which, in a sense, Baylor reflected to himself, it had been.

"On to the Japs!" Joe Junior cried when lunch was done, though in fact one of those Seiko dealers off Dronningen's Gade was Muslim-Indian-looking and the other presumably Near Eastern, as his shop was called The Marrakesh. "They're getting even for V-J Day," Joe liked to say of the Japanese economic triumph — in 1972 even more conspicuous in the free port of Charlotte Amalie than in the U.S. Here one had to look about to find an American-made car, truck, or bus (the few non-Japanese models were mainly Mercedeses); the shop windows were all Sony, Panasonic, Hitachi, Minolta, Nikon, Yamaha, as if Dronningen's Gade were the Ginza. Joe himself, however much he vowed that he bore no grudges from the war, stoutly bought American, at least the big-ticket items, though it wouldn't much surprise him to learn that his Zenith television's innards or his Chevy pickup's dashboard instruments came from Taiwan.

He decided now to have a look at the Texas Instruments pocket calculators he had seen somewhere in the marketplace — "Better check the place of manufacture," Baylor teased — while the women inspected Oriental rugs in a shop just around a corner from The Marrakesh. Lest that name provoke yet more unpleasantness from Jane, Baylor announced that he was going first to the Indian shop, Al Hind, to get their price on the Seiko he had liked in "the other place" — the model with the rotatable bezel. Should we lose track of one another, we would meet down at the ferry dock a bit before four.

He was not all right. In the forenoon his head had seemed to be clearing, but the lunchtime beer made him woozy again, as he had been on the ferry. From the rug place he turned onto the side street where he remembered Al Hind to have been located and found he had confused it with The Marrakesh. Chances were that their prices didn't vary by more than a few dollars; rather than asking directions and wandering about, he decided just to go in and buy the damned watch.

A different salesclerk was on duty: not the lean, light-coffee-skinned fellow with fine white teeth and trim mustache who had showed him watches that morning, but a young woman with handsome, generic third-world features of a sort Baylor had seen before in smart shops in Gibraltar and Tangier, a mix maybe of Berber and Levantine with something farther east and, in this case, perhaps Caribbean as well. When the shop-door tinkled, she looked up from adjusting dials on the inevitable tape player (from which whined Moorish-sounding music), caught sight of him in the wall of filigreed mirrors behind the jewelry counter, and smiled brightly even before turning his way. He specified the make and model of watch he and Juliette had decided on and, satisfied that the price was the same he had been quoted earlier, paid for it in U.S. traveler's checks without further bargaining.

The young woman showed him how to set the date and day of the week (abbreviated by the Japanese manufacturer in both English and Spanish: its Western Hemisphere model) and advised him, in an accent as smooth and as difficult to fix exactly as her lovely features, to let her make the stainless-steel bracelet quite snug, inasmuch as people's wrists "up north" are smaller in wintertime than in summer. Despite elegantly polished long fingernails she did this job expertly herself, there on the glass countertop, removing several links with a pin-punch and needle-nose pliers, fitting the watch to his wrist, replacing one link, fitting again till she was satisfied that the band was neither too tight nor too loose. She was about Juliette's age, maybe a year or two older, and even slimmer than his daughter. Her skin was untanned and flawless, her hair glossy black and lightly scented with something that Baylor decided to remember as jasmine, whatever it might in fact be. Her breasts were tiny but their nipples prominent under her white silk blouse; as she held and turned his wrist to inspect her work, he found himself musing on the disproportion between the small motion it would require for him to caress one of those nipples (three inches from his open left palm), as he suddenly yearned to do, and the large repercussions of so slight a movement.

Over her jasmine-scented head, as she bent to write out his receipt and to staple the spare links into a little envelope, he regarded in the wall mirror the reflection of her slender, paisley-skirted backside and of his own face contemplating it. He looked fifty at least! The plate-glass storefront reflected the reflection: a faint, receding series of old Baylors and of young, unaging women. So demurely yet untimidly did she smile now, so almost affectionately thank him and bid him good afternoon, that he was speechless with stupid love. He could only compress his lips and nod, stuff his folded receipt into a shirt pocket, the link-envelope into his Bermudas, and hurry from the store, shaking some inward head at himself.

In his addlement (he was also trying the Seiko's bezel, to get the feel of it and to refocus his mind) he turned the wrong way, either upon leaving The Marrakesh or at the next corner, which put him into a much narrower "gade" with only one or two shops. There was a rug place, but not the same one: it was open to the cobbled alley like a market stall. The lone old fellow nodding and appraising him from among its piled-up wares looked to Baylor like an Iranian rendition of his late uncle Josh, complete with cigarette holder. A hookah would have been more in keeping with the fellow's turban, the first Baylor had seen in Charlotte Amalie. Maybe this was a back entrance to the Indian place? He thought to retrace his way, but there appeared to be activity ahead, where the alley opened onto a larger gade or market square. Chances were he would see Al Hind up that way, or the Texas Instruments place, and maybe find his womenfolk buying their flour-sack tops.

Instead, he seemed to have strayed into some truly native quarter of Charlotte Amalie, which he did not recall having read of in the cruising guide. Nor were its natives your typical Virgin Islanders. The little city is a free port, more ethnically diverse than Tortola's Road-town or Christiansted in St. Croix; but this square of hardpan and dilapidated market stalls looked (and sounded and smelled) more Maghrebi than Caribbean. There was not another Caucasian face in sight, and most of the denizens wore caftans or djellabas. In the stalls were brass and copper wares and mounded dyes and spices, along with eggs, fruits, vegetables. Goats and sheep huddled near herd-boys here and there in the square itself, where also a turbaned professional storyteller held forth to a circle of listeners, as in the Jmaa el Fna. A snake charmer would not have been out of place there, or a camel. No automobiles or even motorbikes in sight; no streetlights, no sidewalks.

His unusual costume quickly drew small boys and others not so small, speaking Baylor could not tell what language among themselves and, increasingly, to him. As brightly as he could manage, he asked "Dronningen's Gade?" and pointed vaguely across the square. Much language came back, neither yes nor no, by the speakers' looks. Some smaller boys held out soiled hands for money. One touched Baylor's bare knee and laughed sharply with his companions.

"Made a wrong turn, I guess," Baylor said agreeably. A wiry fellow who could have been the brother of our morning taxi driver addressed him volubly and not quite cordially. Baylor's adrenaline stirred. Deciding to appear decisive, he nodded shortly, said, "I'll find my way, thanks," and turned to go back toward The Marrakesh. The boys clamored after and before him. The older fellow strode purposefully in step beside him, speaking sternly and gesticulating with one hand.

Several heavily loaded donkeys now blocked the nearest alleyway, which anyhow didn't look quite like the one he had wandered into the square from. In braided cane saddlebags they carried firewood, cereal grain, silent hens with trussed feet. Their drovers were brown, leather-faced, gray-whiskered old men with bare feet, torn shirts, soiled head-rags. Lean dogs yapped about their dusty ankles like the beggar boys about his. He felt half panicky, and rather more than half when the wiry fellow at his elbow now skipped a step ahead to face him with what sounded like a peremptory demand.

"I'm sorry," Baylor said, clearly but not apologetically. "I don't need anything from you, and I have nothing to give you. Excuse me." He strode on, but the fellow dogged after him, his tone unmistakably abusive now. People turned from their marketing to watch, their faces impassive. Some of the women were veiled! His heart beating faster, Baylor pushed on toward the next alleyway, past bales of silks and raw cotton, stalls of slaughtered fowl, rabbits, lambs. A bloodied butcher called to or at him. The boys around him laughed — and one snatched at his new wristwatch.

"No you don't!" Baylor scolded. The older fellow scolded him right back. To appease him, Baylor reached exasperatedly for a coin, but he found in his change pocket only the stapled envelope of spare watch links. "Here." He thrust it at the ringleader. "That's all you get."

The ploy worked, at least for the seconds it took for the fellow to inspect and rip open the envelope. Baylor stepped past him, the little ones swarming after, demanding their share. Alas, that next alley, now that he could see down it, seemed to lead not into town but to open fields, almost desert-looking, where his annoyers would be more likely to set upon and rob him than they were in a public square. Immediately down from that alley, however, was another, at the corner of which he thought he saw the "Uncle Josh" character standing, beckoning with short motions of his turbaned head. Forcing himself not to run (the fellow with the envelope was angrier than before; he waved the watch links before Baylor's face and cursed, while the boys caught at his shirttails, the legs of his Bermudas, his wristwatch again), Baylor forged on, not even considering why the old rug merchant should prove any less hostile than the others merely because he resembled a good-natured uncle now dead.

But he was. Though the rug stall could not have been the same (it was on a corner, for one thing), the dealer was the man he had passed before, and to Baylor's unspeakable relief he scolded the boys sharply in their language, waved the angry young man away, took Baylor's elbow, and gestured him into his place of business. The boys stood respectfully back. The "cabman's brother" was not so easily put off: he crumpled the torn envelope, threw it at Baylor's feet, and spat after it, rehearsing his grievance (Baylor guessed) to the elder man, who replied more temperately while urging Baylor through the divided counter of the rug stall and toward — welcome sight! — a doorless interior room where more rugs were visible through the portiere.

"Not good to tour souk without guide," his rescuer chided.

"So I've learned!" Baylor's laugh was a touch feverish — and he was not blind to the likelihood that a large tip, or maybe even a small rug purchase, was in the offing. Any port in a storm! As if the merchant's thickly accented English had lifted some spell, the heckler outside now found some English, too, for a final execration as they pushed through the beaded portiere and into the inner shop:

"Go home *New*-York!"

"Mm mm mm," the old man muttered. "You sit for tea. I speak to Muhammud." Gesturing toward yet another, heavier portiere at one side of the little room, he stepped back into the outer stall to reproach in stern but conciliatory Arabic (Baylor supposed) the indignant "cabman."

Mint tea, a scatter-rug souvenir — anything. Eager as he was to make his way back to Dronningen's Gade (he checked his new watch: three o'clock already, or 15 on the international outer dial. The date window read SAB 1; he would have to reset the weekday to English), he would gladly pay his savior's due. He spread the second portiere, expecting a tiny inner sanctum with two hassocks, a hookah, and a chased-silver teapot under a pierced-metal overhead lantern. Instead he saw a larger, brightly lighted display room, the far wall of which was a plate-glass window that gave back his reflection as he entered, in effect, from the rear. Karajas, Tabrizes, Bokharas hung resplendently about. On the street outside . . . tourists! Toyotas! Over near the cash register — from which area sounded incongruous but welcome calypso music — was indeed a teapot on an electric hot plate, tended by a young woman in a bright-red djellaba, perched on a stool. She looked his way and seemed a bit startled not to see the old fellow who no doubt employed her to work the tourist side of his shop while he handled the "native" trade. Although less delicate-appearing than the Seiko salesgirl, she was even more attractive — beautiful, in fact, with striking gray-green eyes and heavy, gleaming auburn hair.

She removed her eyeglasses. "Yes?"

"Yes!" Baylor said enthusiastically, chuckling with relief. "Your father —" He grinned, shook his head in apology, indicated the room behind him. "The gentleman back there. . . ."

She frowned uncomprehendingly. "I can show you something?"

Such eyes! "No, no," Baylor assured her. "I was just . . . passing through and made a wrong turn. Sorry to bother you!" Suddenly it mattered not at all about the tea, the tip, the thanks: that old man was no more going to come through that portiere than Uncle Josh himself from the Other Side.

"No bother," the clerk said mildly as he crossed the room. At the glass front door he turned and called back, "Be seeing you!" His voice sounded half crazed in his own ears. Traffic noise pushed in; the entrance-bell tinkled. The woman's gray-green eyes flashed himward over a tea glass, at whose rim her lips were quizzically pursed.

Over there was Al Hind, the other watch shop! And a few doors farther on, there were stout Betsy Birdsall Behler and slim Juliette, picking up and setting down leather handbags at a sidewalk table. Baylor waved and cried, "Jule?!" When his daughter looked around and made a little wave back, his eyes teared.

"Where've you *been?*" she chided cheerfully when he reached them.

He found himself hugging her, kissing her hair. "Hey!" she protested, laughing, and her aunt Betsy chuckled and said, "Welcome back, stranger!"

Baylor's life had changed.

Jane and Joe, Betsy reported, had finished their shopping and started back to the ferry dock. "It's time we did, too," Juliette opined. She was wearing her new flour-sack top: Molino San Rafael, with a faded blue icon of the grain-bearing saint. Hands on hips, she turned this way and that to model it for her father. He in turn showed off his new watch: "First one I ever picked out for myself!"

"Things here really are a bargain," Betsy declared. "It's a shame I don't need a blessed thing." She had bought souvenir ashtrays for "Dad-Dad" and "Aunt Rachel."

As they strolled together down toward the harbor, Baylor ventured that behind the rug shop they had seen him come out of (which had to have been, he realized now, the same one his wife and daughter and sister-in-law had planned to visit after lunch) was another, very different part of town.

"It's a reg'lar maze, i'n't it?" Betsy agreed comfortably. "A person could meet theirself coming the other way."

Surprisingly, Juliette took his hand and squeezed it, and Baylor understood that he would not try to tell even her, much less his wife, what had happened back there. He himself could not account for it, though as surely as he had known that "Uncle Josh" would not follow him through that second portiere, he knew as well that a helicopter ride, say, over the Charlotte Amalie marketplace would disclose no such exotic square as the one he had just returned from. As to whether, if he and Juliette should go back then and there to that rug store, they would see a portiere in its rear wall, and what they would find if they stepped through it — He checked his watch. They were out of time.

Had he been visited by the first bona fide hallucination of his forty-two years? If so, it was entirely unlike any hashish "pipe dream" or acid vision he had experienced or heard of, more in the nature of an *absence,* he imagined, of the epileptic sort — though an absence preternaturally present and filled. He would ask his doctor friends back in D.C. to arrange whatever neurological testing might reveal whether

his infrequent drug experimenting in the sixties had in any way affected his circuitry, but he knew in advance that the tests would show
nothing.

Yet he knew also that he had been changed — no less profoundly
than his old Bulova, though less conspicuously — and that his life was
about to follow suit, perhaps from the same cause, as if, having been
pulled so deep, he had not altogether resurfaced and never would.

"What took you so long?" Jane asked indifferently as they approached. Beside her, on a bench in the ferry waiting room, Joe Junior
began an account of his own doings since lunchtime.

Clearing customs to reboard *Native Son*, Baylor regarded the familiar stranger regarding him from his passport photo, and the arbitrary
symbols of the name beside it, which with only a slight refocusing of
his mind he could make look as outlandish and unintelligible to himself as Arabic. Juliette wondered whether the perky customs clerk
might be the wife of their forenoon cabbie. Her mother thought the
flour-sack top was a bit on the large side; Juliette agreed but guessed
that it might shrink and really didn't mind either way. As if newly
endowed with genetic-X-ray vision, Baylor felt he could see more exactly than ever what there was of Jane and what of himself in each of
their daughter's speech-acts and gestures, and what of neither of her
parents.

"Anyhow, it was a bargain," Betsy marveled.

With a kindred vision he tenderly regarded them all: his mock-
astonished brother, as deaf in his way as their father, and as much
without guile; Jane Price (she would gladly revert to her "maiden"
name, he knew, when the time came), who would soon enough part
company with the Baylor he had all but become, and he with her.
Mercy on them, every one.

Back aboard *So Far*, he and Juliette made a little happy-hour ceremony of pitching his old Bulova out toward their invisible anchors,
an offering to the spirits of the deep. "Good-bye, dear old watch," he
said. Jane hadn't even asked to see his new one; nor did she or Joe or
Betsy come forward from the sloop's cockpit to see the gold-glinting
talisman arc up and out in the long Caribbean light and then plick
the calm surface of the harbor like an oyster shell. Now the five of
them would confer about what to do tomorrow and the days thereafter: a prospect that Baylor, fingering his pukka-shell necklace and

hearing "Baylor's" words in his head, contemplated with benevolent equanimity.

But if he never told any of those aboard the full story of his third voyage, he would one day write, *to himself Baylor told it over and over and over again.*

Five Interludes

1.

When Somebody, still stranded, wound up the story of his third voyage (a tale abbreviated in its oral presentation and more pitched, he hoped, to its present audience and occasion), Sindbad the Sailor cleared his throat, tapped his tub to rouse the baffled auditors, and said, "Well!

"Well. Very well, now, friends! What do we think of my brother's story? I beg you not to wait upon my opinion, as you have kindly done heretofore before voicing your own, but to speak your mind first and freely."

Ibn al-Hamrā, on his left, had already raised one red-faced finger. Without looking his way, Sindbad patted the fellow's plump near shoulder and declared, "We shall hear my soon-son-in-law's sentiments soon enough, Allah willing. Let us hear some other first, if other there is."

Seven diners frowned at their laps. Of the rest, Ibn al-Hamrā, waiting his turn, made mental notes upon his fingers; Kuzia Fakān, across from Still-Stranded, redrained her empty wine cup, burped politely, and grinned at no one in particular; Yasmīn turned uncertain eyes up-table toward her friend the teller, who shrugged back. Her father regarded them, then said again, "Well! Wine, perhaps, to whet our faculties. Yasmīn?"

Assisted by Jaydā, his daughter made her intricate rounds. At their fourth stop (after Sindbad, the distinguished-looking gentleman on his right, and her prospective fiancé), she bent to whisper into the ear of the beefy, dark-haired fellow who was seated this evening at her own right hand. He looked up wide-eyed (but not yet openmouthed, as was his habit) and pointed to himself in disbelief. But when Yasmīn favored him with a smile and a nod, he cleared his throat as his host had done and, like him, said, "Well."

Going on with her rounds, Yasmīn declared sweetly, "Our faithful Hajj Masūd has something to share with us."

"Yes!" that fellow conceded. "Well."

"Hajj Masūd," Sindbad acknowledged, and with a gesture of his open left hand, he bade him speak.

· "Yes! Well. Allah knows I am no expert in the storytelling way, only a purveyor of fine carpets by appointment to His Excellency our caliph and to the port city of Basra as well, not to mention the potential market in Serendib." He blinked hugely, drew a breath. "I shall not pretend to have understood, and so am in no position to judge, much less to believe, the more fantastic portions of our new comrade's story — which is to say, alas, the bulk of it. But I must speak in praise of the one episode I grasped, that in which the feckless cuckold Bey el-Loor accidentally touches the magic amulet he has purchased unwittingly from an ifritah and is thereby transported from his Never-Never Land to the endlessly fascinating Jmaa el Fna in Marrakesh, the Red City, only to be wizarded promptly back to his joyless kind after that taste of bliss. I particularly commend the portrait of that stern but just rug merchant Sayyid Ankh el-Zhash, whose painful duty it was to expel Bey el-Loor from Paradise, so to speak, before the cuckold could revenge himself upon his unfaithful wife — perhaps by corrupting the morals of those charming Maghrebi beggar boys. The role of rug dealers down through the ages in thus conserving the social fabric, if I may so put it, has not been sufficiently acknowledged hitherto in our literature; I salute Sayyid Still-Stranded for at least attempting to rectify that injustice. I myself have had occasion to do business in the Red City, where I toured the lively Place of the Dead, admired the decorative rotting heads of decapitated malefactors, lost my heart and very nearly my purse to just such winsome scamps as our friend describes, and did sharp business with just such a master rugsman as that Ankh el-Zhash. Indeed, were it not for the presence among us of our host's gracious daughter, for whose unsullied ears the tale is not fit, I could tell you of an adventure that befell me there with a certain woman of the Bedouin who was selling eggs in that very marketplace. . . ."

Touching his forearm, Yasmīn said, "Thank you, dear Hajj Masūd." The rug dealer turned upon the company his look of abashment.

"Allah preserve the Badawiyyat!" cried Kuzia Fakān, and she held out her last-place cup for refilling.

"Allah preserve the women of the Bedouin indeed," Sindbad said, "as I myself could wish to be preserved. Desiccation in their pure desert sunlight turns tart currants into sweet raisins like our Kuzia, whereas marination in the seven brines of the sea turns mild gherkins into sour pickles. But let us hear now some counteropinion, if any there be."

"By Allah, there be!" said Ibn al-Hamrā. He wet his lips so eagerly with wine that even without his fiancée's assistance he managed several purple drops on his clean caftan. Kuzia Fakān rolled her eyes and took another drink. Sindbad gestured for him to proceed.

"Our wise and ever-generous host," declared Ibn, "has schooled us in the art of swallowing the unswallowable. Our capacities enlarged by his example, we have taken unto ourselves not one, not two, but three several moral and aesthetic enormities, served up to us like a serial feast of buzzard barf by an outlander who for reasons of his own has seen fit to assume our host's name, as by his own acknowledgment he has assumed other names in the past.

"But having swallowed the unswallowable, comrades, are we now to digest the indigestible? Ought we not rather to follow our host's example from the second island of his second voyage — Moral Lesson Eight of the twelve given us thus far — and reregurgitate this narrative? Granted (as my colleague Hajj Masūd has observed), there is a sop of Islamic realism among the slop of infidel hashishery — as if one true magic charm could compensate for such false and charmless magic as music issuing from a box, or aerial transport by neither roc nor rug! In the same way we may find the odd scrap of decency floating by like Bey el-Loor's admirable brother's raft, adrift upon a sea of turpitude — as if a turban here, a veil there, could cover the naked immorality of the rest! In place of proper monsters, this interloper gives us monstrous improprieties; in place of straightforward giant serpents, he offers serpentine insinuations.

"What shall we make of his story's hero? Bey el-Loor's wife commits adultery for no better reason than that her husband has disported with other women, but far from halving her with a scimitar, as justice demands, or drowning her in a sack together with a live monkey and a rooster, he forgives her! When the daughter of his infidel loins understandably gives her virginity to a proper Muslim (who, we note with satisfaction, refrains from marrying the unbeliever), Bey el-Loor mildly disapproves, but he seems not to appreciate that the girl's value in the marriage market is thereby so much lowered that he will likely be obliged to sell her off to a white-slaver for whatever he can get. Surely, my friends, we shall now agree that we have heard enough from this narrative quarter. I for one beg our host frankly to call a halt to his so-called brother's so-called stories and get on with us to Serendib!"

Breathing agitatedly, Ibn al-Hamrā nodded his approval of his own proposition. Sindbad repatted his shoulder while looking our man's way. "Perhaps my brother would respond to these hard words?"

Somebody shook his head. "Let the tale stand or fall on its own. Its teller has had his say for this evening."

"Other comments, then?" invited Sindbad down the table. Yasmīn returned to her place and raised her hand, but her father wagged a negative finger at her. Kuzia Fakān flexed a few muscles where she sat, preparing herself to dance. The diners glanced furtively at one another and at her.

"As a matter of fact, yes," presently said the gentleman on Sindbad's right, who looked like a younger Hasīb Alī or an older Hajj Masūd. Pleased, Sindbad cried, "My old and loyal friend Talīb ibn Sahl! The floor is yours; honor us with your opinion."

"Well," Talīb said thoughtfully, "I quite concur with my distinguished colleagues that for recognizability and pungency, the marketplace episode of Sayyid Still-Stranded's narrative stands head and turban above the rest. I shall go so far as to suggest that in stories to come he would do well to build upon this sound foundation and add further touches of a kind with that magic bezel. I myself am partial to talking fish and the granting of extravagant wishes by beholden genies and would be pleased to see such flourishes of verisimilitude in our comrade's next tale.

"As for the obscure stretches of this one and the inexplicable behavior of its principal characters, I believe they are meant to echo the speech and behavior of those fearsome but ingenious apes in Sayyid Sindbad's story: unintelligible to us but not therefore meaningless. I would even venture that the general drift of the stranger's voyages grows ever clearer and increasingly apropos: whereas our host's sea journeys go from this civilized center of the world out to its barbarous margins and come richly back, our guest's do the reverse. We have now seen him for the first time stumble out of Ape-Land for some moments and into such dear realities as the muezzin's morning prayer call and the colorful sayings of rejected solicitors in the Jmaa el Fna. There are even nuggets of true wisdom, such as ought to have pleased our impatient brother Ibn al-Hamrā: Sayyid Ankh el-Zhash's great lesson, for example — 'Not good to tour souk without guide' — deserves to be graved in chalcedony, and when the cuckold repays that good man's kindness by slipping out of the shop's back door without buying so much as a prayer rug, his ingratitude is promptly punished by banishment back to the Island of the Apes, to his virago of a wife and his charming though compromised daughter. Are those not moral lessons?"

He leaned forward to look down-table directly at Somebody the Still-Stranded. "In sum, my friend, while much of what you say is still ape-talk to our ears, your stories appear to be improving in clarity and relevance night by night. If you harbor aspirations in the narrative way, you might consider apprenticing yourself, even at your present age, to one of our professionals, such as the one remarked by Bey el-Loor in the Jmaa el Fna. In time your tales might well approach the charm of theirs, and of our host's."

Both Sindbads bowed to this praise. Without waiting to be told, Yasmīn gratefully refilled the cup of Talīb ibn Sahl. As she did so, however, a dapper, keen-eyed fellow in the fourth place of honor (at her left hand) seconded Ibn al-Hamrā's negative motion. If the prediction of his esteemed fellow import-export merchant Talīb ibn Sahl should prove correct, he declared, then the outlander's fourth

through sixth voyages must fetch him to the gracious house of Sindbad the Sailor — where he already was! "If we are to hear further
adventures of the cuckold Sayyid Bey el-Loor," this critic concluded,
"let those adventures rather fetch him back whence he came, before he
corrupts the morals of this illustrious house as his own household was
corrupted."

"Hear, hear," applauded Ibn al-Hamrā. Somebody, too, nodded.

"Alternatively," proposed Ibn's new ally, "I vote that he produce
for our inspection that magic talisman from Marrakesh. Perhaps if he
rotates its bezel the other way, he will find himself back on the Island
of False Virgins."

"Alī al-Yamān!" protested Yasmīn. But her father, stern-faced, held
up his hand for silence. "You speak of voting," he said to Alī al-Yamān.
"Perhaps, indeed, before Kuzia Fakān delights us yet again, we should
vote on the question of whether tomorrow evening's entertainment
shall continue these narrative preparations for Voyage Seven or steer
some other course." Without consulting the sense of the table —
which would after all have been but voting on whether to vote — he
declared that he, Yasmīn, Kuzia Fakān, his adopted brother, and all
other members of his household would abstain; of the remaining eight
diners, let all in favor of proceeding in their wonted fashion raise their
right hands to Allah the all-knowing. Talīb ibn Sahl did so promptly,
followed by Hajj Masūd, diagonally opposite him. The others considered one another's faces. Presently the man seated between Talīb and
Somebody raised his hand, as did, more timidly, the man between
Hajj Masūd and Kuzia Fakān.

"But I should very much like to see that magic amulet," this last
said.

"As should I," Still-Stranded sighed.

"Opposed?" asked Sindbad. Up went at once the hands of Ibn al-
Hamrā, Alī al-Yamān, and an older fellow on Ibn's left. So meaningfully did those three stare then at the only uncommitted guest (a lean,
pale man about Somebody's age, on Somebody's right) that after some
moments of frowning and tugging his whiskers he half raised his right
hand — at the same time shrugging apologetically at our storyteller,
who smiled and shrugged back.

"We have a tie," observed Sindbad. "Loath as I am to contravene any of my dear friends, I suppose it falls to me to cast the deciding vote."

"No need of that," his daughter declared from her table-end. "This is no tie at all."

Her father raised his eyebrows. "Four–four is no tie? When did Allah change the rules of counting?"

"When He gave His followers the protocols of such feasts as this," Yasmīn asserted. The eight votes, she then smoothly explained, ought no more to be given equal weight than the eight voters, who otherwise (no offense intended) should be stacked up in one another's laps at her father's right hand. Weighted properly, Talīb ibn Sahl's vote should be given eight points, inasmuch as tonight he occupied the seat of honor; that of Ibn al-Hamrā, in the second place, should be counted as seven points, Hajj Masūd's as six, and so forth — down to the vote of the guest in the eighth place (timid Abū Shamāt), which should count as one. By this reasonable reckoning the ayes had it, twenty to sixteen.

More than half the company smiled, none more proudly than the teller of the tale in question and erstwhile author of the Baylor series. Sindbad himself tapped with pleasure his yellow-gold turban, as if to compliment his daughter's resourcefulness. But Ibn al-Hamrā, after busy tabulation on his fingertips and those of the elder fellow at his left, raised his hand and (when recognized by the host) declared to Yasmīn, "Even by your ingenious system of counting, pure milady, it is we nays who have it."

"Light of my heart," dryly asked Yasmīn, "how is that?"

"Because," replied her intended, "the ninth of our company, the venerable and sagacious Hasīb Alī, who until tonight sat always here at our host's seven-point left hand, has voted those points negatively with his feet, if I may so put it. That makes the score twenty-three–twenty against your interloper, O blossom of Baghdad."

Alī al-Yamān, Abū Shamāt, and the old man between Kuzia Fakān and Ibn al-Hamrā all nodded their heads sagely, as did Kuzia until she saw her master's frown.

"Sweet conqueror of my bowels," Yasmīn responded, "my recollection is that when Hasīb Alī awoke last night at the end of our visitor's second voyage, he had only praise for the story of it. If according to your remarkable reasoning his absentee vote is to be counted, it should count in our favor: twenty-seven–sixteen."

All were amused by this sally except him at whom it was directed. Before Ibn al-Hamrā could retabulate a comeback, however, Hajj Masūd, nodding vigorously, said, "By Allah, she has got the better of you, Ibo! And I must say in further support of her position that even if Hasīb had disliked the story of young Bey el-Loor's second voyage, his vote could not fairly be counted tonight upon the third, for I have it on good authority that in withdrawing himself from this company he has also withdrawn his support from our enterprise. Hasīb Alī is no longer an investor in Serendib Limited, and so the vote stands at twenty–sixteen in favor of the stranger's going on with his story."

He beamed at Yasmīn, then at her father — and found the one covering her eyes with her hands, the other raising his to heaven. Among the assembled there was murmuring.

"Jewel of the East!" cried Ibn al-Hamrā to his fiancée, his ruddy grin belying his words: "You have won indeed! On with your endless tale, Sayyid Bey el-Loor! We shall see who's here tomorrow night to hear it, and how the vote goes thereafter!"

"For God's sake, dance," Sindbad the Sailor commanded Kuzia Fakān. "Yasmīn!"

His daughter poured wine, grimly careful not to splash any on her prospective fiancé's caftan. "Allah bless you," murmured grateful Kuzia Fakān to her, and she rose for her performance. Sindbad fixed grave eyes upon Somebody the Still-Stranded, who once more merely shrugged. The tambourinist Fatmah Awād came forward, her instrument sizzling and biffing; the piper-girl did likewise, and the music commenced.

This time neither Yasmīn nor Jaydā excused herself: after a quick whispered conference with Kuzia Fakān, Sindbad's daughter returned to her place, and old Jaydā, surprisingly, seated herself in the place vacated by the dancer and even took an impassive sip of wine under her veil. All but Ibn al-Hamrā, however (and our storyteller), were too preoccupied with Hajj Masūd's news to attend either these remarkable departures from household custom or Kuzia's dance. Under the pipe and tambourine and Fatmah Awād's wild mournful song, Yasmīn spoke in private earnest with Hajj Masūd, her eyes and gestures stern. He nodded in either mock or real astonishment, clapped his brow, turned up his palms. Talīb ibn Sahl consulted the diner on his right, Alī al-Yamān the diner on his left, the others their wine cups. What passed between Sindbad and the veiled Jaydā, who regarded each other without words, Somebody could not suppose.

But Ibn al-Hamrā joyously clapped his hands more or less to the tambourine's beat as the page Salīm and six other male servants, at Kuzia's signal, replaced her master's Tub of Last Resort with the much larger vessel from the courtyard and boosted her up and over and into it. The dancer's splashes revealed it to have been at least partly filled with water for this performance. Within its chest-high walls she danced, accenting Fatmah's rhythms with resonant thumps of her still-slippered feet on the tub's bottom and raps of her knuckles on its sides. Tonight her caftan came off first and was pitched out dripping to Salīm. After an appropriate number of splashy twirls and stomps, her wet slippers followed, then sundry sopping skirts and filmy harem-pants, each caught by the waiting page and displayed suggestively to the distracted guests. Cheered on lustily by Ibn al-Hamrā and politely by Yasmīn and "Bey el-Loor," Kuzia next wriggled out of various che-mises until only a jeweled halter (and, presumably, its lower counter-part) remained. But as she then turned to display her bare arms and shoulders, Talīb and several others bowed their good-nights to Sind-bad, Yasmīn, Jaydā, and still-stranded Somebody, nodded to the per-formers, and rose to leave.

"Gentlemen!" Sindbad protested. "Does none among you wish his laundry done? No need to remove it; simply join our able laundress in her tub!"

"Yallah, Kuzia!" Yasmīn called helpfully, as the busy dancer now slipped out of her halter and tossed it over-shoulder to Salīm.

"Yallah," Somebody seconded. Even Jaydā tapped her wine cup in rhythmic encouragement on the low tabletop. On the tub's far side, Talīb and his companions (Alī al-Yamān from Place Four, and Abū Shamāt from Eight) paused but did not reseat themselves.

"Badawiya-ya-ya!" Ibn cheered or jeered. A trouper to the end, Kuzia Fakān turned to face the remaining guests, grinned deter-minedly, jiggled her sequin-pastied breasts till the water flew, and set-tled lower into the tub for her finale. When Ibn al-Hamrā rose to peek over its side, Jaydā caught the hem of his caftan and peremptorily yanked him back. A splash of red wine slopped onto his chest; he laughed and pointed it out to Sindbad, who merely sighed and tipped his turban tubward. Kuzia groaned, took a breath, and submerged altogether. From the depths then, as the music achieved its dutiful climax, her many-ringed hand appeared with the final undergarment, a glittering bit that instead of tossing she dangled overside like bait. Salīm, on cue, seized its other end and, after a playful tug-of-war, permitted himself to be pulled by its unseen owner into the tub. Piper and tambourinist bowed in unison, winked (one her left eye, one her right), and climbed in after him.

From the vessel's farther side, Talīb ibn Sahl complimented them — "*Mabrouk!*" — but then moved courtyardward in deep conversation with his two companions and Ibn al-Hamrā. Sindbad clutched at his turban and hastened after them. Hajj Masūd and the other three remaining guests rose to follow, despite the beckonings of Kuzia Fakān and her dripping comrades (Salīm included) in the tub.

"My dear Hajj!" implored Yasmīn, and hurrying to his side, she whispered something in his ear, at the same time gesturing tubward.

"Laundry time, everybody!" Sindbad urged, returning to the hall. "Come, Hajj! Come Sīdī, Jafar, al-Fadl!" Jaydā, doing her bit, handed her wine cup to Yasmīn, who merrily dripped a few drops onto Hajj Masūd's caftan sleeve.

"Ah, well, then," that fellow said, and he permitted the musicians to assist him into the tub. The three others obligingly held out their sleeves for Yasmīn's anointing. From out in the dry courtyard Ibn al-Hamrā called, "Till tomorrow, Bey el-Loor!"

"Tomorrow indeed," muttered Sindbad, at the same time encouraging Hajj Masūd's companions to follow their friend's example.

"Good night, all," sighed Yasmīn. Jaydā moved to leave with her, but Sindbad's gold-djellabaed daughter declared that she could in all likelihood find her own way tonight to the apartment in the women's quarters in which she had slept nearly every night since she was born. "Perhaps you should escort instead the unhappy captain of the ship *Sofar*," she suggested. "To his customary chamber."

She then exited, to sounds of dutiful wet merriment from her father's great tub. Jaydā stood by. Somebody looked apologetically to Sindbad, who had returned to his seat at the head of the table, his back to the laundering in progress, and was glumly nursing a final cup of wine. "Go, go," the old man said. "Protect my daughter's honor, while the early rats abandon ship and her future sinks under us like a wakened whale. We'll speak of tomorrow tomorrow."

"Salaam," Somebody said, and he did as bidden.

2.

Installed already in his lamp-lit room and busily re-dressing when her friend arrived with wordless Jaydā, Yasmīn turned to Somebody the Still-Stranded much as young Daisy Moore had once to Simon Behler on the Island of Island Creek, and spoke the first words of French ever uttered by a member of Sindbad's household:

"*Bon ami,* come: we have much business before the morning prayer call."

Her hair was braided up; her djellaba and undergarments lay discarded on the rug. In their place, more or less, she was winding a strip of yellow-gold turban around her lean hips and once between her legs, like a silken diaper.

"Top-*less,*" she proudly pointed out. "Now I am Janeprize, the wife of Sayyid Bey el-Loor, and he will do with me what she would not permit that night aboard *Sofar*. Show me how you did in the days when you loved her."

Used as he was becoming to her whims, our man was still stopped every time by the resplendent first sight of Yasmīn's body. He had presence of mind enough, however, to reply that if she insisted on taking these roles, she would have to show *him* how she imagined, et cetera.

The challenge seemed to please her. Hands on hips, she considered both him and it. From behind him, Jaydā spoke their private language. Yasmīn shook her head, then asked what sounded like a question in the same tongue, to which Jaydā gave some answer.

"What I think," Yasmīn then came closer and declared, "is that when you and Janeprize loved each other as husband and wife, you came together in the light and spoke of other matters, to prolong your pleasure. When you no longer loved each other, you came together in the dark and thought guiltily of your lovers while you did what you did." She placed Somebody's left hand solidly upon her right breast, his right on the hip-knot of her turban. "Just now we love each other. We will speak of other things while you unfasten my top-*less* and I remove your clothes."

This we did, with Jaydā as usual standing by for the most part impassively but volunteering comments or suggestions from time to time in that other language. Yasmīn explained (pausing in the divestment of her "husband" to turn herself around for his review once he had divested her) that this was, in fact, a Cairene dialect that the pair of them had used since her childhood for private communication. We needed to begin our lovemaking promptly, she went on to say — slipping into a modest nightdress now and lying supine, her arms crossed upon her chest — because Bey el-Loor's third voyage had involved him sexually with at least three women: his wife, Janeprize, the spirit-woman Terīfrum Tī-Nech, and his semen-swallowing mistress Terizāh Something-That-Sounds-Like-Bells-Ringing. One after the other, all three would be his again before morning, and allowance must be made for the long recovery time of Sīmon's aging zabb.

"What shall we discuss first, my husband, while you lift my night-dress and touch me here and here, which sets me on fire, and I do this to you but not yet that, lest the game be over before it begins?"

"Hajj Masūd," Somebody breathed. "In the name of Allah, let's talk about Hajj Masūd as if we were sipping mint tea in the courtyard."

Jaydā muttered something from the corner where she had settled. "I *know* that," Yasmīn replied to her: "A proper wife does *this,* not this, which is more in the style of the ifritah Terīfrum Tī-Nech than of Janeprize. But look what Sayyid Bey el-Loor wants to do to me, before he has even done the other things! Is that a proper husband or a camel-driver?"

Hajj Masūd, she then explained, was neither more nor less than what Sīmon had seen: a long-standing admirer of hers and business associate of her father's. His intentions were the best in the world, but he so invariably put his foot in his mouth and let cats out of bags that she ought to have known better than to call on him this evening (*"Bey el-Loor! Husband of my body! Just there!"*). He it was, by the way (she presently went on), who had supplied Jaydā with the rug in which to spirit Sīmon from Basra to Baghdad after our fateful remeeting in the marshy haunts of Mustafā the ex-Navigator — and back again when Sindbad suddenly returned from Voyage Six. He it was also, she did not doubt, who, after the hijacking of the bride-ship *Zahir,* had thought to minimize the damage to her reputation by spreading the story that she had *not* been raped wholesale by the Qeshmi pirates, but probably no more than once or twice, and by their captain. That would be very like dear Hajj Masūd — and would Bey el-Loor now speak to his Janeprize of something else entirely while she floated to the top of Adam's Peak, as she felt herself on the verge of doing?

Sīmon complied, not easily. His "wife's" "top-*less,*" he pointed out, which had joined the rest of her ensemble on the rug nearby, happened to have matched her djellaba, which for the third evening in a row had been of the same color as her father's turban. Was there an explanation?

Jaydā said something sharp.

Breathed Yasmīn, "There is." Her eyes were open and fixed upon Sīmon's, as steady in midascent of that happy height aforementioned as her voice was not: "Until I became the wife of your body . . . I was . . . my father's flesh and blood."

Determinedly we spoke on: of Hasīb Alī's defection from Voyage Seven, which had not been news to Yasmīn and Sindbad but which her father had hoped to talk the old man out of before it was confirmed. Of the possibility that Ibn al-Hamrā would now raise his dowry demands to eighteen or even twenty percent of the profits of Serendib Limited: a further devaluation of Yasmīn's virginity! Of Kuzia Fakān's dance, so unfortunately ill attended, which in Yasmīn's view had been a clever echo of Bey el-Loor's fateful submersion in Soper's Hole. Sīmon thought this interpretation overingenious, but he forbore from saying so because he was preoccupied just then to the point of speechlessness.

"There," said Yasmīn, satisfied, and she slipped out from under him. "Janeprize is pregnant now with our seven children, five of them sons." She pulled the hem of her nightdress back down from under her armpits and demurely put out the lamps, all except one. "We shall sleep awhile, until the zabb of my heart reawakens."

Sleep we did — Sīmon at least, though the word *sons* lodged under his breastbone like a live coal, and his dreams, prompted as they were by the story of Baylor's third voyage, did not soothe him.

An uncertain while later he found himself wordlessly assaulted by an ifritah. Gone were the nightdress and modest mien of "Janeprize";

when he woke enough to grasp what was grasping him — and biting, scratching, poking, pricking, tickling — he saw in the dim light a fury of skin and wild, unbraided hair: Yasmīn's imagination of Teri from Teaneck in Tangier. She was all over him at once; when he protested, a little frantic, "Hey! That *hurts!,*" she thrust her forefinger a whole joint farther in, bit his thigh till surely she had drawn blood, slammed her pelvis hard into his face. "Baylor" fought back; he had known his friend not to be a weakling or sluggard, but her strength and agility nevertheless surprised him, as did the degree of her mock ferocity. We rolled, tumbled, pitched about the room; Jaydā stirred in her corner, drew herself out of harm's way, and murmured approval when, as if furious at Sīmon's still-flaccid tool, Yasmīn pinched its frenum with her teeth until he shouted. Unrelenting, she muffled his outcry with her crotch. He bit her there; she retaliated with a quick trickle in his face and used her finger as she had before but gave over biting and stanched his thigh wound with lips and tongue. Again Sīmon did as he was being done to, not troubling even to moisten his entry first. That hurt her, in a way he had been required to see her hurt more than once before; she gasped into Jaydā's skirts, against which we had by that time rolled. He made at once to withdraw, gently, quickly — but Jaydā herself caught his hand, held it in place, moved it thus and so, and obliged "Bey el-Loor" to press his advantage until "Terīfrum Tī-Nech" gave out a different, longer sound.

Enough theater, he told her then, in effect. Or, if we were going to play this game of erotic recapitulation, let's play it both ways. What partners of Yasmīn's (other than the piratical one just now unhappily evoked) might *he* reenact, beginning with her first? Had that been "dear Hajj Masūd," perhaps?

Jaydā half whispered in Cairene.

"There was no first," prone Yasmīn murmured into those skirts.

"My darling is a virgin," her overseer affirmed, smoothing her charge's touseled hair.

Eyes closed, Yasmīn corrected her. "I never was a virgin. I was deflowered by a mighty ifrit in my mother's womb. He took my maidenhead before it was formed, and his terrible zabb lit a fire in my wâhât that no mortal lover can put out. He made me into an ifritah." She turned her head to glance up at Sīmon. "Terīfrum Tī-Nech?"

He kissed her lightly between the shoulder blades. "That ifritah has now been exorcised, Allah be praised. No more this one and that one: henceforth be you Yasmīn and I Whoever-I-Am."

She did not protest, but announced, "Whoever-He-Is will hold me now while we sleep till his poor cock crows."

Sleep we didn't, however, at least not for long. To Sīmon it seemed that the vessel of his consciousness had scarcely slipped its exotic present mooring when it was recalled by the somnolent voice of Jaydā, speaking now not Cairene but our common tongue:

"Chapter Six of Allah's great tale of Jaydā the Cairene," that voice declared, "its Author has seen fit to divide into two parts, of which the first cunningly precedes the second. That much-violated but still-irresistible flower of the Nile, when last we saw her, had been cured of her monkey-pox, refitted with her third and most convincing maidenhead by the wily artisans of Malabar, and sold to the young but seasoned merchant-mariner Sindbad the Sailor, who knew exactly what he was buying and what use he meant to make of his purchase. To that latter end, one might recall, as we returned together from his famous third voyage he examined me as thoroughly and expertly as if he were the caliph's Chief Inspector of Wâhâts, and while doing so examined the inside of my head as well.

"'Have you observed,' he asked me, 'that the hand with which I am admiring your excellent new equipment is missing portions of both its ring and little fingers?' I answered that while neither digit was presently in my view, I could tell by the feel of the former that only its first joint had been taken. My sojourn with the fishermen-pirates of Zabargad inclined me to think that the barracuda that had bitten it off must have been no more than two feet long and had probably mistaken for a minnow the flash of his signet ring — a gold one, by the feel of it, studded with either turquoise or amethyst.

"'By Allah, young woman,' Sayyid Sindbad cried, 'that is astonishing!' And he told me the story of his interisland tub trip in Voyage One, which had cost him two toes and part of that finger. 'But I see tears in your remarkable eyes,' he then declared. 'Are you weeping for my old injury, or can it be that a mere two thirds of a ring finger discomforts your exquisitely refurbished wâhât?' As to that, I replied, his examination gave me more delight than discomfort, and even far greater discomfort at his hands, so to speak, would give me joy. But by the feel of it, that turquoise-studded gold ring on the finger in question, at least the intaglio cursive *S* of the signet itself, was the work of an accomplished Egyptian goldsmith, most probably from Giza but in any case from no farther down the Nile than my home city. No proper Muslim daughter could be thus reminded of her late father without tears.

"In similar fashion I was able to identify the species of fish that had relieved him of two toes (a small reef shark), and though I misguessed the giant baby buzzards from Voyage Two that had made free with his left pinkie-tip and a portion of his right buttock — I have never known one feathered creature from another — I managed to read my new master's character and certain features of his past by mere visual inspection of his zabb, a skill that I had acquired over the years without trying to and that I was able to put to use in this instance when he dropped his drawers to test me in the matter of his vultured buttock. If he would deign to put that zabb where his ring finger was, I told him, I could read his future as well.

"This he would not do, for the prudent reason given at the end of Chapter Five of Allah's story in progress: time must prove me loyal and uninfected. But so impressed was he by the several talents of that story's main character, that he repeated his promise to reward me well if I would be his eyes and ears in the women's quarters of his new household.

"When his ship at length reached home port, my master left it altogether at the disposal of his faithful captain, Kasīm of Basra, vowing that he himself would never go to sea again. Indeed, so eager was he to put all things nautical behind him that he would not even make the trip from Basra up to Baghdad by riverboat, but packed me and his other treasures on donkey-back to the City of Peace. There he installed me in the empty harem of this house, and though I was not yet twenty years of age, he entrusted me with the selection of the female domestics whom he set about then to hire or purchase as attendants to his bride.

"As to the choice of that lucky woman herself, whose office it would be to bear his children and in all ways so entertain and delight him that never again would boredom tempt him to the salty bosom of the deep: he reviewed the most eligible young women of this city, and after rejecting this one because her character fell short of her beauty, and that one because her beauty was not the equal of her character, and this third because though excellent in both those respects she was of too willful and sharp a temper, and this fourth because she was on the contrary too docile and empty-headed to be interesting, he narrowed the field of his courtship to three and finally to two candidates, high-breasted young virgins so comparably excellent of face and figure — both of them carefully brought up in illustrious households, well versed in the fine and social arts, lively but sweet, firm-charactered but of gentle disposition — that the Prince of Believers himself could not have chosen between them but would have had to marry both.

"This my master was prepared to do, but such an arrangement, though forbidden by neither God nor nature, would have displeased both young women and their families. Having consulted his closest friends and found their opinions as divided as his own, Sindbad was finally driven to ask my advice: which of this pair of prizes, in my judgment, would more likely so please him by night and by day as to cure his wanderlust as completely as my monkey-pox was now cured? I asked him to arrange for me to spend a half hour alone in the company of each, after which I would venture my opinion.

"You must understand that after that thorough shipboard inspection, my master had not touched me further, though by his own acknowledgment I was now cured and available for his pleasure, and though he cannot have failed to observe in our daily consultations on household business that my heart was as much his property as was my new and untried wâhât. Nor did he avail himself of the other women we bought or hired in various domestic capacities or of the dancers brought in from time to time to entertain his guests, though he had been long at sea with no better company than his fellow merchant-traders and assorted ogres, apes, and serpents. It was his program, he confided to me, to starve himself so in this quarter that he would come to the bridal bed like a pious Muslim to the end of Ramadan, his appetite whetted for the feast. I shook my head inwardly at this reasoning, but in the trouble I foresaw therefrom for him, I foresaw opportunity as well as danger for myself, and therefore I kept my own counsel.

"He arranged with the families of the two young women for me to have private interviews with them, in each case representing me as not only his womanservant but also an expert appraiser of jewelry (which in fact I was) whose advice he would rely upon when buying gifts for his bride-to-be and who needed therefore to have a look at and a word with the potential recipient. I saw at once that choosing between these jewels of Islam was like choosing between two matched and flawless specimens from the Valley of Diamonds on Island Two, Voyage Two. Just as I could discern, without seeing directly, that each was blessed with skin like uncurdled cream, breasts and buttocks like canteloupes at their first moment of ripeness, and a wâhât like a fresh mountain spring at which no tongue has sipped, so I could divine without asking directly that each was as eager and able as the other to delight her bridegroom both in and out of bed. If finally, when my master pressed me for my decision, I found a syllable's worth more of praise for Marjānah the daughter of Sīdī Ahmad than for Habībah the daughter of Muīn, it was because, even more than her rival, this Marjānah had been after me for advice on her prospective husband's tastes. From my knowledge of Sindbad the Sailor, would he prefer his wife to entertain opinions of her own or only to echo his? Should she conceal the fact that her father had taught her the intricacies of business, or would it please her husband that she knew such things? If he chose her over Habībah, would I promise to be her friend and confidante and to instruct her in the art of love? For though she had read this and that in the poets and had been told certain things by her mother and other things by her girlfriends and married sisters, she knew nothing in this line at first hand.

"Sindbad was as pleased to receive this report as was I to deliver it, for I saw in that last request, particularly, an opportunity for my own preferment. How had I answered the girl's questions? he wanted to know. As to the first and second, I told him, I had replied that my master was looking for neither a mirror nor a parrot but a wife, who would do well to have knowledge and opinions of her own, but that he was on the other hand not looking for an adversary or a schoolmaster, and so she would do well to put her learning and judgment, like her body, actively at his service when they were desired, and never otherwise. As to that other matter (I told him I had told her), she could depend on me to be her steadfast friend but scarcely her instructor, inasmuch as I was as virginal as herself. 'Can I believe such a thing?' I reported that Marjānah had exclaimed. 'A prize like you, the mere glance of whose eyes must make every zabb in Baghdad stand like a minaret, and he does not mount you five times daily after prayers? What sort of lover is this fiancé of mine?' 'One who readies himself for a feast by fasting,' I told him I told her, 'rather than training for a championship race by riding every mare in his stable into the ground.' I insisted then that she verify my maidenhead (I said to Sindbad) by a simple and harmless procedure I had learned from my mother, which must however be done gently lest it rupture what it had set out to confirm. As she feared she might in her inexperience apply too much force to the verification, I then demonstrated upon her, with my middle finger, exactly the requisite degree of pressure. Laughing and lingering over the job like two schoolgirls, Marjānah and I then and there satisfied ourselves in the matter of each other's virginity and in some other matters, too, which I kept to myself.

"So fired was Sindbad by my edited report of this news that he rewarded me with a complete new wardrobe and married Sīdī Ahmad's daughter as soon as the wedding could be arranged and a king-size sleeping tub constructed in the courtyard for the bride and groom. Though I would have given much to be in her place in that tub on the bridal night, my jealousy was tempered by Marjānah's love and trust, which I found it no chore to reciprocate within the constraints of my pact with my master. The morning after her wedding she flung herself upon my neck with tears of joy and insisted that before I display to the household the bedsheet blazoned with her virgin blood, I must verify the entire absence of what I had previously verified as present; she promised to tell me as I did so every detail of what a man's instrument was like and what tricks it could perform — so much larger and livelier than a girlfriend's finger! — in order that I might not be surprised and alarmed when my turn came. And she was so excited still by her first taste of love that her recounting of it, together with my examination, fetched her for the first time not to Adam's Peak but to Eve's, which she had glimpsed but not managed fully to ascend on her maiden night with Sindbad the Sailor. I assured her that she would do so every night thereafter, now that she knew the way to that summit; nevertheless, she begged me to go the route with her once more to fix it in her mind, and so we spent half the morning laughing and playing again like naughty schoolgirls in the harem, until she bade me stop lest the husband of her body begin to wonder and perhaps grow suspicious at his bride's absence. Was he, by the way, to my knowledge, of a suspicious or jealous nature? She had meant to ask me that question before, and had forgotten to.

"I replied, honestly, that I did not know but would endeavor to find out. Sindbad then summoned me, not Marjānah, to a private audience in his great tub and demanded a full confidential account of his bride's report to me of their wedding night, so that he could verify his own happy impressions and strive to perfect both her pleasure and his own. His delight in her both stung and warmed my heart, as had hers in him. I reported truthfully that his bride had been exalted by her defloration and four subsequent impalements and that tender though she was this morning from that white night, she was eager for tonight and all their nights to come. 'That is well to hear,' Sindbad said, 'for to tell you the truth, though I know well enough that her joy was unfeigned, in none of our five couplings did she reach that height of bliss to which you and I both know a woman can be elevated. In this I was just a touch disappointed, but whether with myself or with beautiful Marjānah I don't yet know.'

"'As to that,' I assured him, not quite honestly, 'she said nothing, for the reason that in her complete innocence she believed her joy complete as well. I cannot easily tell her otherwise while pretending to be more innocent than she; nor need I do so, for from what she reports of the prowess of my master's zabb, it will surely bring her tonight to that joy which you and I have each known separately but of whose existence your Marjānah is not yet aware.' 'May it be so,' said Sindbad, 'for that young woman's beauty and my long abstinence are so well matched that I can think of neither sailing nor selling but only of the sweetnesses of herself. Even to speak of her like this rekindles a fire in me that only she can cool, and that not for long. By Allah, Jaydā, I can't wait for nightfall! Tell Marjānah to make ready for me now; then speak with her privately tomorrow morning as you did today, and afterward speak privately again with me.'

"I did as he commanded, and so excited was my mistress at the prospect of so soon again riding and being ridden by her groom that she quite forgot the question she had asked me about him until I apologized for having forgotten it myself in our interview. 'I mean the question of whether he is by nature a jealous and suspicious man with respect to his wife,' I reminded her, adding that that was after all not the sort of question one could ask him directly — at least, not one in my position. Marjānah, in her perfect innocence, wanted to know why not. Because, I said, such a question might very well inspire the very thing it asked about, might it not? 'How could it do that,' she wondered, laughing, 'unless my husband is jealous and suspicious by nature? A man not disposed to anger will not become angry at being asked whether he is disposed to anger. Really, Jaydā,' she said, 'you know nothing at all about men! Come: brush my hair now before Sayyid Sindbad arrives, and wash me in the places I can't reach for myself. When he finishes with me, I promise to tell you everything that passed between us, so that you can know the secrets of men as I do.'

"To this I said nothing, though I might have said much. That same afternoon in the bridal tub, by her own testimony, Marjānah scaled Adam's Peak once while seated upon Sindbad's lap with her back to his chest and again astraddle him as he stood, both of which positions she demonstrated for my enlightenment with me in the place of my beloved; and that night she reached those heights with him a third time, hind-to on all fours, and almost a fourth time by a means that altogether surprised her, as it entailed no insertion of his zabb at all but only a clever reciprocity of tongues, such as two women might manage quite as readily as a woman and a man.

"'How can that be?' I asked her, as if I hadn't learned how a thousand nights before she did and practiced my learning two thousand times since. And curious as I was to hear how her interrogation of Sayyid Sindbad had gone, I was readier yet to let her show me this new trick she imagined he had invented. In the course of her demonstration, as if by happy accident I easily took her where he had not managed to by that means, and permitted her to take me there as well — my first nonsolitary visit since Sindbad's shipboard inspection of me.

"Thus again we spent half the morning, until our master summoned me to the courtyard to make my report. One glance told me that something was troubling him, even after I had declared that Marjānah had reported only bliss from their connection thus far. That much he had observed for himself, Sindbad replied, except that toward morning, as they had done such-and-such while his tool recovered from so-and-so, he had been unable to fetch Marjānah once again to Paradise or to attain it himself, so distracted had he been by a question she had baldly put to him in the midst of their sport — to wit, was he of a jealous and suspicious nature? At the time, he had been too surprised by the question, and too busy as well, to do more than laugh and mildly chide her for imagining such a thing of him. But why in the world, he demanded now of me, had she asked him that?

"Because, I told him, she was a young and inexperienced but lively and intelligent woman, in love with her husband and naturally curious to know as much as she could learn about him. Now that he mentioned it, I said further, she had asked me the same question about him, both yesterday and today, and I had assured her both times that though my connection with her husband was in no way intimate (alas!), to the best of my knowledge he was free of any such unworthy sentiment as doubts as to her fidelity. By Allah the All-Seeing, I reminded him, he had taken her maidenhead just two nights past and had scarcely given her an hour's rest since! Nor had there been another zabb besides his on the premises since the wedding guests departed. When and with whom could she have been unfaithful, even if, as was unthinkable, she had been so inclined?

"Much relieved, Sindbad said, 'You're right, of course — though none knows better than yourself that ecstasy can be feigned even more readily and convincingly than maidenhood. By Allah, Jaydā!' he cried then. 'I have done nothing day and night but dote upon that woman from the hour she came into this house! Why does she doubt me, unless there's something on her conscience?' I urged him to calm himself while I prepared his bride for their afternoon's dalliance, as I had done the day before. No, he said: he was afraid that if he sent for her now, Marjānah would see at once how distraught he was, how suspicious of her suspicion, et cetera, and that could only cause her pain if she was innocent or put her on her guard if she was not. Besides, in his preoccupation with courtship and marriage he had neglected both his business and his friends in the city. He meant to spend the afternoon making up for that neglect and to bring a few of those friends home for dinner; he would see his bride then.

"Thus begins the end of the marriage of Sindbad the Sailor and of Part One of Chapter Six of Allah's great tale of Jaydā the Cairene. Marjānah wept and tore her garments when she heard that her husband had gone into the city for the afternoon instead of coming to

266

her. She had displeased him with her foolish question, she declared, exactly as I had warned her she might, and no doubt displeased him in their tub-bed as well. His dear zabb had not even risen, she confided to me now, when they played the game of arsey-turvey last night — no doubt because she hadn't known to do that extra little thing I had happened to hit upon this morning when she taught the game to me. We had no time to waste, she said then: I must both prepare her to look her best for the company that evening and take the role of her husband that afternoon so that she could practice how better to please him that night.

"Needless to narrate, despite her apprehensions she was unsurpassable that evening, both for beauty and for wit, and would have been unsurpassable as well in her husband's arms that night had it not been for the fact that he had observed by then, correctly, that every man in the room was smitten by her, and had concluded, incorrectly, that if some one of them was not already her lover, or had not once been, it was only a matter of time till one would be. And the more skillful she became, under my disguised tutelage, at the arts of love — my every lesson taught so cunningly that the pupil believed herself the teacher, and all my tutoring done with no other motive than to give the master of my heart, through his wife, what he would not take from me — the more persuaded he became that some other man was her instructor. Once the seed of his suspicion was well planted, anything Marjānah did sufficed to nurture it. When she wisely ceased to ask whether he was suspicious, he grew more suspicious; if in her ardor she took the initiative in their couplings, he suspected that she was covering her adulterous tracks, and if to allay that suspicion she restrained her ardor, he suspected that she had somehow spent it elsewhere — all because she had once innocently inquired whether he was of a jealous and suspicious nature!

"Readers of Allah's great tale of Jaydā the Cairene may be wondering at this point why Sindbad's jealousy did not fall upon that tale's narrator and principal character, since I was his bride's constant and only companion besides himself and since he knew me to be well versed in the world's wiles. The answer to this question is in several parts, of which the first is that to some extent he did suspect me (or pretended to) of complicity in Marjānah's imagined adulteries, especially when she now became pregnant and he drove us all crazy by imagining that the child in her womb might not be his. In order to extract a confession from me that I had played go-between for Marjā- nah and some one of his business associates, instead of putting me on the rack he took me into his tub, knowing well that I had loved him from the day he purchased me in Beypore, and justifying his behavior on the grounds that he would be a fool to remain faithful to a faithless wife. Thus for the third time, at long last, I lost my maidenhead — for the first time giving it up willingly, to a man I loved — and the joy of that surrender would have been the greatest of my life had I not by that time come much to pity and care for my poor mistress. Not ap- preciating this, Sindbad intended so to play upon my passion for him that I would betray her. Instead, without meaning to do so, he discov- ered to me the real cause of his jealousy, which he himself did not understand.

"As Allah wrote earlier in this chapter, out of my unusually large intimacy with males of every sort and size from all the principal higher species, I had learned to read zabbs the way Gypsies read tea leaves and Chinamen yarrow sticks, only more precisely. From my one and hitherto only glance at my new master's tool, back there on *Zahir*, I had divined among other things that he was not, in fact, of a jealous and suspicious nature. I could therefore have answered Marjānah's question myself before she asked it of her husband, had I not cruelly hoped back then to gain some advantage from her distress; and for months thereafter, having come to love my mistress almost as much as I loved my master, I had berated myself for not having done so. But the instant he fulfilled my dream by plumbing my wâhât almost to its depth, it was as if the scroll of truth had been unrolled before my eyes, and by the same means whereby I had discerned the origin and nature of his signet ring, I now discerned the cause of his causeless jealousy. That diagnosis I might have withheld to my gain, but such was my devotion to both of Yasmīn's prospective parents that I unhesitatingly declared it.

"'In your zabb of zabbs,' I told him as soon as he was securely mounted, 'if not in your heart of hearts, you know as well as I that Marjānah has known no other man than you, nor ever wished to, and that the child in her womb is as exclusively yours as is her heart. Were this not the case, you would long since have said three times to her "I divorce thee" and packed her home to her parents if not to the graveyard. What drives you to torment both her and yourself is not jealousy of your merchant friends but envy of their merchant-voyaging. You long for *Zahir* and the open sea and your old Tub of Last Resort, for new islands and abandonments and rescues, fortunes lost and regained and redoubled, and because you married in vain hope of curing this itch (the strength of which you have kept secret even from yourself), you resent the love that keeps you from your true desire.'

"'By Allah!' he exclaimed at once, and he prematurely fired his charge. 'What you say is true, though until you pronounced it I would have sworn otherwise. I have been a crueler ogre than that cannibal giant of Island One, Voyage Three, who merely killed and ate his victims but never tormented them beforehand. I shall go to Marjānah at once to beg her forgiveness and make amends as best I can!'

"Alas for our lovemaking, this he did, without telling his wife by what means the scales had fallen from his eyes. Marjānah straightway forgave him, and his relief at knowing the cause of his discontent was so great that all his friends remarked upon what a changed man he had suddenly become: the lively and large-spirited Sindbad they had known of old, and whose wedding they had celebrated just a few months past. Thus for a brief while all were happy except Jaydā the Cairene, who had had a sample of what she craved and now therefore craved it all the more.

"Soon enough, however, she was to sample it again, less hurriedly, for it was not long before Sindbad realized that my naming his problem had nowise solved it but only changed its terms. He no longer mistook his wanderlust for jealousy over Marjānah, but once he acknowledged it for what it was, it grew upon him more intensely than had his suspicion. At the same time, now that his eyes were cleared, he loved his wife even more than on their wedding night and could not bear the thought of separation, particularly as she approached her confinement. He briefly considered taking her and the newborn with him aboard *Zahir* once her labor was done, if he could restrain himself even another month before setting out for Basra and Voyage Four — but all his nautical experience taught the folly of that consideration.

"At last he was so at war with himself that again he sought my counsel in his courtyard tub. 'Wise and patient Jaydā!' he saluted me (in his distraction forgetting to add that I was still beautiful as well). 'Once upon a time you told me you could read in a man's zabb not only his character and history, as you have ably proved, but his future as well. Here now is mine, which rightly belongs to your mistress alone but which you must read chapter and verse of for her sake as well as mine. It has told you already how vain was my hope that marriage and fatherhood would cure my wanderlust. Though I love Marjānah and my child-to-come as I love myself, I have sent word to Kasīm in Basra to refit *Zahir* for the fourth voyage of Sindbad the Sailor. You must tell me now whether that voyage will be shorter and safer if I commence it at once or if I wait till after Marjānah's confinement, for in no case can I postpone it further. Remove your clothes, please, open your legs, and make ready to prophesy.'

"'Ruler of my soul!' I replied to him. 'No task could afford me greater joy! But I have no more wish to deceive my mistress than does she to deceive you, and to make a prophecy of such particularity and consequence will require sustained and concentrated effort on both our parts, if I may so put it. You must dip your pen into my inkwell again and again till its screed be scrawled; dot your *bā*s and double-dot your *tā*s, loop your *mīm*s and squiggle your *shīn*s, cross your *khā*s and hook your *zā*s, and recopy any obscure passages till they come clear. Moreover, since you're so impatient to be read, you cannot write in leisurely installments, as does the Author of us all, but rather must ply your quill day and night upon my parchment till we reach the passage in question. Granted that I am yours to inscribe as you see fit, in my opinion Marjānah had better be told — or, rather, asked leave of, since this inscription is in her interest as well.'

"'Pearl of Cairo!' Sindbad exclaimed. 'Wise as you are canny, and honorable as you are wise! Let us tell Marjānah the whole tale thus far, ask her blessing upon its sequel, and get down to it.' This we did, and astonished though she was to hear my hard history — and not a little dismayed at our having hid it from her till now — she accepted that everything we had done had been to the end of keeping her husband home with her. She therefore forgave our deception as she had forgiven Sindbad's jealousy: the bad side of a good coin. And as much as it distressed her to imagine him in another's arms, she was consoled by the fact that those arms would be the same that in months past had so often consoled her, and had cured her husband's doubts about her fidelity. As to the prophetic labor now proposed: if he must make another voyage and leave his family behind, she, too, wished him the shortest and safest of absences from her side, and so she gave our project her reluctant blessing. It did occur to her, however, that a man who took such extraordinary measures as Sindbad had taken, first to verify his bride's virginity and then to guarantee her fidelity, must be — how else to put it? — of a jealous and suspicious nature, my reading of his zabb to the contrary notwithstanding. She hoped my fortune-telling would be more accurate.

"And so it was, though this observation of hers temporarily un-manned Sayyid Sindbad and got our séance off to a lame start. I was obliged to persuade him that zabbs cannot lie, and that therefore his elaborate pretense to Marjānah that I was a virgin proved not that he was of a jealous and suspicious nature but rather that his craving for dry land and a happy marriage had led him to act contrary to his nature, which was essentially trusting though not naive. After some consideration Sindbad declared, 'I accept that. Off with your clothes, and let's get to work.'

"To his disappointment and Marjānah's (if not mine), our first coupling, then and there as soon as she left us to our courtyard soothsay-ing, revealed to me only the outlines of my master's youth, the death of his father, young Sindbad's squandering of his patrimony, and the details of his first voyage, including the ship's bill of lading, the names of her captain and the other merchant passengers, and what meat had been roasting on the shore-side cookfires that waked the whale that was Whale Island. Our second, an hour or so later, did likewise for his second, and our third, after dinner that evening, for his third — dur-ing which, with the excuse of better focusing my wâhât's second sight, I obliged him to recopy twice the episode of his first inspection of me aboard the *Zahir*. A little crossly, Marjānah told me to spend the night with him as well, so that we might get to the future and have done. She was even inclined to remain in the bedroom with us, to make sure we attended strictly to business, but her husband cautioned her against becoming of a jealous and suspicious nature, and I voiced my doubt that successful sooth could be said under such surveillance.

"Strive as we did, however, Sindbad and I, our night's labor brought us no further forward than the present moment of our cou-pling, in which — reading my weary lover's mind through his ex-hausted instrument — I divined that though he was convinced of my abilities vis-à-vis the past, he had all but lost confidence in me with respect to the future, and that one more failure on my part would arouse suspicion on his and jealousy on Marjānah's. Just at first light, therefore, when the muezzin's prayer call detumesced my master and he slipped from me like an anchovy from the fisherman's fingers, I cried, 'There is no god but God, and Mohammed is His prophet, and in that last slight movement of yours, one or the other of Them gave me my first glance into your future!' 'None too soon,' sighed Sindbad. 'Do I leave for Basra this morning or wait until after my son is born?'

"From so tiny a motion of so depleted a zabb, I replied, the most prescient wâhât in Islam could not be expected to read so much as that. What mine had foreseen was merely that he was about to summon Marjānah to our tub after all, remove her nightclothes, and bid her assume the first position for copulation.

"'How could I be about to do such a thing as that?' he scoffed. 'It is true that after the novelty of retracing voyages One through Three with you in this peculiar and dangerless fashion, I found myself wishing I could board Marjānah for Voyage Four, for despite her advanced pregnancy she is as fresh and lively a bottom as my dear *Zahir* was on her maiden voyage, whereas — no slight intended — boarding you is like reboarding the *Zahir* on which I first examined you, or my old Tub of Last Resort: seasoned and seaworthy, tried and true, but tried and tried and tried again. You know as well as I, however, that in Marjānah's condition she cannot in fact be mounted in Position One.'

"'Men may lie or be mistaken,' I maintained firmly, 'but their zabbs cannot. Yours has whispered to me plainly that you were about to summon Marjānah exactly as I have said, whether the rest of you realized it or not. Fetch and strip her, then, as you will, and Allah will show us how to proceed.' 'As *I* will?' he wondered, but fetch and strip her he did, full of sleep and puzzlement though she was, and bade her lie upon her back on the tub floor and prepare to be mounted. 'Dear Jaydā!' she cried to me then, in a voice that I would hear years afterward from her daughter. 'See what my darling means to do with me despite my great belly, which makes the thing not possible! Have you not yet shown him Position Fourteen, or even Twenty-seven, as you once showed me, for occasions like this? And what happened to your prophesying?'

"'Never have I seen the next moment of the future more clearly than at present,' I replied to both of them. And in truth, so beautiful was my mistress naked, even then, in her last weeks and days, that at the sight of her the fine print of Sindbad's scroll of truth rose to uppercase bold before my eyes, and I declared, '*Bism Allah!* Hear and behold! My tongue will now repeat to my mistress in Position One what my master's zabb tells me in Position Three of his love for her. This time, I clearly foresee, he does not intend to make that great declamation into my oasis, as he has done every time so far without our once finding there the prophecy we seek. Allah help me, he means instead to make an inlet out of my outlet and so to force that narrow khawr with the vessel of his husbandly passion that as surely as One and Three make Four, my poor tir'at will be inscribed for weeks to come with every detail of his impending voyage!'

"Said Marjānah with a sigh, 'So be it. Better yours than mine.' As for Sindbad, he acknowledged that once again I had spelled out what he had not known till then were his intentions. We therefore set to as I had foreseen, and if his dhow was not the first to make a dawhat out of the bi'r next door to my wâhât, it was the largest, stoutest, and most fraught. So eloquently did it convey to me his love for Marjānah, and I relay it to her, and her dainty mugharet speak to my tongue of her love for Sindbad, and I relay it to him, that the three of us all too soon climbed Adam's Peak as one, and I was so previsioned both stern and stem that for some moments I left this world altogether.

"'Tell us!' they both demanded of me when I was myself again. 'Are we to name the boy Muhammad or Dū al-Zamān, the Light of the Age? Will his father return quickly and safely from his fourth voyage? Should he set out at once, the sooner to return, or see his son safely delivered before he goes?'

"Ah, handsome listeners asleep in each other's arms, rejoice that you are but minor characters in Allah's great tale of Jaydā the Cairene, for clearly the adversities of its heroine will end only in its final chapter. Here at the close of Chapter Six, Part One, she was so stricken by her double-ended revelation that it took her some while to find her voice again and yet some while longer to sort out what she had seen and think how best to give it tongue. At length, with tears in my eyes, I said to Marjānah, 'Dear milady: your birth-labor will be short and your baby flawless. Beyond that, Allah has not shown me.' And to

Sindbad, 'Dear my master: you will return from Voyage Four as from its predecessors, safely but not soon, your fortune lost but ultimately redoubled. Under no circumstances, however, ought you to leave Marjānah's side before your child has been brought to light, for the time of your waiting will be as short as that of her labor. As for the child at the end of it, a better name for her than either Muhammad or Dū al-Zamān will be Yasmīn. Ask me no more, for before the rest I now draw my veil as Allah has drawn His.'

"Distressed though they were, Marjānah especially, to hear that Sindbad's new voyage would be another long and arduous one, they rejoiced at my forecast of its ending and at my other tidings, ignoring my hint that I had spoken more truly than fully. Even the news of a daughter rather than a son did not dampen their joy. '*Wallahi!*' said Sindbad. 'So it is written and so it shall be! We will lay the keel of Yasmīn's little brother in this same tub when *Zahir* brings me back to Baghdad at last. How can we thank you, faithful Jaydā?'

"I had already drawn my veil, even before I reclothed the rest of my body. But I replied that they could in fact thank me in three ways: first, by Sindbad's setting forth this time in some other vessel than the one that he and I had last returned in and that he had lately compared me to, not altogether flatteringly. Second, by his never again inscribing on my behind what lay before, but rather accepting what was to come as it came. And third, by their loving each other for the remainder of their days as I loved them both, and leaving me to sit in peace on the rest of my previsions.

"Even as we three embraced then for the last time, Marjānah cried out that the time of her labor had come on her. As I foresaw, her pains were brief, and she brought forth a perfect baby girl. All joy, Sindbad kissed his wife and infant daughter and myself as well (through my veil, which I would not remove). He named the child Yasmīn and set out that same day for Basra with his old Tub of Last Resort, his trading goods, and a sealed message from his faithful slave Jaydā the Cairene, to be opened at sea. By the time he embarked, Marjānah was dead of childbed fever, as I had foreseen but not foretold because all the precautions in Islam could not have saved her or stayed him. What was more (as he read in my letter when his hired ship had cleared port and was standing down the Persian Gulf for Muscat), had he remained at home, his daughter would have succumbed as well. He must count on me, I wrote, to bury and mourn his wife with full honor and respect and to raise Yasmīn in her parents' absence as if she were my own, until his fortune found her another mother. Finally, I cautioned him that on this voyage he must be as wary of what he swallowed as on the last he had been of what might swallow him — though I myself could no more explain this warning than I could explain why Allah chose just here, at this unhappy juncture, to end Part One of Chapter Six of His epic of Jaydā the Cairene, whom we now leave weeping with the other domestics of the harem over the dead body of our mistress, even while I stanched with my perfect though milkless breasts the hungry cries of the baby Yasmīn until wet nurses could be fetched to feed her. But end it here He did, for the reason that Part Two, which cunningly follows it, follows it. Now good night."

Yasmīn here paused in her reenactment of "Terizāh" (as she called "Bey el-Loor's" third-voyage mistress), cleared her throat, and whispered, "Good night, dear Jaydā. You were a mother to me indeed, and whatever ills befall your daughter in what follows of this sixth chapter or in the chapters after, they will never be of your doing but rather will come to pass despite your best efforts to shield me from them."

Of this, Sīmon was less than perfectly convinced. But the recipient of Yasmīn's tribute was asnore, and though his lover, too, had seemed to doze through the early history of her father's marriage, she had stirred at about the time of her conception, embraced him tightly through the recital of her birth and orphaning, as if to comfort herself, and left his arms at Sindbad's embarkation on Voyage Four to slip down into her version of young Teresa Anginelli. Sīmon himself was very nearly too absorbed in Jaydā's story (and too needful of sleep) to resume his own, but as his role in this particular episode was passive, requiring only that he stroke his partner's hair while she went about her patient impersonation, he mused, half asleep, upon what he had just learned and what Jaydā's next installment might disclose — until the slowly intensifying excitement down there in "College Park" recalled him to that season of guilty pleasure. Like her original, as she felt him approach climax in the gray first light of morning, "Terizāh" raised to him her great luminous eyes — in their earnestness almost brown instead of green, Italian lapsed-Catholic instead of Muslim Arab — and regarded serenely his self-emptying. But where a muezzin ought to have chided us that prayer was better than sleep, or an ambulance wailed by from the D.C. Beltway, or the East Dorset air-raid siren sounded, we heard instead a knocking and hallooing at the courtyard gate, insistent, unabashed, imperious.

3.

Notwithstanding which, from sheer exhaustion Somebody slept, stirring only slightly at the sensed departure of Jaydā and Yasmīn for their own quarters and at the distant, intermittent hullabaloo. Voices rose and were quieted. Footsteps from somewhere hurried elsewhere. Then either all grew still again or our man's late sleep deepened. His dreams — of the life wherein, in the smithy of imagination, he had forged an identity and found his forging forgery — seemed more real and less remote than the reality Salīm waked him to.

"*Fwff,*" the page said. "Guarding Yasmīn's honor must be sweaty business. This room smells stronger than Sindbad's great tub did when Kuzia Fakān and I were finally let out of it."

Replied Somebody, "You were washed as you worked; my vigil was as dry as it was solitary. I take it your master is ready for our morning interview."

"Sayyid's Tub of Truth is drained now, like his page," Salīm affirmed. "He awaits you in it with his half an arse on his cushion-and-a-half. Here's water to wash with, but don't be long — the fat's in the fire."

He fetched in then a pitcher and basin of what our man hoped, aloud, was not the drainage of last night's frolic, and stood by while Somebody washed up from his own. Despite the page's teasing and prying curiosity — Salīm's eyes flashed about the room and lingered on its occupant's scrubbing — Sīmon let him stay through his toilet, to hear and gauge his gossip. That early-morning noise, he learned, had not been the drunken exit of those lusty rascals al-Fadl, Jafar, and Sīdī Numān, whom Salīm and Kuzia Fakān and Fatmah Awād and Nuzhat the piper had tubbed into the small hours on Sindbad's behalf, to forestall their defection from Serendib Limited. It had been, instead, the arrival of a messenger from another and more formidable

Jafar, surnamed al-Barmakī, grand vizier to Caliph Haroun al-Rashīd himself, the Prince of Believers. And though that messenger's message had been for the ears of Sayyid Sindbad alone, it was already common knowledge among his servants that it expressed the caliph's impatience with Sindbad's delayed departure on Voyage Seven.

"If that is the household's common knowledge," opined Somebody the Still-Stranded, "then we may be sure that the vizier's message had to do with something else — perhaps with new and harsher penalties for those who repeat his confidential dispatches."

To which the page responded, in the experimental tone that Somebody knew from occasions past, "Night after night under Sindbad's nose, while he and Ibo dicker over Yasmīn's virginity and dowry, you and she go at it with Jaydā's connivance, and you did the same through the month of Sha'ban while he was off settling scores in Serendib. Why does he permit this?"

The fellow put his question from safely out of range as they entered the courtyard, where Sindbad's great tub was in its customary place between camel and palm. All the same, he took a quick farther step away when Somebody (to test him) slipped one hand through a side-slit of his caftan, as if to reach for Mustafā's fish-knife but in fact to adjust his drawers. "Perhaps that is the very question asked by Jafar al-Barmakī," our man suggested, "or perhaps his message is the answer to it. More likely, however, it is a sentence of slow castration for those who defame in a single breath their own mothers, their masters, and the caliph's special agents. I shall ask Sindbad the Sailor. Salaam, Brother Sindbad!"

"Salaam, Brother Sindbad!" the call came back, as if echoed from the tub. "Join me here again, please, after dismissing your guide."

"With pleasure. But I believe Sayyid Salīm has a thing to tell and another to ask you before he leaves us."

"Not at all!" the page said at once. "Only to report that the caliph's messenger has been fed and rewarded, and to ask whether I ought not to stand by lest your private conversation be overheard."

Sindbad's head, turbaned this morning in sea-green silk, appeared over the tub's edge. "If you stand by, our private conversation *will* be overheard. You served me well last night, lad; I am mindful of that. Serve me again now by standing watch over yonder, as far from Mustafā as Mustafā is from me. Brother, come aboard."

The page withdrew beyond the camel as instructed. Still-stranded Somebody mounted the dry tub's stile, or boarding ladder, and at Sindbad's invitation cushioned himself opposite his host, who, while offering mint tea and a plate of pastries with pomegranate conserve, asked casually, "You slept well?"

As well as he could, replied our man smoothly, without neglecting his duty to Yasmīn's honor, until this morning's racket woke the whole household.

His host regarded him. "And Salīm will have told you the whole household's opinion — that Haroun has grown impatient with my delays and dispatched that messenger to launch me off to Serendib."

"Salīm has," Somebody acknowledged. "And I have told Salīm that common opinion of that sort is most often common error."

"So it is." Sindbad sighed. "And would it were in this instance. But old Hasīb Alī, it seems, has expressed to Vizier Jafar al-Barmakī the misgivings that led him to withdraw from our enterprise, and the vizier in turn has questioned Ibn al-Hamrā, and to advance his own claims Ibn has neither refuted nor affirmed Hasīb's slanders but has raised his demands to twenty percent of the expedition's profits, along with the rest of Yasmīn's dowry. The upshot is that despite the six several fortunes I have brought into this city, I am ordered to set out on the caliph's embassy to Serendib before the end of Shawwal, or show cause why I should not be charged with fraud."

"To Serendib before the end of this month!" Our man set down his tea glass, aware that his reaction was being carefully observed. "My brother is scarcely dry from his last visit there! And what is this talk of delay, not to mention fraud? Serendib is not a place to be voyaged to on a moment's notice!"

"So I am told," Sindbad said, relieved. "And so I told Haroun when he first commissioned me to return there with his gifts of reciprocity. His reply — the vizier's, rather — was that I could have the whole month of Ramadan to rest and make my plans and gather trading partners. But now he gives me three days to present him with my sailing directions and a timetable for Voyage Seven, with the stipulation and the warning that I spoke of." He regarded his tubmate. "Is this news to you? Do the caliph's agents not speak with one another?"

"What concerns the eye," Somebody replied, "is not always the ear's affair, and vice versa. Moreover, it's common knowledge by now in your household that I am not really the caliph's agent but a nameless impostor who, like a false eunuch in the harem, makes free with what he's set to safeguard. Ask Salīm."

Sindbad scowled. "Salīm's kind tell before they are asked."

"In any case," our man went on quickly, "inconvenient as the vizier's new directive may be, it only presses forward what was already in progress. Three weeks seems time enough to finish commissioning a ship and crew, and as for Yasmīn's marriage, you need only say yes to Sayyid Ibo and the thing is done. But does the caliph appreciate how peculiarly difficult the sailing is to Serendib? Mustafā mu-Allim himself could not easily retrace that route."

Sindbad closed and then opened his eyes. "Have a look at our other Mustafā," he requested quietly, "and see where that shaitan of a Salīm is." Somebody did so, in time to see the page retreating to his assigned distance like a runner caught off base. "Farther, Salīm," he called. "Stand your watch at the gate itself." Sindbad nodded approval, then beckoned our man to sit. "Brother," he said, "there is a time for dissembling and a time for candor. Frankly, what passes between you and my daughter, as long as it does not interfere with my plans for her, is between you and my daughter. As for Ibn's dowry demands, I have my reasons for not yielding too soon, quite apart from what they imply about Yasmīn's honor. My resisting his percentage lends credibility to Serendib Limited and helps encourage the others not to follow Hasīb Alī's bad example — and now Talīb ibn Sahl's, I fear, and perhaps Abū Shamāt's as well. You see how open I am being with you this morning! Time now for you to tell me not what your real name is or how you spend your time after we say good night or what stories Jaydā entertains you with while you entertain yourself but rather . . . what our old friend Mustafā the Navigator, to whom it seems you have been closer than most, has told you about my most recent voyage, to Serendib."

Still-stranded Somebody nodded, deliberately sipped his tea, set down his glass, and fingered his short-bearded chin. "Mustafā the Master Navigator," he declared presently, "to whom several times over I owe my life and whom I revere beyond my own father and all the teachers of my youth, is a man as discreet as he is sea-wise. Despite his vow after your sixth voyage to live in utter isolation from his fellow men, when he recognized me cast away in the Basra marshes he took me in and restored me to life. But of that last voyage of his with you, and of the final fate of the ships *Zahir* and *Shaitan* and their crews, he would say nothing, in keeping with another vow that he had made to you. Salīm tells me, without my asking, that en route home from Serendib you settled certain scores with certain adversaries — but that's Salīm. All I know for certain of your celebrated sixth is that though with Mustafā's assistance you set out properly for Serendib, and with Mustafā's assistance returned, it was not from Serendib that you brought those gifts to Haroun al-Rashīd, for you never reached that fortunate island."

This time Sindbad himself rose with some difficulty from his cushions, grasped the tub's edge with his eight whole and two half fingers, peered overside, and softly cursed. "Here the bastard comes with that damned messenger, just when you and I most need to speak further."

Our man shrugged. "What's the urgency? You have three days to give him your reply."

"Three days," said Sindbad, "during which that moon-faced fellow will be watching and reporting every move I make." He wiped his forehead with his caftan sleeve. "Look here: you said a moment ago that I set out properly for Serendib, but I believe you know that in fact Mustafā and I did not set out for that island at all. Serendib was our name for something else."

"Indeed," said Somebody the Still-Stranded. "And until we have occasion to resume this frank and open conversation, you might tell the vizier's man that the problem of your seventh voyage begins just there. To sail from Serendib to Basra, one sets a course for Basra, but to sail from Basra to Serendib is quite another matter. As we both know, it is in the nature of that elusive island that under no circumstances can it be reached by heading in its direction. Among the other valid reasons for your apparent procrastination is that difficult problem, which you are on the verge of and surely shall succeed in solving, with my assistance and perhaps Mustafā's as well."

"And what is *your* percentage?" Sindbad wondered aloud — but then he replied to his own question, as Salīm announced from camel range his approach with the caliph's vizier's messenger, "No matter, Brother Sindbad: salaam."

4.

Dismissed, our man withdrew to his room, as was now his morning custom, hoping to rebecome, first in sleep and then in written words, the "Baylor" who he had by force of imagination once upon a time become. Dispatched by Jaydā or her son, or perhaps by Sindbad himself, chambermaids had been at work there; he found the place cleaned, aired, and straightened, the bedding freshened, a supply of quills, ink, and paper on the low table near the courtyard window. Weary though he was, the sight of those alternative clean sheets gave him pause: his two roads home to Wherever, until and unless he discovered a third.

Experimentally, he dipped a quill and drew in block capitals the six letters of his more or less established name. The *B* reminded him this morning of Yasmīn's sweet buttocks last night, when at some point in Jaydā's narrative she had turned onto her side, hind-to, and nestled into him. The *A* was the lower half of a short-skirted stick figure, standing assertively with her feet some space apart, as Daisy Moore must have done in 1944 to piss her name in the sand of Island Point; it was the letter she had ended on. The *Y* . . . his current lover's dear initial, to be sure — but by that *BAY* he was at sea, out of analogies, adrift again in home waters and others, brooding upon "Janeprize" and the unhappy last leg of their long connubial voyage.

Under the caps he rewrote the name in script: his professional signature. Its familiar cursive, looping and circling but, like narration itself, always returning to connect the thing behind to the thing before, was so agreeable to the muscles of his spirit that for some while he scribbled on: *Through the first, or "British," half of Baylor's forty-second-birthday gift to himself,* et cetera, word joining word and event event as his script linked letter to letter. What had irrelevantly been in fact, he omitted; what had not been but for design's sake needed to be, he did not scruple to rearrange or invent, until hours and pages later he reached the words *Baylor's Arrested Development Jumps Bail.* There in the early postnoon he came to himself, bade a pained goodnight to Jane Price, to their daughter, to their son (no more lost now than his father), and, marveling that he had got so far in his reretelling without interruption, drew the curtains, turned to those other fresh sheets, and slept.

From near-dreams of near-drownings at the Boundary — Island Point on the Chaptico, Soper's Hole, Adam's Peak — a piping piped him briskly up, gratefully gasping, to and through the surface. Whistled on deck as by a tuneful bos'n, he got breath and bearings: Somebody, he was, or other, still stranded but anyhow alive and not the unluckiest of mortals.

"Come in," he called to Nuzhat, whose piping by now he knew. In she swirled, her music likewise, both dark delights. Without ceasing to play (and all the while glancing busily about the room), she bowed to the bedded one, stepped aside, and skirled a signal toward the corridor from which now came a familiar sizzle-snap.

"Come in, Fatmah Awād," called weary Somebody. She did, her rhythm unbroken, and then bowed bedward like her colleague (sizing up our man, who sat now on his sleeping-couch), stepped to the doorway's other flank, and, with the briefest nod to Nuzhat, switched to fanfare. Smiling, Somebody moved from couch to cushion, put a second in place before him, and bade Kuzia Fakān, "Come, Kuzia, come, for pity's sake. No need for such ceremony between friends."

All the same, that one spun in with a dancer's flourish even as he spoke, and the three made as one a choreographed salaam. "Bravo, then," our man said. "My compliments, too, on last night's dance: your best."

"So far," the dancer agreed, and she sat. "Pearls before porkers, in our opinion. But Yasmīn tells me that you, at least, saw our point: my submersion echoed yours, and all hands got fucked underwater, one way or another." She glanced over her shoulder. Nuzhat and Fatmah Awād, watching each other's faces to stay in sync, announced in unison, "We'll stand watch," and exited in step. Our man nodded and declared, noncommittally, "Another busy night for you."

"*Fuff*," scoffed Kuzia. She conned the room brightly, as had her companions, and even reached to the writing table and picked up a page of script. "Compared to your girlfriend's fiancé, Hajj Masūd and company were no more than a warm-up exercise — but that's enough water sports for this Bedou. Is this your report to the caliph's messenger?"

"Perhaps." He turned the page right side up and pointed to his pen name. "What do these letters tell you?"

"That I can't read Arabic, Sayyid Bey el-Loor, much less Serendibian. What do they tell *you?*"

"Everything except who I am," our man replied, impressed. "In fact, though, this is the name I made for myself, once upon a time."

Examining the symbols, Kuzia declared soberly, "Jaydā says our names are signs of our fate."

"Who can doubt Jaydā? But the trick is to read those signs." For his visitor's amusement, then — but also to harmonize their instruments, as Kuzia herself had put it, for further music-making — Somebody told her what he had imagined not long since in the first two letters: side-turned buttocks (never mind whose) in that *B,* a striding young woman from his "second voyage" in that *A.* . . .

"Aha," quick Kuzia said. "This next then must be Yasmīn."

"How did you know that?" asked surprised Somebody. "Our *Υ* looks nothing like your *yā.*" He drew the Arabic letter, a cobra coiled to strike.

"But it looks like Sindbad's daughter," the dancer replied. Grinning, she traced with her fingernail the Roman letter's fork and stem: "A slitless wâhât with virgin thighs pressed tight. If that brings us to the present, then Bey el-Loor's future must lie in these last three signs. And now that you've taught me the trick of reading from the waist down, I can see pretty clearly what lies ahead for a certain pair of lovebirds. I envy them."

"In the name of Allah, read!"

Kuzia pointed in turn to the *L,* the *O,* and the *R.* "This is the lover's zabb, erect and ready to pierce at last *this,* a certain famous maidenhead. And this is the result: her belly so swollen that she must put her best foot forward to keep her balance."

"For our mistress's sake," Somebody said, "may her future be as you foretell. Thank you for those good wishes, Kuzia Fakān."

"For our mistress's sake," responded Kuzia, "may it be the right zabb when push comes to shove. It's *your* name we're reading, not Yasmīn's, and I'm too new at this game to know for sure what's future and what's past. You may thank me by drawing my name now."

Our man readily did so, but he got no further than *KUZIA* before the dancer said, "Enough. It's just as I suspected." Glumly she pointed to the first two letters. "There I am, climbing into his great tub night after night, trying every trick I know as his famous amulet loses its charm and I lose mine. And here I am now, down on my knees. . . ." She indicated the middle letter: "Am I praying to Allah to make the old tool stand, or presenting myself arse-up, the way he used to like it? Maybe both. In any case, I've one last card to play, and tonight I mean to play it." Turning then to the penultimate letter, she said, "There's the key to my future, right enough, but whether it's pointing up or down, only Allah knows. If it's hanging limp, then there's Yours Truly at the end there, all by her lonesome, pissing letters in the desert like your friend Day-*zee*."

"Bravo again." Somebody applauded and added his hope to hers that that *I* would stand skyward, by whatever charm, or else that that *A* would stand for al-Hamrā, whom, camel-driver or no, one gathered she would settle for if things happened to turn out that way.

The Bedouin, Kuzia Fakān declared, knew how to drive a camel-driver, once they got a secure grip on his reins. But why speak of such daydreams? It was that camel-driver who had Sindbad by the reins, now that Hasīb Alī and those other two had jumped ship, so to speak. There would be no Yasmīn for Bey el-Loor, and no al-Hamrā for Kuzia Fakān: the caliph had called the old man's bluff. Redbeard Ibo would open the bottom of that Υ and get his twenty percent, too, and the likes of present company might as well go water the dunes.

"Our instruments are now in tune," Somebody said. "Let's see whether we can play to our joint advantage. I offer you the information that Sindbad the Sailor has never sailed to Serendib. Is that news to you?"

Kuzia considered his eyes, nodded.

"That name," our man went on, "was what he called his project in Voyage Six: recouping the ransom he had paid to Yasmīn's hijackers and revenging himself on them. I don't know every detail; Ibo must hear none."

Kuzia nodded again. "I suspected this, but till now I knew nothing. The camel-driver shall know less. Then where did that magic amulet come from, if not from the King of Serendib?"

"That is the tune you must play for me."

"I will," the dancer promised, "as best one can who knows only a note or two. But let me offer again my suspicion that Voyage Seven has no more to do with Serendib than did Voyage Six. That's why

Sayyid Sindbad was too alarmed by this morning's messenger to climb me, even though I had roused him for the first time in a month with a charm that I stumbled on by happy accident."

"I had thought to trade news with you, Kuzia, not suspicions," Somebody said. "What was this happy accident? What is this charm? And *what and where is that amulet?*"

Teased Kuzia Fakān, "You speak like a man with Sindbad's problem. And yet every morning lately in Yasmīn's face I see that whatever your problems may be, his is not one of them."

"My problems are three," declared Somebody. "I happen to be in love with this new friend of yours, and more determined than she is that Ibo shall not have her. I want to take her with me back to the Serendib I came from, but I have no more idea of how to get there from here than her father does. Yet instead of helping me find my way by speaking as straightforwardly to me as I'm speaking to you, you do another striptease. Another Kuzia Fakān!"

"Kuzia Fakān," the dancer said calmly, "is who I am. And because I happen to know who I am, I sometimes amuse myself by imitating others. Fatmah Awād says I do Jaydā to perfection, and so last night—this morning, I should say, when Hajj Masūd and his friends had left and the Tub of Truth had been drained and dried and Sayyid Sindbad was snoring away in there — well, Hajj had only stirred me up, as I mentioned before, and since I couldn't get to sleep, it occurred to me to snuggle behind my master and whisper in his ear the way I imagined Jaydā might have done before I took her place, and also to do certain other things in her fashion to see what might happen. If I say so myself, it was a good piece of work, but Sayyid slept right through it. By that time I was half asleep as well, and so I let my imagination wander. All the while holding his mouse in my hand, I did Fatmah Awād; I did Nuzhat; I tried Jaydā again as I thought she might have been years ago, when she was my age. No use: the mouse slept like its owner. Then, just before I dropped off to sleep myself, I remembered some gossip I had heard in the harem once about Sayyid Sindbad's wife, Yasmīn's mother. Even though she died before I was born and I'm not certain of her name, I reckoned that she and Yasmīn must have traits in common, and so by thinking of the daughter I pretended to be the mother, and I whispered and touched him through his sleep in that role. *Abracadabra!* Though the master slept on, the mouse awoke and turned into a mongoose in my hand! At that moment, alas, Allah saw fit to send the caliph's messenger to wake the whole household, and there went my mongoose and the ghost of Yasmīn's mother. But I will raise her again tonight, Inshallah, and we shall see what we shall see. There are your first two questions answered, friend. Do they show you the way to Serendib?"

Somebody shook his head, but to show his gratitude for her candor, he touched the dancer's arm.

"As for that charmless amulet," Kuzia then said, "I'm sorry to report that your guess is as good as mine. He keeps it in a little pouch of calfskin strung from his waist, underneath his drawers, as if it were an extra pair of eggs. But eggs they aren't, neither hen's nor cock's — this much I know from having once grabbed that pouch in the dark, thinking it was the other. What I squeezed, for an instant only, was small and hard and clicky in the hand, like a jeweled necklace or a pendant on a chain. Sayyid then struck my hand away and threatened to sell me to a lepers' brothel if I ever touched that charm again — and there began the decline of its magic powers, for which he blames me."

"Good Kuzia Fakān!" Somebody said warmly. "No more than you do I believe in any other amulet than desire. But we must find out what's in that pouch, if we can do it without packing you off to the lepers." He put both his hands on her shoulders. "The name of Yasmīn's mother was Marjānah. May that name bring you better luck tonight than it ever brought her."

Skeptical but grateful, Kuzia shrugged. "May it indeed."

5.

Sindbad's daughter, not her father, at his nod saluted the company that evening in the banquet hall, her wine cup raised: "Friends assembled! Loyal supporters of my father and canny investors in Serendib Limited! Faithful members of our household and honored new guests! Last but most especially, perspicacious betrothed of my bosom and bowels! Tonight it falls to me to bid you eat and drink and converse unstintingly, without waiting for my father's lead, for we have arrived at that somber midpoint and turning point of his maritime adventures: his fourth voyage. In memoriam whereof, though he

286

would have you make free and merry as always under this roof, he himself will fast and remain silent till he tells his tale. Let us fall to!"

Those who remained did so, with varying degrees of appetite. As had been forefeared, Talīb ibn Sahl, the chief investor in Voyage Seven after old Hasīb Alī, had taken his cue from that gentleman and defected — a loss that still-stranded Somebody felt along with Serendib Limited, for under Yasmīn's scoring system Talīb had been a high-point supporter of his narrative continuance. Gone, too, as foreseen, was the least of Sindbad's investors and Somebody's critics, Abū Shamāt. New to the table (as a seated diner) was Jaydā, in the tenth position, halfway down on Sindbad's left, and new to the company, in the place of honor, at Sindbad's immediate right (which place Ibn al-Hamrā had insisted on giving up to him), was the caliph's vizier's messenger. This was a gray-turbaned, gray-caftaned fellow of indeterminate age and much-pocked face, large of eye and ear and foot, as befit his function, but otherwise as blank as paper awaiting pen, and as silent.

The others, all familiar to our man by now, were in the places they had been assigned the night before, except that he himself had been promoted to the empty eighth (Abū Shamāt's, two down on Yasmīn's left) and Kuzia Fakān to the ninth (beside him and directly across from Jaydā). With this the dancer was delighted, no doubt because it at once confirmed that she was ranked above her predecessor, put her stranded ally on her right flank, and set her in better view than previously of Yasmīn's fiancé. She and he set to with the most conspicuous appetites: Ibn al-Hamrā was clearly triumphant at the new defections, at the appearance on the scene of the caliph's vizier's messenger (who volunteered no other name than that title), and at his own consequent added leverage over his prospective father-in-law. Kuzia all but winked with relish at the red-cheeked apple of her eye as she gorged and guzzled, and she did in fact wink sidewise at Somebody every time silent Sindbad shifted on his cushion-and-a-half. She even managed, it seemed to Somebody, to wink conspiratorially at Yasmīn, but only Ibn al-Hamrā responded in kind. Loyal Hajj Masūd, at Yasmīn's right hand, did his best for appearance' sake to fall to as well, but his heart was not in it; he chewed long before swallowing. Yasmīn did likewise, resplendent tonight in a sea-green djellaba that matched exactly her matchless eyes as well as her father's turban of the day. The remaining investors — Alī al-Yamān on Cushion Four, at Yasmīn's left hand; Sīdī Numān on Five, between Kuzia and the caliph's vizier's messenger; Jafar across from him, on Cushion Six, between Ibn and Jaydā; and al-Fadl on Seven, between Jaydā and Hajj Masūd — ate as circumspectly as they spoke, glancing often at the blank-faced new arrival and at one another. As for Jaydā, she dined as stolidly as she sat, often moving her lips as if narrating to her dinner plate, with accompanying changes of expression.

Stranded Somebody munched and monitored, bethought himself, painfully, of his own fourth voyage. Al-Hamrā it was who through the dinner most often thrust: "High time for us to speak of commissioning and provisioning! What ship, Sayyid? What master? Which of us to sail in her, and when?" Yasmīn would parry: "What? Speak of Seven, when we have yet to resail Four? Light of my liver, you crave your dessert in midmeal!" Or Hajj Masūd: "Why did the Prince of Believers in his wisdom command his vizier to instruct his messenger to return Sayyid Sindbad's answer in three days, if not to give us time to bring the past up to the present before addressing the future?" Sīdī Numān or Jafar would allow thoughtfully, "Indeed, that may be the reason," and the others would exchange glances, and Sindbad shift position, and Kuzia wink at one or another of her winkees, and Ibn al-Hamrā grin and wink, too, but at the caliph's vizier's messenger, and say to Yasmīn, "So be it, Pearl of Pearls: our ears are agape to swallow whatever monsters may attempt to swallow us in this evening's stories."

"Among those who think without speaking," suddenly declared Sindbad toward this uneasy dinner's end, "mind what you swallow, lest you become food for their thought. With this lesson in advance, my friends, and appreciative of your patience, I now break my fast of speech. Yasmīn."

She made her rounds, and after tapping for attention on his Tub of Last Resort — tap tata tap-tap, tap tap — her father began: "Those of you who know me know that just a few years after returning from my third voyage, which I had resolved would be my last, I packed up this steadfast tub and set out from this peaceful city yet again, restless as ever for sharp trading and marine adventure though rejoicing in the pure love of my wife and the birth of my daughter: a blessing to me yet as she was then."

All present drank to this except Yasmīn herself, who fixed her brilliant eyes levelly upon her father.

"Yet not even these blessings," he continued, "could keep me home. No sooner was Yasmīn's birth-cord cut than that other cord pulled me down again to Basra, with a word of advice and a sealed prophecy from a certain young Cairene slave whom I had bought in Beypore at the end of Voyage Three, and whose extraordinary gifts I had so come to admire and trust that I left my wife and infant daughter with full confidence in her care."

Another toast, in which Yasmīn joined, and the recipient, too, as if saluting her former self.

"Her word of advice," grave Sindbad went on, "was to sail this time in some other vessel than my beloved *Zahir*. The sealed prophecy, which I was not to open till the port of Basra had dropped astern, I assumed would explain that warning. If I did not hasten to open it, the reason is that I believed I foreknew its content. The method by which my comely young Cairene used to receive her visions of my future is our secret, but now and then a message would come through so strongly from me to her in our Tub of Truth that its sender became its receiver, so to speak. Moreover, my three previous voyages had yielded, along with three several fortunes, four morals apiece, and though some of those twelve were corrections of their predecessors, all together they gave me ample and hard-won wisdom. *Your fourth voyage,* Jaydā had prophesied, *though ultimately successful, like the others, will be neither short nor easy.* And *Do not sail in your* Zahir. Adding those warnings to each other and to my nautical lesson-book, I concluded that whereas on voyages One through Three my vessels, in one way or another, had lost me, on this one I was fated to lose my vessel.

"Therefore (as on Voyage Three) I hired a ship that to my seasoned eye looked only moderately seaworthy, despite its being larger by half than *Zahir,* and upon it I loaded a comparably larger cargo of stock-in-trade, despite my assumption that I would lose it. These investments I deemed necessary to encourage my fellow merchant traders, for by now I had acquired a reputation for being a fortunate venturer myself, but one whose good fortune was not invariably shared by his companions. As if Allah the All-Powerful were not master of all our fortunes, and such superstitions not arrant blasphemy! Perpend that, comrades.

"With my old captain Kasīm of Basra in command, we then set sail down the tranquil Gulf of Persia. So as not to distract him from his responsibilities, I kept to myself the real reason for our going in a chartered vessel rather than in *Zahir*, declaring instead (and it was true in its way) that the larger ship was required for my larger cargo. This cargo I had chosen, as I had my shipmates, by the proven principles of Voyage Three: it was valuable enough to serve its purpose in the early stages of the voyage but not so precious as to make me inconsolable over its later loss. So confident was I of what Jaydā's sealed message would say that even when Basra dropped below the horizon I did not at once open it, but took what pleasure there was to take in my new companions and in trading for the mere sport of it in the coastal ports along the gulf. And lo, restless as I had been to put Baghdad once again behind me for the zesty melodies of wind and water and the spirited harmonies of haggling, I found my pleasure in that music much diminished this time by thoughts of my wife and child — whom for obvious reasons I had not brought with me. It was more to enjoy a souvenir from home than to have confirmation of my assumptions that at last, in the Hormuz Strait, I unsealed and read Jaydā's prevision."

Here Sindbad paused and, for the first time that evening, drank. His listeners took the opportunity to do likewise, all but Yasmīn, Jaydā, and Somebody the Still-Stranded.

"The words I read," Sindbad then told his cup, "were thunderbolts beside which those that presently wrecked our vessel were no more than the popping vowels of ape-talk on Island One, Voyage Three. Whoever knows me knows those words; whoever does not must excuse my not respeaking them, since I can no more bear to do that than to repeat my lost wife's name. At the mere memory of those words the world still turns blacker before my eyes than in any approaching seastorm. What I cried out as I rent my garments was in no language but that of pain; I so wished to join my wife in death that despite the final warning of that message — to be as wary on Voyage Four of what I swallowed as I had been on Voyage Three of what might swallow me — I literally ate the whole poisonous prediction (which by that time, if accurate, had already come to pass) and rushed to fling myself into the Gulf of Oman.

"From this objective I was restrained by my fellows, who supposed

I had gone mad. Kasīm and the crew, who knew me, imagined that I had espied the first monster of our voyage. In vain they stationed lookouts to confirm my sighting, and would gladly have posted me in that office except that by then I had fallen insensible with grief.

"For several days and nights thereafter I lay like a dead man in my quarters. When at length I regained voice and movement, I tearfully reported to my companions that part of the dreadful prophecy concerning my wife and directed Kasīm to turn the ship homeward. But though I was the largest single investor in the voyage, the other merchants together overruled me, and Kasīm had no choice but to abide by their decision, however reluctantly, even when I added shipwreck to the prophecy. They sympathized with my loss, if indeed I had suffered one, but the words that had so afflicted me were, after all, not a news report from Haroun's town crier, only a Cairene prophecy. If the prophet spoke truly, then what was to happen to my wife had happened, and our returning could not restore her to me; if she spoke falsely, then what was to happen had not happened, and I should punish her on our return. As to the predicted shipwreck, I must excuse them for suspecting that I had added that item for persuasive effect.

"These words of theirs I found as hateful as those I had swallowed. Though I could not gainsay their speakers, I would neither speak nor listen to them thereafter, nor associate with them in any way. In a black fury I withdrew to my cabin and would not even eat what was brought to me, but fed on grief and rage alone while waiting for the typhoon inside me to be matched by one without. A foul and silent while later — during which interval the others traded their goods from port to port and island to island, shaking their turbans at my folly — this came to pass. One afternoon I heard Kasīm, on deck above me, cry, 'Every man for himself! We are lost!' 'So be it,' I said to myself, and I did not even leave my cabin for my faithful tub on the quarterdeck.

"There followed a tempest such as would have sunk even *Zahir,* and which simply splintered our ungainly craft into its component timbers, as if she had been dropped by a roc into the Valley of Diamonds. She did not go down but rather came apart, and so instead of going down with her I found myself astride one of those timbers in midocean, indifferently watching my Tub of Last Resort drift away from me and scarcely caring whether I sank or floated.

"That timber happened to be a large spar, upon which I was soon joined by a number of my fellows, Kasīm included. To none of them would I speak — not even to him, though after my warning he had had no more taste for the voyage than I. When he took command of what was left of the ship and ordered all aboard to paddle with hands and feet toward an island he saw on the horizon, I sat on the aft end of the spar, facing backward, and fed on my resentment as fishes fed upon the digits of the paddlers.

"By the time we reached shore (after a night of paddling toward low watchfires on the island), my sparmates would have no more to do with me than I with them. All had lost toes and fingers; they were prevented from feeding me to their nibblers only by Kasīm's reminding them that I had returned a fair share of myself to Mother Ocean on voyages past and might have useful survival advice to offer in our present stranding, if I could be induced to speak. But when, after lying exhausted on the beach for half a day, we saw the usual odd-looking building in the nearby trees, I still so nursed my grudge that I made no cautionary mention of roc's-egg temples or the dwellings of one-eyed cannibal giants, but kept my own counsel and distance, idly watching for apes to gabble from the trees, giant serpents to hiss from behind boulders, or rocs to swoop from the sky. Instead, we found ourselves corraled, suddenly and silently, by a ring of dark and naked men as wordless as myself. Though they offered no clear threat, so inhuman was their want of speech and gesture, even of expression, that some of my erstwhile colleagues fell to their knees to beg for mercy or commend their souls to Allah; others (notably Kasīm, from habit of command) addressed our surrounders in clear Arabic and other tongues, including the universal language of gestures, to indicate that we were shipwrecked and famished sailors. The naked ones — how can I call them men, who would not register and return such eloquence? — simply herded us buildingward, and this silence, between assemblages of the same species if not of the same race, I found more ominous than the gibber of the apes on Voyage Three, however much it suited my own humor.

"What happened next you will have heard: how we were brought before one who seemed to be the ruler of our captors or rescuers; how he likewise spoke no words but gestured us to sit and help ourselves to a feast of exotic victuals laid out in his banquet hall. Kasīm and the others had no difficulty in understanding this invitation and responding to it; they gorged and gulped, thanking the king and praising Allah between bites and swallows. But though I aped the motions of eating like the others, in fact I hung back once again, out of my ongoing despair and resentment as well as from hard-learned caution and in deference to Jaydā's warning. You might ask, since I cared so little now for my life, why did I not swallow recklessly with the others? The answer is that, first, I had no appetite, and second, if I had lost my taste for life, I was not however altogether indifferent to the manner of my death, and something in the smell of that feast put me in mind of the ogre's den. Day after day I forbore, quite as I had done on shipboard after reading Jaydā's words. The dark, speechless men did likewise, and while I noted their abstinence, they ignored mine, as I was already from my grief the puniest of the lot, and thus beneath their notice.

"Meal by meal, as my fellows swilled like hogs at the trough, they came to speak likewise, their noble though mercantile Arabic transformed into a language of oinks and slurps, farts and belches, as their bodies swelled marvelously, like sausages about to burst their casings. It was not long before they were turned out of the king's hall and into his pasture, where under the silent wardenship of their keepers (whose watchfires were those we had navigated by) they rooted on all fours as contentedly as the livestock they had become. I slipped out with them on hands and knees, swallowed up by the herd, and hid among the hummocks to watch the first brace of them be butchered. Kasīm, as befit his rank among us, was gutted and roasted for the king's table. The chief of the merchants after myself, who by now was the fattest of the lot, the wordless herdsmen made dinner of in their fashion, raw, while his doomed companions imperturbably grazed on.

"That spectacle cured me at last of my resentment and, oddly, of my despair, as well as of any appetite for meat for years thereafter. My appetite for life, however, returned. Inasmuch as my former fellows were beyond rescue, I made shift now to rescue myself, and in doing so regained myself as well. Without difficulty I slipped into the bush, away from those mouths that were no more than maws. Feeding myself at last (on herbs and greens) and talking myself back to life, in a mere six days I made my way to that island's other side. There, on the seventh day, I came upon a people whose civilized work was growing pepper; who never ventured to that island's barbarous other side; who themselves wore clothing over their skin and — wonder of wonders! — spoke not only a language but *my* language. At the sound of it I wept for joy and, swallowing my customary caution, ran calling to them through the pepper plants and rejoined the human race.

"Oh, my friends, what medicine it is to tell our stories! I who had eaten so little but taken in so much now disgorged to the pepper farmers the tale of my shipwreck and my companions' fate, and though that fragment was but the recentest installment of my history, the telling of it made me whole. My old self again, scarred but ready, when the pepperfolk spoke of their king on a neighboring island, I said, 'Of course, of course: let us be off to Island Two, Voyage Four. I shall apply to be your king's registrar of cargoes, and we shall see what we shall see.'

"My new associates were not in fact disposed to take an unscheduled trip to their king's island, this being the peak of pepper season. Moreover, they doubted that any registrar of cargoes was needed in their land, as they were a self-sufficient people who neither imported nor exported anything. Even their pepper was for domestic consumption only. A less seasoned castaway might have despaired at this news: without interisland commerce, how to get home? But I doubted that the pepper people had learned their Arabic directly from Allah himself and guessed therefore that their isolation was less than total. Besides, if they were only half as insular as they claimed, they were bound to be ignorant of many a thing taken for granted by us more traveled folk, and in this I saw opportunity. Indeed, what persuaded them at last to make an inconvenient ferry trip for which I had no money to pay them was their bafflement at my talk of import and export, which they hoped their king or his viziers might understand as they did not. What did they do, I asked them, with their surplus pepper, of which in good years there was bound to be a store? What else, they said, but throw it into the salt sea, as custom decreed? For otherwise there would be no need to plant next year's crop, and they would have nothing to do with their time and skill. Could they not trade that surplus, I asked them, for silks from Al Sin or ivories from Zanj? 'Of those things,' they replied, 'we clearly have no need; otherwise we would know what they were.'

"In short, they took me to their king as an amusing curiosity: one who spoke what sounded to them like Arabic but who was nevertheless in large measure unintelligible. Sure enough, my first hour in their capital city revealed to me a dozen ways to make my fortune. Straw hats these pepper people had, for example, but not turbans, a dozen times more versatile. They had adequate roads and even canals but had never thought of bridges, even to cross the narrowest ditch. They grew excellent grapes but for purposes of intoxication depended upon a crude homegrown bhang, since they had never heard of wine.

"My only problem, it seemed, was to choose from among their ignorances which one to enlighten them on first for best effect, and the solution became obvious when the king and his advisers galloped down to the harbor on horseback, as was their custom, to learn why a pepper boat had returned so early in the season. Excellent horsemen all, with fine mounts, they used bridles but had evidently not heard of saddles and stirrups, and were therefore (as I saw firsthand) often thrown despite their skill. Even as I salaamed before their bareback king, I knew where to begin.

"As all Baghdad has heard, I introduced these people not only to saddles, bridges, turbans, and wine, but also to hookahs, turnspits, hammocks, and a dozen other marvels — including, remarkably enough, pepper mills, of which they knew nothing. Needless to say, I soon became as close to this king as to my royal friend on Island Two of Voyage One, and at his insistence I assuaged my unassuageable bereavement by marrying the most beautiful, rich, and accomplished woman on the island after the queen herself. Yet though it would have been tactless to say so, I longed for my home and the infant daughter I had never seen, and successful as I was at pleasing the court with my several innovations, they brought me no closer to the City of Peace, for the reason that in certain areas the king and his subjects were impervious to novelty. To new contrivances they were quite open, but new concepts were another matter. Import-export trade the king would not hear of; it was contrary to custom and therefore probably impious. Let me show him a better-designed vessel for ferrying peppercorns from the island next door, and he would reward me with ten gold rings (of local manufacture), but I must speak no more of ships capable of venturing beyond the horizon: that was contrary to custom.

"What would have happened, I asked my new bride, if my merchant vessel had survived that storm and put in at Pepper Harbor to do business? Insofar as she could comprehend the idea (and she was by no means dull), it amused her: why should anyone trouble to exchange his dinner for his neighbor's dinner instead of each eating his own? But suppose, I asked her, that I had two dinners and no turban, while my neighbor had two turbans and no dinner? Why, in that case, she supposed (laughing and refilling my cup with new wine), I would first exchange one of my dinners for one of his turbans, and then the pair of us would consult the court physician so that he might cure the madness that had led me to cook two dinners for one person and him to make a turban he didn't need when he hadn't yet got his dinner. In any event, she concluded seriously, exchange with a neighbor was neither unheard-of nor unreasonable, but the same with strangers was strictly contrary to custom.

"Thus we passed some seasons in reciprocal love and benign incomprehension, which Time might have turned corrosive had not catastrophe saved Time time by quickly turning the next page of my story. While I racked my wits in vain to find some way to fetch my wife and myself back to Baghdad (where, I was confident, she would prove to be a fine stepmother to the daughter of whose existence I had not yet seen fit to apprise her), as if inspired by her reference to the court physician, an illness befell both my wife and the wife of my neighbor Zuraik, and I found myself in the presence not of the customary monsters to be expected on a voyage's second island, but rather of a monstrous custom, enforced absolutely by that custom-bound folk. Instead of marrying, as we do, until death do us part (or until the husband repeats three times 'I divorce thee,' whichever may happen first), these people of the peppercorn bound themselves to make that final voyage together as well. When Zuraik's wife succumbed of her illness, her family and neighbors proceeded to the customary place of burial, a large underground cavern in a hill overlooking the sea, into which cavern the dead woman's coffin was lowered on ropes through a small hole, as though down a well. Then, horrible to relate, her perfectly healthy husband — whom I had tried without success to console for his loss with the example of my own bereavement and second joy — permitted himself to be lowered after her with seven loaves of bread and a jug of water, whereafter the rope came up empty and the hole was recapped with its cover-stone.

"'By Allah!' I cried out to those who had lowered him. 'What condolence is this? Why did you not haul that poor fellow back to life, as my shipmates once hauled me, instead of abetting his desperate grief?' Not for the first time, they looked at me as if I were mad and let me know that grief and condolence had nothing to do with what I had witnessed. It was, rather, the custom of the country, decreed by the king himself and from which not even he and the queen were exempt; if my neighbor Zuraik had not voluntarily gone down that hole, he would have been forcibly consigned there.

"How I prayed then for my wife's recovery! But like a popular storyteller, once Allah hits upon a brave effect, He inclines to repeat it. Just three days later I was again a widower, but so overmastered this time were love and loss by terror that when I dashed seaward it was not to drown myself for grief (as my neighbors charitably supposed) but to swim for my life.

"As before, however, I was prevented: to follow my latest late spouse in any but the customary way was contrary to custom. 'Devil take your customs!' I railed at them. 'I am no Peppercornian, but a salty citizen of Baghdad, with three wives and seven children in that city!' To this exaggeration they replied with dignity that it was Allah's custom, not theirs, to allow any Mussulman four wives; theirs was to confer upon me by virtue of my fourth marriage the privileges and duties of a pepper person. Therefore they bound me up despite my struggles and, chiding me for my bad manners, lowered me into that dreadful cavern with my wife's coffin and the customary seven loaves and jug — this last, in token of my many beneficences to their nation, containing wine instead of water.

"One glance around that charnel house of a cavern was enough to send me shinnying up that rope as fast as they paid it out, until in disgust they threw it in after me, capped the hole, and left me to die a most horrid and protracted death in that frightful place. How I cursed the wife I had so lately cherished, for plunging me (through no fault of her own) into a blacker pit than even my first bereavement had! And yet . . . this was a different Sindbad from the feckless fellow whose world had gone death-dark at Jaydā's message. Here was a literal blackness, laid upon me by others, not myself; here was a silence not of the unspeaking but of the unspeakable, and I resolved to escape it somehow, as I had escaped other monstrosities on other islands. I undid my rope, nibbled my bread like a rat in the dark, even sipped my wine, and reviewed in vain the thirteen lessons of my past predicaments for help in this one.

"In that perpetual and fetid blackness, time soon died, as had my neighbor and most immediate predecessor in this vile custom, a robust man carried off by the Destroyer of Delights before he had finished the third of his seven loaves. This I discovered when, by gruesome trial and error, after an indeterminate period of groping among corpses new and old, I became able to move about in that black hole as easily as a blind man in his own house.

"'Unhappy Zuraik!' I addressed him when I found his body atop his wife's coffin. 'Did you die so quickly of the same disease to which our wives succumbed, or of the terror of dying slowly in this place? And has your death but prolonged my own dying, or has it given me more time to find a way back to life?' For now, you understand, I had eleven loaves and two jugs instead of seven and one — enough to keep me nourished for more than a week even after the grave-rats stole their portion.

"I say a week; in fact, I had no way to measure time but by the rhythms of my hunger and my sleep, both of which were no doubt deranged, as, intermittently, was I. But five or six loaves into my confinement I realized that though my cavern was crowded with coffins and bones, they were not so numerous as to comprise the whole dead of Pepper City. Moreover, the coffins were uniformly fine, as were the robes and jewelry of the dead survivors, such as Zuraik. Only the nobler sort of couples, it seemed, embraced their last in this particular hole: the folk of my neighborhood. Along about loaf ten, in a lucid interval, I estimated the population of that neighborhood and its death rate, based upon the passing of my wife and Zuraik's and the state of decomposition of the other uncoffined spouses round about, and calculated a probability of one new burial every eight days. If ten loaves' worth of time had passed since my own interment, either I was eating too much or else Allah was compensating for the irregularity of my wife's having so soon followed Zuraik's.

"Therefore I nibbled my final loaf more sparingly. For if as yet I had no plan for how to escape my fate, I had at least a plan to give myself time to find a plan. Sure enough, not long after my final crumb was eaten, I heard the cover-stone being removed, and once my eyes accommodated to the light I saw a new coffin being lowered amid sounds of mourning, and after it a well-dressed elder lady with her seven loaves and jug. I hid myself behind my own spouse's coffin till the hole was resealed, then armed myself with a leg bone from the nearest skeleton and stalked up behind my new cavemate, who was busy scolding her dead husband. 'See what you've done, Abdul! As if I hadn't warned you a thousand and one times not to walk in the hot sun at your age without your straw hat! Allah forgive me, you are so bullheaded about such things, sometimes it makes me want to kill you!' 'Allah forgive us both,' I said then, and I did her the mercy of cracking her skull with my thighbone club before possessing myself of her loaves and jug.

"In this manner I survived for how long I do not know or wish to know. The Destroyer of Delights being who he is, my provisioning was unpredictable: at one time I had twenty loaves and three jugs and at other times I was down to gnawing bones with my fellow rats, whether because no one in my old neighborhood happened to expire on schedule or because the deceased was a child or an unmarried adult. Even when, as you have heard, I discovered an exit from that cave by following a larger-than-rat-sized animal (a wolf or wild dog, I believe it was, attracted by the smell of carrion to burrow in from the seashore) and found myself on a blinding beach separated from Pepper City by a well-placed mountain — even then, as I had no surf-fishing gear and could find neither freshwater springs nor any edible plant more nourishing than pepper, I returned to the cave for my weekly bread, so to speak. Just as I had at the outset been sickened by the smell and blinded by the dark of that place but had grown in time altogether used to them, so I grew so accustomed to my mode of survival that I cracked my erstwhile neighbors' heads with no more compunction than you would crack a coconut. Indeed, I cannot deny that if the luckless widow happened to be a young woman and my loaf supply was ample, in my desperate new callousness I would help myself to her as well as her provisions until scarcity obliged me to end her shame. And if none of these killings gave me pain, neither did any give me satisfaction, except the last of them.

"As I was once again on an island beach, with the familiar blank sea before me and no monsters behind more dangerous than myself, I took to coldly robbing my necessary victims of their goods as well as their victuals, and to plundering the coffins of their spouses as well. In this way I soon amassed from the accumulated dead a considerable fortune in robes and jewels, which I sorted into piles on the beach while waiting for Allah to send me a passing ship. What He sent me instead, one fine morning, was my trusty old tub, as weathered and barnacled from its sojourn at sea as *Zahir* had been when it rescued me on Voyage Three. I fished it ashore as it fortuitously drifted by, but instead of embracing it like a long-lost friend, I coolly set it aside and went on with my business.

"A thing that puzzled me in that business was that while my death-rate calculations had proved to be close to the mark (as attested by my survival), the number of uncoffined skeletons was so small in comparison to the number of coffins that even after correcting for the unmarried, I judged that the Peppercornian custom of burying the living with the dead could be of no more than a decade's standing. Sure enough, one afternoon when I returned underground to find or await my next week's rations, I heard above me an unusually clamorous mourning, and when the capstone was removed I learned the answer to that puzzle. A coffin richer than any other in the cave was lowered, and after it — objecting as mightily as I had, and like me refusing to undo the rope that he and his loaves were let down by — came my erstwhile benefactor, the king himself.

"'Allah curse you!' he shouted up at his lowerers. 'This is regicide!' 'We are but following Your Majesty's strict order,' one of them called back (I recognized the voice to be that of the king's vizier), 'to which you yourself bound us with the most solemn oaths ten years ago.' 'I was a young and foolish prince back then!' the king protested. 'I wanted to impress my bride with a grander love-gesture than any she had heard of back home on Salt Island, to show her that her bridegroom was a kinglier king than her father! How was I to know that a woman ten years my junior would die before me?' 'We sympathize,

Your Majesty,' replied the vizier. 'Damn you, Tammūz!' the king then shouted. 'I decreed this practice then, and now I undecree it! Haul me up!' 'Decree it you did, Your Excellency,' his vizier called down, 'and your salty young bride was no doubt as impressed by that decree as we were. Your undying love for her killed my mother and a hundred other noble Peppercornians before their time. We would dishonor their memory if we broke the vow you swore us to in your reckless passion for the Salt King's daughter: to see to it that death would no more separate you two than it would separate from that day forward any other Pepper spouses. Having now fulfilled that cruel vow, however, we welcome your rescindment of it. Your Highness may rest assured that he is its last victim.'

"With that, the vizier tossed his end of the rope down into the hole. The king cried up to him, 'Tammūz! My queen was healthy as a horse till just last week! I believe you poisoned her when your own wife took sick, to save your skin!' 'That,' responded the vizier, 'is a sentiment unworthy of the Sultan of Peppercornia. Your Majesty must excuse me for not repeating it to your successor or these noble courtiers. Close the hole, please, gentlemen.'

"With a right goodwill they did, whereupon with like satisfaction I shortened the anguish of the man whose heedless passion had been the death of so many of my neighbors and almost of me as well. His grave-treasure and the queen's completed my fortune. She was indeed a salty, well-born beauty, scarcely stiff in her coffin and withal so fresh in death that it would have embarrassed me to strip and dejewel her had I not by that time passed beyond every civilized compunction. I say no more.

"It pleased Allah then to conclude my season of monstrosity by forthwith sending a merchant vessel past my beach, the first I had seen since my own went down. I hailed it in my customary fashion, turban-on-a-stick, paddled out to it in my tub, and, saying nothing about either the speechless cannibals or the Peppercornians, simply gave its captain to believe that my treasure had been salvaged from the wreck of which in truth I was the sole survivor, and offered to reward him handsomely for coming to my rescue.

"That little speech was my first utterance since the day months past when I had saluted my initial victim in the cave. The captain thanked me but, to my surprise, declined any payment for his act of mercy. 'Men should behave to men as men,' he declared. To this reminder I made silent salaam but to myself remarked, 'Alas, good sir, they do.'

"As this vessel was, like all my rescuers, bound conveniently home for Basra with trading stops en route, the final leg of Voyage Four was as profitable and peaceful for me as had been the last legs of the three voyages before it, except that from time to time the memory of my underground interlude would drive me quite mad. For a whole day, then half a day, then an hour, then half an hour, the good captain or his men would be obliged to restrain me from flinging myself into the sea; and this they gently did, supposing me innocently deranged by mere maroonment. Each time, I offered again in vain to reward them and was told, 'Men should behave to men as men.' By when we reached home port, my mad spells were down to a dark quarter hour every seventh or eighth day, during which I was not responsible for myself. Nowadays they come on me no more than once a season.

"That excellent captain taught me the remaining three lessons of Voyage Four, whose first moral I served up to you at its outset. He was himself a widower who called himself Allim al-Yom, or Navigator of the Day (a surname that we shall, alas, hear more of in voyages Five and Six), and his three rules for daily navigation were the same: first, Men should behave to men as men. Second, Men should behave to men as men. And finally, Men should behave to men as men. Yasmīn."

Replied Sindbad's daughter, "Father," and she rose quietly from her place. Jaydā did likewise, and together they made the wine-cup circuit. In marked contrast to the denouements of Sindbad's previous voyages, this one was met with neither salutes from the listeners nor hearty urgings from the teller to wash down his tale with wine. The host relapsed, grave-faced, into the silence that his account had broken, and from him the guests took their cue. Yasmīn it was who, once her rounds were made, raised her cup high with one emerald-sleeved arm and, emerald eyes flashing down the table's length, by way of toast proposed, "To all men who behave to men as men!"

"Amen," Somebody seconded, and all save pensive Sindbad drank. As that latter contemplated his cup, Ibn al-Hamrā, on his left, proposed in Yasmīn's direction, "To women who behave to men as women!" Only al-Fadl, Jafar, the caliph's vizier's messenger, and Kuzia Fakān joined him. That last then countertoasted, with more success, all men who behaved as men to women — a proposition equivocal enough to raise Hajj Masūd's cup, along with Sīdī Numān's and Alī al-Yamān's, but not those of Jaydā, Yasmīn, Still-Stranded, or (for whatever reason) Sindbad the Sailor. Seeing Yasmīn refrain, the abashed Hajj quickly lowered his cup without drinking.

"To men and women alike," Somebody proposed finally, "who behave to one another as fellow human beings, for we are all strandees together upon this great and monstrous island called the World."

To this even Sindbad nodded assent and sipped; of the others, all drank except Ibn al-Hamrā and his cohorts Jafar and Alī al-Yamān. Yasmīn then turned upon that toast's proposer a smile brighter than every lamp in the banquet hall and declared, "Though the Baghdad that my father came back to was still Baghdad, the Sindbad who returned there from Voyage Four was a stranger to the Sindbad who had set out. This *other* stranger, however — the gentle Sayyid Somebody whom it pleases my father to call his still-stranded brother and whom we have learned to call Bey el-Loor — set out a fourth time from that world whereof we know nothing beyond his telling and wound up here in ours, where he languishes yet. Now we shall hear at last how that accident befell him."

Somebody's Fourth Voyage

Through the first, or "Malaccan," leg of our fiftieth-birthday present to ourselves — a retracing of "Sindbad's" return to Baghdad from a composite of his voyages to the Far East — things have gone about as problematically as we expected. The second leg, to "Serendib," we trust will be another story.

One half of that "we" is our old traveling companion Simon William Behler — a.k.a. "'Simmon," "William Baylor," and more recently the noted New Journalist, no longer new, who signs himself simply "Baylor." The other half? Surprise! "Crazy Daisy" Moore's kid sister, our man's supercapable current bunkmate.

Julia Moore! Shy string-bean Julie from River Boulevard: she of the olive eyes and wheat-bran freckles, orthodontic braces and rapid-fire opp-talk. No nobody herself these days, "J. Moore" in her twenties and thirties established herself as a free-lance photographer and a bit of a daredevil, the Margaret Bourke-White of the Kennedy-Johnson era: not only a forward-area cameraperson in Vietnam and the Middle East but an ardent rock climber, white-water rafter, hang glider, solo sailor. Now in the second half of her forties, she has eased off a bit on the sustained high-exertion stuff but will still go anywhere for a picture; she's a regular in *National Geographic* as well as *Sports Illustrated* and the resurrected *Life* (and in their British, French, and German counterparts), no less a name in her field than Baylor in his, though perhaps less well known outside it. If you know photography, you know J. Moore; you may have heard of Baylor whether you read many books or few.

The two most celebrated living natives of the town of Dorset were not unaware of each other's success. Not only did Baylor note with pleasure J. Moore's photo essays in the magazines, but his family over there — his father and Aunt Rachel while they lived, Mr. and Mrs. Joe Junior thereafter — would occasionally mention Sam Moore's *other* daughter, the one who had made good, and shake their heads over her two elder sisters. Julia Moore's parents, while they lived (and when Mrs. Moore was lucid), and her surviving siblings likewise (Brinsley, the oldest, died in a drunken car-crash not long after *Somebody's Second Voyage*) did the same concerning "Mayor Behler's boy from over in East Dorset, who used to have such a crush on Daise?" Indeed, Daisy Moore herself, after the publication of "William Baylor's" early SF fantasies and historical novels and even more so after "Baylor's" New Journalistic hits, scrawled him cards and letters of congratulation from various places, in which she seldom failed to mention "the *other* great love of [her] life, and that redneck burg's other famous escapee: the jewel of River Boulevard."

These messages came at first from Dorset proper, four of whose five electoral wards were scandalized by Daisy's "running off" in 1962 with an incendiary black civil-rights leader, bearing his child, and dividing her time between Washington, D.C., and Dorset's black Second Ward after her hero abandoned her; later from Havana, whither she defected with her mulatto daughter to protest, by some logic of her own, the growing U.S. involvement in Southeast Asia; later yet from Key West, where, disaffected with Fidelismo, she settled for a time with her Cuban expatriate lesbian lover; next from the Sheppard and Enoch Pratt psychiatric hospital in Baltimore, where she affirmed her solidarity with the resident ghost of Zelda Fitzgerald while lamenting that "Persimmon" had not been her F. Scott; and finally, when the money ran low, from "Eastern Sho' State" (as she gamely called the old asylum on the Chaptico, as if it were a branch campus of the University of Maryland), where her mother had died and whence she fondly chided Baylor for the "fig-leaf liberalism" in his *Esquire* pieces while repeating that he and "J. Moore" were her *dos favoritas* on this dying planet.

"She loved you," Julia Moore told him with a shrug in Andalusia late in '75, when the writer's and the photographer's paths recrossed. "As much as Daise ever loved anybody outside the house. Her thing with the Black Panther wasn't love; it was a political statement. But you were so *green* back then, Bee! Greener than he was black! Daise knew you'd catch up one day and leave her behind, but you had so far to *go!*"

"Yeah, well," B acknowledged, "I went." Indeed, what had fetched him back to the north of Africa and the south of Spain ten years after his initial, life-changing visit to those places was a suspicion that he might no longer be "going" but instead might already have been — that his celebrity might have peaked in '73 with *Baylor's Kid Sister,* a success both critically and commercially, and then turned with the tide of events later that year: the Yom Kippur War and the consequent Arab oil embargo, which, along with the U.S. withdrawal from Vietnam, spelled the real end of the Swinging Sixties. The relative fame and fortune attendant on that book's success had been its author's chief, though inadequate, compensation for sundry losses and failures: the son literally lost in South Vietnam, an MIA; the acrimonious divorce proceedings initiated by Jane Price soon after their Virgin Islands misadventure, both parties' bitterness being exacerbated by the news about Drew and by *BKS*'s climb up the best-seller lists; their daughter Juliette's distancing herself to the Pacific Northwest with her Muslim marine biologist ("Musalām the Mussulman mussel-man," Baylor called him); the petering out of his affair with great-eyed Teresa Anginelli, whose devotion saw him through these traumas and convulsions but who thirsted — forgivably, at age thirty-five — for exactly what her lover was divesting himself of: marriage, parenthood, a house in Bethesda and a condo on the Shore. And beyond all these, a cloud no bigger than the blank sheet of 8½ x 11 in his IBM Selectric: whither Baylor next?

A year passed, then two years, by which point normally he would be winding up Baylor's next big one and have placed half a dozen spin-offs from it in his usual periodicals. In romantic collaboration with Teresa he did a series on the old Italian-American neighborhoods of

Baltimore, Philadelphia, New York, and Boston ("Baylor Goes Italian," sure enough), but it had no more bite than overcooked linguini or the airline in-flight magazine that commissioned it, and he took little pride in the resulting coffee-table book, with its tourist-bureau photographs. Where was *Baylor's Kid Sister*'s big brother?

"Lost in the Virgins, I suspect," he once opined to Teresa Anginelli, "where a wrong turn in Charlotte Amalie can land you in Marrakesh. The guy who came out of that space-and-time warp wasn't the guy who went in."

The trouble with Teresa's reaction to her lover's account of that baffling episode was that she *believed* it, as she believed in ESP and astral projection, whereas Baylor himself believed in nothing more mysterious than hallucination under prolonged stress. But inasmuch as that interlude in the "Jmaa el Fna" of Dronningen's Gade remained as palpable in his memory as any experience in his life — not an "altered perception" but a quite ordinary perception of an unaccountably altered reality — to call it hallucination was tantamount to calling his whole life hallucination, from, say, that scary anchor-line incident in Soper's Hole to the present moment.

"I never resurfaced," he proposed to Teresa Anginelli. "My wife drowned me, and I've lived happily ever after."

"More poetry than truth in that," his friend replied, no doubt wishing he would stop calling that woman his wife. She then added, remarkably, "Maybe it's the *other* Marrakesh you never came back from. Where the hippie girl balled your brains out?"

"Tangier."

"Wherever. You got in, but you never got out, and this Baylor character went on with your story."

When, however, these notions thereafter took possession of our man's imagination to the point of his resolving to do a Theseus-in-reverse — to follow Baylor's thread back into the labyrinth in hope of leading some antecedent out — his friend quietly bade him addio. Such sentimental journeying was best done solo, no? She sensed anyhow that their little intermezzo had about run its course; so did he, if he was honest about it. They had had a real couple of years, but they weren't a real couple. From a certain sentimental revisit of her own she looked up at him, sadly but gamely, and said, "The best-planned lays, as we say in Little Italy, gang aft a-gley. *Capisce?*"

Baylor smoothed her hair.

El Caudillo the Generalissimo Francisco Franco having finally completed his protracted dying, our man tied in a *National Geographic* commission ("Spain's Long Siesta Ends") with a resurrection of William Baylor's abandoned *Court of Lions* project — this version to be narrated in the street-smart style of *Baylor's Kid Sister* rather than the sober cadences of *Zanzibar!* and *The Magnificent* — and, bidding heartfelt *arrivederci* to his dark-eyed friend, set out for Marrakesh by way of Iberia. The solid, self-effacing discipline of old-fashioned journalism he found both bracing and soothing: not Baylor-in-Córdoba but just Córdoba, registered to be sure in the *Geographic's* trademark first-person singular, but by an *I* who unobtrusively asked and listened, who looked but stayed out of the picture. The preliminary legwork, a month of touring and interviewing from La Coruña to Barcelona to Cádiz, went quickly and well; whoever that "I" was, he listened sympathetically to Basque and Catalonian separatists, to aging Falangists still fearful of the Comintern, to U.S. military personnel in Rota and Terrejón, to the popular socialist candidate for prime minister, to teenagers in American-style jeans and hard-rock T-shirts, even (his entrée being the magazine's prestige, not Baylor's own) to the diplomatic tightrope artist King Juan Carlos — a sailing enthusiast who voiced his hope someday to cruise Chesapeake Bay.

Then, greatly impressed by the Spanish people and not displeased with himself, either, he hired a little villa on the Costa del Sol up toward Nerja, which the booming new high rises hadn't yet reached, and settled in to organize his notes (and to work up a handle on *Baylor in the Court of Lions*) before re-viewing the New Spain more selectively with whichever photographer the *Geographic* assigned him.

"Hey there, Persimmon?" The phone call came via satellite from Dulles Airport one Nerja evening as he was eating smoked-mussel *tapas* on his patio, worrying about his daughter (who had announced from Seattle her marriage to Musalām), and admiring a pollution-enhanced Mediterranean sunset: "Guess who!" Grinning all the way, he packed a bag and flew up from Málaga to meet the plane in Madrid, as good a restarting place as any. Tall and pale and rusty-haired, long (and straight) of tooth and limb, gangly still but efficient of movement, in manner still a shade shy but not in act, her eye-corners permanently crinkled from four decades of high spirits, J. Moore was already clicking away at him with her Hasselblad from the far side of customs as he waited to embrace Crazy Daisy's grown-up kid sister.

"Isn't this the *wildest?*" she wanted to know over roast suckling pig at Botín's. Julia Moore was at least as familiar with Madrid as he; both could think of half a dozen less touristy lunch places for toasting their reunion with Codorníu and beginning to catch up on each other's lives while eating their way across post-Franco Spain. But Daisy's kid sister was a fan both of Ernest Hemingway and of Spanish custard, and the novelist James Michener had once mentioned to Baylor that "Hemingway's Favorite Restaurant in Madrid" had renamed one of its desserts Flan Michener in honor of his addiction to it. "I've got so much to *tell* you! You'll have to fight to get a word in edgewise!"

The camera, though, and her appetite and high curiosity took care of that. Julia Moore talked much — about her parents and siblings, her beloved Daisy in particular; about her energetic life since River Boulevard days; about places and politics and photography and flan — but she also plied Baylor with questions ("'Simmon? Simon? Bill? Can't I call you just B?") and, while attending his responses at any length, snapped away at Awakening Spain with her several lenses and took unto herself its cuisine. Once she had reviewed and approved (over Flan Michener) "B's" projected ten-day photo itinerary, she proposed that they hotel themselves promptly to get rid of their bags, then rent a car and shoot a few rolls in the Plaza Mayor and the Retiro to remind her of the feel of Spanish afternoon light, then resume their catching up over a dinner early by Madrid standards, grab a solid night's sleep, and at sunrise tomorrow really get cracking on that agenda.

They did: two singles in a quiet little hotel Baylor knew off the noisy Puerta del Sol; good New Spain shots of kids "break dancing" in the Plaza Mayor and couples necking openly in the park; a many-course seafood dinner in several places that each wanted to show the other. Only the solid night's sleep went by the board; over Fundador and coffee, jet-lagging Julie laughed and listened and talked till midnight (only 7:00 P.M. by her body clock), but good as her word, she rapped on the writer's door at dawn to hustle them out to the Escorial for some Old Spain contrast shots before the sun got high. In the course of that first evening, B spoke in a preliminary way of what he would later come to think of as Somebody's second and third voyages:

his adventures on "the Island" with Daisy Moore and in the Virgins with Jane Price. ("Opp-talk!" crowed delighted Julie over mariscos and Monopole: "OppI'd fopporgoppottoppen oppopptoppalk!") And in a preliminary way he learned in turn that though handsome J. Moore had never married or wished to marry (she guessed old Sam had spoiled all three of his daughters for marriage), she had enjoyed a series of more or less important long-term affairs and — like Daisy, but single-handedly and more successfully — had raised a daughter, in Julia's case sired by a Mexican foreign-service officer early in that series. Conchita Moore was currently a sophomore at the Rhode Island School of Design. Further, that her brothers had all grown up to be respectable burghers who saw to it that their surviving sisters did not want for nieces and nephews, and who in all likelihood hadn't the least suspicion to this day of what it was that had driven Brinsley out of the house and into a lamppost, Daisy over the edge (and away from "'Simmon," without telling him why), and herself, perhaps, into traveling light.

"You had your catalpa tree to escape by," she reminded him (Baylor had forgotten it, as she had forgotten the sisters' opp-talk). "Daisy was my catalpa tree."

"Bee," as his name became the next day, reserved one or two questions in this area for a later time, and the pair set to work. Unlike writers of pure fiction, Baylor was as used to working in collaboration — with photographers, researchers, commissioning editors, even coauthors — as he was to working alone, but not even with Teresa Anginelli had he so enjoyed professional partnership. In truth, good Teresa had been an able but permanent amateur, deferring on almost every journalistic point to her former teacher, for the excellent reason that she knew enough to recognize that his ideas were usually better than hers. J. Moore was a seasoned pro, at collaboration as well as photography. From that first jet-lagged perusal of Baylor's prospectus she clearly grasped the piece's handle and set about efficiently and high-spiritedly to illustrate it in *National Geographic* style: weathered old-timers with Eyes That Have Seen Much, bright-faced children Confronting an Uncertain Future, portentous visual metaphors redeemed by superb photographic composition and exposure.

"Winds of Change, Bee!" she would holler as the windmills of La Mancha hove into view, and together they would quickly choreograph what Baylor came to call "logistically assisted serendipity." A fast phone call to the Club Madrileño de Hang Gliding (with whose membership Julie had "hung out" one afternoon on a previous assignment) set up a perfect Heavy Metaphor shot for later in the day: a colorful flock of young high-tech daredevils circling at the magazine's expense over Don Quixote's slumbering giants. While Baylor made these arrangements by pay-phone from a nearby service station, Julia collared a brace of leathered, crash-helmeted hombres who were refueling their motorcycles — one of them lanky and grizzle-bearded, the other as short and plump as Cochinillo Botín — and, in exchange for picking up their modest gasoline bill, posed them before the famous windmills on their Suzukis: a modern-day knight-errant and squire.

"Let the editors choose," she said, laughing, as their rented Seat zipped south that evening toward Toledo. "Or the caption writers," Baylor replied. "They're the real artists in this operation." Over Quarter-Hour Soup and Partridge Stew Toledaña, among other courses, at Hotel Cardenal in Toledo's Arab Walls, with a soft red wine from nearby Valdepeñas and music from a strolling *tuna universitaria,* they agreed to become less efficient as of the next day; otherwise, at their present rate of progress, they would complete their assignment before they completed their reacquaintance, and neither of them thought that a good idea. Let's hear more about Sister Daisy as Julia's "catalpa tree," for example: Baylor well remembered his old friend's fierce general protectiveness of her younger sister, Daisy's impassioned conviction that "Jule," along with "'Simmon," *mattered,* as she herself did not, and that they two must therefore hold themselves to more rigorous standards than applied to the likes of her. . . .

Julia Moore rolled her olive eyes and responded, not quite to the point, "Ai-yi, those standards!" Had Bee ever known such . . . *Dostoevskian* moral intensity as Daisy Moore's? "Never," he concurred. "I used to fool myself into imagining I knew who I was, and then the Gadfly of Dorset would show me that it was all pretension and affectation."

"*Innocent* pretension and affectation," Julia corrected him, and, grinning, she reached across the table-corner to pat his left hand. "Then she'd lay you, right? To let you know she was deflating you out of love and not out of spite. Me she just hugged and kissed, but she told me all about the Bon Ami business and the Island and Baylor's Kid Sister's grave."

"*Twin* sister," said blushing B, who was also feeling his Valdepeñas and admiring for the manyeth time that day his colleague's full breasts under her khaki work shirt. "Same name as yours, come to think of it: BeeGee-Bijou-Jewel-Jule-Julia."

Daisy's sister applauded. "Bee to Jay in four moves. Are we predestined?"

"*Que será,* et cet. Come to think of it further, I named my only begotten daughter after you, too, without realizing it: Juliette P. Behler. *There's* foreshadowing."

Julia made a mouth, squeezed his hand, and withdrew hers. "There's pretense and affectation, Persimmon. Not particularly innocent."

"And there's deflation," he came back quickly. Just as quickly she smiled and returned, "But not out of spite," and he, teasing, "How can a boy tell for sure?"

The woman sized him up, her face serious but her eyes twinkling. "A boy might need proof, but a man ought to know. Hey, Bee, I thought we'd agreed to slow down!" Taking his hand again, she turned his wrist to check his watch against her own — also a Seiko sports model, not much smaller than his. "Mañana," he reminded her. "Right you are," she agreed, and that being the case, she proposed that they go back to their rooms at the *parador nacional,* which overlooked splendid Toledo from high bluffs across the Tagus, so she could shoot the near-full moon over the city of El Greco. They did; she did; and when Baylor, watching, admiring, and picking up on their earlier dialogue, remarked that the winds of change didn't change *everything* — either for post-Franco Spaniards or for escaped Dorseteers, in whom the proof-needing boy still sometimes dwelt — she grinned, cocked her head a bit behind the camera, held out her hand to him, and said, "Proof time, then, I guess."

Daisy Moore at fifteen had been brown and bony. Her kid sister, three decades later, was white from top to bottom despite her outdoor life, red-haired and lightly freckled likewise, athletically muscled but thickening a bit in middle age at her waist, hips, thighs. Released from their C cups, her breasts seemed to embarrass her: "They're too *big!*" she couldn't help groaning when Baylor first covered them with kisses. Indeed, about sex in general Julia Moore proved to be a touch self-conscious; she went at it with her characteristic combination of shy manner and forthright action. To a woman of her independent spirit, "self-surrender" did not come naturally, and for that very reason it excited her. In making love she preferred a passive role, though there was an alertness, even an energy about her passivity that made it clear it was a role: the tomboy pleased to put on girlishness for her date. In the balcony moonlight her white body all but luminesced, especially after their foreplay worked up a small sweat. "My ass is like *sandpaper!*" she complained when B busied himself in that neighborhood. In truth, she was not the physical specimen that young Teresa Anginelli had been, not to mention Jane Price. But even in Baylor's initial, routine caresses Julia Moore took an uncommonly intense and (as time would prove) unfeigned delight, while his subsequent, less routine ones made her gasp with pleasure. That first night in the aptly named Parador Nacional Conde de Orgaz she climaxed more easily and frequently than any woman our man had ever made love with — so readily, indeed, that "climax" would have been a misnomer had not her peaks, like the Pyrenees, had their own variety. She would continue to do so to Voyage Four's end, and her new lover's pleasure in her pleasure more than compensated for any less-than-perfections in Julia Moore.

They did not catch the next morning's long early light, the photographer's favorite time for outdoor shots. Baylor woke to find his new partner moving naked, white, and quiet about the room, focusing him happily from various angles without clicking the camera's shutter. They made love again, went down to a late breakfast of coffee and *churros,* and came back to make love yet once more, more or less, in *his* room this time, before checking out. "Boyoboy, Bee," Julia sighed atop him, sweeping those breasts slowly back and forth across his face, "did we ever get inefficient." But when, then, decidedly *terminado,* Baylor withdrew in a single slow motion both his spent and tender organ and, from elsewhere, his index forefingertip, she efficiently came one final time.

In Granada that evening (Parador Nacional San Francisco: good view of the Generalife from their double room, but Awakening Spain nowhere in sight) she rummaged through her sparsely packed bag — "Less is Moore," she had quipped in the Madrid airport, clearing customs — and brightly bade him close his eyes just where he stood and . . . open his fly. Gently then she twice circleted his weary instrument with something comparably limp but metallic: a heavy silver I.D. bracelet, its still-blank nameplate dulled with age and a patina of tiny scratches, the same one (he now confirmed when he caught it as it fell to the rug) that Daisy Moore had returned to him on his fourteenth birthday, then impulsively asked him to relend her, some while after, for their next "date" (which turned out to be one of their last) and never got around to rereturning, nor he to asking for it. The fad passed; Daisy began her willful, unexplained withdrawal from him and their high-school friends; before long he found other girls, at once less generous and less exacting.

Having thus boldly made her presentation, Julia Moore declared to him shyly, "Daisy's blessing, I guess; she said to give it back to you if we happened to end up in bed. She's been wishing us on each other since nineteen forty-five, but she never pushed."

Baylor wondered: logistically assisted serendipity? But what he asked was, "Is this what she told you to do with it?"

Strictly her own idea, Julia assured him, chuckling. After growing up on Daisy's accounts of their making out, how could she not think of him as a sex object? In counterinspiration he then ordered her to take her clothes off and "put that trinket where it belongs," though he had no idea where that might be. As he had divined, however, the challenge amused, baffled, intrigued, and excited Julia Moore: she considered aloud and reasoned herself out of the obvious options and some not so obvious, displaying each like an amateur porn model for his delectation while he remained fully dressed and seated like a contest judge. At last he said, "Give it up, Jule; the right answer keeps changing," drew her laughing onto his lap, took the peripatetic talisman from her hand, and, kissing her mouth, cupped it decisively between her legs. Her orgasm was prompt and formidable.

In the event, that bracelet changed hands (and wrists, ankles, pockets, travel bags) as frequently as the lovers changed pet names. Starting there in Granada — where the Alhambra's lions maintained their stony, reproachful silence — they got back down to serious work between their other pleasures, and though they lingered overtime in the Parador Nacional San Francisco in vain hope of rerousing Baylor's muse, by Seville and Córdoba they were back on schedule. B's travel notes grew into text, by turns inspiring J's photographs and taking inspiration from them, so readily that he could scarcely imagine going on to Morocco alone after Spain's Long Siesta reached its end.

Shortly before that, somewhere in Catalonia, he circled back to a subject raised but set aside during their first evening, in Madrid. Granted, the general tenor of Sam Moore's interest in his adolescent daughters had been obvious; at least it was so in retrospect. But forbidden inclinations came in many shades of latency and manifested themselves in sundry forms and to various degrees, and early-teenage girls were not in every instance the most reliable interpreters and reporters of such manifestations. Looking back now as a stable and seasoned adult, to what extent did Julia think her father had . . . acted upon his inclinations? It was something Baylor had wondered about, off and on, for thirty years.

Her expression, wary at the start, grew merrier as he strung his query out. "Why is that important to you, Bee?"

"Not important," he said at once. "Well, a little bit important. Map checking? Focus correction?"

"We think our Bibi wants to know what he's getting mixed up with before he gets any more mixed up."

"You mentioned that Daisy had been your escape route. . . ."

"Not only from Dorset." She shook her head, perked up. "Me he only got his hands on, maybe half a dozen times. 'Look what a big girl our little Julie's getting to be,' that kind of thing. Always with our clothes on, okay? Plus a couple of wandering-ins to pee while I was taking a shower."

Baylor shrugged. His friend went on, her voice still bright but her expression watchful of his: "Dear old Sam. Brinsley he fondled under her nightgown from age twelve on, on his lap in his famous den with his famous brandy snifter, and once he got her to handle his equipment: the illustrated facts of life. It took Brins a while to catch on, Bee, 'cause she was the first and 'cause Sam was always so good-humored and unmenacing about these things. Playful, sweet — even *witty*. In Brins's sophomore year of high school Ma went off to Eastern Shore State for the first time, and Sam came into her room one night with nothing on under his bathrobe and reminded her, half teasing, that we were all counting on her to take Ma's place while she was away. Brins had agreed that if she was grown up enough to have the car she'd been begging for for her sixteenth birthday, she was grown up enough to take on some extra chores around the house."

"But no heavy lifting."

"That's about what Brins told him that night. And lots of nights after."

"She got the car, though," Baylor remembered.

"Of course." Julia frowned in surprise. "The car came before the proposition. My father didn't *rape*, Bee; he seduced. You knew Sam Moore: he was a flirt and a tease, never a bully."

"A snifter."

Julia smiled. "A sweet old snifter. And so easy to say no to that it was hard to say no to him. But Brins finally said no."

"So why'd she leave home?"

"'Cause she told Ma all about it, and Ma got jealous and threw her out. Ma loved Sam Moore to death; the rest of us just loved him a lot. So: there's me, and there's Brinsley."

Like many another through Voyage Four, this conversation took place in a restaurant, in this instance in the uplands behind Barcelona. Julia Moore glanced sidelong at her tablemate, who happened to be fingering the links of their joint I.D. bracelet like worry beads. He raised both it and his eyebrows. She cocked her head. "And there's our dear Daisy," she said. "I got pawed; Brins got fondled; Daisy got fucked. Not in that order."

"Often?"

"How often is often?" Julia considered her own question. "Yeah: often. Daise didn't tell me about it directly at the time, the way she told me about you and her other boyfriends, but I more or less understood what was going on. When I was safely off to college she told me all about it; it was still going on even after Ma died, but I guess not *often* by that time. And after Dad's death she gave me chapter and verse: the whole *Tender Is the Night*. You want chapter and verse?"

Baylor guessed not.

"Thing is," J. Moore went on, "I got these different versions. Daisy's is that she let Sam in to keep him off me. Ma's was that Daise seduced him, the way Brinsley had tried to. Ma actually talked alienation-of-affections and claimed Daisy told her the suit wouldn't stand up 'cause the plaintiff was in the bin. Brins seemed a little jealous herself; she told me Daise always had to go her one better."

"What do *you* think, Jule? Now?"

His long friend considered, cocked her head. "I think I think that the sexual exploitation of human beings is a crime against humanity and that as charming as he was about it, my late father's incest streak was unpardonably exploitative, to put it mildly. Okay? And he *was* charming, Bee. We were all crazy about him, all except Brinsley, and I think her resentment came from her having been crazy about him, too. Sam's to blame, for sure, but everything is true. Daisy balled him to spare me. Did she really have to? I've decided to be grateful anyhow. Ma's accusations were exactly as crazy as Ma was, but what made her crazy? What was cause and what was effect? Daisy *liked* playing wife and mother in that house. Maybe she even needed to feel exploited and doomed, awful as that is to say. Look who she had for a role model!"

She uncocked, then recocked her head. "Samuel Bennett Moore shouldn't have been interested in humping his teenage daughters, nice as he was about it. It screwed us all up, more or less. But long after I was out of the house and Ma was kaput, Daise went on taking care of him. I believe she happened to love old Sam more than she loved her other men, and I can't help thinking that in a different world everybody could've shrugged their shoulders and got on with it."

She considered. "Incest is a loaded word, Bee. *Exploitation* is the crime. Sam should've kept his hands off us till we were our own women. Experienced. Independent. How we handled him then would've been nobody else's beeswax. But don't ask me how I would've handled him, okay?"

Marveled Baylor, "'Nobody's beeswax,'" and he might have declared his love then and there to Julia Moore had not her sister's presence — in the I.D. bracelet, maybe — stopped that precipitateness in its tracks as Daisy herself used to stop him, clutching his arm with one hand and clapping her brow with the other on the corner of High and Holly or halfway across the old Dorset Creek Bridge. Instead, as the pair celebrated the winding-up of their Spanish project with a weekend in Gibraltar (from where, through J. Moore's telephoto lens, they could read the hour on the town clock in Ceuta, across the strait in Africa), he told her in more detail the story of his "third voyage," in particular that disorienting episode in Charlotte Amalie's Dronningen's Gade, her opinion of which he very much wanted to compare to Teresa Anginelli's.

"Cock your head and consider, good friend," he bade her at the story's end. "Where was I?"

Julia Moore's general intention, at this point in our travels, was to make her way back to D.C. and on to something more adventurous, if not more agreeable, than the assignment she was finishing: a solo sail to Hawaii, maybe, or something strenuous in Alaska. But she was in no rush. Baylor's was to cross that nine-mile gap out there between Hercules's Pillars, Gibraltar and Jebel Musa, and to rewind the Moorish invasion of Al-Andaluz — and his own previous, corner-turning sojourn — back to Marrakesh, the Jmaa el Fna. . . . But he was in no rush at all, and kept forgetting, in fact, lately, what the urgency of that pilgrimage had been, if not its point.

Across the gap between them (a table-corner), his friend declared, "Maybe the question isn't *where,* but *who.* However, that's a question I don't take much interest in." Did B remember, by the way, all those books her parents used to press on him, her mother especially, back in his Daisy days? Of course B did, and gratefully: CARE packages from River Boulevard to the culturally undernourished of East Dorset. Why? Oh, Julia had been reminded when she was reading *Baylor's Kid Sister*: the *Thousand and One Nights* business, plus what Daisy had told her about those dandelions on "Bijou's" grave in the Dorset Municipal Cemetery. . . .

"I'd forgotten," B confessed, much stirred. "It was on River Boulevard that I first crossed paths with Scheherazade. Allah bless your poor mother, Ju!"

"And bless Sam, too," his friend insisted, "the most civilized man in Dorset, I'll bet, in most ways. Maybe the only one. He told Daisy those books might help you find out one day who you were. Did they?"

"Allah bless your whole house, J. Moore. Marry me, okay?"

Unsurprised, head duly cocked, she declared, "I'd call us engaged, Bibi. Let's stay that way." Getting back to the subject: what she thought she thought, she said, was that what had happened back there in Charlotte Amalie had doubtless been wished into being by *B's Kid Sister,* which had been very much in gestation at the time, together with the stress of Baylor's failing marriage and Jane Price's equivocal near-drowning of him the evening before. But B had better understand that for his new bunkmate there was not only no other world than this one (and therefore no "boundaries" of the sort he had mentioned) but scarcely any time besides the present. Here, Now, and Tomorrow were her coordinates, and of those she took Tomorrow seriously only because you couldn't pop off in a cruising sailboat from Marina Del Rey to Maui without a bit of advance planning. Would he care to come along? Believe her: if he would rather chase his own tail in Marrakesh, she would truly understand — but from a distance. Either way, he had her blessing.

"But not, as they say," Baylor said, "your heart."

J. Moore winked. "Didn't I tell you? That belongs to Daddy."

In the event, we become a couple but not regularly a team. Engaged indeed, we give no further thought to marriage and prefer as a rule to work on separate projects, though now and then we enjoy a joint commission. Our Arlington townhouse becomes the writer's daily workplace, the photographer's home base between gallivantings everywhere, often of several weeks' duration. The bond between us proves no less strong for its elasticity. In our frequent separations, our missing each other takes the agreeable form of our looking forward, not of our hurrying back; each genuinely misses the other but wants that other to make the most of whatever is in the works, personally and professionally.

For Baylor, at least, one interesting consequence is a prevailing if not quite absolute sexual fidelity, of which no pledges have been exchanged. One evening while J. Moore is off shooting oil rigs on Alaska's North Slope, he gets a call from Teresa Anginelli; she needs a letter of recommendation for her prospective new employer, the National Geographic Society, for whose magazine she aspires to write photo captions. Baylor proposes hand-delivering the letter to her at dinner somewhere in town, and when she teases him over dessert with her version of the song she used to sing after their Tuesday-night class — *Won't you come home, Bill Baylor? Won't you come home?* — they end up in a familiar bed in a familiar College Park apartment. She's doing all right, Teresa supposes; not to worry. She understands things are well with her old evening-school teacher, too, and wonders when there'll be another Baylor book for her to enjoy. It is a sweet and oddly guilt-free evening, but B declines her invitation to stay for breakfast, and declines as well, gently, her subsequent suggestion of another such rendezvous the next time he's "by himself." He enjoys imagining that Julia wouldn't much object, as long as he doesn't get "involved" or bother her with the story. He enjoys his like absence of jealous curiosity regarding her nights away from Arlington; enjoys not exercising his presumable freedom; reckons he must be getting older, maybe even growing up. When he can't be with Julia Moore, he finds, he would as leave be with himself, whoever *that* is becoming.

Not long after our return from Awakening Spain, we visit Daisy together in "Eastern Sho' State." Her building is bright, clean, fairly quiet — not at all the snakepit of Baylor's boyhood imaginings. But Daisy has become not only an old woman but a physical wreck, almost a witch caricature: wild hair, glittering eyes, bad teeth and skin, a too-ready and too-shrill laugh, even a hooked nose complete with hickey. The visit is uncomfortable. She calls him Persimmon and challenges him to tell Julia how he got that name; she teases him about *Lagoon* and Princess . . . Wahoo, was it? Lieutenant Pinkerton? Regarding the pair of us together, she several times declares, "The jewel is in the lotus. Now I can die, right?" And the following winter she is indeed found naked and dead of exposure in the woods of the little island in the mouth of Island Creek, to which evidently she swam one frosty night from the hospital grounds.

At her funeral but seldom thereafter Baylor remeets the brothers Moore, who are as Julia has described them to him: polite, taciturn, unassuming, uninteresting and uninterested. With Julia's daughter, Conchita, on the other hand — a bright and lively black-haired beauty, few of whose genes appear to be her mother's — he gets on warmly and easily in the role of sort-of-stepfather: it revives for him some of the pleasure of seeing his own Juliette into her early-womanhood, with none of the attendant responsibility and mildly nagging guilt.

That young woman's life — as the 1970s run like sand through an egg timer — does not go particularly well, nor does Baylor's career. His daughter and Musalām separate, then divorce: "Irreconcilable cultural differences," Juliette reports from the Strait of Juan de Fuca. Musalām returns east (the American East, not the Middle); Juliette remarries within her own eth but outside her profession — a Seattle divorce lawyer, himself divorced and ten years her senior, to whom Baylor cannot cotton at all — and conceives his first grandchild. Jane Price, remarried also and redivorced, moves out that way to monitor their daughter's pregnancy, an arrangement with which Juliette reports herself not altogether comfortable but willing to go along for her mom's sake. The girl seems to her dad to be not thriving since the loss of her twin brother. B has been half proud, so at least he feels now, of the nonconformist streak that led her into her Muslim alliance, regarding which he set aside his own considerable reservations because Jane Price so flatly opposed the match from the start. He has been more than half proud of his daughter's nontraditional choice of profession. But she is, evidently, not a marine biologist of Musalām's caliber; she complains that federal research-grant money is drying up, though that appears not to be the case for her ex-husband back at Woods Hole. Baylor much wishes that his Juliette were an established, publishing doer of science, if not necessarily a distinguished one; his impression, however, is that she is little more than a lab assistant these days, not at all certain there'll be a place for her in Friday Harbor after her maternity leave and inclined to blame the scientific patriarchy for her unsuccess.

But who is he (he is the first to ask) to tsk? Who is he anyhow? With a few prominent exceptions, the "new journalists" and "nonfiction novelists" do a slow dissolve in post-Vietnam America (Good, pronounces J. Moore, a photographer suspicious of "images" and "names": a little anonymity may be just the ticket to her friend's discovering, belatedly, who he is). Baylor's end-of-the-seventies book is less of an accomplishment than Teresa Anginelli had looked forward to, though its title — *Baylor Won't You Please Come Home?* — has a special voltage for her. A tongue-half-in-cheek social history of the slow dissolve of the New Journalism in Gerald Ford's and Jimmy Carter's America, it fails to recover for its publisher the considerable advance on royalties given to the author, a sum negotiated in the first place only to entice him to leave his old house for a new one on the make. His next book, he knows, must pay its way, or else.

By decade's end, in short, though in other respects a more contented man than he can recall ever having been before, Baylor has unquestionably become the sixties souvenir that he had feared in

Spain he might be becoming. His reading of the cultural-political near future is that the pendulum of taste for what made his name won't swing his way again before 1990 or thereabouts, when, after more than a decade of conservative reaction, the sixties will recycle back into style. Meanwhile . . .

"Meanwhile," Julia Moore one day reminds him — as perdurably handsome a woman at the end of her forties as she was when we first remet — "we never took that sailboat ride we came home from Spain to take."

Well, B acknowledges, that's true. We have chartered nearly every June on the Chesapeake, and Februaried here and there about the Caribbean; together we have done a seagoing photo essay in the North Pacific on the macho whaling-fleet disruptions of the ecological activist outfit called Greenpeace, and another on a convocation of Tall Ships from around the world. But Marina Del Rey to Maui never quite materialized, and J. Moore is itching for some such shared adventure, in part to steer her mate out of his obvious doldrums.

On the other hand, one more middle-aged couple's cruising chronicle would be a less than trail-blazing opus, no? Turns out she has something more ambitious in mind for us, involving not the middle-aged but the Middle Ages. In the course of her professional travels she has caught wind of an exploit-in-the-works that, in her own words, she would *kill* to get the pair of us in on:

To demonstrate the feasibility of the Irish monk Saint Brendan's legendary sixth-century voyage to "The Fortunate Isles" (in a bull's-hide boat, so tradition has it), a canny British adventurer has successfully crossed the North Atlantic westward from Ireland with a crew of four in a thirty-six-foot wood-and-leather coracle. This remarkable feat of research, design, planning, and seamanship the same fellow now means to surpass. Just as Odysseus's mythic wanderings are held by some to be the accretion about a single figure of the actual voyages of ancient Greek mariners, so this Mr. Tim Severin is persuaded on good evidence that the seven voyages of Sindbad the Sailor, as retold by Scheherazade in *The Thousand and One Nights,* are the amplified echoes of actual expeditions to the limits of the known world by Arab maritime traders between the eighth and eleventh centuries. From illuminated manuscripts of the period, Julia Moore has learned, Severin and his associates are working up designs for a careful replica of a medieval Arab trading vessel. If he can find the required funding, he intends to have the vessel built by isolated Arab craftsmen who still employ such ancient methods as sewing ship's timbers together with ropes of coconut fiber — and then, with a mixed crew of Arabs and Europeans, navigate her by medieval techniques from Sindbad's famous starting place (or somewhere farther down the Persian Gulf if international politics rule out Basra), across the Arabian Sea to India and "Serendib" (now Sri Lanka), across the Bay of Bengal to Sumatra and Malaysia, and up the South China Sea all the way to mainland China, the fabled "Al Sin" of Sindbad's time.

"Doesn't that blow you away?" she demands to know. "Was anything ever so tailor-made for Bee and Ju?" She cocks her head. "Scheherazade! *The Next Voyage of Baylor the Sailor,* as photographed by Crazy Daisy's Kid Sister! We gotta be on that boat, Beebs."

"We'll think about it," responds B, to whom for a couple of reasons the idea does not immediately appeal. If this Severin fellow is like your typical modern-day private adventurer, he points out, he will be counting on such media spin-offs as books, magazine pieces, and public-television documentaries to support himself and the project, and will not welcome another pen-and-camera team aboard. What's more, B suspects for reasons given earlier that Baylor the Sailor went down with the ship of *Won't You Please Come Home?,* which sank almost without a trace, and that he oughtn't to be refloated until and unless he undergoes some deep sea-change. Pearls for eyes, coral bones — the works.

"I'm for that," seconds his friend, whose admiration for Baylor's books has never fully extended to his authorial persona. "Ding-dong-bell for old Baylor, as long as *some* things stay the same." Very well, then, she proposes: no Baylor the Sailor. But *somebody's* next voyage, surely — some newbody's maiden voyage, maybe? What likelier locale for a deep sea-change than the Indian Ocean? She'll count on him to work that out; meanwhile, if he'll excuse her, she means to give this bit of serendipity a little logistical assistance via COMSAT, aerogram, even a tête-à-tête with the brainchild's father, if necessary. Every professional intuition tells her that here is something J. Moore and her friend Whoever ought not to miss; every personal intuition tells her the same for "Ju and Bee."

Has B mentioned that he loves this woman? Simon William Behler loves Julia Bennett Moore. We are a couple unlike either him and Jane Price (our man the breadwinner, his mate the homemaker, nest-building together and raising both their fledglings and themselves, up the economic ladder) or him and Teresa Anginelli, say (he the established male lead, she the eternal ingenue). In J. Moore's competent, venturesome company B feels a touch less macho-manly, a touch more passive, more than a touch more humanly himself. By this point in our story we've come to know and respect each other's strengths and weaknesses. Julia Moore, e.g., thrives on physical activity with people but is shy of such social rites as cocktail and dinner parties, which B rather enjoys. He is the more patient and stoical of us, the less daring, the better organized, the more articulate; she's the more logistically inspired, the stronger-feeling and more caring, the less attentive to detail, the better at improvisation, the less serene, the more deeply moral. In our couple-chemistry there is scarcely less sexual passion than there was in Baylor's early marriage or, with its different flavor, his affair with Teresa Anginelli. And there is no less love and rather more adult, unquestioning commitment. As Julia Moore would ask, Okay?

Okay. Half hooked already on his friend's proposal, B stands by while J makes her initial inquiries and finds his apprehensions to have been "spot-on" (she comes away from her transatlantic phone calls mimicking Brit slang). The Sindbad project organizer is polite but both busy and wary: it is *his* voyage, for *his* book, his film, his *National Geographic* piece, etc. A woman crew member, moreover, absolutely will not do, given the large "native" crew he anticipates, with their un-Western notions of gender difference and the primitive conditions of life aboard a crowded Arab boom. Besides, did Sindbad ever sail with a woman aboard?

"Well, he fully *intended* to, coming home from Voyage Four," B points out — promptly to Julia, eventually to Mr. Severin himself, whom we intercept for that purpose on a sponsorship-arranging swing through Washington. The tip comes from T. Anginelli, photo-caption writer at the *Geographic,* and B's information from Mardrus and Mathers's translation of *The Thousand and One Nights,* in which B finds himself reimmersed. "But his new wife on Peppercorn Island up and died on him before he could set sail with her back to Baghdad. She very nearly took him with her instead."

"I'll never do that," oddly promises Julia Moore. Mrs. Sindbad didn't *mean* to, B assures her, and he recounts that ghoulish episode and then gives Mr. Severin and the Sindbad project his best shot when our several paths cross in D.C. Baylor's sense of capital-N Natives (as he declares to the enterprising and engaging younger man over lunch) is that they regard Western professional women as an exotic species not all that different from Western men and somehow exempt from nature's usual and regular sexual distinctions. J. Moore, he attests, has without hassle lived and worked with Natives more capital-N by far than assorted Muslims on location. As for any writing that the project may inspire from the likes of "Baylor," the author guarantees that it will advance the cause rather than compete with its organizer's own anticipated work. An early magazine article or two should attract favorable attention and perhaps additional sponsorship; a Baylor book, if one ensues, he will bind himself to publish only after Severin's account has been safely marketed. Let the gentleman be reminded furthermore that in us he would be getting a publicist and professional photographer who are also competent sailors. . . .

See here, mates, protests, in effect, the lean and cordial professional adventurer: *Lessim!*, as his new Arab sailor friends say — Ease off! He knows who we are, separately and together, and compliments our work: the Greenpeace piece, the Spain piece. But what we're proposing to him simply won't do. His objective is to keep both ship and voyage as "authentic" as possible. He wishes the whole ship's company except himself could be indigenous — cameramen, sound technicians, divers, and scientists as well as deckhands — because experience has taught him that the essential moments of such replicated adventures are those when nothing in sight suggests the Here and Now. But he has already found the perfect sponsor for his project, he's happy to report, the young Sultan Qaboos bin Said of Oman; and that sponsor, though he is as magnanimous as a benevolent genie from *The Arabian Nights,* has stipulated that the voyage must begin during the celebration of his sultanate's tenth anniversary, little more than a year hence. In that short time, Severin must complete the boom's design, find and assemble materials and craftsmen to build it, plan an itinerary both appropriate and feasible, secure governmental permissions where needed (one doesn't simply cruise up to the People's Republic of China, for example), and recruit his crew. Among this last, if only for want of time, he is obliged to depend upon ten or so non-Arab specialists of his acquaintance, including some veterans of his "Saint Brendan" voyage. The cinematographer and still photographer are already signed up.

But see here, mates, he adds, in effect: he doesn't mean to be uncordial. There's nothing to prevent our doing interviews and photo coverage from "outside," if we care to. We can watch the boom's construction and launching and setting out; we can meet it at its ports of call, perhaps even arrange to visit aboard en route, once things are shaken down and the crew is welded into a team. He respects our talents and will value such extra publicity as does not displace his own contracted articles and subsequent book.

"Hell with that," Julia says once we're home, and her disappointed friend agrees. For a while we consider "covering" the Sindbad project from a vessel of our own, buying or chartering a modern sailboat in which to follow Severin's medieval boom from port to port, not competitively but cooperatively. The idea appeals to neither of us.

"Let's scoop the sumbitch," J. Moore next proposes. She means let's let Severin (whom despite her language she not only admires and envies but likes) play Sindbad in his tacky replica with his capital-N Natives and his petrodollar budget; let's us buy ourselves a good secondhand cruising sailboat in Singapore, say, and sail Sindbad's *return* route a full year before Severin sets out. She fetches an atlas: from Singapore through the Strait of Malacca to the western tip of Sumatra for a shakedown, then across to "Serendib" and up the Malabar Coast of India to the Arabian peninsula; two months ought to do it — three, tops — and we can sail up to Oman in time to cover Severin's launch! Okay, so we'll be fiberglass and stainless steel instead of teak logs and coir, Dacron and sextant instead of sailcloth and kamal; we'll be high-tech westward-sailing secular Americans instead of turban-topped eastward-facing Muslims; there won't be those "essential moments" when nothing in view reminds us of the Here and Now. But B knows her line on all that: one can have such moments with a lot less bother just by standing naked in the woods or on a remote enough beach, and to J. Moore's way of thinking they're more than a touch bogus anyhow, like this replica craze that Thor Heyerdahl started with his *Kon-Tiki*. The Here and Now is inside our heads as much as out there, and for J. Moore, at least, it's all there is in any case.

"Let's do it, Bee. After we've scooped Severin on Sindbad we can keep right on to the Mediterranean and do Odysseus or Aeneas, okay? Then we'll do Columbus from the Mediterranean to the Caribbean and Whatshisname from the Caribbean to the Chesapeake — that sixteenth-century Spaniard. What's his name? Never mind. Shit, Bees, let's do it! One last big one before we turn fifty."

Through the first, or "Malaccan," leg of our fiftieth-birthday present to ourselves (B duly wrote in "Baylor's" travel log) . . . *things have gone about as problematically as we expected. The second leg, to "Serendib," we trust will be another story.*

And so it was.

We did it, up to a point. Although the planning and preparation, as we ought to have expected, took longer than we expected, we did it: cleared our calendars, honed our navigational skills and man-overboard routines on the Chesapeake, studied charts and piloting information on the areas we meant to sail through, shopped by mail and telephone through the international brokerages for a suitable boat, saw Conchita Moore safely wed to a Boston architect and Juliette Behler Grossmann roundly reimpregnated by her lawyer husband after the miscarriage of their initial pregnancy. We did it despite the mildly disappointing circumstance that by the time we leased our Arlington town house to a freshman congressman and flew to Singapore to buy a boat, Tim Severin's *Sohar* (named for the Omani seaport traditionally said to have been Sindbad's birthplace) was nearing completion on schedule in the coastal town of Sur, on the easternmost tip of the Arabian peninsula. There would be no scoop after all — but we had long since dismissed that objective as unfair to Severin and unworthy of us, and looked forward to a friendly rendezvous with *Sohar* somewhere along "Sindbad's" route.

We did it, finally, in face of the scary happenstance that Julia Moore — rust-haired, fair-freckled, outdoors Julie — was found in midpreparation to have a class B melanoma smack between her milk-white shoulder blades ("Hardest place to reach with the sun lotion"), the timely surgical removal whereof left her with a fifty-fifty chance of five-year survival. Stoic B was shaken to the soul; not-so-stoic J was stoical: "Fifty-fifty's fifty-fifty, Beeswax, and Here and Now is here and now."

So we did it, with no further comment on metastatic probability but with — for Baylor, anyhow — an entirely new lens upon the world. From harborside quarters in Singapore we quickly narrowed our shortlist of floating possibilities to three boats of comparable suitability. One we eliminated by marine survey (corroded wiring throughout and electrolysis problems with some through-hull fittings); the tie between the remaining two we broke by invoking the old sailor's superstition that it's bad luck to change a boat's name after christening and launch. Both had been built in reputable Taiwan yards and were offered "fully found" and ready to go, but the ketch, though a few feet longer and a few years younger, happened to be named *Moonraker,* and the prospect of repeating so schmaltzy a name in sentence after narrative sentence B found intolerable. Whereas the double-ended, thirty-foot, seven-year-old cutter . . .

"It's an Arabic term for an Arabic legend," he explained to Julia Moore. "Imagine some unobtrusive object — it may take different forms in different epochs — that has the power once your eye falls innocently upon it to gradually take possession of your mind, the way a computer virus gradually takes over the computer's memory bank. Finally you can think of nothing else except that one thing, and you freak out altogether. It might be a paper clip or the ashtray on your desk, or one particular pine tree in a pine forest, or one brick no different from all the other bricks in a building, or an incidental face in a crowd shot. But if it happens to be the zahir, then bingo."

Whether the legend or for that matter the word was authentically Arabic, B couldn't in fact say, but he recapitulated the famous short story of that name by Jorge Luis Borges (in which the zahir is a twenty-centavo coin unwittingly accepted by the narrator, along with other small change, in a Buenos Aires bar) and made bold to explicate it: the aging narrator steps into that bar for a drink en route home from the funeral of a woman whom he loved in his youth; the zahir — so apparently unremarkable but in the event so potent — represents any unexpectedly obsessive image or memory. A youthful romance. A quietly perfect small work of art.

Cancer, we both said to ourselves. "Serendib!" offered smiling Julia Moore, her head cocked. "Sold."

And so we did it: bought, launched, and commissioned *Zahir* (no christening necessary, as she was Chinese/Muslim and already named; we merely toasted her unforgettable handle with Singapore Slings), fitted her with self-steering gear, and provisioned her with one month's supplies, as we had no intention of sailing nonstop through such colorful geography. We ventured out of the famous harbor and back a few times to get the feel of her hull and rig and test all systems; we made wish-us-luck phone calls to our separate daughters; and then we slipped our hired mooring one hazy equatorial A.M., dieseled out through giant tankers and freighters from around the globe, raised all plain sail, hung a hard right at the bottom of Malaysia, and beat into the great Strait of Malacca on a starboard tack against the same northeast monsoon that was driving Tim Severin's *Sohar* down the Arabian Sea from Muscat toward Malabar.

Our thousand-mile "shakedown leg" had two joints: the two-hundred-dred-or-so sailing miles from Singapore to Malacca itself, through the narrowest stretch of what we came to call Tanker Turnpike, and then the six-hundred-odd miles of ever-widening strait from Malacca past Kuala Lumpur to the northwestern tip of Sumatra. There, at the gateway to the Indian Ocean, we planned to rest, regroup, make repairs as needed to boat and crew, and reprovision for the thousand-mile nonstop reach to the port of Matara in "Serendib." Both joints proved to be shakedowns indeed. The first we came to call Breakdown Pass for *Zahir*'s plenteous gear failures, glitches, and crew errors — not many more than we had anticipated for an unfamiliar boat in unfamiliar waters, but a number of them alarming, at night especially, amid such heavy, fast-moving ship traffic in contrary winds and currents. Our nominal watches — four hours on, four shared, four off — nearly never worked out that way; we reached Malacca red-eyed and dizzy from lack of sleep and shaken from half a dozen apparent near rundowns by supertankers plowing toward Japan, our repertory of curses exhausted upon *Zahir*'s inattentive previous owners, upon the manufacturers of sundry items of marine hardware, and upon the oblivious bridge-deck lookouts of assorted merchant shipping, who we concluded must be stoned to the eyes on Sumatran hashish. Any more shaken down, we agreed, and we would be disassembled, but our resourcefulness and stamina had been duly tried along with vessel and gear, and had failed less frequently. Sobered but nowise daunted, after only a brief breather in Malacca — shave and haircut for B, picture taking for J — we addressed the first leg's second joint, through which we hoped to do less motoring and more sailing (even if all to windward), with ampler elbow room and fewer alarms.

This one, however, got itself dubbed Breakaleg Leg, for the squalls that funneled viciously into the strait one after another from the Andaman Sea ("Bahr Kalah Bar" to Sindbad's navigators — the fourth sea of the seven between home and China, China and home). More extended tandem watches, sleepless stretches, navigational crises, plus literal as well as figurative rough going. Knockdowns, green seas crashing aboard, seasickness, lacerations and contusions. By lightning-flash one embattled black night, Allah alone knows where in His exploding ocean, Simon William Behler saw his beloved friend cock her drenched head over-shoulder to shout aft through machine-gun rain (from the foot of the mast, where she was harnessed to the "chicken rails" and struggling with the mainsail she had insisted it was *her* turn to go forward and double-reef): "I love it! I love it! I love it!"

The single-jointed second leg, though — Sumatra to Sri Lanka — proved to be a leisurely foretaste of Paradise, not only by contrast with what we had survived but by any sailing standards. R & R'd per program for a full fortnight just off Sumatra's far end, on the pleasant island of Sabang, we aimed *Zahir* due west, picked up over our starboard beam the steady monsoon winds blowing down from Burma, and reached along day after delicious day, self-steering for Serendib. Modern passage-making sailors seldom touch the helm: on watch we navigated, tended sails, adjusted the wind-vane steering gear, did routine maintenance chores; off watch we exercised and slept, made meals and love, wrote and photographed, read and fished. The occasional squall, like the occasional becalming, we took in stride, seasoned hands now, not troubling our off-watch mate unless things got truly hairy or noteworthy. Mainly we surged and glided on the all-but-unvarying breeze off the Bay of Bengal, escorted by porpoises through blue-and-gold days, planetarium nights. In these two weeks or so — which we wished might never end, so sweet and easeful were they — we became a couple as never before, each depending absolutely now on the other, now on him/herself, and through our shared watches working perfectly together, almost wordlessly: one person in two bodies. By an order of magnitude ours was now the most sane and solid, straight and straightforward, committed and equal connection B had ever been party to. Who anyhow had been this Baylor?

> *Dressed in a little brief authority,*
> *Most ignorant of what he's most assured*
> *(His glassy essence)* . . .

Deep-sixed. Full-fathom-fived.

Was there a book in all this? I scarcely cared. Purged of tentativity — after fifty years! — or all but purged, Simon William Behler in mid–Indian Ocean understood that with Julia Moore he was most himself, or most, at least, on the verge of so becoming: most likely to complete at last the long and undramatic task of learning who he was, perhaps in time to do something worthwhile yet with that hard-won, essential news.

When our dead-reckoning plot showed us to be only a hundred nautical miles from landfall in Sri Lanka, we learned through ham-radio contacts that Tim Severin's *Sohar*, after a sail-replacement stop in Beypore, had rounded the tip of the Indian subcontinent and was currently crossing the Gulf of Mannar, bound like *Zahir* for the south coast of Sri Lanka. The next day we raised that coast, likewise our shatter-proof acrylic wineglasses, and with French champagne bought in Singapore and sipped at tropical world–temperature we toasted what we had found without really looking for it:

"Us," we said, as one.

Another spell of radio fiddling put us in touch directly with *Sohar's* wireless operator. After an exchange of salutations and compliments, with a bit more back-and-forthing we not only arranged a cordial rendezvous in the port town of Galle (which we readily substituted for Matara as our Sri Lankan stop, since getting there would give us two more days of the true Serendib aboard *Zahir*) but received — if we were willing to lay over there till *Sohar* set out again for where we had just come from — an invitation to visit aboard, sail alongside awhile, whatever we pleased. The only stipulation was that J. Moore not wear shorts or other revealing dress.

"Jesus," said Julia, who at the moment was worrying her cancer-conscious friend by wearing nothing but number 10 sun lotion. "Tell him I always sail in long johns under a Mother Hubbard. Purdah.

Anything he wants." The sight of land was already working changes in us, bringing out the professionals. Hello Sri Lanka, farewell Serendib.

We rendezvoused on schedule and more or less reprovisioned *Zahir,* even down to fresh batteries for our trusty Seiko watches, though we were no longer sure wherefore; our adventure seemed done. We admired the remarkable sewn ship *Sohar,* reacquainted ourselves with its intrepid and ingenious skipper, and made friends with his crew, a colorful lot of Omanis, Baluchistanis, Beypore Indians, and Europeans, all wearing the versatile long loincloths called wuzaras. Though the expedition's still photographer was in fact leaving the company at this stop, his replacement was already standing by; nor did J. Moore any longer long, as she once had longed, for that berth. Satisfied that our presence was neither obtrusive nor competitive, *Sohar'*s skipper gave us full access to the boom during its brief layover in Galle and permitted us each some hours aboard during its first days back at sea, while the other of us sailed alongside in *Zahir.* But novel and even exciting as those hours were — with the crew chanting in Arabic at their labors and even the Europeans (except the new hands) looking like grizzled medieval mariners — we had no wish to prolong them. One day more of century hopping, we agreed, and we would forsake the replicated tenth for the all-too-real twentieth and our fifty-fifty chance of five-year survival. Solipsistic or not, we who had given each other so long a leash had come to prefer being alone together (on *Zahir,* at least, unforgettably en route to Serendib) to being with others in the world.

Alas for stirring marine photography, the wind this last day stood as still as time seemed to aboard *Sohar.* All through the crystal night before, we had admired in the Sri Lankan distance the lamps of pilgrims ascending Adam's Peak, where the first man is said by Islamic tradition to have left a giant-size footprint after his expulsion with Eve from Eden. Chagrin, we supposed. In the first calm predawn light, as our little cutter drifted not far from the boom, three times its size, that mountain loomed above the surface haze like an airborne Gibraltar or Dante's Mount of Purgatory as beheld by Ulysses on his final voyage. J. Moore, off watch, clicked away busily across the glassy space from various locations aboard *Zahir.* Then, unexpectedly at that hour, word came from the larger vessel that its navigator was free just now to give our skipper a little lesson in medieval Arab navigation, in which I had expressed some interest, if I happened to be free to dinghy over to *Sohar* while the North Star could still be seen.

"Hey!" my friend protested, not crossly. "Tell that limey we're *both* skippers over here, okay? This tub is an affirmative-action, equal-opportunity cutter; whoever's on watch is the skipper." "I mentioned that, Jule," I said, "but since it happens to be my watch just now and I'm the one officially interested in kamals and azimuths, I guess he means me. Mind?"

Of course she didn't — though it *was* in fact my watch, and this spooky calm was certainly photogenic. But it also left the "skipper" with nothing whatever to do except be technically in charge, and so of course I should go ahead; she would shoot away while minding a store that needed no minding.

I went, via our inflatable dinghy, which since leaving Galle we'd trailed astern to facilitate our shuttling to and from *Sohar*. In air so still that our limp sails hung unluffing, I learned to gauge latitude from Polaris with a little wooden rectangle attached to a knotted string. Each knot, I learned, represented a port of established latitude. Per instructions, I held the "Sabang" knot in my teeth, extended the kamal till the string was taut, then aligned its bottom edge with the northern horizon and its right edge with the azimuth of Polaris. If that star (very near the horizon in any case, this close to the Equator) hung above the kamal, Sabang's latitude lay to the south of us; if below — as in this instance it did, a little — to the north of us. When it rested exactly on the kamal's top edge, *Sohar* and Sabang were on the same parallel of north latitude. There were other, larger kamals for use in higher latitudes (the practical upper limit of the device corresponded, handily, to the northern limit of classical Arab seafaring; lacking chronometers, their navigators could only guess at longitude) as well as other, comparably elegant gadgets and formulations of the same ingenious provenance. With a little wave to *Zahir* (there was J. Moore on our port-side gunwale with her faithful Hasselblad), I went below-decks with my instructor to the navigator's station, redolent of the fermenting vegetable oil in which the aini-wood timbers and their coir stitching had been marinated, to inspect copies of Sindbad-vintage charts and translations of contemporaneous Arab sailing directions for the Bahr Harkand, the Bahr Sulahat, the Bahr Kalah Bar.

"Awesome," I declared, without overstatement — and was at that same moment distracted from my awe at the civilization of medieval Islam by a sudden heaving and creaking of the ship, shouts in Arabic from on deck, and the unmistakable sound of wind in sails and rigging. We clambered up to find all hands busy coping with a strong north breeze from nowhere, the two great settee sails and jib full and drawing, the boom already heeled to starboard and gathering way. The surprised Europeans on deck, like all but one of the "natives," laughed and cheered as they scrambled after lines and loose gear. Only the Omani helmsman, from his vantage point high in the stern at *Sohar*'s ten-foot tiller, seemed alarmed as well as excited; while the others called intructions back and forth and applied themselves to *Sohar*'s many sheets, guys, and braces, he called directly to us in clear (though to me unintelligible) distress, pointing aft off the boom's starboard quarter.

For he alone had seen that fell puff from Polaris strike *Zahir* as well as *Sohar*. Our headsails were furled, but our mainsail had been close-hauled to reduce slatting in the glassy swells. The gust had struck the cutter broad on the starboard beam, and either the bellying of the sail or the sudden heel to port had pitched "the camera lady" overside. "Uh-oh," said my navigation coach. "Your friend's in the water, I'm afraid." To helmsman and crew he called commands in Arabic; I dashed aft, ahead of him, to see where the busy helmsman still pointed with his right arm while bracing his stocky brown body against the huge tiller and keeping an eye aloft at the boom's great press of sails. The slick gray surface had turned as suddenly angry as the sky to eastward, where a huddle of clouds obscured the sunrise. *Zahir*, untended, was looping off downwind; in the hostile reach between us and it I saw Julia Moore's face, a white speck in the building seas, and one white arm holding up her camera. She appeared to be sidestroking toward the cutter, but even had its mainsheet been free, leeway would have carried the boat downwind about as fast as she could swim in those circumstances. As it was, the close-hauled sail would fill, drive the hull along for several lengths, bring the bow to windward, luff, bear off, and fill again.

All this I took in at a glance or pieced together later from that scene photographed forever on my memory. Backing *Sohar*'s sails and bringing the ungainly craft about was going to take a while. My head surging, I hurried for the port-side midships rail, where a boarding ladder ran down to our tethered dinghy — but the distance seemed impossibly far, in the wrong direction, as if I were running from rather than to. In a panic I bolted back, past the grim-faced skipper and the anxious helmsman; vaulted the high aft bulwark between the rudder post and one of the "balconies" hung off either quarter to serve as shower stall and latrine; leaped eight or ten feet feetfirst into the sea, and struck out in what I hoped was still my friend's direction.

This must be told carefully. One is ill advised, as a rule, to go into the water oneself to rescue a person overboard, unless the manned rescue boat is standing by and the person overboard is injured or otherwise needful of additional assistance from the water. Julia Moore and I had conscientiously practiced our man-overboard drills, aboard both our smaller boat in Chesapeake Bay and *Zahir* off Singapore Harbor. They did not apply here. Correct practice, in this instance, called for at least one crewman aboard *Sohar* to be assigned the sole duty of keeping J. Moore in sight — pointing always in her direction as the boom was slowly stopped and brought about — while I and one or two others made haste to fetch her in the inflatable dinghy, on whose transom a small outboard engine was mounted. If the victim needed no immediate postrescue attention, and conditions permitted our going on to overtake the cutter, well and good; otherwise, *tant pis:* better the boat lost than a life, very possibly two lives.

But that was not "the victim" out there; it was Julia Moore, my priceless jewel, in serious trouble, maybe drowning, and canny hands aplenty on *Sohar* were doubtless making ready to do all the above. Like them, I was barefoot and shirtless, wearing only the wuzara I had bought in Galle in imitation of the Omani sailors — in short, unencumbered for swimming, and I was a reasonably strong swimmer, lean and fit from our recent weeks at sea and our earlier months of preparation. My objective, I suppose, was to reach my Julia before the dinghy could and to render assistance, or at least keep her company, until it arrived. But these are reasonings after the fact, as is my assessment of the risks — that with only our heads above water I might be unable to find her in that ever-rougher sea; that a motorized dinghy with a lookout, even given a later start, could probably locate and reach her before I could; and that my additional presence in the water merely doubled the problem: *two* small white faces now for our rescuers to distinguish from the whitecapped seas, keeping one of us in sight while retrieving the other. It was out of pure panic concern for Julia Moore in distress that I jumped, and though the instant I resurfaced I saw the folly of my impulse, I managed after all to reach her side. We are talking not of half a mile but merely of a few hundred feet of rough water — across which, however, I could see my friend only in those moments when neither of us happened to be swallowed by a wave trough. Did she see me? I'm confident she did, for she no longer side-stroked toward our cutter (which by now was far downwind) but bobbed in place and — Allah be praised! — was apparently no longer being more careful of her precious camera than of herself. Moreover, when I was closer and another wave lifted her into view, I saw with enormous relief that unlike me, she was wearing her flotation vest (our rule was to wear one not only in foul weather but anytime either of us was alone on deck). I could almost swear she grinned at me over her shoulder, half scared but half exhilarated, as when she had cried from the foot of *Zahir*'s mast, "I love it!"

"I love you!" I tried to call to her — and took a mouthful of the next wave that crested over both of us.

But when I got my breath back, cleared my eyes, and closed the remaining distance between us, I found her dazed to the point of un-consciousness. The lifevest held her up, her head not cocked now but lolling, her eyes partly open but not evidently seeing, her mouth alarmingly half open, too. Her vest was collarless; the collared kind, which floats an unconscious victim faceup, J. Moore had found too confining for serious photography. Another wave broke over us just as I caught the limp left arm on which she wore our nameless bracelet. When it passed I saw her facedown in the water.

The sea was wild now, and I was winded from exertion and fear, coughing salt water, blinking to clear my eyes. I pulled Julia's head back; my own went under. A wave knocked us apart; I called her name and barely caught the loose cuff of her shirt (long-sleeved, in deference to the "natives"). I neither saw nor heard our dinghy coming, though in that wind and sea it might well have been not far off. Lacking a flotation vest myself, I was not rescuing Julia Moore so much as half clinging to her now to keep myself from going under. *Sohar*, I saw between wave crests, had finally come about, but seemed so far away that I could scarcely imagine I had swum that distance; *Zahir* I could no longer see at all from where I was. I did, however, catch sight at last of the inflatable, bouncing and surfing more or less in our direction, maybe halfway between the boom and us, bobbing in and out of view as Julia's face had done.

It would never reach us in time. I could not be certain that its crew even saw us; often as not it seemed to be off course, maybe headed for our errant boat while searching for us, maybe only coping with the difficult sea. I shouted, a waste of precious breath in that wind; I waved my free arm at them, lost my hold on Julia's sleeve (and very nearly my watch as well, its clasp loosened by my flailing) when the next crest swept by — and, instead of struggling yet again to refind, rereach her, panicked off in the direction of our rescuers.

At this point in many survival narratives comes the spacebreak, the fade; the hero loses consciousness and revives elsewhere. Likewise, often, in the accounts of actual survivors: "Next thing I knew, here I was in this hospital bed." But Simon William Behler remained conscious through another, desperate paragraph, conscious of himself swimming, swamping, struggling not to go under, to the boundaries of his strength and breath and beyond, refinding and relosing both, and himself as well, as often under as upon the surface, wave after wave breaking over a mind mindless of everything now except the panic labor of its body and finally even of that, a drowning animal not quite drowned and then perhaps quite, for the next thing I knew, I knew nothing.

Four Interludes

1.

Silent Sindbad sat. The company likewise, perhaps waiting for Somebody to go on with his story. But what went on was that fellow's pause, even when Kuzia Fakān, on his left, elbowed his ribs.

Most looked then to Yasmīn to commence and lead their critical discussion, as she had done the night before, and perhaps to tally their votes as well. Somebody, too (having smiled and shaken his head absently at Kuzia), turned Sindbad's daughter's way, for a different reason, and for some moments she met his calm gaze calmly.

Of the others, Ibn al-Hamrā regarded the fingers of each of his ruddy hands in turn, counting off one two three and four on his left, then one and two (or five and six) on his right, and nodding to himself with uncordial satisfaction. Old Jaydā regarded Sindbad, who now leaned back against his Tub of Last Resort and not so much regarded as studied his stranded namesake. As for Haroun al-Rashīd's messenger (that is, the emissary of Haroun's vizier, Jafar al-Barmakī), in clear and utter incomprehension he frowned and looked from face to face.

"With my father's permission," Yasmīn now said quietly, "I shall

338

defer tonight to the present mistress of his house, my talented friend
Kuzia Fakān."

Beaming, the dancer raised her long-empty wine cup in salute to
Sindbad's daughter and herself. Sindbad studied Yasmīn for some moments, as he had Still-Stranded, then gave his aquamarine turban a
tiny nod.

"Indeed," Yasmīn went on, rising from her place, "when I have
refilled your thirsty cups, I shall ask you to excuse me from your de-
bate." Accompanied as always by Jaydā, she filled first her father's cup,
then the messenger's. Next, instead of proceeding to her fiancé, in the
second place of honor, she went directly to Kuzia Fakān, at midtable — the lowest-ranking occupied place, since Jaydā had risen from
Seat Ten — and filled both her eager cup and Still-Stranded's, which
Kuzia obligingly held forth in her other hand. Without looking directly at our man, Yasmīn then conferred in busy whispers with the
dancer, who nodded, whispered back, set down the filled cups, said
something with her hands, fished into the neck-opening of her caftan
("*Ya! Ya! Badawiyah!*" cheered Ibn al-Hamrā), and briefly pressed
Yasmīn's free hand between both of hers. Turning then to the company, Kuzia drank off her wine, wiped her lips with the back of one
hand, rose from her place, and, stepping onto the low table, struck a
dancer's preliminary pose.

"Yallah!" Ibn cried again, and he rapped lustily on the table as if on
Sindbad's tub. Two flickers of Kuzia's eyes fetched her accompanists
from somewhere. The tambourinist, Fatmah Awād, took up station at
Jaydā's empty place; the piper, Nuzhat, instrument in hand, stood behind Yasmīn, who herself stood behind Kuzia Fakān's vacated cushion. After a short fanfare, the dancer gestured here, then there and
there, and Yasmīn, instead of leaving the room, spoke as if for her:

"Venerable and dauntless Sayyid Sindbad the Sailor. Distinguished
Commander-of-the-Faithful's Vizier's Messenger. Tireless guests of
our intrepid host. Misfortunate and still-stranded stranger. Gentlemen
and ladies of this house."

She danced more, and Yasmīn translated: "Unaccustomed as I am
to public speaking, I shall not speak publicly but rather will make my
statement in my customary way." Kuzia paused, grinned and nodded
at her spokesperson, then spun nimbly amid the cups and pastry

plates. "In my master's continuing silence," Yasmīn interpreted, "and my two mistresses' . . . abstention? Yes, abstention . . . it falls to me now to invite each of you in turn, in the order of your seating, to air your opinions of Sayyid Bey el-Loor's affecting, even heartbreaking latest story and to cast your allotted votes on the still-open question of its continuance." Kuzia danced a flourish at her accompanists. "My able colleagues, Nuzhat and Fatmah Awād," read Yasmīn, "will tally your votes — Fatmah the ayes, Nuzhat the nays. And my steadfast friend Yasmīn has agreed to postpone her good-night long enough to turn the speech of my body into words . . . as necessary."

All hands applauded. Even silent Sindbad seemed pleased.

"Let us begin," proposed Kuzia/Yasmīn.

"Let us indeed!" cried Ibn al-Hamrā. "Needless to say, pretty Nuz-hat the Nay-Sayer has all seven of my votes." He raised his left thumb. "To begin with —"

A tambourine-snap and Kuzia's hand-clap interrupted him. The dancer then placed a forefinger on his rosy lips and salaamed before Sindbad the Sailor, who shook his head and tipped his turban toward Haroun's vizier's messenger. "What is this?" Ibn complained, but he contented himself with catching and playfully sucking the dancer's ad-monitory finger.

"Our host and master defers to the faithful messenger of Jafar al-Barmakī, Haroun al-Rashīd's all-wise vizier," Yasmīn explained. "As tonight's foremost guest, he it is who should speak first and cast his seven votes as he sees fit. Only then, Lord of Yasmīn's liver, will you and your six votes have their say."

"Queen of my spleen," retorted Ibn, not to Kuzia Fakān. "So be it. That will make the count thirteen for our melodious Nuzhat and zero for our rhythmical Fatmah Awād."

As Allah wills, said Kuzia, in effect. Distinguished messenger, the floor is yours.

That fellow looked on, appreciative, open-faced, and clearly mysti-fied, until Sindbad himself more or less broke his silence to whisper in his ear. "Ah, so," the messenger said then. "Well, now, sayyids, I am only a messenger, and since I have delivered my message this morning, it is not my place to speak further, no, but rather to listen and report. I pray you therefore let me pass, like Sayyid Sindbad, and reserve my vote, at least till I've heard how the more practiced among you go about this business."

"Well spoken," Ibn al-Hamrā declared at once, and once again he ticked his left thumb with his right forefinger. "Now, to begin with —"

"Point of order," Yasmīn objected, using her interpreter's tone, as if the point were being raised by Kuzia Fakān. In the same manner — with Kuzia rapidly translating Yasmīn's words into dance, rather than vice versa — she went on to declare that at this advanced stage of their nuptial negotiations, the Esteemed Sovereign of her Very Saliva must surely be reckoned a member of the household, and as such should disqualify himself, along with his bride-to-be and prospective father-in-law, from voting on Sayyid Bey el-Loor's poignant, gripping tale of love and loss in the romantic Ocean of Al Hind.

The more eloquently to express this procedural point, Kuzia Fakān slipped out of her caftan and danced Yasmīn's proposal before Ibn al-Hamrā in her working costume: sequined bodice and halter, filmy harem pants, and sundry underthings. But Ibn laughed his reddest laugh and replied that not until the jewel was securely in the lotus (to borrow a quaint expression from Bey el-Loor's mad former concubine) would he be an official, nonvoting member of Sindbad's household. Until that happy day and happier night, he was free to protest to Allah's high heaven that the company had been sorely cheated of its promised reward for enduring yet another of the outlander's outlandish and salacious narratives. Did Bey el-Loor not promise us only last night that tonight we would learn how it came to pass that we are afflicted with his society? But far from learning by what means he came here, we have been told only how he left "there" — there where he disported with his mannish, seagoing strumpet, his "Jew-Moor." If we mourn his apparent loss of her, it is because we wish he abode with her yet, far from the City of Peace and the "Here and Now" (as the Moor herself picturesquely put it). This fourth of his baffling voyage-tales he cheats his way out of with a trick no self-respecting Muslim storyteller would stoop to: "The next thing I knew, I knew nothing"! Were we to permit him a fifth, he would not be above beginning it with "The next thing I knew, I found myself aboard Sindbad's daughter's bride-ship," which we now know bore the same unforgettable name as the one that earlier unburdened itself of him.

"May we be as wise as that ship, my friends!" he exhorted the company in conclusion. "Otherwise, far from supplying the missing links between there and here, Bey el-Loor's *sixth* tale will surely begin, 'The next thing I knew, I found myself aboard Sindbad's daughter'!"

At this sally more than one listener smiled. Haroun's vizier's messenger laughed aloud, then saw his host's dark frown and, with his right hand, literally wiped the smile from his own lips. As her fiancé approached his speech's close, Yasmīn moved with the wine jug around the table to stand behind him; when at its end he waggled his eyebrows and held up his cup to her in salute, she emptied that flagon slowly upon his head. Through the burgundy cascade Ibn redly laughed and exclaimed to Kuzia and her comrades, "What laundering you girls must do tonight! Six votes against Bey el-Loor!"

Covering her brow with one hand, as if her head ached, Kuzia Fakān swirled down-table to Nuzhat the piper, then back to thrust her backside six times toward the happily dripping Ibn al-Hamrā. *Peep peep peep,* piped Nuzhat, *peep peep peep,* and Yasmīn (taking a fresh jug from Jaydā) dutifully announced, "Nays, six. Ayes, zero." Moving then, as did the dancer, to the far end of that same table-side, she smilingly filled the cup of her beefy, blank-faced ally there and in her interpreter's voice (while Kuzia salaamed before him) declared, "Hajj Masūd: five votes."

"Hajj Masūd?" That black-bearded fellow turned on his look of astonishment. "Yes! Well! Hajj Masūd, to be sure: that is my name. Now! What does Hajj Masūd think of the story of Bey el-Loor's Fourth Voyage? Well, my friends! Graceful Yasmīn! Supple Kuzia Fakān! Friends one and all!"

Sitting Turk-fashion directly in front of him on the table, Kuzia Fakān drummed her fingers on one knee. Fatmah Awād rustled her suspenseful tambourine. "Our dear friend Hajj Masūd will now speak," Yasmīn prompted.

"Yes, indeed! Well." Blinking as many times as he had votes, he declared that unlike his esteemed friend Ibn al-Hamrā, he himself, Hajj Masūd the rug purveyor, had once again found Sayyid Bey el-Loor's latest story somewhat more pertinent than its predecessors, taken all in all. True, Voyage Four lacked the fine carpets and admirable vendors of Voyage Three, not to mention the winsome beggar boys of the Jmaa el Fna. One might even quibble that for the narrator to promise his listeners a revisit to Marrakesh and then to fly instead, as if by magic carpet, from Al-Andaluz to Serendib, by way of Allah knows where, constituted a breach of narrative contract. But who could resist the appeal of those rugged Omani sailors, especially that steadfast helmsman in his wuzara, or deny the charm of such familiar names as Bahr Kalah Bar, Serendib, Sohar, and that other ship's name that kept slipping his mind, the vessel that Bey el-Loor and his exotic mistress named after Sindbad's own favorite ship . . .

Yasmīn bent to whisper in his ear.

"*Zahir*, of course," said Hajj Masūd. "I can never remember it. Who can deny that in the presence of such landmarks we are nearing home? *My* only real criticism of this story, other than the absence of such heartwarming characters as Ankh el-Zhash, is what strikes me as a lapse of verisimilitude in the portrayal of Bey el-Loor's mixed-breed lover. As has been noted, he calls her his Jew; he calls her his Moor. Yet he gives her milk-white skin, green eyes, and hair as red as Sayyid Ibo's. Has any one among us ever seen a pale-skinned, green-eyed, red-haired Jewish Moor?

"But that I take to be innocent narrative license, as forgivable in measured doses as narrative licentiousness, if I may say so. In conclusion, though I agree with my distinguished critical colleague that tomorrow night's story must not cheat us with such tricks as 'The next thing I knew, I woke to find myself aboard that other . . . whatsitsname? . . . *Zahir*,' I trust good Bey el-Loor to supply us clearly with the missing links between there and here, then and now. In that trust, Hajj Masūd the carpeteer casts his five votes aye. Aye, aye, aye, aye, and aye!"

Five times Fatmah Awād clapped her tambourine, in unison with Yasmīn's applause and the forward thrusts of Kuzia's hips as she danced the tally before Hajj Masūd and her interpreter called out, "Ayes, five!" *Peep peep peep, peep peep peep,* then duly piped Nuzhat: "Nays, six!" Sindbad's daughter beamed encouragingly at our stranded teller — who, however, seemed still adrift in the ocean of his story.

Around the table-foot next to Cushion Four, where from her own place Yasmīn filled the cup of keen-eyed, dapper Alī al-Yamān. Kuzia

343

Fakān spun, slipped off her bodice, and with her haltered breasts made movements that Yasmīn read as "Alī al-Yamān: four votes."

Even as the dancer then salaamed, that fellow briskly declared, "My friends, I'll speech you no speeches. I am a practical sort of fellow who cannot enjoy what he doesn't understand, and however meaningful my left-hand neighbor's ramblings may be to himself and his kind, to me they're ape-talk."

"Yallah!" called Ibn al-Hamrā.

Alī nodded his way. "I grant that what we do not understand, we may accept on faith, if we trust the source; therefore I accept that Adam left his footprint on a certain peak in Serendib because our sacred tradition has it so, and therefore I have accepted also that our resourceful host plans a seventh voyage to that same peak because his wealth attests the success of his first six voyages. But as I know nothing of my left-hand neighbor beyond what I hear from himself and certain others, I see no reason to invest ever more faith in him night after night."

"Four more nays!" called Ibn, and Kuzia, frowning, rose to turn her negative side accordingly. But Alī al-Yamān held up his hand and, looking from face to face, except that of his left-hand neighbor, went on:

"Hear me out, comrades. For this reason I voted Nay last night, and was then outmaneuvered by our resourceful hostess. For this reason I would vote Nay again tonight — but as it happens, I regret to say, my confidence in Serendib Limited has waned to match my confidence in my left-hand neighbor. With respect to both I judge it time to cut my losses, and inasmuch as I shall not rejoin this delightful company tomorrow night or the nights thereafter, it is of no consequence to me whether my left-hand neighbor wakes to find himself in the City of Peace or on Adam's Peak or at the bottom of the sea. In all fairness and indifference, therefore, I shall divide my four votes evenly: two nay, two aye, and good night all."

Amid general consternation he rose and bowed: to Sindbad the Sailor, who nodded gravely, as if to himself; to Yasmīn and to Kuzia's pelvis and rump in turn as they read out Fatmah's and Nuzhat's tallies — "Ayes, seven; nays, eight!" — and even to still-stranded Somebody, who lifted his left hand in mild farewell. But our man's right-hand neighbor, though he left the table, did not yet leave the hall; he stood between Sindbad and Haroun's vizier's messenger, beside the Tub of Last Resort, to watch the outcome.

"Sīdī Numān: three votes." Dancing out of her harem pants as she passed before our storyteller, Kuzia Fakān bowed to the merchant on Cushion Five, between her own vacated place and that of Haroun's vizier's messenger. Her movements before him were as hopeful as Yasmīn's at his side as she filled his cup, for Sīdī last night had cast his vote in Somebody's favor. Tonight, however, he took a pensive draught of his wine, set down his cup, and said, "By what I understood of our foreign friend's story, I was impressed. I extend to him my sympathy for the apparent drowning of his latest unusual concubine. The mixing of breeds, like the mixing of flavors, often makes a more savory dish. Jews and Muslims in particular, like oil and vinegar, each gain piquancy from the other; a woman blended of both must be a delight to her master's tongue.

"I am impressed also, if not equally, by the decision of my friend Alī al-Yamān to join Hasīb Alī, Talīb ibn Sahl, and Abū Shamāt in their withdrawal from Serendib Limited, but in that matter I shall not follow his example, yet. I shall, however, follow his lead in dividing my three votes: one nay, by way of caution to our host's still-stranded namesake not to open his fifth tale tomorrow night as he closed this fourth tonight, with some narrative sleight of hand, but rather to tell us plainly at last how he came from Serendib to here. And two ayes, for that is a passage worth our careful attending if we are ever to get from here to Serendib."

With what chastened gratitude did Kuzia thrust at the assembled first her sequin-fraught pudendum — "Aye aye aye! Aye aye aye! Aye aye aye!" called Yasmīn and Fatmah Awād — and then her likewise glittering rear ("*Ayiyi!*" echoed Ibn as Yasmīn and Nuzhat tallied up the matching nays)! "Nine–nine!"

"My friends," cautioned Somebody the Still-Stranded at this point, "do not expect to hear from me more than I know myself. From the broken bracelet of my voyages, at least one link is lost."

Yasmīn and Jaydā had been circling the head of the table, around behind Haroun's vizier's messenger, Alī al-Yamān, and Sindbad's tub, en route to the merchant Jafar on Cushion Six, while Kuzia Fakān danced the shortcut directly across from Sīdī Numān. At Somebody's words, Sindbad's daughter paused between her father and her wine-soaked fiancé and confidently declared, "This canny Cairene lady who raised me from babyhood has often told me that from scattered pearls a knowledgeable jeweler can infer the string. In the same way, I'm sure, those of us with ears to hear will be able to supply any missing links in either my father's voyages or our stranded guest's."

To this, Kuzia Fakān gave such an artful shake of agreement that her halter-top removed itself and left her breasts covered only by her hands and certain sequined disks. "Sayyid Jafar: two votes."

"As for Jafar," that stern-visaged fellow promptly said — and he covered his cup with one hand to prevent its being refilled — "he feels quite as does his colleague Alī al-Yamān and will follow that colleague's prudent example on both counts. One vote against this so-called second Sindbad's going on with his narratives, which offend both propriety and good sense. One vote in their favor, inasmuch as any who return for yet more must have other motives, which such offense will either strengthen or overwhelm at last."

Cheered Ibn al-Hamrā, "Hear, hear!" and he offered Yasmīn his turbaned head, but she forwent this invitation to rewine him. Jafar raised his hand, stood, and bowed to Sindbad, who seemed still lost in contemplation of the table before him. "It cannot be denied," the merchant went on, "that the food and wine in this house are superior, the entertainment and general hospitality likewise. As for the stories of Sayyid Sindbad the Sailor, they remain as marvel-rich on third and fourth hearings as they were on first, and will no doubt be even richer on fifth and sixth. They deserve to be transcribed for the ages and retold for a thousand nights and a night. But I believe their teller to have been sorely misled by his alleged namesake, and not even our supple Kuzia Fakān can lure me to throw good dirhams after bad. I shall neither listen further to false Sindbads nor invest further in Serendib Limited. Allah bless you all, and good night."

Peep-peep-peep-peep-peep! Peep-peep-peep-peep-peep! piped Nuzhat to the tune of Kuzia's busy rump, while Fatmah Awād after each of these nays tapped off a forward-thrusting aye. "Ten–ten!" announced Yasmīn. Following his leader's example still further, Jafar did not quite leave, but instead stationed himself on the near side of Sindbad's tub and looked with the others to the one remaining voter.

"Our precious al-Fadl," Yasmīn crooned, and she knelt beside Cushion Seven to refill the little man's cup as solicitously as Kuzia knelt before him, moved her hands from her bare breasts to her bare shoulders, and with her whole upper body declared, "One vote," adding, "but what a vote!"

Al-Fadl blinked. Perspired. Began: "I think . . ." His voice failed. He sipped and dripped his wine, worked his jaw-hinge, tried again: "I think I think . . . I think I think I shall follow, in my small way, good Sīdī Numān's example. I mean . . . I think I mean . . . not yet abandoning our enterprise, but dividing my vote: one half yea, one half nay."

Kuzia re-covered one breast and began the tally, but both sides protested this fractioning of the crucial vote. "Come, man!" urged Hajj Masūd at al-Fadl's left elbow, Yasmīn at his right (in Jaydā's empty place), and Sīdī Numān from up and across the table — this last adding that to follow his example truly, al-Fadl ought at least to divide his vote two thirds to one third, giving Still-Stranded the victory by a third of a vote. "A thousand and one nays to that!" cried Ibn al-Hamrā, supported, from both sides of the tub, by Jafar and Alī al-Yamān. "To divide our votes may be all very well, but in the matter of fractioning them, the three of us here have the votes to outvote the two of you — even the three of you, if al-Fadl votes with you on this procedural question."

"Jewel of my lotus," Yasmīn corrected him, "you have no such thing, for unless your nay-saying neighbors have not after all said nay to Serendib Limited, they left their voting privileges on their vacant cushions. But I think that even Sīdī Numān will agree that if single votes are fractioned, we shall never break our tie."

"Agreed indeed," said Sīdī. "Aye or nay, my friend."

All the other voters nodded. Fatmah Awād rolled her tambourine. Al-Fadl sweated. Swiveling before him with her thumbs hooked in readiness under the waistband of her drawers, Kuzia Fakān made it known in the subtle language of dance that he would be rewarded whichever way he cast his vote, but that he must neither fraction it nor abstain. Al-Fadl's eyes grew large; the color left his face; he looked imploringly from our storyteller to Sindbad the Sailor, to Yasmīn, Sīdī Numān, Hajj Masūd. All looked sternly back. At last he whispered or at least mouthed a silent but unmistakable "Nay" and swooned sideways into Yasmīn's arms.

"Eleven–ten!" cheered Ibn al-Hamrā, and he rose to salute the vote

as Kuzia commenced her tally. "The nays have it, and Sayyid Interloper can keep his missing links in his pocket for all we care. Into the
tub with you, Kuzia! Dance for us!"

"Not just yet, O Ruler of my Roost," sweetly but firmly objected
Yasmīn, and she shifted al-Fadl's head from her lap onto Jaydā's cushion. "It is time now for Haroun's vizier's messenger to deliver us his
seven-vote message."

"I suppose it is," that fellow agreed. He held up his cup for refilling
and with the other hand beckoned Kuzia himward. Yasmīn and the
dancer hurried to oblige, but the royal messenger took time to savor
both the wine and Kuzia Fakān's electioneering before he went on:
"And now that I understand the agreeable customs of this house, my
seven votes are easily cast. Of this strange fellow's story I understood
no more than three words in all. Since I am likely to be punished for
reporting such stuff to my master, you young ladies may pipe me three
nays before I say another word."

He sat back, sipped, and watched with satisfaction the rumping
and peeping of those nays. But Ibn al-Hamrā, counting redly on his
fingers, was not pleased, nor was Yasmīn.

"On the other hand," the messenger continued — and Ibn switched
hands accordingly — "the three words I understood, I have often
heard exchanged between my master and *his* master, Caliph Haroun
al-Rashīd, upon whose head may Allah forever smile! I mean the
words *Sohar, Zahir,* and *Serendib.* As for the rest, nonsense or not, I
cannot report to Vizier Jafar al-Barmakī what I myself have not yet
heard, and since Sayyid Sindbad the Sailor has yet to favor me with
his reply to the caliph's message, I cast my remaining votes in favor of
this fellow's going on with his fantastical tale while I await that reply."
He cleared his throat. "My profession teaches that just as many a message makes sense to its sender but not to its receiver, so others make
sense to both but not to the messenger. On, therefore, with your
strange story, Sayyid Whoever-You-Are, and know that whatever I
hear, the vizier hears as well. Aye me four ayes, young ladies."

"No need of that," Yasmīn said with a sigh. "My red and lusty lord
is not the only one among us who can count to fourteen twice. We
are back where we started." So saying, she returned in fact to her place
at the foot of the table, from where she and our storyteller agreed with
their eyes that she had certainly done her best. Kuzia Fakān, mean-

while, having squatted before the caliph's vizier's messenger to drum her disappointed fingers on her disappointed knees, turned now a quarter turn to await orders from her master.

"Perhaps . . . ," said a faint voice down the line — al-Fadl, whom Jaydā had set upright in his own place so that she might retake hers — "I ought to reconsider. . . ."

"Don't trouble yourself," suddenly and clearly said Sindbad the Sailor, entirely wakened from his trance. "This is still my house and household, my table, and my impending voyage to Serendib. Sayyid Sindbad the Still-Stranded is still my brother and still my guest, as are whichever of you choose to return tomorrow night. I shall then retell my fell fifth voyage from first to last, and he likewise his, even if our audience be none but each other and this tub." He rapped upon it. "Nor shall there be any further mincing and haggling, debating and voting, either upon these tales or upon Voyage Seven. Swallow them whole or spit them out, but chew them openmouthed no longer at Sindbad's table. The dance is danced, sirs; I bid you good night."

Without even his usual "Yasmīn," Sindbad then withdrew to the courtyard and climbed the ladder into his great empty sleeping tub, pausing only at its rim to summon Kuzia Fakān with a glance and then lowering himself inside. The dancer happily hurried after him, paused likewise at the ladder-top, turned first to Yasmīn and then to "Bey el-Loor," and to each said with a wink (in the language of her dance), "Aye!" Our storyteller — no expert reader of that tongue — thought he saw her mouth as well what might have been the name *Marjānah!*

Murmuring among themselves, the company dispersed in three several groups. Ibn al-Hamrā, Alī al-Yamān, and Jafar left together, supporting among them the still-apologetic al-Fadl. Likewise exited Hajj Masūd and Sīdī Numān, after a head-shaking short conference with Yasmīn. Nuzhat and Fatmah Awād escorted Haroun's vizier's messenger off, perhaps to join Salīm and the other attendants else-where in the house. Jaydā, Yasmīn, and our storyteller alone remained in their places, silent, until presently from the courtyard tub Sindbad's voice resonated after all:

"Yasmīn."

Without turning her head, she cowled it, called back "Father," and rose at once.

"I need words now with Jaydā," the voice said on. "You yourself will kindly show my bereaved brother to his room."

Black-caftaned Jaydā grunted heavily to her feet. Yasmīn turned her hooded face Somebody's way. "Your will be done."

"See that it is," replied her invisible father.

2.

So bold with her lover in Jaydā's presence, Yasmīn seemed in her absence almost shy. Wordlessly we walked by lantern light up and back through her father's house to the guest apartments near the women's quarters. Her stalemate storyteller took her hand to reassure her and startled her instead. He kissed that hand, held it, but we proceeded then not as man and woman walking hand in hand from banquet hall to bedroom (a thing not often to be seen where we were) but (a sight less rare) as man leading woman by the hand from table to bed. At our corridor's end, in the shadows — was that Salīm? No doubt, and no matter. More ushered than usher, Yasmīn hesitated at the familiar door, as if prepared to say good night there, until her friend opened it and handed her inside.

He waited then for her to initiate what and as she would. She set the lamp down on his writing table and stood by. For the pleasure of seeing her eyes and hair, he slipped back her djellaba-cowl. She regarded him tentatively, then lowered her glance to the light.

He read her sense. This evening's narrative was not the first mention she had heard of "Baylor" and "J. Moore," their lively comradeship and its terrible end. We had had occasion before to review each other's lives: in hesitant bits aboard her bride-ship and through our joint ordeal with the Qeshmi pirates, and more intimately in Yasmīn's rooms through our hidden, healing month of Sha'ban. But those had been reticent allusions, quick takes, glimpses. Tonight, in public and in one piece, she had heard, if not quite the story, anyhow one story of her lover's late love and loss, by which she seemed both touched and distanced. Her previous responses — as to his renderings of "Day-*zee*," "Janeprize," "Terīfrum Tī-Nech," "Terizāh" — would scarcely serve. She waited for him.

And, waiting, happened to touch her fingers to the paper on which she had set the lamp, to the block capitals he had glossed that afternoon for Kuzia Fakān, and Kuzia in turn for him. *"Bey el-Loor,"* she murmured, pleased at her own half-guess, half-recognition, and having thus blessed that equivocal name with her lips, she lightly bent to kiss another blessing upon its letters. "Is this other the name of your lost jewel?"

"It is only our friend Kuzia's," he said. To lighten our air and give the two of us accommodation time, he reviewed for her his musings on the *B* and *A,* then Kuzia Fakān's upon the *Y,* the *L,* the *O,* the *R.* Meant to amuse, they brought tears instead to those djellaba-colored eyes, which, alarmed, he quickly kissed as she had kissed those symbols. "Yasmīn," he told her, "is my jewel."

She shook her head but permitted her tears to be thus stanched, and with some of her customary forthrightness removed and neatly folded her sea-green robe and matching undergarments. Then she turned, not to the bed's edge (where her friend now awaited her pleasure and his consolation) but away from him, back to his writing table (Behold, he could not help thinking as she bent over it: Baghdad's beautifulest *B*). Dipping her left forefingertip three several times into the ink jar, she stood with her back still toward him and her feet apart (Aroused already, he admired Allah's uncrossed *A*) and drew upon herself, out of his sight, three swift strokes.

"Let my lost sisters Day-*zee* and Jay-Moor remain Bey el-Loor's lost jewels," she declared while doing this, "Jay-Moor especially, a bold, free spirit whom I love and envy." Then she turned, arms akimbo, head just slightly cocked, to show him her name's initial letter, his name's third, its three arms drawn from her perfect navel up to her nipples and down to her crotch. "Yasmīn tonight is Sīmon's writing paper. Inscribe yourself on her, and in your writing I shall read our story's next chapter."

That sweet collaboration we forthwith set about, without recourse to further ink or literal quill. So painfully, even in our faint light, did Yasmīn's eyes remind him tonight of "Jay-Moor's" that Sīmon kept his own carefully elsewhere: upon the crux of that *Y,* whose triple arms he retraced with kisses; upon their dainty termination points and the rest of this body so unambiguously Yasmīn's. In lovers' script he wrote upon her his familiar, heartfelt plaint: *My stillborn twin; my first and all subsequent lovers; my wife; my son and daughter, too; my brave and free and latest-lost companion — none is more lost than he who lost you all.*

Whereto, in like language, his living parchment made its like reply: *Whatever has before been written here is no less lost, erased by love. Our page is blank. Write on.*

These salutations exchanged, there followed the body of our text, which, though it comprised but a single word, might be said to have read, *The page that love renews need not be new, nor the pen untried to write with clear new point. Our newly freshened, sweetest page commands, "On me inscribe* Yourself*" — but welcomely supplies, for starting point, its own initial. To which dear* Y *our dedicated pen, replenished, freshly pointed, need but add the word that like that letter fuses two by love's warm confluence into one, mates pen to paper, Sīmon to Yasmīn:* ourself.

Thus glossed, this inscription so soothed both scribe and scribed that history for a while relaxed its hold. We slept.

"Marjānah Marjānah Marjānah," Jaydā's voice incanted some while later in our heads. Our lamp was out; we stirred in each other's arms. The familiar voice complained from the foot of our bed, "He wants a word with Jaydā, declares Sindbad the Sailor, and what does that word turn out to be? *Marjānah!*" After some grumbling in another tongue, she went on in ours, "Every man's key hangs between his legs, and Kuzia Fakān believes she can unlock Sindbad by impersonating Marjānah. Little does she know how little she knows, but she knows she's onto something when our lord and master summons her again tonight into his Tub of Truth, despite this fiasco of an evening. Then he summons me in there, too, the first time in years, and says to me, regarding her, 'This Bedou fly-bait imagines she can please me by imitating my late wife, but as she never had the pleasure of that lady's acquaintance, she might as well be doing Mustafā the camel. Perhaps if you,' he says to me, 'who knew Marjānah better than her husband ever did, were to watch and coach her imitator, she would fail less miserably tonight than she did last night.'"

Yasmīn's body tensed against her friend's. He pressed her head to his shoulder, her groin to the hip against which it rested. Stroking then the small of her back, his hand bumped the speaker's, which was doing likewise as its owner spoke on:

"So he puts her through her paces, and wretched though her imitation is — in her double ignorance of her model — Kuzia Fakān is canny enough to have got hold of something after all. Well: without going half as far as I might have gone, I quickly show her one thing and another that Sindbad himself had no doubt forgotten — not that but this, not there but here, meanwhile doing thus but never so — all things I taught Marjānah herself once upon a time. Then I am obliged to stand by and watch the old goat in a rut such as he has seldom risen to since I first procured that Bedou belly-shaker for his dry-land joy.

"Now then, beautiful and privileged listeners: as everyone knows who has heard Part One of Chapter Six of Allah's great tale of Jaydā the Cairene, its heroine possesses among her many gifts the ability to read men's zabbs as other folk read the Koran. Upon Sayyid Sindbad's, risen from the dead like the Messiah of Unbelievers, I plainly read Part Two of that same chapter of that same tale. Following closely upon Part One, it had to do with our heroine's nearest approach to happiness in the story thus far, and it went as follows:

"When Sindbad the Sailor returned to Baghdad from his horrific fourth voyage (of which he gave a fair account tonight), he found his house no less altered than himself. Hearing of his approach from Basra and not knowing in detail what had befallen him on his long voyage or how he had reacted to my shipboard message about Marjānah's death, I dressed the whole establishment in mourning, even down to little Yasmīn, who by then was two or three years old. Thus we assembled to greet him in the beflowered courtyard, our hearts as full as the fountains and fish pools that in those days graced this place.

"After glowering silently from one of us to another — especially at myself and the daughter whom he had not seen since her birth-day — he declared to us all, 'Men should behave to men as men!' He then picked up Yasmīn (who had even less idea than we what he was saying, but who bravely overcame her fright and kissed her father) and repeated to her that men should behave to men as men. Putting her down, he ordered everyone except Jaydā to return to their usual employment. Me he directed into his erstwhile bridal tub for a private audience. Presently joining me there, he spoke only one word: 'Marjānah.'

"I supposed he wanted from me a full firsthand account of how my hard-won prophecy had come to pass — Marjānah's childbed fever and the rest. But before I got fairly into my preamble, I saw a strange dark look come over him like a roc's wing over the sky. He sprang upon me where I sat, hauled up my skirts and down my drawers, and would have forced my wâhât had it not been brimming already with anticipation. 'Marjânah!' he cried again as he drove in — and now my nether eye read plainly the message of his zabb: how the tidings of Marjânah's death had unstrung his senses for weeks, and how the later horrors of Voyage Four plagued him yet with mad fits from time to time. What exactly those horrors had been — the fate of Captain Ka-sīm and his other surviving shipmates on Island One, his own live entombment on Island Two and the desperate measures by which he had preserved his life, the loss and miraculous recovery of his Tub of Last Resort — I read this first time only in outline, along with the news that in his spells of madness (which by then came on him no more than once a week, for half an hour) he relived both his passion for Marjânah and that baseless suspicion of her fidelity which I had once cured him of. Such a fit (I read further, to my disappointment) was upon him at the moment; he not only invoked his late wife's name but called me by it and vented upon me his conflicting feelings for her. The better to assist their ventilation, I did a thing or two that I had once taught his bride to do, while giving her to believe that she was teaching me. Sure enough, they brought him to a frenzy of coupling, kissing, and cursing his 'darling harlot Marjânah,' after which he quickly recovered his senses.

"In ordinary postcoital Arabic then he thanked me for having seen to his wife's funeral arrangements and for supervising his household and his daughter's upbringing in his long absence — not to mention having given him lifesaving prophetic advice. Any sort of unpleasant treatment I might have just now received at his hands, he warned me, I could expect whenever his madness was on him. But those fits appeared to be slowly abating in frequency and duration, and if I thought myself able to cope with them, he would be pleased to have me manage his household in his presence as I had in his absence.

"How my heart and wâhât together yearned to cry yes at once, without reservation! But my better judgment imposed one condition: he must give me a fair prevision of the arrangement he proposed, and then permit me either to accept it or to decline and take my place instead among his ordinary womenservants. How could he do that, he asked me, when he himself had no clear idea of what he meant to do next with his life? I reminded him of the means whereby I had foreseen certain things before; he reminded me that I had forsworn any future such prophesying and had urged him to accept what was to come as it came. Should I not follow the same advice? Perhaps, I granted, but given his new and unpredictable seizures, if precautions might be taken for his welfare and his daughter's, for example, I wished to foresee and take them.

"'My daughter,' he repeated, as if to convince himself. He then agreed to my condition, on two conditions of his own. First, whatever I might see in the dark well of the future and however I might act upon what I saw there, I must say nothing of it to him — nothing more specific, at least, than 'Mind what you swallow, lest your mind be swallowed' or 'Sail this time in some other vessel than *Zahir.*' Second, I must contrive some way to reinvigorate his instrument of prophecy, which had altogether spent itself on 'Marjānah.'

"That latter requirement I quickly and joyfully fulfilled, for it was not Marjānah or Marjānah's handmaid he was dealing with now, but the central character of Allah's great narrative of the world: Jaydā the peerless Cairene herself. In less time than it takes to say 'Men should behave to men as men,' I had his zabb even readier for Jaydā's bi'r than it had been for 'Marjānah's' wâhât. I assumed the position of prophecy, and without more ado Sindbad the Sailor plumbed the strait passage of things to come, doing to me as men do to men who do to men as men do to women.

"In view of what was thereby previewed by me, however, his other stipulation proved harder than his zabb. My inmost, furthest-seeing eye thus opened, I saw what I saw: what in the weeks and months and years thereafter I would see again, both approaching and come to pass. I keened. Believing he had hurt me, my rider made to dismount, but it was what I saw and could not save us from that hurt. 'Drive in and on,' I bade him, and I keened again. Good as my word, though, I spoke not a syllable of what was revealed to me, but declared myself ready to accept his proposal.

"Thus commenced, despite its darknesses, the brightest interlude in Allah's chronicle of Jaydā the Cairene. She became Sindbad the Sailor's concubine-in-chief, mistress of his house, foster mother of his daughter. Sharing his bridal tub, she shared more fully his hard history, the details of which his zabb inscribed in her as in a logbook, and she came to love and pity him more than herself. Ably, when the fit was on him, she played 'Marjānah' till that fit passed, though she shuddered at what she knew his mad mix of love and rage would lead to. For in those fits he railed not only at his 'faithless wife' but at the doubly innocent Yasmīn as well, calling her no daughter of his at all but the spawn of some nameless interloper upon her shameless mother. Then, when presently the fit passed, there was no more doting father in all Baghdad than Sindbad the Sailor, who claimed to remember nothing of his mad behavior.

"Just a few pages into this interlude, there came one day to our gate, as I foresaw there would, an elder man leading a beautiful boy-child of four or five years and begging an audience with Sindbad. When my master saw him, they fell upon each other's necks in joyous reunion and then spoke together privately at length in his Tub of Truth. That night I learned from the messenger in Sindbad's drawers that the man at the gate was the navigator Mustafā, first officer aboard the ship that had lately rescued Sindbad from Peppercorn Island. That ship's captain, Allim al-Yom (the one who had refused payment for his act of mercy, declaring that men should behave to men as men), had alas just died, leaving behind an orphan son and — having guided his whole life by that virtuous motto — no money for the child's support. Mustafā himself subscribed to that same principle and had therefore taken the child in rather than see him beg on the street, but being unmarried as well as virtuous and poor, and a mariner by profession, he could not provide for the boy. Remembering Sindbad's thwarted wish to reward the good captain who had saved him, Mustafā now presented him with a chance to fulfill that wish.

"'Men should behave to men as men,' Sindbad's zabb told me its owner had affirmed. Extending that precept to boys as well, he forthwith took into his household both the navigator and the orphan child, which latter he consigned to my care, instructing me to behave to the boy thenceforward as to his own flesh and blood.

"Now: this man-child, Umar al-Yom, was indeed as bright and sweet as the morning light that first strikes the caliph's minarets and causes the muezzins to cry out for holy joy. Being so close together in age, he and Yasmīn quickly became as brother and sister and were inseparable. Everyone in the household loved him, from the master to the lowest kitchen slave. Even I, who might have been expected to resent his introduction into the family (and so I did) could not but return the ready and radiant love of Umar al-Yom.

"The hearer of Allah's great tale may wonder, why should Jaydā have harbored any such resentment? Why, because my master's zabb had spoken yet another thing to my wâhât along with its nightly news reports, and when Mustafā mu-Allim the navigator came knocking at our gate with Umar al-Yom, my womb was big already with that utterance. Thus it came to pass that by the time my first- and only-born was born, he had a virtual older brother as well as a true half-sister. All this, mind, I had foreseen with my hinder eye when Sindbad plumbed the Well of Things to Come — this and more besides, despite which I mothered Umar al-Yom as I mothered Yasmīn and — after I had all but followed Marjānah to the grave breech-birthing him — my son, Salīm.

"As for the navigator Mustafā, Sindbad commissioned him to find a new captain for his ship *Zahir,* one as shrewd as he was skillful and as closemouthed as he was shrewd, able both to follow his master's orders and to improvise to advantage when circumstances warranted. *Zahir* itself he intended to refit in certain ways under this captain's direction for a different sort of merchant trading, inspired by his sojourn underground on Island Two, Voyage Four: having accustomed himself there to killing and robbing in order to survive, he had advanced to doing the same in order to prosper. These commissions and intentions Sindbad repeated to me unwittingly in zabb-talk, together with Mustafā's reply: without inquiring into the exact nature of the projected voyage, he believed he could steer Sayyid Sindbad to just the right captain, one Abū Hosayn of Siraf. While men should no doubt behave to men as men, declared Mustafā, the navigator's only job is to navigate — that is, to determine his vessel's position, not its destination, and to plot its course, not judge the reason for the voyage. This he pledged himself to do, out of gratitude for Sindbad's having made a virtual son of Umar al-Yom.

"The new captain was found, as foxy a fellow as his name, and in the years therefollowing he captained *Zahir* on a series of highly profitable short voyages before the long one that Sayyid Sindbad now calls his fifth. Not to put too fine a point on it, Sindbad the Master of Survival had been transformed by his fourth voyage into Sindbad the Predator, Sindbad the Shark, almost into Sindbad the Pirate. I say *almost* because though *Zahir*'s new business was not piracy itself, her new cargoes were pirates' booty, of which Sindbad became the chief importer in the City of Peace. In Qeshm and certain other islands of the Bahr Faris and Bahr Larwi, such goods were cheaply bought wholesale from their barbarous interceptors, who dared not retail them directly. In Baghdad they were readily and dearly sold when their distributor happened to be a man of Sindbad's reputation.

"Our dinner guests were now those merchants who were willing to retail such stock without inquiring overclosely into its origins, together with occasional captains of the sort who supplied *Zahir* with our goods. Truth to tell (I learned from my usual informant), Hosayn the Fox's sailing orders did not prohibit the odd piracy of his own, if our stock-in-trade happened to be scarce at second hand and Sindbad himself happened to be ashore; he was only to spare his employer the unpleasant details of such transactions, so that Sindbad could plausibly deny any charges of complicity. Thus do men behave to men, and if such free and easy society was not the most illustrious in Baghdad, it was one to which Jaydā the Cairene's youthful adventures in Zabargad and elsewhere had quite accustomed her. I presided over the foot of Sindbad's table then as does our Yasmīn now and was his unquestioning ally and confidante as well as his bed-partner and the mother of his son.

"His son! O beautiful and privileged hearers of Allah's epic in progress: who could have guessed, besides the boy's mother and Allah Himself, that my Salīm was Sindbad's son? Unlike Yasmīn, whose father lavished his love upon her when he was himself and cruelly spurned her when he was not, Salīm he neither acknowledged nor denied but took no more notice of than of any other serving-maid's bastard, who might be his own or some scullion's spawn. Granted, the boy was no Umar al-Yom; not even his mother could imagine that. But he was the true get of Sindbad the Sailor by the heroine of this story, and it galled his mother to see his father dandle Yasmīn on his left knee and Umar on his right while I dandled on both of mine the runt Salīm. But presently Sindbad's madness would come upon him; I would shoo the children out of harm's way and for better and worse transform myself into 'Marjānah'; he would bless and abuse both my wâhât and my bi'r; and in those latter depths, when he saw fit to plumb them, I would be reminded of what was to come and reencouraged to bide my time.

"Thus passed ten years of tempered bliss; a dozen; fifteen. While my Salīm skulked and sneaked, my Yasmīn grew from a beautiful child into an even more beautiful young woman, the pomegranate of her father's eye except during his ever rarer (but no less severe) mad seizures. Though she was too loving and charitable a soul ever to scorn outright her nanny's son (and her own unacknowledged half-brother), she could no more take pleasure in Salīm's company than could I, so painfully finer and more akin were her character and Umar's. As for that splendid young man, he had in effect three fathers to Salīm's none, for Sindbad early apprenticed him to Mustafā the Navigator and to Captain Abū Hosayn, both of whom prized him as did Sindbad himself. From every one of his voyages with them, Umar returned yet more handsome and in all ways more appealing than before, and more worldly as well, though with a persisting and endearing innocence that *Zahir*'s peculiar commerce seemed not to touch. Shielded by Mustafā mu-Allim from the true purpose of these brief voyages, he made them as if their single aim was to bring him back with new trinkets and tales of far-off places for Yasmīn's delight; and that young lady thirsted for his return as I did for her father's. A mere seashell fetched home from some desert shore by Umar al-Yom she would prize above any diamond from the Valley of Rocs and Serpents, regretting only that she could not voyage with him to find such treasures.

"Well now, sir and lady: I here confess that much as I loved Umar myself — as who could not, especially one who had mothered him from his childhood and whose affection he repaid as my own child could never? — I grew ever more jealous of his well-justified preferment over Salīm. Yet I bided my time, bided my time, until both my nether and my hinder eye agreed that Part Two of Chapter Six of this story was approaching its disastrous conclusion, which goes as follows:

"There came a long season through which Sayyid Sindbad found himself free of his spells of madness, and this was well, for of late those spells had taken a new and ominous turn. Believe it or not, the beauty of Jaydā the Cairene is not altogether impervious to time, and in his recentest seizures Sindbad had taken to reviling me not only in his customary terms, as the roundheeled strumpet Marjānah, but as the roundheeled *ugly old* strumpet Marjānah, whom he could scarcely bring himself to skewer upon his zabb. And sweet Yasmīn he had come to excoriate (in his fits) not only as her sluttish mother's daughter but as one who, being no kin of his, deserved no better of him than any kitchen wench. Brokenhearted, she would fling herself upon his bosom with appeals to his better nature and protestations of innocence and daughterly love, and I would see in his eye a certain glint that I had first seen in the eyes of the pirate fishermen of Zabargad. Then the fit would pass, together with his memory of it; he would be surprised and pleased to find his darling daughter embracing him, and would wonder solicitously at her tears, which were of pity more for him than for herself.

"Has Allah reported to His listeners that these fits of Sindbad's were for the most part our secret, Yasmīn's and mine? If not, He here does so: even Umar al-Yom was barely aware of them, rapt as he was in his own innocent adorability, his love of sailoring, and his soul mate Yasmīn, who was ashamed to speak of them to him. The rest of the household likewise suspected little or nothing — except perhaps Salīm, whose back-alley nose smelled unsavoriness both where it was and where it was not.

"For Yasmīn in particular, therefore, unable as she was to see as I could the next episode of this tale, it was sweet to imagine that her father was cured at last of his disfiguring affliction and that she and I would be slandered no more with those mad charges, of which I had assured her that her mother was as innocent as herself. As for Jaydā the Cairene, her mention of the Zabargad pirates a moment ago brings her now to the subject of Sindbad the Sailor's fifth voyage. The fact is that what it pleases him to call by that name was originally meant to be merely the next in that series aforedescribed, aboard his beloved *Zahir,* with one difference. Ever more impatient with the wild and untrustworthy pirates who supplied his stock-in-trade, he had in his latest two or three forays been inclined to secure a larger fraction of his merchandise directly, bypassing those unruly middlemen by not only authorizing Abū Hosayn's incidental piracies but supervising them himself; he took care only that young Umar should remain belowdecks with Mustafā through such engagements. In truth, Sindbad had become a pirate at heart, and despite the risk to his reputation he planned this time to make a wholly piratical voyage under the guise of his usual business, hoping to get by with the story that the vessels thus pirated by *Zahir* were themselves pirate vessels, whose cargo he was in effect reclaiming for Haroun al-Rashīd and the City of Peace.

"All this I knew without his having mentioned it to me in words, and realizing that so flimsy a fiction would not go long unexposed, one night I proposed to him — in what we had come to call our Tub of Truth — a cannier lie. If his object was to become his own middle-man, let him give out that his swift and able *Zahir* was to be laid up for extensive overhaul in her captain's home port of Siraf. Let him then hire in Basra, as he had done in days gone by, a larger, slower vessel, put aboard some legitimate trading goods, induce a company of fellow merchants to join him, and make in fact a trading voyage profitable for all, as if for old times' sake. Let him then so arrange matters that en route home up the Gulf of Persia, his profit-laden clunker would be intercepted, perhaps off Siraf, perhaps off Basra itself, by a certain foxy pirate in a certain swift and able ship, and her entire cargo taken, her crew and passengers dealt with as the pirate captain saw fit, and perhaps even the vessel itself scuttled. Let only Sindbad survive to tell the tale, as he had so often done before, reaching Basra perhaps in one of the lost ship's boats, or rescued by another merchant vessel conveniently passing by. He would have lost his goods and his companions and would for the first time have returned to Baghdad empty-handed — and therefore free of suspicion. But not long thereafter, his refitted *Zahir* would serendipitously reappear in Basra, back in business, fetching its owner a treasure from who knew where, the equivalent of his and all his lost companions' lost fortunes put together. . . .

"'Pearl of Cairo!' Sindbad exclaimed upon hearing this plan. 'You have read the fine print of my mind!' I acknowledged that in a manner of speaking, I had — and then I seized the occasion of his gratitude to bring up another matter. Although his daughter and his foster son, Umar al-Yom, had been raised together as sister and brother, I reminded him, in truth they were unrelated by blood and knew themselves so to be. Yasmīn, while unquestionably still virginal, was a ripe young woman nowadays, with breasts and buttocks ready to melt in a lover's mouth. Umar as well, while no doubt still innocent of women, was a young stallion too zabbed and egged to remain innocent much longer. Moreover, it was clear to everyone in the household, with the possible exception of the two young people themselves, that they were either falling in love or had already so fallen. Used though they were to having the same childhood freedom with each other as sibling play-mates, in my opinion they had outgrown that freedom and ought to be separated, as sparks from tinder. Let Umar henceforward pay his court to Yasmīn as a suitor should, I proposed — from a proper re-move, through her father, as other young men of the town had begun to do — and let Yasmīn veil her face in Umar's presence and subdue her free and easy manner with him, lest their intimacy lead to some untoward consequence.

"'Umar and Yasmīn?' Sindbad responded. I saw that the notion took him altogether by surprise and both interested and troubled him. He bade me say and do nothing further in the matter until he had observed the pair together in this new light; he would then confer with me on how best to manage the situation.

"But my earlier proposal, regarding his next voyage, possessed his imagination. While he did not dispatch Umar al-Yom to Siraf along with Abū Hosayn and Mustafā aboard *Zahir*, but instead kept him at home on the pretext of teaching him how ships were leased and stocked for extended trading, the pair of them were so occupied to-gether in Basra that for all Yasmīn and I saw of them, they might as well have been at sea. At one point I could not help complaining to milord that our own Salīm, no less than Umar, could use such tutelage from his father. 'Salīm!' Sindbad exclaimed, altogether incredulous, and for some moments he looked as if he were about to be seized by his first mad fit in half a year. Yasmīn, who happened to be with us, rose — either to forestall him with embraces or to retreat, as the situ-ation might warrant. But then he simply laughed, as though I had been teasing him with that name and epithet — our own Salīm! — not to mention that absurd suggestion. His laughter cut me to my bowels, but I pressed the matter no further and was relieved to see his expression return to normal — except for that certain eye-glint when Yasmīn salaamed before him and kissed his hands.

"Back in the harem, she and I praised Allah for thus sparing both Sindbad and ourselves, and Yasmīn vowed to that deity, now that she was a grown woman herself, never again to let her dear nanny suffer alone her poor father's madness, should his fits ever recur, as I had so often suffered them through her childhood. For this I thanked her, but I kept my own counsel and bided my time.

"Of that last there was little more to bide, inasmuch as Chapter Six, Part Two, had remaining to it at this point but a day and a night. The day (the next after the foregoing) was Sindbad's last in Baghdad before setting out for Basra and Voyage Five, the arrangements for which, both official and secret, were now complete. The trading ship was leased, stocked, and provisioned, and his fellow merchants were forgathered at the port and eager for the voyage, while Abū Hosayn and *Zahir,* under the pretext of laying up in Siraf, stood by there to meet, accompany, and ultimately pluck the fruit when it grew ripe. This last was Sindbad's amendment to my proposal: so as not to keep *Zahir* unprofitably laid up till his return (the date of which not even I could predict, nor plot the fatal rendezvous so far in advance), he planned to make Siraf an early port of call, and there, finding *Zahir* overhauled ahead of schedule, newly armed, and ready for sea, to commission Abū Hosayn to escort the larger merchant ship and 'protect it from pirates' — as the herdsman protects his herd from wolves until it is fattened for slaughter.

"After a farewell dinner that evening (during which a blind man might have seen that Yasmīn and Umar had eyes only for each other and could scarcely bear the thought of their impending separation), Sindbad sent word to the harem that I should join him tête-à-tête in his Tub of Truth. 'Allah's blessing on you, dear Jaydā!' rejoiced Yasmīn, who was with me when smirking Salīm brought this message. It had been long indeed since I was last thus summoned to a night of love (as she supposed), and I heard in her happy sighs a yearning for the time when Umar al-Yom would so summon her. 'May it be,' I replied — but inasmuch as I knew that calamity was about to overtake us, my sigh was less joyful than hers. 'Rub-a-dub dub,' commented Salīm, whose insinuating mouth I bade him go rinse in the hammam.

"When we two were tubbed, Sindbad said shortly, 'I have summoned you for prophecy, not for general dalliance. Kindly assume the vatic position and, as you did once before, without distressing me with details of what lies ahead, give me whatever advice you can for young Umar's preservation and my own on this fifth voyage.' 'I hear and obey,' I said, and did, and was straightway administered such a poke of prescience that tears sprang from all my eyes. 'Speak,' Sindbad commanded. At what I saw ahead from behind I gasped again, then gathered my breath and uttered two prophetic advisories. 'First,' I declared, 'should you find yourself bestrode and all but ridden to earth by some ancient, unshakable hunger, I bid you *feed that rider till he falls of himself from your back.*' What this warning signified was no clearer to the warner than to the warned, but as it appeared to have to do with swallowing (on which subject my earlier advice had proved to be sound), Sindbad perpended it with thanks.

"'Second,' I continued,' — and pray don't ask me the wherefore of it — *do not take with you on this fifth voyage Umar al-Yom*, or any soul else whose life you value.'

"Without bothering to ask what I had bidden him not to, Sindbad here angrily withdrew his divining rod and accused me straight out of falsifying my readings of it in hope of persuading him to leave his dear Umar behind and take with him instead my whelp Salīm, to be educated in the arts of maritime sharp trading and shipwreck survival. 'O more perfidious even than Marjānah!' he railed. 'I need no hinder eye to see the thing clearly! You and your trollop of a daughter are setting your snares for my Umar! You want to pack off old Sindbad and the cur Salīm so that the pair of you can play mare to that young stallion! Confess it, Marjānah: even on our bridal night you were no more a virgin than Yasmīn is now. Your maidenhead was but one more of wily Jaydā's artifices, and your fidelity another!'

"By this point, needless to say, I understood that my well-meant advice had set off that fit we had seen a-building the day before — a fit all the more severe, like the storm that breaks a heat wave, for its being so long overdue. This much I had foreseen, but not the full extent of that storm's fury, which inspired my master now even to the Muslim ritual of unmarrying. 'Foulest of females,' he cried, 'I divorce thee! I divorce thee! I divorce thee! From this moment you are my wife no longer, only a chattel of my harem, and your daughter another — no more kin to me than Jaydā the Cairene. I here consign the pair of you to her wardship: you shall obey her in all things and henceforth come to me only as it shall please me to send for you through her. Begone now, out of my tub and out of my sight!'

"Such was his fury that as he divorced his late wife he tore off his turban and madly exorcised her ghost by snapping it at me like a silken whip, a trick he had perfected in voyages Two and Three for driving off giant buzzards and vipers of moderate dimension. Bare-arsed as I was from prophesying, I felt those silk-snaps no less than his ravings.

As I scrambled into my caftan and out of their range, I heard beyond the tub wall Salīm's familiar snicker and another, equally familiar voice rebuking him. Up the ladder then and into the dry tub to my rescue (as I clambered out and down) came not the brave and stalwart Umar al-Yom — though he surely would have had he not been sleeping like a baby in his own quarters, carried off to dreamland by a single cup of bon-voyage wine — but our even braver because less stalwart Yasmīn. Her surpassing love for both her father and her nanny, which had made her swear to intercede on my behalf should he ever again relapse into his madness, had given her to fear, as I did, that just such a relapse might ensue upon his summons. Boldly therefore she had followed me to the courtyard and stood by in secret near our Tub of Truth — as Salīm was wont to do for less creditable motives — and so got the drift of what passed between us. At the sound of those turban-snaps she rushed to interpose herself for my sake, believing (as the young and good and innocent are prone to believe) that her youth and goodness and innocence could not but prevail over their contraries. Thus Jaydā the Cairene herself once upon a time believed, back in Chapter One of Allah's world-story, until the Zabargad pirates educated her out of this delusion.

"Did I say that Chapter Six, Part Two, here concludes? Then I said truly, for just as Sayyid Bey el-Loor, earlier this evening, piqued his listeners by declaring, 'The next thing I knew, I knew nothing,' so I must report that the next thing Allah's peerless heroine knew, she was in Chapter Seven of her epic tale. Wherein, fearing for her darling Yasmīn's safety, she flies from the courtyard (pausing only to swat her sniggering son), rouses Umar al-Yom from his righteous though wine-induced slumber, urgently dispatches him to rescue her rescuer — and herself withdraws to the security of the harem while what follows follows."

Tense in each other's arms, Jaydā's wakeful listeners bated their breath and listened until we heard her snore. Yasmīn then turned quietly onto her twice-stroked back, did something small with herself in the dark, reached to take her companion's writing hand, and said, "Now I shall read what is written." She snugged that hand against the foot of her self-inscribed Υ. "Here is Baghdad, where Sīmon's sixth and latest voyage has left him stranded. . . ."

"Peace be on this dear place," that voyager affirmed, "this daintiest jewel of a city."

"As Allah wills." From there she drew our hands slowly up the letter's stem toward its fork, declaring, "Kuzia Fakān last night danced a certain dance with my father and contrived to borrow from him, without his lending them, what may be the missing links in Bey el-Loor's story. She has given them to me to return to you, if yours they are."

"Yasmīn!" our man could not help exclaiming — for in her navel his fingertips touched what felt like literal links from some metal band or bracelet. "We must light the lamp!"

"Morning will light it soon enough," she said, pressing his hand against her belly. "And whether or not my father makes a seventh voyage, my Sīmon will. Very soon he will say good-bye to his friend here in the City of Peace." She re-touched "Baghdad" with his fingers, which now held the links, and then retraced with them the stem of the Υ: "From Basra he will set out as if for Serendib" — she traced the Υ's left arm, up to her right breast — "and with the help of these magical links, in some way beyond my understanding" — from her navel again she moved his hand up the Υ's other arm, across her heart — "he will reach his home."

It wanted only her enouncing that destination for our man to realize its emptiness. Pressing the unseen links into her hand now and enclosing that hand in his, on his knees beside her in the dark he declared that there was another, better way to read that letter — a way that did not divide but rather merged us, as the Tigris and the Euphrates flow together into the Shatt al Arab and thence into the Persian Gulf. Moving her hand back down from her left breast toward her navel, he said, "Here is Yasmīn, voyaging through her girlhood into her womanhood and surviving that rough passage." Leaving her hand there, he next moved his own from her right breast toward that same destination. "And here comes Somebody-or-Other, no sooner finding a self for himself than losing it or leaving it behind. At this point here — let's call it the Axis of the World — their separate voyages cast them together." His hand met and clasped hers at that conjunction. "From it we presently set forth, hand in hand." He moved our linked hands down the stem. "And whether our voyage fetches us back to Baghdad or on to Baylorville or down to the bottom of the sea, if we reach it together that place is Serendib."

Yasmīn squeezed our hands between her thighs (returning to him as she did those precious links) and drew Sīmon's face to hers. So ended, where it had begun, this reading exercise.

3.

In his refreshened room that afternoon, while awaiting interruption by Kuzia Fakān and company, Somebody wrote these English sentences, among others:

Between my pen hand and my inkpot, as if transported from that "Jmaa el Fna" in Charlotte Amalie's Dronningen's Gade, lie what we're calling my "missing links." But missing links imply a chain in hand, whereas these present stainless bits are from a missing . . . amulet, let's say: not "Baylor's" nameless bracelet, lost and gone forever with its owner and his beloved Julia Moore, but the faithful keeper of my time, reckoner of my position. From time to time . . .

From time to time, much moved, he paused to touch those linked bits to his lips, his nose, even his tongue, imagining that they bore the savor of at least two lives and worlds. Then he wrote on, for who knows whom: not the story of "Bey el-Loor's" fourth voyage, as told last night up to "The next thing I knew, I knew nothing"; not notes toward the tale he might tell tonight, to whoever might be there to hear, of the next thing Somebody knew after that. He registered, rather, one more found piece of a missing puzzle: this morning's tête-à-tête with Sindbad the Sailor, in their customary conversation place.

The page Salīm, as usual, had brought the forenoon summons. As usual, too, between the writer's room and the deserted courtyard the page attempted to pump dry the summoned by pumping him full. The whole kitchen staff now understood, Salīm insinuated, glancing often at our man's face as he spoke, that Sayyid Still-Stranded and the caliph's vizier's messenger were colleagues, communicating by secret signs down the dinner table as they prepared to expose the grand fraud of Sindbad's next voyage.

"You have found us out!" Somebody exclaimed, as if consternated. "A sharp fellow like you would do well in the vizier's service! Was it our wine-cup signals you deciphered, or the code of our votes? And does Sayyid Sindbad suspect us?"

"You tease me," Salīm replied. "But I know what I know, and if you don't soon spring your trap, Sayyid Ibo will spring it for you. Even Hajj Masūd can't be fooled forever; soon there'll be no chickens left for Sindbad to pluck."

"Or to divide his profits with," Somebody suggested instead. "We believe your father knows what he's doing."

"My father!" The page spat on the ground and, in vulgar but sub-dued Arabic as the pair approached the camel Mustafā and the lad-dered courtyard tub, swore that he aspired one day to fist-fuck Sindbad the Sailor in his half an ass for all the father that man had ever been to him.

Said Somebody, "Filial love takes many forms. Good morning, Brother Sindbad!"

"Brother Sindbad!" the old man's voice called back from inside the tub, hollowly but cordially. "Kindly join us here while Salīm kindly waters Mustafā."

The page made a fist of his left hand, extended it tubward, and thrust into it the thumb of his right before moving off. Still-Stranded Somebody mounted the ladder and found his namesake turbaned in resplendent ultramarine, and not alone. Cross-legged to the left of him sat black-veiled and -caftaned Jaydā, as impassive as always. Prostrate before him, Kuzia Fakān was busily kissing the tub floor between his feet. Both of her arms were stretched before her, and old Sindbad gripped her firmly by both wrists. She waggled her costumed backside high, as if in desperate greeting.

"Be seated, Brother! Over here, perhaps." Sindbad tipped his tur-ban toward the vacant cushion on his right quarter rather than the one opposite him, from which Kuzia evidently had been drawn. As won-dering Somebody sat, the dancer rolled her eyes in an uncertain signal and rekissed the floor.

"Well, now," Sindbad said. "Jaydā reports that my daughter's honor was so closely guarded through the night that she's sleeping still."

Her guardian made a small salaam of acknowledgment. Kuzia Fakān rapped her forehead on the floor until her master let go of one wrist to silence her. Head pressed to the floor, she mouthed in Some-

body's direction something silent, urgent, but alas unintelligible. Sindbad next declared that as for himself, despite last evening's defection
of several more investors in Serendib Limited and the prospect of further such defections to come as certain poisonous slanders got about;
and despite the pressure on him from Haroun al-Rashīd, by way of
his vizier, by way of his vizier's messenger, to reply forthwith to the
caliph's directive; and despite the prospect of banishment if not death
should he fail to come up by tomorrow with a final sailing plan (of
which, he candidly admitted, he had in fact not even the hint of a
beginning); and despite the regrettable circumstance of his being
obliged to chop the hands off a certain thieving whore of a dancer and
to sell the rest of her to the keeper of the Baghdad lepers' brothel for
stealing a certain small treasure from him yesterday and attempting to
steal a greater one early this morning — despite all these considera-
tions, he found himself in good humor. For when she was not busy
being a common thieving Bedou whore, Kuzia Fakān was an *un*common thieving Bedou whore, and last night (her final night in his
house), before she attempted the impermissible and was subsequently
revealed to have done the unpardonable, she had contrived with the
aid of Jaydā's coaching and her own native desert wit to delight him
in a fashion in which and to a degree that he had not been delighted
for a good many years — so much so that notwithstanding the Islamic
justice that he must now inflict upon her (and that Haroun might
soon inflict upon him) nothing could altogether dampen his spirits
this excellent morning. "Peace, therefore, Brother," he concluded,
"and the blessings of the day be on you."

"On yourself as well," replied Still-Stranded. "Likewise upon these
canny and formidable women of your house." Without asking then
why exactly he had been summoned to this domestic business —
which his host's manner and Kuzia's face-talk told him was, though
serious, rather less dire than it sounded — he declared straightway
that it was himself who must be disciplined for theft. "The hand that
took these links from you," he said, and he displayed them in his open
palm, "was the one you hold. But the arm was this that now returns
them. Kuzia Fakān acted on my orders."

"Yours!" But Sindbad seemed to Somebody not altogether surprised, just as his threat of punishment had seemed less than literal.
Nor did he move immediately to reclaim the missing watch-bracelet

links. Our man deposited them near his slippered feet; Kuzia kissed them welcomely, then picked them up between her lips and, like an obedient puppy, placed them in the hand her master presently extended. "And whose right arm are you, of which this Bedou is the hand? Vizier Jafar al-Barmakī's, or that of Haroun himself?"

Our man responded simply that those links came from where he himself came from and were his only present link thereto. In hope of reachieving their source, he must know where and how his host had come by them. Only with that knowledge might he — just possibly — be of assistance in Sindbad's present plight as well as his own.

Scowling and murmuring, the old man now briefly inspected the bits of steel in question. Evidently satisfied, with surprising quickness he then lifted one buttock (the less-cushioned left) and thrust them under it. "Not content to be my brother," he grumbled to Jaydā or to himself, "he would be my son as well."

As Somebody considered that remark, his host pronounced a conditional reprieve for Kuzia Fakān: he bade Jaydā take her back into the harem for further instruction of a particular sort and to fetch her back to revisit him later in the day, before the evening's feast and exchange of tales. Should she improve yet more upon her last performance and complete the restitution that his brother had begun, he might even pardon her offense.

"Fountain of mercy!" the dancer duly cried.

Said Sindbad the Sailor, "Don't speak to me of fountains," and — bidding Somebody to remain with him and Jaydā to clear her snooping son from the courtyard — he dismissed the two women.

"What then shall we speak of?" our man asked presently. "Serendib, perhaps? Where I come from, we say of situations like yours that *the clock is running* . . . by which is meant, let's say, Allah's hourglass."

As if to his beard, Sindbad responded, "Mine has all but run. I am an old man, easily baited if not so easily bested. Serendib for me is no brine-soaked island but some dune-girt oasis five hundred parasangs from the nearest sea. To live out my last years in bone-dry peace in such a desert wâhât, with none to attend me but Jaydā and my daughter . . . I would trade all this." Without raising his eyes, he indicated with a wave of one hand his tub and, presumably, the house and household therearound. "Let younger Sindbads feed themselves to Allah's sharp-toothed swimmers," he went on. "The only seventh voyage *I* crave is aboard the camel Mustafā, with the crew aforementioned, to some such arid Serendib."

He glanced up shortly at his listener, who ventured in reply that such an inland trek was in secret fact the very voyage that his host and "brother" had all along been planning — perhaps dispatching a decoy ship from Basra on a wild-goose chase to "Serendib" while he absconded with the bulk of his partners' capital? In this reading (our man ventured further), the whole protracted dowry negotiation with Ibn al-Hamrā, for example, was no more than a diversion. If Sindbad was less than devastated by the recent defections from Serendib Limited, was that not because he was more than desperate over Haroun's having called his bluff, and was prepared to settle now for merely escaping the caliph's wrath? With full saddlebags, to be sure, and agreeable company. . . .

Sindbad sighed. "Whoever you are, you are indeed my brother." But even while sighing, he flashed Somebody a reappraising glance; then, rather than asking the price of confidentiality and possible assistance, he waited, as if to hear it.

"A moment ago you called me your would-be son," our man said instead. "How is that?"

For the first time in this interlude, Sindbad smiled. "Because if you came from where Kuzia stole those links from, my son you'd be. But ask me no further questions on that head," he added sternly, "or I'll bid you good day until this evening."

"Then I can do nothing for either of us."

"As Allah wills. The blessings of the day be on you."

Sindbad's stubbornness, however, seemed clearly experimental. "'The day,'" Somebody repeated, "*al yom*. My fifth-voyage tale this evening ends with *al layl*, the night. Will yours begin with al-Yom?"

The old man's startlement appeared authentic, his groan sincere. "Umar! That shaitan of a godchild, who played all his fathers false!" Presently he let go of his beard, recomposed his turban and himself, and declared that while he would no more repeat that false son's name in public than repeat the name of that despicable Qeshmi pirate Sahīm al-Layl (and was therefore obliged, whenever he recounted his fifth voyage, to speak more or less figuratively), if his brother insisted on hearing in confidence the literal and sorry truth about Umar al-Yom — and would press him no further in the matter of those metal trinkets — he would tell it.

Still-stranded Somebody shook his head. Regarding those links, he regretted to say, he had no recourse but to press, press, press, to the end of the chapter and beyond, or else fling himself into the Shatt al Arab. He could promise no more than to postpone further pressing till after the telling of this other tale, in which he might be said to have an official interest, as he understood it to involve the honor he was pledged to protect: Yasmīn's.

"It most certainly does that," dour Sindbad acknowledged. "But give me your word that what I say will remain within this tub."

"So be it; and let this tub be where the tale begins. I've heard from here and there how the boy Umar came into your household, and how you kindly raised him as if he were your own son and Yasmīn's brother. . . ."

"Men should behave to men as men," Sindbad said gloomily. "What else have you heard?"

"How he took to sailoring, like his father and his foster father, and how he looked forward to his first real trading voyage with you. Perhaps you can begin with the night before that voyage, here in this tub."

Once again, nodding, Sindbad assessed his tubmate's tone and face. Then he told this tale:

The night before any voyage, he had learned from experience, was normally a restless one for him. Was everything in order? Would he ever see his home and friends again, and if so, after surviving what perils? Through the night before Voyage Five, however, he slept like a newborn, or as his sturdy but sensitive godson was wont to do after but a single glass of wine. There had indeed been good wine at the farewell banquet earlier that evening, and despite Sindbad's making free with it (for he did not permit himself wine at sea), he had not failed to notice that his daughter seemed even more distressed at her "brother's" imminent departure than at her father's, and that Umar's eagerness for his first major voyage was tempered by the prospect of a long separation from his "sister." As the young pair were not in fact blood relatives, and as Sindbad loved them equally, the happy thought had occurred to him (he said) of perhaps marrying Yasmīn to Umar al-Yom when the time came — maybe when Voyage Five was safely behind them.

Furthermore, though it had been his practice ever since Voyage One, in order to compose his spirit for the rigors ahead, to sleep alone in his Tub of Truth just before setting out for Basra with his Tub of Last Resort, that practice did not forbid a little good-night sport — provided in this instance by his then favorite, Jaydā. Already by that time she was no longer the Cairene beauty he had fetched home from Voyage Three: bearing and nursing the whelp Salīm, in particular, had taxed her charms. But in the dark (if Sindbad might speak so freely), she had still an uncanny knack for impersonating other women, her younger self included. In this specialty, as Still-Stranded had lately heard him attest, the dancer Kuzia Fakān was no slouch, either, but her bedtime improvisations could not fetch tea for Jaydā's in her prime. On the evening in question, as a bon-voyage gift, the Cairene had done to a T Sindbad's late beloved wife, of whom Somebody had heard in the tale of Voyage Four. Sindbad could have sworn she was Marjānah's ghost, come back full-fleshed as his virgin bride! Even the tricky business of a maidenhead Jaydā had managed with more than usual cunning, along with Marjānah's winsome combination of shy modesty and eagerness to please. . . .

All this was by way of accounting for his uncharacteristically solid slumber on the night in question, for if "Marjānah" was as spry and fresh as on their wedding night, her bridegroom was not the lusty young Sindbad who had survived Voyage Three but rather a weary, wine-drowsed old shark not many years younger than the one now speaking. His every appetite presently sated, "the next thing he knew," he was being gently shaken awake (from dreams of beautiful Marjānah and her look-alike daughter) by the whelp Salīm and eager young Umar, the latter declaring that it was time to set out for Basra and their great adventure.

"How I loved that boy!" Sindbad here exclaimed. "The image of myself at his age, ready to seize life by the turban and ride adversity like a Bedou horseman! What hopes I had in him for my elder age, what trust! A trust that (unknown to me, despite certain ugly insinuations from Salīm, which I dismissed) he had already betrayed!"

En route down to the port, however (he presently continued), the lad was not his usual sunny self; even at the time it seemed to Sindbad that something heavy was on the young man's mind, which he wished to speak of but found it difficult to broach. For his part, Sindbad, too, had had a disagreeable announcement to make. Perhaps his stranded brother had heard that Voyage Five, like its predecessor, had not been sailed in the redoubtable *Zahir*: following certain warnings and premonitions that experience had taught him to trust, Sindbad had leased a larger though less able vessel for the trading voyage proper and had commissioned *Zahir* as an armed escort at least through the gulfs of Persia and Oman, which were every year more infested with pirates. Such was Umar's love for him (so Sindbad had believed) that not until they reached their first port of call — Persian Siraf, halfway down the Gulf, where *Zahir* waited to join them — did he have the heart to tell the boy that he was transferring him there to the escort vessel for the remainder of the voyage, and even then he shied from telling him the reason, for he knew that to Umar al-Yom the prospect of shipwreck (which Sindbad foresaw) would be but one more splendid adventure, the more so at his foster father's side.

And so indeed Umar protested, without Sindbad's even having mentioned shipwreck specifically, when the time came to set out from Siraf. As much as he loved Mustafā mu-Allim and *Zahir*, Umar declared, he loved Sindbad many times more, and would as leave stay behind in Siraf, or even make his way home to Baghdad, as not sail at his mentor's side, in whatever vessel and through whatever tribulations, learning from him the subtle art of survival with profit.

At that mention of home and Baghdad, Sindbad had nodded to himself, knowing well what the real attraction of that place was for Umar. It occurred to him then (as he set aside once more Salīm's troublemaking innuendos) that perhaps what had been bothering the young man lately was the prospect both of having to explain that he had fallen in love with his adopted "sister" and of asking his "father" for permission to marry her. As Sindbad had not yet consulted Yasmīn's feelings on the matter, he said nothing of it to Umar (and would in any case have withheld his consent till the voyage's end, even if the young man had raised the subject); he overrode his objections, ordered him aboard *Zahir*, and refused to hear more on the matter.

In every subsequent outbound port of call, when the two ships moored together, Umar stubbornly repeated his request; Sindbad stubbornly denied it without explanation (lest rumors reach his fellow merchants of their expected fate); and the young man grew ever more downcast and sullen. At one point Mustafā mu-Allim even came over from *Zahir* to intercede on Umar's behalf and was reminded by his employer that the navigator's responsibility was position-fixing, not crew assignment. One final time Umar made his plea — at the port of Kulam Mali, at the southern tip of Al Hind, just prior to the little convoy's long leg across the Bahr Harkand to the Bahr Salahat — and was again refused.

Now it happened that a few of the merchant traders, whether they were unused to the rigors of voyaging or simply unlucky, had fallen ill on the outbound passage and either had died at sea or were put ashore at Kulam Mali to recover; their places were filled by other Muslim traders in that port who were eager to try their fortunes farther east. Among this number was a cowled and muffled young man who no sooner came aboard than he retired below, claiming seasickness even before the ship made sail, and remained abed there, the butt of his fellows' jokes, until the merchantman and its escort were well out to sea. Just about then the two ships were separated by the first serious storm of the voyage, and though *Zahir* was nowhere to be seen when that storm passed, and Sindbad trembled for its welfare and Umar's, he comforted himself that there was no sign of floating wreckage, either, and that his less seaworthy merchant vessel had survived. All the same, when several days went by with no sight of *Zahir* on any horizon, he withdrew to his quarters and prayed aloud to Allah to preserve from harm his dear son Umar al-Yom.

Thereupon the seasick young merchant rose up from his berth nearby, disclosed himself to be that same Umar, begged Sindbad to pardon his ruse on the grounds that its motive was loving, and in one burst confessed his love for Yasmīn and begged for Sindbad's permission to marry her. Overjoyed to see him safe, the older man embraced the younger at once before scolding him roundly for his disobedience and impertinence. He explained to Umar then why he had assigned him to *Zahir* and why the boy must return to that vessel as soon as the ships refound each other. Meanwhile, so as not to arouse the other merchants' misgivings, he must remain incognito but position himself as near Sindbad as possible at all times, repeating like prayers the sixteen lessons of voyages One through Four and hoping to rendezvous with *Zahir* before the inevitable disaster overtook them. As for that other matter, to teach the lad yet another lesson, Sindbad steadfastly refused to discuss it until and unless they safely regained Baghdad.

As he had anticipated, the young man was undaunted by the prospect of nautical catastrophe. But chagrined though he obviously was not to have his marriage proposal ratified on the spot, he agreed to abide by Sindbad's stipulations. There followed the several celebrated episodes of Voyage Five proper, which our narrator said he would pass over here, inasmuch as he would be rehearsing them tonight. He did assert, however, that when the party made landfall at the usual uninhabited Island One of every voyage, and came upon the usual windowless dome that was in fact a roc's egg, it was Umar al-Yom, not the naive merchants, who rashly smashed it and slaughtered the near-hatchling inside for the ship's meat locker. Given that none besides his mentor knew better than Umar the peril of this folly, Sindbad could only conclude that in his eagerness the boy had broken the egg deliberately to precipitate the omelet of adventure. Sindbad himself fled at once back to the ship and his tub, entreating Umar (within the constraints of the latter's incognito) to do likewise, but the young man smilingly declined and stayed behind with the other merchants to butcher the giant chick.

For the first time then it occurred to Sindbad, he declared, to wonder about his protégé's motives — the more so when, back aboard at last with his terrified companions as the chick's vengeful parents circled overhead with huge boulders in their talons, Umar still refused the Tub of Last Resort and stood by a spare plank instead, at the opposite end of the deck. As Allah would have it, the ensuing bombardment sank not only the fleeing ship but, for the first time, the faithful tub as well. Sindbad himself, needless to say, survived; likewise Umar, lashed to his plank but sorely roc-rocked. All the others drowned.

The young man's subsequent behavior, Sindbad even yet endeavored to persuade himself, must be attributable to his injuries. When the veteran survivor, dazed by the furious bombardment and the loss of his trusty tub, swam gratefully over to that plank to preserve his own life and assist his injured ward, Umar actually struck and kicked him away, cursed his very beard and turban, and swore by Allah he would have Yasmīn to wife — over her father's dead body, if need be!

And so he might have, Sindbad said, had those injuries not carried the day. Himself weakening fast from immersion and shock, Sindbad clung as best he could to one end of the plank, enduring both physical and verbal abuse from that least expected of sources until at last, to save his own life, he was obliged to promise Yasmīn to Umar in exchange for a more secure survival perch. Almost grudgingly the young man agreed, and thus they drifted for three uneasy days, Umar growing ever weaker while Sindbad, an old hand at this mode of seafaring, regained his strength. When at length the boy had clearly passed the point of posing any threat to him, Sindbad declared, in effect, "Ungrateful fellow! It was your late father, Allim al-Yom of blessed memory, who taught me that men should behave to men as men. In honor of him and that precept, I forgive you this shameful episode on the grounds of your injuries, and I pray that Allah will do likewise. It goes without saying, however, that the promise you extorted from me is null and void. I intend to do my utmost to save your life as well as my own, and never to mention this interlude again — but perish the thought of your ever having my Yasmīn!"

To this, with what proved to be his last breath, the young man laughed and replied that as to that, he had already had Sindbad's daughter masthead to keel and stem to stern on the eve of this same voyage, so basting and infusing her with the nectar of his zabb that even as he now spoke she was doubtless belly-full of him in Baghdad. So saying, he died, and though at his taunt the world turned nearly as black before Sindbad's eyes as before Umar's, the older man managed before fainting to cut loose his godson's lifeless body and bind himself to the plank with those same lashings. "The next thing he knew," he said, he was reviving on the paradisical beach of Voyage Five's Island Two, almost ready to believe that all that had transpired since the roc wreck, perhaps even since the storm, was an evil dream inspired by Salīm's malicious mutterings.

There followed the rest of Voyage Five, whereof more tonight: his encounter with the Old Man of the Sea, his eventual rescue by a landing party from *Zahir*, and the voyage's profitable completion in that vessel. Through it all, Sindbad said, he sustained himself with the presumption that Umar al-Yom's dreadful words, like his atrocious behavior, had been the effect of injuries that had left him not himself.

To *Zahir*'s captain and navigator he affirmed that his godson had jumped ship in Kulam Mali, not to make his way home to Baghdad, as they had supposed, but to be with his foster father, and that he had alas gone down with the merchant vessel that Sindbad had tried to keep him from: a story true enough of the young man whom they had all so loved. Thus Sindbad both pretended to mourn his loss and truly did mourn it, but he ended *Zahir*'s voyage some months short of its maximum profitability in order to get back to Baghdad and put his mind at ease regarding his daughter.

Once home, he straightway summoned both Jaydā and Yasmīn to the Tub of Truth. Whether because rumor had preceded him from Basra or because Jaydā had foreseen the news, there was no need for Sindbad to inform them of Umar's fate; the two women, already dressed in black, were red-eyed from mourning. Instead, he demanded directly of his daughter (no use doing so of the wily Cairene or her spawn) that she look him in the eye and say whether she was still virginal.

"Of course my darling is still virginal!" Jaydā replied indignantly. "Why should she not be?" But Yasmīn only stared at him, her whole expression (Sindbad said) declaring otherwise.

When he regained his voice, her father next asked her whether she had been forced.

"Why, certainly she was forced!" Jaydā cried at once. "Can anyone imagine that my darling would yield her flower willingly before her wedding night?"

Her eyes never faltering, Yasmīn admitted, "The thing you speak of happened with my consent. I did not resist."

Only when Sindbad next demanded "Where is the child?" did his daughter turn away, to weep on Jaydā's shoulder. There was no child, her guardian reproved him; the whole unfortunate indiscretion and its consequences were past and private history, of which no one beyond present company need ever know — just as the perpetrator himself might well not have known, so out of his head had he been with wine when he forced Yasmīn.

"No man will ever force me!" Yasmīn cried again, even as Sindbad groaned, "He knew, all right! He knew! And will your royal bridegroom not know as well, on your wedding night?"

He then informed them bitterly that en route home from the Sea of Pearls he had stopped at his birthplace, the port of Sohar, and had been so well received there by the young Omani prince Jabāl, who was preparing to make a state visit to Baghdad, that he had every hope of soon returning that hospitality. Until now, he had even dared hope as well that the handsome young bachelor prince (who was said to be scouting all Islam for a bride) might look favorably upon Yasmīn. But why should royalty give a second glance to shopworn merchandise?

Yasmīn only wept for her lost "brother"; Jaydā answered firmly, "Leave everything to me." But though for Sindbad's diversion she soon after found in the slave market the frisky young Bedou dancer Kuzia Fakān, her master was scarcely placated until the following year, when Prince Jabāl not only fell in love per program with Yasmīn but was so desirous of marrying her that he was willing to go against his vizier's advice and accept no further verification of his fianceé's maidenhood than Jaydā's oath. A dowry was arranged to the satisfaction of both parties; by quiet decree, the name Umar al-Yom was forbidden to be mentioned in the house. The good ship *Zahir,* with her faithful captain Abū Hosayn and navigator Mustafā, was recommissioned to ferry the bride, her attendants, and half her dowry down the Gulf to her wedding and her new home. So as not to jeopardize their safety, her father (applying now the twenty lessons of his five voyages) made ready to follow after, fingers crossed, in a second vessel with the remaining portion of the dowry — and then disaster, like a mighty roc rock in Qeshmi pirate form, removed to the realm of grim nostalgia all concern for such niceties as the success of Yasmīn's reconstructed innocence.

"Such is the honor that you have, in your fashion, kindly been safeguarding," Sindbad concluded bitterly to Somebody the Still-Stranded, "and that Ibn al-Hamrā has been negotiating for in complete though delicate bad faith: an honor compromised, to put it mildly, long before the Shark of Qeshm devoured it utterly."

"Be that as it may," our man replied, "it is Allah's truth — as I've told you before but you have chosen not to believe — that that shark never took one bite. Look here, Brother Sindbad: you think no more of Sayyid Ibo than I; you would need to despise your daughter to marry her to him, on whatever terms. But in truth you love her almost as much as I do."

"You!"

"And in fact, as you've all but acknowledged, the dowry game with Ibn al-Hamrā is no more than bait for Serendib Limited — a bait that lures fewer fish each night." Straight out, then, to astonished Sindbad's further astonishment and even, a little, his own, he proposed that he himself marry Yasmīn. Moreover, that he himself, "Sindbad the Still-Stranded" — in the company of his bride and with the advice and assistance of Mustafā mu-Allim — skipper Sindbad the Sailor's next and seventh voyage, to Serendib.

Incredulous, his host exclaimed again, "You!"

"Myself. Sell your house and goods, Brother, and fill your camel-bags as you please. Give me and Mustafā just enough to build and equip a small boat especially for carrying Haroun's embassy-gift to Serendib. Return your investors' money and keep their goodwill; I believe Yasmīn and I can explain things to the caliph's satisfaction. Or make off with their money, if that better pleases you, and disappear into the Sahrā al Hijārāh with Jaydā and Kuzia Fakān for company. . . ."

"You!" Sindbad repeated, frowning but (Somebody noted, and now makes written note of) no longer altogether disbelieving his ears. Indeed, this time he added, as if grudgingly, "And what dowry would *you* demand?"

Our man pointed unhesitatingly at Yasmīn's father's crotch. "The thing that those links came from, if it is still in working order."

Not merrily, Sindbad laughed. "Allah be praised, my zabb and eggs are still in working order! Sufficiently so, at least, that I'm not yet ready to make a gift of them to any son-in-law for my daughter's entertainment! Ibn himself has yet to demand *that* bride-price!"

But it was clear enough to still-stranded Somebody that his host understood what was being asked for. "Consider this, Brother. What you take to be an amulet may be in fact a key: the key to my returning to where I came from. I've yet to find the door, not to mention its lock, but with the key perhaps I can at least sail off in search of them. The amulet *you* need is dry desert air and the caliph's pardon for deceiving him. There is no other."

To which Sindbad shortly replied, "As regards my needs, it is not for my brother to describe and prescribe. But you're right in saying that there is no such amulet as the one you believe I believe in; there are only those bits of metal that Kuzia stole and you kindly returned.

I keep them about me as a souvenir of my recentest voyage: my sixth, on which I lost *Zahir* but quite avenged my daughter's honor."

And on that surprising note (Somebody noted at this writing's end), *Sindbad ended, and would say no more.*

4.

Having considered through that afternoon, among other troubling matters, the discrepant versions he had heard of Sindbad's fifth voyage and the events immediately preceding it, our narrator waited for Salīm to summon him as usual to the evening's feast; he had questions for that page. But it was Kuzia Fakān and comrades who, when the time came, came to fetch him. Sizzle-snap: Fatmah Awād spun in, salaamed, stood by. Close behind piped noodling Nuzhat and did likewise. The dancer herself then hauled herself unceremoniously into the room and plopped onto a cushion.

"Dinnertime," she announced, glumly massaging her legs. "Let's fill our bellies before the roof falls on our heads."

By which she meant (Somebody learned as the four of them made their musical way down through the courtyard to the banquet hall) that for everyone except Sayyid Ibn al-Hamrā things appeared to be moving from bad to worse. There were new defections, perhaps many, from the ranks of investors in Serendib Limited. Rumor now had it not only that Sindbad's projected seventh voyage was a swindling fraud but that his sixth had not been what he claimed it was, either, and perhaps the earlier ones as well. Rumor had it further that the caliph was about to seize the old man and confiscate his property; Haroun's vizier's messenger was now insisting on a full response to his master's message by dawn tomorrow.

"On the other hand," Somebody pointed out, "Kuzia Fakān is still here with us instead of in the lepers' brothel, and every new defection moves her higher up the table. The next thing we know, we'll see you dining in Brother Sindbad's lap."

Tambourine and pipes applauded, but Kuzia declared that she had done time enough today already in that seat of honor, with such mixed results that she had all but given up trying to understand where she stood, so to speak. Having been rescued in the forenoon by present company (for which Allah bless him!) and sent back to the harem for "further instruction" from Jaydā, she had been resummoned just an hour or so past to what by then was her Tub more of Artful Simulation than of Truth. There she had "done" the late Marjānah so thoroughly and cunningly as to half fool even herself into believing she was Sindbad's bride. Really, at the risk of boasting, she would have thought her master so roundly Marjānah'd that he'd have made her a gift of his eggs themselves if she had asked for them, not to mention any leathern accessories hanging thereabout. She had expected him to be so altogether wâhâtted that she could have made off with his very zabb, the way she had made off with certain oversatisfied customers' purses back in her apprentice days. Instead, alas, the old scoundrel had been so preoccupied — apparently with whatever had passed between himself and his "brother" in the interim between her tubbings — that far from being transported to Serendib, he was by turns amused and mildly annoyed by her virtuoso performance. He had both applauded the refinements of her impersonation and criticized its unavoidable shortcomings. Her figure, for example, he had complained, was all wrong: Marjānah, like her daughter, Yasmīn, had had small breasts, slim-boyish hips, and a tight little rump, not the moon-melon opulences above and below Kuzia's muscled Equator. Granted, he had been much roused for the couple of minutes that were all he could lately manage — but for that he credited his amulet at least as much as her skill, and he had so carefully guarded that treasure that she not only hadn't a second to snatch it but couldn't even *find* it, either by sight or by feel. She was persuaded now, Kuzia declared, that Sindbad had deliberately permitted her to steal those few links last night in order to see whether she would do so and to discover who wanted them and why.

"Somehow or other," she concluded as they approached the hall, "you've managed both to disarm him and to put him on his guard. Even Jaydā agrees that by rights he ought to be terrified of the caliph's anger and alarmed at the way his pigeons are flying the coop before their feathers are plucked. He ought to be packing me off to the lepers and gelding you for stealing Sayyid Ibo's fiancée. . . ." The piper and the tambourinist cut their eyes his way; steadfast Somebody did not react. "And he *is* distressed by all these things," Kuzia went on, "now and then, for moments at a time. But then he sighs or smiles to himself; instead of cutting off my hands, he waves me away and talks to that camel or to his own beard, telling them the same old stories he tells anyone who'll listen. And his audience has never been smaller than it looks to be tonight." She made an artful pirouette and bow. "That's what we came to tell you, Sayyid Bey el-Loor."

Somebody thanked her, earnestly, for having done her best on his behalf at such considerable risk. He declared his hope and hunch that whether or not he had advanced her position with Sindbad the Sailor, he had at least not further distanced it. "It may be," he acknowledged finally, with a sigh, "that my brother really doesn't have the thing I'm after, after all. Even if he does, it's so slender a straw that only a drowning man would grasp at it. So: let's eat and drink, as you suggested, before we all go under."

Entering the tapestried and incensed hall, they found Sindbad seated as always before his smaller tub, blue-turbaned still and in deep harangue with Ibn al-Hamrā (on Cushion Two, as before, at the host's left hand, counting off vehement points on his fingers before the old man's beard while Sindbad shook his head). On Cushion One once again sat the caliph's vizier's blank-faced messenger, looking about him with pursed lips and twiddling his cup. As usual, at the low board's foot sat Sindbad's daughter, djellabaed tonight in resplendent ultramarine to match her father's headgear. She was in earnest conference with her faithful standby on Cushion Three, Hajj Masūd, who looked to Somebody to be trying hard to swallow the unswallowable, but upon our man's entrance she turned and smiled, made as if to rise and greet him, then reseated herself with a bona fide blush and merely gestured instead toward Cushion Four, immediately on her left. But as he bowed to the company and sat, to everyone's startlement she openly clasped his hand.

Thus were filled the table's head, four corners, and foot. All six of the remaining cushions were empty: not only Alī al-Yamān, Jafar the merchant, and al-Fadl had absented themselves (as they had severally declared or, by last night's votes, implied their intention of doing), but, it appeared, Sīdī Numān as well, whose three votes had been two ayes for "Bey el-Loor" against one cautionary nay. Had he, too, Somebody wondered, had second thoughts concerning Serendib Limited? Here and there around the walls stood Jaydā, smug Salīm, and now the three entertainers, along with sundry serving-people, awaiting their instructions.

Yasmīn released Somebody's hand and observed brightly to her father, "Our friend Sayyid Sīdī appears to have been delayed." So fresh was her face, our man reflected, that one would have thought she had slept as profoundly through the night as young Umar al-Yom was reported to have done after a single cup of wine. Though the deep-sea blue of her robe disquieted him — Caribbean, Serendibian blue, a color to drown in — and could not much have pleased her hydrophobic father, either (whose own blue turban was safely out of its wearer's sight), Somebody believed he had never seen the woman more beautiful, and that was saying much.

Red Ibn, who had reddened further at sight of that unprecedented handclasp, gleefully seconded her: "In my opinion we ought not to fast until Sīdī's arrival, or we'll starve to death. But I suppose we must vote on that, as on other issues."

"Sovereign of my spittle," Yasmīn smoothly reminded him, "you have forgotten my father's ban last night on all such democracy. Shall we begin?" This last was asked of Sindbad, who left off contemplating her as raptly as our man had been doing and bade Kuzia Fakān, to her large surprise and joy, to take the fifth place, alongside Haroun's emissary. The sixth, across from her, he then assigned to Jaydā, as expressionless as ever. The two women exchanged a glance: Kuzia shrugged; Jaydā nodded. The seventh place, next to Hajj Masūd, went now to Fatmah Awād, who had to be coaxed by Yasmīn and Kuzia to join the entertained instead of entertaining. Likewise suddenly shy Nuzhat, who when Sindbad ordered her to Cushion Eight (on Somebody's left) would no more put down her pipe than Fatmah unclutch her tambourine.

"Be it understood," Sindbad said to them, "that when Sīdī Numān or any others arrive, your places are theirs. Meanwhile, be still and be silent."

There remained the middle place on each side and, except for anonymous kitchen folk, none but Salīm left standing. Sindbad winced; Jaydā fixed her eyes on him sternly; Ibn grinned his redmost. With a short gesture of his left hand Sindbad motioned the page to Place Ten, beside his now beaming mother, and bade Yasmīn pour the wine. But "Why not over there," Salīm boldly complained, pointing to Seat Nine, "where nobody is? Is Salīm less to you than nobody?"

Replied Sindbad, glowering, "That place is reserved for Kuziạ Fakān, who will give up her present seat to Sayyid Sīdī when he arrives. Is Salīm less to me than my light-footed and lighter-fingered Kuzia? We shall see." As if the evident debacle of Serendib Limited had perversely relieved him, with something like his earlier cheerful authority he then commanded certain servants who were standing by to bring in the final dinner guest from the courtyard. They bowed, stepped out, and duly returned with the camel Mustafā and feed-buckets full of straw and water, which they placed on the ninth cushion, between Nuzhat and Kuzia Fakān. "Now our party is complete," Sindbad declared, challenging with his smile Salīm and Ibn al-Hamrā especially. "Gentlemen and ladies: fill your bellies before my stranded brother and I fill your ears."

Mustafā had not waited for that invitation. His table-neighbors, Nuzhat and Kuzia Fakān, shifted their cushions toward Somebody and the messenger, respectively, to avoid the beast's dribble. The others more or less delicately fell to, attempting as well to make conversation. Hajj Masūd and Yasmīn, in particular, strove to speak normally of market prices and the weather. But quite apart from the camel's masticating presence, the dinner company was too uneasy an assortment for easy talk, and what its number bespoke too ominous for appetite. Before long, conversation trailed off, and eating, too, when presently Mustafā saw fit to fart. By the second course (a couscous) only Ibn al-Hamrā and the camel still trenchered. The others one by one gave over even toying with their food; they washed their fingers and either sipped their wine or sat with hands lapped.

"Well," Yasmīn said to the room. "No doubt it's better that men should behave to animals as men than to men as animals. But enough is enough." All eyes followed her then to the table's head, even indifferent Mustafā's. Did Somebody see her once-more-mesmerized father silently mouth the name Marjānah? Five raps she rapped for attention upon the Tub of Last Resort; one would have more than served for all except Sindbad the Sailor, who however by Rap Three was nodding in cadence with the count. Promptly upon Knock Five, without preamble, he launched his tale:

"Among the outbound cargo of my fifth voyage were sixteen hard-learned lessons — four from each of my previous times out — plus a certain fresh prophetic caution from my Tub of Truth. But among the new maxims I brought back, the first of tonight's tale will be this: Experience teaches us . . . to mistrust her lessons. See how well Sayyid Ibn al-Hamrā has learned it already: he now licks pigeon gravy from the fingers with which he used so redly to inscribe these morals! And this voyage's second lesson will be: The foretellings of true prophets necessarily come true, but in ways that not even they can foresee.

"For all the usual reasons plus some others, when I had dwelt enough years here in the City of Peace to put even the horrors of Voyage Four more or less behind me and to see my daughter cross the threshold from girlhood to young-womanhood, I once again defied both common sense and the teachings of experience and betook my-self down to Basra, provisioned with my sixteen lessons and this dark advice from soothsaying Jaydā, which can stand as my tale's third moral, or Lesson Nineteen of the lot: He who finds himself ridden by a hunger both ancient and unshakable can only feed that rider till he falls of himself to earth.

"What did it mean? I refer you to the lesson immediately before it.

"My trusty *Zahir* being laid up for repairs and unsuited anyhow to the voyage in prospect, I found me in Basra a vessel commodi-ous enough for both my trading stock and the freight of my expe-rience. For servants I took only the more expendable of my slaves; for companion-passengers — perpend this, Son-in-law! — I chose a handful of merchants willing both to take their chances with Sindbad the Survivor and to pay their freight up front, in cash. And for ship's officers (my usual and regular being with *Zahir*) I chose men disposed to heed the voice of my experience.

"So as not to waste time, then, once we were clear of the Gulf of Persia and in open sea, I instructed the captain to put in at the first uninhabited island we might happen upon, even if we needed neither water nor food, and this he did. Why so, my companions demanded to know, when except for fresh poultry our meat lockers were still amply stocked, and where in the absence of inhabitants there was no profit? 'Trust my experience,' I told them. 'How shall we do that,' they then taunted, 'when your experience tells you that this island is unin-habited, whereas even from our anchorage we can see an alabaster temple-dome in the woods just behind the beach?'

"I, too, of course, had not only espied that same dome but recognized it at once as just another giant roc's egg. This information I kept to myself, even when the captain apologized for having thought the island uninhabited and offered to go look for another. 'This one will do nicely,' I said. A party of taunters then lightered ashore to do business with the temple folk; I remained aboard and made ready my faithful tub. Finding neither worshipers nor for that matter doors or windows in their infidel temple, the disappointed merchants vented their spite on it with stones. When eventually the great shell cracked and a giant roc chick thrust forth its leg, they were at first frightened, then fascinated, then fulsome in their praise of my perspicacity. How canny my experience had made me, they marveled, not only to know the island uninhabited despite appearances to the contrary, but to direct them to the only larder item in short supply! They fell upon the hatchling, reduced him to poultry parts, and boated back to boast of their adventure and apologize for having doubted me.

"I accepted their apologies and — so as not to be washed up on that same island after the disaster I knew to be winging our way — bade the captain make sail at once and clear the harbor while those merchants set about their guileless barbecue. Just as I anticipated, before the first great drumstick was half roasted on the afterdeck, the sun disappeared behind double clouds, each of which was a vengeful roc parent bearing in its talons a rock larger than the holy Ka'ba, and bent on repaying in kind and with interest those who had cast the first stones.

"'Only two shots,' I worried to myself, remembering the many such missiles those one-eyed giants on Island One, Voyage Three, had required to sink us. 'May their aim be good.' And so it was, inasmuch as the giants had been hurling at us from the shore, at unaccustomed range and without depth perception, whereas all birds are practiced at hitting their targets from above. The first alone of those airborne mountains would have done for us had not the captain taken masterful evasive action. Even so, the splash all but swamped us, and it opened such a moment's hole in the ocean that I saw its deepest tenants gasp for watery breath and crabs scuttle for cover across the naked floor. Down then came the second, and by steadying with my long experience the helmsman's frightened hand, I contrived to keep our vessel in position to receive the full strike of it on that taffrail barbecue — not to mention the rudder, the tiller, the poopdeck itself, the helmsman, and indeed the whole aft half of the ship. She went down like the stone that sank her, and for all intents and purposes — which is to say, *my* intents and purposes — I was once again the sole survivor.

"A pity, to be sure, but — perpend this, Son-in-law! — Fate is Fate howsoever we diddle her. I had for example taken equal measures to stay the steersman and to preserve my life-tub, but though the former succeeded, the latter failed. That tub of mine, which I had come to trust, depend upon, and even love, was lost and gone from me (the one you see behind me is a replica: a Tub more of Verisimilitude than of Truth, and of Next Resort more than Last), and I mourned it as one might mourn . . . a lost child. In its place on Allah's ocean was but a single plank, to which was lashed a dead survivor, so to speak, never mind his name: a fellow whose luck had proved unequal to his foresight. I welcomed his companionship, inasmuch as experience had taught me that the fare for my upcoming passage to Island Two must be paid to the fish in toes and fingers. Better his than mine, which were already in less than full supply.

"Thus, after the usual hard solo interisland crossing, I reached the usual paradise and thanked Allah by giving my sharp-finned escorts a handsome tip: the remaining remains of my late plankmate. I even presumed to imagine that Jaydā's prophecy was safely thus fulfilled, for that plank had indeed been beset by an appetite as ancient and unshakable as any: the hunger of God's creatures for one another, which hunger I had escaped by gorging them rather than myself. Starving, I now nibbled cautiously at the golden fruits everywhere about me, among silver streams and jewel-like birds and flowers, taking care not to eat enough to make myself palatable. I lit no watchfires, lest the island be a sleeping whale; I looked out for monocular ogres, enormous serpents, wrathful rocs, gibbering apes, speechless cannibals, and other such of Paradise's familiar hazards. Had I found evidence of any, I would have taken routine precautions and settled down to much-needed sleep, but finding none (nor any diamonds, either), I was much perplexed and anxiously on my guard through that whole first night on Island Two, Voyage Five.

"Only the next morning, when I ventured inland to a crystal pool at the base of a waterfall and saw sitting therebeside a humanlike creature robed in stitched fig leaves, did I relax and tell myself that here at last was the monstrosity I needed to get on with my story: Nemesis

Overcome, King's Favor Bestowed, then Rescue, New Fortune, and Home. To my disappointment, however, a closer look revealed my monster-designate to be just another castaway like myself, only older — *so* like myself, indeed, that when he turned his sea-seasoned face my way it was as if I looked into time's mirror and saw either my long-dead father or myself many voyages hence, wrapped head to toe in Experience's leafy lessons and grown so wise willy-nilly as to be rendered mute.

"'Venerable father!' I saluted him, speaking figuratively. 'What misfortune has stranded you here with me?' In truth, I had better asked the opposite, for the misfortune turned out to be not the father's but the son's. The ancient beckoned me nearer and in the soundless tongue of hand-signs begged me to carry him across that mirror-pool to feed upon certain fruits hanging near the falls. They had caught my hungry sense as well: just ripened, sweet, tender, of a sort at once familiar to my eye yet foreign to my tongue, which craved them all the more for their being out of ready reach and for the flowers whose perfume advertised their savor. 'Aha,' I said, respectfully teasing him. 'Our limbs fail sooner than our lusts, and young legs are obliged to carry old desires.' Although my experience in voyages Three and Four cautioned against strangers who hungered speechless, in this oldster's plight I could not but see myself some shipwrecks hence, and so it was by way of being my future that like a dutiful son I shouldered toward its heart's desire. In that clear pool I saw me carrying myself ever deeper, step by step, until the human Sindbad who speaks words like these and behaves to man as man was all but submerged, and the blind old craving on his back — ageless, tireless, wordless but alas not toothless — had its way with that young vine.

"You all have heard what followed — how when presently I unpooled myself and bade the old chap alight so that I could proceed uncumbered to my own, more temperate nourishing, he gripped my head near to cracking between his thighs and gobbled on; how when then in angry fright I tried to cast him off me, he choked me senseless with one hand while still gorging with the other. I recovered to find the sweet vine stripped of fruit and flower and leaf alike, my rider still aboard and spurring me for more. All day he drove me like a beast of burden through Paradise's orchards, kicking my gut while stuffing his. At nightfall he rode me insensible to earth, nor could I shake free of him even when he seemed to sleep, for his fig-leaf frailty masked a stallion's strength. Worse than a slave, worse than a donkey, I was but his walking prop and privy, on which he voided the unspeakable wastes of his appetite. So debased did I become after weeks of this that between furtive scroungings to keep myself alive I prayed for the Severer of Societies to take me out from under my foul rider — and only then, in the formulation of that prayer, did I recognize the terms of Jaydā's prophecy.

"But how unhorse by overgorging this ape of appetite, who so crammed his maw through every waking hour that I soon became a walking dunghill? A staggering one, I should say, for the burden of his gluttony at length so weakened me that I could scarcely stand, and down the road I saw the day when exhaustion must end my story. Meanwhile (so cling we limpetlike to life even as we pray to die), as my rider happened one afternoon to be ravishing a field of wild grape and gourd, it occurred to me to postpone death for one paragraph with wine. While the old one on my back was at his insensate gobbling and voiding, I surreptitiously juiced a quantity of those grapes into one of those gourds, stoppered it with my next-to-last clean scrap of turban, and left it to ferment in the sun. Sure enough, when some days later I staggered with him that way again — on all fours now, my last legs long gone, like the lower animal I had become — Allah had worked His natural magic upon that juice, which then worked its own on me. When I had drunk enough, my weightsome rider grew as light as my head; I not only stood once more erect like the man I had rebecome, but laughed aloud at what beshat me, and even danced under my afflictions like the younger man I had once been. I shouted God's praises till the mountaintops replied, and when my ancient demon pounded my skull for his portion, I passed up the gourd and cried, '*Yallah,* foul fartsome father! Drink till your wicked old thirst is drowned, and then piss me such a river as will raft me home!'

"Of this, to be sure, he comprehended not a syllable, but he needed no instruction to guzzle God's support for the insupportable — after which he flung the empty gourd half a parasang across the glade, let go a shriek of joy and both his sphincters, and slipped senseless from my stinking shoulders like a shriven sin. All but levitating with relief, I straddled *him* now and, still laughing like the drunken sailor I just then was, relieved myself further till I seemed to float above him in an antic dream. With the first rock that came to hand — smaller than the ones that had undone our ship but larger than those that had undone the egg of its undoing — I scrambled his skull as my wine had done his brains. 'No mercy on your filthy soul!' I cried, my own soul even lighter now than my body. Then, as we happened to have ended our connection where it began, at that limpid pool, after weeping at what it showed me of myself I bathed clean in it till its waters were fouled past all reflection.

"As fatherless and free again as Adam, with a final scrap of sea-blue turban as my fig leaf I ran to Mother Ocean's edge and there frightened speechless a party of fellow sailors come ashore from their anchored craft for fresh fruit and water. When presently we both regained our Arabic, they said they had mistaken me for the much-dreaded Old Man of the Sea, from the legendary grip of whose loins no mariner, once seized, had ever freed himself. And I told them, in more detail than they could doubt, how the very man whom they had taken for that fell gripper had sprung that grip and unstrung those treacherous loins forever.

"What matter who those seamen were, where bound and why and in what vessel? It was enough that they were fellow men: young men of the sea, to whom I clung fast till Paradise dropped safely astern. Never mind that in the rest of Voyage Five I learned to turn pebbles into coconuts and coconuts into pearls, and once again came back to Baghdad richer than ever — and with the prospect, moreover, of a princely bridegroom for my pearl of a daughter. Never mind either that just as Allah's right hand can turn sour grapes into sweet wine and paupers into princes, His left as lightly unturns them: the turn of Voyage Five, and of this tale and its teller, was turned unreturnably in that paradisiacal moment of my back's unmonkeying, when I laughed heavenward through the shit, pissed on my pisser, and came back clean and mother-naked to the sea's salt bosom.

"*Clean*, I say — and in truth, comrades, I so laved myself back there in Eden's pool, diving under again and again and scrubbing till my head was clear equally of wine and dung — that I felt washed clean of Experience itself and all its tricky lessons. But if that bath soaked nineteen such away, it also anointed me with traces of a twentieth, which I here pass on but will neither complete nor gloss: He who, to cleanse himself, fouls the mirror that has showed him foul . . .

"Yasmīn."

But Sindbad's daughter, as a rule the very spirit of replenishment, did not promptly this time rise on her father's cue to refloat the company's suspended doubt. Indeed, she appeared to still-stranded Somebody to be on the verge of falling over in her place. Upon Sindbad's meeting the Old Man of the Sea she had closed her eyes, and had not reopened them while that hard rider bestrode his mount. At his fall and death she began to sway slowly on her cushion, as if in prayer; at the mention of the pool befouled by cleansing she opened her eyes wide; and the coupled syllables of her name would have felled her had not Hajj Masūd on one side and Somebody on the other steadied her between them. But refill the cups drained by that narrative she could not. Again her father spoke her name, more in piteous declaration than in command: "Yasmīn." On a signal from Jaydā, Kuzia Fakān went around to pour from the older woman's jug. At the table's foot they bent together to whisper to Sindbad's daughter; she shook her head, but permitted her cup to be refilled with Allah's Helper and then drank it off.

Complained then Ibn al-Hamrā across the table to Haroun's vizier's messenger, "You may report to your master that our host's travel stories have turned into parables that honest businessfolk can make neither heads nor tails of, and their morals into riddles instead of lessons." Then down the table, laughing, he called, "Hold her, Hajj! That is as near to Serendib as you'll ever come, and nearer by a table's length than I. It's we who have been ridden down the path, night after night, by a certain pair of ancient mariners, and got our caftans fouled with their fairy tales. I say let's get ourselves out from under, as Sīdī Numān and the others have done, and go hammam ourselves clean of these naughty dreams!" Still grinning, however, he took Kuzia's pouring hand as she filled his cup, and saw to it that wine spilled down the front of his caftan. "Try this," he advised the moon-faced messenger with a wink. "It's the only piece of their code I've cracked, and the tub it leads to is one more of laundering sport than of laundered truth."

At these radical pronouncements even the page Salīm seemed startled, if also mischievously pleased. Nuzhat and Fatmah Awād dared not turn their heads from their laps, but they nonetheless cut their eyes alertly here and there. Jaydā and Kuzia Fakān stopped stock-still; Yasmīn hid her face in Hajj Masūd's shoulder. Sindbad the Sailor turned our-manward in sober silent question, as if to say, "There we have it, Brother: bluff called, gauntlet thrown, Allah's sky about to fall. What now?"

Only the camel Mustafā chewed on, indifferently.

Somebody's Fifth Voyage

"Truth," I said, echoing Ibn al-Hamrā. "Yes. That is what any shall hear who'll stay to hear me. Not that Sindbad the Sailor has spoken falsely of his fifth voyage, but by his own acknowledgment there are truths that must be approached as one approaches Serendib: by indirection."

My own fifth voyage, however, I went on, turned out to coincide with Ms. Yasmīn's first, of which I meant to give now a plain and literal account: how the ship *Zahir*, carrying bride to royal bridegroom, fell prey to certain pirates not through disastrous mischance, as though the island of Qeshm in the Hormuz Strait were some anti-Serendib, but rather through deliberate, accurate, and malevolent navigation into their waiting hands.

"Stop there, Brother," Sindbad commanded me. "This is a story that we will not hear."

"Indeed not," Hajj Masūd agreed at once, with none of his usual hem and haw. "In the name of Allah, tell some other!"

"*Any* other," Jaydā seconded, surprisingly: the first words I had heard her speak aloud in general company. Even Kuzia Fakān shook

her head in disapproval. But Ibn al-Hamrā clasped his hands in car-
mine satisfaction and declared, "I think we *shall* hear this one! It's the
first by this fellow that I've looked forward to!" And when I made a
small, ironic salaam of acknowledgment, he added, speaking to Sindbad, "Indeed, sir, I so anticipate this story that if we are denied it, I
don't see how I can in good faith continue my engagement to your
stainless daughter and my support of your seventh voyage — not even
for thirty percent of the proceeds."

Yasmīn raised her sorrowed face from Hajj Masūd's shoulder to cry,
"Thirty percent!"; then she reclosed her eyes and returned her brow
to its comforter. Mustafā made a noncommittal camel-sound.

I affirmed that for the sake of its bearing upon that enterprise —
but even more for its bearing upon Sindbad's daughter's reputation —
my tale ought to be heard. Together with its sequel, I said, it was the
story that I had come back to this house to tell.

"Came *back!*" Ibn clapped his hands on his knees, grinned grimly at
Salīm, and glared down-table. "Mark what he said, Hajj! I knew it!"

You know nothing, I said to him, yet. But while there is surely no
reason why the woman who will become my story's main character
should not be excused from hearing her indignities rehearsed, so resolved am I to tell this tale that if I am forbidden to tell it here and
now, I will find some way to tell it to Haroun al-Rashīd himself.

"You have found that way," suddenly declared the caliph's vizier's
messenger, and he beamed around the room. "You clever gents may
think me camel-dumb, and in fact I am neither scholar nor poet nor
astronomer. *This* fellow's stories, in particular" — he tipped his turban meward — "are all algebra and abracadabra to me. But like Bedouin horses, we royal messengers are bred to our business, and we
pass down from father to son our peculiar talent for messengering.
Does the paper need to understand what's written on it? It need only
take the ink without smear or smudge, and for faithful impression you
will look far to find my like in the City of Peace. Everything said in
my presence from the moment I arrived in this hospitable house to
the moment I leave it at dawn tomorrow will be repeated as faithfully
to Vizier Jafar al-Barmakī as if you gentlefolk had written it word-
for-word upon my skin, and then rerepeated to the caliph as may be
called for. Here, for example, is Sayyid Sindbad, just a moment ago:
Stop there Brother this is a story that we will not hear. And Sayyid

Whoeverheis: *Truth yes that is what any shall hear who'll stay to hear me.*
And Mistress Kuzia last night, as read off by Mistress Yasmīn: *Unaccustomed as I am to public speaking I shall not speak publicly but rather make my statement in my customary way,* et cetera — as I shall make mine to my master the vizier. Allah forfend, however," he concluded with a bow to Sindbad, "that the guest give orders to the host. If Sayyid forbids that this tale be told, I can report to the vizier only that Sayyid forbids this tale to be told."

"By God and so you shall," Sindbad exclaimed, "for I will ink that message on your skin in truth! *Sayyid forbids this tale to be told!*"

"And Sayyid's daughter," Yasmīn now declared, "respectfully but firmly entreats her father to change his mind." She retook my right hand in her left and in unwavering voice went on: "Not only did this man witness at first hand everything that happened to me from the hour we fell together into the pirates' trap until the hour I was ransomed and he was not; he was also instrumental in preserving what is called my honor, though he could do nothing to save my reputation. If he may not tell that story tonight, in the presence of this company and especially this unerring messenger, I will go myself to Jafar al-Barmakī and petition him to let us tell it together to the Prince of Believers."

Sindbad seized his own beard and set down his wine cup hard. "Here is the end of religion! Guest threatens host, and daughter father! You!" he cried to still-standing Jaydā and Kuzia Fakān. "Take your places and give orders to your master, as every slave should! Then let the camel drive his driver, and good night all!"

But despite his show of indignation and his no doubt real enough concern, the old man seemed to me not a little pleased as well — with his daughter, with the prospect of the tale (the gist of which I had outlined to his disbelieving ears that first forenoon in the Tub of Truth), and even with its prospective teller — as if things were proceeding after all per a certainly desperate and risky but just possibly successful strategy of his own. I was not surprised, then, when after further scowling and humphing at his empty cup he raised his eyes to me and commanded, as if grudgingly, "Tell."

Thank you.

The next thing I knew, I was sorry to have to say last night, *I knew nothing*. And of what happened between that next thing and the next thing I knew after it, I know little more.

"I knew it!" Ibn al-Hamrā complained happily.

When Simon William Behler was a boy in East Dorset, Maryland, in the American 1930s and '40s, he rocked himself to sleep long past the age for such childishness. The next thing I knew after I knew nothing, I was rocking myself awake, remembering my baby twin, my playmate and soul mate and first loss, and a certain boundary or launching game I used to play we played. Then I understood myself to be in a shipboard berth, full-grown, at sea, amid a muted babble of tongues and the belowdecks smell of oiled wood, ship's stores, and sweat. I stopped still, opened my eyes, and reflexively focused on my wristwatch, still marking patient time. I even reset its rotating bezel, just as reflexively, back up to twelve, at the same moment remembering that I had very nearly lost that watch and registering that my berth was not the snug forward vee of our stout little *Zahir*. . . .

Then I all but drowned in memory: Captain Tim Severin's *Sohar* and our cutter *Zahir* becalmed on the glass-green Indian Ocean below Sri Lanka; the sudden squall from nowhere while "J. Moore" was photographing us; my frantic and vain attempt to rescue her; my abandonment of that attempt and panicked effort to save myself instead. The accidental unclasping of my watchband and my unreasoning last effort not to lose *that*, too. The exhaustion. The going under.

With a groan I bolted up, went dizzy, was steadied by a brown-skinned, turbaned and wuzaraed crewman who said "Tamoun," *good* — one of the few dozen words of Arabic I understood. With him were others, all likewise browned and weathered and similarly costumed (as for that matter was I, more or less), mildly curious, and apparently cordial. They smiled, nodded, said things I couldn't make out to one another and to me. Shifting with the ship's motion, sunlight filtered through overhead grates and hatchways; water rustled at the planks. I had been rescued, then, after all, by *Sohar*'s crew, and was back aboard that sturdy replica, under way.

Urgently I asked the man steadying me, "Where's the lady with the camera? Where's *Zahir*?" I made the motion of shutter-clicking and repeated the name *Zahir*. Pleased, the fellow nodded and said something to one of his comrades, who then leisurely moved off and up a companionway ladder. "Captain Severin?" I tried next, and then, "Any English?" — for on my several visits belowdecks on *Sohar* I had always seen a few Anglo faces among the mix of Omanis, Malaccans, Baluchistanis, and others. Here I saw none. I was given some calm, unintelligible reply and was asked questions in return, which I couldn't make out.

A trembling seized me: fatigue, sinking grief, and mounting apprehension, together with the stifling heat and smell of the crew's quarters — even more cramped than I recalled *Sohar*'s far-from-commodious hold as being. By the time that other crewman returned — not with Captain Severin but rather with a white-bearded, somewhat portly, and wise-appearing Arab whose good-humored expression and gently teasing manner reminded me of my late uncle Josh — I was verging on nausea and panic. *Sohar,* I repeated, beginning to fear that this was after all not *Sohar. Zahir,* the camera lady, Captain Severin, Sindbad's voyages resailed. . . .

At these cues they variously nodded, shook their heads, looked questioningly at one another, and replied with questions and comments that were unintelligible to me. The "Uncle Josh" fellow, in particular, appeared to recognize my language problem and to sympathize with my distress; he spoke slowly and patiently to me, articulated his Arabic with care, repeated key phrases and embellished them with gestures. At the name *Zahir* he smiled, nodded, and patted the nearest ship-timber, as if to say "That's right." *Sindbad* fetched a nod from him, too, together with a gesture that seemed to include the vessel, its whole company, and himself, and then a finger pointed astern and the word *Basra. Sohar* got another nod of recognition and a finger-point forward. But *Severin* drew a blank, as did *Sri Lanka, Serendib* . . . and *Julia Moore.*

My Julia! I stood too quickly, swayed, steadied myself, then pushed through them to the companionway ladder and clambered up, followed already by merry admonitions. One glance around the deck told me that this was not Tim Severin's *Sohar* but a larger vessel of the same general sort: an Arab boom, her crew, officers, and passengers evidently all "native." In addition to the barefoot, bare-chested, turbaned and loinclothed sailors working on deck and below, I saw on the boom's high poop a dark and commanding figure, clean-caftaned like "Uncle Josh." With him, besides the helmsman, was a slender woman in a red djellaba, who despite her veil and hood appeared not only to be listening attentively to what the smiling "officer" was saying, but to be asking questions of him as well, pointing to this or that item of the ship's rig. It even seemed to me (as my heart surged) that she was insisting on trying the great tiller herself, to the helmsman's large though respectful amusement and the officer's mild but likewise respectful disapproval.

"Julia!"

The hatch I had emerged from was well forward, a forecastle companionway; "Uncle Josh" and the off-watch sailors were right behind me up the ladder, talking busily among themselves but politely standing by to see what entertaining thing I might do next. At my aftward cry and bolt, however, they and their comrades quickly restrained me. I was scolded by many voices at once in excited Arabic; "Uncle Josh" shook his head and waggled his finger sternly.

"Julia Moore!" I shouted again, for I could well imagine my friend's gritting her teeth and — once she had seen to it that I was in good hands — taking the veil if necessary to satisfy local proprieties and get done what it was quite like her to want to do: try steering the ship herself. The deck officer called forward something sharp; the young woman (not as tall as my Julia, I strickenly saw now, though awfully like her in that determination to get her hands on the tiller) glanced at me but then quickly took advantage of the officer's distraction to brush the steersman's hands away and manage the helm herself. As I was taken below I saw her nodding at the officer's expostulations or instructions, steadying the massive tiller with both hands and one shoulder while the regular helmsman stood by with folded arms and a wide grin. The cowl of her djellaba had fallen partway back; her hair was dark, not copper-red.

I was roundly rebuked by "Uncle Josh" and ordered unambiguously to remain in the fo'c's'le and commit no further such mad breaches of discipline. Very pointedly, though still patiently, the old fellow signed to me that my next impropriety would get me a flogging. In his harangue I heard often the names Sindbad, *Zahir,* Sohar . . . and Yasmīn.

Plainly then he demanded to know mine, and (not for the first time), he expressed curiosity about my wristwatch, as did the crewmen. They were fascinated by its sweep second hand, as if they had never seen such a marvel before, and for all my near-vertiginous distress I noticed that neither this obviously senior fellow nor the ordinary crewmen wore watches, whereas all but the poorest of *Sohar's* deckhands, though not given to measuring time by the minute, like the Europeans aboard, had sported Japanese quartz-crystal jobs with (I had reminded myself at the time) what were, after all, Arabic numerals. *Behler,* I told him: *Behler, Behler, Behler.* I firmly refused to open the clasp and remove the instrument for their closer inspection, as they urged me to do and even tried with gentle insistence to do for me, but I let them watch the red pointer go around until, overcome by new despair, I fell back groaning into the berth assigned me, shut my eyes tight, and — grasping my watch wrist as if my right hand were a rescuer's — rocked in black misery from side to side.

That misery's details are beside our point. I did not die of it, though it lives on with me. The red hand of my watch went around, and the two white ones as well, against despair's black face, until I "came to myself," as our language puts it. In time, with the help of my forbearing shipmates and that firmly solicitous elder officer, I took up the large work of piecing together my situation (while also doing ship's work with the crew), though the largest piece of it mercifully eluded me for some while and thus preserved my sanity. Our dealings with Muslim tradespeople in Malacca, Sabang, and Galle (How that *our* cuts through me still!), along with our preparatory homework for cruising through Arab waters and our visits aboard *Sohar,* had taught J. Moore's mate more than a few dozen words of Arabic after all, nautical Arabic especially; and desperate necessity is an able language coach. I learned that I had been fished unconscious . . . and alone . . . from the sea by order of Mustafā mu-Allim (the "Uncle Josh" character), who, though he was only the ship's navigator, happened to be the senior officer on deck when the lookout spotted me. With great difficulty, owing to the dizzying coincidence of names, I got it eventually straight that the rescuing vessel was indeed not Captain Severin's *Sohar,* of which the crew knew nothing, but a larger clone of it named, incredibly, *Zahir,* bound from Basra for — incredibly! — the Omani port city of Sohar, the shipowner's birthplace and the site of his daughter's upcoming wedding to one Prince Jabāl. This was the young lady I had glimpsed and rudely called to, the one at the mention of whose name the crewmen rolled their eyes, in admiration of her beauty and in amusement at her willfulness. She and her chaperone and entourage were billeted in the after cabins and were not supposed to show themselves on deck, but this Yasmīn was irrepressible; it would not surprise good Mustafā to see her climb the mainmast itself.

"She may climb mine," one sailor sighed, and he was chided by the navigator.

In our communication the gaps were unavoidably large and many. Such terms as *replica* and *commemorative reenactment* were leagues beyond my Arabic then. But I knew from Severin that descendants of the medieval Arab boom and other fiber-sewn vessels were still to be found here and there in Arab waters (though I had heard of none on this scale). Moreover, and alternatively, the elegance of *Zahir*'s trappings, the apparent absence of commercial cargo, the frequent occurrence of the name Sindbad, and the clearly celebratory aspect of the voyage in progress gave me to imagine that this might be, if not some all-Arab version of Severin's project, then some other sort of programmatic anachronism. My mentor Mustafā even used a kamal to measure latitude.

I found it in me therefore to hope against all odds that since it was not *Sohar*'s inflatable tender that had rescued me, perhaps it had managed instead to reach and rescue Julia Moore. Somehow Severin's ship and this one had missed seeing each other in the squall; in that fast outboard dinghy his crew might even have caught up with our runaway cutter and taken it in tow. But me they would by now have long since given up for lost; they would return grieving Julia to the port of Galle, with or without our boat, or arrange for her transfer to another vessel, so she could make her way home and go on with her life — though it would not surprise or displease me if that intrepid woman, after notifying what remained of my family and collecting herself, decided to go on with our voyage single-handed, as it were in my honor.

So ran my early reveries. Urgently, as best I could, I told Mustafā what might just possibly have happened and asked him to have *Zahir*'s radio operator try to raise *Sohar* or, failing that, get word to our families of my rescue and of Julia's undetermined status. By neither speech nor hand-sign nor drawing could I make this request understood, though not only Mustafā but the deckhands as well got the general drift of my plight: my woman lost overside in a squall, myself almost likewise in an unsuccessful rescue attempt, my ship either lost also or lost track of. They seemed able to sort out even the confusing coincidence of ship names and the remote possibility (remote since they had seen no sign of other vessels when they picked me up) that *Sohar* had retrieved the woman and sailed on. Women, they agreed unanimously, were much comfort ashore but bad luck on shipboard; they would all be relieved when this particular voyage was done and they could return to their usual, less decorous seafaring. Meanwhile, as several of them had lost shipmates, too, and all had experienced Allah's maritime fury, they sympathized.

"Let me speak to the captain," I next begged Mustafã, though he assured me that he had already relayed my story to that sayyid, Abū Hosayn. He also puzzled, as did I, over what appeared to be one vast discrepancy in my account, as he understood it: had I not said that this misfortune befell me in the great ocean south and east of Al Hind? But we were nowhere near that ocean, nowhere near that land, both of which Mustafã knew well from previous voyages. We were in no ocean at all, only the Bahr Faris, the Gulf of Persia, which he could navigate blindfolded. Impossible, I said, and I gave him *Sohar*'s approximate latitude and longitude at the time of the accident, just off the southeast coast of "Serendib." Those coordinates evidently meant nothing to him, but for all I knew, "local" Arab navigators in 1980 might be ignorant of or indifferent to Greenwich meridians and parallels, just as Mustafã seemed to get along handily with neither sextant nor chronometer nor — so far as I had so far seen — even a steering compass.

This positional mystery got me what my unintelligible radio plea had not: a brief interview with the captain and a look at what passed for the ship's navigational station. Abū Hosayn — that same dark, long-nosed fellow, about my age, whom I had seen deferring uncomfortably to the young woman on the afterdeck — I found aloof, indifferent, even impatient: as deaf to me in his way as my father had been in his, but without Joseph Behler's passive benevolence. Like Mustafã, he could not be made to understand what I meant by such terms as *radio* or *wireless*; unlike Mustafã, he could not be bothered with my plight. *Zahir* had paused in its important delivery mission in order to save my life, his whole manner said; I could best express my gratitude by working out my passage and disturbing no further the ship's officers and passengers. In Sohar I would be put ashore to fend for myself and look for someone who could understand my language. Mustafā cued me to salaam and press no further.

As to the "nav station": down an aft companionway, near what looked to be the captain's quarters, was a simple table above a chest in which Mustafā kept charts, dividers, rulers, kamals and sandglasses of various sizes, and other instruments whose use I couldn't guess. The charts were meticulously hand-drawn, gridded in a manner unfamiliar to me, and absent any compass roses marked in degrees. The place-names and annotations were in Arabic script, which I could not then read. Whether local trading vessels still preferred such charts to modern hydrography, or whether *Zahir*'s "commemorative reenactment" was simply being carried further than Tim Severin's, I could not get clear (*Sohar* had been equipped with radio, compass, sextant, chronometer, and up-to-date Admiralty charts). I saw immediately, however, that while the overall landmasses on the larger-scale charts were inaccurately shaped and imprecisely positioned — these were copies, I supposed, of medieval originals — the smaller-scale coastal charts were impressively detailed. I would presently learn that as a mu-allim, or master navigator, Mustafā knew them all by heart, as he knew the stars, and almost never consulted them except to show the ship's position to others, as he now showed it to me.

It made no sense. We were not in the Indian Ocean, not in the Bay of Bengal, not even in the Arabian Sea. According to Mustafā's dead-reckoning plot, we were in the lower portion of the Persian Gulf, paralleling the coast of Iran, reaching east-southeast and about to bear east and then north of east into the Strait of Hormuz! He showed me Basra, *Zahir*'s home port, and Sohar, our destination, where the toe of the Arabian peninsula is bathed by the Gulf of Oman. I showed him, on his largest-scale chart, the (misshapen) subcontinent of India, or "Al Hind"; Ceylon/Sri Lanka/"Serendib" was not drawn in, but I put my finger on where it should have been and on the approximate spot nearby where Julia Moore and S. W. Behler had gone separately overside: fifteen hundred miles away!

Genies, Mustafā amiably supposed; magic carpets. It was clear to me that he knew exactly where he was; he could name every feature of the featureless coast that now and then hove into sight off our port beam, and could show each to me on his charts. It was clear to him that I knew approximately where I had been (I was able now to show him what passed for Malaysia and Sumatra — "Kalah Bar" and "Al Zabag" on his chart — and our *Zahir*'s route through the Malaccan Strait and across to its rendezvous, though what exactly we had been doing there he couldn't comprehend). But how I had got from there to here neither of us could imagine.

"Trouble yourself no more with that," Mustafā recommended. "Strange fish swim in Allah's ocean, and strange things happen upon its surface. Of your life before we found you, who knows or cares now but God? You were born last week, full grown, in the Bahr Faris. You are alive and healthy. The sun rises and sets, the fixed stars are in their places, and you seem to know their names and how to read a chart. Perhaps you can assist me; my eyesight is not what it used to be."

Thus it came to pass that though no one could have been more lost than I (who did not yet know just how lost I was, or I would have gone screaming mad), I became *Zahir*'s assistant navigator. The young man who had formerly held that position had, I gathered, been lost at sea some while before I had been found; with my scanty Arabic, I could not yet make out whether the accident had happened on this voyage or some previous one, nor whether my predecessor had been Mustafā's son or one whom the old man had loved like a son. In either case, I was the beneficiary of that misfortune. The stars were indeed still in their places, like steadfast friends, and bore the same names for me as for Mustafā: Aldebaran, Betelgeuse, Mizar, Rigel and Regulus, Deneb, and the rest. I knew the fundamentals of azimuth-sighting with the kamal; once I had gotten some sense of Mustafā's units of measurement, with the aid of my watch I could make considerably more accurate time/speed/distance calculations than he could; and though his intuitive allowances for the effects of wind and current on the ship's course were incomparable, I was able to show him how to plot these in vector diagrams. In a matter of hours he entrusted me with taking bearings for triangulation of our distance offshore; within a few days — after I had demonstrated such tricks as "doubling the angle on the bow" with the sort-of-pelorus that he used in lieu of a hand-bearing compass — he left the navigation of the ship in my hands when he was off watch or had other duties to attend to.

Although I was still in a condition of sustained psychological shock, the useful work of reckoning our position, together with Mustafā's kindness and my special status as his assistant, was some balm to my distress. Moreover, the same language difficulty that left uncertain the circumstances of my predecessor's fate delayed my realizing what on some final level I cannot credit yet: where I was (and am), not in charted space but in recorded time. Our charts, my own eyes and bearings, and my mentor all agreed that we were approaching the Hormuz Strait; quite aside from how I had got there, I wondered where the oil rigs were, and the supertankers and other large shipping bound into and out of the Persian Gulf. From time to time I would see a lateen or settee sailing rig more or less like ours; where were the diesel freighters, the motorized trawlers, the naval patrol craft? As best I could then, I asked, but my best was not good enough to make my questions or Mustafā's responses understood.

On his tongue my name became the more or less Turkish/Tunisian and viceregal "Bey el-Loor"; the ship's company (excepting Captain Abū Hosayn, an altogether preoccupied fellow, who ignored me) seemed to find that name's vague distinction appropriate to my general foreignness. However, they were seafarers, not unaccustomed to dealing with outlanders; once my nautical competence had been demonstrated, they accorded me a standing somewhere between the officers and the deckhands. In the performance of my navigational duties I was given free run of the vessel except for the captain's cabin aft and the passengers' quarters, which occupied most of *Zahir's* midsection. Several times a day (and whenever I awoke off watch and found myself, impossibly, where I was) I would be seized with a panic desperation, and feel tempted almost to throw myself back into the sea, in hopes of reviving on the track I had somehow lost. Impossible, impossible — and I did not yet realize the worst of it. I would give my head a violent shake; I would hear myself involuntarily groan aloud. Then Mustafā's calm hand, or some other shipmate's, would steady me, supposing it was only my lost woman that I grieved for, and not my lost self as well.

To keep myself from dwelling upon those losses to the point of vertigo, I did my best to concentrate on reckoning our course and improving my Arabic. I tried to savor, rather than go dizzy at, the absence of anything "modern" except my wristwatch and the contents of my head. And I counted the days between our present position and our destination, where I hoped to be able at least to clarify my situation and get word of it to my daughter and to Julia Moore's.

That same counting and course plotting revealed something amiss in our progress and gave me incidentally a second, closer look at our chief passenger. By my reckoning, confirmed by Mustafā, we had cleared the little island of Forūr and were bearing just a touch north of east toward Ras Musandam, the very toenail of the Arabian boot, about a hundred miles ahead. There we would turn south-southeast for the run to Sohar, another hundred and fifty miles on. *Zahir*'s average speed in a fair breeze — which I measured in the literal knots of an improvised string-and-woodchip taffrail log, with the aid of my Seiko's sweep second hand — was in the neighborhood of four knots, meaning a daily run of between eighty and a hundred nautical miles when the wind was steady. We were no more than two days, then, from Ras Musandam, and another two, or three at most, from the port of Sohar and "civilization." But even allowing for periods of calm or light or adverse wind, we were not making nearly the distance we ought to be. On a night when we should have covered forty miles, we covered fifteen; a leg that should have fetched us from the islet of Tunb to within sight of Cape Musandam fetched us instead to the island of Hengām, some twenty miles to the northwest, just below the much larger island of Qeshm, which dominates the Hormuz Strait.

Upon noticing this latter oddity I went up on the afterdeck (Captain Hosayn being in conference below with Mustafā), took a few relative bearings by a method I had devised, which involved sighting across the rotatable bezel of my watch, checked with the helmsman — and found him steering almost 45 degrees to the north of our plotted course! Astonished, I pointed this out to him. Captain's orders, he told me: he had been steering that northeasterly course through his whole trick at the helm and was to maintain it until we raised the little island of Lārak, on Qeshm's far end.

Why so, I asked, when the Musandam cape lay southeast? Captain's orders.

As I made my puzzled way back toward the chart table to log our new position, I heard a woman's scolding voice amidships and another, pleasanter, saluting me: "Sayyid Survivor! Helper of Mustafā!" It was the young woman in the red djellaba, being hectored for her forwardness by an older woman in black. I salaamed, then approached at her request. Her duenna said something dismayed in Allah's direction, which sounded like my late aunt Rachel's "*Hwell!*" Both women were veiled, but now I saw close up the younger one's luminous green eyes and glowing dark-brown hair, and I scented as well the floral perfume appropriate to her name. Bereft though I was, the surviving male animal in me could not help registering that from the bridge of her nose upward, at least, Prince Somebody's bride-to-be was a striking beauty, and I found most winsome (and painfully reminiscent of my Julia's) the spiritedness that alarmed her chaperone and amused the crew.

She wanted, it turned out, two things. First, to express her sympathy for my having lost my ship and my wife (as the story went by the time it reached the women's quarters) and her gratification that Allah had at least seen fit to spare myself; her family were celebrated voyagers, she said, and she, too, had lost dear ones at sea. And second, to see at first hand the curious navigational device that she had several times observed me using, inasmuch as she was much interested in all things nautical. Hoping I had understood her correctly, I thanked her for her concern, apologized for my minimal and halting Arabic, wished God's blessing upon her upcoming marriage, and did my best to demonstrate how one could use an ordinary analog wristwatch to help estimate not only speed but distance run and relative bearings. I found her a quick study indeed, this Yasmīn, surprisingly familiar (for a sequestered Muslim woman) with navigational matters, though even more surprisingly *un*familiar with the watch's basic function: measuring time! In what dark, superconservative Islamic time warp did these people live? Their names were Arabic, not Persian; *Zahir's* home port was Iraqi Basra, not Abadan in the regressive Iran of the Ayatollah Khomeini. I supposed there must be enclaves of studied antimodernity throughout Islam; for that matter, the language barrier, though becoming daily more penetrable, might still be concealing from me some important circumstance of this nuptial voyage: a systematic imitation, perhaps, not only of medieval Arab seafaring but of the medieval Arab mind-set and worldview?

She had to try the thing herself. As I held my arm athwartships to align twelve o'clock on the dial with *Zahir's* bow, she rotated the bezel until its zero mark pointed at Hengām, just forward of our port beam now. The angle, I showed her, was twelve minutes on the watch face, or forty-eight minutes counted clockwise; at six degrees per minute, the island's relative bearing could be expressed either as 288 degrees or as 72 degrees off the port bow. She understood that with two such bearings on different landmarks, we could fix *Zahir*'s position on the chart; her brother (was it?) had once explained that procedure to her. It delighted her now to be shown that with a second bearing on the first landmark, taken after a carefully measured interval of time, we could determine the ship's speed as well.

To take that second bearing she pushed back her djellaba-hood and pressed her veiled cheek to the back of my hand. I felt her breath there; her fragrant auburn hair tumbled loose. The chaperone quietly wailed; a nearby deckhand muttered something wry; there was tittering from the companionway to the women's quarters, where now I saw other youthful veiled faces watching us. Yasmīn turned her remarkable eyes to one after another of them, silencing each in turn with frowning dignity, then smiled those eyes at me and went back to her close sighting.

"Twenty . . . *minutes* this way now," she reported of Hengām Island, "or forty that way, yes?"

Sharply behind me, from the quarterdeck, came Abū Hosayn's rebuking voice. Yasmīn, facing me to sight aft again across the watch dial, could see him as I could not. Unruffled, she called back without raising her head, "I am learning where you're taking us, Sayyid Captain!" Then to me: "Times six gives two hundred forty degrees, yes? Or one hundred twenty off the port bow. This gentleman will be my navigation teacher," she declared smoothly to Mustafā, who had hurried usward from Abū Hosayn. "He knows things that [*a name I could not catch: Omar?*] never told me of."

"If Sindbad's daughter will not be discreet," Mustafā reproved me some while later, "then you must be all the more so. The captain is not pleased."

"What is this 'Sindbad's daughter' business?" I asked him, in effect. "What's going on here? And why isn't the captain sailing the courses we lay out for him?"

The first of those questions I had asked before, but I had not been able to follow Mustafā's reply. In only the few intervening days, however, my constant language practice and closer bond with my mentor had improved our communication enough for me to make out now that the young woman's father and owner of our vessel was indeed a wealthy Baghdad merchant trader of that name. (Many a modern-day Greek, I reminded myself, is named Aristotle; why should not an Iraqi oil and shipping magnate assume the name of his famous seagoing forebear and carry out this elaborate charade on the occasion of his daughter's wedding? But that idea was not yet within my power to express for Mustafā's verification.) As I had seen, the woman was willful, even wayward. Mustafā disapproved of her behavior, not only on strict Muslim principle but also — so I learned when I gently teased him on that score — because her waywardness had contributed to the downfall of the young man whom she had spoken of as if he were her brother, and whom Mustafā now spoke of, his eyes moistening, as if he were a lost son. This was my unlucky predecessor; let his fate stand as a lesson to me. Whatever it was that had happened — Mustafā would speak no further of it — had been the end of the young man and, I gathered, had cast some shadow upon the upcoming marriage as well. In unacknowledged compensation, Yasmīn's dowry had been made so unusually large that two ships were required to carry it to the Sohari prince Jabāl: *Zahir* was the first of these, and the bride's father would soon follow in the second.

It was easy enough to imagine, in a general way, what had likely happened between the young people; to press Mustafā for details (had there been an accidental pregnancy, or was it sufficient in "Sindbad's" Muslim fundamentalist household for the couple to have enjoyed an illicit flirtation?) would have been tactless and ungrateful. The other of my questions, concerning *Zahir*'s position, distressed him less, though he was clearly unhappy about it. Our job as navigators, Mustafā reminded me (as if to remind himself), was to apprise the captain of the ship's position and recommend the course to be steered for the next way point toward our destination. If Abū Hosayn chose to steer some other course or to reach the destination via other way points or even to change our destination, that was not our concern, as navigators, so long as we were kept informed of such changes for position-fixing purposes.

"But I have *not* been kept informed," I complained to him, and I showed him on our chart how my dead-reckoning tracks (more carefully plotted than his because my time/speed/distance estimates were better) had had to be wildly corrected when visual fixes had shown me our actual position. Much impressed by the chart work, Mustafā nevertheless reminded me that I was only the assistant navigator. I put my hands on his shoulders. "My friend," I told him, "I don't know where I am or how I got here, but I know that I owe my life and my sanity to you. You have assisted me so much; how can I be your assistant, if you keep from me what I need to know?"

He pondered this, stroking his beard and reexamining my DR plots: their running fixes, lines of position, and neatly entered courses, times, and distances run. "What you do with that instrument on your arm is marvelous," he said. "I myself am too old now to learn it, but how I wish you could have taught it to Umar al-Yom!"

I registered my predecessor's name and returned the compliment: what Mustafā managed with the kamal, and by merely looking at the stars, wave patterns, and shorelines, without aid of sextant, compass, chronometer, or written calculations, was tantamount to magic. Had this misfortunate Umar been his son, or the captain's, or the shipowner's?

Mustafā shook his head and, there being no pressing navigation work for us just then, bade me come sit with him for some minutes far forward in *Zahir*'s bow, on the pretext of reviewing our charts. There he told me of the kindly old captain Allim al-Yom, from whom he himself had learned the art of navigation, and who happened to have rescued Sayyid Sindbad the Sailor from Peppercorn Island on that celebrated adventurer's fourth voyage. How that gentle old fellow, at his death, had left an orphan son, whom Mustafā had first taken into his care and then arranged a better situation for in the house of this same Sindbad, in whose service Mustafā, too, had subsequently plied his nautical skills. How he and Sindbad and Captain Abū Hosayn and everyone else — Yasmīn included, it would appear — had loved the young man, each in his or her way, until Umar's apparent loss in the wreck of Sindbad's chartered auxiliary cargo vessel in Voyage Five, which wreck Sindbad alone had once again survived. Finally, how the pity of that loss had been given a bitter turn by unsubstantiated rumors in the household of a falling-out between foster father and son just prior to or during that fatal voyage. Mustafā claimed to know for a fact that Umar had aspired to marry Yasmīn — whose brother he had been raised as but to whom he was in fact unrelated by blood or law, and who unquestionably had reciprocated his feelings — and that Sindbad had seemed at first to approve but then later opposed the match, evidently because his ambitions for his daughter were more elevated. But a further ugly rumor — also unsubstantiated, mind, and denied within the household — had it that Yasmīn had given herself to Umar just prior to Voyage Five, and that when that fact had come to light after the lad's reported death, she had not denied her duenna's claim that the young man had forced her. Hence Mustafā's coolness toward the young woman, which he granted might be unfair but which he could not help feeling, so had he loved Umar al-Yom. And there was no doubt that Prince Jabāl's vizier had been most unhappy at having to take the word of Yasmīn's duenna, of all people, on the bride's virginity, instead of corroborating it in the customary fashion, with suitable inspectors from the prince's own retinue. Moreover —

"Wait a minute!" I pleaded, in effect, and ignoring the whole romance of star-crossed lovers, I tried once again to express my bafflement at the way Mustafā spoke of this "Sindbad" and his serial voyages and shipwrecks as if we were in Scheherazade country. He had no idea what I meant. I pressed on in my stumbling Arabic, not for more details of Umar Whatshisname or beautiful Yasmīn and her father but — tapping my wristwatch — what is this called in Arabic? Not *hourglass,* surely! Have you truly never looked upon its like? How is it we've seen no large motor vessels in all this time? No airplanes? What year is this? Have you really never heard of the United States of America?

It was very difficult to put such questions without a bilingual dictionary. Mustafā seemed to think I was alluding to rocs and island-sized whales (about both of which he was skeptical, despite his master's tales), to Champa and Al Sin and similarly exotic places beyond even his far-ranging ken. Like the seasoned navigator he was, he steered our talk back to where it had last been mutually comprehensible. He, too, was uneasy about Captain Hosayn's behavior: he had sailed many times under that officer's curt but competent command and had been party to more than one bit of business that he himself deplored and wished the boy Umar had not witnessed. In all such cases, however, there had at least been no question of Sayyid Sindbad's approval, and never had there been cross-purposes between navigator and captain, or such discrepancy as existed now between courses plotted and courses sailed. It was precisely that that had led Mustafā this day to confront Abū Hosayn in his cabin, where the captain had informed him brusquely that rather than sailing directly to Sohar from Ras Musandam, as originally planned, *Zahir* would stand by off the northeast tip of Qeshm, between the islands of Lārak and Hormuz, and rendezvous there with an armed vessel dispatched by Prince Jabāl to escort his bride and her dowry safely down the Gulf of Oman to Sohar. When Mustafā had then pointed out that we would be lingering at our peril in the very neighborhood that we ought to be passing through as quickly as possible — the pirate-troubled Strait of Hormuz — and had wondered further just how and when this ill-advised change of plans had come down from their master or up from the prince, Abū Hosayn had instructed him to mind his own duties or risk being relieved of them.

"And mind them I shall," my mentor concluded, "as I hope you will, too. But let us keep a weather eye on things, as navigators should, for something here is not as it ought to be."

Sure enough, all the next night and day, as I wrestled in wretched vain with the questions of where I "really" was and how I had got there, we sailed back and forth along a north-south line between that pair of little islands while Abū Hosayn scanned the southern horizon for another vessel. The whole crew grew uneasy; even the bride-to-be (whom I regarded with mild new interest in the light of what I had heard, finding it hard to imagine her falsely defaming a lover to protect herself, so rich in character were those green eyes) demanded to know why we were marking time in these notorious waters, like chickens promenading between two fox-holes. The simile was hers and involved a play on the captain's name, to which Abū Hosayn did not take kindly. But when with respectful apologies he commanded her and her duenna to retire immediately to their quarters and remain there until after our rendezvous with the prince's escort vessel, she insisted that he tell her when and by what means her father had changed *Zahir*'s sailing orders without apprising her.

"Sail ho!" our lookout called just then. "Take her below, Mustafā," the captain ordered at once, and Mustafā nudged me to assist him. But even as we salaamed before Yasmīn's defiant eyes and Mustafā urged her sternly to heed advice given for her own safety, she narrowed those eyes to westward, in the direction of Qeshm, and declared to him, "That is not the ship that my fiancé sailed to Basra in, Mustafā. Prince Jabāl's *Sohar* had a single jib, cut low; that one has double headsails. And it is not approaching from the Gulf of Oman."

I saw the old fellow look astarboard, where she was looking, and not like what he saw there any more than did she. "In Allah's name, get yourself below," he urged her again, in a different tone. "Try to calm the others, and pray for our safe deliverance." This time she went, without further protest, herself urging her already wailing duenna to cease her racket and help her reassure the other women. The older woman's alarm had indeed spread quickly to the deckhands — all of whom now watched a gaily festooned vessel about the size of ours bear swiftly down upon us from the west — and also to the women's quarters, from where (though those therein could see nothing) came already the first notes of what would soon become a frantic chorus. But the captain, undismayed, ordered us *not* to bear off and run for safety but to luff up, take in sail, and make ready to greet Prince Jabāl's boarding party.

"This does not smell right," Mustafā confided to me, and, boldly for him, he went aft to confront Abū Hosayn. As our steersman headed up and our crew dropped sail, I saw the sailors murmur to one another and touch their knife handles, one of which thrust forth from the sash of every man's wuzara except mine. Mustafā, agitated, pointed out to our captain this and that detail of the approaching vessel, whose crew were already assembling in her bow and along the nearer rail — some of them, it appeared to me, waving swords! Abū Hosayn, though he seemed to me not altogether easy himself, remained deaf to the navigator's expostulations and finally ordered him off the afterdeck. Now the other vessel began making her turn to heave alongside. Like *Zahir*, she bore not a trace of the twentieth century about her: no radio or radar antennae, no outboard engine on her tender, not even a binnacle before the helmsman; no binoculars among the deck officers, no T-shirts, jeans, or fisherman's caps, only turbans, wuzaras . . . and now scimitars everywhere!

Returning to my side, Mustafā muttered, "If that is Prince Jabāl of Sohar, then I am the Commander of the Faithful." From his own belt he drew a curved, horn-handled dagger and pressed it into my hand. "I'm too old for them to bother with, Bey el-Loor," he told me. "You are not." He then urged me back toward the midships companionway leading to the women's quarters. "Do what you can for the green-eyed one. Umar loved her, to his cost, and I loved Umar."

By now, instead of breast lines being cordially passed from vessel to vessel, grapnels had been thrown from the approacher and made fast. Most of *Zahir's* crew, uncertain of whether to assist or resist the operation, stood by; a few discreetly withdrew to the opposite bulwark. Abū Hosayn and our first mate strode forward to greet the overtaker's chief deck officer — and no sooner reached the midships rail than they were seized by half a dozen bearded roughnecks and stripped of the weapons they had not drawn. The teller of this tale had had, as it happens, the extraordinary good fortune (given the catastrophic decades through which he'd lived) never to have seen with his own eyes a fellow human done mortal violence to. Now in an instant I was shocked and sickened to see *Zahir's* mate stuck through with a scimitar from belly to back and dumped overside, spurting and howling: the signal, it seemed, for the others to swarm aboard and hack away at any deckhands who dared stand fast.

After the first few, none did, but those two or three bloody minutes supplied me with a lifetime's worth of what good luck had theretofore spared me. Terrified myself, and nowise prepared to die defending anyone on that ship except myself and maybe Mustafā, I retreated with him as far as the midships companionway, the hatch of which I found shut fast and bolted from inside when I tried to open it in search of cover. There Mustafā's grip recalled me to my purpose, but I shall not say that I would have remained there in Yasmīn's defense — what was "Sindbad's daughter" to me, back then, when I was grieving so for Julia Moore? — had not the situation at that point taken a sudden turn.

"These are common pirates!" Mustafā exclaimed, to me and some crewmen nearby. "If we're all dead men, in Allah's name let's die like living ones!" To shame and inspirit us then, he snatched the nearest deckhand's dagger (the fellow relinquished it readily) and charged at an approaching, scimitar-wielding pirate. Frightened though I was, I found myself hurrying after him; others of our crew, as well, moved forward in a hesitant but desperate phalanx.

"Stop there, Mustafā!" Abū Hosayn called then, and having been released by the men who had murdered our first mate, he interposed himself between the old navigator and the pirate who waited to slaughter him — but who for some reason did not take that opportunity to butcher our captain instead. Indeed, all the invaders now kept their places, their blades at the ready, instead of swarming upon us, and permitted Abū Hosayn to announce that in the face of overwhelming superiority of arms, to prevent unnecessary loss of life he was surrendering *Zahir* to the attackers who had deceived him under guise of Jabāl's emissaries.

Behind him now, as we assimilated this announcement, stepped (with a limp) a lean, clean-caftaned fellow from the other vessel, obviously a chief officer, the lower half of whose face was covered by a wrap of scarving like a Bedou horseman's in a sandstorm. From between his fierce-appearing bodyguards he leaned forward to say something to Abū Hosayn, who then begged Allah's forgiveness and ours for his misjudgment and informed us that we were at the mercy of Captain Sahīm al-Layl of Qeshm, who knew of our mission and our cargo. That that cargo was now that captain's prize, together with our passengers, may Allah preserve them, certain of whom Sahīm intended to hold for ransom. That any of us who were interested in dying miserably for those passengers' sake would be given that privilege at once if we did not immediately drop our weapons and move to the foredeck; otherwise, except for the two or three sailors needed to replace recent casualties among the pirate crew, we and *Zahir* would be released without further harm to return to Basra with Captain al-Layl's ransom demands.

Dirks and daggers clattered to the deck — all except Mustafā's, with which he seemed ready to attack Abū Hosayn even as he stared, as if transfixed, at the scarf-faced officer behind. A pirate raised his scimitar. Having myself dropped my mentor's knife readily along with the others, I stayed the old navigator's hand. He turned his eyes dumbly to my grip on his forearm, then flung down his borrowed dagger and stalked away, mumbling to himself. The scarf-faced officer nodded. His guard put down the sword.

Thus we surrendered without real resistance to the pirates who had allegedly duped our captain, and even in retrospect this seems to me to have been a prudent move, though I suspected at once and would soon learn for certain that Abū Hosayn was party to the plot. As things stood, the mate and two of our seamen had been killed, presumably

415

to demonstrate the pirates' seriousness (but I suspect, too, that the mate, like Mustafā and me, had guessed at our captain's complicity); and what subsequently happened to most of the women was atrocious. But Sahīm al-Layl's *Shaitan* was faster than *Zahir* and would presently have overtaken us even if Abū Hosayn had in good faith fled at the first sight of her; the pirates outnumbered us, and though to my surprise they had no firearms, our knives were nonetheless no match for their cutlasses and scimitars. In short, what happened to *Zahir*'s women would have happened in any case once we had sailed into that trap, while our men would have quickly died had they resisted, instead of being spared along with Sindbad's ship for the purpose of negotiating his daughter's ransom.

Those women's fate, all except Yasmīn's, is quickly told and best told quickly. After the shroud-faced pirate captain, in conference with our shamefaced one, had impressed into his service the replacements he needed to fill out his crew, all of our deckhands and officers — Mustafā and Abū Hosayn included — were herded under guard into *Zahir*'s forecastle. The companionway to the women's quarters was then forced, as were, soon after, most of the women themselves, whom the pirates appropriated as their plunder along with the chests filled with Yasmīn's dowry. In both cases the loot was first hauled on deck and roughly inventoried: the rich chests of silks and jewels were tallied up, reclosed, and dispatched into *Shaitan*'s hold; the women —weeping, praying, clinging to one another for support — were stripped of their veils and sorted by Sahīm al-Layl into three categories. The half dozen serving-maids were given to the crew, or more exactly to a kind of bos'n or warrant officer in charge of the crew, who forbade any laying-on of hands until the distribution was completed. The half dozen bridesmaids, distinguishable by their richer costume as the daughters of well-to-do families, were rapidly scrutinized by the captain, who then gave one to each of his two lieutenants and ordered the four others confined under close guard for ransoming by their families — whose names he would determine and daughters' ransoms fix before releasing *Zahir* on its new errand.

There remained the prize and her chaperone — whom I had heard Mustafā refer to as Jaydā the Egyptian. Heretofore I had seen this black-robed personage do little more than wring her hands in operatic despair at her charge's forwardness, as if to make it clear that she had done all a duenna reasonably could and was not to be held further responsible. In the face of this genuine threat, however, there was nothing operatic about her response: her voice preceded her up the companionway, threatening Yasmīn's handlers in language as strong as any pirate's. After her curses came not the curser but the cursed: the first of those two lieutenants, whom the captain had assigned to bring forth Sindbad's daughter. His turban was in disarray, and he was bleeding about the face and onto his linen blouse, which had been ripped or slashed; in the hand that he gripped with both of his own as he climbed on deck and pulled her up after him, Yasmīn clutched yet the knife she had cut him with. She herself, it almost seemed — still kicking and biting at his arm through her disheveled white veil — pulled up after her the second officer, whose task it was to keep her other hand away from that knife while shielding himself from her kicks. *She fought like a wildcat,* the cliché goes, common to those novels called "bodice rippers." I have never seen a wildcat fight, but on the day when I see one go at her unlucky captors with hands, feet, teeth, and utter disregard for consequences to herself, I will say that that wildcat fought like Sindbad's daughter.

And close after that hapless second officer came the shrill-cursing Cairene, buffeting his head and shoulders not only with imprecations but with a hammered-copper teapot and — once the three were more or less on deck — kicking, too, at the groin he turned from Yasmīn's kicks. The pirate crew were much amused by this spectacle, which their captain quickly put an end to by assigning their bos'n and one or two others to help subdue the chaperone, disarm both her and Yasmīn, and bind the latter's wrists with a length of soft cord provided by the captain himself. Taking care to avoid her flailing feet, one of the lieutenants retrieved her knife from the deck and presented it to Sahīm al-Layl, who inspected its jeweled handle attentively. The other made now as if to strip away the captive's veil for his commander's benefit — and found the point of that knife pressed to his gullet. He backed off a step, smiled, salaamed.

"Go to my cabin," I heard the captain say then to Jaydā, using the plural imperative, and he gestured to his men to unhand both women. The chaperone shrugged them away and drew herself up straight but offered no further resistance; Yasmīn, however, once unrestrained, bolted. Sahīm al-Layl himself adroitly caught her by the shoulder of her robe and said something to her that I could not hear; Jaydā hurried over and spoke into the white cowl of her ward's djellaba, at the same time putting straight its dishevelment. The captain pointed with the jeweled knife to *Shaitan*'s aft companionway, toward which Sindbad's defeated daughter, her wrists bound fast, now let herself be led by her comforter and her limp-gaited captor, like an animal on a silken leash. A wail rose from the four bridesmaids held for ransoming, and another sort of cry from the pair assigned to other duty, as the two lieutenants herded all six across the ships' mated gunwales to their separate fates. With the half dozen serving-women no such niceties were observed. The instant their officers stepped from *Zahir* onto *Shaitan,* the pirate sailors fell upon their shrieking victims and upon one another as well, for order of possession. And the teller of this tale, who through fifty years of a sordid century had managed never to witness sexual violence, either, now beheld . . .

What I beheld, and what would be mere prurience to recount. Ask, rather, How came it to be that I was there to behold it, and those other matters just narrated, instead of locked in *Zahir*'s fo'c's'le with brooding Mustafā and my other shipmates? It was because Sahīm al-Layl had ordered Abū Hosayn to deliver over to him not only two able-bodied seamen but a hand with navigational skills as well, to replace one lost in a recent accident. But not the oldster who had come at him with a dagger; that one was clearly a troublemaker. "The tall one yonder, then," Abū Hosayn had offered, nodding meward with some satisfaction. "The outlander. May you make good use of him."

Thus did I pass from I knew not where (except on Mustafā's hand-drawn charts) to I knew not where, gratified to have been so far spared, more anxious about my own fate than about that of Sindbad's daughter and her retinue, sorrowful indeed at my separation from kindly Mustafā, my link to the strange world in which I found myself — and chagrined to the point of tears at this new diversion from my reaching Sohar and "civilization." For despite the mystery (still unresolved) of my losing consciousness off Sri Lanka and regaining it in the Persian Gulf, I had by no means yet accepted the greater — indeed, the unacceptable — mystery of my transportation in time. Though every passing day aboard *Zahir* and now aboard *Shaitan* brought new evidence to the contrary, like a shipwrecked sailor to a plank I clung to my belief (by now an ever more desperate hope) that

I was in some technological backwater, one of those third-world pockets where things are still done as they have been done for centuries.

Among those things, alas, is rape: not only the repeated sexual as-
sault before my eyes of Yasmīn's serving-women by the pirate crew,
but also the homosexual rape of the two young seamen pressed into
service from *Zahir*, as well as, one had to presume, other assaults in
progress belowdecks. This essential violation I was spared, at least for
the present, no doubt because though my body was lean and fit from
sailoring, my years made me fortunately less attractive than their other
victims to the pirates, men mostly in their twenties and thirties. Likewise spared, I learned presently, were the duenna Jaydā and — for a
different reason, and at least for a while — those four of Yasmīn's
bridesmaids.

When the deckhands had taken their initial pleasure, on orders
from the two lieutenants (who had clearly had theirs as well), the
abused women were sent below — all but one, that is, who chose to
leap into the sea rather than endure more of the same — and the violated men put to work with their violators preparing to separate the
ships and get under way. *Zahir*'s officers (which is to say, Abū Hosayn,
Mustafā, and a bos'n, the first mate having been murdered earlier)
were released to hear the terms of ransom, which they were to carry
back to Baghdad and the hostages' families: for the lives of the womenservants, such-and-such an amount, to be delivered by *Zahir*, without
armed escort, to this same place of rendezvous not later than such-
and-such a date. For the life if each of the six bridesmaids, a specified
higher amount, and for the life of Sindbad's daughter, a considerably
higher amount yet: the other half of her sumptuous dowry. For the
bridesmaids' unviolated "honor" in addition to their lives, exactly
double that earlier figure — and here the ransom terms and their proposer's good faith, so to speak, turned equivocal, for this second figure
was applied to all six of the bridesmaids, two of whom had presumably been forced already by the lieutenants who relayed these terms
from Sahīm al-Layl's cabin. In token of the kidnappers' earnestness, if
not of their trustworthiness, they counted out to Abū Hosayn one at
a time the six veils torn from those bridesmaids' faces, naming in turn
the family to which he must deliver each along with the ransom demands. I saw the lieutenants smirk as they added the fifth and sixth
veils to the first four.

And for Yasmīn's honor, inviolate? No one put the question, but at this juncture one of the lieutenants stepped over to *Shaitan*'s aft companionway, said something, was told something, and came back followed by black-clad Jaydā. "For Sindbad's daughter's honor preserved along with her life," the lieutenant announced, smiling that same unpleasant smile, "we demand the total value of her dowry over again; whether it comes from her distinguished father or from her royal fiancé is of no concern to Captain Sahīm al-Layl. If they offer only *half* again her total dowry, her life will be spared but she will be enjoyed by every officer on this ship, in order of descending rank. If the ransom is less than that, all the crew will take their turn as well before she is released." This said, he gestured to Jaydā, who withdrew Yasmīn's white veil from a fold of her caftan, presented it to Abū Hosayn, and, as he took it, raised her own veil and spat in his face.

The two ships were then separated, as were I and my benefactor Mustafā. I had no more chance to say a proper good-bye to him than I had to Julia Moore, much less to try one last time to explain to him where I had come from and how to get word of my fate to my family, from Basra or Baghdad. We looked at each other from rail to rail across the widening gap of water as the crews of both vessels made sail. I raised my hand in some sort of farewell salute; Mustafā nodded, deep in thought, it seemed to me, while clearly acknowledging that he, too, had valued our association. Then I saw him being summoned to *Zahir*'s afterdeck by Abū Hosayn, presumably to lay a course homeward, back up the Bahr Faris. Concerned as I was for my own welfare among the pirates, I was concerned for his as well, for he and I knew almost for certain what the rest of *Zahir*'s company (except, it now appeared from her behavior, the duenna Jaydā) did not: Abū Hosayn had betrayed his employer and prearranged his vessel's interception by the Qeshmi pirates. The old navigator might be indispensable in guiding *Zahir* home, but as the ship neared Basra, would the captain not be obliged to buy Mustafā's silence — not a likely prospect! — with a share of the ransom proceeds that he had doubtless been promised by Sahīm al-Layl, or else ensure that silence by other means?

From these therapeutic worries, which at least distracted me from my own situation, I was recalled by one of the young lieutenants, who as best as I could make out (his accent was different from Mustafā's) ordered me aft to confer with the captain. It occurred to me to pretend to understand even less of his language than I had learned — a stratagem remembered from some forgotten novel or movie — in hope that my captors might speak unguardedly in my presence. At the same time, I had to take care not to exasperate them. In as fellow-officerlike a tone as I could manage, I replied first in English, then in deliberately lame Arabic, that I knew more about the language of ocean navigation than about the local speech, and I asked him to repeat what he had said. He did, more loudly and with gestures, adding more or less to himself that it was to be expected of that fox Abū Hosayn that he would hand over his troublemakers and incompetents. He snatched my sleeve, as if to drag me aft; counting on the respect that I had learned Arab sailors accord to master navigators, I took the gamble of scolding him sharply in English, pulling my sleeve free with as senior a frown as I could muster, and striding ahead toward the captain's companionway instead of being led there.

The tactic seemed to work. But because it would soon enough become apparent that I was no Mustafā mu-Allim, after pausing at the companionway, permitting the lieutenant to announce "Sayyid Bey el-Loor the Navigator," and being summoned below, I took a different line with the captain himself.

His face still scarfed, Sahīm al-Layl sat at a table spread with charts, kamals, and such in his small but comfortably appointed cabin, into which light filtered from overhead gratings on the afterdeck. On a couch across from him Jaydā comforted Sindbad's daughter, who — though moist-eyed and unveiled now except by the cowl of her djellaba (with which Jaydā stanched her charge's tears and more or less covered the lower half of her face) — did not appear to me to have suffered any further indignity yet than being kidnapped and deprived of her veil. Despite her tears (which were not copious), Yasmīn's expression and manner remained more defiant than self-sorrowing. Her hands had been freed, and there was no evidence of a struggle in the cabin; indeed, her hair and clothing were in better order now than they had been after her tussle on *Zahir*'s deck. She brushed away Jaydā's ministrations, and when the captain courteously invited her to reveil herself in my presence, she pushed back her cowl instead and glared full-faced — and astonishingly beautiful — at the pair of us.

After a moment the captain said quietly, "As you will." In his curious voice — distorted either by the scarf or by some other impediment — he then suggested that Jaydā draw the curtains that had been rigged to screen their couch from the rest of the cabin (which included a matching couch on the opposite side) if the women wished to have some privacy while he and I discussed navigational matters. She made to do so, but Yasmīn stayed her, never moving those arresting green eyes from Sahīm al-Layl. Again the captain regarded her for some moments before turning to me.

Among the items on the chart table was that jewel-handled knife with which Yasmīn had resisted the two lieutenants. The captain turned it between his fingers and, through the interview that followed, as often studied it as me.

"You were the assistant of that old troublemaker who navigates *Zahir*."

In the best Arabic I could manage, I acknowledged that I was and went on to praise Mustafā mu-Allim as the gentlest, kindest, bravest benefactor one could wish for, as well as a master among navigators. The captain heard me out without comment, then in that same difficult voice asked, "How did you come to be the old devil's assistant? By your look and speech you are not of any Muslim nation, and you are of an age to have assistants of your own."

I nodded. "Mustafā had a young helper whom he prized like a son but lost to the sea. Another sea washed me to him from another realm, and he was merciful enough to rescue and teach me despite my age. Not all sons are young, Sayyid Captain."

This observation seemed not to displease him. He invited me to tell my story briefly, and as briefly as I could I did, hoping to win his sympathy for my limitations in the way of language and local navigational skills, perhaps to learn more yet of my own circumstances, and maybe even to appeal to him to assist in my repatriation. Pirate or no, face-scarfed or no, by his words and manner Sahīm al-Layl impressed me as being potentially more approachable than Abū Hosayn. For all her own unenviable situation, Yasmīn, too, attended my story, which she was hearing for the first time other than as ship's gossip aboard *Zahir*. She even supplied me from time to time with a word I lacked, shrewdly guessing it from context. Each time she did so, the captain regarded her over his scarf. So beautiful was she, and so selfless and courageous and in every way appealing were her efforts on behalf of one who could be of no imaginable use to her, that it occurred to me to worry that such forwardness might put her own best interests at risk. Her duenna seemed to share this apprehension; at every helpful intercession by Yasmīn she twitched her disapproval and glanced ever more fearfully at our captor. But Sindbad's daughter would not be deterred. At my recitation's end, when I tried briefly to indicate my desperate puzzlement at hearing such epithets as "Sindbad's daughter" and at seeing about me nothing in the way of aircraft, motor vessels, radios, or even steering compasses and wristwatches, while she could not supply Arabic names for those devices or even guess at what I meant by them, she urged her kidnapper to trust in my sincerity. Her father, she declared, had reported no less wondrous phenomena on his five famous voyages — giant birds, fish the size of islands — and just as he had brought home to Baghdad fist-sized gemstones to support his claims, so I had demonstrated for her that magical last-mentioned instrument, with which she had seen me make navigational calculations more accurate even than Mustafā's.

As grateful as I was for her support, I regretted her mentioning this item, which I had hidden in my wuzara upon the pirates' boarding *Zahir*, lest they steal it from me. There was nothing for it now but to produce the watch and explain its functions. Sahīm al-Layl set down the knife to examine it; he attended my — and Yasmīn's — account of its powers (clearly as novel to him as they had been to her and my former shipmates), tried the bracelet on his wrist (which was too thin to accommodate it, I was relieved to see), and then, as I'd feared, placed the watch on the table before him instead of returning it to me. Picking up the jeweled knife again, he told me that he, too, was a competent navigator, if not quite a mu-allim like my former master. He would be pleased to have *Shaitan*'s new assistant navigator demonstrate the device's workings in the weeks ahead, as we patrolled the area and waited for *Zahir*'s return. On the mystery of my translation to the Bahr Faris from wherever I had been before, he had no comment, except to say that most people would doubtless choose life in a strange place over death in a familiar one. The marvels I spoke of he neither questioned nor took much interest in: though younger than me by nearly twenty years, he had seen a few things in Allah's ocean and ashore as well that he himself could scarcely credit, much less expect others to believe. The fact was that neither he nor I nor Sindbad's daughter — nor even Sindbad's daughter's chaperone, he presumed to add, though she was reputed to have prophetic powers — a year ago would have imagined himself or herself in the cabin of a Qeshmi pirate ship, whether as captive, captor, or captain. But here we were and would be for some time, during which he had other work for me in addition to helping him with *Shaitan*'s navigation — work that my age and circumstances and demeanor inclined him to entrust to me, even though I was a stranger, rather than to his lieutenants.

This speech was by far the most extended I had heard from Sahīm al-Layl, who seemed in general to find speaking painful. The women, too, I guessed, had not heard that much from him thitherto, or else his words this time for some reason particularly disturbed them. Yasmīn's expression became concerned, puzzled, frowning; as I bowed acknowledgment of what I had little choice but to accept, I saw her touch Jaydā's forearm and exchange a troubled glance with her.

The captain stood and gimped over to them, holding the jeweled knife by its blade. Yasmīn, her eyes showing her alarm, shifted back a bit on the couch-cushion, closer to her protector. I considered retrieving my watch, but remembering Sahīm's sudden threat to the lieutenant who had offered to unveil Sindbad's daughter, and the quickness with which he had stopped her subsequent flight, I feared he might pin my hand to the table with that knife. Speaking still to me, but addressing his words sarcastically to Yasmīn, he asked, "How can anyone find it strange to hear men speak of Sindbad the Sailor, whose five voyages are famous throughout Islam and even beyond? Or of his daughter, the flower of Baghdad, as renowned for her intelligence and character as for her beauty?"

Yasmīn drew up her cowl and turned away, behind Jaydā's shoulder. I said nothing but felt and shared her apprehension — at the same time wondering, ever more despairingly, why they spoke of this Sindbad exactly as if he were the legendary original. And why — a much smaller matter — five voyages instead of the celebrated seven?

Speaking now directly to Yasmīn and holding the knife out by its point, the captain asked, "Where did you get this?"

Almost in a whisper, Sindbad's daughter answered, "A beloved friend gave it to me, years ago."

"For what purpose?"

"To defend my . . . *self* with," Yasmīn said, hesitating over the object, "should such self-defense become necessary."

"Allah forfend!" cried Jaydā.

The captain ignored her. "And did she show you how to use it, this friend?" he pressed Yasmīn. "I believe she must have, judging from your work on Mudyī al-Dīn. Answer me promptly."

Still speaking into Jaydā's shoulder, Yasmīn replied, "My friend was not a she. It was . . . my brother, whom I loved greatly, and who taught me many things not usually taught to girls."

"Your brother. Where is this greatly beloved brother now, when you most need his protection?"

Her duenna, embracing her, answered scoldingly (but with a peculiar emphasis), "The poor boy was lost at sea on Sayyid Sindbad's fifth voyage, while assisting Mustafā mu-Allim, and was *never heard from again*. Have pity on this child, in Allah's name!"

The captain here took his own, more formidable dagger from his belt and, to my considerable surprise, handed it to me. "Two strokes of this," he declared, "can relieve a man of his zabb and his tongue and leave him mute at both ends. It can also cut an old woman's lying throat if she does not move now to that other couch and sit there quietly under your guard."

"*Ai yi!*" Jaydā wailed, and she hugged Yasmīn more tightly. "Here is what I feared!"

A flick of Sahīm's left hand ordered me to my work. "Forgive me, lady," I said to the duenna. "I have no choice."

"Nor I nor she!" the woman cried. "Allah have mercy!" But she let go her embrace and shuffled cross-cabin, with myself following reluctantly. One glance I had of Yasmīn — wide-eyed, grim-mouthed, clutching her djellaba at her throat and at her pressed-together knees — and of the captain proffering the jeweled knife.

"Defend your *self* as your brother taught you," I heard him command her, "for I intend to find out now whether Prince Jabāl's bride is the virgin she claims to be."

"The end of religion!" Jaydā wailed, pressing her clasped hands to her veil and rocking back and forth. "The end of the world!"

I stood over her with Sahīm's dagger as instructed, neither daring to watch nor wishing to see the struggle that I now heard behind me — and that my prisoner alternately closed her eyes to and followed with sharp attention, shifting her position as necessary to get a better view. From Yasmīn came not a sound except quick breaths and sudden steps and lunges; the same from her threatener as the pair evidently feinted, dodged, and jockeyed for advantage, except that from time to time I heard from Sahīm an ironic "*Yallah!*" or "*Shabash!*" as, presumably, Yasmīn thrust. It occurred to me that she might turn the dagger on herself, or try to. But when I hazarded one look over-shoulder I saw her half-crouched between couch and table like a seasoned knife-fighter, her left hand up and open to parry her attacker's grabs, her knife poised underhanded out of reach, close to her chest, her cowl flung back again, her eyes positively blazing. Sahīm, barehanded, lunged. I believe I saw Yasmīn thrust, but Jaydā's accompanying howl recalled me to my duty. Behind me then I heard an urgent, grunting scuffle; the combat was obviously joined. The chart table got bumped hard. I heard the strugglers battle our way, then back, and then fall grunting upon their couch. Now, surely, I could back up a few steps and retrieve my watch. . . .

But then Sindbad's daughter screamed, and screamed again, joined this second time by Jaydā. My blood prickling, I turned in fearful expectation of seeing either the rape-in-progress of a brave woman who had been kind to me or else the worse evil — no denying it — of her having managed after all to find her target, thereby leaving both of us in the vengeful hands of *Shaitan*'s lieutenants and crew. Whatever I hoped for her, what I saw was Yasmīn sitting again on the couch-edge, rumpled but far from raped, screaming yet again and turning her face from her assailant, who once again stood before her. He, too, was disheveled, his scarf and turban both having been knocked loose. With his back toward us, he held Yasmīn's knife-hand high and firmly by the wrist with his own right hand; his left, with which he would cover his face, she clutched just as firmly with her left. He being larger and stronger, his arm movement raised her to her feet; they turned a cross-armed quarter turn before she dropped the knife and they released each other. Yasmīn fled to the waiting Jaydā and buried her face in the duenna's lap. Sahīm al-Layl, straightening his turban, turned usward what was still unscarfed: a nose and mouth shockingly misshapen by the scar of one long cut grotesquely healed, disfiguring an otherwise handsome face. He bent with difficulty to retrieve the jeweled knife and, carrying it again by the blade, limped as far as the chart table and reoffered it with a frightful semblance of a smile.

"You learned your lessons well, little sister. Keep this, in case your protector needs protection."

As he rescarfed his disfigurement, Sindbad's daughter flung herself weeping at his knees. But the name she cried (more as if for pardon than for another sort of mercy) was not "Sahīm!" but — incredulously, hysterically — "Umar! Umar! Umar!"

There ends, almost, the fifth voyage of Somebody the Still-Stranded, who only in the next weeks began truly to comprehend the awful magnitude of his stranding. I was appointed Yasmīn's warden and guardian as well as *Shaitan*'s second navigator; assisting the captain in both capacities, I came to know more of both my beautiful, distressful fellow captive and our extraordinary captor, of whom I shall say this much here:

The young sailor who, under the name Sahīm al-Layl, had quickly risen through the ranks of local pirates to become the captain of *Shaitan* and the scourge of the Hormuz Strait was the very fellow who, under the name Umar al-Yom, had been raised as Sindbad the Sailor's foster son, Yasmīn's much-beloved brother, and the protégé of both Mustafā mu-Allim and Sindbad's captain, Abū Hosayn. With them, in his young-manhood, he had made a number of brief trading voyages in the Persian Gulf before setting out in a party of two ships on Sindbad's longer, ill-fated fifth voyage. In the course thereof he had indeed been lost at, but not to, the sea; like Sindbad, but unknown to Sindbad, he had managed to survive, though not unscathed. Just as his foster father had paid a survival tax to Allah of sundry digit joints and half a buttock, so the once handsome and gentle Umar, whether in his struggle to survive among the Hormuz pirates and eventually to gain ascendancy over them or in some other fashion, had suffered not only the disfiguring face wound whose scar we had seen but another, private, elsewhere, known not even to his lieutenants, and yet a third, nonphysical, which had inspired his new name, his ferocious piracy, and a craving for revenge against the house of which he had once been the favorite son: the house of Sindbad the Sailor.

They were a sharklike lot, *Shaitan*'s crew and officers — violent, rapacious, and not to be trusted — and Sahīm maintained his authority over them by frequent demonstrations of his own ferocity and cunning. Fights among the crew were common, even before the captive women inflamed them further, and were typically settled with knives, often by the lieutenants or the captain himself. Just such squabbles, and not storms or disease or ship-to-ship combat, had accounted for the losses made good by myself and other members of *Zahir*'s crew. The lot of the serving-maids was unspeakable; that of the bridesmaids merely somewhat less so, for not only did the two lieutenants eventually avail themselves of the four whose "honor" was supposedly being preserved for higher ransom, but while they were doing so one drunken night, the bos'n and another crewman made free with the lieutenants' designated concubines, and the ensuing bloody free-for-all had to be put down with masterful sword-and-knife-work by Sahīm himself. But one of those lieutenants in particular seemed eager to play the same trick on his captain that the bos'n had played on him, and so whenever Sahīm was elsewhere on the ship, Jaydā and I had to watch constantly lest that fellow slip into the aft cabin and try to force Sindbad's daughter. . . .

Who they all assumed, of course (as did most of Baghdad when *Zahir* brought home the ransom news), was faring no better at the captain's hands than were her bridesmaids at the hands of his lieutenants; and for at least three reasons Sahīm was at pains to give credence to this fiction. In the first place, knowing his lieutenants, he reasoned that a Yasmīn believed to be already much violated by himself would be somewhat less of a prize for them than one whose "honor" was being carefully preserved (though they still would covet on principle the captain's sexual property, as the crew had coveted theirs). Second, it was a matter of piratical pride among them to indignify the women whose virtue was officially being ransomed, and in this, as in knife wielding, a captain who failed to set an example for the others would suffer serious loss of face, so to speak. On this point Sahīm al-Layl was especially sensitive owing to the nature of his second physical wound, about which his lieutenants knew only that it had left him with a slight limp but no loss of agility in close-quarters combat. Of this I shall say no more here than that he could not have deflowered the flower of Baghdad even had he wanted to — at least not in the way customary among men who behave as men to women.

But for a third reason — related to that third, nonphysical scar that he carried from the fifth voyage of Sindbad the Sailor — Sahīm/Umar did *not* wish to rape his foster father's daughter, with whom he had been raised as if he were her twin or slightly older brother. He wished only to ravish and despoil her "good name," as (he insisted) she had despoiled his, and to find out why and on whose behalf she had done that incomprehensibly vicious, altogether uncharacteristic thing. The details of all this I would not learn fully until my own sixth voyage, as you shall hear them on that voyage's retelling tomorrow night. Suffice it here to say that though there came to be heard from Sahīm al-Layl's cabin — day after day and night after night, beginning with those first sounds of struggle and screams of recognition just narrated — the same female entreaties and cries of pain and shame that issued in greater number from the lieutenants' quarters and greater yet from where the serving-maids were confined, in fact these were a sore half masquerade. Yasmīn's entreaties were not for the captain's mercy but for his forgiveness, if not his forbearance; the pain was for what Umar al-Yom had suffered in becoming Sahīm al-Layl; the shame was Yasmīn's overwhelming remorse for having contributed, however unintentionally, to that suffering. But far from laying rapacious hands on her himself, he saw to it that the left thumb of one who would (that sly lieutenant) and the zabb of another (the bos'n) were fed to the fish between Hengām and Tunb. Thanks to his sword, my borrowed dagger, and Yasmīn's own feisty blade, when we finally rerendezvoused weeks later with *Zahir,* collected the ransom, and released the hostages, although the others had been raped repeatedly and several were pregnant, Sindbad's daughter reboarded her father's ship no less "virginal" (if considerably less innocent) than she had left it.

Of that transfer I shall speak tomorrow, for it began my sixth voyage, not ended yet. In my manifold capacities as Yasmīn's warden/guardian and Sahīm's assistant navigator and trusted deputy, I came to know and respect both captive and captor and to serve as the link between them in ways that even Jaydā, who had raised them both as children, could not. They trusted me, perforce, in their differing fashions and with different things, and I strove not to betray their trust. About them both and their past connection I learned some, but not yet all, for each was possessed of a fierce self-respect and sense of privacy. My young captain's trust in me I was obliged in one important matter to reciprocate (as in another, in time to come, I would Yas-mīn's): knowing how beyond all reason I prized my wristwatch — all the more as I began to understand my real situation — Sahīm seques-tered it as a final insurance that I would do neither more nor less than his bidding. For my navigational chores, in which he took a lively interest, he lent it back to me but then promptly reclaimed it and (as it was too large for his wrist, and his crew were a pack of thieves) hid it elsewhere on his person. He would return it to me without fail, he promised, when my work for him was done.

As it turned out, repatriating Sindbad's daughter and her abused companions was not the last of that work. Indeed, inasmuch as Sahīm al-Layl was very much a man of his word and *I have not got back that watch to this hour,* I conclude that my work for him remains even now somehow incomplete. But among the several innocences lost aboard *Shaitan* was this final one of mine: in my frequent conversations with Sahīm concerning that watch and related matters, and my occasional like ones with Sindbad's daughter through our joint captivity in *Shai-tan's* aft cabin, I began to comprehend at last (if scarcely to accept) that off "Serendib" I had lost not only my beloved Julia Moore and all my former selves but the very world in which they and I had lived, together with my daughter, my grandchild-in-the-womb, my brother, my town and time and native tongue — my whole world. The time came when Sindbad's daughter, contrite but unconfessing, defamed but not "deflowered," was ransomed and released. Her erstwhile cap-tor, by no means gloating over his revenge, gimped and bittered among his sacks of gold and hatched febrile further schemes. But her sometime warden, sometime protector, sometime confidant and more, whoever that sometime somebody was, remained . . . still stranded.

Three Interludes

1.

"... *still stranded*," the caliph's vizier's messenger echoed, as if to himself, and to himself nodded that Somebody's tale was now faithfully registered. Sindbad, in turn — disconcerted though he seemed by the narrative — appeared to register this registration. Slowly, then, for best effect, he turned from his right-hand neighbor to his left- and drew himself up to direct at Ibn al-Hamrā a glare of triumphant inquiry.

"Very well," that fellow grumbled — and on cheeks and brow so already red, how to detect a blush? "Thirty percent was a trifle over. Twenty, shall we say, and no questions asked?" But his prospective father-in-law had already turned away to watch Kuzia Fakān as she rose from her place.

"Fifteen, in the name of Allah!" Ibn urged. "My original and final offer: fifteen percent, your daughter's maiden self, and no further story-criticism! Perhaps I can talk Sīdī Numān and al-Fadl into rejoining us. . . ."

But already Fatmah Awād was sizzling her tambourine. Kuzia stepped onto the low table as if to dance, with her own wine cup in one hand and in the other, from the place to the right of her, the camel Mustafā's, unsipped-from. To Fatmah's *tap tata tap-tap* she crossed before her approving master and emptied both upon Ibn's head, completing what he himself had initiated pages past. Then, however, she curtsied before him, set down the cups, took both his hands to raise him up, and said, "Off we go, my friend, to the Tub of Truth-Too-Late."

Nuzhat piped up to join them, beckoning under the camel's knobby legs for Haroun's vizier's messenger to come along. Right readily that fellow excused himself to do so; he salaamed to the company, bade all good night and good-bye (as he would be leaving first thing in the morning to make his report), and let Nuzhat tweet him off, chanting over her minor melody the opening words of Somebody's fifth voyage: "*Truth yes that is what any shall hear who'll stay to hear me. . . .*"

"Twelve and a half?" Ibn al-Hamrā inquired of Sindbad's indifferent sea-blue turban. As the four moved off, rhythmic Fatmah rose to go with them but looked lingeringly down at her left-hand dinner companion, Hajj Masūd, whom through the evening's voyage-tales she had been admiring less and less furtively. *Will you not come, too?* her tambourine asked for her. The rug merchant stirred and stood, blank-faced, as if to do so, but he then called after the caliph's vizier's messenger to halt and hear what Hajj Masūd had to say.

"And what does Hajj Masūd have to say?" he demanded of the company and himself. Crossing behind Yasmīn, he put his right hand on her left shoulder, his left on Somebody's right. "Hajj Masūd," he began — and then he picked up *their* joined hands in both of his, kissed those hands, and declared to that four-hand clasp that in the judgment of Hajj Masūd, purveyor of fine carpets, more questions about these two fifth voyages remained unanswered than there were seats at Sayyid Sindbad's ever-gracious table, plus original investors in Serendib Limited, plus voyages of Sindbad and Somebody combined. If he, Hajj Masūd, carpeteer designate to the caliphate of Serendib, had happened instead to be Haroun al-Rashīd, Commander of the Faithful, he would be passing curious to know, for example, just how that dear lad Umar al-Yom (whom the speaker himself fondly remembered) came to become the dreadsome and disfigured Sahīm al-Layl, and what exactly his grievance was against the house in which he had

grown up like a graceful date palm. How came it to pass that Abū
Hosayn foxed his foxy master, and that the so-canny Jaydā, with her
formidable and hard-proved prescience, failed to foresee this connivance and thereby protect her ward from those piratical conspirators,
not to mention from whatever had earlier beclouded this admirable
young woman's name and fame? He, Hajj Masūd, had more than once
wondered about that. How had good Mustafā mu-Allim, with his
dangerous knowledge of *Zahir*'s betrayal, fared upon that vessel's return to Basra and its rereturn to the Hormuz Strait? Why was he not
here with us now to tell his own tale, in the place of this imperfectly
silent beast who bore his name?

"To conclude," he declared, "Hajj Masūd respectfully declares in
the presence of Jafar al-Barmakī's messenger that these twin tales, their
tellers, and their principal characters all want steeping in the Tub of
Truth: not to launder out indelicacies but to scrub away false cosmet-
ics and true discrepancies until their veritable complexions are
revealed.

"Such tubbings, however, are not the business of Hajj Masūd, old
friend of and supplier of carpets to this house. What shines clearly to
him through all these questions and contradictions, like a light across
dark waters, is the spirit and beauty of his host's daughter, together
with the worth of her stranded companion-in-distress — whose testimony in the matter of Mistress Yasmīn's intactness Hajj Masūd elects
not to question further. Allah bless and preserve you both and give you
good-night, as does Hajj Masūd."

Yasmīn kissed his hand as he had kissed hers and another's. Fatmah
Awād then led him off, or made happily to do so, but he paused near
the table's head to salaam before the host. Sindbad, however, had gone
back to stroking and stroking his beard, as he had done through
Somebody's tale. All but oblivious of Hajj Masūd, he looked now at
that tale's teller, now at his daughter, now at Jaydā. More than at any
of these, though, he fixed his gaze upon some middle distance, as if
his table's centerpiece were some vision of Serendib. When at length
Hajj fell in behind the pleased tambourinist, the camel Mustafā fell in
behind both, stirred perhaps by some recollection of caravanseries past.
Salīm, nudged by his mother, reluctantly detoured the animal out into
the sandy court. Jaydā herself, however, stolidly remained in her place
even when Yasmīn now rose from hers, still holding Somebody's

hand, and led him straightforwardly from the hall with neither explanation nor good-night. Glancing back, he saw the old man turn from his reverie to watch them go; saw Jaydā watch Sindbad watch, and (as more than once aboard Captain Sahīm al-Layl's *Shaitan*) heard her grunt in real or feigned dismay the Arabic equivalent of his late aunt Rachel's "*Hwell!*"

No sex in this interlude. Under the dark shadow of our evening's tales, how go at it, who had been so programmatically gone at?

Besides (Yasmīn reported, once we were bedroomed and restlessly secure in each other's arms), "Sīmon's" lover's menses had come on her that morning, just at early prayer call. All day, until dinnertime, she had suffered from cramps and nausea, to which for some reason she had been prone every second month since Jaydā had terminated her accidental pregnancy years ago, during her father's fifth voyage. Now the discomfort had largely passed, if not her wistful half regret that she was not once more pregnant, this time by her comrade Sīmon, her Bey el-Loor. Nor had her rueful conviction passed that Allah's will was for her never again to conceive, a fate that she accepted as deserved, but sadly.

"There is no God . . . ," her friend began.

"Allah forgive me," she affirmed. "I believe that."

And so we made love by merely holding each other skin to skin through this Arabian night — one of us, at least, reliving through those skins as though in a sustained and vivid dream what we had been obliged by "Sahīm al-Layl" time after time to do before his eyes (and the wailing-but-ever-watchful Jaydā's) in the after cabin of *Shaitan*. So much had Umar al-Yom loved this Yasmīn, so much did he love her still despite his anger and bafflement, that he had cut short her pleading for his forgiveness back on that day of his first unscarfing, had rescarfed himself and thickly, through that veil, declared, "As Allah and this stranger are my witnesses, Yasmīn, I loved you!"

"As they are mine," she had cried, still shocked, "I loved you, poor brother! What cruel thing happened to your dear face?"

"What happened happened," he replied, "thanks to you and your father. And not only to my face. What cruel thing happened to your heart and soul," he then demanded in return, "to make you say I forced you in Sindbad's courtyard?"

"I never said that!" Yasmīn protested, and she snatched up her knife from the chart table. "No man will ever force me!" Her duenna heatedly seconded her denial, adding that when the secret could be kept no longer and Umar was thought sunk and drowned, her charge had only with the greatest reluctance acknowledged that on the night before Sindbad's fifth voyage, she and her "brother" —

"Allah smite me if we did!" *Shaitan*'s captain cried — convincingly, so it seemed to his navigator. "Much as we both desired it!"

Sindbad's daughter's eyes filled up; her knife-hand faltered. On her behalf, Jaydā scolded, "One glass of wine, Umar, and you were too drunk to know what you were doing? What with all her heart but against her better judgment this child let you do, before you sailed off to Allah knows where? Double shame! — for that's a gift no woman can give twice, in the ordinary way. And when you plucked her flower, you sowed your seed, which then for shame's sake we weeded out when we learned its sower was lost at sea. What a curse is wine, which the Prophet wisely forbids His believers to enjoy, though we do so nonetheless."

"Shaitanas!" Our captor was obliged to steady himself against the chart table. "Devils and liars, your whole house! Acknowledge before Allah and this stranger that I never touched you in that way!" Approaching Sindbad's daughter then, in a steadier voice he declared, "Jaydā is Jaydā, who says what she says. Your father is your father, who does what he does and did what he did. But who is Yasmīn, whom I thought I knew as I know myself? For whose sake did you sacrifice Umar al-Yom?"

Her reply was a movement so swift that had Sahīm's not been swifter (as if he had anticipated hers) she would, I quite believe, have put that knife into her breast. Quickly and efficiently this time, Sahīm disarmed her, while the duenna duly shrieked and the astonished other witness to this melodrama looked on appalled. Umar/Sahīm now held the knife and Yasmīn's arm as well. She pressed her face into his chest and implored him to take his revenge on her if he would not permit her to take it on herself. Instead of doing so at once, he demanded again to know who among her several Baghdad suitors could have been so much dearer to her than himself, when he had imagined that he had no serious rivals at all.

"One glass of wine!" Jaydā wailed — almost as if to cue her charge.

It was Yasmīn, released, who now steadied herself against the chart table, shrugging off Jaydā's words and ministrations. As evenly as she could, she declared that for having permitted her most precious friend to bear that blame (though at first she had hoped that their impending marriage might cover her shame, and later had thought him lost at sea, and never had supposed that he would suffer her father's wrath), she would never forgive herself and was remorseful unto death — might it come soon, and at his hands! Believing him dead, she had mourned him, had accepted her father's anger at herself, and had permitted Sindbad and Jaydā to redirect her life anyhow they pleased, for she herself had taken little further interest in it. That said (she said), she would say no more — nor need he threaten Jaydā for information, for that lady knew nothing more on this subject than the outlander Sayyid Bey el-Loor.

"But *you* know!" had cried bescarfed Sahīm al-Layl. "You and one other, unless you deflowered yourself and blamed Umar!" He brandished the jewel-handled knife. "Tell me!"

To this threat Yasmīn responded by boldly opening the neck of her djellaba and baring her throat and chest to the blade.

"She was forced, Umar!" Jaydā protested. "What could the poor child do? And yourself so gone in wine that you remembered nothing!"

Ignoring her, Sahīm said to Yasmīn, "Your cruelty has made me cruel, little sister, and you no longer have your brother's knife to defend your *self* with. Tell Sahīm al-Layl who it was that you loved so much more than Umar, or you shall be forced indeed."

"The end of religion!" Jaydā wailed. But Sindbad's daughter's lips remained as firmly sealed as her eyes remained fixed upon her threatener, who now ordered alarmingly (in what in time we would come to call his "Sahīm voice"), "Off with her djellaba, Bey el-Loor. The rest as well."

"The end of the world!" Jaydā cried. Yasmīn's eyes filled, but there was in them also now that willfulness that had been apparent in several other situations. To Sahīm's navigator's immense relief, before he was obliged to proceed with his captain's orders their subject carried them out herself, deliberately and unhurriedly, assisted by her fretting but ever-ready duenna. Her djellaba and underthings removed (all of the same sea-blue she had worn this evening, as if in commemoration), she stood unnervingly before us in the moving squares of light from overhead, apprehensive but regal, her chin high, her arms crossed under her perfect breasts; and now it was Sahīm al-Layl whose tears ran.

"Tell me, Bey el-Loor: wine or no wine, could any man look upon this and forget it? Will you ever, though you live another half hundred years?"

In simple truth I shook my head: no evading that pronoun now, because though what followed I did perforce, it was I who did it, under whatever name.

"Walk around her!" Sahīm ordered me. Then "Turn for us, Shaitana!" he ordered her. "Show us what Umar al-Yom is supposed to have seen in his cups in Sindbad's courtyard and quite forgotten!"

"You never could hold your wine," Jaydā reproved him, fussing with her charge's hair even as — dutifully, sorrowfully, yet defiantly — Yasmīn turned.

"And not only to have seen" — Sahīm almost wept — "but to have touched, as you shall now unless she tells us who touched her that other time! Touch her, Navigator, and say whether your hands will forget her even on your deathbed!"

To those flashing eyes, when she would not speak, I murmured, "Allah pardon me, young lady; I have no choice."

"For pity's sake, Umar," Jaydā scolded, "do the thing yourself, as a pirate should! Keep our shame in the family!"

Sahīm made an angry sound. Yasmīn said nothing. Never removing her eyes from our captor, she flinched at but did not flee from my reluctant touch. By way of indirect reply to Jaydā's exhortation, then, he commanded me, "Do exactly now as I say, Sayyid Survivor, or you will lose *your* zabb, too. . . ."

At this least equivocal remark thus far upon his second wound, Yasmīn made a stricken moan, her duenna a louder one. Bend her forward over that chart table, I was ordered next: facing his way, so that (if she would not speak immediately and truly) he could watch those beautiful but perfidious eyes while I —

"No, Umar, in the name of Allah!" Jaydā protested. "She is reflowered for Prince Jabāl, who need know nothing of what happened between you two in Baghdad!"

"Reflowered!" Tears ran freely into Sahīm's scarf. Most bitterly, then, his voice regained, he declared that not for a king's ransom, much less a princess's, would he have the prince know what had happened that night in the City of Peace between Sindbad's daughter and his foster son: namely, an impassioned but chaste farewell and a loving pledge of faith until Umar's return from Sindbad's fifth voyage, when they hoped to marry with his consent! Not for the world would Sahīm al-Layl or his navigator redo what Umar al-Yom had never done; he would yield that privilege to the prince — if, after his fiancée's ransoming, Jabāl still wanted it. Instead (unless she spoke at once) . . .

She did not. Literally before her eyes upon that chart table then he laid the little knife that he had presented to her (he reminded her now, as if for my information) that same fateful night, in token of their vow, as he escorted her back toward the harem from the house's courtyard — in his blindness imagining her distress to be over their impending separation, and her desire to be for himself, not for a scapegoat for her shame. She had even challenged him to lend her his *other* blade, of which this one was the emblem! Now (unless she spoke as ordered) she would have neither the one nor the other, but instead . . .

Yasmīn closed her eyes, and Sahīm al-Layl gruffly gave me my next, very specific orders.

Through what followed, and what followed what followed, that knife was never out of Sindbad's daughter's reach, and (once his first commands had been carried out) Sahīm, as if daring her, no longer kept his hand upon it. At any time Yasmīn could have chosen to cut short her degradation by cutting short her life, or in an access of humiliation could have assaulted with it either the engineer of her shaming or its reluctant agent. But after that second disarming, despite her tormented tormentor's demands, threats, taunts, and dares, she appeared to be no longer tempted to it, any more than to confession. That knife lay like a weight upon those charts over which at his command she silently bent herself to be . . . not redeflowered, exactly (Jaydā, at his order, disconcertingly reported to him from her position of vantage beside me what precisely was taking place, all the while wailing to Allah, soothing her ward, and complaining that pirates were no longer what they had once been), and not by the man held to have been her original deflorator. At his later command (and to my enormous alarm) she even held that knife in her right hand while kneeling before me on the cabin floor to carry out yet other of his punishing orders. The jeweled handle itself she was more than once obliged, supine, to touch herself with just so until a certain result was achieved (and echoed by her duenna). And at the deepest, hardest, most hurtful of my obligatory penetrations, to my horror she snatched the blade up — but only to bite down upon the flat of it to keep herself from crying out. Jaydā did so in her stead, just as I, in Sahīm al-Layl's. . . .

These things and others like them took place nearly every day and night of our weeks aboard *Shaitan* as we prowled the strait and sailed up the Persian Gulf as far as the islets of Forūr and Sīrrī to reintercept *Zahir*, whose foxy captain Sahīm did not trust to return directly to our intended place of rendezvous. "I am profoundly sorry," I would declare to Yasmīn each time our master set us once more to his shameful work, "to have to do this, under these circumstances." "You are doing it on pain of death," Sahīm would interject. "Why apologize? One cup of wine, we're told, and you'll quite forget all this." Presently he commanded me to cease my apologizing, but I could not lay hands upon that lovely person without murmuring, in my still-awkward Arabic, "Forgive me." To which Sindbad's tight-lipped daughter made no reply except with her extraordinary eyes, which she fixed (in whatever spirit) upon the man who could neither kill nor forgive her.

Lay hands upon her I did, and more, and she likewise me, at our tyrannical director's joyless direction: this way, that way, every way but one, the main and basic between women and men. It was therefore quite literally the case — when at last *Zahir* reappeared and the huge ransom was paid over and the much-abused hostages were repatriated and the other things that happened happened — that if Sindbad's daughter had been a virgin at her kidnapping, she would have been one, in the technical sense, upon her release. For that, we suppose, Allah be praised — but we shall let some other praise Him.

Now along the man's whole length the sleeping woman stirred. "Sīmon" realized that he, too, had lightly dozed. But though his *Shaitan* recollections were no dream — what had happened had happened — he cannot say for certain that what happened next this night between us did not take place in one of those way stations between awakeness and oblivion. We were who and where we were: Sīmon and Yasmīn, in his dark bed in her dark house. Directly into his near ear she seemed to whisper *Must we have that watch?* and to answer, before he could, *We must, and will.* He knows that what happened next truly happened, not long after: we were waked, or rewaked — he was, at least — by Jaydā's not-quite-noiseless entry. We heard the familiar black rustle of her skirts as she crossed usward, and felt her sit on Yasmīn's side of our low bed. Sīmon then heard the two women exchange three quiet sentences in their private language: to him, Jaydā's first had the sound of a short and neutral declarative statement, and his darling's, next, that of an even shorter question, to which Jaydā's reply was not much more than a word. Did the duenna then rise and go, and Yasmīn slip lightly from his arms to follow? He believes so but cannot thereto swear, for like Sindbad among the sea grapes of Island One, Voyage Two, our weary narrator just here drowned in sleep.

2.

> *Till age thirteen I thought it was a hose.*
> > *Devil take it!*
> *No other use for it could I suppose,*
> > *Devil take it!*
> *I pissed on fires and flowers; I spanned*
> *Such liquid lengths, my scores still stand.*
> *I peed my full name in the sand!*
> > *The Devil take it.*

So sang Sindbad from his Tub of Truth, Somebody wrote that afternoon, *this forenoon, when I went unsummoned to our usual tête-à-tête.*

He had awakened stranded still (Simon William Behler-Baylor, Bey el-Loor, B-Bibi-Bill, 'Simmon-Sīmon-Somebody) and, finding himself alone, had assumed that his current lover, saddened by last evening's reminders of *Shaitan* and her misfortunate "brother," Umar al-Yom, had returned with Jaydā sometime before dawn to nurse her sorrows in her own apartment of the harem. He reslept; redreamed with painful clarity the world he had drowned from; rewoke to the

440

impossible one whereof and wherein he writes these words. As best as he could judge in his watchlessness, the hour when Salīm or Kuzia Fakān usually came with Sindbad's summons had passed. Presently therefore he made his own, now-familiar way to the arid courtyard, where, not far from the great tub, he found a fresh-caftaned Kuzia feeding straw to Mustafā the camel and chatting in Bedou dialect with that animal.

To the approacher she cheerfully complained, "I had thought my camel-tending days behind me!" Cupping one hand beside her mouth then to make sure her voice carried to the tub, she added that no working musician ought to be up and about before midmorning in any case, and that playing laundress again to Ibo's wine-stains should have entitled her to sleep till noon, along with Nuzhat and Fatmah Awād. However, having found herself second-winded by her labors in the Tub of Truth-Too-Late, she had made her way in the smallest hours to the Tub of Truth, thinking that perhaps her standing with Sindbad was restored (as it certainly was with Ibn al-Hamrā) and that he might fancy her company in the last interval before the caliph's vizier's messenger left to deliver his fateful message. In fact, she went on (still delivering her own message tubward in a raised voice, though our narrator was beside her now), she had come as the hopeful bearer of not-bad news: Yasmīn's fiancé was half persuaded now that his intended, against all odds, might be actually virginal after all, and that if *that* unlikelihood proved to be the case, then her father's projected seventh voyage might just possibly be no fiction, either. Despite the wholesale defections now being reported to the caliph, Ibn himself shrewdly hoped to buy his way back into Serendib Limited even for as small a share of its take as seven percent, and Kuzia had fed these hopes of his in her own hope of raising her stock with her master. She had wanted to report all that, she now loudly reported, along with her belief that she was in a better position than Jaydā, for example, to act as go-between in Yasmīn's dowry negotiations.

"But before I got as close to that tub as you and I are now," she called to the man standing next to her, "I heard sounds of manly joy from inside it such as Ibo himself had not been moved to. And between them," she added in a voice meant for Somebody's ears alone, "certain womanly yips and yelps that I recognized as Jaydā's famous imitation of the late lamented Mrs. Sindbad. Devil take it, I said to myself: the old witch has managed somehow to out-Marjānah me! *So roll the dice of Allah,*" she declared (in her louder voice again) that she had declared to herself at the time. "I left milord to his lusty pleasures and hauled back sleepless to the harem. Then, just after prayer call, I heard certain camel distress cries that only we Bedouin can hear, the way they say a mother hears her baby's breathing from the next room: it was this fellow Mustafā here, complaining that Salīm and his breakfast were nowhere in sight. Well, my friend: that's a sound no desert girl can turn her back on, and so once again I said good night to sleep and did what Allah and His creature will thank me for, if no one else. Not a sign of Salīm, and Haroun's vizier's messenger has no doubt gone off with a message that you would think might scare the drawers off Sayyid Sindbad. But when his loyal concubine, dancing girl, dowry negotiator, wine-stain laundress, and camel groom peeked into that tub a few minutes ago — just to make sure nothing was amiss, it was so quiet in there compared with before — I found that sly old survivor snoring away, all by his lonesome!"

"Mm hm," Somebody said.

"He snores no longer," Sindbad's voice called from the tub. "Nor sleeps, either, with such a muezzin to call him awake." The old man's head, deep-indigo-turbaned, appeared now at the tub's edge, smiling broadly. So vigorously then did he shake himself awake that his silver beard hung over the wooden rim. "But what a sleep, dear Kuzia and Brother Sindbad! I haven't drowned so in that element since my seagrape grove of Island One, Voyage Two. Come inspect my back, friends, and see whether it's not overgrown with rocks and trees from so sound a sleep, like Whale Island on my maiden voyage! But now I'm awake, so at least it seems to me, and ready to ride out tonight's shipwreck in my Tub of Last Resort. Where is that moon-mugged messenger, did you say?"

"Long gone with his tattling of mass defection," Kuzia replied, and she gave Mustafā a smart snout-smack when he made to schmoozle his gratitude.

"Good riddance. And Salīm the Slippery?"

"Gone with him, I don't doubt," the dancer said, "to chatter like a parrot to Jafar al-Barmakī."

"Better news yet! Let the pair of them sing two-part inventions from all the minarets of Baghdad. Hand up my sand-pot, Kuzia."

The dancer did so, and as he made his splashless water thereinto, her master exclaimed again (out of view), "By Allah, what a sleep! Now, as the mountain came to Mohammed, let shipwreck come to Sindbad, who is too old to go to it." Finding himself still urinating, he sang then those verses aforequoted.

"You seem ready enough to ride that shipwreck out," Somebody commented from the court. Finally finished, Sindbad sighed with satisfaction, handed back the wet-sand vessel, thanked Kuzia Fakān for her morning news report and her loyal ministrations (which he promised would not go unrewarded, particularly if she now fetched tea), and to our man responded — bidding him into Truth's dry tub — that since the very first island of his very first voyage he had always been ready for the worst.

"But come, Brother Bey el-Loor," he said when Kuzia had gone off with the sand-pot and the two men were seated as usual. "Now that all Baghdad has heard your farfetched stories, perhaps you have lost interest in their much-compromised current heroine and are ready for some new game?"

Surprised, Somebody could reply only, "Not at all, Sayyid."

"For if you have," Sindbad went right on, "now is the time to get out from under, so to speak. I didn't need Kuzia Fakān to tell me that for one reason or another your rival has chosen to incline to believe your story and has all but apologized for his dishonorable presumption; he is more eager than ever to have Yasmīn, even at less than a ten-percent share of Serendib. Indeed, when the story of your fifth voyage gets about, it may be that many a rat will want to reboard our sinking ship despite the caliph's vizier's messenger's message."

Somebody cocked his head. "Then your troubles are over, are they not? Ibn marries Yasmīn, and off you sail to Serendib with your fellow merchants and the caliph's blessing, while I rejoin my fellow beggars at your gate."

In mock dismay Sindbad raised his hands. "What gratitude would that be to the man who turned our fortune's tide? It's time for me to thank you, Brother, and to discuss seriously those proposals that you surprised me with this time yesterday. Where's our tea?" He pulled himself up to look for Kuzia's return and, whether or not he saw her, was moved to sing a second stanza across the courtyard:

> *At age fourteen I found its second use,*
> > *Devil take it,*
> *And reveled three full years in self-abuse,*
> > *Devil take it!*
> *At risk of going blind or mad*
> *I whacked away like every lad*
> *And circle-jerked right round Baghdad.*
> > *The Devil take it!*

"As I gather boys did where you hail from as well, eh? We thank you, Kuzia," he said over the tub's edge, and he handed down a tea tray. "*I* thank you; my brother thanks you; Mustafā thanks you. Leave us now, please, with our thanks."

"*Pouf*," Somebody heard the dancer reply.

"The long and the short of it," Sindbad said, chuckling — as he reseated himself carefully on his cushion-and-a-half and gestured for our man to pour — "is that we accept, we accept, we accept! Ibn al-Hamrā may go and sing for his supper; Yasmīn is yours to marry, with my blessing. The fact is, I've dispatched the vizier's messenger back to his master with word that you and your colleague Mustafā mu-Allim, if that old fellow is still alive and willing, will build and sail a special craft, based on your personal knowledge of Serendib and its peculiar waters, for the purpose of delivering the caliph's gift to the king of that island and establishing trade relations there. In return for underwriting the cost of this trial voyage, the original investors in Serendib Limited will hold exclusive trading rights between that caliphate and this, to their certain enrichment and Haroun's as well. You and Yasmīn may honeymoon in Basra at my expense while your ship's a-building; I myself would happily join you there were it not for the circumstance that that city is a seaport and ipso facto within sight of the sea. When you and Mustafā set sail, Yasmīn will rejoin her family here to await your safe return, and on that happy day this house will become hers and yours. With the caliph's blessing I'll retire with Jaydā or some other to the wâhât of my dreams, somewhere in the empty reaches of the Sahrā al Hijārāh, and there end my travels and my days. Agreed?"

Our man salaamed. "May all that my brother envisions come to pass. But he omits two details. If your stranded namesake is to become your son-in-law and your surrogate in Serendib, then my bride must sail there with me. And you must return to me the amulet you took somehow from Sahīm al-Layl, who took it from me. Without my watch, I can't navigate to Hormuz, much less to Serendib."

Right through this double demand Sindbad shook his head; at its end he declared, "If those are the conditions of our success, Brother, then we are, as the sailors' saying goes, futtered in the fo'c's'le. As to that latter item: I can't give you what I've told you repeatedly I do not have. From Sahīm al-Layl of accursed memory I took nothing, alas — not even his life, which another robbed me of robbing him of. And as to the former, how can you speak of sailing off with my daughter, after what the sea has done to her already? By your own account a drowned lover was your ticket from Serendib to the City of Peace. If you need another for the return fare, for God's sake take Nuzhat or Fatmah Awād! Take my Kuzia, even, who is obviously pleased with you — but Yasmīn, never!" He shifted his seat. "Let's speak openly. My daughter has been yours already and nightly in my house. She shall be yours night and day in Basra until the hour you sail, and yours again in *your* house — this one — when you return, until the Destroyer of Delights and Severer of Societies has his way with one or both of you. But go to sea with you she shall not. And I have no *watch!*"

Somebody set down his teacup and regarded his host eye to eye. "As between the perils of Serendib and those of this house, your daughter can make her own decision. But if there is no watch, sir, there can be no seventh voyage."

"I have not got it, have not got it, have not got it!" Sindbad repeated, as if by the Muslim rule of three. "Not it nor any other amulet, often though I've wished for one in recent years. As the poet sings memorably of his zabb in the third stanza:

> *At seventeen it came into its prime,*
> *Devil take it!*
> *I humped my father's maids and concubines,*
> *Devil take them!*

> *It rose and fell and stood and stood*
> *Through years of love's apprenticehood*
> *With women good and not so good —*
> *The Devil take it!*

"After which, in his fourth, much to my point, he declares:

> *Three decades of virility ensued,*
>   *Devil take them!*
> *Through which I wooed and wed and sailed and screwed,*
>   *Devil take it!*
> *Lover, husband, sire, and stud,*
> *As I sailed on to widowerhood*
> *My purse enlarged — but not my pud,*
>   *The Devil take it!*

"Which, needless to add, in time he did," Sindbad concluded, "amulet or no amulet. If you haven't yet discovered what I speak of, one day you will."

Taking care not to hide his annoyance altogether, Somebody now said, "As it offends my ear to hear you play so lightly on the name *Shaitan*, so it offends my sense of courtesy to say you're lying in this matter, as in the matter of Serendib. But I confess my suspicion that in marrying me to your daughter and then packing me off with Mustafā on the caliph's errand, you hope to do more than save Yasmīn's face and the rest of your own backside. By withholding my watch, you guarantee the failure of a voyage that at best has little enough chance of success. Mustafā and I will be lost at sea, as Umar al-Yom was supposed to have been. Yasmīn will achieve the honorable estate of young-widowhood and continue to grace her father's table. Serendib then becomes a dead issue, and Sindbad the Former Sailor retires in peace and honor to the bosom of his family. No, Sayyid! No watch, no seventh voyage."

Sindbad likewise then duly permitted his face to redden, his eyes to flash. "So be it, then, by Allah: no Yasmīn and no Voyage Seven!" He waggled a finger from the hand with fewer than five. "Too many times I have sat patiently in this tub while you've insinuated what now you've declared outright. I have long since acknowledged to you privately that what I call Serendib was in fact my voyage of revenge against those who played me false, and that if there exists any literal island of that name, I have yet to be washed up on its shores. But however figurative my accounts may be of voyages Five and Six, I support my fictions with souvenirs of substantial fact, whereas *your* fantastical tales have no more to support them than the words of their telling. Who and what are you, if not a clever and lucky drifter from Allah knows where, who talked himself into Mustafā's confidence aboard *Zahir* and into Sahīm al-Layl's and my daughter's aboard *Shaitan* — Devil take it! — just as you later talked your way into mine?"

He moderated his voice. "For your services to Yasmīn during her captivity I am not ungrateful. She herself has well rewarded them, right under my nose, and I have not only overlooked that affront to my honor but offered to reward you further with my consent to your marriage. But it does not follow that I believe your stories, Brother; or even if I did, that I imagine you to have the slightest chance of getting back to where you claim you came from; or even if you had, that I would permit my only true child to take that chance with you. In my time I have acted monstrously now and then for survival's sake, but I am no monster: for all I know, you'll sail off with my daughter to whatever infidel port you actually hail from and there sell her into concubinage in exchange for another trinket like the one you lost. Which, then, is Sindbad the Swindler: myself or you?"

Summoning all his resolution, Somebody said, "You, Brother, if you believe those unpleasant suppositions and deny that you have my watch in the calfskin pouch you wear between your legs."

Was the old fellow's surprise feigned? His amusement seemed real enough when now he declared, "It's not a swindler but a fool who believes whatever he hears from the women of this house." Easing up his right buttock, with a quick movement under his caftan he produced and held forth a fawn-colored sack the size and shape of an actual human scrotum. "This legendary pouch came from no calf but from a treacherous pup who carried his natural male eggs in it till Prince Jabāl relieved him of that burden." In a more confidential tone he added, "Around it, believe it or not, like a silver purse string, he wore that magical ticking device that you call a *watch*, the like of which no Mussulman had ever seen before, fastened by its cunning bracelet.

Once Jabāl had fed those puppy eggs and their owner to the sharks, he cured their pouch to carry that odd instrument: a double souvenir of his revenge on Sahīm al-Layl. When then not long afterward I had mine on *him,* Jabāl bargained for his life by offering me that amulet, whose potency he had supposed from where he found it. He lost that bargain as he'd lost Yasmīn, and after my return from Voyage Six I wore this souvenir — not because I put much faith in magic charms but because for all I knew it might have some power despite my skepticism. As the poet explains in his fifth stanza:

> *By my fifties and my sixties, its poor power*
> *(Devil take it!)*
> *Had declined to once a week from once an hour.*
> *Devil take it!*
> *The toothless wolf still drools at sight*
> *Of frisking lambs, but cannot bite —*
> *Nor any amulet cure his plight:*
> *The Devil take it!*

"And take it he did, Brother, the thing you're after, just last night. Or more exactly, I presented it to him, for the following reason:"

After the story of Somebody's fifth voyage, Sindbad went on, he'd had cause to suspect that between last night's good-nights and this morning's prayer call a second attempt would be made — whether by Kuzia Fakān again or by some other — to steal from him that souvenir of his own sixth, whereof he meant to tell the tale tonight. As it happened (and as Somebody had perhaps observed), Jaydā had lingered behind when the company dispersed, and though Sindbad no longer trusted her or anyone as he once had done, he had not refused her request to sleep beside him in the Tub of Truth. To test his suspicions, then, when the time was ripe he had feigned a spell of madness — one of those "Marjānah fits" that had served him well on certain past occasions — and sure enough, his old mistress and her shaitan of a son had done precisely what he'd anticipated, Salīm materializing from the nearest dark corner as was his wont. What they sought, however, Sindbad had already that evening delivered secretly for safekeeping to Haroun's vizier's messenger, to be presented to his master's master by way of surety for Voyage Seven: a token from its Serendibian skipper, Sindbad's new prospective son-in-law! All the robbers had got for their pains was that token's bracelet, which Sindbad had detached and left in the pouch to lure them on. Their victim, on the other hand (by a means that he would not divulge but that "Bey el-Loor" could surmise from Jaydā's nocturnal narratives), had gained from this transaction a prophecy of things to come, which was so to his liking that he forgave the prophet her transgression as he had earlier forgiven Kuzia's. At the foiled Salīm he had merely laughed.

"As for that clever bracelet," he concluded cheerfully, "if it should find its way into your hands, as would not surprise me, I make you a gift of it, Brother, and of this pupskin pouch to put it in, which now holds only those extra links that Jabāl found on Sahīm al-Layl, and that Kuzia stole for you once before, and that you kindly returned to me. Take them and my daughter to boot! May you have better use of them all than I ever had, and a merry wedding and a bon voyage — but not with Yasmīn. For anything further in the way of navigational aids, you must apply to the Commander of the Faithful and to Allah Almighty."

He concluded his conclusion: "As for yours truly, the fact of the matter is, this so-called amulet never worked, even with its original contents in place. Who could mistake Time, the great depotentiator, for an aphrodisiac? On the contrary: Sindbad the Sometime Sea-Stallion has been all but impotent since Voyage Five, and is as ready now to retire from boarding women as he is from boarding ships. The only wâhât I crave is the literal sort, out yonder in the dear dry desert — whereto, as aforedeclared, I shall withdraw on the day after you set sail for Serendib. For the poet concludes truly, does he not:

> *Another well-shaped breast and soft round rump?*
> > *Devil take them.*
> *Old Zabb won't blink at what once made him jump,*
> > *Devil take him.*
> *He can but* write, *no longer stand,*
> *And writes in short-, not in longhand.*
> *One final S pissed on the sand —*
> > *Then the Devil take it!*

"And so good morning, Brother," he said finally (*Somebody wrote*). "Regarding Yasmīn and my conditions, kindly give us your answer before this evening. She has already given me hers."

3.

Naming the container for the thing once upon a time contained, Somebody wrote: *Poor Sahīm's balls — Umar's! — if these were those.*

He had checked his impulse to fling at its giver that atrocious gift and instead had pocketed it back to his quarters to see whether in fact . . . and in fact found it to appear to be the grisly thing Sindbad had said it was, and its present contents to be as advertised: on his writing table now lay the three links that Sahīm had one day obliged his navigator to remove from the watchband, to size it down to his own smaller wrist. How that fellow had ever worn it around his scrotal sac was another, more pathetic question: until Sindbad's secondhand account confirmed that Sahīm had actually done so, "Bey el-Loor" had thought that claim to be another of his captor-friend's bitter jokes during Somebody's sixth voyage.

Those links retrieved, what to do with their horrid purse? When the time came, he decided, he would recycle it to the sea, which had received already the rest of its first owner's mortal body — at the hands of Prince Jabāl of Oman, it now seemed, though the story was less than clear.

World-girdling solvent (Somebody mused, and wrote), *in which the antecedent of* myself, *like old Ulysses on his final cruise, will doubtless one day find solution.*

With or without Yasmīn? Sindbad had said that she'd already given her answer even before still-stranded Somebody, there in the Tub of Truth, had promptly repeated his: with Julia Moore surely dead, himself lost who knows how, marry Sindbad's daughter he would, with joy and gratitude, at any time and by any rite, and count himself among Earth's favored. But unlike Ibn al-Hamrā's, *his* dowry terms were nonnegotiable: on the day when Mustafā mu-Allim should declare him and his new craft ready, he would set out for "Serendib" (a code word for him as it had been for Sindbad the Sailor, but with a less grim reference), sans armed escort or any other crew than his able bride, if she would go with him. If she would not, or if Haroun al-Rashīd would not return to him the instrument that was, however insufficient in itself, nonetheless indispensable to that voyage attempt, he would abandon his last, farfetched hope of reachieving the world and time he had fallen from; he would abide with Yasmīn wherever she chose — Baghdad, Basra, or the bottom of the sea — even if he did no more with the years remaining to him than scribble out the story of his love and of the six voyages that had led him to her. *The latest whereof* (he presumed and wrote), *my prospective father-in-law and I will tonight each tell a tale of, if only to Allah, the other, and the courtyard camel.*

And therewith, inconclusively, their forenoon interview had ended.

"By all indications," Kuzia Fakān now interrupted him to report, "your audience will be half of Baghdad." Somebody's blood had surged with hope that the approaching footsteps were Yasmīn's; so as not to distress her with further reminders of *Shaitan,* he had quickly hidden the awful amulet pouch under the bedcovers. But having skirled in with sleep-eyed Nuzhat and Fatmah Awād, the dancer confirmed Sindbad's prediction that last evening's new story of Yasmīn's hostagehood and ransoming had gotten around; it was widely suspected that its teller really was from Serendib, if not from somewhere even more wondrous, and that Bey el-Loor's and Sindbad's joint strategy all along had been to shake out the doubters from Serendib Limited in order to minimize the division of the profits. The original investors all now wanted to buy back in, Kuzia understood, as did many others who had been skeptical before. They believed that inasmuch as Sindbad was not fleeing for his life to the Sahrā al Hijārāh, the caliph must have sent secret word of his approval — or else, more likely, Haroun had been party to Sindbad's plan from Page One, with Sayyid Bey el-Loor as his agent.

"Which is all very well for *you* clever chaps," she granted. "But what's to become of us simple, hardworking sex-slaves and entertainers, I'd like to know, now that Sayyid Sindbad has given away his amulet and told his zabb in six stanzas to rest in peace?"

"I suspect," Somebody replied, "that there may be yet a seventh stanza to that ode, just as I know for sure there's many a card yet to be played in the game of Sindbad's seventh voyage." Merely to tally the unresolved mysteries in and discrepancies between the accounts of his and Sindbad's fifth voyages, he declared, as well as certain events therebefore and thereafter, would require more fingers and toes than remained to Yasmīn's father. Be it understood, however, he assured her, that though except for Yasmīn's love he himself was as wealthless a beggar as he had been upon his arrival in Baghdad, he and his presumable fiancée would never turn their backs on Kuzia Fakān, should her master turn his.

Tambourinist and piper applauded this pledge with their respective instruments. The dancer nodded, pressing her veil between her lips, then said, "To think I once turned my bum to you! If I ever do that again, my friend, it's yours." Her black eyebrows smiled. "But you won't be needing it."

Our man then asked, "Where is Yasmīn? Why hasn't she told me what she told her father? Why has she kept herself to herself all day?"

Nothing unusual in that latter matter, Kuzia ventured: women had other things to do besides wait on men. "As to those earlier questions, I could say that your girlfriend is the sort whose monthlies sweep down like a sandstorm that brings the whole caravan to a halt. But I suspect that she's getting herself together for your engagement party tonight, while honoring the old custom of keeping herself from your view until that party begins."

An old custom (Somebody noted after his visitors left to make their own preparations) *that I suspect our Kuzia of improvising on the spot.*

Her news report and accompanying forecast, however, proved accurate enough. Through an oddly solitary rest-of-the-afternoon our man made sentences until his muse grew weary; then he exercised his body, logy from days of relative inaction; then, restless, he prowled the premises and found the house staff (all but still-missing Salīm) even busier than usual making ready the evening's feast. Elaborate decorations were being hung in courtyard and banquet hall, food was being prepared, dancer and accompanists were in rehearsal and not to be bothered — but there was no sign of Yasmīn, Jaydā, or Sindbad, and two smiling but absolute guards denied access to the women's quarters. Next, then, for the first time since he had interrupted his host's end-of-Ramadan banquet, he felt an urge to venture out into the city, fabulous and squalid, whose streets and alleys he had learned the hard way: a Baghdad not out of *The Arabian Nights* but in it. Through the closed courtyard gate, however, he was hailed by such a press of beggars and gentry alike ("Yo there, Sindbad the Shusher!" called one of the former, whom our man recognized as the porter who had rented him the burden for his masquerade; and among the latter, was that not venerable Hasīb Alī, the first to defect?) that he retreated to his quarters, where presently he washed himself, dressed in the best and cleanest caftan from the wardrobe-chest early provided him, and waited.

As in the forenoon, so now again, unusually, no summons came, though from courtyard and feast hall he heard ever-growing sounds of sociality. When his stomach and the fall of light outside indicated what, watchless, he could only suppose — that the hour for dining in Sindbad's house had come — with an inward frown he went out and down alone.

The sandy court was as festive with lanterns and guests as if a caravan had just arrived. Between the Tub of Truth, near which browsed the camel Mustafā, and the feast-hall door, where merry Sindbad stood forth in an indigo caftan to match his turban, a considerable company was foregathered. As if in reunion they salaamed and embraced one another and their host; among them moved house-servants with large trays of small delicacies, while from the throng outside the gate new arrivals were admitted by the page Salīm, himself returned not only to the household but, it surprisingly appeared, to his former standing. Within the gathering Somebody recognized one after another of the original investors in Serendib Limited: not only old Hasīb Alī, but Sīdī Numān, Jafar, al-Fadl, Talīb ibn Sahl — even timid Abū Shamāt, along with steadfast Hajj Masūd and undiscourageable Ibn al-Hamrā. They clapped one another's shoulders; they confided; they exclaimed. There they all were, and there were Kuzia Fakān, Fatmah Awād, Nuzhat — but where was Yasmīn? Where Jaydā? And what exactly was going on?

Now Fatmah caught sight of our man's approach, tapped Nuzhat's elbow with her tambourine, and rattled for general attention while the piper fanfared and the dancer hurried to notify the host. Somebody found himself their focus: all turned himward, and way was made for portly Sindbad to stride forth with arms extended, saluting as well as announcing, "My son-in-law!"

There were salaams from right and left, even from the likes of Talīb ibn Sahl, the next to defect after Hasīb Alī. Only the beet-faced Ibn al-Hamrā hung back. Somebody returned the salutes uneasily and permitted Sindbad's embrace, but to that deep-purple turban muttered, "Where's Yasmīn? What about my conditions?" Sindbad raised a brief forefinger, then turned to the assembled, ended the fanfare with a gesture of his maimed left hand, and bade all please to follow him now into the dining hall, and there kindly to await their place-assignment according to the custom of his house.

"Permit me to review that custom," he said when the company had entered and were standing about the main and side tables, all bright-lanterned and beflowered (Somebody noted that Hasīb and Ibn gravitated toward Sindbad's end of the main table, Hajj Masūd toward what customarily was Yasmīn's, al-Fadl and Abū Shamāt toward their former positions halfway between). "Old friends and new, partners major and minor; the steadfast, the wavering, the reconverted — in my house all shall be fed." Sindbad smiled. "Clearly, however, not all of us can sit on the same cushion, any more than every suitor can win the fair maiden or all parties to a shipwreck emerge the sole survivor."

He waited for the duly appreciative murmur to subside, and the knowing nods and wry smiles. "As you are aware," he then went on, "mine is a table with no foot, but rather with a head at each end and its tail amidships, so to speak, like the sort of beast one might expect to find on Island Two of any major voyage. Tonight, however, that second and fairer head, together with her intended, are by way of being our guests of honor and shall sit at my right and left hand — Yasmīn at my right, when she appears, for the reason that (as all of you have seen) since my return from Voyage Six my daughter has *been* my right hand. At my left, it goes without saying, shall sit her new prospective bridegroom, my namesake and erstwhile brother, now to be my son-in-law and the intrepid captain of a voyage such as not even Sindbad the Sailor ever purposely undertook: the man we have come to know as Sayyid Bey el-Loor and may now call Sindbad the Soon-Unstranded!"

He raised his short-fingered hand to still the general applause, from which only Ibn al-Hamrā abstained. "And in Yasmīn's customary place at our table's other head shall preside tonight, as so often in years past, my longtime companion and adviser, sometime soothsayer, and the virtual mother of my daughter, the peerless Cairene Jaydā. Will these most-honored persons please assume their places."

As of the three only our narrator was present, with considerable misgivings he permitted himself to be salaamed on every side and escorted to his place by winking Salīm. Indeed, it was those knowing winks, together with Sindbad's late imperturbability and the general air of certain people's being in the know, that persuaded Somebody to contain for the present his urge to halt the proceedings until he and Yasmīn and her father could confer and agree in detail upon what exactly was taking place, and on what terms. His strong sense was that the latter two of these had already done so.

His lips pursed, bowing with dignity, Hasīb Alī shifted discreetly down-table on one side, and Ibn al-Hamrā on the other. At the same time they sized up the next-ranked places, at what tonight would be Jaydā's right and left hand, as if debating whether to move obviously into position there or wait to be next-named. The other guests quietly reshuffled themselves correspondingly.

"As is well known," Sindbad resumed, "our seating now proceeds according to an order of distinguished contribution and loyalty to our enterprise. In the third place, therefore" — already Hasīb Alī was nodding in acknowledgment — "who more deserves to sit, for his unshakable fidelity to this house and to the project of Voyage Seven, than Sayyid Hajj Masūd?"

"Hajj Masūd, did he say?" exclaimed Hajj Masūd, pointing to his own chest and looking about as if astonished. "Hajj Masūd the rug merchant, is it? But Allah is all-knowing!" And he seated himself on his assigned cushion, behind which he had been standing all along, and waved a salute up-table to still-stranded Somebody, who was pleased to return it. Again Hasīb Alī nodded, perhaps less vigorously but no less courteously, and, raising his eyebrows at Ibn al-Hamrā, this time moved unambiguously toward the next place, opposite Hajj Masūd. But florid Ibn was already there and would not budge, though his salaam to the older man could not be faulted.

"The fourth place, at Jaydā's cunning left hand," Sindbad declared — and here his announcement-in-progress was for the first time underscored by Fatmah's tambourine, as Hasīb and Ibn discreetly pressed shoulder to shoulder — "shall be graced this evening by one whose investment in our enterprise, of its own kind, can scarcely be said to have its equal. I refer of course to that most light-footed and -fingered flower of the desert, Kuzia Fakān."

"Hear, hear!" Somebody cheered in Arabic, himself cheered to see that if this ritual had been as carefully prearranged as he now suspected, here was a bit of its choreography that was unanticipated by the dancer, if not by her associates. Blushing, protesting, apologizing to the men who wonderingly made way for her, Kuzia was half ushered, half forced to her seat by grinning Nuzhat and Fatmah Awād. Hajj Masūd generously saluted her with his wine cup.

"See here, Sayyid Sindbad!" Hasīb Alī called up-hall. "It seems your purpose is to chastise those of us who, not without reason, came to lose confidence in your next voyage and to withdraw our support from it. . . ."

Ibn al-Hamrā interrupted him to observe, "Not all who lost confidence withdrew their support, even when they lost much else as well." He then nudged closer to Cushion Five, up next to Yasmīn's designated place.

"Be that as may," Hasīb continued, "*my* purpose is to apologize publicly to you and this company for having doubted Serendib Limited and for leading others to share my doubt. We accept our chastisement and reaffirm our support of Voyage Seven."

A chorus of fellow ex-defectors seconded this declaration. Sindbad nodded at them severally, repeated his earlier welcome, and pledged again that all would be seated and fed. Hasīb moved confidently to where Ibn already was now poised, and made a curt salaam of invitation to him to give way. But the younger man stood fast.

"To the fifth place," serene Sindbad said, "I invite nimble Kuzia's steadfast associate. . . ."

"And he accepts your invitation!" cried beaming Ibn, displaying to Kuzia Fakān and to Sindbad his spotless caftan-front, ready for wining. "What laundry she and I have done together!" But as he stepped in front of Hasīb Alī to seat himself, Sindbad finished: "Fatmah Awād."

She had been rattling a fanfare; rattled herself by this unexpected distinction, she lost her beat. Giggling, Nuzhat pushed her to her place, then froze in midgiggle when Sindbad quickly added, "And *her* indispensable accompanist, our delightful Nuzhat, shall sit sixth."

"We have the idea," said Ibn al-Hamrā. Himself forcing a chuckle now, he escorted the embarrassed piper around behind Sindbad to her place on Somebody's left, then beckoned to the page Salīm. "This way, Sayyid Salīm! Let me usher you to Hajj Masūd's right hand! It is last night all over again," he informed Hasīb Alī and the others, "as you would recognize had you not deserted us."

Salīm readily appeared from somewhere to accept the privilege, but Sindbad stayed him with one waggled forefinger and nodded to Kuzia

Fakān, who, crosslegged on Cushion Four, made a megaphone of her cupped hands and let go a strange high call that startled all the room. In from the courtyard promptly trotted Mustafā the camel, looking about for his summoner. With Bedou chirrups, clicks, and clucks, Kuzia directed him to Cushion Seven, next to an astonished-looking Hajj Masūd.

More gravely now, "Very well, sir," Ibn said. "Let us follow your principle to the last detail, so as not to lose the interest. Take the eighth place, Salīm, and I'll sit below you in the ninth."

"You shall not," Sindbad declared, "nor Salīm, either."

"Salīm ninth, then, Devil take it! Myself tenth and last!"

Sindbad shook his head. "No, my friend. Salīm saw fit to abandon our ship last night; he must work his way back aboard as best he can, with the others who did likewise before him. You yourself, on the other hand, though you did your redfaced best to scuttle Serendib Limited, never quite left it; and while your presumptions regarding my daughter do you no credit, nevertheless you bargained for her when no other gentleman would. Have her you shall not, but at my table you'll always have a place, if scarcely the highest. Be seated where you are, sir, and not a seat lower."

"Well!" Looking at once complimented and reprimanded, Ibn seated himself on Cushion Eight, nodded greetings to the other seated guests, and smacked his lips at Kuzia Fakān, on his right.

With difficult dignity, Hasīb Alī now speculated aloud that the remaining two places must be reserved for representatives of those who, like himself, had turned their backs on Sindbad's seventh voyage and now repented that turning: Abū Shamāt, perhaps, in the ninth place, who though he had been the last to join the original company and the smallest investor therein, had also been the last to leave it? The standees greeted this suggestion merrily, clapping the little man on his flustered shoulders.

"And I myself, it seems," Hasīb went on, "must humbly take the lowest place, as the first to abandon the enterprise that I was the first and largest supporter of — which support, I might add, I not only reoffer but am prepared to increase. May I presume your assent, Sayyid?" he all but demanded of the host. "Or am I to yield my place to your page and go round with the wine?"

Before Sindbad could reply, Nuzhat the piper (looking courtward from her place) piped; across from her, Fatmah Awād at once took up and sizzled her tambourine. The host turned to the doorway, through which now entered black-caftaned, black-veiled Jaydā. The room went silent. Once inside, the duenna turned and stepped back to let Yasmīn pass before her. In forget-me-not-colored djellaba and white veil, Sindbad's daughter did so; whether by prearrangement or by prophecy, she moved directly and wordlessly to Cushion One, and Jaydā then to her assigned place at the table's far end. To both, Sindbad salaamed. Jaydā responded with a nod; Yasmīn made no acknowledgment, but kept her eyes fixed upon her declared fiancé, and he his, questioningly, upon her.

To Hasīb Alī then Sindbad once again affirmed that in his house none went unfed. "You shall dine with us, Sayyid Hasīb; likewise you, Talīb ibn Sahl, and Alī al-Yamān, Sīdī Numān, Jafar, al-Fadl, Abū Shamāt, even slippery Salīm. Welcome back to my house, sirs, all of you — but not to my table."

A touch more loudly, over ground-sounds of abashment, he went on: "Five nights ago I seated here a nameless beggar, whom now I embrace as my son-in-law, my namesake indeed, and captain of my seventh voyage. Tonight I will seat two more such before any of you. Let Salīm fetch in the first brace of hungry wretches he finds at my gate to take these last two places. The rest of you may seat yourselves if and as you will at these side tables, where I wish you good appetite."

Amid the murmursome smiles and frowns of the seated and the unseated (even Mustafā gave his head a shake, as if in wonderment), Salīm presently led in two cowled and skulking fellows in ragged djellabas, one of them lean, the other not. As if ashamed to show their faces in such high company, they drew their hoods close; they salaamed abjectly to Sindbad, to the more or less amused other guests, to the page who ushered them, even to the heedless camel. Between them then ensued a little dumb-show over which would sit where, each deferring elaborately to the other. Finally the leaner of the pair accepted Cushion Nine; the plumper salaamed even to him (Somebody caught a glimpse of two dark-bearded, sooty faces, but their eyes were not the red and weary eyes of derelicts) and all but groveled around the table-head toward the tenth place. Between Fatmah Awād and Yasmīn, however, he paused and fumbled in the tatters of his robe ("Scratch your lice elsewhere, fellow!" Hajj Masūd scolded from down-table, to general laughter); therefrom he drew a dirty knotted rag and presented it to Sindbad's daughter. Yasmīn neither flinched from him, as did the tambourinist, nor acknowledged the gift, which, however, she permitted him to place before her. Still-stranded Somebody, speaking as one who had himself been poor and worse than poor, thanked the fellow on behalf of his fiancée and himself.

Bowing and scraping, the beggar scuttled on around to his place. Nuzhat wrinkled her face and shifted away. Salīm made a mock salaam as he seated him. Mustafā turned his muzzle disdainfully toward his other neighbor, Hajj Masūd. But it was the plump beggar himself, surprisingly, who, once settled in his place, clapped his soiled hands with satisfaction and in a clear voice called to Sindbad the Sailor: "Let the feast begin!"

"By Allah," said Ibn al-Hamrā more or less across the table to Hajj Masūd. "Here is a beggar even more presumptuous than the one who interrupted us five nights past."

"Indeed, Ahmad," the lean other beggar, on Ibn's left, agreed, "we must remember our place among these gentlefolk. It is not for us to give commands — especially before we've toasted the bride-and-groom-to-be."

"Your pardon, Aslān," the plump one begged, "and yours, sayyids all." But then he presumed further by raising his cup and declaring up-table, "To the young lady and her lean and lusty gentleman! She is a filly fit for an emir, and her rider looks like one who won't lose his seat at the first jump."

Protested Hajj Masūd, "You go too far, sir!" But Sindbad, with no more than a nod, raised his own cup to join the salute, and the others followed, including Yasmīn and even, with a sigh, Ibn al-Hamrā. Still-stranded Somebody was the last to drink, so many were his unanswered questions yet. But Yasmīn's eyes would not be denied; he raised his cup to them and to hers. Never moving those eyes from his, she lifted her veil enough to sip with him, and he understood that whatever its destination or fate, his next voyage was already under way.

Without rebuking the beggars, Sindbad then signaled the servants to their work, and the feast proceeded, with toasts to the engaged (proposed most often by plump Ahmad and lean Aslān) between every course. At the two side tables, once the investors had accepted both their penance and their absolution, the conversation grew merrier with each cup of wine. At the main table, however, except for strained banter between Ibn al-Hamrā and Hajj Masūd and discerning compliments from the two beggars on the quality of the food, the diners seemed busy with their private thoughts. When at last Salīm went around with sweets and small cups of strong mint tea, the side-table diners turned expectantly in their host's direction. But it was the lean beggar Aslān who spoke, much in the manner of Somebody five nights since:

"Gracious Sindbad," he saluted, "whom men call the Sailor! You have invited us all-but-nameless beggars into your house and seated us among your family, giving us pride of place even over your former and newly dedicated friends! You have fed us like sultans, not least with the sight of your celebrated daughter and her fortunate fiancé — may Allah grace their marriage bed! We whose profession is begging beg you now one further alm: regale us with the full story of those wondrous half dozen voyages that brought you to your present estate, and that the very birds of Baghdad rehearse to one another in the trees! Then we shall count ourselves rich beggars indeed!"

To which plump Ahmad added, "Let us hear as well the fantastical voyages of your son-in-law-designate and successor to your helm, in particular his accounts of Serendib: a round dozen stories to round out this feast!"

Remarked Ibn al-Hamrā to Hajj Masūd, "Here is a test of dedication indeed." And to the returned defectors he called ironically, "Welcome back, brothers!"

Sindbad, however, shook his head. "We have resailed those waters enough, my friends, each voyage more amazing and harrowing than the ones before. Let my namesake (whom I now trust to carry on my name) tell as he will; for my part, I shall recount only my sixth and recentest voyage, the one to what we're calling Serendib. And my telling will be brief, for this is a night of celebration, and the sixth voyage of Sindbad the Sailor was so grim that like my fifth, it must be glanced at sidewise and told edge-on if it is to be borne at all."

Though he had the house's attention, he rapped solemnly six times on the Tub of Last Resort before proceeding. An additional low *pfft* from Kuzia Fakān turned even the camel's head tale-tellerward.

"Those who know me," Sindbad then declared to the brace of beggars, "— the people of my household and the old friends and new partners who fasted with me through Ramadan and, in ever-diminishing number, feasted with me through the week since — have heard this story already in its figured form. In that form only will I represent it now, together with a sample key for its unlocking.

"The tale begins thus: always before, what sooner or later drove me from the pleasures of Baghdad to the perils of the sea was boredom with the rich fruits of my voyaging — a devilish itch once more to trade sharply with exotic customers, to lose my way and my fortune and then regain both by Allah's grace, my wits, and the resourceful application of the lessons of my previous voyages. Of these lessons, by the time I tell of, I had come to accumulate no fewer than twenty (though three of the four from Voyage Four were the same, and Lesson Four of Voyage Five was incomplete) — enough wisdom, one would imagine, to guide a man unerringly to his final port and more than satisfy those who, like Sayyid Ibn al-Hamrā, demand a moral for every story. Indeed, so adept had I become at drawing instruction from my adventures that Lesson One of Voyage Six may be said to have been taught and learned even before I went down for the half-dozenth time to the port of Basra. Perpend it, shipmates: He who goes to sea merely in order to go to sea shall find himself . . . at sea.

"But consider: when men speak of themselves as being 'at sea,' we understand them to mean at sixes and sevens, do we not? Their way lost? Thus 'finding oneself at sea' actually signifies *losing* oneself in that element. With that key as our polestar, so to speak, we can embark upon our story as I embarked upon Voyage Six — not because I was once again weary of the City of Peace but rather because I so loved it, and was so altogether weary of the sea, that the sight one day of a group of merchants joyously arriving home from a trading voyage overwhelmed me with the desire to know that joy again: the joy of return to terra firma, for which the prerequisite goes without saying.

"What further proof could one ask that I had indeed, as I remarked last night, been washed clean of Experience itself (figuratively speaking) on Voyage Five? In any case, fired by this novel motive, I caused my trusty old *Zahir* (which, to tell the truth, had lost her charm for me between voyages Five and Six) to be refitted for her new mission: the speedy accomplishment of self-loss in order to reereach my starting place. With shrewd Abū Hosayn at the helm, wise Mustafā mu-Allim

461

at the kamal, and for company a few diehard fellow merchants who little suspected my true purpose, I set forth down the Gulf of Persia, not for any place marked on Mustafā's charts of Allah's seven seas, but for that elusive goal aforegiven.

"How to attain it? I let my captain scratch his wily turban league after league over that question, until all familiar landmarks had long since disappeared astern. Finally, in proper nautical frustration, he tore that silken wrapper from his head and for very despair flung it over-side, declaring us lost. Yasmīn."

At this familiar summons, Sindbad's daughter for the first time turned her face from Somebody's, not to her father but down-table, to Jaydā, who rose at once and went around with Kuzia Fakān to replenish all the cups except our man's, which Yasmīn, taking Kuzia's flagon, herself reached across her father's place to fill. Sindbad then proceeded:

"Had Abū Hosayn attended as had I the lessons of our prior voy-ages together, he would have understood the peculiar utility of tur-bans for venturers into the unknown: I refer of course to Lesson Two, Voyage Two. As well throw your head to the scaly ones, comrades, as the scarf that covers it! I affected to share his marine dismay but was in my secret heart much pleased, for in the dramaturgy of voyaging, if I may so put it, he had without knowing it importantly advanced the action. Seafaring and storytelling alike teach us that certain linkages, once established, may become reversible as to cause and effect. Does not Lesson One, Voyage Three, instruct us not only that where dia-monds abound one must watch for serpents, but vice versa? In the same way, so often had I seen one captain after another tear turban in the teeth of tempest that, though the sea was dish-calm and the sky cloudless when Abū Hosayn deep-sixed his, I quickly climbed into my Tub of Last Resort and awaited the narrative consequences.

"None too soon! For the skipper's silk had scarcely scarfed the sur-face when, in lightninglike succession, there appeared off to starboard a sheer mountainous island and off to port a veritable typhoon, the latter whereof promptly dashed *Zahir* against the former. As we are speaking in figures, I shall call the mount that wrecked us Adam's Peak. Those of us who survived collision with it did so by dint of clinging to its lowermost crags until the tempest spent its fury — whereupon we dog-paddled to the nearest beach and fell dog-weary on it, little suspecting (all save myself, that is, and just possibly Mustafā) that we were stranded on the shore of Serendib!

"Now, my friends: who who has heard my sea tales has not long since learned that once a castaway has been duly cast, his first concern must be in the matter of swallowing and being swallowed, and his second (inseparable from the first) with minding the distinction between things spoken, things unspoken, things unspeaking, and things unspeakable? Yet not a few of my costrandees, in the teeth of experience, so to speak, finding themselves on a beach so bestrewn with the cargo of shipwrecks past that it more resembled a Baghdad souk than a desert isle, fell upon this windfall wealth like the merchants they were, divided it among themselves against the day of their rescue, and, having judged from the number of wrecked vessels that nautical traffic in our neighborhood must be heavy, did not bother to ration what food and drink we had salvaged from *Zahir,* but gorged as if in celebration of our imminent retrieval. Yasmīn."

This time Sindbad's daughter merely lifted her cup to her lover, and he his to his, while Jaydā and Kuzia made their rounds.

"Needless to say," Sindbad went on, "starvation reached them before rescue, for though indeed another ship or two sailed by in the weeks that followed, and those of us with turbans duly waved for pickup, the new arrivals foundered as had we on that tricky coast and only increased our hungry number. Moreover, a fearsome colic soon hastened the effects of malnourishment and taught the surviving survivors Lesson Two of this sixth voyage, to wit: What battens in Baghdad may kill in Calicut, or Al Zabag, or Serendib.

"I speak in figures, but their deaths were literal and daily. To spare myself the spectacle, while they buried one another and reapportioned to no purpose the spoils of the departed, I set about as usual to reconnoiter and assemble materials for raft or tub as the occasion might warrant. I also hid my share of *Zahir*'s provisions well out of view, sipped and nibbled only enough to keep myself alive, and wasted no energy in squabbling over merchandise for which there was no customer except the Destroyer of Delights. Though my explorations turned up no monsters other than that ever-present one, I discovered a remarkable river whose current ran counter to all others of my experience — that is to say (speaking figuratively), from mouth to head rather than vice versa. Inasmuch as out there beyond the mouth lay only shipwreck, castaway's colic, and starvation, my experience suggested that this riverine anomaly might prove to be of more value to the advancement of my story than would the gemstones and precious metals that happened to cover the streambed.

"All the same, having learned on Voyage Five the capital lesson that Experience teaches us not to swallow her instruction before well chewing it, I kept my own counsel, bided my time, and helped bury my erstwhile companions one by one, beginning with the turbanless Abū Hosayn, until none remained save myself and faithful Mustafā. A man as sea-wise and experience-fraught as I, my old navigator had each morning since our stranding wandered off alone down the beach in one direction as soon as I wandered off in the other. No more than I had he deigned to scrabble like the others for distressed merchandise; nor did I ever see him eat or drink. Like me, he was thus spared the fatal colic, and so I did not doubt that he, too, had stashed his rations for the long haul. For all I knew, he had perhaps discovered a reverse estuary of his own, the counterpart of mine; in any case, like me he was keeping himself to himself, returning only at afternoon's end from his reconnoitering, as I from mine, to help inhume the day's dead. The morning after we laid the last of our shipmates to rest, we salaamed to each other as usual, praised Allah in unison for the wondrous obscurity of His blessings, bade each other good day, and wandered off in our respective directions. I went to my back-flushing riverside, he no doubt to his; perhaps like me he ate the final morsel of his secret store and laid the final plank of his raft of last resort (for carrying river freight, no tub can match a raft). Unlike me, however, he did not return that evening to our common strand; nor when I went down-beach to look for him could I find any trace of his cache of food, his raft, his river, or Mustafā himself.

"My friends: to lose one's way is one thing; to lose the unerring finder of one's way, another. I was no stranger to being lost, but had I this time lost my navigator, or he me? Although Mustafā and I had come to steer contrary courses, always till now they had ultimately reconverged. Not in all my strandings had I ever felt so desolate! I went so far as to dig my own seaside grave, lay myself in it, curse all twenty-two lessons of my five and a half voyages for having led me to this pass, and close my eyes to die, trusting Allah's trade winds to cover my body as in time past they had covered my business losses. Yasmīn.

"Instead," Sindbad went right on, "I slept like a newborn and woke ditto, snugly blanketed in windblown beach-sand up to my chin but not yet to my turban and fired with new purpose by Lesson Twenty-three, which had come to me like a missive from Allah Himself just prior to my waking: *Sole-survivorship,* it reads, *is finally a one-man job.* Instead of despair at Mustafā's absence, I felt a grand relief at being once more the only comber of the beach. Without further ado I freighted my raft with as many bales of fine jetsam and baskets of snake-free river-gems as it could safely carry and poled myself out upon that in-flowing current. Rivers no less than stories, I said to myself, have their beginnings, their middles, and their ends. Of this river and this voyage-tale I knew and was quite done with the beginning; now as I approached their middle (figuratively speaking, a great dark cavern at the foot of Adam's Peak, into which both stream and story now swept me willy-nilly), I commended my soul to Allah and recited that wise poet who wrote:

> *Nothing not yet written shall surprise you.*
> *Every story has been told.*
> *You've heard them all; their plots are old —*
> *Yet of your own, no poet can apprise you.*

"And that other, no less wise, who proposed:

> *If from Nowhere Island's shore you can't depart,*
> *Voyage inward, to its isolated heart.*
> *Your own is no less lorn: It may be bound*
> *Out by sailing in, the long way round.*

"Soon enough, in those black onrushing depths, I wished myself back in my sunny beachfront grave. But I had made my irreversible narrative move, and having made so many such before, instead of tearing my turban in suspense I belted myself securely with it to the raft of dramatical profluence and refell into a sleep that this time seemed to me to last a thousand nights and a night. Yasmīn."

To everyone's surprise — not least her father's, so it seemed to Somebody the Still-Stranded, but who could tell when that tricky teller was truly caught off guard? — Sindbad's daughter this time promptly and clearly responded, not with wine but with the following declaration to the company:

"Friends and other guests: my father's figured fable has it that from this indeterminate slumber he wakes to find himself and his raft moored peacefully in a quiet inland meadow-pond surrounded by friendly Indians and Abyssinians. He believes himself to be dreaming — and who can doubt that he is? — for they address him sweetly in dreamlike tongues of which he comprehends not a word. Experience has taught him, however, to be vigilant even in his dreams, especially in the presence of incomprehensible discourse, and so though they beckon with seductive hospitality, he stays put on his figurative raft with his figurative freight in this figurative meadow-pond until someone salutes him in perfect though figurative Arabic and explains across the little space between them that they have rescued and moored him but, so as not to frighten him, have let him sleep on. 'Better a man wake himself,' this fellow declares — as if offering Lesson Twenty-four (which, figuratively, he is) — 'than be waked by strangers.'

"Figuratively awake now, my father lets them take him to their caliph, who in effect explains to him that this figurative island is known as Serendib and that the office of King's Favorite is currently vacant. My ever-resourceful sire straightway applies for it by gifting the caliph with half a raftload of shoreside and streambed booty. Impressed though he is by this munificence, the caliph lets him know that the decision will be a close one, inasmuch as the *other* front-running candidate has made him a much smaller but rather more impressive application gift, which moreover touchingly comprised the fellow's total wealth except for loincloth and turban, both badly soiled: a magical bracelet this gift is, which, if worn on the wrist, merely measures time and assists in navigation (arts of no particular interest to Serendibians), but if worn on or near a man's eggs, allegedly promotes the sportive function of his zabb. 'Aha!' my father says he says upon hearing this. 'My rival for the post of Your Favorite can be none other than my faithful old sidekick Mustafā mu-Allim, to whom I loaned that amulet (for future navigational purposes only) shortly after our shipwreck, when I found it among the general jetsam on your shore. So delighted am I to learn that my comrade remains among the living that I shall happily share my office with him.'

"And so it comes to pass, the story goes, that the two old shipmates are reunited and share almost equally the caliph's favor. By some means that he will no more divulge than will my father his, but that are doubtless no less figurative, Mustafā has navigated his submontane way to the heart of Serendib, carrying with him nothing but that remarkable gadget figuratively found upon that island's shore. I say *almost equally* because though there is no Muslim of more exemplary character than Mustafā mu-Allim, he is a man of few words, and those invariably literal, whereas my father is one of many and figurative. Not surprisingly, therefore, Sayyid Sindbad's tales of maritime adventure and of the urban splendors of Baghdad endear him to the caliph, who has scarcely imagined that Allah's world extends beyond Adam's Peak.

"I speak figuratively.

"Being Sindbad the Sailor, my father soon divines that his narrative prospects lie less in the tales of his five and a half voyages than in panegyrics on the City of Peace and the sundry excellencies of its caliph, the very Prince of Believers, Haroun al-Rashīd. These he sings to the end of the chapter, figuratively speaking, until the caliph of Serendib declares his resolve to send a goodwill emissary to this most sagacious and powerful fellow king and assigns my father that mission. Ever mindful of his comrades' welfare, so this story has it, my father insists that Mustafā accompany him, adding, moreover, that he will be obliged to borrow back that magical timepiece-amulet-gift to reach his destination. After due consideration the caliph not only restores to his new ambassador, by way of advance salary, a king's ransom's worth of the riverine jewels my father had rafted in from the coast, but assembles a ship's cargo of three times that value as a gift to the Commander of the Faithful, plus the usual flawless virgin sex-slave and, to abet her defloration as well as guarantee the embassy's success, the magic thingamabob — and here we are."

Muttered Sindbad the Sailor, "Yasmīn." But his daughter's forthright and efficient conclusion of his tale was applauded, most heartily by the beggars Ahmad and Aslān. Yasmīn now rose from her place, moved behind her frowning father, silenced the applause with six smart raps (*tap tata tap-tap, tap*) upon his Tub of Last Resort, then stood between him and it, with her hands firmly upon his shoulders, and said on:

"Of this particular version of this particular tale of this particular voyage, one might well ask, for example, 'How did the caliph's favorites contrive to build a seagoing vessel in that inland capital and drive it under that mountain against that black onrushing current to that colicky though opulent coast and thence to Basra and home?' Such questions, I submit, are of a literal character inappropriate to a figurative story. Adverting to the pond-side wisdom of Lesson Twenty-four, however — 'Better a man wake himself,' et cetera — I would add this corollary: If a man decline to wake himself, better that his loved ones wake him than that he slumber on to his hurt or be rudely roused by some extrafamiliar. Permit me now therefore to speak literally."

"Yasmīn," her father repeated, without looking up. "No."

"Yes!" the two beggars surprisingly cried as one, and the company at large took up their cry, especially Ibn al-Hamrā, the page Salīm, and the investors at the two side tables. Mustafā the camel appeared to nod as well, though his movement may have been a mere shift of cud; likewise, gravely, our new narrator's new fiancé. Yasmīn registered with an emerald glance this last nod only, drew a deep breath through her perfect nostrils, and declared:

"Of my three several engagement-and-dowry negotiations, only this latest, to my friend Sayyid Sīmon-the-Not-Yet-Unstranded, may be said to have been cloud-free — though even over it there hangs the unresolved question of that time machine you have just heard tell of: its present whereabouts and the contingency upon it of our honeymoon seventh voyage. My next-prior affiancement, to Sayyid Beetface Camel-Driver, was most marvelously shadowed, as all Islam knows, by the equivocal circumstances of my hostagehood and my exorbitant ransoming therefrom: a tale our household heard afresh last night and the rest of Baghdad, we may assume, no later than noon today.

"But even my original betrothal, to the handsome, wealthy, and doubtless virile young Prince Jabāl of Oman, was blemished by a gentlemen's disagreement between my father and the prince's vizier concerning the attestation of my maidenhood — a disagreement not without consequences in the sequel. To put it briefly and literally, Jabāl's vizier insisted that my virginity be ascertained by female inspectors from the prince's staff, as is the custom among civilized royalty before a dowry contract is drawn. My father, however, distempered by the trials of Voyage Five, refused the on-site inspection of my intactness by any except my lifelong chaperone, Jaydā, out of his private conviction that on the very eve of his fifth embarkation I had given

468

'myself' (by which the whole world means my maidenhead) to my childhood companion Umar al-Yom — whom in very truth I loved in those bygone days and wished to wed."

She looked down for some moments at her father's indigo turban before continuing, her eyes agleam with tears. "Umar: what shall I say? When we were children together, I loved him not only as my brother but as my surrogate, free to do a hundred boyish things that I longed to do as well but was forbidden to by custom. I loved him also as my accomplice, who in secret taught me how to ride a horse and use a knife, throw a ball and tie useful knots and do half a hundred other of those hundred boyish things. So close were we in this that I half regretted it when with the passing of our childhood I saw Umar's love for me change character, and mine for him — though I had been warned by Jaydā how nature works on young men and women, and I understood that Umar was even less a blood relative of mine than Salīm, my opposite: a boy whom nature meant to be a girl.

"Need I add, to this company, that Umar's till-then-brotherly affection was all the more important to a motherless girlhood beclouded by the several long absences of the man whom I admired most in the world: my father? And beclouded yet further by the intermittency of that father's love for me, owing to the shock of my mother's childbed death and the other shocks his flesh proved heir to? With Jaydā's help I came not only to understand his troubled feelings but to love him all the more for them and to do my utmost to secure his love for me — and in this I often succeeded. In particular I used to hang upon the tales of his voyages, wrecks, and rescues, which I could not hear retold too often. I would have given anything to sail with him, not as an idle passenger but as a working deckhand. Indeed, it was my enthusiasm in this quarter that inspired Umar's; he became a sailor because I could not. Yet compared to my salty father that lad was a landlubbing cherub, a roebuck fawn, while the other men I knew were less than that. My half-brother, Salīm? A wily urchin, all whine and skulk. Mustafā mu-Allim? A gentle old gelding, kind but neuter. Abū Hosayn? More weasel than fox; him I mistrusted even before he surrendered *Zahir* without a fight, and despised thereafter even before I learned that he was Sahīm al-Layl's accomplice. Even Prince Jabāl, when the time came, seemed to me but a self-smitten peacock like my other official suitors, neither as handsome-sweet as dear Umar had been nor as resourceful and commanding as Sindbad the Sailor: the best I could say for the Prince of Oman was that for an arrogant young cock, he was not unacceptable, and that on balance, under the then circumstances, I looked forward to our marriage — not least because it involved a sea voyage, such as I had longed for all my life.

"As for women, I might as well add, the two whom I most admired in my girlish years I never knew: my mother, Marjānah, because she had so altogether possessed my father's heart; and young Jaydā, whose earlier life had been as adventureful as mine was secluded. To these now I would add a third, whom, too, I know only by hearsay: my new fiancé's lost friend 'Jay-Moor,' in whose world at least some women have the freedom that none has in ours.

"All this is by way of suggesting who it was who did what she did on the eve of my father's fifth voyage; who it was who later sailed off down the Persian Gulf to marry Prince Jabāl and fell instead into the clutches of the Qeshmi pirates. To return to that famous fifth, which was to be my friend Umar's first of any consequence: what would I not have given to trade places with him? For I regarded myself as his equal in resourcefulness and courage and his superior in shrewdness, quite able to manage both my father's ever more erratic behavior (since Voyage Four) and the hazards of the sea. On the fateful night in question, when, long after the bon-voyage banquet, Jaydā was summoned to the Tub of Truth, I secretly followed after, as I had vowed to do, in case she needed protection from one of her master's lamentable and all but unpredictable mad rages, which came over him willy-nilly like typhoons. When I reached the courtyard, however, and approached the notorious tub, what I heard instead (for the first time in my life) were the unmistakable sounds of ardent coupling, which — as I have vowed to speak not only literally but candidly — much stirred my bosom with warm thoughts of Umar al-Yom, for I was no longer a child.

"I made wistfully to leave my dear nurse and even dearer sire to their last such pleasures until his return. But as I withdrew toward the harem I was alarmed to hear after all the flare of my father's anger, directed not at Jaydā but, in the sudden onset of one of his seizures, at the 'Marjānah' who he was given to fancy had come back to him from the grave. There followed the whip-snaps of his turban, a cruel application he had learned for that versatile garment along with its many lifesaving ones, and across the moonlit court I saw my poor chaperone scramble for safety. Gathering my courage, I interposed myself as I had vowed to do, braved that silken whip, and literally wrestled my mad father back into the tub, using certain holds . . . that Umar had taught me. Soon enough his fit passed; he nodded off like a troubled babe, and I kissed his brow as an exhausted mother would her tempestuous child's and then left him to his prevoyage slumber.

"A short while later, recovering my composure before returning to my own interrupted sleep, I was surprised under the courtyard palms by Umar himself, who had been obliged to retire early from our farewell banquet by reason of his incapacity in regard to wine, a standing joke in our house: a single bon-voyage toast had been enough to undo him. Now, however, though still a touch groggy, he was hurrying at Jaydā's summons either to rescue me from some unspecified danger in the courtyard or to awaken my father for their predawn departure for Basra; he himself was not quite sure which. I assured him that I was in no peril, as he could see for himself — only somewhat shaken . . . by an evil dream that had spoiled my sleep. And I teased him about his susceptibility to wine: I myself had drunk several such toasts to his maritime safety, I said, with no worse effect than warm thoughts of his dear person and even warmer wishes that I could be his shipmate on Voyage Five.

"At this my beloved friend quite came to himself, so I thought, and our farewells grew unexpectedly tender. Alone in that moon-washed space, we tearfully embraced, kissed each other good-bye, and pledged marriage upon his safe return: a match that we imagined (despite Jaydā's apprehensions to the contrary) my father would rejoice in, though we had not yet spoken of it to him. In token of this pledge, I here acknowledge, we would then and there have exchanged that intimate gift which no lovers can give twice, had not Umar been unmanned by virtue if no longer by wine, and had not I been . . . what I then was. Instead we sealed our troth with more ordinary blood, drawn with a more ordinary gift: a beautiful little jewel-handled knife that Umar then gave me to defend my honor with for him, if necessary, until he returned to defend it forever after.

"As much as I loved my friend and admired that little knife (as keen of edge and handy as it was handsome), I asked him with what he meant to defend his own honor, in extremis: with his blade of love, perhaps, of which I took this to be the emblem (and which I was quite confident would not fail us once we were wed)? Let him leave me *it* for my comfort and protection in this harmless house, I fretted, and keep its symbol for his own out there in the parlous world. Better yet, let him stay behind in Baghdad, I went so far as to propose, and lend me the zabb of which this blade was the jeweled sign, so that I myself might daringly ship out with Sindbad the Sailor!

"Patient Umar soothed me with more embraces and promises that we two would one day sail together as husband and wife. Over my objections, then, he escorted me safely back to the harem (what need had I of escort, I pouted, when I had his blade and his lessons in its use to guarantee my safety?). At its entryway we kissed good morning, for it was by then nearly prayer-call time — and that was the last I ever saw of my dear honest Umar, who when I saw him next was neither Umar nor dear nor mine, though unshakably honest still. One way or another, Umar al-Yom was lost on Voyage Five, from which my un-sinkable father returned with a princely fiancé for his daughter, among his other hard-won riches — and there followed the verification prob-lem of which I have spoken.

"In the event, so considerably did Prince Jabāl desire Sindbad's daughter to be his bride that he overrode his vizier's objections and accepted Jaydā's word for my pristinity, requiring only that for his reputation's sake, my dowry be doubled. What will a loving sire not do for his only daughter? Mine, whose marine experience had made him a master of the arts of not-swallowing and not-being-swallowed, swallowed hard, agreed to the prince's escalated terms, assembled my dowry in two ships, and freighted the first moiety down the gulf — along with myself, Jaydā, and my bridesmaids and attendants — aboard his trusty *Zahir,* under his trusted captain Abū Hosayn. The second installment was to follow in another vessel, along with my fa-ther, as soon as word reached him of my safe arrival in the port of Sohar, his own birthplace and the prince's capital. As everybody knows, however, that voyage was forestalled by *Zahir's* 'interception' off the island of Qeshm and its distressing consequences, which my current fiancé rehearsed both eloquently and diplomatically last eve-ning for those with ears to hear.

"For those without, the long and short of it is that my hijacker, the fearsome pirate Sahīm al-Layl, proved to be none other than the lost

Umar al-Yom, very much the worse for his several mishaps on Voyage Five. These he charged as much to my account as to my father's, for my having let him be falsely named (when word reached Baghdad of his loss at sea) as my deflorator on the eve of that voyage. By way of revenge on the pair of us, Umar/Sahīm had conspired with Captain Hosayn to steer the bride-ship into his clutches, to the end of ruining my father with a staggering ransom for what men call my honor, and of ruining me by ravishing not my person directly but my reputation.

"This latter objective, despite my best initial efforts with the knife that he himself had given me, he accomplished through the helpless instrumentality of my fellow prisoner, to whom here and now I solemnly pledge my troth."

"Hear, hear," affirmed again Aslān and Ahmad, followed, amid much murmuring, by the others. Sindbad himself nodded sober, impassive assent. Having smiled magnificently upon her incumbent fiancé, Yasmīn then went on:

"There remain two things for me to tell concerning *Zahir*'s interception by the Qeshmi pirates. The first is that Jaydā's stories of her own remarkable young-womanhood, which I heard almost from my own babyhood, had prepared me (insofar as any woman can be prepared) for that particular category of misfortune. Though I naturally feared the pain and shame of being savaged, as she had been, by a series of rough, foul-smelling brutes, I was determined from the hour we left Basra to use my wits and my knife as might be necessary and — like her and like my father — above all to survive. Hence my fury when Abū Hosayn surrendered *Zahir* without a proper fight, and hence also my limited sympathy for those of my handmaidens who did likewise to their ravishers or who on the contrary chose suicide before dishonor — as if it were dishonorable of *them* to be overpowered and victimized! That is one reason why, through my long and grievous ordeal in *Shaitan*'s captain's cabin, I did not after my initial impulse use Umar's jeweled knife upon myself. Why, on the other hand, after my first disarming by 'Sahīm al-Layl,' I chose not to try it further upon him (when in fact it lay never far from hand throughout my indignifying) is another story, to be read perhaps between the lines of this.

"The second thing that has not yet been literally said is that Prince Jabāl's thwarted vizier played a role in all of this. When my desperate father quite reasonably asked the prince to contribute to my ransom (which, remember, was half again my escalated dowry for my life alone, and double that amount for my equivocal virtue's being at least technically preserved), on his vizier's shrewd advice Jabāl not only declined but insisted that if our nuptials were to proceed, my ransomed virginity must be reattested, this time by his own Inspectress of Maidenheads.

"Needless to say, my father indignantly rejected this affront to his honor and mine (as would I have, had he not). Some while later, moreover, we came to learn that Abū Hosayn and the prince's vizier had further plotted, upon *Zahir*'s delivering that sky-high ransom, to double-cross Sahīm al-Layl, divide the treasure between themselves, and ferry me and my bridesmaids not home to Baghdad but on to Sohar, to be bound over into the ranks of Jabāl's concubines!"

Here Yasmīn moved from behind her nodding father to stand behind Somebody the Still-Stranded. Placing her hands upon his shoulders as she had upon Sindbad's, she concluded, "How *that* plot was scotched, and what followed its scotching, is the literal story of Voyage Six — not only the sixth voyage of Sindbad the Sailor but that as well of my most dear friend and ex–fellow captive: my unwilling past assailant, my more than willing present lover, and my future husband if he be willing. . . ."

She bent to kiss that fellow's lucky crown half a dozen times and as if to it chanted, more softly but still clearly, for all to hear, "Sīmon, Sīmon, Sīmon. Sīmon. Sīmon. Sīmon!"

Somebody's Sixth Voyage

"Her future husband, if *she* be willing," I repeated after Yasmīn, and placing my hands upon hers where they still rested on my shoulders, I pledged before all gods from Allah to Zoroaster my love and troth to Sindbad's daughter and my hope to sail with her for Serendib on the caliph's errand and our own.

This declaration was received with general approval — except, surprisingly, from the pair of beggars at midtable. Aslān, the leaner, appeared to reckon carefully upon his fingertips, as Ibn al-Hamrā had done when tallying the lessons of Sindbad's early voyages. His plump companion studied him while the others toasted my heartfelt profession.

From down-table, Hajj Masūd observed ironically, "Something troubles our distinguished new guests."

"By Allah, it does," Aslān acknowledged, "grateful though we are to sit in this handsome house, and fervently though we wish God's blessing upon our host's long-suffering and altogether desirable daughter. Among these several stories there are discrepancies that even

475

an undeserving beggar finds it hard to swallow. Is that not so, Brother Ahmad?"

"It is, in truth," his fellow sternly agreed, and then he inquired, "What are they, Brother Aslān?"

"Oh, well, to take but a single example: Sayyid Sindbad's daughter — whom may Allah bless and fructify! — has acknowledged that on the eve of her distinguished father's fifth voyage she volunteered her maidenhead to her longtime friend and childhood companion, Umar Whatshisname, or in any case would not have withheld it from that worthy but wine-sensitive fellow, whom her duenna later charged with having forcibly snatched it. Yet both Mistress Yasmīn and her strapping new fiancé have reported that that lucky first possessor of her person (if such he was, as it now appears he was not) later not only denied his extraordinary good fortune but elaborately revenged himself upon her for her having named him as its recipient! Wine or no wine, Sayyid Ahmad, I find that troubling."

"No less do I," the other beggar affirmed. "And yet no more so than its sequel, wouldn't you agree? I mean that mysterious story-between-the-lines, which, if we were to hear it, might explain why that wretched pirate's delicious victim, once she had recognized her captor, first begged his pardon, then turned her knife upon her toothsome self, and thereafter submitted without further struggle to her alleged indignification at his hands, via the lucky fellow who now pledges her his troth. One is tempted impudently to observe that she accepted his punishment of her as if it were merited!"

"Succinctly put, Ahmad!" Aslān commended. "Nor is that the end of it, alas —"

But here Hajj Masūd broke in to exclaim, "By Allah, that *is* the end of it, or may Hajj Masūd never sell another carpet in this life!" He rose to his point. "*At Sindbad's table all shall be fed,* so our host has declared and more than demonstrated. But must every beggarly appetite there be catered to? Hajj Masūd says let there be no further public discussion of Mistress Yasmīn's past misfortunes, on this happy night of her third engagement! Or fourth, if we count young Sayyid Umar al-Yom as her first."

Across-table from him, amid the dutiful approbation of this sentiment, Ibn al-Hamrā grinned at his neighbor Kuzia Fakān and held up all ten of his fingers, evidently proposing to reraise his percentage. The dancer playfully but firmly interlaced her fingers with his and drew their clasped hands to her lap. The beggar Aslān, however, undeterred, pointed out to the company that he and his companion were but digesting aloud, so to speak, what Yasmīn herself had forthrightly served up.

"Allah in His wisdom has assigned us the role of beggars," he concluded, "and thereby spared us the necessity of worrying about whether to invest our fortunes in Sayyid Sindbad's seventh voyage (whoever skippers it) when so much remains obscure concerning his sixth and even his fifth."

At the side tables, especially, this observation caused some stir; Ibn al-Hamrā now flashed to Hajj Masūd first those original ten fingers and then two more. At the same moment Yasmīn squeezed this narrator's shoulders from behind, and her father looked meward, as if for reply.

"The tale of *my* sixth voyage," I therefore announced, "may cast some light upon those obscurities, though I cannot say it will resolve the questions that trouble our new guests. On the contrary, it may highlight those and even show forth others. But as the woman whom I admired and came to love on that same sixth voyage has chosen to speak at once literally and discreetly of her tribulations in the course of it, so shall I, of hers and mine alike."

I then reminded those present who had not been so last night that my own *fifth* voyage had begun in the fo'c's'le of the now-notorious *Zahir,* where I seemed to have revived into this improbable world after drowning in my scarcely more probable own; it had ended in the captain's cabin of the infamous *Shaitan,* in the unwilling embraces (I now made clear) of my now willing fiancée, under the vengeful orders of Sahīm al-Layl and the helpless but ever-watchful eyes of Cairene Jaydā.

"A lucky fate, our beggar guests have called it, and Allah knows there are worse fates — Yasmīn's, for one, and Sahīm al-Layl's, for another — but few more complex, I think, than mine there." I had lost my life's uncertain first half century and those I had shared it with. I could nowise account (cannot yet: the thing is unaccountable) for where I found myself or who quite the self was that I found there, doing what I was obliged to do with the multiply tormented daughter of . . . Sindbad the Sailor! So I was supposed to believe and could

477

finally neither doubt nor assimilate: as if I had been reborn, full-grown and middle-aged, between two random pages of *The Thousand and One Nights*! I was at sea both literally and figuratively, plotting *Shaitan*'s position with the aid of my borrowed-back wristwatch while desperately searching for clues to my own position. Still shocked by the loss of Julia Moore, I had been freshly shocked by the several atrocities I had witnessed and was now party to. Inclined to sympathy for (and scarcely in a position to blame) the plucky young woman who had befriended me and whom now I had no choice but to abuse, I was not without sympathy as well for her abuser and mine when I saw what pain his vengeance cost him and began to comprehend its motive.

Most of all, however (I now confessed), I reserved my sympathy for myself — the sometime Simon William Behler of East Dorset, Maryland, now become "Bey el-Loor" of "Serendib" — and resolved to survive by whatever means among these exotic folk until I could redetermine who and where I was and find my way back to where my life had strayed off the charts. To this end I did (as gently as possible) what I was obliged to do, navigated to the best of my ability, stayed clear of *Shaitan*'s barbarous crew, and endeavored to win the confidence both of "Sindbad's daughter" (and her watchful duenna) and of Captain Sahīm al-Layl.

In the former enterprise, as might be expected, I had small success. Though when opportunity permitted I made it clear to both women that I would much prefer to be back in "Serendib," in the company of my lost friend, than here in God knew where, required to maltreat a splendid young woman for whom I felt mainly compassion, it was scarcely to be hoped that she and her chaperone would welcome my company in the intervals between its being forced more or less obscenely upon them. Indeed, Jaydā was once even moved to scold me — in midnevermindwhat, before the weeping eyes of our taskmaster — for wishing myself out of a position that Prince Jabāl of Oman and many another would kill to replace me in, and, furthermore, for doing the indecent thing I was in obligatory process of doing to her poor darling without compensating for my victim's discomfort by simultaneously doing at least thus-and-so — as her own very first pirate-rapists had thoughtfully done long ago in Geziret Zabargad. . . .

With Sahīm, on the other hand, I was more successful. As we patroled the Hormuz Strait and up the gulf halfway to Basra on the lookout for *Zahir*'s return with our hostages' ransom, there was not a great deal to occupy us beyond managing and maintaining our ship, violating our prisoners per assignment, and guarding them vigilantly against abuse by other than their designated violators. He and I therefore found ample time to converse. Inasmuch as my Arabic was ever improving, and Sahīm's other shipmates were so brutish a lot, and he was as curious about the world I had floated in from with my magical navigation tool (which presently he adjusted to his wrist and kept jealously on his person except when I required it for my work) as was I about him and the misfortunes that had transformed Umar al-Yom into Sahīm al-Layl, we came as close to being friends as two can when one has absolute power over the other.

Thus I verified that my ex-protector and mentor aboard *Zahir*, Mustafā mu-Allim, had been Umar's as well in years past, and before that his father's navigator. And that when that kindly captain (Allim al-Yom) died, Mustafā himself had brought the orphan boy into the house of the wealthy merchant-trader Sindbad, who had been taught by Umar's late father that men should behave to men as men. I learned further of that childhood friendship we have all since heard of, between the orphan lad and his foster sister, which had then ripened into another kind of feeling as the young people themselves ripened out of childhood. Umar himself had recognized this emotional sea-change (Sahīm told me) only when his virtual "mother," Jaydā, brought the subject up and warned him to dismiss it from his heart, inasmuch as his "father," Sindbad, would not be pleased to learn of it. Yasmīn, he discovered presently, had been likewise informed and instructed by her guardian, whose wisdom in such matters the young people accepted and virtuously agreed to be guided by, despite their private opinion that Sindbad (between his occasional mad fits, at least) would more likely delight in the prospect of their eventual marriage. The young woman permitted herself dutifully to receive the formal attentions of sundry other suitors; the young man strove to concentrate upon seafaring. But the more Umar was separated from his long-time playmate and dearest friend — by brief but frequent voyages with his foster father and his "uncles," Mustafā and Captain Abū Hosayn — the more his love for Yasmīn grew, until at last he resolved to broach with Sindbad the subject of marriage, as tactfully as he could, sometime during the upcoming long trading voyage for which the household was making ready: Sindbad's fifth such, Umar's first beyond the familiar Bahr Faris.

On the eve of that voyage (or more exactly, the evening before Sindbad and Umar went down from Baghdad to Basra to board their hired vessel), there had taken place the now notorious bon-voyage feast in this very hall, during which, by his own acknowledgment, Umar drank off a single cup of red wine — ostensibly to the voyage's success, privately to the success of his planned marriage proposal — and was characteristically so undone thereby that, to the household's general amusement, the servants were obliged to carry him off to bed. The next thing he knew, he declared to me, he was being roused from a deep sleep by Jaydā, who bade him hurry to the courtyard tub and waken Sindbad for the early start they two had agreed upon. Though the stars over Baghdad told his sailor's eye that morning prayer call was still hours off, he groggily collected himself and set about to do as bidden, unsure by that time whether Jaydā had actually appeared and said what she'd said or whether he had dreamed himself awake — and unable to ask because by then the woman had disappeared.

Making his way to the Tub of Truth, he found his benefactor peacefully asleep in it, murmuring Yasmīn's mother's name. By this time convinced that the hour was premature and that Jaydā's visitation had been the last effects of that cup of wine, he recrossed the court toward his quarters and to his astonishment found Yasmīn herself sitting quietly under a date palm, wiping her eyes with the cowl of her djellaba.

Gentlemen and ladies: my fiancée (my muse as well) has authorized me to repeat Sahīm al-Layl's version of what ensued, inasmuch as Umar al-Yom can never again speak for himself. Imagining that she was distressed by their impending separation (that version has it), the young man hurried to comfort her. "Lend me that jewel-handled knife you've taught me the uses of," Sahīm told me Yasmīn begged Umar. "There is one thing or another I must do with it before dawn." She would not say what or why, but as he knew her to be no trifler, with deep misgivings he fetched forth that knife, wondering darkly whether some manservant of the house (the page Salīm, perhaps, whom Umar had never quite understood or trusted, or one of her official suitors) had offered to molest her. In full possession of his faculties now, as her hand closed on the dagger handle he suddenly feared her intention, though he could not imagine her reason, and seized the blade. His right hand cut and bleeding, he then wrestled the knife from her (not easily, Sahīm told me aboard *Shaitan*; as I had seen, she was a savvy scrapper, and he recalled his wound's smearing blood on his friend's djellaba). Their urgent grappling, to his surprise, turned into a no less urgent embrace, in the struggling course of which she made clear her desire that he himself impale her — not this time in the heart — upon his blade-not-made-of-steel (which had never yet been unsheathed for its manly purpose), if he was so determined to deny her the other.

But again he denied her, so Sahīm al-Layl swore to me — both because he truly wished to deflower his bride per custom on their wedding night and proudly display love's crimson banner to the morning household, and because his dismay at her earlier gesture had altogether unmanned him. There followed the exchange already narrated by my fiancée, quite as reported to me by Captain Sahīm: her keeping the literal blade as an emblem of the figurative (after pledging never to use it except in self-defense); her distractedly challenging him to lend her both, to fare forth with on Voyage Five in his stead if she could not sail at his side; and their final tender farewells at the harem gate — during which, it must be added, she is said to have declared to him repeatedly and tearfully, "I love you, sweet Umar, but you have failed me tonight." And when he assured her that he would never touch wine again, and that they would surely marry upon his return, she replied without confidence, "May that come to pass."

Much moved by his friend's distraught behavior, Umar then went back to the Tub of Truth to wake his "father" (since by now it was almost muezzin time) and found him already awakened by Salīm and out of sorts. All the way to Basra, this story has it, Sindbad scolded Umar for oversleeping on that important morning; because the young man dared not acknowledge what he had been busy with and was never an able liar, he accepted that false blame. Far from being appeased, however, Sindbad seemed to Umar to grow ever more testy as their hired vessel made its way from Basra to Persian Siraf, there to rendezvous with the recommissioned *Zahir*. It became evident to the young man that something more than his tardy appearance at the Tub of Truth (which in fact, Sahīm said, had not been tardy at all; the page's had been early) was troubling his benefactor — something involving Umar himself and Yasmīn. He feared that Sindbad might somehow have overheard and misinterpreted their courtyard scuffle, but lest he needlessly incriminate them both, he was afraid to bring the subject up, much less express his wish to marry the girl whose brother he had been raised as but was not.

In Siraf, to his bitter disappointment, Sindbad assigned him to the escort ship, ostensibly to spare him the shipwreck that was so often his own fate but actually (Sahīm believed) as a further discipline for some still-unspecified offense. In despair Umar consulted Mustafā mu-Allim, confessed the whole story, and begged for the old man's help. His "uncle" sagely advised him to keep both his feelings for Yasmīn and his marriage plans in his seabag until the voyage's homeward leg, if for no other reason than that given Sindbad's parlous record, there was always the possibility that on this fifth adventure his luck would run out and no fatherly permission would be required.

"Allah forfend!" Umar had cried, horrified. Straightway then, just before the two ships left Siraf, he gathered his courage and against Mustafā's advice (and Jaydā's earlier warning) declared frankly to his foster father his love for Yasmīn, his conviction that it was reciprocal, and his hope for Sindbad's blessing upon their marriage at the voyage's end. He did this (so Sahīm reported to me) precisely *lest* Allah not see fit to spare Sindbad the Sailor yet once again, but his benefactor, far from being pleased, forbade him ever to speak thenceforth of such virtual incest, a crime against Allah, and brusquely ordered him back to *Zahir*.

Umar was heartsick, Sahīm said. Mustafā counseled patience.

At Kulam Mali, however, at the lower extremity of the subcontinent of Al Hind, just before the little convoy set out for the fabled regions of Al Zabag and Kalah Bar, Sindbad surprisingly reversed his order and bade Umar join him incognito on the larger, slower hired vessel. He was to represent himself as a rich young merchant, new to the business; the disguise would permit Sindbad to teach his foster son the ins and outs of sharp trading while at the same time giving the pair of them the advantage of appearing to compete with each other and their fellow merchants even as they secretly collaborated on the most profitable deals. They might also discuss further the matter that

Umar had mentioned in Siraf, which Sindbad allowed he had perhaps condemned too precipitately.

This proposal troubled Mustafā and was by no means altogether clear to Umar, but so overjoyed was the young man at Sindbad's apparent change of heart that he changed ships at once, reciting to himself the sixteen lessons of his benefactor's first four voyages and resolving to lose no opportunity to show his prospective father-in-law (now mine) how thoroughly he had learned them:

Voyage One, Lesson One: *Some shores may be less solid than the sea.*

1:2: *A dream long dreamed may grow a real geography, unsuspected by the dreamer, etc.*

1:3: *The castaway who would become King's Favorite must not only abandon hope but feed a portion of himself to his ultimate devourers.*

1:4: *He who would regain his lost goods does well to become registrar of cargoes.*

Voyage Two, Lesson One: *Sleep is a soporific with respect to salvation; in Paradise, do not doze off.*

2:2: *God gave men heads not only for wearing turbans on, and conversely.*

2:3: *Where diamonds abound, so surely shall serpents.*

2:4: *What goes down may come up.*

Voyage Three, Lesson One: *Where no diamonds are, there may be serpents nonetheless.*

3:2: *Be not the plumpest chicken in the coop, etc.*

3:3: *Discourse that makes no sense may not be nonsense, etc.*

3:4: *Better to speak the unswallowable and swallow the unspeakable than be swallowed by either.*

Voyage Four, Lesson One: *Among those who think without speaking, mind what you swallow, lest you become food for their thought.*

4:2: *Men should behave to men as men.*

4:3: *Men should behave to men as men.*

4:4: *Men should behave to men as men.*

There followed Voyage Five proper: in the figured version, Sindbad's encounter with the Old Man of the Sea. But as Sahīm al-Layl reported it to *Shaitan*'s new navigator, what happened literally was this: after a storm had separated the merchant vessel from its escort and fetched it to that voyage's Island One, Umar at first wondered why Sindbad didn't warn the reckless merchants not to vandalize the alabaster dome that Umar himself had quickly recognized, from his guardian's stories, to be a roc's egg. On the contrary, he saw Sindbad slip away from the landing party without a word and row himself alone back to the moored ship in one of the two boats they had come ashore in. After due reflection he decided that so great was his "father's" confidence in him after all that Sindbad was depending on him to urge the merchants to bring about their own destruction: a prerequisite for his and Sindbad's moving on together to Island Two. He therefore steeled himself and not only cast the first stone but insisted to his companions — when they became alarmed at the giant chick's stirring in its broken shell — that they *not* retreat posthaste but slaughter the roc child for the ship's larder. Reluctantly they agreed, and to give the roc parents time to discover and revenge their loss, Umar drew out the process of butchering and of ferrying chick parts and shipmates, a few at a time, back to their vessel. When only himself, one fellow merchant, and one roc drumstick remained on the beach, he saw the mother ship making sail and weighing anchor, even as the mother roc blackened the sky to westward; only by dint of the most furious rowing was he able to overtake the vessel before it sailed off to certain destruction without him!

For this adroit bit of applied vicarious experience he rather expected Sindbad's compliments. But he found his mentor already secured on the foredeck in the Tub of Last Resort, busily pretending to bathe himself and all but ignoring his ward's urgent request to join him. Umar could not deny, however, the sagacity of Sindbad's grumbled observation that such a move would arouse suspicions of one sort or another; he therefore stationed himself near a spare spar in the vessel's waist while the rocs accomplished their boulderment of ship, crew, and passengers, destroying every one and even the theretofore unsinkable tub, until no one remained both afloat and alive except himself (by that time turbaned to his spar) and his erstwhile benefactor, injured and barely conscious — which benefactor's past kindnesses the young man was gratified now to be able to repay by lashing Sindbad to the spar in his place and clinging alongside as best he could through the several days and nights customarily required to float from first to second islands.

It was an interval all the more arduous, Sahīm al-Layl recalled, for the delirium brought on by Sindbad's injuries (one of his legs appeared to be sprained, if not broken, and he was conscious only intermittently) — a delirium in which he uttered shocking things about his daughter and his foster son. Excusable though Umar found these slanders to be in Sindbad's fevered state, he was much relieved to drift ashore at last on the paradisiacal Island Two, where he secured his nearly comatose spar partner on the palm-shaded beach and foraged inland for food and water to revive them both. No alabaster domes this time — nor monsters, either, so far as could be seen — but among the wild orchids and bird-of-paradise blossoms he discovered a crystal spring ringed with unfamiliar but appetizing fruits. Pressing though his own needs were in that line, he would sample neither until reassured by Sindbad that they were safe. To that end he hurried back to the beach, fetched the older man up onto his shoulders, and carried him dazed and raving to that orchard pool, even wading chin-high into it so that his passenger could reach and gobble the tenderest fruit.

This Sindbad did, ravenously, and he guzzled the pristine water in cupped-handfuls, whereupon Umar permitted himself a few lifesaving sips and nibbles as well. To his dismay, however, when he offered to lay the old man down to rest at poolside, Sindbad clamped his injured legs tight about his porter's neck, pounded his head, and not only cursed him more vilely than ever (with scurrilous reference to Yasmīn) but, as the water and fruit ran through him, befouled Umar literally as well as verbally. Nor would he release his grip even when night fell, but rode the young man to earth and snored and gripped and farted relentlessly till dawn, when he cursed the poor fellow awake, pissed down his neck, and pounded him back to his portering.

Thus passed an obscene interval of which Umar himself lost measure but which he endured for his beloved's sake as well as her feverish father's and his own. Messy trial and error taught him presently a trick to ease his ordeal: in empty gourds he fermented wild grapes to make a crude wine, which, though it grievously loosened his rider's sphincters, loosened his cruel grip, too, if supplied in quantity after sunset. Then Umar could lay his taskmaster gently down to sleep, wash himself in the no-longer-crystalline pool, stretch his weary muscles, and — with no need of wine to aid him or any wish for that treacherous elixir after his bon-voyage experience — sleep soundly until Sindbad reclimbed him and hammered him awake.

At no time, Sahīm al-Layl told me, did Umar imagine Yasmīn's father's hard treatment of him to be anything but the effect of fever, though Sindbad's legs appeared to give him pain no longer, and the nature of his curses — that "brother" and "sister" had shamelessly gone at it right under their father's nose; or that Umar had incestuously forced Yasmīn, whose plundered honor would not go unavenged — cast a troubling retrospective light upon Sindbad's behavior back on Island One. Umar bore his burden stoically, kept himself alive as best he could, fermented a steady supply of the wine that indirectly afforded him his only respite, and even commenced work on a larger replica of the lost Tub of Last Resort, though his cooperage was much impeded by Sindbad's fists and bowels.

A late afternoon came when Umar saw a ship approaching the island and joyfully recognized it as *Zahir*. Per Lesson Two, Voyage Two, he waved his turban, but his signal went either unseen or unheeded. As well as he could with his difficult burden, he scrabbled after driftwood for a bonfire, upbraiding himself for not having done so earlier. The day was fast fading, and even with his half-completed tub thrown in for good measure, he feared *Zahir* would sail out of view before he got a proper blaze going. His only chance, he decided, was to get out from under by the usual means and thus free himself to feed and fan the fire; so deranged was his terrible rider, however (Sahīm said), that he stubbornly refused this time to take the proffered gourd, declaring his belief that Umar had poisoned the wine to rid himself of the only obstacle between his zabb and his sister's wâhât. Such were his terms, and since *Zahir* bade to disappear with the twilight, there was nothing for it but that Umar drink some of the wine himself, despite his pledge to Yasmīn, to demonstrate its harmlessness. "More!" his rider insisted. "A man could sip cobra venom in that piddling amount and suffer no worse than a headache."

And so he drank more, and the next thing he knew (said Sahīm al-Layl), it was the middle of the next morning, and Umar al-Yom's head ached indeed, and his face and crotch, too. Coming painfully to his senses, he found himself no longer on the beach but almost buried in a pile of forest litter beside that once-pure woodland spring. He ventured to touch his throbbing groin and to his horror discovered that he had been crudely bandaged there with his own turban, more stained with blood by far than Yasmīn's djellaba after their courtyard scuffle. And under that bandage, though what hereabouts are called his eggs remained to him, what hereabouts is called his zabb did not.

With a howl he dragged himself to the pool and, washing his nether wound therein, was further horrified by the reflection of a face that he could scarcely recognize from the nose down, so mutilated was it: as if whoever had taken his manhood had made to take his tongue as well, and had abandoned the attempt only after much hack and slash. When his nausea and general shock permitted, he made his way beachward and there found the ashes of his signal fire, with many footprints round about, but no sign of Sindbad or *Zahir*.

Umar's first thought (Sahīm swore) was that that vessel had been commandeered by some of those pirates with whom, between voyages Four and Five, his foster father had regrettably established an increasing commerce; that in the manner of such desperadoes they had seen but ignored his daytime rescue signal and instead sent a night raiding party ashore to see what booty they might claim. Finding no prize beyond the helpless owner of their stolen ship, they had either murdered him or taken him hostage, then done their wanton knife-work on his wine-drugged companion as on a hapless roc chick and left him for dead. Despite his dreadful injuries, as soon as he was able he combed the island, wine-gourd in hand, calling in vain for Sindbad. Finding no trace of him, he flung into the sea that veritable poison which had unmanned him before any pirate's knife and left him unable to defend either himself or his fevered foster father.

How many despairing weeks or months went by before another ship passed and rescued Umar al-Yom, Sahīm al-Layl could by no means guess. His wounds healed; their scars remained; thinking miserably of Yasmīn, he scarcely cared whether he lived or died. From his rescuers, for his own sake, he concealed his emasculation, and for their sake veiled his facial disfigurement with a turban-scarf. Painfully he retrained his damaged mouth and tongue to speak; for his other loss there was no remedy. En route back up the Persian Gulf, off the island of Qeshm, the ship was taken by the same sort of pirates he imagined to have taken *Zahir*. In his general fury Umar fought them so bravely that after they had dispatched every one of his shipmates they offered to spare his life if he joined their crew — and only then (said Sahīm al-Layl) did he truly realize that regardless of Sindbad's fate there was nothing left for Umar al-Yom in the City of Peace, to which out of habit he had been making his way. Better that his beloved think him dead than see him as he now was! And so he not only joined the pirates but (in part to conceal and compensate for his emasculation) by dint of his reckless ferocity quickly earned their respect and worked his way up through their lawless ranks.

All the same, he remained concerned about Yasmīn's welfare and Sindbad's fate — about the latter more particularly when he gathered from the pirate leaders that *Zahir* was once again operating out of Basra under the command of Abū Hosayn, who was reestablishing connections with a rival band of pirates from Qatar! "Sahīm" (as Umar had taken to calling himself, to protect the memory of the man Yasmīn had loved) volunteered to win that profitable business for his new comrades if they would put him in the way of this Abū Hosayn, whose favorite apprentice he declared himself once to have been. To this end they set him ashore by night near Basra — as the teller of this tale will subsequently be set by Sahīm al-Layl himself, when the narrative returns to its narrator — agreeing to retrieve him there after two weeks.

His actual intentions (Sahīm told me) were to put behind him the practice of piracy, which had soon disgusted him, and, after learning what had happened to his feverish foster father and whether Yasmīn and Jaydā were in financial need, perhaps to join his "uncle" Mustafā aboard *Zahir* and live out his blighted years incognito as an ordinary sailor. Finding the old navigator not aboard, however, and judging it best (for the first time in his life) to approach wiliness wilily, he applied to Abū Hosayn and stated his business as one who, before he had become a pirate himself with the up-and-coming Qeshmis, had suffered at the hands of whoever those other pirates or mutineers were who had seized control of *Zahir* during the fifth voyage of Sindbad the Sailor and perhaps kidnapped that famous fellow himself, under the pretext of rescuing him, after the shipwreck of his hired vessel. How had Abū Hosayn managed to regain command, "Sahīm" asked respectfully, and what had been Sayyid Sindbad's fate?

Puzzled and wary, Abū Hosayn assured the scarfed stranger that at no time during Sindbad's fifth voyage had *Zahir* been under any other command than her present captain's. That by prior arrangement, after the two ships were separated by foul weather *Zahir* had sailed from shore to desert shore on the lookout for waving turbans, and by Allah's grace had thus managed once again to rescue her owner, in reasonable health and spirits despite his latest harrowing maroonment. But that Sindbad had been, also once again, the sole survivor of his hired ship's roc-rock wreck, in which, alas, his adopted son had perished along with all other hands. The lad had been duly mourned by *Zahir*'s captain and navigator as well as by her owner and, Abū Hosayn presumed, her owner's family — though he himself had not been up to Baghdad since their after-all-profitable return from Voyage Five. Now, as to the proposed little side business with the pirates of Qeshm rather than those of Qatar: not impossibly something might be arranged, if the terms were irresistible. . . .

Hurrying next in great confusion to Mustafā mu-Allim, whom he found in the old man's marsh-side hut, Sahīm first got confirmation of Hosayn's startling report and then revealed himself (and his facial wounds only, out of some final pride) to this oldest and closest of his mentors. After weeping for joy at Umar's survival and in shocked pity for his disfigurement, Mustafā told him a more alarming story yet: though he could not attest the thing firsthand, he had heard rumors from the page Salīm of an ugly turmoil in Sindbad's house, where all mourning for Umar al-Yom had been cut short for the reason that that young man, before sailing off on Voyage Five and being lost in the roc wreck, had betrayed the family's trust by seducing, perhaps even forcing, Sindbad's daughter! The matter was being hushed up and was not, Mustafā acknowledged, altogether clear: one rumor had it that Jaydā had been obliged to correct an accidental consequence of Yasmīn's defloration by her foster brother; yet another maintained on the contrary that the young woman's new fiancé, Prince Jabāl of Oman, was entirely satisfied that she was virginal and had concluded arrangements for their marriage. Mustafā's stern present advice was that whatever had or had not happened, Umar should steer clear of Sindbad's household and its ever more erratic master. Even the Qeshmi pirates, in his opinion, were safer shipmates.

At this report (Sahīm reported), day turned to night before Umar's eyes — an experience he would remember when he came to choose his full new name. Base and baseless though the rumored charges against him were, however (he insisted), if Sindbad had got wind of them in Basra just before embarking for Siraf, it would cast some light upon his subsequent behavior toward the young man whom he had once taken such pride in: Sindbad must have yearned to disbelieve the page's insinuations (or whoever's) and yet — knowing Umar's feelings for Yasmīn — feared they might be true, and thus, in his feverish condition on Island Two, had savagely avenged his honor and Yasmīn's.

But that that splendid young woman could make such slanderous charges against anyone, least of all himself, or permit others to, was quite unthinkable, and so against Mustafā's urging Umar went up to Baghdad after all to find out the truth for himself. Disguised as a crippled beggar (not much acting was required, as his wounds had left him lame), he hung about this neighborhood in hopes of waylaying and interrogating the page Salīm. Instead, he was able one afternoon to accost Jaydā herself in an alleyway between this house and the marketplace and reveal himself to her. That ordinarily imperturbable woman fell faint to the ground; fortunately she was without the attendants who usually helped her with such chores, and so Umar was able to calm her alarm without attracting undue notice and to tell her quickly all that had happened to him, as well as at whose hands (he was now nearly certain) and for what probable though utterly false cause.

"Dear boy!" Sahīm told me Jaydā had then cried to him. "Leave this city as quickly as you can and never come back, or your life will go the way of your luckless zabb!" *She* quite understood and in large measure forgave what had happened between him and his foster sister, she declared: young people will go at it. She even held Sindbad himself somewhat responsible, for not heeding earlier the same warnings she had given Umar and Yasmīn and taking more care to separate spark from tinder, so to speak. But all that was water down the Tigris now, and had better be left so. She and Yasmīn had truly mourned Umar's reported loss at sea, as (for appearance' sake) had Sindbad; better he *had* been lost, Jaydā felt obliged to say, than suffer what he had suffered and then come back to reopen, to no purpose, those barely closed wounds! His and Yasmīn's lapse had been successfully kept from public knowledge; the girl was in strict seclusion while preparations were completed for her brilliant marriage. Though Sindbad's wrath had been more or less assuaged by a new young Bedou mistress whom Jaydā herself had procured to distract him, her own status in the house was unfairly much diminished by the episode, as witness her having to go to market without assistance. What could possibly be gained by Umar's turning up now, alive but far from intact, just when a fragile peace had been restored to the household? If he needed money to get back to Basra and the open sea, Jaydā was confident that she could secretly convey to him any reasonable amount. . . .

"Shaitana!" Sahīm told me Umar had found himself cursing her, to his own dismay; but at the same moment he realized that Jaydā must only be repeating what Yasmīn — inexplicably! — had told her. Weeping, he apologized, then reported in detail everything that had happened between him and Yasmīn in the courtyard on that fateful night, and insisted that Jaydā take him at once to Sindbad's daughter; or better yet, to father and daughter together, so that he might confront his erstwhile beloved and, though nothing could restore his manhood, at least restore his reputation and perhaps learn on whose behalf he had been falsely accused by the unlikeliest of false accusers.

Impossible, Jaydā insisted in turn (quickly recovering her composure, Sahīm remarked): for one thing, Sindbad was so anxious to get his daughter's marriage safely consummated before Prince Jabāl's vizier could invent further conditions that he would be mortally furious at Umar's disruptive reappearance. Everyone would suffer, and no one benefit — for what good was a clear reputation to a dead man? Moreover, while she did not doubt that Umar honestly believed himself innocent of "Yasmīn's" charges, Jaydā said (which, be it noted, the girl had made or at least had acquiesced to most reluctantly and tearfully, under great stress, and only when the evidence of her fall could no longer be concealed), she, Jaydā, was less certain that he was actually so. As Umar himself had acknowledged, Sindbad's daughter was the last person in Islam to besmirch another's character, least of all her dearest friend's; and he could not deny that wine had always played the Devil with him. . . .

This observation so enraged him (Sahīm said) that once again day turned to night before his eyes. With the greatest difficulty he restrained himself from striking the woman who had raised him from babyhood, and whose determination, once her mind was made up, he was well acquainted with. Much as she loved and pitied him, Jaydā declared, and painful though it was for a mother to choose among her own children, so to speak, she felt her first responsibility to be to his foster sister, whose story, true or not, Jaydā had no choice but finally to accept.

"Then let me at least hear that story from her own lips!" Umar was reduced to pleading. The old woman considered, then acknowledged that on her ward's behalf she had not only attested Yasmīn's virginity for Prince Jabāl but was in the process of restoring it, both physically and spiritually, in time for Yasmīn's bridal voyage to Oman aboard *Zahir* at the year's end. That was a process both arduous and delicate (as well as secret), which Umar's reappearance would spoil irremediably. Whatever the facts of the case, however, she *did* pity his condition. If Umar would vow to her not to reveal his presence in Baghdad or even the fact of his having survived Voyage Five, she would arrange for him to hear Yasmīn herself affirm her account of that voyage's eve — but only if he pledged further to go his poor zabbless way thereafter and leave Sindbad's household in whatever peace Jaydā could contrive for it.

As this was the best bargain he could strike, Umar agreed (Sahīm said), though he could no more imagine not confronting Yasmīn with the cruel falsity of her charges than he could imagine her actually making them. At Jaydā's direction, therefore, he followed her to the shop of Sayyid Hajj Masūd, the distinguished rug merchant and trading partner of Sindbad's, who was to deliver a number of his finest carpets to Basra for loading aboard *Zahir* as part of Yasmīn's dowry as soon as the bride-to-be had completed her selection. While Jaydā distracted the proprietor's attention, Umar rolled himself up in one particular wine-dark Bokhara in a small roomful of carpets set aside for Yasmīn's final inspection — which, he then heard Jaydā promise Hajj Masūd, would take place as arranged . . . the following forenoon.

All that evening, that night, and next morning, then, he was obliged to hold both his peace and his water in that most strait and stifling hiding place. As the teller of this tale can attest from firsthand later experience, he could scarcely breathe there, much less move his limbs, particularly when, at Jaydā's instruction, several other rolled carpets were laid atop his, no doubt to ensure his concealment. Unable to tell night from day, he could not reckon how often he dozed off or for how long, his muscles ever more cramped, his head ever dizzier for want of fresh air and proper blood circulation, his mind spinning dark ruminations: Yasmīn *had* entertained other, tentatively official suitors after Jaydā's insistence that "brother" and "sister" be separated; to hide the depth of their abiding love, they had made some dutiful show of other interests and had had less opportunity than before to confide in each other. Moreover, he had been off voyaging from time to time. . . . But notwithstanding her unusual behavior on the eve of Voyage Five, she was Yasmīn, Yasmīn, Yasmīn!

The hour came at last when through his misery he heard Hajj Masūd welcome Jaydā back to his premises along with "the blushing bride," whom he affectionately scolded for having lately so hidden herself from her old friends. Umar's nerve ends leapt at hearing then the voice he treasured above all other human voices quietly thank her father's partner for his concern and kindness. At Jaydā's insistence, Hajj Masūd left the two women alone to review their list of carpets to be shipped down to Captain Abū Hosayn. With much womanly camaraderie (on Jaydā's part in particular) they speculated as to whether the young Omani prince would prefer for his bride's boudoir this beautiful little specimen from Al Sin, with its delicate floral pattern on a cool blue field, or this large Herīz, with its warmer earth tones. For their initial lovemaking, of course, Jabāl would require a white silk sheet for postcoital display — and once again Jaydā assured her charge that she need have no concern in that quarter if she followed those few simple precautions they had so often rehearsed. But for subsequent bedroom sport Yasmīn would need to balance the softer nap of the Chinese carpet against the superior stain-concealing qualities of the Persian.

"I have had my fill of concealing stains," Umar heard his once-beloved reply, wearily. "If Jabāl still wants me after our wedding night, let him soil every rug in Sohar with our juices. These carpets are his, not mine, and the same is true of my body. Choose whatever pleases your eye, Jaydā."

"Just listen to you!" the older woman chided — and she plunked herself down on the rolled Bokhara in which she knew Umar to be hidden. In a more subdued voice then she declared, "If Umar had kept his hands in his own pockets instead of yours, there would be no need for all this legerdemain. But instead of thanking me for repairing the damage, your father blames me for leaving the two of you alone that night in the courtyard to make your good-byes. And you behave as if you're going to the executioner instead of to a lusty young bride-groom as handsome as he's rich. Allah help us all!"

"Where was Allah's help when my poor brother drowned?" Yasmīn inquired, and Umar's heart leapt as he himself could not. But Jaydā then scolded her in a pointed whisper, "If you must go against your father's orders and speak of that boy at all, why do you insist on still calling him your brother? That makes his forcing you a crime against nature instead of just a young man's drunken rashness."

"No man will ever force me!" Yasmīn cried — no doubt to her duenna's satisfaction. "Not Umar nor Jabāl nor any other! I would put this blade in his heart or my own before I allowed such a thing! *Nothing happened to me in that courtyard that night without my consent.*"

"And you seem determined to announce it to all Baghdad!" Jaydā reproved her. Then in a lighter tone, while moving from carpet to carpet, she added, "Very well: you took advantage of the poor boy's drunkenness to make free with his dear little zabb — not so little by that time, I daresay. May you have as much sport with Prince Jabāl! What about this Tabrīz over here, which Hajj Masūd is so proud of?"

As if repeating a lesson, Yasmīn said, "My brother and I were drunk that night on nothing but each other's kisses. What happened happened, what did not did not, and for each of us there followed what followed, by Allah's will and my father's. I shall go to my husband with no regrets except for Umar's death — and take with me that Ta-brīz, that Herīz, and that blue Chinese as well, along with all the ones we chose before. Enough of this."

Hearing these declarations from Yasmīn's own lips, Sahīm al-Layl told me, Umar al-Yom would for the third time have seen day turn to night had his position allowed sight of daylight at all. Whether from the shock of her words (despite the fondness of their tone) or from want of air, he literally knew no more until he found himself in the captain's cabin of *Zahir*, at quayside in Basra. The longshoremen had found him unconscious in one of the rugs they were loading into the ship's hold and brought him to Abū Hosayn as a would-be stowaway; the captain had recognized the enterprising young Qeshmi pirate and (saying nothing to Mustafā mu-Allim) revived him to learn what was what.

The end of this chapter of Sahīm's story, up to the beginning of ours together, is quickly told. Yasmīn's unwitting confession worked changes on the young man's heart and mind as considerable as those that Sindbad (he was now certain) had worked upon his body on Island Two, Voyage Five. Confident now that Yasmīn, against his whole sense of her, had so wished to conceal an infidelity with someone else (but whom? All candidates seemed equally out of the question) that she had falsely implicated the once-beloved whom she thought lost at sea and unable to defend himself, he determined to revenge himself upon the household. To begin with, he repeated the Qeshmis' business proposal to Abū Hosayn, adding that its terms would be even more favorable if the transactions could be kept hidden from Sindbad. "That might be managed," Abū Hosayn allowed. Sahīm then hinted that having just completed some secret reconnoitering in Sindbad's house on behalf of Prince Jabāl's vizier, he hoped soon to approach *Zahir*'s captain with an audacious but far more lucrative proposition, the nature of which he was not yet at liberty to disclose.

"Airy talk from a man of no authority," Abū Hosayn replied. "Send your captain to me, if he means business." "That I shall," Sahīm promised; "meanwhile, let my proposals be strictly between you and me." "You have made me no proposals yet, young fellow," Abū Hosayn observed; "you have only proposed to do so. Get along with you, now."

Going then to Mustafā's hut, Sahīm embraced him and declared, without explanation, "You have not seen Umar al-Yom, Uncle, and you never shall again. Umar did not return from Voyage Five, because he was lost before that voyage began. Say nothing of this meeting."

"As Allah wills," agreed Mustafā, shaking his head.

At the end of his allotted fortnight, then, Sahīm kept his rendezvous with the Qeshmi pirates, changed his surname from al-Yom to al-Layl to mark the three occasions when day had turned for him into night, and boldly proposed to his captain that instead of doing business with Sindbad the Sailor, they intercept the bride-ship *Zahir* for plunder, rape, and ransom. When that fellow demurred — on the grounds of Sindbad's growing reputation as the most dangerous man in the Persian Gulf — Sahīm al-Layl promptly organized a mutiny of his shipmates, sharked the captain, took command of the vessel (which he renamed *Shaitan*) himself, redemonstrated his ferocity in a number of bloody raids upon the rival pirates of Qatar, established a secret connection with Abū Hosayn at great profit to that crafty fellow, and (seeing to it that their plan was hidden from Mustafā as well as from Sindbad) arranged for *Zahir,* its cargo, and its passengers to fall afoul of *Shaitan* off Qeshm.

There we sailed now, back and forth across the Hormuz Strait, ever on the lookout for *Zahir*'s return, while in bits and pieces I heard the above story from my captor-commander and, in the narrative pauses, apologetically did everything he required of me in this "first island," as he called it, of his revenge. Why did he not trust Abū Hosayn to bring the ransom directly to Qeshm? Because, Sahīm told me, he had learned not only that mentor's lessons but his character. It would not surprise him if Sindbad sent *Zahir* ahead as a decoy and then ambushed *Shaitan* with an armed convoy; nor would he be surprised if Abū Hosayn attempted to double-cross both parties to the hostage transaction by sailing off with the ransom to Al Dibajat or Serendib. And sure enough, when the evening came on which our lookout espied what Sahīm and I agreed must be *Zahir* on the southeast horizon, she was standing full sail past Qeshm for Ras Musandam. By morning, I calculated, she would have rounded that cape into the Gulf of Oman, headed for who knew where, were it not that *Shaitan* was better sailed and (thanks in part to my watch, whose dial glowed in the dark) better navigated.

Unlike the first, this second interception was authentic, though as soon as we drew close enough in the failing light for Abū Hosayn to recognize us, he ordered *Zahir*'s sails struck, saluted Sahīm al-Layl as one might a younger brother, and blamed his vessel's equivocal position on its navigator. That old fellow, he smoothly confided — one Mustafā — had become altogether undependable at his trade, though he was less of a danger in other ways than his captain had expected. Lest the old man report to Sindbad the truth about *Zahir*'s original "capture," Abū Hosayn had duly threatened him with death and at the same time promised him a certain share of the profit, and to both Mustafā had been indifferent: the navigator's job, he had stubbornly insisted, had to do with where, not why. He had not even stepped ashore in Basra when *Zahir* arrived with its dreadful news, much less gone tattling off to Sindbad; nor had he objected in the least to navigating the ransom back to Qeshm — but clearly his skills were not what they had been when he had earned the proud title of mu-Allim.

Sahīm said nothing, but as he looked about for armed escort vessels I saw his right eyelid twitch in a way that I had learned meant anger. Quickly then Abū Hosayn proposed that instead of returning the hostages to Baghdad, we sail both vessels right on down to the Omani port of Sohar, where Prince Jabāl's vizier — with whom Hosayn, too, had been in touch, inspired by Sahīm's remark at their second tête-à-tête in Basra — would give them half of the enormous ransom if they delivered Yasmīn and her bridesmaids to the prince's concubinery. Who but a fool would refuse such an opportunity?

"Neither of us is a fool, I daresay," Sahīm replied. "But we Qeshmi pirates pride ourselves on giving value for money. The sort of thing you propose is bad for repeat business, and I am not done yet with Sayyid Sindbad the Sailor, though I have quite had my fill of his daughter." In an unmistakable tone then he bade *Zahir*'s captain take tea with *Shaitan*'s first mate on the afterdeck while he and I had a private word with that undependable old navigator. Abū objected; the mate's hand drifted to his dagger. Sensing his position and no doubt playing for time to assess it, *Zahir*'s captain salaamed and permitted himself to be led aft.

Sahīm then ordered me to lock his cabin for Yasmīn's protection, and with a bodyguard of our less untrustworthy shipmates, together we warily boarded *Zahir* and sought out Mustafā mu-Allim. We found the old man working by lamplight at his charts, updating *Zahir*'s plotted position by a convenient method that I myself had taught him in return for the many things he had taught me. There followed a reunion among the three of us of such warmth as I need not here describe: if Mustafā was pleased to see me again, in no worse shape than before, he was overjoyed to reembrace Sahīm al-Layl, whom at our previous maritime encounter he had scarcely dared believe to be the same misfortunate Umar al-Yom who had declared himself lost "before Voyage Five began." And my own heart was the more full for returning to the vessel and the man who, for better or worse, had fished me into the world wherein I speak these words.

To us both, then, when he had regained his voice, Mustafā confirmed that Abū Hosayn had once again ignored his navigator's instructions and this time steered *Zahir* for the Musandam cape rather than for Qeshm — the opposite of what he had done before, but with a like objective.

"I am more saddened than surprised to learn that," Sahīm said, "for he, too, was my teacher. But so was Sayyid Sindbad, whom I think of now as the Grand Shaitan himself."

"May you have savored your revenge," said Mustafā, without conviction. "Losing his fortune to a pirate instead of to a shipwreck pained Sindbad as much as losing his daughter's marriage prospects."

Sahīm replied that as I could attest (and I here do), he had savored nothing of what nevertheless he had exquisitely exacted and meant now to exact yet further, in the "second island" of his revenge.

We three then went on deck and together recrossed to *Shaitan*, where by the garish light of oil torches Sahīm assembled the officers and crew of both vessels and, bidding them bear communal witness that the Qeshmi pirates were as good as their word, proceeded with the formalities of exchange. To begin with, he flabbergasted Abū Hosayn (surprised already to see us on such cordial terms with *Zahir*'s "incompetent navigator") by announcing publicly that before the house of "Sindbad the Satan" had turned bright day into dark night, Sahīm al-Layl had borne the name Umar al-Yom.

"Allah forgive me!" *Zahir*'s captain cried. "If I had known *that —*"

"You would have steered the very course you steered," Sahīm responded, "as you would steer it yet if I let you sail off with our ransomed hostages. For that you should be sharked — or, worse, sent back to suffer Sindbad's wrath for having twice betrayed him. But as you were once my instructor in seamanship, you shall now serve as my apprentice in leniency — and as my lieutenant." He then appointed Mustafā to be *Zahir*'s captain and directed him in that capacity to produce first the ransom for Yasmīn's womenservants, while *Shaitan*'s bos'n fetched up from the fo'c's'le those much-abused folk themselves. Bedraggled and wild-eyed, some weeping, others stony-faced, one or two laughing and kissing their captors good-bye, they were one by one released as the proper sum was counted out. Next came payment for the lives only of the six bridesmaids, who were led forth from the midships cabin in their now soiled djellabas and, after showing their faces to Captain Mustafā for identification (and to Jaydā as well, fetched up for that purpose from *Shaitan*'s locked after-cabin), permitted to reveil themselves. As to the additional ransom for their virginity, Sahīm collected it peremptorily for the four who had been kept under more or less scrupulous guard. In the other two cases (those of his lieutenants' unwilling concubines), he transferred the money to the women themselves and gave each her choice: to return with that sum to her family, acknowledging her defloration, or to submit to private inspection by Jaydā and make whatever arrangement she saw fit with her inspector. One, wailing for shame, chose the former course, the other the latter: in whispered conference she and Jaydā went down briefly into *Shaitan*'s midships cabin; when they emerged a few minutes later, the cowled young woman was led off to her companions on *Zahir* while Jaydā, to the sailors' amusement, presented the ransom bag to Sahīm, raised her eyes solemnly to heaven, and announced to all hands that Tufhah was every bit as virginal as the Christian Mary. The officer whose property she had been protested this insult to his virility; Sahīm placated him with what remained of Tufhah's hymen-price.

Next came the penultimate ransom, for Yasmīn's life. When the leathern sacks of coin and caskets of jewels had been assembled on *Zahir*'s gunwales at Mustafā's direction and counted over at Sahīm al-Layl's by his grudging new lieutenant, Abū Hosayn, I was ordered to fetch the hostage and her duenna and escort them back to the erst-while bride-ship. But upon my unbolting the aft-cabin companion-way, Yasmīn stepped forth at once in the same spotless white djellaba and veil she had worn at her capture. The sailors, still merry at the verification of Tufhah's honor, fell silent and made respectful way for her when, ignoring us all, she strode directly to Mustafā, threw back her cowl, and removed her veil. The old man averted his eyes and declared quietly, "The daughter of Sindbad the Sailor has been re-turned alive into her father's keeping."

"Allah be praised!" Jaydā cried, and she hurried to her side while at Sahīm's orders I went to help *Shaitan*'s officers transfer the ransom from *Zahir*'s gunwale to ours. For a long moment Yasmīn turned her face — still unveiled, uncowled, uncowed — to her scarfed and pensive captor's; for a moment less long he returned her unblinking stare, then averted his eyes like Mustafā.

"Dear dead Umar," his victim said, perhaps too softly for him to hear. "Because you stayed her hand that night in the courtyard, your Yasmīn killed herself in a different way. Now Sahīm al-Layl has killed my Umar, and I can mourn him all over again. May Allah forgive both of us."

"Veil yourself!" Jaydā fretted, and she made to do the job for her. But it was I upon whom Yasmīn now fixed her extraordinary gaze for some terrible seconds; I at whose feet she flung her veil when for the thousandth time I said, "I'm sorry," and for the thousand-and-first, "I'm sorry!"

Then only did she raise her cowl and withdraw belowdecks to comfort her sisters-in-misery. Jaydā, however, who started to go with her, was called back by a clearly shaken Sahīm al-Layl and publicly authorized to relay to her ward the same options he had given those two bridesmaids, as proof that the former Umar al-Yom, unlike certain of his teachers and certain of his victims, was as good as his word: if Yasmīn wished to maintain that she had brought her maidenhead aboard *Shaitan* and was departing now without it, let Jaydā attest the loss and return that specific portion of her ransom to Sayyid Sindbad. If, on the other hand, for the sake of her regrettably delayed wedding plans or her future prospects, she wished her duenna to swear otherwise, she was at liberty to forfeit the ransom and do so.

"I am sorry to have to say this," the honorable Mustafā put in here, "but it's only fair to report what Abū Hosayn knows very well: as soon as they heard of *Zahir*'s hijacking, Prince Jabāl and his vizier in effect canceled the wedding by making impossible stipulations, and they refused to contribute to Sindbad's daughter's ransom on the grounds that she could not imaginably now still possess the thing required of a royal bride. Yasmīn ought to reckon that circumstance into her decision."

"I told you the old fool was not to be relied upon," Abū Hosayn muttered to Sahīm al-Layl. "There goes a nice bonus back to Baghdad." But without even consulting Yasmīn, Jaydā proclaimed indignantly to all hands that that piddling princelet of a Jabāl and his eunuch vizier could presume and stipulate and cancel and disengage to their wretched hearts' content. She herself had examined Sindbad's daughter's virtue at the time of her affiancement and pronounced it unsullied: as fresh and untried a wâhât as had ever awaited princely penetration. Throughout their entire sojourn aboard *Shaitan*, moreover, Yasmīn had not been out of her duenna's sight for an eye-blink's time, and as Allah was her witness — not to mention Sayyid Bey el-Loor the Navigator — not a zabb had pierced that pearly portal. Barring some further misfortune between here and home, Sindbad's daughter would return to Baghdad no less virginal than she had left it.

This proclamation was greeted with hoots and catcalls by *Shaitan's* crew especially, every man of whom had heard issuing from their captain's cabin over the days and weeks past the proclaimer's exclamations of woe and vain appeals for Sahīm to have mercy on Yasmīn — not knowing that it was I who implemented his punishing orders and that those orders scrupulously spared the orifice in question, at cost to every other. To reinforce their mistaken impression, Sahīm ostentatiously salaamed to Jaydā, fished a handful of coins from the final ransom bag, and presented them to the duenna with ironical thanks for her having so responsibly safeguarded her charge's wâhât from piratical violation. He further presented her with that little jewel-handled dagger, to be returned to its owner for her self-defense lest some other try what Captain Sahīm al-Layl had refrained from. The balance of the maidenhead ransom, he declared, we would keep — as we had kept the balance of Tufhah's after disbursement of fees and commissions.

Embracing Mustafā but speaking for all to hear, he concluded, "Tell Sayyid Sindbad the Sometime Sailor that Umar al-Yom has had his pleasure and his revenge."

"Poor boy!" I heard the old man reply, not for general hearing. "When did revenge ever fail to breed revenge, so long as men behave to men as men?"

The two ships then unrafted and went their separate ways — which for a time, as shall be seen, were quite the same way. But if by insuring that Yasmīn's reputation had been forever besmirched, Sahīm had achieved the joyless "second island" of his revenge, his navigator (the still-stranded speaker of these words) was far from approaching any comparable station of his sixth voyage. I repeat: for Sindbad's beautiful daughter through her ordeal I had felt considerable sympathy, however equivocal remained the events of "Tub Night" (as Sahīm and I came to call the eve of Sindbad's fifth voyage). For Sahīm as well — he who had paid so dearly for a deed of which he still swore himself to be innocent and for which he had inflicted such unsatisfying vengeance in return — I continued to feel a large measure of pity admixed with my puzzlement and appall. But at no time had I ceased to wonder what in Allah's name (so to speak) had happened to Simon William Behler, once of East Dorset, Maryland, in the fiftieth-or-so year of his life and the nineteen-hundred-eighty-first of the Christian Era, evidently to strand him not only in medieval Islam but in one of the crown jewels of its literature? And to my redoubtable Julia Moore, and to my daughter, Juliette (perhaps by now delivered of her child), and for that matter to such sometime players in my life story as my stolid brother, my former wife, my several friends and professional colleagues? In all the time since my reviving in *Zahir*'s fo'c's'le, remember, I had set foot neither literally nor figuratively on solid ground. My last, ever-fainter hope of orientation if not of "rescue" was to get myself to some island of historical certainty — a city, for example, unequivocally Basra, Baghdad, Abu Dhabi, Abadan — and there either refind at last the world I had lost (complete with U.S. consulate, I hoped) or find undeniably that it and I had lost each other.

For this reason I was at first as gratified as Abū Hosayn was uneasy at Sahīm's decision to "shadow" *Zahir*'s homeward voyage despite the danger of our falling into some trap set by Sindbad or our pirate rivals from Qatar, perhaps in concert. It was to protect Yasmīn and her companions from further piracy that we all but escorted our former hostages home; but Abū Hosayn so feared an ambush that as best as his compromised position allowed, he argued for our running to Oman and dividing "our" ransom with Prince Jabāl in return for that prince's granting us piratical privileges in the Hormuz Strait. Sahīm ignored him, in a way that told me, if not Abū Hosayn, that his lieutenancy was more precarious than he supposed.

On the other hand, our captain denied my respectful request to be relieved of my post and put ashore at Basra in hopes of finding what I sought. "In the first place," Sahīm said, "you won't find what you're after in that town, which I know as intimately as you now know our friend Yasmīn. What you'll find there instead is a painful death at the hands of Sindbad's people for doing what you did to his lying daughter, even though you did it at my order. In the second place, your absence would leave me no one to talk to except myself, and no navigator except Uncle Abū the Fox, whom I wouldn't trust to navigate me to the chamberpot. Why don't we sail for Serendib instead?"

He was serious, more than not. Sometime the next day, by my

reckoning, *Zahir* would reach Basra with the hostages. Shortly thereafter (by Sahīm's reckoning), Yasmīn's formidable father could be expected to embark upon a voyage of revenge, just as Mustafā had
predicted. Having exacted his own revenge — and seen its victim
safely home — Sahīm had no further interest in that quarter, nor any
relish, either, for returning to Qeshm and routine piracy to increase
his now enormous fortune. Truth to tell, he told me, he had lost interest in being Sahīm al-Layl. As he could no more return to being
Umar al-Yom than I could return to being whoever it was that I had
once been, it had occurred to him to sail with me to the place I called
Serendib, which every sailor had heard legends of but which none he
knew had ever visited. Perhaps my magical instrument could navigate
us there?

Sahīm's inclination toward this project was not intense; he simply
had nothing more diverting to do with what remained of himself and
his life. For me, on the other hand, his startling suggestion opened
promising possibilities, quite apart from whatever we might find upon
a literal landfall at the port of Galle in Sri Lanka, whence "my" *Zahir*
had set out in the company of Captain Tim Severin's *Sohar* to retrace
"Sindbad's" voyages. So long a journey could not be undertaken without periodic stops for reprovisioning; with Sahīm's new wealth, once
we were clear of the Hormuz Strait we would be welcomed in any
port. Somewhere along that way, surely — perhaps in the busy strait
itself, which I had several times approached but not yet actually
traversed — I would see what I'd been disappointed not to see thus
far in the Bahr Faris, or Persian Gulf: some unmistakable sign of my
century.

Thus my ever more desperate rationalizing as we retraced our
course down the whole length of the now familiar gulf without my
seeing so much as an outboard engine, a T-shirted fisherman, or a pair
of sunglasses, not to mention oil-drilling rigs, supertankers, and over-
flying aircraft. As day after day of southeasting passed and we reapproached the neighborhood of Qeshm and Ras Musandam, Abū
Hosayn increasingly turned his attention to me, whom he had scarcely
deigned to notice theretofore. Speaking always out of Sahīm's hearing
and feeling his way carefully, he first complimented my navigational
skills and praised the seamanship and general cunning of our captain,

whose nautical education he felt privileged to have overseen on Sindbad's behalf in the years before Umar's misplaced passion for Yasmīn
had turned foster father and foster son against each other.

I shrugged my eyebrows and busied myself with chart-work.

What trouble women were, Hosayn continued in our next such
one-way conversation, especially aboard ship! If he remembered correctly, on the occasion when he had rescued me from the sea, I had
lost my woman and my vessel together; in his opinion they ought
always to be kept apart. Look now what had become of the formidable
Sahīm al-Layl, so lately the terror of the Bahr Faris, whose revenge
upon Sindbad's daughter had been as clever a piece of business as he,
Abū Hosayn, had ever arranged — though he had not at the time
guessed its true motive any more than he had guessed the up-and-
coming young pirate's true identity. Would he imaginably have tried
to outfox his favorite protégé?

I went on with my kamal-work.

Very well, he acknowledged next: that misjudgment had cost him
his share of the hostage-ransom and led to his present humiliation —
the master overmastered by the student! Yet contrary to God's order
though his position was, it troubled him less than the mortal risk at
which we all were being put by Sahīm/Umar's obvious loss of mental
balance. Having satisfied his vengeful lust upon Sindbad's daughter
(whether justly or unjustly, Abū would not presume to say) and ru-
ined her father into the bargain, the man had come within an isba of
getting us all killed by following *Zahir* back to Basra! And now he
meant to carry us out into Allah's ocean, not with any sensible aim
such as trade, piracy, or even further revenge, but in mere whimsical
pursuit of that sailors' mirage called Serendib — of whose particulars
the many fo'c's'le fantasies agreed on but one: it could never be
reached by plotting a course directly for it, but only by sailing in good
faith for elsewhere and losing one's bearings. In Abū Hosayn's opinion, Umar/Sahīm had quite lost his. Did I not agree?

If that was so, I replied, then perhaps we were on course after all
for Serendib.

Though he must have seen that he was getting nowhere with me,
as we rounded the Musandam cape his agitation so grew that he approached me once again and proposed outright that if only for the
sake of Sahīm al-Layl, of whom I was obviously as fond as he himself

had long been of Umar al-Yom, he and I should divert *Shaitan* from its present southeasterly course and sail due south toward Sohar. Under certain little islands just past the cape, he happened to know, Prince Jabāl's vizier had stationed a vessel to receive Sindbad's ransom money, his daughter, or both — whichever Abū Hosayn was able to deliver, either alone or in league with Sahīm al-Layl. The deliverers' reward would be half the ransom, plus a fair slave-price for Jabāl's new concubine if she was part of the package, plus exclusive piracy rights in the Hormuz Strait. Though we were considerably behind schedule and lacking the woman, so great was Jabāl's desire for Yasmīn's wâhât and his vizier's for her ransom that Abū Hosayn thought it likely the vessel would still be on station; if not, we could sail directly to Sohar and complete the business there. We would divide our reward three ways, guarding our friend Sahīm's share for him until the best physicians in Oman had cured his madness. Or if I agreed that his case was past curing, we could help ourselves to his share as well. . . .

I pretended enough interest to ask how he meant to take *Shaitan* south when our intended course down the Gulf of Oman was southeast, as far from Jabāl's navy as we could steer. Did he suppose that our unhappy colleague had so lost his bearings as not to know which way his ship was bound?

His expression more wolf's than fox's, Abū Hosayn replied, "A clever navigator can accomplish much when his captain is belowdecks. And my sense of our shipmates is that they would not be entirely displeased if you and I were to confine him there — for his own good, as Allah is our witness! — and save them from this fool's errand. Their pleasures are in Qeshm and the Bahr Faris, not the open ocean."

I pointed out to him that only in the open ocean, out of sight of landmarks, was such a navigational deception as he proposed likely to succeed, whether practiced by the navigator upon the captain or vice versa — as witness how quickly Mustafā mu-Allim had recognized that *Zahir* was off course. All fox now, Hosayn responded that one day's southing would do the job if we moved promptly, before *Shaitan* was well out into the Gulf of Oman. In keeping with his surname and his disposition, Sahīm was on deck mostly at night, leaving the daytime watches to his junior officers; if we ran south from dawn to dusk tomorrow, we ought to raise Jabāl's vizier's island station. Or we could simply bolt the aft companionway and assume command of the ship.

As it was clear to me that I was in far greater danger from Hosayn than from al-Layl, I temporized by suggesting that we attempt the deception first and resort to mutiny only when it failed, as sooner or later it was bound to. Meanwhile, he could discreetly sound further the sentiments of the crew, and I could plot the required false bearings on our charts. But it was to be understood, I insisted (in order to make my assent more credible) that Sahīm's life would be spared, as he had spared mine, and his share of our reward held in trust for his recovery.

"Done, as Allah is my witness," vowed Abū Hosayn. "For though he has made a target of his archery teacher, I love him still."

That evening, as soon as I could safely do so, I reported these conversations to Sahīm, who received them with neither surprise nor anger, only a listless sigh. "He was indeed my teacher," he acknowledged, "as was Sindbad. It saddens me that he failed to learn his lesson when I forgave his first attempt to fox me." He instructed me then not only to consent to the ruse but to alter our course for the proposed rendezvous at once, as soon as Abū Hosayn went off watch, and (with the aid of my luminescent instrument) to sail it all through that night rather than next day. He would attend to the rest, with no more joy but a good deal less pain than he had settled scores with Sindbad's daughter.

And so it came to pass before morning that the old lieutenant, not the young captain, found himself seized, bound, gagged with his turban, and placed under guard in Sahīm's cabin, where he was presently visited by the ship's barber-surgeon while the captain announced — to my dismay and the crew's delight — that our Serendib plan had been merely a test of their loyalty, which they had passed but their lieutenant had failed. After a certain little business at certain little islands just ahead, we would return to Qeshm, distribute the crew's share of our booty, and sign on whoever wished to sail for our next destination. Very much the cunning pirate captain again, Sahīm then gave them intructions greatly to their liking for the upcoming rendezvous, should it actually take place.

It did, and what ensued must please those who believe that men ought to do to men as they have been, rather than as they would be, done to. By extraordinary fortune we found Jabāl's vizier's pilot boat not only on station in the expected neighborhood but carrying a high deputy of the vizier himself, sent up from Sohar to review the situation and decide whether to recall the vessel or dispatch it to Qeshm to learn how the ransoming had gone and perhaps negotiate a deal with Sahīm al-Layl concerning passage rights through the Hormuz Strait. Sahīm welcomed this deputy and his bodyguards aboard, entertained them on deck, and reported that while his senior colleague, *Zahir's* former captain, was unfortunately indisposed due to recent surgery, he was pleased to send news to Prince Jabāl that *Shaitan* had made off with both the ransom and the principal hostage. We were prepared to pay half the former for exclusive piracy privileges between Ras Musandam and Qeshm, and to make Jabāl a goodwill gift of the latter — admittedly somewhat the worse for wear, but still a worthy addition to the prince's harem.

The deputy could scarcely believe his ears; he would have done well not to. Overjoyed, he asked to see for himself the money and the celebrated young woman — whom his master the vizier had given him to understand had been of questionable purity even before her hijacking. "You shall not only see both for yourself," Sahīm promised, "but count out the ransom with your own hands and examine the woman likewise, however you please and for as long as you like. Both are in my cabin, under the protection of a eunuch." Bidding me accompany them, he then led the excited deputy aft. When the guards made to go with us, however, Sahīm whispered something in the deputy's ear, to which that flush-faced fellow responded by indignantly ordering them to remain on deck, so as not to anger their prince by witnessing the examination that he alone had been deputized to carry out. ("The woman is bound and blindfolded," Sahīm later told me he had whispered. "Whatever you do to her she will blame on me, and Jabāl need never know otherwise.")

All the same, en route with us down the companionway ladder the deputy worried, "Where is that eunuch guard you spoke of?"

"He awaits your pleasure," Sahīm replied, drawing his knife. "Close our hatch, Bey el-Loor, and our guest will open Sayyid Abū Hosayn's."

I take no satisfaction in narrating what followed: how, at the signal of the closed aft hatchway, the deck crew drew their cutlasses and obliged the deputy's bodyguards to stand by in the pilot boat's tender. How Prince Jabāl's indignant but terrified representative, on pain of castration, was made to perpetrate upon the helpless and already egg-less Abū Hosayn, whose wound was bandaged but would never heal, the same outrage that I had been obliged to perpetrate upon an earlier sufferer of Sahīm's justice, similarly bent forward over *Shaitan*'s chart table. How when this "inspection of our gift to Prince Jabāl" had taken place, inspector and inspected were delivered together to the bodyguards' boat, to the considerable amusement of our crew. "Another eunuch to watch over the prince's harem," Sahīm declared to them. "Let's get ourselves back to Qeshm and then on to Serendib." But how, even as we weighed anchor and before our guests' tender had reached its mother ship, we saw Abū Hosayn, his arms and mouth still bound, dumped unceremoniously overside by the deputy's guards.

So much for him, as they say in *The Thousand and One Nights* at such narrative moments. For this narrator's part, I had become sickened by all these plots and passions; sickened, too, by the unswallowability of what every passing day told me must be my position, without ever explaining how it had come to be so. Whoever I was, I was sick of being that person here, in these fantastic and volatile but helpless circumstances. Turning away from the spectacle of Abū Hosayn's drowning — which the crew cheered merrily and Sahīm al-Layl watched with rueful satisfaction — I could almost have wished that my own had not been interrupted (if that is what happened) so long . . .

Ago, I was about to say, out of an unshakable habit of mind, though if I was where I appeared to be, the term had lost its meaning. Of such vertiginous logic or illogic I was also sick; that evening, more determined than ever to find some irrefutable confirmation of my circumstances, I once again begged Sahīm either to set out promptly for "Serendib" or to put me ashore in any major port city whose name I knew, so that I could attempt reconnection with what I am obliged to call *my past*.

By this time he and I had exchanged enough amiable night-sailing conversation for him to understand (as well as anyone in his position could) what I was referring to. For some while he did not respond; I had studied his moods enough to imagine that he was reflecting upon his own situation and next move as well as upon mine, and not without sympathy. Instead of replying directly to my appeal, he presently asked me what was done in Serendib with a man who had lost his manhood to the knife, or whose face had been chopped into such a hash that he must veil it like a woman's? Were such nonmen set to guard other men's harems, or buggered and dumped into the sea like Abū Hosayn?

As his question was clearly half rhetorical, I went into no detail about genital prostheses, hormone therapy, and cosmetic surgery, but gave him simply to understand that the medical arts where I came from could work virtual miracles in cases like his for those who could afford them. Sahīm reached under his wuzara, fetched out my watch, and contemplated its faithfully glowing face. "Have you ever seen me drunk with wine, Bey el-Loor?"

"I have not seen you so much as taste it. The Prophet himself was no more abstemious."

"And yet more than once, in days gone by, Umar al-Yom was drunk as a Christian after a single cup, just as Jaydā and Yasmīn attested. No doubt he said and did things of which he was no more aware the next day than of an unremembered dream."

Seeing his line of thought, I pointed out that the problem with "Tub Night" was not that he remembered nothing, but that he distinctly and in detail remembered otherwise than Sindbad's daughter.

"That is well observed. And yet unlike Jaydā, who is what she is and says what she says, our friend Yasmīn has never to my knowledge spoken less than truthfully on any serious matter, whatever the consequences to herself. Whom on earth can she have been protecting at my expense when she thought me dead, and be protecting so dauntlessly yet, despite all? Honesty has always been a passion with her."

Aware of the voltage on his every utterance of her name, I kept to myself the reflection that Sindbad's daughter had seemed ready enough to deceive Prince Jabāl in the matter of her virginity. Perhaps that subject had lost its seriousness for her for having been made so much of by everyone else.

"How I loved that woman, Bey el-Loor!" Sahīm exclaimed quietly. In hopes of returning him to my subject, I said nothing, but it was clear to me that he had his verb tense wrong. "Tell me truly," he then demanded. "Have you ever had connection with one more beautiful?"

"Never," I said, truthfully, and presumed to add, "Nor ever enjoyed the connection less."

Sahīm nodded, then presently said, "You shall have your wish of a while ago, my friend — though I warn you that unless some genie has changed the world since I left it, what you seek is neither in Basra nor in Baghdad."

He went on to affirm (though it was obvious enough) that he could not get Sindbad's daughter off his mind. It was easier for him to accept what her father had done to him — the old fellow being known to be dangerously erratic since his fourth voyage — than what Yasmīn had done, even though she had believed him dead when she did it. The woman had in effect acknowledged her guilt by begging his forgiveness; she had attempted to take her own life — if not in the courtyard long ago (when he had thought her despairing at their separation!), then unequivocally in *Shaitan*'s cabin — and afterward had maddeningly suffered his obscene punishment as no more than her due. The mystery was driving him to distraction. Before we set out for parts unknown, therefore, he felt compelled to risk yet another voyage up the Bahr Faris, under the excuse of determining how his revenge on the house of Sindbad was working out and what else might be afoot there.

More specifically, he recalled from his youth that Sindbad's household customarily spent the month of Rajab (just now ending) in a pleasant seat on the Shatt al Arab below Basra, dealing with shipfitters and maritime agents of various sorts, before returning to Baghdad for Sha'ban and the holy month of Ramadan. Sahīm proposed to put me ashore there as a castaway, keeping my wristwatch as surety against my return. For the whole month of Sha'ban, while reconnoitering the household on his behalf to see how Yasmīn and her father fared after her ransoming, I would be free to investigate both the port and the capital city for some means of communicating with the world I had lost. He, meanwhile, would lay up in Qeshm to give his crew shore leave, reprovision *Shaitan,* and recruit volunteers for an extended ocean voyage. In the dark of the moon before Ramadan he would return to Basra at risk of interception by the caliph's coast guard and stand for a week off the place where I had been put ashore. If I appeared and reported to him, my watch would be mine again, and I would be free either to return ashore with it or to sail with him for Serendib. If I did not (for whatever reason), he would make his way there, or wherever, without me — much missing my company and conversation. Agreed?

"Agreed," I said at once.

"There is one difficulty," Sahīm said then, and though his mouth was scarfed, his eyes smiled. "For your own safety I want you to approach Sindbad's household as a half-drowned castaway, narrowly escaped from the despicable pirate Sahīm al-Layl. But you have no talent for dissembling. Let's see how far you can swim."

Over the next days, to the crew's amusement and over my protests (the Persian Gulf being almost as rich in sharks as the Red Sea), we found out. Measuring time and distance with my watch, as I had taught him to do, Sahīm would order me overside whenever the wind was gentle and oblige me to swim in *Shaitan*'s wake to the point of exhaustion, while oarsmen rowed a tender alongside to watch for sharks and to retrieve me when my strength was gone. Additionally, he halved my rations to trim me to my role, though my long season at sea had already made me as brown and lean as sun-dried beef.

"Why not kill me outright," I complained from the water, "and go ashore yourself, as you did once before?" I was not so ingenuous, however, as to let myself truly reach the point of exhaustion before feigning that condition, especially since the oarsmen's orders were to "let me drown a bit" at the end of each exercise before rescuing me.

"If Sindbad should catch you in any condition better than half dead," Sahīm explained from the taffrail, "he'll know I sent you." And he added, cryptically, "You have done my office already with our friend Yasmīn; it may be that you'll need to do it again. Swim, swim."

And as if he knew very well that I had been reserving a bit of my strength, when the dark night came for *Shaitan* to heave to off the Shatt al Arab, Sahīm accompanied the four oarsmen who rowed me well up into that broad waterway. Though I could see next to nothing, he steered us confidently along a featureless marshy shore, then far out into the channel and yet farther upstream, carefully measuring the distance with my watch. At a certain point he bade the crew ship their oars and asked whether I could see a tiny light low on the northeast shore, like a fallen star of faint magnitude.

"No."

"It is there. Swim to it, Bey el-Loor, and return our friend's veil to her." That small white garment (which I had retrieved from *Zahir*'s deck and Sahīm had morosely claimed as a souvenir) he now tied around my left wrist in the dark. "I'll look for you here one month from tonight."

"I see no light."

"Upstream at sea level, just under Algol the Demon Star: as bright and steady as Yasmīn's heart. Navigate by it, my friend, and Allah help you. Swim!"

I swam — and swam. The water was mercifully calm and warm, the waterway empty. My heart had sunk earlier at the absence of industrial shipping in this very artery of Iraq; it sank now at the absence of any sign of shore, of anything. A dozen strokes and I lost *Shaitan*'s tender; turning to look for it, I lost my bearings and could only guess which way I had been directed. No light was yet visible to me on shore. I could see the point of Sahīm's bitter joke about Yasmīn's constancy, if he was making one (Algol, in the constellation Perseus, is an eclipsing binary), but not the point of his drowning me — unless his own tormented heart had come to begrudge me what he himself had ordered me to do to Sindbad's daughter. Nor could I find Algol, though intermittently through the clouds I made out one or another of the Perseid constellations or the Dippers and corrected my course as best I could northeastward. I swam, rested, swam, swam, farther than I ever had behind *Shaitan,* and only as I approached the limit of my strength did I begin to see, or think I saw, a tiny light, low and impossibly distant on the water ahead. I swam and floated, changed strokes to use different muscles, grew chilled despite my exertions and the mild water, lost sight of that light and refound it, never brighter. Swam.

I speak these words, and so must have managed once again not quite to drown. Mindless from exhaustion, I came at very long last indeed to muddy shallows and mucked myself lightward belly-down across odorous flats like the first amphibian. There was no *next thing I knew*; I knew I had not lost consciousness this time, only come perilously near the end of it. I knew I was not crawling back into "my" world from the world of Sindbad the Sailor, only — but never more welcomely — from sea onto land for the first time since Julia Moore and I had set sail from "Serendib." I knew (or at least supposed) that Sahīm al-Layl had after all not meant to drown me, only to make convincing my castaway's credentials, for though I could no longer see the light that he had known was there to guide me, I came to the stucco walls of the isolated shoreside house that it must have shone from. Aching, shivering, faint, I hauled myself to its massive wooden gate; I rapped and pleaded in Allah's name, *rap tata tap-tap,* and, when that deity did not respond, with the last of my last strength called out, "Yasmīn!"

She was asleep (I would learn later), her duenna not — or else that name, spoken by a male voice, waked and alarmed her. Instead of sending to learn who spoke it, she trudged herself to the gate's inside and asked. I recognized her raspish voice and, scarcely believing my luck, cried, "Good Jaydā, for God's sake help me! I'm the navigator Bey el-Loor, escaped from *Shaitan,* half drowned and freezing!"

Full of suspicion, she obliged me to repeat my name several times through a small grilled window in the gate; also the name of the ship I had jumped, its captain, that captain's name before he had been a captain, how I came to be where I was, and what I wanted from her at that black hour.

"A dry corner to sleep in," I begged, "and a crust of bread in the morning, as Allah lives!"

She supposed I had come with my band of brigands to kidnap and abuse them all again while Sayyid Sindbad was off a-voyaging to Serendib. I perpended that datum — at once concerned for Sahīm's sake and wondering why I should care in the least what happened to him — and swore I was alone, harmless, helpless, suffering from exhaustion and exposure, at her mercy. Not so, Jaydā suggested: my cohorts were hiding in the marsh nearby, ready to rush the gate as soon as she unbolted it and rape and pillage the household. So our dialogue went until, my teeth chattering, I could do no more than moan and fist the door. Unknown to me, Jaydā had drawn out her interrogation in order to rouse the one servant at her disposal (her son, the page Salīm, whose office it was to mind the gate but who had slept soundly through my first calls) and dispatch him to fetch rope and a lantern. These she passed through the inward-opening grille and obliged me first to show her my face in the lamplight, then to show that I was alone and weaponless, then to sit on the ground outside and tie my ankles together with one end of the rope, and finally to pass the free end back inside through the reclosed grille for her to secure before her two scimitared eunuch guards (so she swore) opened the gate just far enough for me to thrust my hands inside for tying.

Only then, when the gate was refastened behind me, would she unbind me and give me bread and water and a dry rug to sleep on; but come morning I must begone.

These elaborate precautions I excused on the grounds of Jaydā's *Shaitan* experience and her master's absence. Not without misgivings, but fearing hypothermia if I remained any longer outside, I did all she required. When my hands were duly bound, however (by whom, I could not see), and I was at last permitted to shuffle on bare knees through the partly opened gate, I found no armed guards, only the black-veiled duenna and a wary young manservant holding the lamp that I had returned upon their first opening the gate a hand's width. He slammed and rebolted it; she fell upon me like a vengeful ifritah, cuffing, clawing, kicking me to the ground, and crowing, "Now we'll see who does what to whom! Wake your sister, Salīm! Tell her to come look at the fine coney we've caught for her!"

As I did not know then who "Salīm" was, I was too far gone in dismay and pain to register the phrase *your sister* and relate it to Sindbad's daughter. I know now that after her first alarmed surprise at learning who and in what state I was, resourceful Jaydā had quickly seen an opportunity to improve her standing in Sindbad's household, much diminished (as was her master's estate) since Yasmīn's ransoming. He blamed her for not having foreseen and forewarned him of *Zahir*'s hijacking — "As if it's the well's job to carry water to the bucket!" I would later hear her complain. Even the young Bedou dancing girl she had procured for him had not assuaged Sindbad's disgruntlement; Jaydā and Yasmīn were virtually exiled from the Baghdad establishment while he prepared grimly for Voyage Six, amid dark hints that if he did not both recoup his lost fortune and exact his revenge, they would suffer worse. Hence Jaydā's joy at the prospect of delivering to him upon his return, for the most exquisite retribution, the very instrument of his daughter's humiliation and his own. "What times we'll have!" she exulted, pummeling and spitting on me while I did my best to shield my face and crotch. "Sharp knives and boiling oil! A red-hot sword down your gullet and another up your fundament!"

I had thought I would never reach shore; now I wished I had not. But stronger than fear, pain, dismay, stronger even than despair was merciful exhaustion, which came to my rescue before "Salīm's sister" could.

Rescue me she did, however, unknown to me and much against the inclination of her chagrined, exasperated, but finally subservient duenna. Sore consciousness returned to me on a proper couch in a comfortably appointed room, my arms and legs unbound, my body cleaned of mud and spittle, my wet wuzara replaced by soft coverlets, my worst contusions soothed with compresses, my reviving monitored indifferently by Sayyid Salīm, who some while after daybreak said, "He's awake now."

"Leave us, then," replied a voice I knew, in a tone more restorative than ten compresses for its absence of malice. "But tell Jaydā please to wait at the door in case I need her."

There was warm bread, warm tea, warm sunshine in the window — and a familiar jewel-handled knife on the tea tray, within its owner's ready reach. There was Yasmīn, cowled and veiled and wary, her green eyes large with pained wonder but clear of wrath, not to mention vengefulness. "Ignore Jaydā's threats," she advised me — and now I saw that in her hands she held the veil I had swum with on my wrist. "You did nothing to me that you were not obliged to do, except apologize." The recollection filled her eyes with tears, which she stanched with that second veil. "When you can talk," she went on presently, when *she* could, "tell me truthfully why you came here with this. Did you really escape from poor Umar, or did he send you?"

"Both," I said at once, and as soon as I was able, I told her the full story: Umar's version of "Tub Night" and of her father's fifth voyage, wherein Sindbad himself had been the monstrous Old Man of the Sea; Umar/Sahīm's ongoing love and bafflement and rage; his mutilation and transformation; his eavesdropping at that rug merchant's shop with Jaydā's connivance; his collusion with Abū Hosayn and Hosayn's with Prince Jabāl's vizier; his revenge upon that pair — and the frustrate desperation that had led him back virtually to the doorstep of his tormentor and victim and had dispatched me across that doorstep on his business as well as my own.

"I'm supposed to report to him how badly your reputation has been damaged," I said, "and whether you've told your father that Umar al-Yom was innocent. But I half suspect that what he really wants to believe is Jaydā's version of that night. Then he could feel guilty twice over, return the ransom, beg your forgiveness and your father's, too, and accept his condition as deserved. As is, he's miserable."

Instead of registering dismay at any of this, Yasmīn regarded her lap. "What do *you* think happened, Sayyid Bey el-Loor?"

"Why should I care?" I almost wept. "I'm fifty years old. I've lost everything I value, including a daughter your age. I don't know where I am or how I got here. All I want is to find an American embassy to get me back home."

The young woman nodded, then raised her beautiful eyes to me in a serious new way. "What will you do there, without your woman-friend? But that's not for me to wonder." All bright purpose now, she tucked away her knife (wrapped in the veil I'd brought her) and declared, "Here is what I think, Bey el-Loor: we go to Baghdad tomorrow, and you shall come with us. If my father were there, he would kill you on principle, but he and Mustafā and *Zahir* have gone to sea again and will not be back soon. You have all of Sha'ban to do your business and Umar's before *Shaitan* returns for you, and I'll help you with both if you'll ask me nothing further ever about what you and Umar call Tub Night — though I can tell you now that nowhere in the City of Peace have I ever seen or heard of such things as that navigation machine you used to wear on your wrist. But you shall observe that for yourself, as you shall observe me and my situation to your heart's content. At the month's end you may swim back to *Shaitan*, if you have not already swum back to where you came from, and report what you wish to my poor lost brother."

Inspired by her plan, she pulled off her other veil, asking herself, "Why do I wear this in your presence, when you've so often seen much more than my face? Look at me, Bey el-Loor! You and I shall be friends, as Umar and I once were. I'll show you my world and my strange place in it while you tell me about yours. But never speak to me of what happened between us aboard *Shaitan* or ask me questions I don't wish to answer."

Those were promises easily made and kept. If I was distressed at Yasmīn's confirmation that her Baghdad was not after all the modern capital of Iraq, I was overjoyed by her offer of assistance and friendship, much moved by her lack of vindictiveness, and — though still

rich in questions and reservations — struck afresh by her beauty. By
her enterprise, too, and her resourcefulness. Calling in Jaydā (who
affected consternation at seeing her unveiled), Yasmīn candidly announced her plan: to smuggle me not only into her father's principal
house but into her private apartment in its harem, from which I could
safely observe both her life in the household, on Umar's behalf, and
the city round about, on my own. But the page Salīm must know
nothing of the matter, she declared, or all Baghdad would hear of it.

"What madness is this?" Jaydā protested. "How can such a thing
be done?"

"By the same clever means that you employed to carry poor Umar
to Basra from Hajj Masūd's rug shop," Sindbad's daughter replied
pointedly, "without bothering to tell me how you had tricked both
him and me."

"Allah forgive me," Jaydā said with a shrug. "The knife was at my
throat."

"As it was at our friend's here when he did what he did," Yasmīn
reminded her, and she smiled at me warmly through fresh tears. "For
which reason I forgive him, as I forgive you but not myself. Tell Salīm
I've sent our visitor back into the marsh he crawled from, and let's be
off to Baghdad."

To Baghdad I went, not on a flying carpet but inside a tightly rolled
one, by upstream barge and donkey-back, over what uncomfortable
period of time I could not measure, to the house in which I speak
these words and to the strangest, sweetest lunar month of my half
century, which I here compress into a few pages:

My rescuer happened, at the time just narrated, to be on the verge
of menstruation. To this circumstance she would attribute, when I
came to know her better, both her ready tears in the scene foregoing — as if the matters spoken of were not cause enough for tears! —
and the fact that except for that brief unveiling I scarcely *saw* her
(though I spoke with her often) during my first few days in Baghdad.
Having been rugged into her rooms — evidently by night and by
three or four grunting women, who complained, "What's *in* here,
Jaydā?" — I was unrugged at last, in total darkness, by Yasmīn herself
and alone, though Jaydā (she let me know) stood by always either just
outside or just inside the door. I was of course never to speak above a
whisper; a strange male voice would bring the harem down on our

heads. For my discomfort in transit she apologized; such of my needs as food and drink, wash-water and clean linens and chamberpot, she and Jaydā would minister to, and supply whatever else I required or requested. For the first few days, until she could make proper arrangements, I would have to forgo physical exercise beyond quiet calisthenics there in the room. As soon as possible she would find a way for me to make surreptitious excursions into the city in pursuit of my personal business; meanwhile, she would inquire of her father's associates whether Baghdad contained such a thing as an embassy from the island of America. As for Umar/Sahīm's business: through a grilled window overlooking the central courtyard I would be able to observe by daylight and evening lantern-light the house's routine and her current role in it, which each night, when the household had retired and she could visit me unnoticed, she would also provide me with a full account of and answer my questions about. Given the nature of the situation, she could not (she said levelly) provide me as well with one of the slave women to attend to my physical gratification, as her hospitable father would do if I were his official houseguest; and needless to say, my least gesture of that kind toward her would be met with the jewel-handled knife and a general alarm. But if there was anything further I required . . .

"Pen and paper," I surprised her by replying at once, "and a copy of *Kitab Alf Laylah Wah Laylah*." With herself as my Scheherazade, I explained, I wanted to hear on location, as it were, in the language that I had learned pretty well to speak but could not yet read, the famous tales of Sindbad the Sailor and what Yasmīn might have to say about them. And because in my other life I had been not exactly a teller of tales but a successful reporter of my own adventures (none of which compared with what had happened to me since my rescue by the bride-ship *Zahir*), it had occurred to me that if I was going to be in more or less solitary confinement for a while, here was my first opportunity to rebegin the journal I had lost with my own *Zahir* off "Serendib." Although I would likely be articulating my predicament for no reader except myself, it would give me some comfort to resume the professional habit of registering my experience in written words.

There was, clearly, something queer in all of this — in Yasmīn's elaborate combination of restrictions, precautions, and risk-taking solicitousness, and in my more than patient acquiescence to a confining and potentially dangerous arrangement. "Umar's business" (which I had thought would anger her) she could readily have dealt with in a single conversation back in Basra; there was no need for her to *show* me her compromised position in the household since her ransoming. And my own concerns she could better have addressed by bidding me good-bye and turning me loose in the city, to confirm for myself what world and time I was astray in. Her fascination with my two requests was genuine: though she had not heard of *The Book of the Thousand and One Nights* (and she was a well-educated woman, versed in both the Koran and secular literature), she knew a number of the stories from it, not the Sindbad tales ("How can there be tales of my father's seven voyages," she asked, "when he's only now making his sixth?") and not the story of Scheherazade herself and King Shahryar, which moved her to tears of admiration when I recounted it for her, but the beast-fables and other older items in Scheherazade's repertoire, some of which were to be found in the book she brought me instead, an Arabic translation of the eleventh-century Sanskrit *Kathā Sarit Sāgara,* or Ocean of Story. As for my own authorhood, although she had only my word for it (and though "Baylor's" fame "back there" had been less than immense), it gave me a considerable new status in her eyes. Raised as she had been in a culture in which autobiography was all but unknown, she found the idea of publishing one's rather ordinary adventures and misadventures (even of the more intimate sort), as if they were exemplary, for the entertainment of strangers, not self-evidently admirable; with only a little prompting, however, Yasmīn came to see in it the possibility of experience's imaginative redemption (into art, I presumed to say), and thereby, perhaps, of its vindication.

So far, so good: she *was* genuinely intrigued by all of this, and she drew me out, as far as our time and circumstances permitted, on the outlines of what I have since called my several "voyages." I in turn was intrigued to hear from her (and to see through my window grille) more of the house and history of her formidable father: the tales he — and Jaydā — had told her of his fabulous first three voyages, his traumatic and life-changing fourth, his allegorical, equivocal fifth; also her own constrained girlhood under Jaydā's tutelage and her thwarted wish to hazard forth like her father and her "brother." Unobserved, I observed for myself the uneasy relations among Sindbad's new favorite, Kuzia Fakān, her predecessor Jaydā, and Yasmīn — who, to placate her father's creditors, presided over his ever-hospitable table in his present absence. I saw, as well as heard from her, how they all treated her respectfully, sympathetically, even admiringly . . . as irreparably soiled merchandise of unusually high quality. On that basis, she gave me uncomplainingly to understand, she would be auctioned off, one way or another, upon her father's return from "Serendib," to whoever would marry her after her presumable but unmentionable rape by the Qeshmi pirates. All this I saw and heard, along with the abundantly flowing fountains, strutting peafowl, and elaborate gardens of Sindbad's house, the eloquent performances of his dancers and musicians (who rehearsed daily in that Gulistan of a courtyard, where I could watch them), and his celebrated Tub of Truth. I learned which of the dinner guests was the obliging rug merchant Hajj Masūd, which the wealthy and cautious elder Hasīb Alī, which the aggressive parvenu Ibn al-Hamrā. Yasmīn in turn learned sketchily of tidewater Maryland, of "Baylor's" profitable misadventures in North Africa and southern Spain, of the further attrition of his innocence in the Virgin Islands, and rather more of his subsequent, ultimate loss, between his *Zahir* and hers, of all that had then to him mattered — and there we were.

There we were, conversing in murmurs hour after hour, night after night, through a darkness that would have been total if not for the slowly waxing moon of Sha'ban. Respectful of Yasmīn's ground rules, neither by gesture nor by inquiry did I trespass, stirred though I was in my singular loneliness by the gracious sight of her moving daily about the courtyard, balancing the uneasy tensions among herself, Jaydā, and Kuzia Fakān, dealing deferentially yet spiritedly with her father's associates — and then slipping silently into "my" room when all were abed to sit over by the grilled window, her face and caftan filigreed by moon-shadow, to hear what I had written that day, and speak and listen, ask and answer. Scheherazades both, I told her we were, yarning till just before early prayer call, but to our narratives rather drawn than compelled; in a certain danger but under no particular threat; by turns teller and told.

"And Jaydā is our Dunyazade," Yasmīn said, laughing for the first time in our conversation, "hearing and seeing everything from the foot of the bed. You're supposed to beg for more, my sister!"

Almost invisible by the door, Jaydā sniffed and said nothing. To myself, as the moon waxed nightly brighter upon my beautiful visitant, I reflected that there was yet another difference between Scheherazade's situation and ours. To speak of it would have been to transgress the bounds I had agreed to, but just as the moonlight defined the window grille by illuminating what was not it, so our nightly narratives, exchanged in ever growing confidence and trust, by scrupulous avoidance defined two subjects much on our minds, and they in turn implied a third. The first of these — and the least among my own concerns, for it concerned me least — remains a mystery yet to the "present" speaker of these words (though not to their later writer): what exactly had happened between Yasmīn and Umar al-Yom out in that courtyard back on "Tub Night"? Whom had she later protected from her father's anger by permitting Umar to be blamed, when she thought him lost at sea? And why had she not since her ransoming confronted Sindbad with his crime against his evidently innocent foster son, if indeed (as appearances argued) she had not?

The second subject more and more possessed my reflections as I watched, listened to, and whispered with the young woman who sat by then so easily an arm's length from me in our moonlit tête-à-tête: how I had, after all — though under duress, against both our wills — repeatedly, by moonlight, lamplight, daylight, in the captain's cabin of *Shaitan,* seen what I'd seen, done what I'd done . . . and, human animal, felt what I'd felt. I had been invariably as gentle as Sahīm al-Layl would permit me to be: apologetic, appalled, in no way "responsible," as I knew she knew. How did she feel about me now, I wondered, concerning that? (This was the third subject.) She had "rescued" and spared me in the Basra marshes; she had gone and was going the extra parasang to accommodate my "business" (though neither of us, for the present, pressed the matter of her turning me loose in Baghdad to search for the U.S. embassy). Along with her expectable and well-justified shock at that interlude, as along with mine on her behalf, could it be that, now that we knew each other better and so obviously trusted, respected each other . . . ?

Midway through the second week of my sequestration, as she recounted mutedly her girlhood disappointment at being obliged to stay behind with Jaydā in Baghdad while Umar went down for the first time to Basra to go to sea with her father, without thinking I sympathetically touched Yasmīn's bare forearm. She recoiled as if from a burn. Jaydā hissed warning. But when I apologized at once, Yasmīn apologized in turn and, remarkably, went so far as to take the offending hand in her own before resuming her story — to which I could scarcely then attend, so distracted was I by our skins' reunion. The night after that, as I happened to be explaining (as delicately as I could manage) how "Crazy Daisy" Moore had come to call me by the nickname Persimmon, or merely 'Simmon, Yasmīn again caught up my hands in hers, first one and then the other. At once smiling and (to my astonishment) weeping moonlit tears that had little to do with my story, she pressed our hands to her cheeks and echoed, "Sīmon. Sī-mon." Again, from somewhere behind me, Jaydā sibilated.

But as if her new name for me had turned some key, Yasmīn not only kept my hands clasped tight but regarded me through her tears in a different way and made as if to draw me to her. In the event, as I was the heavier and surprised into immobility, it was herself she drew, from her cushion onto me and mine, repeating, "Sīmon! *Sīmon!*" Before I could embrace I was embraced, kissed before I could kiss — Jaydā already bewailing, from her station, the imminent undoing of her artful reconstruction-work. Fearful still of my position, respectful of my young friend's feelings, and not a little overwhelmed, I gladly yielded her the initiative until Yasmīn made it wordlessly clear that Jaydā's minatory presence notwithstanding, I was to take it — take . . . what Sahīm, though demanding so much else, had forbidden.

And so I took; Yasmīn likewise. And we gave, the pair of us — Yasmīn as if releasing something long reserved, though not likely for its present recipient. Then we rested and (myself hardly believing) regave, retook, as I for one had not since who could measure when — until, near moonset, one or both of us gave forth such a cry of pleasure that to cover it, Jaydā howled over us from the dark doorway like a moonstruck hound. Her baying roused the courtyard peacock, who returned a raucous trumpeting that roused the roosters round about, and they their farther neighbors, until all Baghdad resounded with our joy.

Well. Fifty then, no younger now, I had and have done, been, and known what and whom et cetera; was neither innocent nor cynic; remained no less lost for being so extraordinarily found. Though certain subjects were still taboo to speech (and upon the others, from that night forward, fewer words were spent), from our bodies' dialogue all curbs were raised. So fluently did they converse as Sha'ban waxed resplendent that whatever Yasmīn's feelings and despite the un-healed wound of my losing Julia Moore, for the fourth time in my five decades I found myself in love.

Which circumstance posed a problem even as our moon, contrary to our passion, began noticeably to wane. Never mind, for the present, I said to Yasmīn, the United States embassy (in my heart I knew there was none in this Baghdad), the world I had fallen out of, my concerns and griefs and problematical identity therein, the metaphysics of my fall. Whoever and wherever I was, here I was, in my life's early autumn, in love with Sindbad the Sailor's daughter. Of what concern to me was her equivocal past, for which she had paid dearly enough? With her consent, I went so far one night as to declare, I meant to put my case — *our* case — to her father man to man upon his return, and with or without his blessing to go on somehow with our story.

Once more that peacock's sleep was rent as Yasmīn, not this time in delight, joined her cry to Jaydā's. Simplest of Sīmons, invincibly naive, incorrigibly romantic! To Tub Night and *Shaitan* days was forthwith added a third taboo, much more difficult to abide: no fur-ther mention of Sindbad's "blessing" — Allah spare us! — or of her-and-my "future" beyond her father's return from Voyage Six or the onset of Ramadan, whichever came first. Deservedly or not, she had been through much, as had I. Although a fair part of her ordeal had been at my involuntary hands, she had respected and admired me be-fore, after, and even in course of that ordeal, which, one way and another, had brought her during our recent intimacy to feel . . . what she now felt for me. But this present idyll, two-thirds run, was all our future; seize the night, she bade me, and waste not another of its precious minutes in foolish talk of her father's "blessing"!

In this matter she was unrelenting; in every other so altogether winsome that my remaining days under her roof were all-but-unen-durable anticipations of our nights. If I wrote at all, it was of but one subject. If from my inkwell a genie had sprung to offer me transpor-tation home, I'd have accepted on one condition only, absent which I would have bidden him, "Back to your well, sir: if my Julia is no more, I have no home but Sindbad's daughter." To spend yet more time with me, in Sha'ban's last week Yasmīn feigned illness — specifically, pre-menstrual malaise of such bed-confining severity that Jaydā alone of the household was permitted access to her. Our last three days like one long night, we loved and slept, played, and talked wide-openly of everything . . . except the main things.

The sixth voyage of Sindbad the Sailor was by far his shortest. In midembrace on a certain afternoon we heard across the courtyard the page Salīm announce sardonically to Kuzia Fakān and the others that the master of the house had already rereached Basra, once again wealthy, once again shipless, once again his voyage's sole survivor, except perhaps (it was uncertainly reported) for Mustafā mu-Allim. Yasmīn closed her eyes, covered my ears, and bade me carry on with our story, not just then of the verbal kind. Simon William Behler made a decision, of which he did not speak. Yasmīn likewise; or rather, she bade Jaydā in their private language to act upon the decision that she had made some days, perhaps weeks, before. Moments later she was overtaken in unequivocal fact by what she had been feigning, and by its attendant discomforts.

The sixth voyage of still-stranded Somebody was likewise his briefest, however long its story; would seem so to its sailor and recounter, at any rate, even had it lasted ten thousand nights and a night. In fact it ended on this last one, last of Sha'ban. Silenced by Salīm's news and Yasmīn's menses, we took time out from our wordless narrative for tacit tea, fetched in as usual by expressionless Jaydā. Into my glass whereof, as I cannot say I hadn't half expected . . .

Still to be told is what Mustafā mu-Allim, though sworn to silence, confided to "Bey el-Loor" of Sindbad's sixth voyage, in bits and pieces through the hungry month of Ramadan, while once more following Captain Allim al-Yom's cardinal rule of human conduct by fish-chowdering me back to wretched consciousness:

How the redoubtable *Zahir*, refitted for corsairing and crewed largely by out-of-work pirates from Qatar, serendipitously came upon *Shaitan* between Kharg and Qeshm (a sluggish, ill-sailed *Shaitan*, it seemed to Mustafā) and, per program, made ready to feign surrender, though in truth she was massively armed and ready. How, to their surprise, the Qeshmis fled — not for their home base but down-gulf, toward the Hormuz Strait — and were not only quickly overtaken but as quickly overwhelmed by Sindbad's Qataris, who were eager to settle scores with their competitors. How, however, they discovered their victims to be not Sahīm al-Layl and company but none other than Prince Jabāl and his vizier, commanding a prize crew from the prince's navy. Outraged by Sahīm's outraging of his vizier's deputy, Jabāl had led a large Omani task force to clear the strait of pirates and had successfully destroyed the Qeshmis, their base, their formidable but unexpectedly listless captain, and all their ships except *Shaitan,* onto which trophy they had loaded the entire confiscated pirate treasury, including Yasmīn's dowry and double ransom. So rich was the haul that prince and vizier had transferred themselves to the prize-ship to oversee its delivery to Sohar; but only the night before *Zahir*'s arrival on the scene, a terrific squall had separated the overburdened *Shaitan* from her escorts, leaving her alone just long enough for lucky Sindbad to complete his revenge and make his getaway.

How Yasmīn's former fiancé had bargained vainly for his life in exchange for a certain potency-amulet that he had taken from the late Sahīm al-Layl, together with the testicles that that already-dezabbed pirate had girded with it. No deal, had said Sindbad — all the more readily when Mustafā recognized that amulet as one whose demonstrable potency was of a different character. How then (the luckless Omanis planked and sharked), at risk of being overtaken at any moment by Jabāl's navy, Sindbad had insisted against Mustafā's advice that three quarters of the booty be then and there transferred to *Zahir*; he could neither abide, he said, to step aboard the vessel of his daughter's ruination nor on the other hand trust any except himself and Mustafā to steer his treasure home. The remaining quarter — a fortune in itself — he had generously awarded to the Qataris among his crew, together with the ship *Shaitan* and (as if the boon were his to dispense) full piracy rights in the Hormuz Strait, which he himself had no intention ever again of traversing. Not bothering to tell them what only he and Mustafā had learned from shit-frightened Prince Jabāl — that the Omani task force was regrouping just over the southern horizon — he salaamed them off in that direction and himself ran north with Mustafā and *Zahir*'s skeleton crew of three Persians from Siraf.

How *Shaitan* has not been heard from since, nor is likely ever to be.

How that trio of Sirafis, alas, almost within sight of Basra and their journey's end, had together succumbed to "a mysterious sea-distemper," leaving old Sindbad not only the sad responsibility (munificently discharged since) of consoling their families with the sailors' back wages plus a handsome bonus, but also the quite impossible job of bringing *Zahir* into harbor, by night, under full sail in a strong following breeze, single-handed except for his even older navigator. Unable between them to manage tiller, sails, and anchor tackle on so sizable a vessel, they could wait for neither daylight, calmer air, nor assistance; it required the pair of them simply to steady the helm against broach and capsize. As it was infeasible for them to lower sail or reverse course, they had either to charge full-tilt into the harbor and ram the first convenient breakwater, wharf, or moored vessel, or else run *Zahir* hard aground somewhere in the marshes near the port.

"Aground, aground," Sindbad had ordered, inasmuch as the harbor proper was deep enough to sink in. "If I could run her straight into the Sahrā al Hijārāh, I would do it." Who else but Mustafā mu-Allim, however, could have picked out in that black waterway a certain faint low longshore gleam and plowed *Zahir* neatly into a mud flat at the virtual front door of her owner's marsh-side establishment? Though the impact brought down the ship's mainmast and sprang half her bottom seams, it left her high and almost dry and doubtless salvageable had not Sindbad resolved to let her rot right where she rested (once her cargo was off-loaded), a memorial to his six voyages and an admonition against any seventh.

How her navigator, unnecessarily sworn to silence and offered any emolument he wished (up to twenty-five percent of the voyage's net profit after the reimbursement of Sindbad's ransom-creditors), had asked for two things only: his master's leave to retire from navigation to the life of a hermit salt-marsh fisherman, and that minuscule odd amulet-machine that poor "Sahīm al-Layl" had taken from a nameless outlander (who claimed to have fetched it from "Serendib"), Jabāl from Sahīm, Sindbad from Jabāl — so that he, Mustafā, might spend his last years studying its construction and true operation. "No," had replied Sindbad, whom one might almost suspect of coveting automatically anything desired by those he respects. "That amulet I intend as a gift to the Commander of the Faithful." "As Allah wills," said Mustafā, shrugging, and uninterested in other compensation, he set off for his solitary hut not far up-marsh.

How Sindbad the Sailor then returned in lonely triumph to the City of Peace with his splendid treasure and his no less splendid (though figurative) story of the voyage to Serendib, his adventures in that magic isle, and the magnificent gift — of jewels, robes, rare unguents, inlays, ivories — entrusted to him by its caliph for Caliph Haroun al-Rashīd. In the face of such munificence, who would incline to credit niggling rumors from Oman, Siraf, Qatar?

How, however, that gift did *not* include, nor Sindbad's story so much as mention, a certain exotic thingamabob, allegedly an amulet, believed in some quarters to recharge declining male sexual potency.

How then its new possessor, restored to his household just in time for Ramadan, drained his ponds and fountains, sanded his gardens, throttled his peafowl, cactused and cameled his courtyard, plowed his Bedou mistress till he tired of her and began once more to lust for his long-late wife Marjānah, and opened negotiations for the marriage of his daughter to the redoubtable, crimson-visaged entrepreneur Ibn al-Hamrā. To whom also he confided a tremendous new investment opportunity: Voyage Seven, back to Serendib on what would almost certainly be the caliph's orders despite Sindbad's own inclination, for the purpose of establishing diplomatic and trade relations between Baghdad and that fabulous, elusive land. . . .

No: the somebody whose "hows" those are to narrate in firsthand detail is our host (and his retired navigator), not he whose lover named him Sīmon, Sīmon, Sīmon; who, from mint tea handed him by her, revived stark naked in a tidal marsh, on an unrolled carpet on a spot of dry beach ensconced by cattails and spartina and lapped by the olive shallows of a wide, sun-bright estuary on which nothing moved but wavelets. No people, buoys, boats in that sparkling, sharp-focused scape; it could have been East Dorset or Iraq, the Chaptico or China, in any century since the last ice age. My head's inside was similarly, almost preternaturally (and precariously) clear; likewise, for some moments, *cueless*. Then all came back and down.

"Bhang," opined gentle Mustafā. "A skillfully measured potion, in your tea. Try this instead." Yasmīn's wine-dark Bokhara — our "magic carpet" — was now on the mud floor of his hut beside the Shatt al Arab, this narrator still on that carpet, my senior ex-colleague beside me with mullet soup in lieu of Ramadan harira. "Allah understands," he assured me, with respect as much to our bending the dietary rules as to what had befallen myself, Umar/Sahīm, and the worthiest master navigator who ever behaved to humans humanly. Over the next weeks, while I regathered strength, purpose, and even some composure by assisting him with his nets, we exchanged our stories. Mustafā showed me the grounded wreck of *Zahir,* already stripped of every usable bit of gear by the Basra fishermen. I showed him the spot not far away where I had crawled ashore on miserable Umar/Sahīm's errand and been carpeted off to Paradise, whose serpent I neither knew nor much cared about except for that poor dead fellow's sake, and truth's.

"It's time I met Sayyid Sindbad the Sailor," I told Mustafā. "He and I have business."

"Wrap yourself in this mullet net instead," my benefactor wryly recommended, "and let me fling you directly into the gulf to drown. It will save you another trip up and down the Tigris."

Yet up that ancient waterway I went and, six evenings and voyage-tales ago, reached this house's gate with nothing to my name besides love, despair, and one of Mustafā's fileting knives to defend my "self" with. I sang my lament. Was paged. Was plied.

Here I am.

Two Interludes

1.

By all the diners at Sindbad's side tables and most of those at his main, "Bey el-Loor's" latest story was received with watchful whispers or watchful silence: watchful of the latter table's "two heads," Sindbad and Jaydā, regarding each other level-gazed and expressionless in the face of "Sīmon's" surely damning disclosures; watchful of Yasmīn, who had literally and proudly stood behind her lover through his tale, her hands upon his shoulders, and who at his final "Here I am" (when also he leaned his head back against her forget-me-not djellaba and again took her hands in his) embraced him unabashedly from behind and laid her cheek upon his hair. Mustafā the camel perhaps had nodded off in place; not so the two beggar guests, though time and again in the course of Somebody's sixth voyage they had nodded meaningly at each other. Indeed, it was plump Ahmad (between the sleeping beast and Nuzhat the piper) who broke the restive silence:

"Before I say anything further —"

"Before you say anything further," Hajj Masūd interrupted him from down-table, "Hajj Masūd advises you to say nothing further. Otherwise he himself — purveyor-designate of carpets to the Caliph

529

of Serendib by order of Caliph Haroun al-Rashīd, on whom be peace! — Hajj Masūd himself will carpet the pair of you back to the alleyway you crawled from!"

"Foolish man, be silent!" lean Aslān commanded, to everyone's surprise, while Ahmad rose from his cushion as red with wrath as Ibn al-Hamrā was with wine. Their suddenly imperious manner stirred the room. Ahmad now began unwinding his filthy turban; by when Aslān had hurried around the table to assist him, all could see a fine purple silk one underneath, secured with a flashing jewel. Fatmah Awād could not stifle a discreet tambourine-sizzle of admiring awe, at which Aslān nodded approval while removing his own soiled topknot to reveal a gleaming saffron one under it. Handing both rags to Salīm (who stepped to take them as if cued), with Fatmah's tambourine accompaniment Aslān then assisted his companion out of his raveled robe — under which Ahmad wore one fit for an emir at least — and permitted Salīm to help him off with his own, discovering one scarcely less resplendent. Off then, with a flourish of Nuzhat's pipe atop Fatmah's fanfare, came the plump beggar's unbarbered and doubtless louseful beard, and Aslān's as well, to reveal glistening, short-trimmed black ones: the beards and imposing visages of . . .

"Caliph Haroun al-Rashīd and his grand vizier, Jafar al-Barmakī!" Yasmīn whispered to still-stranded Somebody, and then she joined the astonished room (Hajj Masūd most especially) in general salaam. Though he lacked the reflexes of servility, her fiancé more or less prostrated himself with the others; but he risked a peek in time to see the vizier make a sign to Salīm just as the caliph bade the company resume their places — even Sindbad and Jaydā, who tried vainly to exchange theirs with their unexpectedly distinguished guests, and the two musicians, who were unable to reseat themselves beside such eminence until reinstructed.

"Do kindly remove *that* one, however," Aslān/Jafar commanded of no one in particular, with a nod at the now snoring camel. Kuzia Fakān promptly snapped the beast awake with claps of her finger-cymbals and, herself unmoving, with Bedouin *pssts* and tongue-clicks talked him out of the hall as she had earlier talked him in. The momentarily vanished page now reappeared from the kitchen bearing two pairs of bejeweled slippers and a water basin; with triumphant side glances at Jaydā and Sindbad he set about washing the bare feet of caliph and vizier.

"Hear me, Commander of the Faithful!" Sindbad began. But the caliph promptly cut him off:

"Call us rather the Dispenser of Denouements," he advised in the royal plural. "We have listened and heard enough: our messenger's full and faithful message this morning; this page's confidential embellishments of that text this forenoon; and the mattersome, intriguing, and entertaining, though lengthy, stories told tonight — whose several discrepancies we are now prepared to resolve and their several tellers judge. Are we not, Jafar?"

Resettling himself across-table from the caliph, the vizier replied, "We are, sire, once the peerless daughter of our ever generous host refills our cups and we hear the testimony of two final witnesses to that catenation of events conveniently labeled Tub Night by our visitor from Serendib." He nodded Somebodyward.

"Well, then," the caliph said.

"I hear and obey," said Sindbad's daughter, and with Jaydā's assistance she went around with the wine in her customary fashion, except that (eyes lowered) she filled first the caliph's cup, next his vizier's, next her fiancé's, and only then served her father and completed the usual order. Haroun, our narrator observed, followed her movements with a connoisseur's appraising admiration, of which Yasmīn seemed not unaware. To Salīm then, who was standing behind the camel's vacant cushion as if tempted to seat himself at the caliph's left hand, Jafar said curtly, "First witness: speak, boy."

The page swallowed. "I . . ." Yasmīn just then reached his place (the last in her rotation but for that of expectant Ibn al-Hamrā) and paused. Hajj Masūd obligingly handed Salīm the camel's cup, which the page held forth in two hands. Yasmīn poured, her eyes as steady upon him as his hands were not upon that cup.

"I," he said again, and as if encouraged by the sound of that pronoun, he thumped his chest with one hand and repeated it to the room: "I! I, Salīm — under protection of the Prince of Believers On-whombepeace — I, here, declare . . ." He drew breath. "That I despise every member of this household, without exception! Beginning with *you!*" He pointed to his father. "And you and you!" indicating his mother and his half-sister, now back at their places. "But not excepting all you others who've treated me like camel-flop under your slippers every day of my life! Shaitan take all of you, including that mangy Mustafā!"

Haroun, who had not once glanced at the page, here raised his eyebrows at Jafar, who said to Salīm, "The Prince of Darkness will take *you* first, surely, for presuming to speak so to your own parents though they be devils themselves. Tell us of Tub Night now, or be silent."

Salīm's hand shook wine over the cup's edge. He swallowed air. "That one, too, I hated: Umar the Yum-Yum!" At impassive Sindbad he railed, "You should have taken *me* to Basra with you that morning!"

"Enough, by Allah," Haroun commanded. "Call the other witness, Jafar."

But the vizier once more warned Salīm sternly: "Your next word off the subject will be your last to this assembly, fellow. Tub Night!"

The page gripped his cup and, as if to it, said shakily, "That night, sayyids, after the household had celebrated *his* leaving for his fifth voyage and taking Umar the Peacock with him instead of me, and Umar the Peacock had been carried off drunk after one cup of wine, and Sindbad the Stonehorse had taken my mother into that hideaway of his to do their tricks together —"

The caliph rumbled. His vizier raised a warning forefinger.

"That night," Salīm resumed, less agitatedly, "standing watch in the courtyard as I always do, out of sight, the better to see sneakers and snoopers before they can see me —"

Haroun cleared his throat.

"— I saw *him*," the page said, pointing to Sindbad, "in one of his famous fits, driving *her*" — pointing to Jaydā — "from that famous tub with snaps of his famous turban, snap snap snap —"

"Which famous tub?" Jafar interrupted him to ask. "This one here looks scarcely big enough for two people and a turban."

"No, Sayyid: I mean that great one out in the courtyard, from which *she* came scrambling out just as *she*" — he pointed to Yasmīn — "came running from the shadows to put herself between *him* and *her*. She caught hold of his snapping turban and said something I couldn't hear and led him back up and into the tub while *she* ran off calling for Umar Yum-Yum, who must have been dead asleep from his sip of wine, for he was a long time coming to anybody's rescue, and by the time he got himself down to the courtyard, the trouble was over: *he*" — Sindbad — "was snoring away like a camel inside his tub, and *she*" — Yasmīn — "was cooling her heels under the date palm beside the central fountain, which had running water in it in those days, which is why I couldn't hear what she'd said to *him* earlier. Now along comes Yum-Yum rubbing his eyes and scratching his crotch and looking up at the sky, and he all but stumbles over *her,* as she's no doubt waiting for him to come out and count stars with her, and I saw the pair of them then talking and touching and frisking under that date palm, and when they went off at last toward the harem together I ran to wake *him* to show him what his pets were up to, right under his nose. But by the time I'd shaken him awake enough to listen, here comes Umar the Peacock, claiming *he'd* come to waken him and go off voyaging. . . ."

"Zabb?" asked the vizier sharply. "Wâhât?"

"Your pardon, Sayyid Vizier?"

"You saw you saw you saw," Jafar pressed, "but what did you see? Were those two young people wrestling over a jewel-handled knife, or did they come down to zabbs and wâhâts? And if the latter, did he force her gate, or did she welcome him in? The penalty for lying to the caliph is slow disembowelment."

Salīm's cup trembled, but his voice did not. "I saw what I saw," he insisted.

"Then you saw nothing useful to this inquiry," Haroun himself declared, speaking as if to Jafar. "Go mind that camel, and see to it that you're here at noon tomorrow to see your reward for so much seeing. Call the other witness, Jafar, and see to it that he's more di-verting and less of a diversion than this one was."

"*She,* sire," the vizier amended him, and as Salīm exited with sniffs of satisfaction at his father's and half-sister's backs, Jafar asked for and received the caliph's permission to interrogate the next witness rather than invite another such impertinent spiel.

"It has not escaped the Commander of the Faithful," he then ob-served to the company, "that Yasmīn's duenna played a more than minor part in the events of the night in question, not to mention in many events leading up to and following that night. It appears to the caliph that it was Jaydā the Cairene, for example, who first put into her charges' heads the idea that they might be in love with each other, and then reported her fears in that quarter to her master, at a time when she was jealous of the boy Umar's preference over her own son. Jaydā it was (the caliph notes) who by everybody's testimony did alif bā tā and thā jīm hā and the rest of her alphabet of thises and thats, about one or two of which the caliph would hear more." Turning then to Jaydā, the vizier said, "Slow disembowelment, woman, without respect for age or sex, if you do not now tell the caliph truly and simply where you ran to from the so-called Tub of Truth on the night in question, when Sindbad's daughter bravely interposed herself to save you from her father's turban-snaps."

Closing her eyes and rocking on her cushion, Jaydā cried, "As Allah is my witness, sayyids, I ran to fetch Umar to rescue my rescuer, just as Salīm said! Ai, the lot of us poor women, to be disemboweled without respect —"

"Sayyid Sīmon Bey el-Loor," Jafar quickly put in, "has reported that the pirate Sahīm al-Layl maintained that under his former aspect as Umar al-Yom, he was awoken that night by your instructing him merely to go waken Sayyid Sindbad for the journey down to Basra, without mentioning the trouble in progress or any other urgency."

"Let Umar dare say that to my face!" Jaydā cried. "I, who raised him as if he were my own!"

"We shall not wait for his testimony," the vizier said dryly. "Why did you not go with him back to the courtyard, to see Yasmīn safely to the harem once she had been rescued from her fitful father?"

This question was received with due nod and murmur from the company. But Jaydā replied promptly and proudly, "Because, masters, what Sayyid Sindbad and myself had been about earlier in that same tub was *prophecy,* a business of which the uninitiated know nothing whatever. Before his Marjānah-fit (as we call his unhappy seizures since Voyage Four) came on him, my master and I had done what was required to show me the future, and in that prevision I had seen that my darling Yasmīn was in no danger from her father's cruel turban, and that she could manage the situation without assistance — as in fact she did."

Haroun himself, nodding as if impressed, nevertheless inquired via his vizier, "If that is what you foresaw, madam, why did you run off calling for Umar to come rescue Sindbad's daughter?"

Jafar bowed in salute to the question's pertinence. But Jaydā unhesitatingly responded, "Why else, sire, except that it was foreseen that I would do so? But Allah knows all! Just as it was foreseen that Umar would find his sister weeping under that date palm because she'd not been blessed with a zabb and eggs so that she could go to sea with him! Oh, she was a tomboy, that one, Allah bless her! I well recall —"

"Madam Duenna," Jafar interposed, "where *did* you go, then, after waking young Sayyid Umar for either one thing or the other?"

"Back to the harem, to be sure," Jaydā said, "as I had foreseen I would, to await my girl's return. And there I waited, sayyids, and waited more, until at last I dozed off — as who would not have, so long did it take Umar to rescue Yasmīn and Yasmīn to be rescued! My thought was that the boy's cup of wine had passed through him at last, and that brother and sister were comforting each other with fond farewells and innocent whatnot under that date palm. But a duenna is a duenna, sirs, asleep or awake! When my dear one came back to her room at last, I could read in the book of her sighs and sniffles that she was now a woman, if you take my meaning. 'Were you forced?' I asked her, knowing very well she had not been, despite her bloody djellaba-lap. 'Forced!' cries she, and she shows me Umar's jewel-handled knife: 'I would cut the eggs off any man who tried to force me!' And she could likely do it, too, masters, for Umar had taught her well. 'Only look at you!' I said. 'We'll tell your father you were forced.' For I had foreseen, sirs, that her roll in the hay with Umar was not to be the end of their story. 'Is my father so easily fooled, Jaydā?' she asks me — *laughing*, mind you, though not a bit happily. 'All men are,' I tell her, and she bids me speak no more of forcing and fooling, inasmuch as whatever had happened had happened and was done with.

"So off go Sindbad and his pet on their famous fifth voyage, while my Salīm and we womenfolk stay home and make the best of our unprivileged lot. Sure enough, my darling misses her next two monthlies and begins to swell. 'What now, young lady?' I ask her, and she tells me she's of half a mind to sail away by herself to some desert island and bear the child and raise it herself as she wishes *she'd* been raised: a free spirit, whether girl or boy. But she knew such a thing was impossible in her circumstances, and so she gave me leave to do whatever I saw fit; she no longer cared.

"And so Jaydā did and did, good sirs, just as Jaydā has ever done and done: I did this and I did that, said alif bā tā and thā jīm hā to keep this house together. I cured Yasmīn's morning sickness and found my old master a frisky new tubmate fresh from the desert to appease his temper at what I confessed to him that Umar had done, and at the same time I grieved as much as any at that poor boy's loss at sea, even though he had taken my Salīm's place. And then I saved him from certain death when it turned out that only a certain part of him was lost at sea and the rest come back to Baghdad; and I played peacemaker between Kuzia Fakān and Yasmīn, who declared that she was jealous of Kuzia on my account; and I played matchmaker with young Prince Jabāl and persuaded Yasmīn to let me put her in the way of as good a maidenhead as the one she'd lost, and then when things went amiss in the Bahr Faris I did my best to comfort my darling girl while Sayyid Sīmon Bey el-Loor did what he had to do at the naughty orders of Sayyid Sahīm al-Layl, who was poor Umar in disguise. And after that I helped Yasmīn smuggle that same Sayyid Sīmon into the harem for the month of Sha'ban and back out again for Ramadan; and after that I helped Sayyid Sindbad make arrangements for her with Sayyid Ibn al-Hamrā —"

"Jafar!" Haroun here broke in. "This bawd so sets our teeth on edge that we would choose slow disembowelment for ourself and for you as well over hearing any more of her story!"

"Allah forfend we should hear another syllable from her," the vizier said smoothly. "Be seated, woman, while we turn our interrogation to your master."

But the caliph declared, "There will be no further interrogation, at least not tonight, in our presence. Disembowel this jade of a Jaydā with perfect slowness if she does not appear tomorrow at noon to hear from us the end of her story. As for our host," he went on, still addressing Jafar, "whose generosity toward us after each of his several voyages has been surpassed only by his generosity toward himself, we would eagerly suffer impalement before sitting through another of his fanciful sea yarns. What we require at this late hour is not interrogation but music, to accompany our dispensation of denouements."

"Who shall gainsay the King of the Ages?" Jafar asked rhetorically, and he whispered into the right ear of Fatmah Awād, seated at his left.

With a pleased nod Fatmah relayed his instructions across-table to Nuzhat in the language of tambourines, and Nuzhat piped the message diagonally down-table to Kuzia Fakān. "We hear and obey!" cried Kuzia. Already vibrant of hip and belly as she rose from Cushion Four, she stepped onto the table in front of Jaydā, doffed her outermost robe, and salaamed before Haroun al-Rashīd, her finger-cymbals accenting Fatmah's rhythm. In her most articulate body-Bedouin then, accompanied ardently by her colleagues and encouraged by approving nods from caliph and vizier, she danced out Haroun's not-uncomplicated first pronouncement, as murmured by the caliph and given strong voice by Jafar al-Barmakī:

"By the authority vested in him by fate and by Allah to bid and forbid between man and man," this pronouncement ran, "Caliph Haroun al-Rashīd now dispenses as follows: the extraordinarily green-eyed, steadfast, prevailingly high-principled, eloquent, much-mishandled but nonetheless uncommonly desirable daughter of Sindbad the Sailor, though she would grace the caliph's own harem like a jewel from Island Two, Voyage Two, he herewith gives in marriage, if she be still willing, to the worthy Sayyid Sīmon Whatshisname from the Blessed Isle of Serendib, if *he* be still willing — their union to be consummated or reconsummated, as may be, this very night, and preparations for their joint embassy to Serendib on the caliph's behalf to be launched tomorrow or at the latest the day after, when other denouements shall have been dispensed by the Prince of Believers in this gracious hall. Be you both still willing, the caliph inquires, now that you and we have heard all that we have heard? We see that you are and here pronounce you husband and wife, et cetera et cetera. May Allah bless and fructify your union."

So defiant earlier in the evening, Yasmīn at the caliph's question appeared to consult her father with those aforecited eyes, just as her bridegroom consulted her with his. Sindbad closed his own eyes and nodded assent to the pronouncement. His daughter returned her gaze to her husband, and Haroun's vizier spoke on:

"The caliph further declares the issue of Mrs. Sīmon Somebody's maidenhood, its history and present state, to have been, though tiresome, so central to the complex and discrepancy-fraught narrative now approaching its climax and resolution that in lieu of further testimony upon the question (which the caliph is persuaded will lead only to additional contradictions, digressions, and culs-de-sac), *he himself,* in the awful majesty of his person and his entire distrust of the bawd Jaydā, will upon the close of this pronouncement adjudge the hymenal state of Sindbad's daughter — a judgment whereof there shall be no appeal by any party and whereof the merest questioning shall be rewarded with leisurely immersion in boiling palm oil."

Somebody frowned at this, and his new father-in-law likewise, and Jaydā pulled her black cowl close about her face. Hajj Masūd gave his beard an apprehensive tug, picked up by Kuzia Fakān and amplified in her dance. Salīm and Ibn al-Hamrā smiled and smiled. But Yasmīn changed neither her expression nor the focus of her gaze.

"On the other hand," Jafar continued, "the caliph cordially invites wagers before the fact as to his finding in this delicate matter and appoints his vizier, Jafar al-Barmakī, to hold in trust all sums so wagered for appropriate disbursement after the caliph's determination. We now pause briefly in middispensation to accept and record such wagers."

This by no means simple article of Haroun's pronouncement Kuzia danced out directly in front of Ibn al-Hamrā, with such perspiring eloquence that that plum-phizzed fellow was moved to cry, "My whole investment in Serendib Limited says that Sindbad's daughter is no more virginal than myself!"

From the courtyard doorway Salīm laughed and jeered, "After what we've heard from the bride and groom themselves, who'll bet against you?"

"Who else but the bride's father?" Ibn replied triumphantly. "Didn't he pay two fortunes to his Qeshmi friends for preservation of the very item in question, and then dangle it before me like a sugar-tit before a suckling all through our dowry negotiations? Let Sindbad match my wager with a thirty-percent share of Serendib Limited!"

Fatmah tambourined a pensive pause as vizier and caliph nodded to each other and turned to Sindbad. But from the table's other head, from Jaydā's cowl, there now came strange, crowlike cries in what sounded to our narrator like the language spoken between his new bride and her duenna: *"Oppabroppa! Koppadoppabroppa!"* Not even Kuzia Fakān's polyglot midsection could translate, but Sindbad nodded and declared to Jafar al-Barmakī, "What you hear is the very tongue of prophecy. I accept the terms of Sayyid Ibn al-Hamrā's wager."

"Done," the vizier affirmed, "and gallantly. The caliph presumes that there are no further bets?"

There appeared to be none, unsurprisingly, from either the main or the side tables. But having danced Haroun's presumption (which required but two accented twitches of left buttock and right breast), Kuzia Fakān was inspired to a remarkable unaccompanied solo burst, directed principally toward Haroun and Jafar but with gestures as well toward Ibn al-Hamrā (his caftan-bib in particular), Yasmīn, Sindbad, and even the bridegroom, to whom it seemed almost as if she were spelling out with her supple body the letters of his name. Nuzhat giggled into her pipe. Fatmah Awād applauded tambourinely.

"What did she say?" Haroun demanded of Jafar. As Fatmah whispered in the vizier's ear, Kuzia salaamed down-table and seated herself, smiling, not back on Cushion Four but directly facing Ibn al-Hamrā — in fact, upon his empty dessert plate.

"Kuzia Fakān," Jafar reported, "of the noble and restless Bedouin, seconds her master's wager upon his daughter's virginity and begs the caliph to marry her to the merchant Ibn al-Hamrā if she and her master win that bet."

"Done." Haroun approved. "And if she loses?"

Without turning her head or torso, Kuzia followed a quick tattoo of her finger-cymbals with a thrust of her dessert-plated rump. Fatmah whispered; Jafar nodded and declared, "If she loses her wager, Kuzia Fakān will either launder Sayyid Ibn's caftans till the end of the story or do whatever else it may please the Dispenser of Denouements to command of her. Well proposed, say I."

"And done," said the caliph, already rising from his place and beckoning to both Yasmīn and her husband. Observed Jafar, "There are things that one can prove possession of only by losing them. The Commander of the Faithful now bids that more wine be served while he retires with the bride and groom to make his adjudication." He himself then — as Yasmīn promptly stood to go and her troubled husband uncertainly rose to follow — moved behind Fatmah Awād to retrieve from Sindbad's daughter's cushion the knotted rag that "Aslān" and "Ahmad" had presented to her upon their arrival in the hall. "The wedding gift," he said, re-presenting it with a bow not to the newlyweds but to his master the caliph, whom then he followed as Haroun al-Rashīd followed us — unlikely foursome! — led by bride leading groom by the hand from dining hall to bridal chamber.

At its threshold, Jafar (who had moved ahead of us en route, as if he knew the way) halted and bowed again. Yasmīn stepped unhesitantly inside. Hesitant indeed, her husband nevertheless presumed to move ahead of the caliph, wondering whether some Arabian Nights variety of le droit du seigneur was in the offing and whether the penalty for resistance would be slow disembowelment or palm-oil parboiling, and was gratified not to find himself seized and hauled from the room. His bride stood quietly at his lamp-lit writing desk.

"Sit," the caliph said kindly — to both of us, it seemed — and with a small grunt and less small sigh seated himself plumply on one corner of our memoryful Bokhara. When we had taken our places at the two opposite corners, and Jafar his station, at Haroun's direction, at the fourth, the caliph handed the husband of us that knotted rag.

"Our congratulations upon your marriage. Open and inspect, please."

Scarcely daring to hope . . . yet there it was, bandless but still ticking, faithfully registering the hour as either 0220 or 1420 on some WED 27. At the sight of it, tears sprang to our bridegroom's eyes; likewise and more so to our bride's when he offered it for her inspection and she kissed its familiar crystaled face.

"May it steer you both safely to Serendib," the caliph wished us when we had much thanked him, and Jafar added, "Kindly bring us back several such navigation amulets when you return."

"Now, then," Haroun harrumphed, looking first to his vizier and then, severely, to Yasmīn.

"Indeed," murmured Jafar al-Barmakī.

Yasmīn's eyes flashed. She tucked her legs under her a touch more tightly; then, a little, untucked them; then, with only the briefest proud side glance at her husband (to whom it occurred, bizarrely: *But she's menstruating!*), untucked them quite, as if to bid Haroun al-Rashīd as he had bidden us: Open and Inspect.

The Commander of the Faithful immediately smiled his satisfaction, shook his head, and sighed again, saying to both of us, "Such customs are regrettable, but the people are the people. Jafar al-Barmakī will duly proclaim to all Baghdad that Sindbad's daughter, by our personal certification, came to her bridal bed a virgin. We now leave to the pair of you what really matters: seeing to it that she's not one still by morning prayer call."

"Thy will be done!" my wife whispered gratefully, and she turned to her husband, radiant. That much-but-not-entirely-relieved chap concurred, "We hear and obey." Caliph and vizier nodded and rose to leave us. But then it occurred to Haroun to ask, "Was there not a bracelet of some sort for that amulet? We should like to see it."

The bracelet, I explained, was missing, except for two or three spare links — whose present location and container I now suddenly remembered with appall.

"It is missing no longer," Yasmīn declared, reaching into the bosom of her djellaba. "It was to be my wedding gift to my husband." She fetched it forth but at the sight of it — a simple band of stainless-steel links — could not not sob. I hurried to embrace her and was gratified to be permitted to.

"What is the trouble?" the caliph wondered. His vizier supposed discreetly that the price of that bracelet's retrieval had perhaps been high. Moving doorward, he wished us white nights and golden days until the Destroyer of Delights and Desolater of Dwelling Places collected from us the debt all creatures owe their maker.

"No more tears!" Haroun commanded, joining him. "If the goods are good, then the price is the price. See to it that those missing links are in place by tomorrow noon and that bracelet clasped as you must clasp each other now, and Devil take the price! It's paid, we presume, and we bid you good night, and there's the end of it."

But it was not, though caliph and vizier left us then to make their proclamation to the company. Still tearful, Yasmīn moved from carpet-corner to bed-edge to fit the bracelet onto the watch — very possibly sitting, it pained her husband to note, directly upon the awful link pouch that he had thrust out of sight there when Kuzia Fakān had visited him that afternoon. It was the memory of Umar al-Yom, he presumed — and Sahīm al-Layl, and *Shaitan* — together with the strain of the evening's narratives, that now overburdened her.

When he made again to comfort her, she managed to say, "Wear this and nothing else, husband, while you deflower your virgin bride."

The thing would not clasp, I was obliged to tell (and show) her, without the links removed by our late friend Umar/Sahīm. "And we *have* those links," I decided to acknowledge, "but it's better not to ask where they came from and where they are."

"As you wish," Yasmīn replied. "Don't ask your wife then how she came by the bracelet, either. That way neither of us will be deflowered, and tomorrow the caliph can annul our marriage."

Her meaning, please? Stroking thoughtfully her startled husband's unclasped watchband, she said, "Yasmīn and Sīmon are one person now. Should that person keep secrets from himself?"

To myself I reflected that dark ones indeed were still being kept from me. All the same, sitting beside her on the bed and making soft love to her neck-nape with one thumb and two fingers as she did likewise to my open bracelet clasp, Sīmon told Yasmīn the full story of those missing links: how, Sahīm al-Layl's wrist having been less thick than Bey el-Loor's, he had bidden me remove them, and to assure my service had thereafter kept the watch always on his person except when I was actually navigating. How I had thought it but another of his bitter jokes when he had speculated on its possible potency and had pretended (so I'd supposed) to consider wearing it where it might regenerate his corporal losses.

"Umar . . ." My bride could say no more.

How, then, this very afternoon her father had told me of his premonition yesterday that a second attempt would be made last night to steal his "amulet"; how he had forestalled that theft by sending the watch, belatedly, to Haroun al-Rashīd via the caliph's vizier's messenger and then had tricked the would-be thief — not Kuzia Fakān this time, he'd reported, but Jaydā, assisted by Salīm — by substituting the bracelet for the watch in that atrocious pouch he wore between his legs. How, finally, so pleased had he been by whatever it was that Jaydā had prophesied in the course of his feigned "Marjānah-fit" —

"*Feigned?*" Yasmīn all but screamed at me.

— that he had excused the theft, sung to me a six-stanza ode to impotence, declared his retirement from sexuality, and made me a mocking gift of Umar/Sahīm's pouch — empty now but for those spare links overlooked by the thieves. I would prefer not to show her it, I said.

Yasmīn pressed her fingernails into my wrist. "Show me it!"

Most reluctantly, I did.

"Empty it," she whispered.

Gingerly indeed, I loosened its silk drawstring and shook three links onto my palm. She held out hers — for those links, I assumed, and I offered them, making to put their revolting container out of view.

"Not them!" Indifferent to those bits of metal, she snatched up the empty, fawn-soft scrotal sac of the manifoldly maltreated Umar al-Yom, also Sahīm al-Layl, and pressed it repeatedly to her lips, kissing it as if it were, after all, a sacred amulet.

"Poor innocent!"

I thought she meant *him*. But now she kissed me, almost violently, and pushed and pulled us down onto the bed, and kept her mouth pressed against mine while her hands — *both* hands, I noted, and I praised Allah that she had let fall that pouch — groped under my caftan and her own djellaba. Very well: I groped, too — and bolted upright at what I felt, and turned into serious contest what in my innocence I had taken for nuptial foreplay. I forced her knife-hand away and downward, dislodging en route the soft pad of folded cotton that Yasmīn used by way of "sanitary napkin." She managed a wrist-twist sufficient to scratch herself inside one thigh; whether she had counted on my stopping her there I might subsequently wonder but would never ask. When I threw a leg over hers to help immobilize her, I, too, felt the blade. But I had her pinioned now, and I kissed and kissed her face as she had kissed that other thing.

In and from that strained embrace there followed my own latest "defloration": my wife's half-muttered, half-whispered account of how young Umar al-Yom had *never* been her lover — not first, not ever — nor had any other of her young suitors. How not Jaydā's and Sind-bad's son but Sindbad's daughter (with Jaydā's full assistance) had, by false prophecy and drastic other means, attempted last night to steal or bribe from her father the necessary though insufficient instrument of my rereaching home — and had got only its bracelet for her pains.

By story's end its teller's grip had eased; its shaken hearer's, too, once I had secured that jewel-handled blade. Yasmīn now opened her djellaba and pointed imperiously to her heart, much as she had done aboard *Shaitan*. I kissed her breast instead; put the knife, the watch, the spare links, the pouch, the story, all out of harm's (and harming's) way, over on my writing table; stanched our lightly bleeding scratches with the bedsheet. Almost defiantly, her entire person asked, What next? To which my whole though still-stunned self responded: Love.

2.

Love we made, as awkwardly and tenderly as two virgins. Then sank into deep but uneasy sleep, down almost to the Boundary. Then found ourselves just before daylight coupling again, this time with more ardor than tenderness and not awkwardly at all. Exactly where one might have expected a muezzin cry, siren blast, or peacock call, in through our doorway mumbled . . . Jaydā! One of us sprang from love to naked anger, and from the bed; the other stayed him.

"She's my Jaydā still, Sīmon. I was never innocent."

"Her doing!" I protested. "And your crazy father's!"

Jaydā stood by. Yasmīn shrugged her whole splendid body as she sat up, saying, "Even if his fits were feigned, who took advantage of whom? He's Sindbad the Sailor, Sīmon, and Jaydā is Jaydā, and Yasmīn is Yasmīn. The only innocent in this house was Umar, and I loved him to death. Now there's you."

Announced Jaydā, "They want to see the sheet."

"Show it." The two of them stripped it from the bed, in the gray light admiring together the magnitude and splendor of its stains. Such a bride! Such a bridegroom! The most wine-spoiled of Ibn al-Hamrā's caftans, they agreed, paled before our bridal sheet, which Jaydā promised to display in the courtyard like a victory flag.

"Won't your father be pleased!" she thrilled; then she clucked her tongue. "And isn't he the sly one, pretending to *feign* his fits!" With a nod to her ward's near-speechless spouse, she exited with the trophy.

Opined Yasmīn (down Turk-fashion on our rug again now, adroitly refitting the three "missing links" to their bracelet), "If Jafar al-Barmakī were to ask her, Jaydā would swear to Allah she brought Kuzia Fakān into this house to keep my father away from me, because whether *he* knew it or not, *she* knew what he'd be wanting in return for that ransom." By dint of considerable effort, I said nothing. My bride continued, "Nobody loves and hates Sindbad the Sailor as much as Jaydā does, except maybe me, and we both knew that I was her best link to him because of *my* link to Marjānah. Who doesn't play double games, Sīmon? Even with himself?"

Her husband tapped his chest.

"Yes, well, maybe," Yasmīn granted. "But your old friend Day-*zee* did, for certain. Now, then, speaking of links . . ." As confident as that lovely clerk had been in the Marrakesh watch shop somewhere near Dronningen's Gade in Charlotte Amalie, she closed the bracelet clasp around my wrist: a perfect fit. Crossing her forearms then under her breasts, she cocked her head to inspect, to approve, and to ask, "Is it Serendib for Sindbad's daughter, or the Sahrā al Hijārāh?"

To which her husband replied that she was her father's daughter no longer. She was her husband's wife, and I her husband.

Her glance flicked away, then returned steadfast. "Husband me, then, my friend, whether to Serendib or to the Destroyer of Delights. And I will wife you to your famous Boundary and beyond."

Called the caliph's vizier's moon-faced messenger late that forenoon from Sindbad's courtyard: "*Resolutions here! By order of Caliph Haroun al-Rashīd, Prince of Believers and Dispenser of Denouements, all surviving principals in the several voyage-tales of Sindbad the Sailor and Still-Stranded Sīmon Bey el-Loor shall now assemble to hear their endings, happy and otherwise!*"

And at local noon exactly — which was to say, as exactly as the venerable Mustafā mu-Allim could determine with instruments older than the Seiko Quartz Sports 100 that our narrator there recalibrated to his former mentor's "Mark!" — the caliph, in his own person, spoke.

Over the courtyard gate our "bridal banner" hung, remarked and admired by various of the household and pointed out by the street-side crowd as they said things to one another behind their hands. At Yasmīn's insistence, she and I came from our rooms dressed in triumphant red, she in the djellaba she had worn at Ramadan's end, I in matching caftan. Before the gate, beneath the validated banner, semi-circled by prayer rugs and standing people, the great Tub of Truth had, we saw, been inverted into a dais, upon which the smaller Tub of Last Resort, fetched from the banquet hall and similarly inverted, made a backless throne. There in full robes of state sat Haroun al-

Rashīd. His vizier's familiar messenger stood behind him, the vizier himself down on his right. Two other figures attended the dais: just before the caliph, brandishing an enormous polished and jewel-studded scimitar, a heavy-muscled, fierce-mustachioed fellow whom Yasmīn identified to her husband as Haroun's celebrated sword-bearer and bodyguard, Masrūr; and cross-legged on the ground at the caliph's left, a disheveled, red-eyed, swag-bellied scamp whom I presumed to be Haroun's other legendary sidekick, the poet-jester Abū Nuwās. Round about stood the summoned principals of these stories (those still living and on this side of the Boundary, in Sindbadland), together with all investors past and present in Serendib Limited. In their center, facing Masrūr, black-turbaned Sindbad bent his head and stroked and stroked his beard, and black-cowled Jaydā kept her own counsel. The sight of them dizzied our narrator: the man had *pretended to feign* his mad incestuous attacks? But then I caught sight of old Mustafā catching dim-eyed sight of me and beaming from the courtyard margin as if he had achieved a tricky landfall exactly per plot. I hurried to him; we embraced; he even put by his grudge against Yasmīn, seeing our happiness, and permitted her to embrace him as well. The vizier's messenger had expressed him up from Basra, Mustafā said, and he had much to tell us. We too him, said we; there would be time.

"Be seated all," that messenger bade the company. "At local noon exactly, as determined by the peerless Mustafā mu-Allim together with Sayyid Sīmon Bey el-Loor, captain of the caliph's new expedition to Serendib, the Commander of the Faithful will address this company in his aspect of Dispenser of Denouements."

All sat upon the prayer rugs except Mustafā and me (my ex-mentor already explaining to me, sotto voce, how we would proceed with the business at hand) and Abū Nuwās, who, having sat while the others stood, now perversely struggled to his feet as the rest did contrariwise. On the dais, in a square of sunlight at the caliph's feet, Mustafā set up a small contraption of ancient design (lately modified by himself, he would tell me later): half sundial and half pelorus, by the look of it. He aligned it thus-and-so, sighting on a minaret here, a sun-shadow there; he adjusted the angle of its gnomon, rotated some sort of scale until this matched that, then held up one bony forefinger as the needle-thin shadow crept toward a certain . . .

"Mark!" he bade me crisply, as by sunlight, moonlight, and starlight he had done a hundred times before on *Zahir*'s deck. But this time, instead of logging with my watch the precise moment of his celestial sight, I clicked into motion the hands that I had preset to 12:00:00. We reembraced. Led by Yasmīn, the bystanders applauded.

The caliph spoke: "It is the custom of this house, as demonstrated last evening to all here, for its master and host to seat his guests at table in an order corresponding —"

"Devil take it, most high and excellent Excellency!" Abū Nuwās broke in, at the same time stifling a belch and pointing across the courtyard. "There is an infidel who dares to stand and stare like a camel while the caliph speaks!"

Haroun's face flashed his anger, as much at the interrupter as at the cause of his interruption. Masrūr shifted his awful scimitar and turned menacingly to the poet while we others looked where that poet was pointing: at the camel Mustafā, idly browsing oleander beside the dry central fountain. Remarked the vizier Jafar al-Barmakī (himself now seated on the dais at Haroun's right hand), "There are two such. With the caliph's leave I'll instruct the Bedou dancer to deal with *that* camel and Masrūr to deal with this one" — pointing to the poet.

"Done," said Haroun al-Rashīd. Kuzia Fakān, without even turning toward the courtyard, gave two shrill whistles and three sharp clucks, and the camel settled to his knees. Abū Nuwās made a sideshow of doing likewise, salaaming abjectly before the great bodyguard's upraised sword. "Enough," Haroun said. But the irrepressible poet, seating himself now comfortably on the ground with the inverted Truth-Tub for a backrest, presumed to improvise:

> *Before her desert songs*
> *As before her dunes and hollows —*
> *Sahl, Sahrā, Sarīr, Wâdi, Wâhât! —*
> *Man and beast alike must squat,*
> *In hope that whatso follows*
> *Will be that wherefor he longs.*

"But Allah is merciful," he added.

"So this time shall we be," Haroun allowed, "but perhaps not next. Be warned." To the amused company then he resumed: "Today, however, Sindbad the Sailor cannot perform his customary office, nor ever henceforth in this house, alas, for the reason that his manifold offenses — against his delectable daughter and others, not excluding ourself — oblige us to declare all his property forfeit, together with his life. Both are to be considered in escrow against their disposition later in the denouement-luncheon to which we here invite you all. You shall take your places in the banquet hall as we now assign them, along with preliminary judgments where appropriate. Those not singled out for mention may dispose themselves as they wish at the side tables — excepting the camel Mustafā, who shall dine where he now sits, in company with the prince of poets, Sayyid Abū Nuwās. As for the main table, proceeding from the lowest cushion to the highest, we pronounce as follows . . ."

He leaned toward his vizier, who whispered into his ear while consulting a paper withdrawn from his robe. At Haroun's beckon the messenger bent to listen, too, and then announced on the caliph's behalf, "*Sindbad the Sailor* we find guilty of certain offenses too heinous to speak of and of others atrocious but speakable, not least among them lying allegorically to the caliph regarding his voyage to Serendib and sequestering for his own lascivious use the extraordinary souvenir of that place that he was duty-bound to present to the Commander of the Faithful. Also deceiving the caliph and sundry other investors into supporting his fraudulent projected seventh voyage. Also jealously unzabbing and otherwise disfiguring his then-innocent and evidently admirable foster son, Umar al-Yom. Also shamefully neglecting his illegitimate and unlovable but nonetheless natural son, Salīm, who, though certainly no prize, deserved better from his father. Also very possibly even conspiring with the late unlamented Captain Abū Hosayn to have his own daughter kidnapped by the late pirate Sahīm al-Layl in order to divert from the late Prince Jabāl of Oman that virgin bride's munificent dowry and the young woman herself, both of which said Sindbad begrudged him and coveted."

Abū Nuwās whistled appreciatively. From behind us, Mustafā mu-Allim muttered, "That was what I had in mind to tell you, when the coast was clear. No matter now, I suppose."

"Of this last offense," the messenger proclaimed on, "nothing further shall be said unless the caliph chooses to say it. On the strength of the others alone, however, we here condemn Sindbad the Sailor to Cushion Ten at his own table and, after lunch, to death, by whichever means and at whatever place and hour his aggrieved daughter shall elect. We recommend to her attention slow flaying with dull knives, leisurely impalement, gradual immersion in hot palm oil, and consignment into the Tigris in a sack containing a live cock and a disgruntled ape, but the choice shall be hers alone. To your place, sir."

"I should say so," Abū Nuwās commented, tsking his tongue.

"Allah knows all," Sindbad said, and he obediently rose to go. Ignoring me, he fixed his eyes briefly and neutrally upon Yasmīn's as he passed us. She met them no less neutrally. Behind him trudged Jaydā, murmuring to herself, until Masrūr interposed his sword between them like a railway-crossing gate. Declared the caliph then to her (having attended his vizier and nodded to the messenger, who spoke for him), "As for you, Jaydā the Cairene: your loyalty to your master is at once your offense and its mitigation. In the name of it, in ways that shall not here be spoken of, you have played bawd with the girl entrusted to your care. And in more other ways than the caliph has fingers to count them on, not to mention your master, you have lied and tricked and cheated and mixed false prophecy with true to the ends of maintaining your place in Sindbad's esteem and advancing the interests of your whelp of a son. Inasmuch as you did all of this, however — including the deception of your master himself — out of a perverted fidelity of a sort that, unperverted, is approved by both Allah and the caliph, your punishment shall be your reward for that devotion, and vice versa: whatever the fate elected by Sindbad's daughter for her father, you shall share it equally. Meanwhile, we cheerfully condemn you to Cushion Nine, above and across from him."

Haroun nodded. Abū Nuwās shook his head admiringly at the catalogue of Jaydā's offenses. Masrūr lifted his formidable crossing gate. Still murmuring, the duenna trudged on. But now the messenger said, "Wait." The gate came down. There was a conference on the dais, after which the messenger announced further to Jaydā, "Your miserable son, the page Salīm — whether rendered miserable in your womb by God's design, or subsequently by his father's despisement — shall have as his sole reward for a lifetime of sneak and snoop and skulk and scurry, but rarely of any real harm to anyone, the satisfaction of sitting one place above his putative father at the celebratory luncheon following and completing this preliminary dispensation. To your place on Cushion Nine, wretched boy, to queen it over your naughty sire; and your mother to Cushion Eight."

Queening indeed, Salīm went, with a particular buttock-flick at Abū Nuwās when that poet saluted him in street-hustler's Arabic. But Jaydā, who had lingered behind to hear this pronouncement, made bold to plead — speaking to Abū Nuwās, of all people, as if not daring to address herself higher — that on this special occasion her son be given precedence for once over both of his parents. The poet turned his palms up to Masrūr, who in turn shrugged his scimitar at Jafar al-Barmakī, who raised his eyebrows at Haroun al-Rashīd, who considered for no more than a moment before instructing the messenger to proclaim to Jaydā, "Let perversity be disciplined perversely. It shall be part of your punishment to be seated as aforeassigned, one place above your son and two above your lord, on Cushion Eight. Go."

She went (Salīm had preceded her already); and now it was Haroun who spoke to Jafar, and Jafar to his messenger, who announced, "We are weary already of this slow-moving denouement and have seven places yet to assign! Let there be music."

Having consulted the paper in his left hand, Jafar spoke to Masrūr, who cantilevered his scimitar in the direction of Fatmah Awād. Instantly that tambourinist tambourined: first a tentative fanfare as she looked about for her colleagues, then a tremolo of alarm when Haroun himself beckoned her to rise and come forward, at the same time messaging the messenger.

"Fatmah Awād," that fellow duly declared, "whose rhythms are as true and unfaltering as the stars in their courses or the hands of Captain Bey el-Loor's magical *watch*: as of this hour you are Sindbad's tambourine-slave no longer. We assign you instead to the rhythmic service of one whose loyalty to this house has been as steadfast as your instrument."

"Not Jaydā!" Fatmah could not help protesting.

"Certainly not," the caliph assured her through his vizier's messenger, who then said, "Sayyid Hajj Masūd: we invite you to escort your new servant to Cushion Seven of our main table and to take your own well-merited place beside her on your usual Cushion Three. We invite you further to marry this rhythmical young woman, with our blessing and an appropriate caliphly gift to serve as her dowry, but we do not insist upon your doing so if you have sufficient wives already or prefer to enjoy her rhythms otherwise. In either case, as your loyalty to Sindbad was ever on his daughter's behalf and did ourself no injury, we here reaffirm your purveyorship of carpets to the caliphate of Serendib."

"Hajj Masūd?" that fellow asked, incredulous. Clutching the neck of his caftan, he half rose and looked about, as if for confirmation that he was himself. "Hajj Masūd, by order of the caliph?"

He could say no more, nor stand nor sit, until Abū Nuwās took it upon himself to grasp Fatmah Awād's elbow and, shaking her tambourine hand in step, lead her ceremoniously to her new master and bid her march him to their places. As she did so — happily indeed, but with wistful glances at Nuzhat and Kuzia Fakān — the poet boldly observed to Jafar al-Barmakī that for so accomplished a musician to be thus separated from her band was as much punishment as reward. The vizier straightway consulted the caliph, who replied through his spokesman, "Before this denouement is done, that band's bond shall be rebound. Music!"

Merrily then Fatmah danced Hajj Masūd tableward, her tambourine accompanied now by Nuzhat's flute and Kuzia Fakān's finger-cymbals. That was more like it, the caliph made known, and now he bade Kuzia dance out her own reward for services well rendered in Sindbad's household and bets shrewdly placed last night. "On that occasion," his messenger said for him as she salaamed her way to the dais, "we pronounced our pronouncements in Arabic and you translated us into the Bedouin of your body. Please you now to speak your wishes with that body, and Jafar al-Barmakī will render you into Arabic."

Replied Kuzia's hips and cymbals, "We hear and obey!" The vizier raised his eyes to Allah. Vigorously and expressively then the dancer danced from our blood-stained bedsheet to its red-robed stainers; then from the caliph on his tub-throne to crimson-faced Ibn al-Hamrā, before whom she mimed the pouring of wine on head and caftan-front, its intimate laundering, and percentage figures ranging from a low of five to a high of thirty. Her performance concluded with a shrill of Nuzhat's pipe, a bravura flurry of buttocks and finger-cymbals, and the dancer's artful collapse into Ibn's plump lap. Throughout, Jafar watched and whispered to Haroun, who now nodded to the messenger.

"We here proclaim this supple Bedou a free woman and the hands-down winner of her wager with Sayyid Ibn al-Hamrā," that last announced, "as the banner behind us unequivocally attests. With an appropriate caliphly gift by way of dowry, we here wed Kuzia Fakān to that same sayyid, who, if he has a wife already, now has two, and if he has none, now has the equivalent of the Muslim's lawful four. We pronounce you husband and wife and bid you take your places on cushions Six and Five, respectively."

Danced frowning Kuzia: Respectively? Whether, like Jaydā, not presuming to address herself directly to the dais, or else trusting Abū Nuwās to read her movements more accurately than the vizier, she elaborated her question bodily before that poet. "Run that last line by me again," he demanded with a lip-lick, and when she had done so he conveyed to Jafar her wish not to be set above her new husband: let him take the higher cushion, herself the lower. Ibn beamed. Haroun nodded but then consulted his vizier's paper and himself gave voice to his anticipation of sitting on Cushion One between two beauties: on his right hand Kuzia Fakān and on his left, at the table's head, Sind-bad's daughter, now Sayyid Sīmon Bey el-Loor's wife. Let the dancer therefore lead her husband to the lower place as instructed, for today's denouement purposes only, and thereafter defer to him as Allah or-daineth proper.

"There remains Cushion Four," the messenger went on on Haroun's behalf, "across from Sayyid Hajj Masūd at the table's Second Head — where our distinguished emissary from Serendib shall of course pre-side as the South Pole of our hospitality to his bride's most attractive North. On that fourth cushion, at his left hand, shall sit his rescuer and mentor, Mustafā mu-Allim, whom we here appoint to advise upon and oversee the construction at our expense of whatever vessel Captain Bey el-Loor requires for his upcoming voyage."

As this proclamation was duly applauded, Jafar conferred further with Haroun, who bade the messenger add, "To said Mustafā, for his decades of accurate navigation and of behaving to men as men, we further award a delightful young mate to pipe him through his voy-age's final leg: the melodious Nuzhat."

She coughed in midcadenza. "Sayyids!" protested Mustafā; humbly thanking then the caliph, the vizier, the suddenly much-distraught messenger, Masrūr the sword-bearer, Abū Nuwās, and the piper her-self, he begged to be excused, this late in his travels, from the respon-sibility of behaving as a man to so young a woman, or for that matter to any other. By his reckoning, he was not so much on his voyage's final leg as on his own last legs; having contrived to reach safe harbor after so many and perilous passages, he declared, he was content now to cast his net for nothing more frisky than marsh minnows.

"Your wisdom extends beyond pilotage," Haroun said approvingly, and he bade his relieved messenger bid Nuzhat pipe the good man to his place, without further obligation.

"By Allah, master!" cried Abū Nuwās. "Award her to me, and she'll have manly words to fit her womanly music!" As she passed he made an impudent grab at her, which Nuzhat adroitly dodged and smartly parried with a flute-crack on his knuckles. "You go too far, Abū!" the messenger scolded him, speaking this time for himself. Nuzhat paused in her piping to curtsy and favor him with such a smile of appreciation that the vizier whispered to the caliph, who whispered to the messenger, whose moon-face reddened with pleasure like Ibn al-Hamrā's as, between clearings of his throat, he announced it to be the caliph's wish, if it be Nuzhat's wish, as it was most certainly his own most ardent wish . . .

"I do," piped the piper, and with a new lilt to her music, she fluted Mustafā into the banquet hall.

Whereinto now Haroun al-Rashīd himself escorted Yasmīn, and conferred with her gravely as they went; and Jafar al-Barmakī ushered the bridegroom, whose eyes remained ever on his bride while he attended and nodded at the vizier's confidences. After us came mighty Masrūr and tiptoeing Abū Nuwās (who pretended to sneak in behind the sword-bearer, against the caliph's orders), and after them Haroun's vizier's messenger, already conning the hall for his new companion. From one of the several smaller tables beside the famous main one, she piped a greeting his way, and there he joined her, as did the sword-bearer and the still-clowning poet. Those not already in their places then assumed them, per the caliph's vizier's seating plan: at the main table's head, radiant Yasmīn, and at its other pole her husband; at Yasmīn's right, the Commander of the Faithful; at her left, his grand vizier. At our narrator's right, steadfast Hajj Masūd, still thumping his chest in happy incredulity; at my left, Mustafā (whom I myself would have assigned to Hajj's place even at the cost of separating the rug man from his rhythmical friend). From the fifth place, at the caliph's right, Kuzia Fakān devoured with grinning eyes her flush-faced spouse across from her at the vizier's left, on Cushion Six. Blissful Fatmah Awād marked time in the seventh place, beside her new master. Across from *her,* at Mustafā's left on Cushion Eight, disapproving Jaydā resolutely shook her cowl while Salīm, beside her in the ninth position, gloated openly cross-table to where sat — with scowling dignity after all, in the last place at his own board — black-turbaned Sindbad the Sailor.

Evidently the caliph's kitchen staff had descended earlier upon the house, for as soon as we were all seated Haroun nodded at Yasmīn, who mildly said, "If my husband pleases, I shall order our first course served."

"Wine, too!" called Abū Nuwās, who then shushed the vizier's messenger as if the call had been his.

"So be it," I said. "Inshallah — though I see in the doorway one diner yet to be seated."

It was the other Mustafā, come to join the party. "There shall he stay," declared Haroun, "with an impudent poet to block the threshold that neither of them may cross. See to that, Masrūr. And let there be wine now."

Once the poet had been repositioned in the doorway and the wine and seven kinds of dates served around by handsome servers from the caliph's retinue, Haroun proposed a surprising first toast: not to us but "To the voyages of Sindbad the Sailor, who, though he has been a liar, a fraud, a betrayer of trust, an abuser of those whom he ought most to have protected and nurtured, a murderer, and worse, has also been beyond question an intrepid voyager, a sharp trader, an ingenious and resourceful survivor, a fetcher of six several fortunes into the economy of our caliphate, a perennially hospitable and lavish host, and a tireless teller of his voyage-tales, both literal and figurative."

"We'll drink to that," Abū Nuwās affirmed from the threshold, and (as the caliph looked from face to face around the table) all did, including Sindbad himself and even I, when I saw Yasmīn unhesitatingly set our example. "Hear, hear!" applauded Hajj Masūd, and he was echoed by Hasīb Alī and other erstwhile investors in Serendib Limited. But no sooner had we put down our cups than Haroun said next, "That same Sindbad shall now hear the particulars of his death sentence."

Except for a single pleased whimper from Cushion Nine, the room went silent. Almost brow to brow, my wife conferred with Jafar al-Barmakī, who then left his place to cross behind her and whisper to the caliph. Haroun frowned, reconsulted Yasmīn, then shrugged and nodded to his vizier, who, returning to his place but still standing, announced, "Surpassing her steadfastness, beauty, and intelligence is the condemned man's daughter's mercy. The caliph has sentenced her father to death, and the caliph's sentence may not be unsentenced. But it is the discretionary judgment of the wife of Captain Bey el-Loor that that sentence be executed as follows: Sindbad the Sailor shall die of old age in the desert fastness of the Sahrā al Hijārah, whereto we order him fetched forthwith. More particularly, he shall sit in his waterless Tub of Last Resort with a certain empty amulet pouch ever before his eyes to remind him of his iniquities, the aforecited tub itself to be placed inside the so-called Tub of Truth and transported to the centralmost wâhât of the aforecited desert. There in strict banishment from this caliphate the condemned shall live out his days with no company beyond his natural son, Salīm, the bawd Jaydā, and the camel Mustafā, and to their wishes defer in every matter large and small, on pain of simultaneous slow impalement and disemboweling if he show his turban ever again in Baghdad or Basra while he lives."

"So be it," affirmed Haroun, "for while it is a more merciful fate than I had in mind, it cannot but be sore punishment for a sinful old sailor to end his days so far from the sea. Said sentence shall commence between the final course of this luncheon and the initial of this evening's dinner."

"Ungrateful girl!" Jaydā scolded, straight-faced beneath her cowl. Salīm, on the other hand, evidently as ignorant as the caliph of what had for some time been his father's professed retirement-wish, all but crowed his joy. Yasmīn's eyes smiled at mine. Sindbad himself only nodded his turban and observed, as if resignedly, that there is no god but God and that Mohammed is His prophet.

"On whom be peace," the caliph duly added. "What further, Jafar?"

The vizier leaned over to reconfirm something with my wife, then declared, "The culprit's voyage-tales, on the other hand—which we regard as the only part of him worth preserving—we request Sayyid Captain Bey el-Loor to inscribe at his leisure for the caliph's archives, and to carry them to Serendib as well, should he and his bride achieve that happy landfall."

"Done," I readily agreed.

"And your own six voyages, too," Yasmīn added, "if you would please your bride."

Before I could reply, Haroun asked, "Shall there be soup?"

Yasmīn smiled my way. "My husband willing."

Said I, "Let there be soup."

"And more wine, Brother!" Abū Nuwās called from the doorway.

"Also wine."

When the most delicious harira in Islam had been served and eaten, and more wine poured, and more conferring accomplished at the table's head, Jafar al-Barmakī announced from his cushion, "The caliph next decrees that all the wealth and property of Sindbad the Sailor — excepting the aforedispensed bastard, bawd, camel, and tub-within-tub — now belong to his daughter, in partial recompense for the here-unnamed abuses that she has suffered more or less voluntarily at his hands from time to time. Into the casuistry of those abuses, not to mention the fact itself, we will neither inquire further nor brook further inquiry by others. What happened happened; what did not did not. To mitigate the taint thereof, however, the caliph here decrees that Yasmīn is *not* Sindbad's daughter, nor Sindbad Yasmīn's father, this decree to be retroactive to the moment of her conception." To Yasmīn herself then he said, "This house and all its contents are yours. The house near Basra and its contents are yours. The remains of the ship *Zahir* and whatever goods your former father has laid up in vaults and warehouses here and there—all are yours."

"And what is mine is my husband's," Yasmīn replied. "We accept the caliph's gift with thanks."

"Enjoy it with Allah's blessing and ours," Haroun bade both of us, "until the Destroyer of Delights and Sunderer of Societies et cetera. Let there be couscous."

"And wine!" called Abū Nuwās.

There were both, of a quality not inferior to that of the barley soup. Following our enjoyment of them the caliph made known his wish that Captain and Mrs. Sīmon Bey el-Loor proceed as soon as convenient with Mustafā mu-Allim to our establishment near Basra for the honeymoon purpose of planning, preparing, and embarking upon Voyage Seven. Should that voyage succeed, it was his wish that we attempt in due time to return, bringing with us news of his fellow caliph's welfare plus a number of magical timepieces such as mine for himself and his retinue. And should that return voyage succeed as well, it was his hope that we would thenceforth alternate our years between this caliphate and that, overseeing their regular commerce.

It wanted only the quick conference of our eyes for Yasmīn to respond for both of us, "We hear and shall obey, God willing."

"Grilled pheasant, then," Haroun ordered. "Rabbit kabobs."

"Wine," ordered Abū Nuwās.

"Done." "Done."

"It is our wish finally," the vizier said on behalf of the caliph after these had been served, enjoyed, and cleared, "that the three households of sayyids Hajj Masūd, Ibn al-Hamrā, and our messenger often intervisit and be the caliph's frequent guests as well, so that for years to come we may enjoy the eloquence of Kuzia Fakān's dancing to the music of her inspired accompanists. And it is our command that they treat us now to another of their performances."

Tap tata tap-tap, Kuzia's finger-cymbals replied at once. *Tap tap,* affirmed Fatmah's tambourine. Which was to say (piped Nuzhat from her side table), *We hear and obey!*

We it was then who heard and saw the remarkable Dance of Denouements: how with the several and independent though profoundly interrelated motions of her limbs and digits, eyebrows and buttocks, ears, navel, and every other movable appurtenance, Kuzia Fakān bodied forth the dramaturgy of closure. After only the swiftest of choreographical synopses of my disruption of Sindbad's end-of-Ramadan feast, his proposal and my counterproposal, our subsequent alternating voyage-tales and the interstitial thickenings of plot and subplots, before our eyes Kuzia danced the rising action to its climax, adroitly interweaving exposition with complication of the conflict. There in her hips *Shaitan* intercepted *Zahir* and was itself fatally overtaken by Jabāl's navy, while a single earlobe recapitulated Allah's Great Tale of Jaydā the Cairene. There between Kuzia's shoulders I was rugged into Yasmīn's apartment and back out to the Basra marshes, stoned on bhang; her eyelids and belly told of my return in poor-porter guise to sing my lament and raise the dramatical stakes. Came next the grand reprise of that foreshadowing, done with double-breasted variations on the ground-theme of her buttocks: the Commander of the Faithful and his vizier, in beggars' garb, manifesting themselves to us last night, declaring Yasmīn and her lover wed, the bride intact, our union triumphantly consummated. With what subtlety and pacing then, before each present player in our plot, Kuzia danced out his/her just deserts: these raised up, these brought low, these paired with those, justice done (both retributive and distributive), catharsis catharsed, epiphany epiphed, dramatic tension resolved, ground-situation altered meaningfully and irreversibly.

Shabash, Fatmah Awād: well done! *Mabrouk*, Nuzhat: good show! Brava, brava, Kuzia Fakān!

"Wine!" Abū Nuwās cheered from the threshold.

Sweat-soaked and breathless, Kuzia sprawled athwart the table, her head in her beaming husband's lap and her articulate but narratively exhausted bare brown feet upon her cushion opposite. That being at the caliph's right hand, when he had done applauding her performance he stroked her instep with that hand and said, "In the three hundred sixty-five pleasure domes of our harem there is not one pair of feet so skillful as these. We expect to attend them from time to time in nights to come."

"They hear and obey," Kuzia assured him with all ten toes. "Do they not, my husband?"

"As Allah lives," Ibn al-Hamrā carminely acknowledged.

Haroun nodded. "Then we now pronounce this denouement dispensed. There remains its implementation, the details of which we leave to our vizier and other lieutenants." Jafar al-Barmakī, still smiling on his cushion beside Ibn al-Hamrā, snapped his fingers once, and a number of splendidly armed guards materialized where just a moment before the table-waiters had been arrayed. Abū Nuwās rolled from the doorway in mock terror before them. Vizier and caliph rose together, and from the side table likewise Masrūr the sword-bearer and the moon-faced messenger.

"We bid you all good afternoon," said Haroun al-Rashīd. "Fare you well, Captain Bey el-Loor and most green-eyed Yasmīn. Sayyids and ladies all, farewell, and even you, Sindbad the Sailor. Before evening prayer call, begone from here — and fare you well."

"Not yet!" cried Abū Nuwās from the floor. The caliph rounded upon him sternly. Guards stirred; Masrūr handled his scimitar. But the poet rose swaying to his feet, lifted his wine cup, and declaimed:

No last word without a period.
No dessert without mint tea.
After the Ending comes the Wrap-up;
After Haroun al-Rashīd comes me

"to toast your sundry denouements as follows: All please rise."

We did, and whether the poet's inebriation was real, feigned, or feignedly feigned, he balanced himself down the main table's length as if walking a beam and raised his cup to each of us in turn — beginning with myself, to whom he said somewhat cryptically:

"*You will find your Serendib . . . under a blue wuzara!*"

Then, to Mustafā mu-Allim: "*If your needle won't point north, sail south.*"

To Hajj Masūd and Fatmah Awād: "*Bang tambourine till you wear your carpets through.*"

To Jaydā, with a thrust of his pelvis: "*Your future I foresee in yonder camel's hump.*"

To Salīm, with another: "*Buggee now shall bugger be!*"

To Sindbad: "*In quicksand slowly shall the sinful sailor sink.*"

Then, over Sindbad's head to Nuzhat's and Haroun's vizier's messenger's side table: "*Piper play new pipe and messenger message till you both be winded.*"

Next, to Kuzia Fakān and Ibn al-Hamrā: "*The wandering Bedou will give him red horns to match his cheeks.*"

Relapsing more or less into meter then, to Yasmīn:

> *May you lose it twice again twixt lunch and dinner*
> *And hang more such pretty laundry on the line.*

And finally, inspired by that rhythm back to rhyme and raising his cup to Allah:

> *May our caliph and his vizier live forever,*
> *And Abū Nuwās have one more cup of wine!*

Somebody's Next Voyage

What do we imagine we're doing, really, Yasmīn and her "Sīmon Bey el-Loor," in Basra and in Baghdad, through the busy honeymoon season that follows the caliph's dispensations?

Sindbad the Sailor, when Haroun and all guests have gone, withdraws wordlessly to his Tub of Last Resort (replaced right side up now in the courtyard, inside the Tub of Truth) and will have nothing further to do with the story of his life. He neither turns a hand to prepare for his imminent exile nor stays others from preparing for him as they wish. Jaydā and Salīm energetically do so, the duenna lamenting her fate to Allah and the world while busily ordering the house servants to pack this and that, the page bustling importantly about and smirking that who can no longer pitch (we approximate the Arab proverb) must catch. The three musicians, too, busy themselves in the harem, packing their belongings and kissing one another, tearful but eager to commence their separate next chapters.

As for us: between that midday and the evening meal, just as Abū Nuwās has proposed, we lose and find ourselves in each other at least once again, if perhaps not twice. Then toward afternoon's end we reappear, rerobed at Yasmīn's suggestion in sea-blue, to bid due fare-wells. Salīm we find dressed like a Bedou sheik and already mounted upon the camel Mustafā; he gives imperious commands to a troop of porters sent by the grand vizier to rig the Tub of Truth with carrying poles, like a sedan chair, and see to its portage. They go about their work indifferent to his strutting.

"Won't you ride in there, too?" Yasmīn asks Jaydā.

With some asperity the duenna replies, "As *he* wishes." She does not mean her son.

Yasmīn reminds her, "You're to give the orders," and her old nurse responds, "*You* may turn the world upside down, Miss Wear-the-Pants. I've ordered him to order me."

"I'll say good-bye, then, Jaydā. To him, too. Lift me, please, Sīmon."

Salīm taunts, "He has seen enough of you."

Declares Yasmīn, "That is no longer for him to say." Not at all eagerly, her husband interlaces his fingers to give her a step up into the outer tub and stands by uncomfortably with sphinx-faced Jaydā when the blue djellaba disappears over its edge.

Presently from his camel-perch Salīm hoots, "*Yallah*, Bey el-Loor! If you saw what I see!"

"You see nothing," Yasmīn's twice-tubbed voice replies. "You see a dutiful ex-daughter bidding her ex-father farewell forever."

"I see what I see," Salīm gloats. Another silent minute passes before our blue-cowled bride reemerges and matter-of-factly bids, "Off to the desert with him, Jaydā." To her husband then, "Which way to Serendib?"

"South, to begin with," offers Mustafā mu-Allim, who has agreed to stay to dinner with us even though he's far too full of Haroun's denouement-lunch to eat anything more that day. "All voyages begin at Basra."

"To Basra, then, yes? As soon as possible."

We watch the little caravan leave the courtyard for the Sahrā al Hijārah. Of her officially former father Yasmīn reports, "I tied Umar's pouch to his forehead like a Jew's phylactery. He's pretending to be-lieve that it will lead him to Marjānah."

"Or pretending to pretend," her husband uneasily reminds her. Then, though our intention is to repair promptly with Mustafā to the house near Basra in pursuit of the caliph's directive, after a high-spirited dinner and affectionate farewells to Nuzhat, Fatmah Awād, and Kuzia Fakān (and their companions, the vizier's messenger, Hajj Masūd, and even Ibn al-Hamrā), Yasmīn proposes that we restore the courtyard gardens and refill its ponds and fountains to their "Sha'ban" splendor before closing the place down for our voyage.

In truth there is no hurry, and so we do. Indeed, so frequent is our traffic between the seaport and the capital, the boatyard and Haroun's palace, that in the year that follows we maintain both of Sindbad's former establishments with a cook and caretaker and commute between them while preparing with Mustafā for the vague adventure to come. As those preparations mature, we decide that upon our departure we will make an outright gift of the Baghdad house to Hajj Masūd and Fatmah Awād (our frequent guests at both places, as are Nuzhat and her moon-faced friend; also Kuzia Fakān, when she is not dancing to the caliph's tune — and, yes, even Ibn al-Hamrā) and of the Basra place to Mustafā.

"Hajj Masūd?" that worthy exclaims. "Sindbad's house to Hajj Masūd the rug merchant?" Fatmah discreetly rustles her ever-present tambourine. "And to his devoted companion?" the rug man adds. But they will accept the gift only with the grateful stipulation that they maintain it in trust for us for ten years or until our return from Serendib, whichever comes earlier to pass, or — Allah forfend! — until news arrives of our loss at sea. Mustafā, likewise, declines with thanks the marsh-side house near Basra, for reasons not dissimilar to those that led him to decline the caliph's offer of Nuzhat. But he fully approves of our amended proposal (to be implemented by Jafar al-Barmakī) to convert the place into a haven for derelict sailors, with a light ever burning at its seaward gate to guide them thither.

The vizier himself becomes a periodic caller upon us and the sympathetic monitor of our project, whose peculiar nature and difficulty he seems quite to appreciate. It is all very well for Yasmīn to prove to be a quick learner of navigation and the fine points of sailing, and a ready student of English, too. All very well for Sīmon Bey el-Loor and company to attempt something like the reverse of many seagoing replicas: not an ancient design constructed with modern materials but, of necessity, vice versa, insofar as is permitted by its chief designer's limited grasp of naval architecture and Mustafā's of "modern" design concepts — though his general boat-building sense is superb. And all very well, of course, for our man in the interstices of love and boat-work to write out fuller accounts of Sindbad's six voyages and his own, interweaving among them the story of his unaccountable season in the house and world of Sindbad the Sailor, in the caliphate of Haroun al-Rashīd.

"But what, really," Jafar asks us one cordial evening, "do you imagine yourselves to be doing?"

What he means is that by now there can be no serious doubt as to which side of that hypothetical Boundary Sayyid Sīmon is on. There is no "U.S. embassy" around some corner of Haroun's Baghdad (Jafar has had the whole city checked for us); no rug-shop passageway from the "Jmaa el Fna" of this world back to the "Dronningen's Gade" of that. If the odd vessel under our construction should, by improbable hazard, survive the Persian Gulf and the Arabian Sea, then the Serendib whose Adam's Peak we'll raise will *be* Serendib, will it not? Not some "Sri Lanka" on the Boundary's farther side. Nevertheless we busily love and plan, put our affairs conscientiously in order, and work and play through our honeymoon year as if in a sustained and vivid dream.

"Why do you not simply stay here?" the vizier goes so far as to inquire of us, or propose. "From what Sayyid Sīmon has reported, I find his Serendib to be after all not so blessed a place as one had imagined, and his station in it to have been at best equivocal. Sayyid himself is no longer a young man. Sindbad's fortune will last the pair of you more than a lifetime, and you enjoy the caliph's favor as well as Allah's. I believe I can explain diplomatically to the Commander of the Faithful why your good-faith intentions are literally impossible of accomplishment. . . ."

To which our narrator replies, Thanks, but no: Yasmīn's world is truly not his, nor his hers; if we can't intervisit between them, we'll try to reach some third that's neither — an island as far out of her time as out of his, where nothing fixes us in any world except Nature's — and there improvise our own world out of elements from all three.

"*Misl al kikāyat*," in Jafar's opinion. "All fanciful-romantic enough, no doubt, for a time — though why one would flee voluntarily from the most civilized city in Islam I cannot imagine. But soon enough, my friend, you'll be a truly old man, and your green-eyed partner, believe it or not, an old woman, though always younger than yourself, and you'll find yourselves craving if not requiring the comforts of Baghdad. What's more, it may be that Allah will bless you with children. How will you educate them properly, out there on some faraway island?"

Quickly, emphatically, and not quite to the point, Yasmīn declares, "There will be no children." Both men turn to her. "Let's speak only of the voyage," she quietly requests.

"Well," her husband replies to Jafar, "I suppose we'll navigate that stretch of it when the time comes." So the three stroll outside through the ultramarine evening to the specially constructed ways on the marsh flat where Bey el-Loor once crawled from the Shatt al Arab like the first amphibian, and they admire the sturdy ketch-rigged vessel there a-building, its salty sheer and tumble home, deep keel and long, low cabin trunk: a scaled-up, Arabized version of Simon Behler's memory of Captain Joshua Slocum's famous *Spray,* in which that doughty New Englander in the 1890s made the first known solo circumnavigation of the globe. But even as the vizier commends its unusual lines, and compliments Mustafā and the workmen, and presents the captain-designate with a new token of the caliph's encouragement (a jeweled dagger larger than Yasmīn's, to replace the fish-fileting knife that our man has carried with him through many a chapter), he shakes his head and again wonders aloud, "What exactly is it that you imagine you're going to do?"

The day arrives that we have been neither hastening nor postponing, neither particularly fearing nor, by this time, particularly anticipating: when there is nothing further to be done in the way of preparation for our voyage. *Zahir 3* has been named and numbered; whichever of its predecessors ought properly to be thought of as the first and which the second, we agree that this is the third and "christen" it with the Arabic numeral, not the Roman. It has been launched, sea-tried, modified here and there, retried, commissioned, provisioned. Our literal and psychological mooring lines have been singled up; the season is favorable, the weather fair. It is either go or stay.

Our friend Kuzia Fakān, as it happens, is just then visiting (with, yes, Ibn al-Hamrā, a contented though no less florid fellow these days, at peace with himself and us) and has brought us a gift of two matching gold rings in token of her own impending journey and new life-venture: with the caliph's reluctant blessing the couple are opening a jewelry shop in Cairo, a long-standing ambition of Kuzia's that her husband is shrewdly bankrolling to get her away from Haroun's palace. To Bedouin Kuzia, our open sea is as uninviting as the desert she came from; even Baghdad has come to seem to her a provincial backwater compared to what Jaydā has endlessly told her in time past about the souks and bazaars of Cairo. Ibo smiles, reddens, nods. Our rings are inscribed with charms in both Arabic and Roman letters (the goldsmith was from Alexandria), meant to keep their wearers afloat and in love forever — or more precisely, until the Destroyer of Delights makes his inevitable visit, may it be not soon. We have taken the visitors for a little day-sail, much to Kuzia's discomfiture; now the guests have stepped gladly back onto the dock, but the hosts lounge on awhile, idly yet edgily, in *Zahir 3*'s varnish-gleaming cockpit. Yasmīn twists and twists her new ring upon her finger; her husband is moved to wonder, uneasily, Is she going to *remove* it?

Instead, from somewhere under the sea-blue wuzara she has taken to wearing like any male sailor or longshoreman, she suddenly withdraws her own bejeweled, now-famous knife — our man's blood surges — and with one surprising stroke cuts the ketch's forward spring line.

"*Yallah!*" cheers one of the dockhands who are standing by (as are Kuzia Fakān, Ibn al-Hamrā, Mustafā mu-Allim, and others), and as if on signal he casts off the bow line he has just secured. Quick-thinking Kuzia takes up the cry — "Yallah!" — and other hands cast off our aft spring and stern lines, leaving *Zahir* tethered by a single breast line.

Laughing, its official captain protests, "Hold on! I've got things to work out yet with Ankh el-Zhash!"

Such has become our affectionate nickname for Mustafā — who, however, hunkering gravely on the pier just beside our cockpit, affirms with a nod of his turban Yasmīn's resolve. "There is nothing more to be worked out. Your wife is right; the tide runs. Shall I not cast off?"

For all of several seconds, "Sīmon" considers. Rather than drawing his own new blade then, he quietly orders, "Breast line away," and fetches the fall of it aboard like his own umbilicus. As *Zahir 3* gently drifts clear, the couple embrace in the cockpit, acknowledging goodbyes from the dock. Yasmīn steps then smartly to the tiller, beautifully laminated of ebony and poon; her husband to the hempen halyards, to raise the clean canvas mainsail on its varnished gaff.

"*Allah 'l-mueen!*" calls Kuzia Fakān across the widening space: "God will help!"

To himself, as the sail fills and the ketch gains steerageway, our man says, "Yes, well."

These mismatched but perfectly suited, more or less married lovers: what do they imagine they're doing? I see them clear the port of Basra and stand down the Bahr Faris, "shaking down" their craft and settling into the rhythms of aboard-ship life. I see them pass white-knuckled through the vicinity of Qeshm, through the Hormuz Strait, into the Gulf of Oman. With great good fortune they manage not to fall afoul of pirates; they cope successfully with squalls and sundry small-to-medium-size mishaps, as if Allah really were monitoring and gracing them. They grow seasoned and ever cannier in the ways of their vessel, the sea, each other. For Yasmīn, particularly, such self-reliance and freedom of action is paradise, however rough the going. As necessary they put ashore to rewater, reprovision, and make repairs; Yasmīn's pleasure then is to pass as a remarkably pretty sailor boy, catamite no doubt to *Zahir*'s lean and grizzled skipper. They make their way down the Arabian Sea, through the Lakshadweep Islands and along the Malabar Coast; I see them reaching on the northeast monsoon winds day after jewel-starred night, a trying but exhilarating magic-carpet ride southeast toward the tip of India.

It will be in that neighborhood, I expect — where the parallels of North Latitude dwindle toward 0° and the meridians of East Longitude approach that of Adam's Peak — that *Zahir 3* meets the truly life-threatening storm that all sailors dread but must expect sooner or later to confront: the one to survive which depends as much upon sheer good luck as upon seaworthiness in the vessel and good seamanship in the crew. By this time Sīmon Bey el-Loor is by way of being a master of the art of shorthanded small-boat sailing, and Yasmīn at the very least a sailor first-class, able within her not inconsiderable strength to do anything her husband can do in the management of their vessel. They function together superbly. But they are without radio, weather service, hydrographic charts, compass, and sextant, not to mention loran, SatNav, and the rest. They are without weather-proof sails and lines, aluminum spars, stainless-steel standing rigging and stanchions and lifelines, high-efficiency bilge pumps, inflatable life raft, Emergency Position Indicating Radio Beacon. Their Personal Flotation Devices are segmented vests of cork and sailcloth designed by Sīmon and fabricated by Nuzhat, as gifted with the needle as with her flute; even a few weeks of the tropical marine environment has riddled them with rot and mildew.

What concerns me most, however, is their vessel. Not its low-tech, high-maintenance materials: sailors for centuries made do with wood and hemp, cotton and bronze; Josh Slocum's *Spray* was built of nothing more durable. But the design . . . Simon William Behler knows himself to be no naval architect; a seasoned sailor but only a knowledgeable novice at marine design and construction, he has endeavored to meld his experience of modern materials and his memory of traditional designs with the very different conceptions and experience of medieval Arab shipwrights. *Quixotic* is the kindest adjective for anyone's venturing offshore in the product of that combination, and yet *Zahir 3* has nearly three thousand nautical miles under her keel by the time she leaves the Maldive Islands astern, points her bowsprit due east toward "Serendib," and meets the tremendous storm head-on. But not even "quixotic" will do to describe (nor would even steel and state-of-the-art synthetics suffice to achieve) the goal of navigating the Boundary between Yasmīn's world and her husband's, between "Sīmon Bey el-Loor" and Simon William Behler.

Sindbad's daughter knows what *she's* doing: she is sailing with her chosen mate, wifing him to wherever, exactly as she pledged on their wedding night. But what does her husband imagine he's doing? Where does he imagine he is? Who?

Whatever he imagines, the storm is real, and though the couple struggle with it heroically through a day and a night and another day, as night refalls I see reality overwhelm them and their craft. In the mad wind and seas, knockdown follows knockdown; *Zahir 3* is pitchpoled, rolled, dismasted, pooped, swamped, and ultimately sunk. Can "our man" have imagined that things would turn out otherwise? As the possible long shot, perhaps (whatever "otherwise" might have led to), but I credit Simon William Behler with understanding that the more likely end of his seventh voyage would be something like this, the classic Sindbad situation: once again derelict in Allah's ocean, bruised and battered, hungry, thirsty, spent, but no bones broken, no blood to fetch the sharks even sooner — and not alone: a pair of lovers clinging to a shattered spar (they tie themselves turban-fast to it through the storm's tag end), with no land in sight, no food no water no hope of rescue, the only questions what form of death will reach them first and which of them earlier. In the long history of seafaring, how many luckless sailors have shared their extremity! Time to turn our narrative eyes away and hope their agony will be brief.

But "Luckless!" Yasmīn protests when, after black hours of immersion, her mate mutters something like the above in the course of lamenting that he has brought her to this pass. "How many lovers have the good luck to end their story together?" If in fact this *is* the end (she goes on to say as her failing strength permits); but don't all the lessons of a certain old sailor's voyages teach that what has befallen us is merely the prerequisite to reaching Island One, Voyage Seven? Our story isn't over; only its beginning is.

Et cetera, through that night's dark end, doubtless only to buoy her friend's spirits and her own, and he loves her all the more for that. Nevertheless, he's sinking: exhaustion, hypothermia even in so warm an ocean, despair (Where did he imagine he was? What doing?). The wind has mercifully blown itself out. The night sea calms. There are stars, whose names they know.

The woman embraces the man, in part for warmth's sake, and speaks on softly, a shivering Scheherazade, as he rocks with her in the swell and floats in and out of consciousness. She even *teases* him: she is his lost "Jay-Moor" swum back to him by "logistically assisted serendipity." She is his lost "Day-*zee*" leading him back to their bower on the Island of Island Creek. She is Princess Wakini of that long-ago Lagoon. . . .

Unless he's dreaming, he hears her say presently that she sees a single small light to eastward, low on the horizon. *My watch dial,* he thinks he replies: *five* A.M. No, she insists: it's the beachfires of pilgrims, she bets, making ready to climb Adam's Peak in the first dawn. He himself sees nothing; can no longer speak; is not this time "drowning into sleep" but, surely, sleeping into his drowning.

"I see our island, Sīmon!" she almost whispers. She has unbound herself now, stripped off even her blue wuzara to free herself for the swim. Now she's unbinding him. She turns his watch-wrist her way; our gift-rings tap.

"Time," she says, and she turns the bezel of his watch. "Follow me now, my darling. Let go. Let's go."

She herself has already done so: let go of their spar, of him. She moves off gently toward what she says she sees in the gray blush eastward. But she's smiling back his way, her green eyes urging him to follow.

More easily than he had ever imagined, he does.

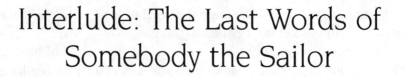

Interlude: The Last Words of Somebody the Sailor

"Well, so," said Simon Behler to himself: *"I've been stranded with less."*

For this time — though once again naked, salt-soaked, sunburnt; again sore-muscled, ache-jointed, daze-headed, also ungroomed un-barbered unoriented and all but out of breath — I was blessed not only with my watch (its hour disjoint from the overhead sun, its date some summer-weather WED 31) but with a gold ring to press my cracked lips to and turn upon its brine-swollen finger. I took on faith, of necessity, the charmed letters graved inside: love's initials in two scripts.

Where was I beached this time, then, in hand-me-down but stub-bornly serviceable birthday suit? Some marshy lowland: brown sand, tall green spartina, brown and green cattails; estuarine-olive water, brackish, tepid, tranquil. Air subtropical, but as in a temperate-zone midsummer. Trees nonequatorial: white cedar, black locust, sweet-gum, loblolly pine. *So far, so good,* said (as it were) my old hand's eye. Nothing to be seen in the way of beachfire, pilgrim, peak, not to men-tion my young heart-, soul-, and shipmate. No sign of buoy, boat, building, bridge — but there a blue heron stalked, there an osprey wheeled; that was a red-winged blackbird's rasp, a mockingbird's cadenza.

Understanding thereby where (mid-East-Coast-North-American tidewater cove) more clearly than when how why or who, in time I grunted myself together, picked myself up, and gimped me up-shore on waking legs, perhaps to meet . . . whomever: my Chesapeake Athene or Nausicaä-on-the-Chaptico; my East-Dorset, fin-de-siècle Whomever. What would be my initial time-fix, I managed to wonder: crabber's johnboat? Discarded Sheik condom or Camel cigarette pack? Full name spelled out on beach in urinary cursive? Or, after all, just around the next point, an alabaster roc dome, shoal of jewels, lost late-life love with matching ring?

None of the above. Instead, half buried in the sand ahead, where creek debouches into river at the Island Point day beacon, a little canister as red and yellow as Howard Garton's old Bellanca. Smiling but in no hurry, I retrieved my Bon Ami: not the modern redesign, but the classic container of my boyhood.

Almost empty, but not quite. *Hasn't scratched yet.*

Well, I would return it, one way or another. If my dead reckoning was right, behind a certain creek-mouth islet not much farther on was the Eastern Shore Asylum, which no doubt would welcome me as one of its strays if I swam over: a semicentenarian buck-naked but for wristwatch, ring, and forty-year-old can of patent cleanser. Or I might reverse course, wander back down-shore, river-bridgeward, past Dorset General and up the white-clapboard, silver-mapled streets of home. In those years when I used now and then to slip by moonlight into East Dorset from my back bedroom via my catalpa-tree "escape route," had I returned by the same trunk and limbs? *Naked stranger enters second-story bedroom in broad midday via Chinese Cigar tree:* another shortcut to asylum.

Or I could take the third way, yes: up-creek in my brother's ever-leaking initiation-skiff as far into my place of origin as I could get till I was got: bail my way past the old tomato canneries, crab pickeries, oyster shuckeries and tideside shacks to the neglected plot at that place's head and heart. I would ground my vessel on a nearby flat and scale the rusty chain-link fence along Cemetery Ave. I'd find the family, take my ease there among the dandelions with

THE DESTROYER OF
DELIGHTS

or,

The Familiar Stranger

From her absence in my story's wrap-up, its narrator concludes, *we may infer that old Scheherazade achieved her narrative end. Okay?*

Pleat-skirted or not, sleek-nyloned, auburn-haired or not — and stethoscoped, green-tunicked, multifunction-digitaled — his audience he now recognizes to have been all along his oldest friend.

Okay, she says, and sighs, and then brilliantly smiles: lost sister Bijou, green-eyed BeeGee; fellow ovum, comrade, pal; come to . . . play a game with him, one of their old ones; tell *him* a story; let him know his real and first and final name.

The poor devil down the hall has howled himself out.

Remember how it was? she says, familiar stranger: In the spaceship, weightless, making ready to go Outside? You went first, you always thought, but *I* was the one; *I* went first. I know the way. Follow me, now:

Two. One.